Archaeologist and anthropologist **Steven Erikson** is the bestselling author of the genre-defining The Malazan Book of the Fallen, a multi-volume epic fantasy that has been hailed a masterwork of the imagination and one of the top ten fantasy series of all time. The first novel in the series, *Gardens of the Moon*, was shortlisted for the World Fantasy Award. He has also written several novellas set in the same world. *Forge of Darkness* is the first Kharkanas novel and takes readers back to the origins of the Malazan world. *Fall of Light* continues this epic tale. A lifelong science fiction reader, he has also written fiction affectionately parodying a long-running SF television series and *Rejoice*, a novel of first contact. *The God is Not Willing* is the opening chapter in a new sequence – The Tales of Witness – and is set in the world of the Malazan Empire, ten years after the events recounted in *The Crippled God*.

Steven Erikson lives in Victoria, Canada. To find out more, visit www.steven-erikson.org – and you can also find him on Facebook: Steven Erikson – Author

www.penguin.co.uk

Acclaim for Steven Erikson's
THE MALAZAN BOOK OF THE FALLEN

'Erikson is an extraordinary writer . . . my advice to anyone
who might listen to me is: treat yourself'
STEPHEN R. DONALDSON

'Give me the evocation of a rich, complex and yet ultimately
unknowable other world, with a compelling suggestion of intricate
history and mythology and lore. Give me mystery amid the grand
narrative . . . Give me a world in which every sea hides a crumbled
Atlantis, every ruin has a tale to tell, every broken blade is a silent
legacy of struggles unknown. Give me, in other words, the fantasy
work of Steven Erikson . . . a master of lost and forgotten
epochs, a weaver of ancient epics'
SALON.COM

'I stand slack-jawed in awe of *The Malazan Book of the Fallen*.
This masterwork of the imagination may be the high
watermark of epic fantasy'
GLEN COOK

'The most masterful piece of fiction I have ever read. It has
single-handedly changed everything we thought we knew about
fantasy literature and redefined what is possible'
SF SITE

'Rare is the writer who so fluidly combines a sense of mythic power
and depth of world with fully realized characters and thrilling action,
but Steven Erikson manages it spectacularly'
MICHAEL A. STACKPOLE

'Erikson's magnum opus, *The Malazan Book of the Fallen*,
sits in pole position as the very best and most ambitious
epic fantasy saga ever written'
PAT'S FANTASY HOTLIST

'This is true myth in the making, a drawing upon fantasy to recreate
histories and legends as rich as any found within our culture'
INTERZONE

'Arguably the best fantasy series ever written. This is of course
subject to personal opinion . . . but few can deny that the quality
and ambition of the ten books that make up *The Malazan
Book of the Fallen* are unmatched within the genre'
FANTASY BOOK REVIEW

Midnight Tides
A Tale of the
Malazan Book of the Fallen

STEVEN ERIKSON

PENGUIN BOOKS

TRANSWORLD PUBLISHERS
Penguin Random House, One Embassy Gardens,
8 Viaduct Gardens, London SW11 7BW
www.penguin.co.uk

Transworld is part of the Penguin Random House group of companies
whose addresses can be found at global.penguinrandomhouse.com

First published in Great Britain in 2004 by Bantam Press
an imprint of Transworld Publishers
Bantam edition published 2005
Penguin paperback edition published 2024

A CIP catalogue record for this book
is available from the British Library.

ISBN
9781804995525 (B format)

Typeset in Goudy by Falcon Oast Graphic Art Ltd.
Printed and bound in Great Britain by Clays Ltd, Elcograf S.p.A.

The authorized representative in the EEA is Penguin Random House Ireland,
Morrison Chambers, 32 Nassau Street, Dublin D02 YH68.

Penguin Random House is committed to a sustainable future
for our business, our readers and our planet. This book is made
from Forest Stewardship Council® certified paper.

To Christopher Porozny

Acknowledgements

Deepest appreciation to the old crew, Rick, Chris and Mark, for the advance comments on this novel. And to Courtney, Cam and David Keck for their friendship. Thanks as always to Clare and Bowen, to Simon Taylor and his compatriots at Transworld; to Steve Donaldson, Ross and Perry; Peter and Nicky Crowther, Patrick Walsh and Howard Morhaim. And to the staff at Tony's Bar Italia for this, the second novel fuelled by their coffee.

Contents

Tiste Edur Villages

Forts (Letherii)

Cities & Towns

MERUDE Tiste Edur Tribes

Border

Breed Bay

DEN-RATHA

Tund

MERUDE

BENEDA

SOLLANTA

ARAPAY

HIROTH

CALASH SEA

Reach Inlet

Fent Reach

FIRST MAIDEN FORT

The Reach

HIGH FORT

Trate

SECOND MAIDEN FORT

Trate Inlet

Katter R.

Katter

Catch

Lookout MTNS.

Moss R.

Saltsong's Reach

THIRD MAIDEN FORT

Dresh

First Reach

Awl

Lan

Cargo

Tulamesh

Brous R.

Brous

Rennis

Almas

TISTE EDUR LANDS and NORTH·LETHER FRONTIER

Tundra

I C E

F I E L D S

FORT SHAKE

The Manse

East Shake R.

White Point

Five Points

BRANS KEEP

To Letheras

N

0   50   100   150

leagues

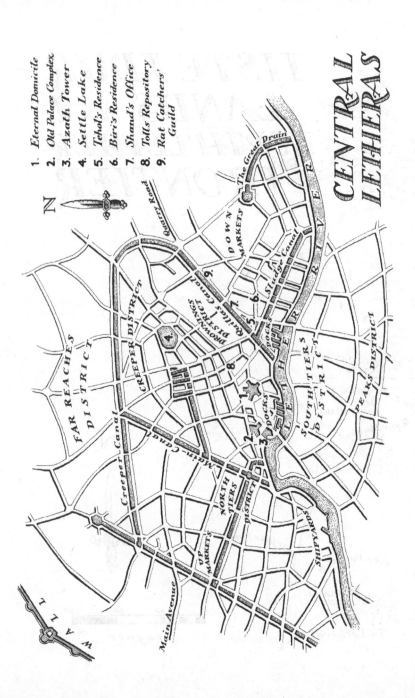

CENTRAL LETHERAS

1. Eternal Domicile
2. Old Palace Complex
3. Azath Tower
4. Settle Lake
5. Tehol's Residence
6. Biri's Residence
7. Shand's Office
8. Tolls Repository
9. Rat Catchers' Guild

DRAMATIS PERSONAE

THE TISTE EDUR

Tomad Sengar, patriarch of the Sengar Bloodline
Uruth, matriarch of the Sengar Bloodline
Fear Sengar, Eldest Son, Weapons Master of the Tribes
Trull Sengar, Second Son
Binadas Sengar, Third Son
Rhulad Sengar, Fourth and Youngest Son
Mayen, Fear's Betrothed
Hannan Mosag, Warlock King of the Six Tribes
  Confederacy
Theradas Buhn, Eldest Son of the Buhn Bloodline
Midik Buhn, Second Son
Badar, an unblooded
Rethal, a warrior
Canarth, a warrior
Choram Irard, an unblooded
Kholb Harat, an unblooded
Matra Brith, an unblooded

LETHERII SLAVES AMONG THE TISTE EDUR

Udinaas
Feather Witch
Hulad
Virrick

THE LETHERII

In the Palace

Ezgara Diskanar, King of Letheras

Janall, Queen of Letheras

Quillas Diskanar, Prince and Heir

Unnutal Hebaz, Preda (Commander) of Letherii army

Brys Beddict, Finadd (Captain) and King's Champion, youngest of the Beddict brothers

Moroch Nevath, a Finadd bodyguard to Prince Quillas Diskanar

Kuru Qan, Ceda (Sorceror) to the King

Nisall, the King's First Concubine

Turudal Brizad, The Queen's First Consort

Nifadas, First Eunuch

Gerun Eberict, Finadd in the Royal Guard

Triban Gnol, Chancellor

Laerdas, a mage in the Prince's retinue

In the North

Buruk the Pale, a merchant in the north

Seren Pedac, Acquitor for Buruk the Pale

Hull Beddict, Sentinel in the north, eldest among the Beddict brothers

Nekal Bara, a sorceress

Arahathan, a mage

Enedictal, a mage

Yan Tovis (Twilight), Atri-Preda at Fent Reach

In the City of Letheras

Tehol Beddict, a citizen in the capital, middle among the Beddict brothers
Hejun, an employee of Tehol
Rissarh, an employee of Tehol
Shand, an employee of Tehol
Chalas, a watchman
Biri, a merchant
Huldo, an establishment proprietor
Bugg, Tehol's servant
Ublala Pung, a criminal
Harlest, a household guard
Ormly, Champion Rat Catcher
Rucket, Chief Investigator, Rat Catchers' Guild
Bubyrd, Rat Catchers' Guild
Glisten, Rat Catchers' Guild
Ruby, Rat Catchers' Guild
Onyx, Rat Catchers' Guild
Scint, Rat Catchers' Guild
Kettle, a child
Shurq Elalle, a thief
Selush, a Dresser of the Dead
Padderunt, assistant to Selush
Urul, chief server in Huldo's
Inchers, a citizen
Hulbat, a citizen
Turble, a citizen
Unn, a half-blood indigent
Delisp, Matron of the Temple Brothel
Prist, a gardener
Strong Rall, a cut-throat
Green Pig, an infamous mage of old

OTHERS

Withal, a Meckros weaponsmith
Rind, a Nacht
Mape, a Nacht
Pule, a Nacht
The One Within
Silchas Ruin, a Tiste Andii Eleint Soletaken
Scabandari Bloodeye, a Tiste Edur Eleint Soletaken
Gothos, a Jaghut
Rud Elalle, a child
Iron Bars, a soldier
Corlo, a mage
Halfpeck, a soldier
Ulshun Pral, an Imass

PROLOGUE

The First Days of the Sundering of Emurlahn
The Edur Invasion, the Age of Scabandari Bloodeye
The Time of the Elder Gods

FROM THE TWISTING, SMOKE-FILLED CLOUDS, BLOOD rained down. The last of the sky keeps, flame-wreathed and pouring black smoke, had surrendered the sky. Their ragged descent had torn furrows through the ground as they struck and broke apart with thunderous reverberations, scattering red-stained rocks among the heaps of corpses that covered the land from horizon to horizon.

The great hive cities had been reduced to ash-layered rubble, and the vast towering clouds above each of them that had shot skyward with their destruction – clouds filled with debris and shredded flesh and blood – now swirled in storms of dissipating heat, spreading to fill the sky.

Amidst the annihilated armies the legions of the conquerors were reassembling on the centre plain, most of which was covered in exquisitely fitted flagstones – where the impact of the sky keeps had not carved deep gouges – although the reassertion of formations was hampered by the countless carcasses of the defeated. And by exhaustion. The legions belonged to two distinct armies, allies in this war, and it was clear that one had fared far better than the other.

The blood mist sheathed Scabandari's vast, iron-hued wings as he swept down through the churning clouds, blinking nictitating membranes to clear his ice-blue draconean eyes. Banking in his descent, the dragon tilted his head to survey his victorious children. The grey banners of the Tiste Edur legions wavered fitfully above the gathering warriors, and Scabandari judged that at least eighteen thousand of his shadow-kin remained. For all that, there would be mourning in the tents of the First Landing this night. The day had begun with over two hundred thousand Tiste Edur marching onto the plain. Still . . . it was enough.

The Edur had clashed with the east flank of the K'Chain Che'Malle army, prefacing their charge with waves of devastating sorcery. The enemy's formations had been assembled to face a frontal assault, and they had proved fatally slow to turn to the threat on their flank. Like a dagger, the Edur legions had driven to the army's heart.

Below, as he drew closer, Scabandari could see, scattered here and there, the midnight banners of the Tiste Andii. A thousand warriors left, perhaps less. Victory was a more dubious claim for these battered allies. They had engaged the K'ell Hunters, the elite bloodkin armies of the three Matrons. Four hundred thousand Tiste Andii, against sixty thousand Hunters. Additional companies of both Andii and Edur had assailed the sky keeps, but these had known they were going to their own deaths, and their sacrifices had been pivotal in this day's victory, for the sky keeps had been prevented from coming to the aid of the armies on the plain below. By themselves, the assaults on the four sky keeps had yielded only marginal effect, despite the Short-Tails being few in number – their ferocity had proved devastating – but sufficient time had been purchased in Tiste blood for Scabandari and his Soletaken draconean ally to close on the floating fortresses, unleashing upon them the warrens of Starvald Demelain, and Kuralds Emurlahn and Galain.

The dragon swept downward to where a jumbled

20

mountain of K'Chain Che'Malle carcasses marked the last stand of one of the Matrons. Kurald Emurlahn had slaughtered the defenders, and wild shadows still flitted about like wraiths on the slopes. Scabandari spread his wings, buffeting the steamy air, then settled atop the reptilian bodies.

A moment later he sembled into his Tiste Edur form. Skin the shade of hammered iron, long grey hair unbound, a gaunt, aquiline face with hard, close-set eyes. A broad, downturned mouth that bore no lines of laughter. High, unlined brow, diagonally scarred livid white against the dusky skin. He wore a leather harness bearing his two-handed sword, a brace of long-knives at his hip, and hanging from his shoulders a scaled cape – the hide of a Matron, fresh enough to still glisten with natural oils.

He stood, a tall figure sheathed in droplets of blood, watching the legions assemble. Edur officers glanced his way, then began directing their troops.

Scabandari faced northwest then, eyes narrowing on the billowing clouds. A moment later a vast bone-white dragon broke through – if anything, larger than Scabandari himself when veered into draconean form. Also sheathed in blood . . . and much of it his own, for Silchas Ruin had fought alongside his Andii kin against the K'ell Hunters.

Scabandari watched his ally approach, stepping back only when the huge dragon settled onto the hilltop and then quickly sembled. A head or more taller than the Tiste Edur Soletaken, yet terribly gaunt, muscles bound like rope beneath smooth, almost translucent skin. Talons from some raptor gleamed in the warrior's thick, long white hair. The red of his eyes seemed feverish, so brightly did it glow. Silchas Ruin bore wounds: sword-slashes across his body. Most of his upper armour had fallen away, revealing the blue-green of his veins and arteries tracking branching paths beneath the thin, hairless skin of his chest. His legs were slick with blood, as were his arms. The twin scabbards at his hips were empty – he had broken both weapons, despite the weavings of sorcery invested in them. His had been a desperate battle.

Scabandari bowed his head in greeting. 'Silchas Ruin, brother in spirit. Most stalwart of allies. Behold the plain – we are victorious.'

The albino Tiste Andii's pallid face twisted in a silent snarl.

'My legions were late in coming to your aid,' Scabandari said. 'And for that, my heart breaks at your losses. Even so, we now hold the gate, do we not? The path to this world belongs to us, and the world itself lies before us ... to plunder, to carve for our people worthy empires.'

Ruin's long-fingered, stained hands twitched, and he faced the plain below. The Edur legions had re-formed into a rough ring around the last surviving Andii. 'Death fouls the air,' Silchas Ruin growled. 'I can barely draw it to speak.'

'There will be time enough for making new plans later,' Scabandari said.

'My people are slaughtered. You now surround us, but your protection is far too late.'

'Symbolic, then, my brother. There are other Tiste Andii on this world – you said so yourself. You must needs only find that first wave, and your strength will return. More, others will come. My kind and yours both, fleeing our defeats.'

Silchas Ruin's scowl deepened. 'This day's victory is a bitter alternative.'

'The K'Chain Che'Malle are all but gone – we know this. We have seen the many other dead cities. Now, only Morn remains, and that on a distant continent – where the Short-Tails even now break their chains in bloody rebellion. A divided enemy is an enemy quick to fall, my friend. Who else in this world has the power to oppose us? Jaghut? They are scattered and few. Imass? What can weapons of stone achieve against our iron?' He was silent a moment, then continued, 'The Forkrul Assail seem

22

unwilling to pass judgement on us. And each year there seem to be fewer and fewer of them in any case. No, my friend, with this day's victory this world lies before our feet. Here, you shall not suffer from the civil wars that plague Kurald Galain. And I and my followers shall escape the rivening that now besets Kurald Emurlahn—'

Silchas Ruin snorted. 'A rivening by your own hand, Scabandari.'

He was still studying the Tiste forces below, and so did not see the flash of rage that answered his offhand remark, a flash that vanished a heartbeat later as Scabandari's expression returned once more to equanimity. 'A new world for us, brother.'

'A Jaghut stands atop a ridge to the north,' Silchas Ruin said. 'Witness to the war. I did not approach, for I sensed the beginning of a ritual. Omtose Phellack.'

'Do you fear that Jaghut, Silchas Ruin?'

'I fear what I do not know, Scabandari ... Bloodeye. And there is much to learn of this realm and its ways.'

'Bloodeye.'

'You cannot see yourself,' Ruin said, 'but I give you this name, for the blood that now stains your ... vision.'

'Rich, Silchas Ruin, coming from you.' Then Scabandari shrugged and walked to the north edge of the heap, stepping carefully on the shifting carcasses. 'A Jaghut, you said ...' He swung about, but Silchas Ruin's back was to him as the Tiste Andii stared down upon his few surviving followers on the plain below.

'Omtose Phellack, the Warren of Ice,' Ruin said without turning. 'What does he conjure, Scabandari Bloodeye? I wonder ...'

The Edur Soletaken walked back towards Silchas Ruin.

He reached down to the outside of his left boot and drew out a shadow-etched dagger. Sorcery played on the iron.

A final step, and the dagger was driven into Ruin's back.

The Tiste Andii spasmed, then roared—

—even as the Edur legions turned suddenly on the

23

Andii, rushing inward from all sides to deliver the day's final slaughter.

Magic wove writhing chains about Silchas Ruin, and the albino Tiste Andii toppled.

Scabandari Bloodeye crouched down over him. 'It is the way of brothers, alas,' he murmured. 'One must rule. Two cannot. You know the truth of that. Big as this world is, Silchas Ruin, sooner or later there would be war between the Edur and the Andii. The truth of our blood will tell. Thus, only one shall command the gate. Only the Edur shall pass. We will hunt down the Andii who are already here – what champion can they throw up to challenge me? They are as good as dead. And so it must be. One people. One ruler.' He straightened, as the last cries of the dying Andii warriors echoed from the plain below. 'Aye, I cannot kill you outright – you are too powerful for that. Thus, I will take you to a suitable place, and leave you to the roots, earth and stone of its mangled grounds . . .'

He veered into his draconean form. An enormous taloned foot closed about the motionless Silchas Ruin, and Scabandari Bloodeye rose into the sky, wings thundering.

The tower was less than a hundred leagues to the south, only its low battered wall enclosing the yard revealing that it was not of Jaghut construction, that it had arisen beside the three Jaghut towers of its own accord, in answer to a law unfathomable to god and mortal alike. Arisen . . . to await the coming of those whom it would imprison for eternity. Creatures of deadly power.

Such as the Soletaken Tiste Andii, Silchas Ruin, third and last of Mother Dark's three children.

Removing from Scabandari Bloodeye's path his last worthy opponent among the Tiste.

Mother Dark's three children.

Three names . . .

Andarist, who long ago surrendered his power in answer to a grief that could never heal. All unknowing that the hand that delivered that grief was mine . . .

24

Anomandaris Irake, who broke with his mother and with his kind. Who then vanished before I could deal with him. Vanished, probably never to be seen again.

And now Silchas Ruin, who in a very short time will know the eternal prison of the Azath.

Scabandari Bloodeye was pleased. For his people. For himself. This world he would conquer. Only the first Andii settlers could pose any challenge to his claim.

A champion of the Tiste Andii in this realm? I can think of no-one . . . no-one with the power to stand before me . . .

It did not occur to Scabandari Bloodeye to wonder where, of the three sons of Mother Dark, the one who had vanished might have gone.

But even that was not his greatest mistake . . .

On a glacial berm to the north, the lone Jaghut began weaving the sorcery of Omtose Phellack. He had witnessed the devastation wrought by the two Soletaken Eleint and their attendant armies. Little sympathy was spared for the K'Chain Che'Malle. They were dying out anyway, for myriad reasons, none of which concerned the Jaghut overmuch. Nor did the intruders worry him. He had long since lost his capacity for worry. Along with fear. And, it must be admitted, wonder.

He felt the betrayal when it came, the distant bloom of magic and the spilling of ascendant blood. And the two dragons were now one.

Typical.

And then, a short while later, in the time when he rested between weavings of his ritual, he sensed someone approaching him from behind. An Elder god, come in answer to the violent rift torn between the realms. As expected. Still . . . which god? K'rul? Draconus? The Sister of Cold Nights? Osserc? Kilmandaros? Sechul Lath? Despite his studied indifference, curiosity finally forced him to turn to look upon the newcomer.

Ah, unexpected . . . but interesting.

Mael, Elder Lord of the Seas, was wide and squat, with deep blue skin that faded to pale gold at throat and bared belly. Lank blond hair hung unbound from his broad, almost flat pate. And in Mael's amber eyes, sizzling rage.

'Gothos,' Mael rasped, 'what ritual do you invoke in answer to this?'

The Jaghut scowled. 'They've made a mess. I mean to cleanse it.'

'Ice,' the Elder god snorted. 'The Jaghut answer to everything.'

'And what would yours be, Mael? Flood, or . . . flood?'

The Elder god faced south, the muscles of his jaw bunching. 'I am to have an ally. Kilmandaros. She comes from the other side of the rent.'

'Only one Tiste Soletaken is left,' Gothos said. 'Seems he struck down his companion, and even now delivers him into the keeping of the Azath Tower's crowded yard.'

'Premature. Does he think the K'Chain Che'Malle his only opposition in this realm?'

The Jaghut shrugged. 'Probably.'

Mael was silent for a time, then he sighed and said, 'With your ice, Gothos, do not destroy all of this. Instead, I ask that you . . . *preserve*.'

'Why?'

'I have my reasons.'

'I am pleased for you. What are they?'

The Elder god shot him a dark look. 'Impudent bastard.'

'Why change?'

'In the seas, Jaghut, time is unveiled. In the depths ride currents of vast antiquity. In the shallows whisper the future. The tides flow between them in ceaseless exchange. Such is my realm. Such is my knowledge. Seal this devastation in your damned ice, Gothos. In this place, freeze time itself. Do this, and I will accept an indebtedness to you . . . which one day you might find useful.'

Gothos considered the Elder god's words, then nodded. 'I might at that. Very well, Mael. Go to Kilmandaros. Swat down this Tiste Eleint and scatter his people. But do it quickly.'

Mael's eyes narrowed. 'Why?'

'Because I sense a distant awakening – but not, alas, as distant as you would like.'

'Anomander Rake.'

Gothos nodded.

Mael shrugged. 'Anticipated. Osserc moves to stand in his path.'

The Jaghut's smile revealed his massive tusks. 'Again?'

The Elder god could not help but grin in answer.

And though they smiled, there was little humour on that glacial berm.

* * *

1159th Year of Burn's Sleep
Year of the White Veins in the Ebony
Three years before the Letherii Seventh Closure

He awoke with a bellyful of salt, naked and half buried in white sand amidst the storm's detritus. Seagulls cried overhead, their shadows wheeling across the rippled beach. Cramps spasming his gut, he groaned and slowly rolled over.

There were more bodies on the beach, he saw. And wreckage. Chunks and rafts of fast-melting ice rustled in the shallows. Crabs scuttled in their thousands.

The huge man lifted himself to his hands and knees. And then vomited bitter fluids onto the sands. Pounding throbs racked his head, fierce enough to leave him half blind, and it was some time before he finally rocked back to sit up and glare once more at the scene around him.

A shore where no shore belonged.

And the night before, mountains of ice rising up from the depths, one – the largest of them all – reaching the surface directly beneath the vast floating Meckros city.

27

Breaking it apart as if it were a raft of sticks. Meckros histories recounted nothing remotely like the devastation he had seen wrought. Sudden and virtually absolute annihilation of a city that was home to twenty thousand. Disbelief still tormented him, as if his own memories held impossible images, the conjuring of a fevered brain.

But he knew he had imagined nothing. He had but witnessed.

And, somehow, survived.

The sun was warm, but not hot. The sky overhead was milky white rather than blue. And the seagulls, he now saw, were something else entirely. Reptilian, pale-winged.

He staggered to his feet. The headache was fading, but shivers now swept through him, and his thirst was a raging demon trying to claw up his throat.

The cries of the flying lizards changed pitch and he swung to face inland.

Three creatures had appeared, clambering through the pallid tufts of grass above the tideline. No higher than his hip, black-skinned, hairless, perfectly round heads and pointed ears. Bhoka'ral – he recalled them from his youth, when a Meckros trading ship had returned from Nemil – but these seemed to be muscle-bound versions, at least twice as heavy as the pets the merchants had brought back to the floating city. They made directly for him.

He looked round for something to use as a weapon, and found a piece of driftwood that would serve as a club. Hefting it, he waited as the bhoka'ral drew closer.

They halted, yellow-shot eyes staring up at him.

Then the middle one gestured.

Come. There was no doubting the meaning of that all-too-human beckoning.

The man scanned the strand again – none of the bodies he could see were moving, and the crabs were feeding unopposed. He stared up once more at the strange sky, then stepped towards the three creatures.

They backed away and led him up to the grassy verge.

Those grasses were like nothing he had ever seen before, long tubular triangles, razor-edged – as he discovered once he passed through them when he found his low legs crisscrossed with cuts. Beyond, a level plain stretched inland, bearing only the occasional tuft of the same grass. The ground in between was salt-crusted and barren. A few chunks of stone dotted the plain, no two alike and all oddly angular, unweathered.

In the distance stood a lone tent.

The bhoka'ral guided him towards it.

As they drew near, he saw threads of smoke drifting out from the peak and the slitted flap that marked the doorway.

His escort halted and another wave directed him to the entrance. Shrugging, he crouched and crawled inside.

In the dim light sat a shrouded figure, a hood disguising its features. A brazier was before it, from which heady fumes drifted. Beside the entrance stood a crystal bottle, some dried fruit and a loaf of dark bread.

'The bottle holds spring water,' the figure rasped in the Meckros tongue. 'Please, take time to recover from your ordeal.'

He grunted his thanks and quickly took the bottle.

Thirst blissfully slaked, he reached for the bread. 'I thank you, stranger,' he rumbled, then shook his head. 'That smoke makes you swim before my eyes.'

A hacking cough that might have been laughter, then something resembling a shrug. 'Better than drowning. Alas, it eases my pain. I shall not keep you long. You are Withal, the Swordmaker.'

The man started, and his broad brow knotted. 'Aye, I am Withal, of the Third Meckros city – which is now no more.'

'A tragic event. You are the lone survivor . . . through my own efforts, though it much strained my powers to intervene.'

'What place is this?'

'Nowhere, in the heart of nowhere. A fragment, prone to wander. I give it what life I can imagine, conjured from memories of my home. My strength returns, although the agony of my broken body does not abate. Yet listen, I have talked and not coughed. That is something.' A mangled hand appeared from a ragged sleeve and scattered seeds onto the brazier's coals. They spat and popped and the smoke thickened.

'Who are you?' Withal demanded.

'A fallen god . . . who has need of your skills. I have prepared for your coming, Withal. A place of dwelling, a forge, all the raw materials you will need. Clothes, food, water. And three devoted servants, whom you have already met—'

'The bhoka'ral?' Withal snorted. 'What can—'

'Not bhoka'ral, mortal. Although perhaps they once were. These are Nachts. I have named them Rind, Mape and Pule. They are of Jaghut fashioning, capable of learning all that you require of them.'

Withal made to rise. 'I thank you for the salvation, Fallen One, but I shall take my leave of you. I would return to my own world—'

'You do not understand, Withal,' the figure hissed. 'You will do as I say here, or you will find yourself begging for death. I now own you, Swordmaker. You are my slave and I am your master. The Meckros own slaves, yes? Hapless souls stolen from island villages and such on your raids. The notion is therefore familiar to you. Do not despair, however, for once you have completed what I ask of you, you shall be free to leave.'

Withal still held the club, the heavy wood cradled on his lap. He considered.

A cough, then laughter, then more coughing, during which the god raised a staying hand. When the hacking was done, he said, 'I advise you to attempt nothing untoward, Withal. I have plucked you from the seas for this purpose. Have you lost all honour? Oblige me in this, for you would deeply regret my wrath.'

'What would you have me do?'

'Better. What would I have you do, Withal? Why, only what you do best. Make me a sword.'

Withal grunted. 'That is all?'

The figure leaned forward. 'Ah well, what I have in mind is a very particular sword . . .'

BOOK ONE

FROZEN BLOOD

There is a spear of ice, newly thrust into the heart of the land. The soul within it yearns to kill. He who grasps that spear will know death. Again and again, he shall know death.

Hannan Mosag's Vision

CHAPTER ONE

Listen! The seas whisper
and dream of breaking truths
in the crumbling of stone

Hantallit of Miner Sluice

Year of the Late Frost
One year before the Letherii Seventh Closure
The Ascension of the Empty Hold

H*ere, then, is the tale. Between the swish of the tides,
when giants knelt down and became mountains. When
they fell scattered on the land like the ballast stones of
the sky, yet could not hold fast against the rising dawn. Between
the swish of the tides, we will speak of one such giant.
Because the tale hides with his own.*

And because it amuses.

Thus.

In darkness he closed his eyes. Only by day did he elect
to open them, for he reasoned in this manner: night defies
vision and so, if little can be seen, what value seeking to
pierce the gloom?

Witness as well, this. He came to the edge of the land
and discovered the sea, and was fascinated by the mysterious fluid. A fascination that became a singular obsession
through the course of that fated day. He could see how the

35

waves moved, up and down along the entire shore, a ceaseless motion that ever threatened to engulf all the land, yet ever failed to do so. He watched the sea through the afternoon's high winds, witness to its wild thrashing far up along the sloping strand, and sometimes it did indeed reach far, but always it would sullenly retreat once more.

When night arrived, he closed his eyes and lay down to sleep. Tomorrow, he decided, he would look once more upon this sea.

In darkness he closed his eyes.

The tides came with the night, swirling up round the giant. The tides came and drowned him as he slept. And the water seeped minerals into his flesh, until he became as rock, a gnarled ridge on the strand. Then, each night for thousands of years, the tides came to wear away at his form. Stealing his shape.

But not entirely. To see him true, even to this day, one must look in darkness. Or close one's eyes to slits in brightest sunlight. Glance askance, or focus on all but the stone itself.

Of all the gifts Father Shadow has given his children, this one talent stands tallest. Look away to see. Trust in it, and you will be led into Shadow. Where all truths hide.

Look away to see.

Now, look away.

The mice scattered as the deeper shadow flowed across snow brushed blue by dusk. They scampered in wild panic, but, among them, one's fate was already sealed. A lone tufted, taloned foot snapped down, piercing furry flesh and crushing minute bones.

At the clearing's edge, the owl had dropped silently from its branch, sailing out over the hard-packed snow and its litter of seeds, and the arc of its flight, momentarily punctuated by plucking the mouse from the ground, rose up once more, this time in a heavy flapping of wings, towards a nearby tree. It landed one-legged, and a moment later it began to feed.

The figure who jogged across the glade a dozen heartbeats later saw nothing untoward. The mice were all gone, the snow solid enough to leave no signs of their passing, and the owl froze motionless in its hollow amidst the branches of the spruce tree, eyes wide as they followed the figure's progress across the clearing. Once it had passed, the owl resumed feeding.

Dusk belonged to the hunters, and the raptor was not yet done this night.

As he weaved through the frost-rimed humus of the trail, Trull Sengar's thoughts were distant, making him heedless of the forest surrounding him, uncharacteristically distracted from all the signs and details it offered. He had not even paused to make propitiation to Sheltatha Lore, Daughter Dusk, the most cherished of the Three Daughters of Father Shadow – although he would make recompense at tomorrow's sunset – and, earlier, he had moved unmindful through the patches of lingering light that blotted the trail, risking the attention of fickle Sukul Ankhadu, the Daughter of Deceit, also known as Dapple.

The Calach breeding beds swarmed with seals. They'd come early, surprising Trull in his collecting of raw jade above the shoreline. Alone, the arrival of the seals would engender only excitement in the young Tiste Edur, but there had been other arrivals, in ships ringing the bay, and the harvest had been well under way.

Letherii, the white-skinned peoples from the south.

He could imagine the anger of those in the village he now approached, once he delivered the news of his discovery – an anger he shared. This encroachment on Edur territories was brazen, the theft of seals that rightly belonged to his people an arrogant defiance of the old agreements.

There were fools among the Letherii, just as there were fools among the Edur. Trull could not imagine this broaching being anything but unsanctioned. The Great Meeting was only two cycles of the moon away. It served neither side's purpose to spill blood now. No matter that the Edur would be right in attacking and destroying the intruder ships; the Letherii delegation would be outraged at the slaughter of its citizens, even citizens contravening the laws. The chances of agreeing upon a new treaty had just become minuscule.

And this disturbed Trull Sengar. One long and vicious war had just ended for the Edur: the thought of another beginning was too hard to bear.

He had not embarrassed his brothers during the wars of subjugation; on his wide belt was a row of twenty-one red-stained rivets, each one marking a coup, and among those seven were ringed in white paint, to signify actual kills. Only his elder brother's belt sported more trophies among the male children of Tomad Sengar, and that was right and proper, given Fear Sengar's eminence among the warriors of the Hiroth tribe.

Of course, battles against the five other tribes of the Edur were strictly bound in rules and prohibitions, and even vast, protracted battles had yielded only a handful of actual deaths. Even so, the conquests had been exhausting. Against the Letherii, there were no rules to constrain the Edur warriors. No counting coup. Just killing. Nor did the enemy need a weapon in hand – even the helpless and the innocent would know the sword's bite. Such slaughter stained warrior and victim alike.

But Trull well knew that, though he might decry the killing that was to come, he would do so only to himself, and he would stride alongside his brothers, sword in hand, to deliver the Edur judgement upon the trespassers. There was no choice. Turn away from this crime and more would follow, in waves unending.

His steady jog brought him past the tanneries, with their troughs and stone-lined pits, to the forest edge. A few Letherii slaves glanced his way, quickly bowing in deference until he was past. The towering cedar logs of the village wall rose from the clearing ahead, over which woodsmoke hung in stretched streams. Fields of rich black soil spread out to either side of the narrow, raised track leading to the distant gate. Winter had only just begun to release its grip on the earth, and the first planting of the season was still weeks away. By midsummer, close to thirty different types of plants would fill these fields, providing food, medicine, fibres and feed for the livestock, many among the thirty of a flowering variety, drawing the bees from which honey and wax were procured. The tribe's women oversaw the slaves in such harvesting. The men would leave in small groups to journey into the forest, to cut timber or hunt, whilst others set out in the Knarri ships to harvest from the seas and shoals.

Or so it should be, when peace ruled the tribes. The past dozen years had seen more war-parties setting out than any other kind, and so the people had on occasion suffered. Until the war, hunger had never threatened the Edur. Trull wanted an end to such depredations. Hannan Mosag, Warlock King of the Hiroth, was now overlord to all the Edur tribes. From a host of warring peoples, a confederacy had been wrought, although Trull well knew that it was a confederacy in name only. Hannan Mosag held as hostage the firstborn sons of the subjugated chiefs – his K'risnan Cadre – and ruled as dictator. Peace, then, at the point of a sword, but peace none the less.

A recognizable figure was striding from the palisade gate, approaching the fork in the trail where Trull now halted. 'I greet you, Binadas,' he said.

A spear was strapped to his younger brother's back, a hide pack slung round one shoulder and resting against a hip; at the opposite side a single-edged longsword in a leather-wrapped wooden scabbard. Binadas was half a head taller than Trull, his visage as weathered as his buckskin clothes. Of Trull's three brothers, Binadas was the most remote, evasive and thus difficult to predict, much less

39

understand. He resided in the village only infrequently, seeming to prefer the wilds of the western forest and the mountains to the south. He had rarely joined others in raids, yet often when he returned he carried trophies of coup, and so none doubted his bravery.

'You are winded, Trull,' Binadas observed, 'and I see distress once more upon your face.'

'There are Letherii moored off the Calach beds.'

Binadas frowned. 'I shall not delay you, then.'

'Will you be gone long, brother?'

The man shrugged, then stepped past Trull, taking the westerly fork of the trail.

Trull Sengar moved on, through the gate and into the village.

Four smithies dominated this inland end of the vast walled interior, each surrounded by a deep sloping trench that drained into a buried channel that led away from the village and the surrounding fields. For what seemed years the forges had rung almost ceaselessly with the fashioning of weapons, and the stench of heavy, acrid fumes had filled the air, rising up to coat nearby trees in white-crusted soot. Now, as he passed, Trull saw that only two were occupied, and the dozen or so visible slaves were unhurried in their work.

Beyond the smithies ran the elongated, brick-lined storage chambers, a row of segmented beehive-shaped buildings that held surplus grains, smoked fish and seal meat, whale oil and harvested fibre plants. Similar structures existed in the deep forest surrounding each village – most of which were empty at the moment, a consequence of the wars.

The stone houses of the weavers, potters, carvers, lesser scribes, armourers and other assorted skilled citizens of the village rose round Trull once he was past the storage chambers. Voices called out in greeting, to which he made the minimal response that decorum allowed, such gestures signifying to his acquaintances that he could not pause for conversation.

The Edur warrior now hurried through the residential streets. Letherii slaves called villages such as this one *cities*, but no citizen saw the need for changing their word usage – a village it had been at birth, thus a village it would always be, no matter that almost twenty thousand Edur and thrice that number of Letherii now resided within it.

Shrines to the Father and his Favoured Daughter dominated the residential area, raised platforms ringed by living trees of the sacred Blackwood, the surface of the stone discs crowded with images and glyphs. Kurald Emurlahn played ceaselessly within the tree-ringed circle, rippling half-shapes dancing along the pictographs, the sorcerous emanations awakened by the propitiations that had accompanied the arrival of dusk.

Trull Sengar emerged onto the Avenue of the Warlock, the sacred approach to the massive citadel that was both temple and palace, and the seat of the Warlock King, Hannan Mosag. Black-barked cedars lined the approach. The trees were a thousand years old, towering over the entire village. They were devoid of branches except for the uppermost reaches. Invested sorcery suffused every ring of their midnight wood, bleeding out to fill the entire avenue with a shroud of gloom.

At the far end, a lesser palisade enclosed the citadel and its grounds, constructed of the same black wood, these boles crowded with carved wards. The main gate was a tunnel formed of living trees, a passage of unrelieved shadow leading to a footbridge spanning a canal in which sat a dozen K'orthan raider longboats. The footbridge opened out onto a broad flagstoned compound flanked by barracks and storehouses. Beyond stood the stone and timber longhouses of the noble families – those with blood-ties to Hannan Mosag's own line – with their wood-shingled roofs and Blackwood ridgepoles, the array of residences neatly bisected by a resumption of the Avenue, across yet another footbridge to the citadel proper.

There were warriors training in the compound, and Trull

41

saw the tall, broad-shouldered figure of his elder brother, Fear, standing with a half-dozen of his assistants nearby, watching the weapons practice. A pang of sympathy for those young warriors flickered through Trull. He himself had suffered beneath his brother's critical, unrelenting eye during the years of his own schooling.

A voice hailed him and Trull glanced over to the other side of the compound, to see his youngest brother, Rhulad, and Midik Buhn. They had been doing their own sparring, it seemed, and a moment later Trull saw the source of their uncharacteristic diligence – Mayen, Fear's betrothed, had appeared with four younger women in tow, probably on their way to the market, given the dozen slaves accompanying them. That they had stopped to watch the sudden, no doubt impromptu martial demonstration was of course obligatory, given the complex rules of courtship. Mayen was expected to treat all of Fear's brothers with appropriate respect.

Although there was nothing untoward in the scene Trull looked upon, he nevertheless felt a tremor of unease. Rhulad's eagerness to strut before the woman who would be his eldest brother's wife had crept to the very edge of proper conduct. Fear was, in Trull's opinion, displaying far too much indulgence when it came to Rhulad.

As have we all. Of course, there were reasons for that.

Rhulad had clearly bested his childhood companion in the mock contest, given the flushed pride in his handsome face. 'Trull!' He waved his sword. 'I have drawn blood once this day, and now thirst for more! Come, scrape the rust off that sword at your side!'

'Some other time, brother,' Trull called back. 'I must speak with our father without delay.'

Rhulad's grin was amiable enough, but even from ten paces away Trull saw the flash of triumph in his clear grey eyes. 'Another time, then,' he said, with a final dismissive wave of his sword as he turned back to face the women.

But Mayen had gestured to her companions and the party was already moving off.

Rhulad opened his mouth to say something to her, but Trull spoke first. 'Brother, I invite you to join me. The news I must give our father is of grave import, and I would that you are present, so that your words are woven into the discussion that will follow.' An invitation that was normally made only to those warriors with years of battle on their belts, and Trull saw the sudden pride lighting his brother's eyes.

'I am honoured, Trull,' he said, sheathing his sword.

Leaving Midik standing alone and tending to a sword-cut on his wrist, Rhulad joined Trull and they strode to the family longhouse.

Trophy shields cluttered the outside walls, many of them sun-faded by the centuries. Whale bones clung to the underside of the roof's overhang. Totems stolen from rival tribes formed a chaotic arch over the doorway, the strips of fur, beaded hide, shells, talons and teeth looking like an elongated bird's nest.

They passed within.

The air was cool, slightly acrid with woodsmoke. Oil lamps sat in niches along the walls, between tapestries and stretched furs. The traditional hearthstone in the centre of the chamber, where each family had once prepared its meals, remained stoked with tinder, although the slaves now worked in kitchens behind the longhouse proper, to reduce the risk of fires. Blackwood furniture marked out the various rooms, although no dividing walls were present. Hung from hooks on the crossbeams were scores of weapons, some from the earliest days, when the art of forging iron had been lost in the dark times immediately following Father Shadow's disappearance, the rough bronze of these weapons pitted and warped.

Just beyond the hearthstone rose the bole of a living Blackwood, from which the gleaming upper third of a longsword thrust upward and outward at just above head height: a true Emurlahn blade, the iron treated in some manner the smiths had yet to rediscover. The sword of the

Sengar family, signifier of their noble bloodline; normally, these original weapons of the noble families, bound against the tree when it was but a sapling, were, after centuries, gone from sight, lying as they did along the heartwood. But some twist in this particular tree had pried the weapon away, thus revealing that black and silver blade. Uncommon, but not unique.

Both brothers reached out and touched the iron as they passed.

They saw their mother, Uruth, flanked by slaves as she worked on the bloodline's tapestry, finishing the final scenes of the Sengar participation in the War of Unification. Intent on her work, she did not look up as her sons strode past.

Tomad Sengar sat with three other noble-born patriarchs around a game board fashioned from a huge palmate antler, the playing pieces carved from ivory and jade.

Trull halted at the edge of the circle. He settled his right hand over the pommel of his sword, signifying that the words he brought were both urgent and potentially dangerous. Behind him, he heard Rhulad's quickly indrawn breath.

Although none of the elders looked up, Tomad's guests rose as one, while Tomad himself began putting away the game pieces. The three elders departed in silence, and a moment later Tomad set the game board to one side and settled back on his haunches.

Trull settled down opposite him. 'I greet you, Father. A Letherii fleet is harvesting the Calach beds. The herds have come early, and are now being slaughtered. I witnessed these things with my own eyes, and have not paused in my return.'

Tomad nodded. 'You have run for three days and two nights, then.'

'I have.'

'And the Letherii harvest, it was well along?'

'Father, by dawn this morning, Daughter Menandore will have witnessed the ships' holds filled to bursting, and the

44

sails filling with wind, the wake of every ship a crimson river.'

'And new ships arriving to take their places!' Rhulad hissed.

Tomad frowned at his youngest son's impropriety, and made his disapproval clear with his next words. 'Rhulad, take this news to Hannan Mosag.'

Trull sensed his brother's flinch, but Rhulad nodded. 'As you command, Father.' He pivoted and marched away.

Tomad's frown deepened. 'You invited an unblooded warrior to this exchange?'

'I did, Father.'

'Why?'

Trull said nothing, as was his choice. He was not about to voice his concern over Rhulad's undue attentions towards Fear's betrothed.

After a moment, Tomad sighed. He seemed to be studying his large, scarred hands where they rested on his thighs. 'We have grown complacent,' he rumbled.

'Father, is it complacency to assume the ones with whom we treat are honourable?'

'Yes, given the precedents.'

'Then why has the Warlock King agreed to a Great Meeting with the Letherii?'

Tomad's dark eyes flicked up to pin Trull's own. Of all Tomad's sons, only Fear possessed a perfect, unwavering match to his father's eyes, in hue and indurative regard. Despite himself, Trull felt himself wilt slightly beneath that scornful gaze.

'I withdraw my foolish question,' Trull said, breaking contact to disguise his dismay. *A measuring of enemies. This contravention, no matter its original intent, will become a double-pointed blade, given the inevitable response to it by the Edur. A blade both peoples shall grasp.* 'The unblooded warriors will be pleased.'

'The unblooded warriors shall one day sit in the council, Trull.'

'Is that not the reward of peace, Father?'

Tomad made no reply to that. 'Hannan Mosag shall call the council. You must needs be present to relate what you witnessed. Further, the Warlock King has made a request of me, that I give my sons to him for a singular task. I do not think that decision will be affected by the news you deliver.'

Trull worked through his surprise, then said, 'I passed Binadas on the way into the village—'

'He has been informed, and will return within a moon's time.'

'Does Rhulad know of this?'

'No, although he will accompany you. An unblooded is an unblooded.'

'As you say, Father.'

'Now, rest. You shall be awakened in time for the council.'

A white crow hopped down from a salt-bleached root and began picking through the midden. At first Trull had thought it to be a gull, lingering on the strand in the fast-fading light, but then it cackled and, mussel shell in its pallid beak, sidled down from the midden towards the waterline.

Sleep had proved an impossibility. The council had been called for midnight. Restless, nerves jangling along his exhausted limbs, Trull had walked down to the pebble beach north of the village and the river mouth.

And now, as darkness rolled in with the sleepy waves, he had found himself sharing the strand with a white crow. It had carried its prize down to the very edge, and with each whispering approach, the bird dipped the mussel shell into the water. Six times.

A fastidious creature, Trull observed, watching as the crow hopped onto a nearby rock and began picking at the shell.

White was evil, of course. Common enough knowledge. The blush of bone, Menandore's hateful light at dawn. The

46

sails of the Letherii were white, as well, which was not surprising. And the clear waters of Calach Bay would reveal the glimmer of white cluttering the sea bottom, from the bones of thousands of slaughtered seals.

This season would have marked a return to surplus for the six tribes, beginning the replenishment of depleted reserves to guard against famine. Thoughts that led him to another way of seeing this illegal harvesting. A perfectly timed gesture to weaken the confederacy, a ploy intended to undermine the Edur position at the Great Meeting. *The argument of inevitability. The same argument first thrown into our faces with the settlements on the Reach. 'The kingdom of Lether is expanding, its needs growing. Your camps on the Reach were seasonal, after all, and with the war they had been all but abandoned.'*

It was inevitable that more and more independent ships would come to ply the rich waters of the north coast. One could not police them all. The Edur need only look at other tribes that had once dwelt beyond the Letherii borderlands, the vast rewards that came with swearing fealty to King Ezgara Diskanar of Lether.

But we are not as other tribes.

The crow cackled from atop its stone throne, flinging the mussel shell away with a toss of its head, then, spreading its ghostly wings, rose up into the night. A final drawn out cawl from the darkness. Trull made a warding gesture.

Stones turned underfoot behind him and he swung about to see his elder brother approaching.

'I greet you, Trull,' Fear said in a quiet voice. 'The words you delivered have roused the warriors.'

'And the Warlock King?'

'Has said nothing.'

Trull returned to his study of the dark waves hissing on the strand. 'Their eyes are fixed upon those ships,' he said.

'Hannan Mosag knows to look away, brother.'

'He has asked for the sons of Tomad Sengar. What do you know of that?'

47

Fear was at his side now, and Trull sensed his shrug. 'Visions have guided the Warlock King since he was a child,' Fear said after a moment. 'He carries blood memories all the way back to the Dark Times. Father Shadow stretches before him with every stride he takes.'

The notion of visions made Trull uneasy. He did not doubt their power – in fact, the very opposite. The Dark Times had come with the rivening of Tiste Edur, the assault of sorceries and strange armies and the disappearance of Father Shadow himself. And, although the magic of Kurald Emurlahn was not denied to the tribes, the warren was lost to them: shattered, the fragments ruled by false kings and gods. Trull suspected that Hannan Mosag possessed an ambition far vaster than simply unifying the six tribes.

'There is reluctance in you, Trull. You hide it well enough, but I can see where others cannot. You are a warrior who would rather not fight.'

'That is not a crime,' Trull muttered, then he added: 'Of all the Sengar, only you and Father carry more trophies.'

'I was not questioning your bravery, brother. But courage is the least of that which binds us. We are Edur. We were masters of the Hounds, once. We held the throne of Kurald Emurlahn. And would hold it still, if not for betrayal, first by the kin of Scabandari Bloodeye, then by the Tiste Andii who came with us to this world. We are a beset people, Trull. The Letherii are but one enemy among many. The Warlock King understands this.'

Trull studied the glimmer of starlight on the placid surface of the bay. 'I will not hesitate in fighting those who would be our enemies, Fear.'

'That is good, brother. It is enough to keep Rhulad silent, then.'

Trull stiffened. 'He speaks against me? That unblooded . . . *pup*?'

'Where he sees weakness . . .'

'What he sees and what is true are different things,' Trull said.

'Then show him otherwise,' Fear said in his low, calm voice.

Trull was silent. He had been openly dismissive of Rhulad and his endless challenges and postures, as was his right given that Rhulad was unblooded. But more significantly, Trull's reasons were raised like a protective wall around the maiden that Fear was to wed. Of course, to voice such things now would be unseemly, whispering as they would of spite and malice. After all, Mayen was Fear's betrothed, not Trull's, and her protection was Fear's responsibility.

Things would be simpler, he ruefully reflected, if he had a sense of Mayen herself. She did not invite Rhulad's attention, but nor did she turn a shoulder to it. She walked the cliff-edge of propriety, as self-assured as any maiden would – and should – be when privileged to become the wife of the Hiroth's Weapons Master. It was not, he told himself once again, any of his business. 'I will not show Rhulad what he should already see,' Trull growled. 'He has done nothing to warrant the gift of my regard.'

'Rhulad lacks the subtlety to see your reluctance as anything but weakness—'

'His failing, not mine!'

'Do you expect a blind elder to cross a stream's stepping stones unaided, Trull? No, you guide him until in his mind's eye he finally sees that which everyone else can see.'

'If everyone else can see,' Trull replied, 'then Rhulad's words against me are powerless, and so I am right to ignore them.'

'Brother, Rhulad is not alone in lacking subtlety.'

'Is it your wish, Fear, that there be enemies among the sons of Tomad Sengar?'

'Rhulad is not an enemy, not of you nor of any other Edur. He is young and eager for blood. You once walked his path, so I ask that you remember yourself back then. This is not the time to deliver wounds sure to scar. And, to an unblooded warrior, disdain delivers the deepest wound of all.'

49

Trull grimaced. 'I see the truth of that, Fear. I shall endeavour to curtail my indifference.'

His brother did not react to the sarcasm. 'The council is gathering in the citadel, brother. Will you enter the King's Hall at my side?'

Trull relented. 'I am honoured, Fear.'

They turned away from the black water, and so did not see the pale-winged shape gliding over the lazy waves a short distance offshore.

Thirteen years ago Udinaas had been a young sailor in the third year of his family's indenture to the merchant Intaros of Trate, the northernmost city of Lether. He was aboard the whaler *Brunt* and on the return run from Beneda waters. They had slipped in under cover of darkness, killing three sows, and were towing the carcasses into the neutral Troughs west of Calach Bay when five K'orthan ships of the Hiroth were sighted in hard pursuit.

The captain's greed had spelled their doom, as he would not abandon the kills.

Udinaas well remembered the faces of the whaler's officers, the captain included, as they were bound to one of the sows to be left to the sharks and dhenrabi, whilst the common sailors were taken off the ship, along with every piece of iron and every other item that caught the Edur's fancy. Shadow wraiths were then loosed on the *Brunt*, to devour and tear apart the dead wood of the Letherii ship. Towing the other two sows, the five Blackwood K'orthan ships then departed, leaving the third whale to the slayers of the deep.

Even back then, Udinaas had been indifferent to the grisly fate of the captain and his officers. He had been born into debt, as had his father and his father before him. Indenture and slavery were two words for the same thing. Nor was life as a slave among the Hiroth particularly harsh. Obedience was rewarded with protection, clothing and a dwelling sheltered from the rain and snow, and, until recently, plenty of food.

50

Among Udinaas's many tasks within the household of the Sengar was the repair of nets for the four Knarri fisherboats owned by the noble family. Because he had been a sailor, he was not permitted to leave land, and knotting the nets and affixing weight-stones down on the strand south of the river mouth was as close as he ever came to the open waters of the sea. Not that he had any desire to escape the Edur. There were plenty of slaves in the village – all Letherii, of course – so he did not miss the company of his own kind, miserable as it often was. Nor were the comforts of Lether sufficient lure to attempt what was virtually impossible anyway – he had memory of seeing such comforts, but never of partaking in them. And finally, Udinaas hated the sea with a passion, just as he had done when he was a sailor.

In the failing light he had seen the two eldest sons of Tomad Sengar on the beach on the other side of the river mouth, and was not surprised to hear the faint, indistinguishable words they exchanged. Letherii ships had struck again – the news had raced among the slaves before young Rhulad had even reached the entrance of the citadel. A council had been called, which was to be expected, and Udinaas assumed that there would be slaughter before too long, that deadly, terrifying merging of iron-edged ferocity and sorcery that marked every clash with the Letherii of the south. And, truth be told, Udinaas wished them good hunting. Seals taken by the Letherii threatened famine among the Edur, and in famine it was the slaves who were the first to suffer.

Udinaas well understood his own kind. To the Letherii, gold was all that mattered. Gold and its possession defined their entire world. Power, status, self-worth and respect – all were commodities that could be purchased by coin. Indeed, debt bound the entire kingdom, defining every relationship, the motivation casting the shadow of every act, every decision. This devious hunting of the seals was the opening move in a ploy the Letherii had used

51

countless times, against every tribe beyond the borderlands. To the Letherii, the Edur were no different. *But they are, you fools.*

Even so, the next move would come at the Great Meeting, and Udinaas suspected that the Warlock King and his advisers, clever as they were, would walk into that treaty like blind elders. What worried him was all that would follow.

Like hatchlings borne on the tide, the peoples of two kingdoms were rushing headlong into deep, deadly waters.

Three slaves from the Buhn household trotted past, bundles of bound seaweed on their shoulders. One called out to Udinaas, 'Feather Witch will cast tonight, Udinaas! Even as the council gathers.'

Udinaas began folding the net over the drying rack. 'I will be there, Hulad.'

The three left the strand, and Udinaas was alone once more. He glanced north and saw Fear and Trull walking up the slope towards the outer wall's postern gate.

Finished with the net, he placed his tools in the small basket and fastened the lid, then straightened.

He heard the flap of wings behind him and turned, startled by the sound of a bird in flight so long after the sun had set. A pale shape skimmed the waterline, and was gone.

Udinaas blinked, straining to see it again, telling himself that it was not what it had appeared to be. Not that. Anything but that. He moved to his left to a bare patch of sand. Crouching, he quickly sketched an invoking sigil into the sand with the small finger of his left hand, lifting his right hand to his face, first two fingers reaching to his eyes to pull the lids down for a brief moment, as he whispered a prayer, 'Knuckles cast, Saviour look down upon me this night. Errant! Look down upon us all!'

He lowered his right hand and dropped his gaze to the symbol he had drawn.

'Crow, begone!'

The sigh of wind, the murmur of waves. Then a distant cackle.

Shivering, Udinaas bolted upright. Snatching up the basket, he ran for the gate.

The King's Meet was a vast, circular chamber, the Blackwood boles of the ceiling reaching up to a central peak lost in smoke. Unblooded warriors of noble birth stood at the very edge, the outermost ring of those attending to witness the council. Next, and seated on backed benches, were the matrons, the wedded and widowed women. Then came the unwedded and the betrothed, cross-legged on hides. A pace before them, the floor dropped an arm's length to form a central pit of packed earth where sat the warriors. At the very centre was a raised dais, fifteen paces across, where stood the Warlock King, Hannan Mosag, with the five hostage princes seated around him, facing outward.

As Trull and Fear descended to the pit to take their place among the blooded warriors, Trull stared up at his king. Of average height and build, Hannan Mosag seemed un-prepossessing at first glance. His features were even, a shade paler than most Edur, and there was a wide cast to his eyes that gave him a perpetually surprised look. The power, then, was not physical. It lay entirely in his voice. Rich and deep, it was a voice that demanded to be listened to without regard to volume.

Standing in silence, as he did now, Hannan Mosag's claim to kingship seemed a mere accident of placement, as if he had wandered into the centre of the huge chamber, and now looked about with a vaguely bemused expression. His clothing was no different from that of any other warriors, barring the absence of trophies – for his trophies, after all, were seated around him on the dais, the first sons of the five subjugated chiefs.

A more concerted study of the Warlock King revealed another indication of his power. His shadow reared behind him. Huge, hulking. Long, indistinct but deadly swords gripped in both gauntleted hands. Helmed, the shoulders angular with plates of armour. Hannan Mosag's shadow wraith bodyguard never slept. There was, Trull reflected, nothing bemused in its wide stance.

Few warlocks were capable of conjuring such a creature when drawing from the life-force of their own shadows. Kurald Emurlahn flowed raw and brutal in that silent, ever-vigilant sentinel.

Trull's gaze fell to those of the hostages facing him. The K'risnan. More than representatives of their fathers, they were Hannan Mosag's apprentices in sorcery. Their names had been stripped from them, the new ones chosen in secret by their master and bound with spells. One day, they would return to their tribes as chiefs. And their loyalty to their king would be absolute.

The hostage from the Merude tribe was directly opposite Trull. Largest of the six tribes, the Merude had been the last to capitulate. They had always maintained that, with their numbers approaching one hundred thousand, forty thousand of which were blooded or soon-to-be-blooded warriors, they should by right have held pre-eminence among the Edur. More warriors, more ships, and ruled by a chief with more trophies at his belt than had been seen in generations. Domination belonged to the Merude.

Or it should have, if not for Hannan Mosag's extraordinary mastery of those fragments of Kurald Emurlahn from which power could be drawn. Chief Hanradi Khalag's skill with the spear far outweighed his capacity as a warlock.

No-one but Hannan Mosag and Hanradi Khalag knew the details of that final surrendering. Merude had been holding strong against the Hiroth and their contingents of Arapay, Sollanta, Den-Ratha and Beneda warriors, and the ritual constraints of the war were fast unravelling, in their place an alarming brutality born of desperation. The ancient laws had been on the verge of shattering.

One night, Hannan Mosag had walked, somehow

unseen by anyone, into the chief's village, into the ruler's own longhouse. And by the first light of Menandore's cruel awakening, Hanradi Khalag had surrendered his people.

Trull did not know what to make of the tales that persisted, that Hanradi no longer cast a shadow. He had never seen the Merude chief.

That man's first son now sat before him, head shaved to denote the sundering from his bloodline, a skein of deep-cut, wide scars ribboning his face with shadows, his eyes flat and watchful, as if anticipating an assassination attempt here in the Warlock King's own hall.

The oil lamps suspended from the high ceiling flickered as one, and everyone grew still, eyes fixing on Hannan Mosag.

Though he did not raise his voice, its deep timbre reached across the vast space, leaving none with the necessity to strain to hear his words. 'Rhulad, unblooded warrior and son of Tomad Sengar, has brought to me words from his brother, Trull Sengar. This warrior had travelled to the Calach shore seeking jade. He was witness to a dire event, and has run without pause for three days and two nights.' Hannan Mosag's eyes fixed on Trull. 'Rise to stand at my side, Trull Sengar, and relate your tale.'

He walked the path the other warriors made for him and leapt up onto the raised dais, fighting to disguise the exhaustion in his legs that made him come close to sagging with the effort. Straightening, he stepped between two K'risnan and positioned himself to the right of the Warlock King. He looked out onto the array of upturned faces, and saw that what he would say was already known to most of them. Expressions dark with anger and a hunger for vengeance. Here and there, frowns of concern and dismay.

'I bring these words to the council. The tusked seals have come early to the breeding beds. Beyond the shallows I saw the sharks that leap in numbers beyond counting. And in their midst, nineteen Letherii ships—'

'*Nineteen!*'

A half-hundred voices uttered that cry in unison. An uncharacteristic breach of propriety, but understandable none the less. Trull waited a moment, then resumed. 'Their holds were almost full, for they sat low in the water, and the waters around them were red with blood and offal. Their harvest boats were alongside the great ships. In the fifty heartbeats that I stood and watched, I was witness to hundreds of seal carcasses rising on hooks to swing into waiting hands. On the strand itself twenty boats waited in the shallows and seventy men were on the beach, among the seals—'

'Did they see you?' one warrior asked.

It seemed Hannan Mosag was prepared to ignore the rules – for the time being at least.

'They did, and checked their slaughter . . . for a moment. I saw their mouths move, though I could not hear their words above the roar of the seals, and I saw them laugh—'

Rage erupted among the gathering. Warriors leapt upright.

Hannan Mosag snapped out a hand.

Sudden silence.

'Trull Sengar is not yet finished his tale.'

Clearing his throat, Trull nodded. 'You see me before you now, warriors, and those of you who know me will also know my preferred weapon – the spear. When have you seen me without my iron-hafted slayer of foes? Alas, I have surrendered it . . . in the chest of the one who first laughed.'

A roar answered his words.

Hannan Mosag settled a hand on Trull's shoulder, and the young warrior stepped aside. The Warlock King scanned the faces before him for a moment, then spoke. 'Trull Sengar did as every warrior of the Edur would do. His deed has heartened me. Yet here he now stands, weaponless.'

Trull stiffened beneath the weight of that hand.

'And so, in measured thought, such as must be made by a king,' Hannan Mosag went on, 'I find I must push my pride to one side, and look beyond it. To what is signified. A thrown spear. A dead Letherii. A disarmed Edur. And now, I see upon the faces of my treasured warriors a thousand flung spears, a thousand dead Letherii. A thousand disarmed Edur.'

No-one spoke. No-one countered with the obvious retort: *We have many spears.*

'I see the hunger for vengeance. The Letherii raiders must be slain. Even as prelude to the Great Meeting, for their slaying was *desired*. Our reaction was anticipated, for these are the games the Letherii would play with our lives. Shall we do as they intended? Of course. There can be but one answer to their crime. And thus, by our predictability, we serve an unknown design, which shall no doubt be unveiled at the Great Meeting.'

Deep-etched frowns. Undisguised confusion. Hannan Mosag had led them into the unfamiliar territory of complexity. He had brought them to the edge of an unknown path, and now would lead them forward, step by tentative step.

'The raiders will die,' the Warlock King resumed, 'but not one of you shall spill their blood. We do as predicted, but in a manner they could not imagine. There will be a time for slaughter of the Letherii, but this is not that time. Thus, I promise you blood, my warriors. But not now. The raiders shall not know the honour of dying at your hands. Their fates shall be found within Kurald Emurlahn.'

Despite himself, Trull Sengar shivered.

Silence once more in the hall.

'A full unveiling,' Hannan Mosag continued in a rumble, 'by my K'risnan. No weapon, no armour, shall avail the Letherii. Their mages will be blind and lost, incapable of countering that which arrives to take them. The raiders will die in pain and in terror. Soiled by fear, weeping like children – and that fate will be writ on their faces, there for those who find them.'

Trull's heart was pounding, his mouth bone-dry. A full

unveiling. What long-lost power had Hannan Mosag stumbled upon? The last full unveiling of Kurald Emurlahn had been by Scabandari Bloodeye, Father Shadow himself. Before the warren had been sundered. And that sundering had not healed. It would, Trull suspected, *never* be healed. Even so, some fragments were vaster and more powerful than others. Had the Warlock King discovered a new one?

Faded, battered and chipped, the ceramic tiles lay scattered before Feather Witch. The casting was done, even as Udinaas stumbled into the mote-filled barn to bring word of the omen – to warn the young slave woman away from a scanning of the Holds. Too late. *Too late*.

A hundred slaves had gathered for the event, fewer than was usual, but not surprising, since many Edur warriors would have charged their own slaves with tasks of preparation for the anticipated skirmish. Heads turned as Udinaas entered the circle. His eyes remained fixed on Feather Witch.

Her soul had already walked well back on the Path to the Holds. Her head drooped, chin between the prominent bones of her clavicles, thick yellow hair hanging down, and rhythmic trembling ran through her small, child-like body. Feather Witch had been born in the village eighteen years ago, a rare winter birth – rare in that she had survived – and her gifts had become known before her fourth year, when her dreams walked back and spoke in the voices of the ancestors. The old tiles of the Holds had been dug up from the grave of the last Letherii in the village who'd possessed the talent, and given to the child. There had been none to teach her the mysteries of those tiles, but, as it turned out, she'd needed no instruction from mortals – ghostly ancestors had provided that.

She was a handmaid to Mayen, and, upon Mayen's marriage to Fear Sengar, she would enter the Sengar household. And Udinaas was in love with her.

Hopeless, of course. Feather Witch would be given a husband from among the better born of the Letherii slaves, a man whose bloodline held title and power back in Letheras. An Indebted, such as Udinaas, had no hope of such a pairing.

As he stood staring at her, his friend Hulad reached up and took his wrist. Gentle pressure drew Udinaas down to a cross-legged position amidst the other witnesses.

Hulad leaned close. 'What ails you, Udinaas?'

'She has cast . . .'

'Aye, and now we wait while she walks.'

'I saw a white crow.'

Hulad flinched back.

'Down on the strand. I beseeched the Errant, to no avail. The crow but laughed at my words.'

Their exchange had been overheard, and murmurs rippled out among the witnesses.

Feather Witch's sudden moan silenced the gathering. All eyes fixed upon her, as she slowly raised her head.

Her eyes were empty, the whites clear as the ice on a mountain stream, iris and pupils vanished as if they had never been. And through the translucence swam twin spirals of faint light, smeared against the blackness of the Abyss.

Terror twisted her once-beautiful features, the terror of Beginnings, the soul standing before oblivion. A place of such loneliness that despair seemed the only answer. Yet it was also the place where power was thought, and thought flickered through the Abyss bereft of Makers, born from flesh yet to exist – for only the mind could reach back into the past, only its thoughts could dwell there. She was in the time before the worlds, and now must stride forward.

To witness the rise of the Holds.

Udinaas, like all Letherii, knew the sequences and the forms. First would come the three Fulcra known as the Realm Forgers. Fire, the silent scream of light, the very swirl of the stars themselves. Then Dolmen, bleak and root-less, drifting aimless in the void. And into the path of these

59

two forces, the Errant. Bearer of its own unknowable laws, it would draw Fire and Dolmen into fierce wars. Vast fields of destructions, instance upon instance of mutual annihilation. But occasionally, rarely, there would be peace made between the two contestants. And Fire would bathe but not burn, and Dolmen would surrender its wandering ways, and so find root.

The Errant would then weave its mysterious skein, forging the Holds themselves. Ice. Eleint. Azath. Beast. And into their midst would emerge the remaining Fulcra. Axe, Knuckles, Blade, the Pack, Shapefinder and White Crow.

Then, as the realms took shape, the spiralling light would grow sharper, and the final Hold would be revealed. The Hold that had existed, unseen, at the very beginning. The Empty Hold – heart of Letherii worship – that was at the very centre of the vast spiral of realms. Home to the Throne that knew no King, home to the Wanderer Knight, and to the Mistress who waited still, alone in her bed of dreams. To the Watcher, who witnessed all, and the Walker, who patrolled borders not even he could see. To the Saviour, whose outstretched hand was never grasped. And, finally, to the Betrayer, whose loving embrace destroyed all it touched.

'Walk with me to the Holds.'

The witnesses sighed as one, unable to resist that sultry, languid invitation.

'We stand upon Dolmen. Broken rock, pitted by shattered kin, its surface seething with life so small it escapes our eyes. Life locked in eternal wars. Blade and Knuckles. We are among the Beasts. I can see the Bone Perch, slick with blood and layered with the ghost memories of countless usurpers. I see the Elder, still faceless, still blind. And Crone, who measures the cost in the scrawling passage of behemoths. Seer, who speaks to the indifferent. I see Shaman, seeking truths among the dead. And Hunter, who lives in the moment and thinks nothing of the consequences of slaughter. And Tracker, who sees the signs of the unknown, and walks the endless paths of tragedy.*

The Hold of the Beast, here in this valley that is but a scratch upon Dolmen's hard skin.

'*There is no-one upon Bone Perch. Chaos hones every weapon, and the killing goes on and on. And from the maelstrom powerful creatures arise, and the slaying reaches beyond measure.*

'*Such powers must be answered. The Errant returns, and casts the seed into blood-soaked earth. Thus rises the Hold of the Azath.*

'*Deadly shelter for the tyrants, oh they are so easily lured. And so balance is achieved. But it remains a grisly balance, yes? No cessation to the wars, although they are much diminished, so that, finally, their cruel ways come into focus.*'

Her voice was like sorcery unbound. Its rough-edged song entranced, devoured, unveiled vistas into the minds of all those who heard it. Feather Witch had walked from the terror of the Beginnings, and there was no fear in her words.

'*But the tread of time is itself a prison. We are shackled with progression. And so the Errant comes once more, and the Ice Hold rises, with its attendant servants who journey through the realms to war against time. Walker, Huntress, Shaper, Bearer, Child and Seed. And upon the Throne of Ice sits Death, cowled and frost-rimed, stealer of caring, to shatter the anxious shackles of mortal life. It is a gift, but a cold one.*

'*Then, to achieve balance once more, is born the Eleint, and chaos is given flesh, and that flesh is draconic. Ruled by the Queen, who must be slain again and again by every child she bears. And her Consort, who loves none but himself. Then Liege, servant and guardian and doomed to eternal failure. Knight, the very sword of chaos itself – 'ware his path! And Gate, that which is the Breath. Wyval, spawn of the dragons, and the Lady, the Sister, Blood-Drinker and Path-Shaper. The Fell Dragons.*

'*One Hold remains . . .*'

Udinaas spoke with the others as they whispered, 'The Empty Hold.'

61

Feather Witch tilted her head suddenly, a frown marring her forehead. '*Something circles above the Empty Throne. I cannot see it, yet it . . . circles. A pallid hand, severed and dancing . . . no, it is—*'

She stiffened, then red spurted from wounds on her shoulders, and she was lifted from the ground.

Screams, the witnesses surging to their feet, rushing forward, arms outstretched.

But too late, as invisible talons clenched tighter and invisible wings thundered the dusty air of the barn. Carrying Feather Witch into the shadows beneath the curved ceiling. She shrieked.

Udinaas, heart hammering in his chest, pushed away, through the jostling bodies, to the wooden stairs reaching to the loft. Splinters stabbed his hands as he clawed his way up the steep, rough-hewn steps. Feather Witch's shrieks filled the air now, as she thrashed in the grip of the unseen talons. *But crows have no talons—*

He reached the loft, skidding as he raced across its uneven planks, eyes fixed on Feather Witch, then, one step from the edge, he leapt into the air. Arms outstretched, he sailed over the heads of the crowd below.

His target was the swirling air above her, the place where the invisible creature hovered. And when he reached that place, he collided hard with a massive, scaled body. Leathery wings hammered wildly at him as he wrapped his arms tight about a clammy, muscle-clenched body. He heard a wild hiss, then a jaw snapped down over his left shoulder. Needle-like teeth punched through his skin, sank deep into his flesh.

Udinaas grunted.

A Wyval, spawn of Eleint—

With his left hand, he scrabbled for the net-hook at his belt.

The beast tore at his shoulder, and blood gushed out.

He found the tool's worn wooden grip, dragged the hooked blade free. Its inner edge was honed sharp, used to trim knots. Twisting round, teeth clenched in an effort to ignore the lizard jaws slashing his shoulder again and again until little more than shreds remained, Udinaas chopped downward to where he thought one of the Wyval's legs must be. Solid contact. He ripped the inside edge of the blade into the tendons.

The creature screamed.

And released Feather Witch.

She plummeted into the mass of upraised arms below.

Talons hammered against Udinaas's chest, punched through.

He slashed, cutting deep. The leg spasmed back.

Jaws drew away, then snapped home once again, this time round his neck.

Net-hook fell from twitching hand. Blood filled his mouth and nose.

Darkness writhed across his vision – and he heard the Wyval scream again, this time in terror and pain, the sound emanating from its nostrils in hot gusts down his back. The jaws ripped free.

And Udinaas was falling.

And knew nothing more.

The others were filing out when Hannan Mosag touched Trull's shoulder. 'Stay,' he murmured. 'Your brothers as well.'

Trull watched his fellow warriors leave in small groups. They were troubled, and more than one hardened face revealed a flash of dismay when casting a final parting glance back at the Warlock King and his K'risnan. Fear had moved up to stand close by, Rhulad following. Fear's expression was closed – nothing surprising there – while Rhulad seemed unable to keep still, his head turning this way and that, one hand dancing on the pommel of the sword at his hip.

A dozen heartbeats later and they were alone.

Hannan Mosag spoke. 'Look at me, Trull Sengar. I would

you understand – I intended no criticism of your gesture. I too would have driven my spear into that Letherii in answer to his jest. I made sore use of you, and for that I apologize—'

'There is no need, sire,' Trull replied. 'I am pleased that you found in my actions a fulcrum by which you could shift the sentiments of the council.'

The Warlock King cocked his head. 'Fulcrum.' He smiled, but it was strained. 'Then we shall speak no more of it, Trull Sengar.' He fixed his attention next upon Rhulad, and his voice hardened slightly as he said, 'Rhulad Sengar, unblooded, you attend me now because you are a son of Tomad . . . and my need for his sons includes you. I expect you to listen, not speak.'

Rhulad nodded, suddenly pale.

Hannan Mosag stepped between two of his K'risnan – who had yet to relinquish their vigilant positions – and led the three sons of Tomad down from the dais. 'I understand that Binadas wanders once more. He knows no anchor, does he? Ah, well, there is no diminishment in that. You will have to apprise your brother upon his return of all that I tell you this night.'

They entered the Warlock King's private chamber. There was no wife attending, nor any slaves. Hannan Mosag lived simply, with only his shadow sentinel for company. The room was sparse, severe in its order.

'Three moons past,' the Warlock King began, turning to face them, 'my soul travelled when I slept, and was witness to a vision. I was on a plain of snow and ice. Beyond the lands of the Arapay, east and north of the Hungry Lake. But in the land that is ever still, something had risen. A violent birth, a presence demanding and stern. A spire of ice. Or a spear – I could not close with it – but it towered high above the snows, glittering, blinding with all the sun's light it had captured. Yet something dark waited in its heart.' His eyes had lost their focus, and Trull knew, with a shiver, that his king was once more in that cold, forlorn place. 'A gift. For the Edur. For the Warlock King.' He was silent then.

No-one spoke.

Abruptly, Hannan Mosag reached out and gripped Fear's shoulder, gaze sharpening on Trull's older brother. 'The four sons of Tomad Sengar shall journey to that place. To retrieve this gift. You may take two others – I saw the tracks of six in my vision, leading towards that spire of ice.'

Fear spoke. 'Theradas and Midik Buhn.'

The Warlock King nodded. 'Well chosen, yes. Fear Sengar, I charge you as leader of this expedition. You are my will and shall not be disobeyed. Neither you nor any other in your party must touch the gift. Your flesh must not make contact with it, is that understood? Retrieve it from the spire, wrap it in hides if that is possible, and return here.'

Fear nodded. 'It will be as you command, sire.'

'Good.' He scanned the three brothers. 'It is the belief of many – perhaps even you – that the unification of the tribes was my singular goal as leader of the Hiroth. Sons of Tomad, know that it is but the beginning.'

All of a sudden a new presence was in the room, sensed simultaneously by the king and the brothers, and they turned as one to the entrance.

A K'risnan stood in the threshold.

Hannan Mosag nodded. 'The slaves,' he muttered, 'have been busy this night. Come, all of you.'

Shadow wraiths had gathered round his soul, for soul was all he was, motionless and vulnerable, seeing without eyes, feeling without flesh as the vague, bestial things closed in, plucking at him, circling like dogs around a turtle.

They were hungry, those shadow spirits. Yet something held them back, some deep-set prohibition. They poked and prodded, but did nothing more.

They scattered – reluctantly – at the approach of something, someone, and Udinaas felt a warm, protective presence settle at his side.

Feather Witch. She was whole, her face luminous, her grey eyes quizzical as she studied him. 'Son of Debt,' she said, then sighed. 'They say you cut me free. Even as the Wyval tore into you. You cared nothing for *that*.' She studied him for a moment longer, then said, 'Your love burns my eyes, Udinaas. What am I to do about this truth?'

He found he could speak. 'Do nothing, Feather Witch. I know what is not to be. I would not surrender this burden.'

'No. I see that.'

'What has happened? Am I dying?'

'You were. Uruth, wife to Tomad Sengar, came in answer to our . . . distress. She drew upon Kurald Emurlahn, and has driven the Wyval away. And now she works healing upon us both. We lie side by side, Udinaas, on the blood-soaked earth. Unconscious. She wonders at our reluctance to return.'

'Reluctance?'

'She finds she struggles to heal our wounds – I am resisting her, for us both.'

'Why?'

'Because I am troubled. Uruth senses nothing. Her power feels pure to her. Yet it is . . . stained.'

'I do not understand. You said Kurald Emurlahn—'

'Aye. But it has lost its purity. I do not know how, or what, but it has changed. Among all the Edur, it is *changed*.'

'What are we to do?'

She sighed. 'Return, now. Yield to her command. Offer our gratitude for her intervention, for the healing of our torn flesh. And in answer to the many questions she has, we can say little. It was confused. Battle with an unknown demon. Chaos. And of this conversation, Udinaas, we will say nothing. Do you understand?'

'I do.'

She reached down and he felt her hand close about his – suddenly he was whole once more – and its warmth flowed through him.

He could hear his heart now, thundering in answer to

that touch. And another heart, distant yet quickly closing, beating in time. But it was not hers, and Udinaas knew terror.

His mother stepped back, the knot of her brow beginning to unclench. 'They approach,' she said.

Trull stared down at the two slaves. Udinaas, from his own household. And the other, one of Mayen's servants, the one they knew as Feather Witch for her divinatory powers. The blood still stained the puncture holes in their shirts, but the wounds themselves had closed. Another kind of blood was spilled across Udinaas's chest, gold and glistening still.

'I should outlaw these castings,' Hannan Mosag growled. 'Permitting Letherii sorcery in our midst is a dangerous indulgence.'

'Yet there is value, High King,' Uruth said, and Trull could see that she was still troubled.

'And that is, wife of Tomad?'

'A clarion call, High King, which we would do well to heed.'

Hannan Mosag grimaced. 'There is Wyval blood upon the man's shirt. Is he infected?'

'Possibly,' Uruth conceded. 'Much of that which passes for a soul in a Letherii is concealed from my arts, High King.'

'A failing that plagues us all, Uruth,' the Warlock King said, granting her great honour by using her true name. 'This one must be observed at all times,' he continued, eyes on Udinaas. 'If there is Wyval blood within him, the truth shall be revealed eventually. To whom does he belong?'

Tomad Sengar cleared his throat. 'He is mine, Warlock King.'

Hannan Mosag frowned, and Trull knew he was thinking of his dream, and of his decision to weave into its tale the Sengar family. There were few coincidences in the world. The Warlock King spoke in a harder voice. 'This Feather

Witch, she is Mayen's, yes? Tell me, Uruth, could you sense her power when you healed her?'

Trull's mother shook her head. 'Unimpressive. Or . . .'

'Or what?'

Uruth shrugged. 'Or she hid it well, despite her wounds. And if that is the case, then her power surpasses mine.'

Impossible. She is Letherii. A slave and still a virgin.

Hannan Mosag's grunt conveyed similar sentiments. 'She was assailed by a Wyval, clearly a creature that proved far beyond her ability to control. No, the child stumbles. Poorly instructed, ignorant of the vastness of all with which she would play. See, she only now regains awareness.'

Feather Witch's eyes fluttered open, revealing little comprehension, and that quickly overwhelmed by animal terror.

Hannan Mosag sighed. 'She will be of no use to us for a time. Leave them in the care of Uruth and the other wives.' He faced Tomad Sengar. 'When Binadas returns . . .'

Tomad nodded.

Trull glanced over at Fear. Behind him knelt the slaves that had attended the casting, heads pressed to the earth and motionless, as they had been since Uruth's arrival. It seemed Fear's hard eyes were fixed upon something no-one else could see.

When Binadas returns . . . the sons of Tomad will set forth. Into the ice wastes.

A sickly groan from Udinaas.

The Warlock King ignored it as he strode from the barn, his K'risnan flanking him, his shadow sentinel trailing a step behind. At the threshold, that monstrous wraith paused of its own accord, for a single glance back – though there was no way to tell upon whom it fixed its shapeless eyes.

Udinaas groaned a second time, and Trull saw the slave's limbs trembling.

At the threshold, the wraith was gone.

CHAPTER TWO

Mistress to these footprints,
Lover to the wake of where
He has just passed,
for the path he wanders
is between us all.

The sweet taste of loss
feeds every mountain stream,
Failing ice down to seas
warm as blood
threading thin our dreams.

For where he leads her
has lost its bones,
And the trail he walks
is flesh without life
and the sea remembers nothing.

Lay of the Ancient Holds
Fisher kel Tath

A glance back. In the misty haze far below and to the
west glimmered the innermost extent of Reach
Inlet, the sky's pallid reflection thorough in disguising that black, depthless water. On all other sides, apart
from the stony trail directly behind Seren Pedac, reared

jagged mountains, the snow-clad peaks gilt by a sun she could not see from where she stood at the south end of the saddle pass.

The wind rushing past her stank of ice, the winter's lingering breath of cold decay. She drew her furs tighter and swung round to gauge the progress of the train on the trail below.

Three solid-wheeled wagons, pitching and clanking. The swarming, bare-backed figures of the Nerek tribesmen as they flowed in groups around each wagon, the ones at the head straining on ropes, the ones at the rear advancing the stop-blocks to keep the awkward conveyances from rolling backward.

In those wagons, among other trade goods, were ninety ingots of iron, thirty to each wagon. Not the famed Letherii steel, of course, since sale of that beyond the borders was forbidden, but of the next highest quality grade, carbon-tempered and virtually free of impurities. Each ingot was as long as Seren's arm, and twice as thick.

The air was bitter cold and thin. Yet those Nerek worked half naked, the sweat steaming from their slick skins. If a stop-block failed, the nearest tribesman would throw his own body beneath the wheel.

And for this, Buruk the Pale paid them two docks a day.

Seren Pedac was Buruk's Acquitor, granted passage into Edur lands, one of seven so sanctioned by the last treaty. No merchant could enter Edur territory unless guided by an Acquitor. The bidding for Seren Pedac and the six others had been high. And, for Seren, Buruk's had been highest of all, and now he owned her. Or, rather, he owned her services as guide and finder – a distinction of which he seemed increasingly unmindful.

But this was the contract's sixth year. Only four remaining.

Maybe.

She turned once more, and studied the pass ahead. They were less than a hundred paces' worth of elevation from the treeline. Knee-high, centuries-old dwarf oaks and spruce flanked the uneven path. Mosses and lichens covered the enormous boulders that had been dragged down by the rivers of ice in ages past. Crusted patches of snow remained, clinging to shadowed places. Here the wind moved nothing, not the wiry spruce, not even the crooked, leafless branches of the oaks. Against such immovable stolidity, it could only howl.

The first wagon clattered onto level ground behind her, Nerek tongues shouting as it was quickly rolled ahead, past Seren Pedac, and anchored in place. The tribesmen then rushed back to help their fellows still on the ascent.

The squeal of a door, and Buruk the Pale clambered out from the lead wagon. He stood with his stance wide, as if struggling to regain the memory of balance, turning with a wince from the frigid wind, reaching up to keep his fur-lined cap on his head as he blinked over at Seren Pedac.

'I shall etch this vision against the very bone of my skull, blessed Acquitor! There to join a host of others, of course. That umber cloak of fur, the stately, primeval grace as you stand there. The weathered majesty of your profile, so deftly etched by these wild heights.

'You – Nerek! Find your foreman – we shall camp here. Meals must be prepared. Unload those bundles of wood in the third wagon. I want a fire, there, in the usual place. Be on with it!'

Seren Pedac set her pack down and made her way along the path. The wind quickly dragged Buruk's words away. Thirty paces on, she came to the first of the old shrines, a widening of the trail, where level stretches of scraped bedrock reached out to the sides and the walls of the flanking mountains had been cut sheer. On each flat, boulders had been positioned to form the full-sized outline of a ship, both prow and stern pointed and marked by upright menhirs. The prow stones had been carved into a likeness of the Edur god, Father Shadow, but the winds had ground the details away. Whatever had originally occupied these two flanking ships had long vanished, although the bedrock within was strangely stained.

The sheer walls of rock alone retained something of their ancient power. Smooth and black, they were translucent, in the manner of thin, smoky obsidian. And shapes moved behind them. As if the mountains had been hollowed out, and each panel was a kind of window, revealing a mysterious, eternal world within. A world oblivious of all that surrounded it, beyond its own borders of impenetrable stone, and of these strange panels, either blind or indifferent.

The translucent obsidian defied Seren's efforts to focus on the shapes moving on the other side, as it had the past score of times she had visited this site. But that very mystery was itself an irresistible lure, drawing her again and again.

Stepping carefully around the stern of the ship of boulders, she approached the eastern panel. She tugged the fur-lined glove from her right hand, reached and set it against the smooth stone. Warm, drinking the stiffness from her fingers, taking the ache from the joints. This was her secret, the healing powers she had discovered when she first touched the rock.

A lifetime in these hard lands stole suppleness from the body. Bones grew brittle, misshapen with pain. The endless hard rock underfoot soon sent shocks through the spine with each step taken. The Nerek, the tribe that, before kneeling to the Letherii king, had dwelt in the range's easternmost reach, believed that they were the children of a woman and a serpent, and that the serpent dwelt still within the body, that gently curved spine, the stacked knuckles reaching up to hide its head in the centre of the brain. But the mountains despised that serpent, desired only to drag it back to the ground, to return it once more to its belly, slithering in the cracks and coiled beneath rocks. And so, in the course of a life, the serpent was made to bow, to bend and twist.

72

Nerek buried their dead beneath flat stones.

At least, they used to, before the king's edict forced them to embrace the faith of the Holds.

Now they leave the bodies of their kin where they fall. Even unto abandoning their huts. It had been years ago, but Seren Pedac remembered with painful clarity coming over a rise and looking upon the vast plateau where the Nerek dwelt. The villages had lost all distinction, merging together in chaotic, dispirited confusion. Every third or fourth hut had been left to ruin, makeshift sepulchres for kin that had died of disease, old age, or too much alcohol, white nectar or durhang. Children wandered untended, trailed by feral rock rats that now bred uncontrolled and had become too disease-ridden to eat.

The Nerek people were destroyed, and from that pit there would be no climbing out. Their homeland was an overgrown cemetery, and the Letherii cities promised only debt and dissolution. They were granted no sympathy. The Letherii way of life was hard, but it was the true way, the way of civilization. The proof was found in its thriving where other ways stumbled or remained weak and stilted.

The bitter wind could not reach Seren Pedac now. The stone's warmth flowed through her. Eyes closed, she leaned her forehead against its welcoming surface.

Who walks in there? Are they the ancestral Edur, as the Hiroth claim? If so, then why could they see no more clearly than Seren herself? Vague shapes, passing to and fro, as lost as those Nerek children in their dying villages.

She had her own beliefs, and, though unpleasant, she held to them. *They are the sentinels of futility. Acquitors of the absurd. Reflections of ourselves forever trapped in aimless repetition. Forever indistinct, for that is all we can manage when we look upon ourselves, upon our lives. Sensations, memories and experiences, the fetid soil in which thoughts take root. Pale flowers beneath an empty sky.*

If she could, she would sink into this wall of stone. To walk for eternity among those formless shapes, looking out, perhaps, every now and then, and seeing not stunted trees, moss, lichen and the occasional passer-by. No, seeing only the wind. The ever howling wind.

She could hear him walking long before he came into the flickering circle of firelight. The sound of his footfalls awakened the Nerek as well, huddled beneath tattered furs in a rough half-circle at the edge of the light, and they swiftly rose and converged towards that steady beat.

Seren Pedac kept her gaze fixed on the flames, the riotous waste of wood that kept Buruk the Pale warm while he got steadily drunker on a mix of wine and white nectar, and fought against the tug at one corner of her mouth, that unbidden and unwelcome ironic curl that expressed bitter amusement at this impending conjoining of broken hearts.

Buruk the Pale carried with him secret instructions, a list long enough to fill an entire scroll, from other merchants, speculators and officials, including, she suspected, the Royal Household itself. And whatever those instructions entailed, their content was killing the man. He'd always liked his wine, but not with the seductive destroyer, white nectar, mixed in. That was this journey's new fuel for the ebbing fires of Buruk's soul, and it would drown him as surely as would the deep waters of Reach Inlet.

Four more years. Maybe.

The Nerek were mobbing their visitor, scores of voices blending into an eerie murmur, like worshippers beseeching a particularly bemusing god, and though the event was hidden in the darkness beyond the fire, Seren Pedac could see it well enough in her imagination. He was trying, only his eyes revealing his unease at the endless embraces, seeking to answer each one with something – anything – that could not be mistaken for benediction. He was, he would want to say, not a man worthy of such reverence. He was, he would want to say, a sordid culmination of failures – just as they were. All of them lost, here in this cold-hearted world. He would want to say – but no, Hull Beddict never

74

said anything. Not, in any case, things so boldly ... vulnerable.

Buruk the Pale had lifted his head at the commotion, blinking blearily. 'Who comes?'

'Hull Beddict,' Seren Pedac answered.

The merchant licked his lips. 'The old Sentinel?'

'Yes. Although I advise you not to call him by that title. He returned the King's Reed long ago.'

'And so betrayed the Letherii, aye.' Buruk laughed. 'Poor, honourable fool. Honour demands dishonour, now that is amusing, isn't it? Ever seen a mountain of ice in the sea? Calving again and again beneath the endless gnawing teeth of salt water. Just so.' He tilted his bottle back, and Seren watched his throat bob.

'Dishonour makes you thirsty, Buruk?'

He pulled the bottle down, glaring. Then a loose smile. 'Parched, Acquitor. Like a drowning man who swallows air.'

'Only it's not air, it's water.'

He shrugged. 'A momentary surprise.'

'Then you get over it.'

'Aye. And in those last moments, the stars swim unseen currents.'

Hull Beddict had done as much as he could with the Nerek, and he stepped into the firelight. Almost as tall as an Edur. Swathed in the white fur of the north wolf, his long braided hair nearly as pale. The sun and high winds had darkened his visage to the hue of tanned hide. His eyes were bleached grey, and it seemed the man behind them was ever elsewhere. And, Seren Pedac well knew, that place was not home.

No, as lost as his flesh and bones, this body standing before us. 'Take some warmth, Hull Beddict,' she said.

He studied her in his distracted way – a seeming contradiction that only he could achieve.

Buruk the Pale laughed. 'What's the point? It'll never reach him through those furs. Hungry, Beddict? Thirsty? I

75

didn't think so. How about a woman? I could spare you one of my Nerek half-bloods – the darlings wait in my wagon.' He drank noisily from his bottle and held it out. 'Some of this? Oh dear, he hides poorly his disgust.'

Eyes on the old Sentinel, Seren asked, 'Have you come down the pass? Are the snows gone?'

Hull Beddict glanced over at the wagons. When he replied, the words came awkwardly, as if it had been some time since he last spoke. 'Should do.'

'Where are you going?'

He glanced at her once more. 'With you.'

Seren's brows rose.

Laughing, Buruk the Pale waved expansively with his bottle – which was empty save for a last few scattering drops that hit the fire with a hiss. 'Oh, welcome company indeed! By all means! The Nerek will be delighted.' He tottered upright, weaving perilously close to the fire, then, with a final wave, he stumbled towards his wagon.

Seren and Hull watched him leave, and Seren saw that the Nerek had returned to their sleeping places, but all sat awake, their eyes glittering with reflected flames as they watched the old Sentinel, who now stepped closer to the fire and slowly sat down. He held out battered hands to the heat.

They could be softer than they appeared, Seren recalled. The memory did little more than stir long-dead ashes, how-ever, and she tipped another log into the hungry fire before them, watched the sparks leap into the darkness.

'He intends to remain a guest of the Hiroth until the Great Meeting?'

She shot him a look, then shrugged. 'I think so. Is that why you've decided to accompany us?'

'It will not be like past treaties, this meeting,' he said. 'The Edur are no longer divided. The Warlock King rules unchallenged.'

'Everything's changed, yes.'

'And so Diskanar sends Buruk the Pale.'

76

She snorted, kicked back into the flames an errant log that had rolled out. 'A poor choice. I doubt he'll remain sober enough to manage much spying.'

'Seven merchant houses and twenty-eight ships have descended upon the Calach beds,' Hull Beddict said, flexing his fingers.

'I know.'

'Diskanar's delegation will claim the hunting was unsanctioned. They will decry the slaughter. Then use it to argue that the old treaty is flawed, that it needs to be revised. For the lost seals, they will make a magnanimous gesture – by throwing gold at Hannan Mosag's feet.'

She said nothing. He was right, after all. Hull Beddict knew better than most King Ezgara Diskanar's mind – or, rather, that of the Royal Household, which wasn't always the same thing. 'There is more to it, I suspect,' she said after a moment.

'How so?'

'I imagine you have not heard who will be leading the delegation.'

He grunted sourly. 'The mountains are silent on such matters.'

She nodded. 'Representing the king's interests, Nifadas.'

'Good. The First Eunuch is no fool.'

'Nifadas will be sharing command with Prince Quillas Diskanar.'

Hull Beddict slowly turned to face her. 'She's risen far, then.'

'She has. And for all the years since you last crossed her son's path . . . well, Quillas has changed little. The queen keeps him on a short leash, with the Chancellor close at hand to feed him sweet treats. It's rumoured that the primary holder of interest in the seven merchant houses that defied the treaty is none other than Queen Janall herself.'

'And the Chancellor dares not leave the palace,' Hull Beddict said, and she heard the sneer. 'So he sends Quillas.

A mistake. The prince is blind to subtlety. He knows his own ignorance and stupidity so is ever suspicious of others, especially when they say things he does not understand. One cannot negotiate when dragged in the wake of emotions.'

'Hardly a secret,' Seren Pedac replied. And waited.

Hull Beddict spat into the fire. 'They don't care. The queen's let him slip the leash. Allowing Quillas to flail about, to deliver clumsy insults in the face of Hannan Mosag. Is this plain arrogance? Or do they truly invite war?'

'I don't know.'

'And Buruk the Pale – whose instructions does he carry?'

'I'm not sure. But he's not happy.'

They fell silent then.

Twelve years past, King Ezgara Diskanar charged his favoured Preda of the Guard, Hull Beddict, with the role of Sentinel. He was to journey to the north borders, then beyond. His task was to study the tribes who still dwelt wild in the mountains and high forests. Talented warrior though he was, Hull Beddict had been naive. What he had embraced as a journey in search of knowledge, the first steps towards peaceful co-existence, had in fact been a prelude to conquest. His detailed reports of tribes such as the Nerek, and the Faraed and the Tarthenal, had been pored over by minions of Chancellor Triban Gnol. Weaknesses had been prised from the descriptions. And then, in a series of campaigns of subjugation, brutally exploited.

And Hull Beddict, who had forged blood-ties with those fierce tribes, was there to witness all his enthusiasm delivered. Gifts that were not gifts at all, incurring debts, the debts exchanged for land. The deadly maze lined with traders, merchants, seducers of false need, purveyors of destructive poisons. Defiance answered with annihilation. The devouring of pride, independence and self-sufficiency. In all, a war so profoundly cynical in its cold, heartless expediting that no honourable soul could survive witness.

Especially when that soul was responsible for it. *For all of it.*

And to this day, the Nerek worshipped Hull Beddict. As did the half-dozen indebted beggars who were all that was left of the Faraed. And the scattered remnants of the Tarthenal, huge and shambling and drunk in the pit towns outside the cities to the south, still bore the three bar tattoos beneath their left shoulders – a match to those on Hull's own back.

He sat now in silence beside her, his eyes on the ebbing flames of the dying hearth. One of his guards had returned to the capital, bearing the King's Reed. The Sentinel was Sentinel no longer. Nor would he return to the southlands. He had walked into the mountains.

She had first met him eight years ago, a day out from High Fort, reduced to little more than a scavenging animal in the wilds.

And had brought him back. At least some of the way. *Oh, but it was far less noble than it first seemed. Perhaps it would have been. Truly noble. Had I not then made sore use of him.*

She had succumbed to her own selfish needs, and there was nothing glorious in that.

Seren wondered if he would ever forgive her. She then wondered if she would ever forgive herself.

'Buruk the Pale knows all that I need to learn,' Hull Beddict said.

'Possibly.'

'He will tell me.'

Not of his own volition, he won't. 'Regardless of his instructions,' she said, 'he remains a small player in this game, Hull. Head of a merchant house conveniently placed in Trate, with considerable experience dealing with the Hiroth and Arapay.' *And, through me, legitimate passage into Edur lands.*

'Hannan Mosag will send his warriors after those ships,' Hull Beddict said. 'The queen's interest in those merchant houses is about to take a beating.'

'I expect she has anticipated the loss.'

The man beside her was not the naive youth he had once been. But he was long removed from the intricate schemes and deadly sleight of hand that was so much the lifeblood of the Letherii. She could sense him struggling with the multiplicity of layers of intent and design at work here. 'I begin to see the path she takes,' he said after a time, and the bleak despair in his voice was so raw that she looked away, blinking.

He went on, 'This is the curse, then, that we are so inclined to look ahead, ever ahead. As if the path before us should be any different from the one behind us.'

Aye, and it pays to remind me, every time I glance back.

I really should stop doing that.

'Five wings will buy you a grovel,' Tehol Beddict muttered from his bed. 'Haven't you ever wondered how odd it is? Of course, every god should have a throne, but shouldn't it also follow that every throne built for a god is actually occupied? And if it isn't, who in their right mind decided that it was worthwhile to worship an empty throne?'

Seated on a low three-legged stool at the foot of the bed, Bugg paused in his knitting. He held out and examined the coarse wool shirt he was working on, one eye squeezing into a critical squint.

Tehol's gaze flicked down at his servant. 'I'm fairly certain my left arm is of a length close to, if not identical with, that of my right. Why do you persist in this conceit? You've no talent to speak of, in much of anything, come to think of it. Probably why I love you so dearly, Bugg.'

'Not half as much as you love yourself,' the old man replied, resuming his knitting.

'Well, I see no point in arguing that.' He sighed, wiggling his toes beneath the threadbare sheet. The wind was freshening, blessedly cool and only faintly reeking of the south shore's Stink Flats. Bed and stool were the only furniture on the roof of Tehol's house. Bugg still slept below, despite the sweltering heat, and only came up when his work demanded light enough to see. Saved on lamp oil, Tehol told himself, since oil was getting dreadfully expensive now that the whales were getting scarce.

He reached down to the half-dozen dried figs on the tarnished plate Bugg had set down beside him. 'Ah, more figs. Another humiliating trip to the public privies awaits me, then.' He chewed desultorily, watching the monkey-like clambering of the workers on the dome of the Eternal Domicile. Purely accidental, this exquisitely unobstructed view of the distant palace rising from the heart of Letheras, and all the more satisfying for that, particularly the way the nearby towers and Third Height bridges so neatly framed King Ezgara Diskanar's conceit. 'Eternal Domicile indeed. Eternally unfinished.'

The dome had proved so challenging to the royal architects that four of them had committed suicide in the course of its construction, and one had died tragically – if somewhat mysteriously – trapped inside a drainage pipe. 'Seventeen years and counting. Looks like they've given up entirely on that fifth wing. What do you think, Bugg? I value your expert opinion.'

Bugg's expertise amounted to rebuilding the hearth in the kitchen below. Twenty-two fired bricks stacked into a shape very nearly cubic, and indeed it would have been if three of the bricks had not come from a toppled mausoleum at the local cemetery. Grave masons held to peculiar notions of what a brick's dimensions should be, pious bastards that they were.

In response to Tehol's query, Bugg glanced up, squinting with both eyes.

Five wings to the palace, the dome rising from the centre. Four tiers to those wings, except for the shoreside one, where only two tiers had been built. Work had been suspended when it was discovered that the clay beneath the foundations tended to squeeze out to the sides, like closing a fist on a block of butter. The fifth wing was sinking.

'Gravel,' Bugg said, returning to his knitting.

'What?'

'Gravel,' the old man repeated. 'Drill deep wells down into the clay, every few paces or so, and fill 'em with gravel, packed down with drivers. Cap 'em and build your foundation pillars on top. No weight on the clay means it's got no reason to squirm.'

Tehol stared down at his servant. 'All right. Where in the Errant's name did you come by that? And don't tell me you stumbled onto it trying to keep our hearth from wandering.'

Bugg shook his head. 'No, it's not that heavy. But if it was, that's what I would've done.'

'Bore a hole? How far down?'

'Bedrock, of course. Won't work otherwise.'

'And fill it with gravel.'

'Pounded down tight, aye.'

Tehol plucked another fig from the plate, brushed dust from it – Bugg had been harvesting from the market leavings again. Outwitting the rats and dogs. 'That'd make for an impressive cook hearth.'

'It would at that.'

'You could cook secure and content in the knowledge that the flatstone will never move, barring an earthquake—'

'Oh no, it'll handle an earthquake too. Gravel, right? Flexible, you see.'

'Extraordinary.' He spat out a seed. 'What do you think? Should I get out of bed today, Bugg?'

'Got no reason to—' The servant stopped short, then cocked his head, thinking. 'Mind you, maybe you have.'

'Oh? And you'd better not be wasting my time with this.'

'Three women visited this morning.'

'Three women.' Tehol glanced up at the nearest Third Height bridge, watched people and carts moving across it. 'I don't know three women, Bugg. And if I did, all of them arriving simultaneously would be cause for terror, rather than an incidental "oh by the way".'

'Aye, but you don't know them. Not even one of them. I don't think. New faces to me, anyway.'

'New? You've never seen them before? Not even in the market? The riverfront?'

'No. Might be from one of the other cities, or maybe a village. Odd accents.'

'And they asked for me by name?'

'Well, not precisely. They wanted to know if this was the house of the man who sleeps on his roof.'

'If they needed to ask that, they *are* from some toad-squelching village. What else did they want to know? The colour of your hair? What you were wearing while standing there in front of them? Did they want to know their own names as well? Tell me, are they sisters? Do they share a single eyebrow?'

'Not that I noticed. Handsome women, as I recall. Young and meaty. Sounds as though you're not interested, though.'

'Servants shouldn't presume. Handsome. Young and meaty. Are you sure they were women?'

'Oh yes, quite certain. Even eunuchs don't have breasts so large, or perfect, or, indeed, lifted so high the lasses could rest their chins—'

Tehol found himself standing beside the bed. He wasn't sure how he got there, but it felt right. 'You finished that shirt, Bugg?'

The servant held it out once more. 'Just roll up the sleeve, I think.'

'Finally, I can go out in public once more. Tie those ends off or whatever it is you do to them and give it here.'

'But I haven't started yet on the trousers—'

'Never mind that,' Tehol cut in, wrapping the bed sheet about his waist, once, twice, thrice, then tucking it in at one hip. He then paused, a strange look stealing across his features. 'Bugg, for Errant's sake, no more figs for a while, all right? Where are these mountainously endowed sisters, then?'

83

'Red Lane. Huldo's.'

'The pits or on the courtyard?'

'Courtyard.'

'That's something, at least. Do you think Huldo might have forgotten?'

'No. But he's been spending a lot of time down at the Drownings.'

Tehol smiled, then began rubbing a finger along his teeth. 'Winnin' or losin'?'

'Losing.'

'Hah!' He ran a hand through his hair and struck a casual pose. 'How do I look?'

Bugg handed him the shirt. 'How you manage to keep those muscles when you do nothing baffles me,' he said.

'A Beddict trait, dear sad minion of mine. You should see Brys, under all that armour. But even he looks scrawny when compared to Hull. As the middle son, I of course represent the perfect balance. Wit, physical prowess and a multitude of talents to match my natural grace. When combined with my extraordinary ability to waste it all, you see, standing before you, the exquisite culmination.'

'A fine and pathetic speech,' Bugg said with a nod.

'It was, wasn't it? I shall be on my way now.' Tehol gestured as he walked to the ladder. 'Clean up the place. We might have guests this evening.'

'I will, if I find the time.'

Tehol paused at the ragged edge of the section of roof that had collapsed. 'Ah yes, you have trousers to make – have you enough wool for that?'

'Well, I can make one leg down all the way, or I can make both short.'

'How short?'

'Pretty short.'

'Go with the one leg.'

'Aye, master. And then I have to find us something to eat. And drink.'

Tehol turned, hands on his hips. 'Haven't we sold

virtually everything, sparing one bed and a lone stool? So, just how much tidying up is required?'

Bugg squinted. 'Not much,' he conceded. 'What do you want we should eat tonight?'

'Something that needs cooking.'

'Would that be something better when cooked, or something that has to be cooked?'

'Either way's fine.'

'How about wood?'

'I'm not eating—'

'For the hearth.'

'Oh, right. Well, find some. Look at that stool you're sitting on – it doesn't really need all three legs, does it? When scrounging doesn't pay, it's time to improvise. I'm off to meet my three destinies, Bugg. Pray the Errant's looking the other way, will you?'

'Of course.'

Tehol made his way down the ladder, discovering, in a moment of panic, that only one rung in three remained.

The ground-level room was bare except for a thin mattress rolled up against one wall. A single battered pot rested on the hearth's flatstone, which sat beneath the front-facing window, a pair of wooden spoons and bowls on the floor nearby. All in all, Tehol reflected, elegant in its severity.

He swung aside the ratty curtain that served as a door, reminding himself to tell Bugg to retrieve the door latch from the hearth-bed. A bit of polishing and it might earn a dock or two from Cusp the Tinkerer. Tehol stepped outside.

He was in a narrow aisle, so narrow he was forced to sidle sideways out to the street, kicking rubbish aside with each step. *Meaty women . . . wish I'd seen them squeezing their way to my door.* An invitation to dinner now seemed essential. And, mindful host that he was, he could position himself with a clear view, and whatever pleasure they saw on his face they could take for welcome.

The street beyond was empty save for three Nerek, a

mother and two half-blood children, who'd found in the recessed niche in the wall opposite a new home and seemed to do nothing but sleep. He strode past their huddled forms, kicking at a rat that had been edging closer, and threaded his way between the high-stacked wooden crates that virtually blocked this end of the street. Biri's warehouse was perpetually overstocked, and Biri viewed the last reach of Cul Street this side of Quillas Canal as his own personal compound.

Chalas, the watchman of the yard, was sprawled on a bench on the other side, where Cul opened out onto Burl Square, his leather-wrapped clout resting on his thighs. Red-shot eyes found Tehol. 'Nice skirt,' the guard said.

'You've lightened my step, Chalas.'

'Happy to oblige, Tehol.'

Tehol paused, hands on hips, and surveyed the crowded square. 'The city thrives.'

'No change there . . . exceptin' the last time.'

'Oh, that was a minor sideways tug, as far as currents go.'

'Not to hear Biri talk of it. He still wants your head salted and in a barrel rolling out to sea.'

'Biri always did run in place.'

Chalas grunted. 'It's been weeks since you last came down. Special occasion?'

'I have a date with three women.'

'Want my clout?'

Tehol glanced down and studied the battered weapon. 'I wouldn't want to leave you defenceless.'

'It's my face scares 'em away. Exceptin' those Nerek. Got past me, those ones did.'

'Giving you trouble?'

'No. The rat count's way down, in fact. But you know Biri.'

'Better than he knows himself. Remind him of that, Chalas, if he starts thinking of giving them trouble.'

'I will.'

Tehol set out, winding through the seething press in the

square. The Down Markets opened out onto it from three sides; a more decrepit collection of useless items for sale Tehol had yet to see. And the people bought in a frenzy, day after blessed day. *Our civilization thrives on stupidity.* And it only took a sliver of cleverness to tap that idiot vein and drink deep of the riches. Comforting, if slightly depressing. The way of most grim truths.

He reached the other side, entered Red Lane. Thirty strides on and he came opposite the arched entrance to Huldo's. Down the shadowed walkway and back into the courtyard's sunlight. A half-dozen tables, all occupied. Repose for the blissfully ignorant or those without the coin to sample the pits in Huldo's inner sanctum, where various sordid activities were conducted day and night, said activities occasionally approaching the artistic expression of the absurd. One more example, Tehol reflected, of what people would pay for, given the chance.

The three women at a table in the far corner stood out for not just the obvious detail – they were the only women present – but for a host of subtler distinctions. *Handsome is . . . just the right word.* If they were sisters it was in sentiment only, and for the shared predilection for some form of martial vigour, given their brawn, and the bundled armour and covered weapons heaped beside the table.

The one on the left was red-haired, the fiery tresses sun-bleached and hanging in reluctant ripples down onto her broad shoulders. She was drinking from a clay-wrapped bottle, disdaining or perhaps not understanding the function of the cup that had accompanied it. Her face belonged to a heroic statue lining a colonnade, strong and smooth and perfect, her blue eyes casting a stony regard with the serene indifference of all such statues. Next to her, and leaning with both forearms on the small tabletop, was a woman with a hint of Faraed blood in her, given the honeyed hue of her skin and the faint up-tilt of her dark eyes. Her hair was either dark brown or black, and had been tied back, leaving clear her heart-shaped face. The third

87

woman sat slouched back in her chair, left leg tipped out to one side, the right incessantly jittering up and down – fine legs, Tehol observed, clad in tight rawhide, tanned very nearly white. Her head was shaved, the pale skin gleaming. Wide-set, light grey eyes lazily scanning the other patrons, finally coming to rest on Tehol where he stood at the courtyard's threshold.

He smiled.

She sneered.

Urul, Huldo's chief server, edged out from a nearby shadow and beckoned Tehol over.

He came as close as he dared. 'You're looking . . . well, Urul. Is Huldo here?'

The man's need for a bath was legendary. Patrons gave their orders with decisive brevity and rarely called Urul over for more wine until the meal was finished. He stood before Tehol now, brow gleaming with oily sweat, hands fidgeting over the wide sash of his belt. 'Huldo? No, Errant be praised. He's on the Low Walk at the Drownings. Tehol, those women – they've been here all morning! They frighten me, the way they scowl whenever I get close.'

'Leave them to me, Urul,' Tehol said, risking a pat on the man's damp shoulder.

'You?'

'Why not?' With that, Tehol adjusted his skirt, checked his sleeves, and threaded his way between the tables. Halting before the three women, he glanced round for a chair. He found one and dragged it close, then settled with a sigh.

'What do you want?' asked the bald one.

'That was *my* question. My servant informs me that you visited my residence this morning. I am Tehol Beddict . . . the one who sleeps on his roof.'

Three sets of eyes fixed on him.

Enough to make a stalwart warlord wilt . . . but me? Only slightly.

'You?'

88

Tehol scowled at the bald woman. 'Why does everyone keep asking that? Yes, me. Now, by your accent, I'd hazard you're from the islands. I don't know anyone in the islands. Accordingly, I don't know you. Not to say I wouldn't like to, of course. Know you, that is. At least, I think so.'

The red-haired woman set her bottle down with a clunk. 'We've made a mistake.'

'I'm sorry to hear that—'

'No,' the bald woman said to her companion. 'This is an affectation. We should have anticipated a certain degree of ... mockery.'

'He has no trousers.'

The dark-eyed woman added, 'And his arms are lopsided.'

'Not quite accurate,' Tehol said to her. 'It's only the sleeves that are somewhat askew.'

'I don't like him,' she pronounced, crossing her arms.

'You don't have to,' the bald woman said. 'Errant knows, we're not going to bed him, are we?'

'I'm crushed.'

'You would be,' the red-haired woman said, with an unpleasant smile.

'Bed him? On the roof? You must be insane, Shand.'

'How can not liking him be unimportant?'

The bald woman, the one named Shand, sighed and rubbed her eyes. 'Listen to me, Hejun. This is business. Sentiments have no place in business – I've already told you that.'

Hejun's arms remained crossed, and she shook her head. 'You can't trust who you don't like.'

'Of course you can!' Shand said, blinking.

'It's his reputation I'm not happy with,' said the third, as yet unnamed, woman.

'Rissarh,' Shand said, sighing again, 'it's his reputation what's brought us here.'

Tehol clapped his hands. Once, loud enough to startle the three women. 'Excellent. Rissarh with the red hair.

Hejun, with Faraed blood. And Shand, no hair at all. Well,' he set his hands on the table and rose, 'I'm content with that. Goodbye—'

'Sit down!'

The growl was so menacing that Tehol found himself seated once more, the prickle of sweat beneath his woollen shirt.

'That's better,' Shand said in a more mellow tone. She leaned forward. 'Tehol Beddict. We know all about you.'

'Oh?'

'We even know why what happened happened.'

'Indeed.'

'And we want you to do it again.'

'You do?'

'Yes. Only this time, you'll have the courage to go through with it. All the way.'

'I will?'

'Because we – myself, Hejun and Rissarh – we're going to be your courage. This time. Now, let's get out of here, before that server comes back. We've purchased a building. We can talk there. It doesn't smell.'

'Now that's a relief,' Tehol said.

The three women rose.

He did not.

'I told you,' Hejun said to Shand. 'It's not going to work. There's nothing left in there. Look at him.'

'It'll work,' Shand said.

'Hejun is, alas, right,' Tehol said. 'It won't.'

'We know where the money went,' Shand said.

'That's no secret. Riches to rags. I lost it.'

But Shand shook her head. 'No you didn't. Like I said, we *know*. And if we talk . . .'

'You keep saying you know something,' Tehol said, adding a shrug.

'As you said,' she replied, smiling, 'we're from the islands.'

'But not *those* islands.'

'Of course not – who'd go there? And that's what you counted on.'

Tehol rose. 'As they say, five wings will buy you a grovel. All right, you've purchased a building.'

'You'll do it,' Shand insisted. 'Because if it comes out, Hull will kill you.'

'Hull?' Finally Tehol could smile. 'My brother knows nothing about it.'

He savoured the pleasure, then, in seeing these three women knocked off balance. *There, now you know how it feels.*

'Hull may prove a problem.'

Brys Beddict could not hold his gaze on the man standing before him. Those small, placid eyes peering out from the folds of pink flesh seemed in some way other than human, holding so still that the Finadd of the Royal Guard imagined he was looking into the eyes of a snake. *A flare-neck, coiled on the centre of the river road when the rains are but days away. Up from the river, three times as long as a man is tall, head resting on the arm-thick curl of its body. 'Ware the plodding cattle dragging their carts on that road. 'Ware the drover stupid enough to approach.*

'Finadd?'

Brys forced his eyes back to the huge man. 'First Eunuch, I am at a loss as to how to respond. I have neither seen nor spoken with my brother in years. Nor will I be accompanying the delegation.'

First Eunuch Nifadas turned away, and walked noiselessly to the high-backed wooden chair behind the massive desk that dominated the chamber of his office. He sat, the motion slow and even. 'Be at ease, Finadd Beddict. I have immense respect for your brother Hull. I admire the extremity of his conviction, and understand to the fullest extent the motivation behind his . . . choices in the past.'

'Then, if you will forgive me, you are further down the path than I, First Eunuch. Of my brother – of my *brothers* –

91

I understand virtually nothing. Alas, it has always been so.'

Nifadas blinked sleepily, then he nodded. 'Families are odd things, aren't they? Naturally, my own experience precludes many of the subtleties regarding that subject. Yet, if you will, my exclusion has, in the past, permitted me a certain objectivity, from which I have often observed the mechanisms of such fraught relationships with a clear eye.' He looked up and fixed Brys once more with his regard. 'Will you permit me a comment or two?'

'Forgive me, First Eunuch—'

Nifadas waved him silent with one plump hand. 'No need. I was presumptuous. Nor have I explained myself. As you know, preparations are well along. The Great Meeting looms. I am informed that Hull Beddict has joined Buruk the Pale and Seren Pedac on the trail to Hiroth lands. Further, it is my understanding that Buruk is charged with a host of instructions – none issued by me, I might add. In other words, it is likely that those instructions not only do not reflect the king's interests, but in fact may contradict our Sire's wishes.' He blinked again, slow and measured. 'Precarious, agreed. Unwelcome, as well. My concern is this. Hull may . . . misunderstand . . .'

'By assuming that Buruk acts on behalf of King Diskanar, you mean.'

'Just so.'

'He would then seek to counter the merchant.'

Nifadas sighed his agreement.

'Which,' Brys continued, 'is itself not necessarily a bad thing.'

'True, in itself not necessarily a bad thing.'

'Unless you intend, as the king's official representative and nominal head of the delegation, to counter the merchant in your own way. To deflect those interests Buruk has been charged with presenting to the Edur.'

The First Eunuch's small mouth hinted at a smile.

Nothing more than that, yet Brys understood. His gaze travelled to the window behind Nifadas. Clouds swam

92

blearily through the bubbled, wavy glass. 'Not Hull's strengths,' he said.

'No, we are agreed in that. Tell me, Finadd, what do you know of this Acquitor, Seren Pedac?'

'Reputation only. But it's said she owns a residence here in the capital. Although I have never heard if she visits.'

'Rarely. The last time was six years ago.'

'Her name is untarnished,' Brys said.

'Indeed. Yet one must wonder . . . she is not blind, after all. Nor, I gather, unthinking.'

'I would imagine, First Eunuch, that few Acquitors are.'

'Just so. Well, thank you for your time, Finadd. Tell me,' he added as he slowly rose, indicating the audience was at an end, 'have you settled well as the King's Champion?'

'Uh, well enough, First Eunuch.'

'The burden is easily shouldered by one as young and fit as you, then?'

'Not easily. I would make no claim to that.'

'Not comfortable, but manageable.'

'A fair enough description.'

'You are an honest man, Brys. As one of the king's advisers, I am content with my choice.'

But you feel I need the reminder. Why is that? 'I remain honoured, First Eunuch, by the king's faith, and of course, yours.'

'I will delay you no longer, Finadd.'

Brys nodded, turned and strode from the office.

A part of him longed for the days of old, when he was just an officer in the Palace Guard. When he carried little political weight, and the presence of the king was always at a distance, with Brys and his fellow guardsmen standing at attention along one wall at official audiences and engagements. Then again, he reconsidered as he walked down the corridor, the First Eunuch had called him because of his blood, not his new role as King's Champion.

Hull Beddict. Like a restless ghost, a presence cursed to haunt him no matter where he went, no matter what he did. Brys remembered seeing his eldest brother, resplendent in the garb of Sentinel, the King's Reed at his belt. A last and lasting vision for the young, impressionable boy he had been all those years ago. That moment remained with him, a tableau frozen in time that he wandered into in his dreams, or at reflective moments like these. A painted image. Brothers, man and child, the two of them cracked and yellowed beneath the dust. And he would stand witness, like a stranger, to the boy's wide-eyed, adoring expression, and would follow that uplifted gaze and then shift his own uneasily, suspicious of that uniformed soldier's pride.

Innocence was a blade of glory, yet it could blind on both sides.

He'd told Nifadas he did not understand Hull. But he did. All too well.

He understood Tehol, too, though perhaps marginally less well. The rewards of wealth beyond measure had proved cold; only the hungry desire for that wealth hissed with heat. And that truth belonged to the world of the Letherii, the brittle flaw at the core of the golden sword. Tehol had thrown himself on that sword, and seemed content to bleed to death, slowly and with amiable aplomb. Whatever final message he sought in his death was a waste of time, since no-one would look his way when that day came. No-one dared. *Which is why, I suspect, he's smiling.*

His brothers had ascended their peaks long ago – too early, it turned out – and now slid down their particular paths to dissolution and death. *And what of me, then? I have been named King's Champion. Judged the finest swordsman in the kingdom. I believe I stand, here and now, upon the highest reach.* There was no need to take that thought further.

He reached a T-intersection and swung right. Ten paces ahead a side door spilled light into the corridor. As he came opposite it a voice called to him from the chamber within.

'Finadd! Come quick.'

Brys inwardly smiled and turned. Three strides into the

spice-filled, low-ceilinged room. Countless sources of light made a war of colours on the furniture and tables with their crowds of implements, scrolls and beakers.

'Ceda?'

'Over here. Come and see what I've done.'

Brys edged past a bookcase extending out perpendicularly from one wall and found the King's Sorceror behind it, perched on a stool. A tilted table with a level bottom shelf was at the man's side, cluttered with discs of polished glass.

'Your step has changed, Finadd,' Kuru Qan said, 'since becoming the King's Champion.'

'I was not aware of that, Ceda.'

Kuru Qan spun on his seat and raised a strange object before his face. Twin lenses of glass, bound in place side by side with wire. The Ceda's broad, prominent features were made even more so by a magnifying effect from the lenses. Kuru Qan set the object against his face, using ties to bind it so that the lenses sat before his eyes, making them huge as he blinked up at Brys.

'You are as I imagined you. Excellent. The blur diminishes in importance. Clarity ascends, achieving pre-eminence among all the important things. What I hear now matters less than what I see. Thus, perspective shifts. The world changes. Important, Finadd. Very important.'

'Those lenses have given you vision? That is wonderful, Ceda!'

'The key was in seeking a solution that was the antithesis of sorcery. Looking upon the Empty Hold stole my sight, after all. I could not effect correction through the same medium. Not yet important, this detail. Pray indeed it never becomes so.'

Ceda Kuru Qan never held but one discourse at any one time. Or so he had explained it once. While many found this frustrating, Brys was ever charmed.

'Am I the first to be shown your discovery, Ceda?'

'You would see its importance more than most. Swordsman, dancing with place, distance and timing, with

95

all the material truths. I need to make adjustments.' He snatched the contraption off and hunched over it, minuscule tools flicking in his deft hands. 'You were in the First Eunuch's chamber of office. Not an altogether pleasing conversation for you. Unimportant, for the moment.'

'I am summoned to the throne room, Ceda.'

'True. Not entirely urgent. The Preda would have you present . . . shortly. The First Eunuch enquired after your eldest brother?'

Brys sighed.

'I surmised,' Kuru Qan said, glancing up with a broad smile. 'Your unease tainted your sweat. Nifadas is sorely obsessed at the moment.' He set the lenses against his eyes once more. Focused on the Finadd's eyes – disconcerting, since it had never happened before. 'Who needs spies when one's nose roots out all truths?'

'I hope, Ceda, that you do not lose that talent, with this new invention of yours.'

'Ah, see! A swordsman indeed. The importance of every sense is not lost on you! What a measurable delight – here, let me show you.' He slid down from the stool and approached a table, where he poured clear liquid into a translucent beaker. Crouched low to check its level, then nodded. 'Measurable, as I had suspected.' He plucked the beaker from its stand and tossed the contents back, smacking his lips when he was done. 'But it is both brothers who haunt you now.'

'I am not immune to uncertainty.'

'One should hope not! An important admission. When the Preda is done with you – and it shall not be long – return to me. We have a task before us, you and I.'

'Very well, Ceda.'

'Time for some adjustments.' He pulled off the lenses once more. 'For us both,' he added.

Brys considered, then nodded. 'Until later, then, Ceda.'

He made his way from the sorceror's chamber.

Nifadas and Kuru Qan, they stand to one side of King Diskanar. Would that there was no other side.

The throne room was misnamed, in that the king was in the process of shifting the royal seat of power to the Eternal Domicile, now that the leaks in its lofty roof had been corrected. A few trappings remained, including the ancient rug approaching the dais, and the stylized gateway arching over the place where the throne had once stood.

When Brys arrived, only his old commander, Preda Unnutal Hebaz, was present. As always, a dominating figure, no matter how exalted her surroundings. She stood taller than most women, nearly Brys's own height. Fair-skinned, with a burnished cast to her blonde hair yet eyes of a dark hazel, she turned to face him at his approach. In her fortieth year, she was none the less possessed of extra-ordinary beauty that the weather lines only enhanced.

'Finadd Beddict, you are late.'

'Impromptu audiences with the First Eunuch and the Ceda—'

'We have but a few moments,' she interrupted. 'Take your place along the wall, as would a guard. They might recognize you, or they might assume you are but one of my underlings, especially given the poor light now that the sconces have been taken down. Either way, you are to stand at attention and say nothing.'

Frowning, Brys strode to his old guard's niche, turned about to face the chamber, then edged back into the shadows until hard stone pressed against his shoulders. He saw the Preda studying him for a moment, then she nodded and swung to face the doorway at the far corner of the wall behind the dais.

Ah, this meeting belongs to the other side . . .

The door slammed open to the gauntleted hand of a Prince's Guardsman, and the helmed, armoured figure of that man strode warily into the chamber. His sword was still in its scabbard, but Brys knew that Moroch Nevath could draw it in a single beat of a heart. He knew, also, that

Moroch had been the prince's own candidate for King's Champion. *And well deserved too. Moroch Nevath not only possesses the skill, he also has the presence* . . . And, although that bold manner irritated Brys in some indefinable way, he found himself envying it as well.

The Prince's Guard studied the chamber, fixing here and there on shadowed recesses, including the one wherein Brys stood – but it was a momentary thing, seeming only to acknowledge the presence of one of the Preda's guards – and Moroch finally settled his attention on Unnutal Hebaz.

A single nod of acknowledgement, then Moroch stepped to one side.

Prince Quillas Diskanar entered. Behind him came Chancellor Triban Gnol. Then, two figures that made Brys start. Queen Janall and her First Consort, Turudal Brizad.

By the Errant, the entire squalid nest.

Quillas bared his teeth at Unnutal Hebaz as would a dog at the end of his chain. 'You have released Finadd Gerun Eberict to Nifadas's entourage. I want him taken back, Preda. Choose someone else.'

Unnutal's tone was calm. 'Gerun Eberict's competence is above reproach, Prince Quillas. I am informed that the First Eunuch is pleased with the selection.'

Chancellor Triban Gnol spoke in an equally reasonable voice. 'Your prince believes otherwise, Preda. It behoves you to accord that opinion due respect.'

'The prince's beliefs are his own concern. I am charged by his father, the king, in this matter. Regarding what I do and do not respect, Chancellor, I strongly suggest you retract your challenge.'

Moroch Nevath growled and stepped forward.

The Preda's hand snapped out – not to the Prince's Guardsman, but towards the niche where Brys stood, halting him a half-stride from his position. The sword was already in his hand, and its freeing from the scabbard had been as silent as it had been fast.

Moroch's gaze flashed to Brys, the startled expression giving way to recognition. The man's own sword was but halfway out of its scabbard.

A dry chuckle from the queen. 'Ah, the Preda's decision for but one guard is . . . explained. Step forward, if you please, Champion.'

'That will not be necessary,' Unnutal said.

Brys nodded and slowly stepped back, sheathing his sword as he did so.

Queen Janall's brows rose at the Preda's brusque countermand. 'Dear Unnutal Hebaz, you rise far above your station.'

'The presumption is not mine, Queen. The Royal Guard answer to the king and no-one else.'

'Well, forgive me if I delight in challenging that antiquated conceit.' Janall fluttered one thin hand. 'Strengths are ever at risk of becoming weaknesses.' She stepped close to her son. 'Heed your mother's advice, Quillas. It was folly to cut at the Preda's pedestal, for it has not yet turned to sand. Patience, beloved one.'

The Chancellor sighed. 'The queen's advice—'

'Is *due respect*,' Quillas mimed. 'As you will, then. As you all will. Moroch!'

Bodyguard trailing, the prince strode from the chamber.

The queen's smile was tender as she said, 'Preda Unnutal Hebaz, we beg your forgiveness. This meeting was not of our choice, but my son insisted. From the moment our procession began, the Chancellor and I both sought to dissuade him.'

'To no avail,' the Chancellor said, sighing once more.

The Preda's expression did not change. 'Are we done?'

Queen Janall wagged a single finger in mute warning, then gestured to her First Consort, slipping her arm through his as they left.

Triban Gnol remained a moment longer. 'My congratulations, Preda,' he said. 'Finadd Gerun Eberict was an exquisite choice.'

Unnutal Hebaz said nothing.

Five heartbeats later and she and Brys were alone in the chamber.

The Preda turned. 'Your speed, Champion, never fails to take my breath away. I did not hear you, only . . . anticipated. Had I not, Moroch would now be dead.'

'Possibly, Preda. If only because he had dismissed my presence.'

'And Quillas would have only himself to blame.'

Brys said nothing.

'I should not have halted you.'

He watched her leave.

Gerun Eberict, you poor bastard.

Recalling that the Ceda wanted him, Brys swung about and strode from the chamber.

Leaving behind no blood.

And he knew that Kuru Qan would hear the relief in his every step.

The Ceda had been waiting outside his door, seemingly intent on practising a dance step, when Brys arrived.

'A few fraught moments?' Kuru Qan asked without looking up. 'Unimportant. For now. Come.'

Fifty paces on, down stone steps, along dusty corridors, and Brys guessed at their destination. He felt his heart sinking. A place he had heard of, but one he had yet to visit. It seemed the King's Champion was permitted to walk where a lowly Finadd was not. This time, however, the privilege was suspect.

They came to a pair of massive copper-sheathed doors. Green and rumpled with moss, they were bare of markings and showed no locking mechanism. The Ceda leaned on them and they parted with a grinding squeal.

Beyond rose narrow steps, leading to a walkway suspended knee-high above the floor by chains that reached down from the ceiling. The room was circular, and in the floor were set luminous tiles forming a spiral.

The walkway ended at a platform in the chamber's centre.

'Trepidation, Finadd? Well deserved.' Gesturing, Kuru Qan led Brys onto the walkway.

It swayed alarmingly.

'The striving for balance is made manifest,' the Ceda said, arms held out to the sides. 'One's steps must needs find the proper rhythm. Important, and difficult for all that there are two of us. No, do not look down upon the tiles – we are not yet ready. To the platform first. Here we are. Stand at my side, Finadd. Look with me upon the first tile of the spiral. What do you see?'

Brys studied the glowing tile. It was large, not quite square. Two spans of a spread hand in length, slightly less so in width.

The Holds. The Cedance. Kuru Qan's chamber of divination. Throughout Letheras there were casters of the tiles, readers of the Holds. Of course, their representations were small, like flattened dice. Only the King's Sorceror possessed tiles such as these. With ever-shifting faces. 'I see a barrow in a yard.'

'Ah, then you see truly. Good. An unhinged mind would reveal itself at this moment, its vision poisoned with fear and malice. Barrow, third from last among the tiles of the Azath Hold. Tell me, what do you sense from it?'

Brys frowned. 'Restlessness.'

'Aye. Disturbing, agreed?'

'Agreed.'

'But the Barrow is strong, is it not? It will not yield its claim. Yet, consider for a moment. Something is restless, there beneath that earth. And each time I have visited here in the past month, this tile has begun the spiral.'

'Or ended it.'

Kuru Qan tilted his head. 'Possibly. A swordsman's mind addresses the unexpected. Important? We'll see, won't we? Begins, or ends. So. If the Barrow is in no danger of yielding, then why does this tile persist? Perhaps we but witness what is, whilst that restlessness promises what *will* be. Alarming.'

'Ceda, have you visited the site of the Azath?'

'I have. Both tower and grounds are unchanged. The Hold's manifestation remains steadfast and contained. Now, drag your gaze onward, Finadd. Next?'

'A gate, formed of a dragon's gaping jaws.'

'Fifth in the Hold of the Dragon. Gate. How does it relate to Barrow of the Azath? Does the Gate precede or follow? In the span of my life, this is the first time I have seen a tile of Dragon Hold in the pattern. We are witness – or shall be witness – to a momentous occasion.'

Brys glanced at the Ceda. 'We are nearing Seventh Closure. It *is* momentous. The First Empire shall be reborn. King Diskanar shall be transformed – he shall *ascend* and assume the ancient title of First Emperor.'

Kuru Qan hugged himself. 'The popular interpretation, aye. But the true prophecy, Finadd, is somewhat more . . . obscure.'

Brys was alarmed by the Ceda's reaction. Nor had he known that the popular interpretation was other than accurate. 'Obscure? In what way?'

'"The king who rules at the Seventh Closure shall be transformed and so shall become the First Emperor reborn." Thus. Yet, questions arise. Transformed – how? And reborn – in the flesh? The First Emperor was destroyed along with the First Empire, in a distant land. Leaving the colonies here bereft. We have existed in isolation for a very long time, Finadd. Longer than you might believe.'

'Almost seven thousand years.'

The Ceda smiled. 'Language changes over time. Meaning twists. Mistakes compound with each transcribing. Even those stalwart sentinels of perfection – numbers – can, in a single careless moment, be profoundly altered. Shall I tell you my belief, Finadd? What would you say to my notion that some zeroes were dropped? At the beginning of this the Seventh Closure.'

Seventy thousand years? Seven hundred thousand?

'Describe for me the next four tiles.'

Feeling slightly unbalanced, Brys forced his attention back to the floor. 'I recognize that one. Betrayer of the Empty Hold. And the tile that follows: White Crow, of the Fulcra. The third is unknown to me. Shards of ice, one of which is upthrust from the ground and grows bright with reflected light.'

Kuru Qan sighed and nodded. 'Seed, last of the tiles in the Hold of Ice. Another unprecedented appearance. And the fourth?'

Brys shook his head. 'It is blank.'

'Just so. The divination ceases. Is blocked, perhaps, by events yet to occur, by choices as yet unmade. Or, it marks the beginning, the flux that is now, this very moment. Leading to the end, which is the last tile – Barrow. Unique mystery. I am at a loss.'

'Has anyone else seen this, Ceda? Have you discussed your impasse with anyone?'

'The First Eunuch has been informed, Brys Beddict. To ensure that he does not walk into the Great Meeting blind to whatever portents might arise there. And now, you. Three of us, Finadd.'

'Why me?'

'Because you are the King's Champion. It is your task to guard his life.'

Brys sighed. 'He keeps sending me away.'

'I will remind him yet again,' Kuru Qan said. 'He must surrender his love of solitude, or come to see no-one when he glances your way. Now, tell me what the queen incited her son to do in the old throne room.'

'Incited? She claimed the very opposite.'

'Unimportant. Tell me what your eyes witnessed, what your ears heard. Tell me, Brys Beddict, what your heart whispered.'

Brys stared down at the blank tile. 'Hull may prove a problem,' he said in a dull voice.

103

'This is what your heart whispered?'

'It is.'

'At the Great Meeting?'

He nodded.

'How?'

'I fear, Ceda, that he might kill Prince Quillas Diskanar.'

The building had once housed a carpenter's shop on the ground floor, with a modest collection of low-ceilinged residential rooms on the upper level, reached via a drop-down staircase. The front faced out onto Quillas Canal, opposite a landing where, presumably, the carpenter had received his supplies.

Tehol Beddict walked around the spacious workshop, noting the holes in the hardwood floor where mechanisms had been fitted, hooks on walls for tools still identifiable by the faded outlines. The air still smelled of sawdust and stains, and a single worktable ran the full length of the wall to the left of the entrance. The entire front wall, he saw, was constructed with removable panels. 'You purchased this outright?' he asked, facing the three women who had gathered at the foot of the staircase.

'The owner's business was expanding,' Shand said, 'as was his family.'

'Fronting the canal ... this place was worth something ...'

'Two thousand thirds. We bought most of his furniture upstairs. Ordered a desk that was delivered last night.' Shand waved a hand to encompass the ground level. 'This area's yours. I'd suggest a wall or two, leaving a corridor from the door to the stairs. That clay pipe is the kitchen drain. We knocked out the section leading to the kitchen upstairs, since we expect your servant to feed the four of us. The privy's out in the backyard, empties into the canal. There's also a cold shed, with a water-tight ice box big enough for a whole Nerek family to live in.'

'A rich carpenter with time on his hands,' Tehol said.

'He has talent,' Shand said, shrugging. 'Now, follow me. The office is upstairs. We've things to discuss.'

'Doesn't sound like it,' he replied. 'Sounds like everything is already decided. I can imagine Bugg's delight at the news. I hope you like figs.'

'You could take the roof,' Rissarh said with a sweet smile.

Tehol crossed his arms and rocked on his heels. 'Let me see if I understand all this. You threaten to expose my terrible secrets, and then offer me some kind of partnership for some venture you haven't even bothered describing. I can see this relationship setting deep roots, given such fertile soil.'

Shand scowled.

'Let's beat him senseless first,' Hejun said.

'It's simple,' Shand said, ignoring Hejun's suggestion. 'We have thirty thousand thirds and with it we want you to make ten.'

'Ten thousand thirds?'

'Ten peaks.'

Tehol stared at her. 'Ten peaks. Ten *million* thirds. I see, and what precisely do you want with all that money?'

'We want you to buy the rest of the islands.'

Tehol ran a hand through his hair and began pacing. 'You're insane. I started with a hundred docks and damn near killed myself making a single peak—'

'Only because you were frivolous, Tehol Beddict. You did it inside of a year, but you only *worked* a day or two every month.'

'Well, those days were murderous.'

'Liar. You never stepped wrong. Not once. You folded in and folded out and left everyone else wallowing in your wake. And they worshipped you for it.'

'Until you knifed them all,' Rissarh said, her smile broadening.

'Your skirt's slipping,' Hejun observed.

Tehol adjusted it. 'It wasn't exactly a knifing. What terrible images you conjure. I made my peak. I wasn't the first to ever make a peak, just the fastest.'

'With a hundred *docks*. Hard with a hundred levels, maybe. But docks? I made a hundred docks every three months when I was a child, picking olives and grapes. Nobody starts with docks. Nobody but you.'

'And now we're giving you thirty thousand thirds,' Rissarh said. 'Work the columns, Beddict. Ten million peaks? Why not?'

'If you think it's so easy why don't you do it yourselves?'

'We're not that smart,' Shand said. 'We're not easily distracted, either. We stumbled onto your trail and we followed it and here we are.'

'I left no trail.'

'Not one most could see, true. But as I said, we don't get distracted.'

Tehol continued pacing. 'The Merchant Tolls list Letheras's gross at between twelve and fifteen peaks, with maybe another five buried—'

'Is that five including your one?'

'Mine was written off, remember.'

'After a whole lot of pissing blood. Ten thousand curses tied to docks at the bottom of the canal, all with your name on them.'

Hejun asked in surprise, 'Really, Shand? Maybe we should get dredging rights—'

'Too late,' Tehol told her. 'Biri's got those.'

'Biri's a front man,' Shand said. 'You've got those rights, Tehol. Biri may not know it but he works for you.'

'Well, that's a situation I've yet to exploit.'

'Why?'

He shrugged. Then he halted and stared at Shand. 'There's no way you could know that.'

'You're right. I guessed.'

His eyes widened. 'You *could* make ten peaks, with an instinct like that, Shand.'

'You've fooled everyone because you don't make a wrong step, Tehol Beddict. They don't think you've buried your peak – not any more, not after this long with you living like a rat under the docks. You've truly lost it. Where, nobody knows, but somewhere. That's why they wrote off the loss, isn't it?'

'Money is sleight of hand,' Tehol said, nodding. 'Unless you've got diamonds in your hands. Then it's not just an idea any more. If you want to know the cheat behind the whole game, it's right there, lasses. Even when money's just an idea, it has power. Only it's not real power. Just the *promise* of power. But that promise is enough so long as everyone keeps pretending it's real. Stop pretending and it all falls apart.'

'Unless the diamonds are in your hands,' Shand said.

'Right. Then it's *real* power.'

'That's what you began to suspect, isn't it? So you went and tested it. And everything came within a stumble of falling apart.'

Tehol smiled. 'Imagine my dismay.'

'You weren't dismayed,' she said. 'You just realized how deadly an idea could be, in the wrong hands.'

'They're all the wrong hands, Shand. Including mine.'

'So you walked away.'

'And I'm not going back. Do your worst with me. Let Hull know. Take it all down. What's written off can be written back in. The Tolls are good at that. In fact, you'll trigger a boom. Everyone will sigh with relief, seeing that it was all in the game after all.'

'That's not what we want,' Shand said. 'You still don't get it. When we buy the rest of the islands, Tehol, we do it the same way you did. Ten peaks . . . *disappearing*.'

'The entire economy will collapse!'

At that the three women all nodded.

'You're fanatics!'

'Even worse,' Rissarh said, 'we're vengeful.'

'You're all half-bloods, aren't you?' He didn't need their answers to that. It was obvious. Not every half-blood had to *look* like a half-blood. 'Faraed, for Hejun. You two? Tarthenal?'

107

'Tarthenal. Letheras destroyed us. Now, we're going to destroy Letheras.'

'And,' Rissarh said, smiling again, 'you're going to show us how.'

'Because you hate your own people,' Shand said. 'The whole rapacious, cold-blooded lot of them. We want those islands, Tehol Beddict. We know about the remnants of the tribes you delivered to the ones you bought. We know they're hiding out there, trying to rebuild all that they had lost. But it's not enough. Walk this city's streets and the truth of that is plain. You did it for Hull. I had no idea he didn't know about it – you surprised me there. You know, I think you should tell him.'

'Why?'

'Because he needs healing, that's why.'

'I can't do that.'

Shand stepped close and settled a hand on Tehol's shoulder. The contact left him weak-kneed, so unexpected was the sympathy. 'You're right, you can't. Because we both know, *it wasn't enough.*'

'Tell him our way,' Hejun said. 'Tehol Beddict. Do it right this time.'

He pulled away and studied them. These three damned women. 'It's the Errant's curse, that he walks down paths he's walked before. But that trait of yours, of not getting distracted, it blinds both ways, I'm afraid.'

'What do you mean?'

'I mean, Shand, that Lether is about to fall – and not through my doing. Find Hull and ask him – I'm sure he's up there, somewhere. In the north. And, you know, it's rather amusing, how he fought so hard for your people, for every one of those tribes Lether then devoured. Because now, knowing what he knows, he's going to fight again. Only, this time, not for a tribe – not for the Tiste Edur. This time, for Lether. Because he knows, my friends, that we've met our match in those damned bastards. This time, it's the Edur who will do the devouring.'

'What makes you think so?' Shand demanded, and he saw the disbelief in her expression.

'Because they don't play the game,' he said.

'What if you're wrong?'

'It's possible. Either way, it's going to be bloody.'

'Then let's make it easier for the Tiste Edur.'

'Shand, you're talking treason.'

Her lips pressed into a thin line.

Rissarh barked a laugh. 'You idiot. We've been doing that all along.'

Errant take me, she's right. 'I'm not convinced a host of barbaric Edur overlords will do any better.'

'We're not talking about what's better,' Shand said. 'We're talking about revenge. Think of Hull, of what was done to him. Do it back, Tehol.'

I don't believe Hull would see it that way. Not quite. Not for a long, long time. 'You realize, don't you, that I've worked very hard at cultivating apathy. In fact, it seems to be bearing endless fruit.'

'Yes, the skirt doesn't hide much.'

'My instincts may be a bit dull.'

'Liar. They've just been lying in wait and you know it. Where do we start, Tehol Beddict?'

He sighed. 'All right. First and foremost, we lease out this ground floor. Biri needs the storage.'

'What about you?'

'I happen to like my abode, and I don't intend to leave. As far as anyone else is concerned, I'm still not playing the game. You three are the investors. So, put those damned weapons away; we're in a far deadlier war now. There's a family of Nerek camped outside my house. A mother and two children. Hire them as cook and runners. Then head down to the Merchant Tolls and get yourselves listed. You deal in property, construction and transportation. No other ventures. Not yet. Now, seven properties are for sale around the fifth wing of the Eternal Domicile. They're going cheap.'

'Because they're sinking.'

'Right. And we're going to fix that. And once we've done that, expect a visit from the Royal Surveyor and a motley collection of hopeful architects. Ladies, prepare to get rich.'

Looking for solid grounding? Bugg's Construction is your answer.

Until the flood sweeps the entire world away, that is.

'Can we buy you some clothes?'

Tehol blinked. 'Why?'

Seren stared down. The valley stretched below, its steep sides unrelieved forest, a deep motionless green. The glitter of rushing water threaded through the shadows in the cut's nadir. Blood of the Mountains, the Edur called that river. *Tis'forundal*. Its waters ran red with the sweat of iron.

The track they would take crossed that river again and again.

The lone Tiste Edur far below had, it seemed, emerged from that crimson stream. Striding to the head of the trail then beginning the ascent.

As if knowing we're here.

Buruk the Pale was taking his time with this journey, calling a halt shortly after midday. The wagons would not tip onto that rocky, sliding path into the valley until the morrow. Caution or drunk indifference, the result was the same.

Hull stood at her side. Both of them watched the Tiste Edur climb closer.

'Seren.'

'Yes?'

'You weep at night.'

'I thought you were asleep.'

He said nothing for a moment, then, 'Your weeping always woke me.'

And this is as close as you dare, isn't it? 'Would that yours had me.'

110

'I am sure it would have, Seren, had I wept.'

And this eases my guilt? She nodded towards that distant Tiste Edur. 'Do you recognize him?'

'I do.'

'Will he cause us trouble?'

'No, I don't think so. I believe he will be our escort back to Hiroth lands.'

'Noble-born?'

Hull nodded. 'Binadas Sengar.'

She hesitated, then asked, 'Have you cut flesh for him?'

'I have. As he has for me.'

Seren Pedac drew her furs tighter about her shoulders. The wind had not relented, though something of the valley's damp rot now rode its bludgeoning rush. 'Hull, do you fear this Great Meeting?'

'I need only look back to see what lies ahead.'

'Are you so sure of that?'

'We will buy peace, but it will be, for the Tiste Edur, a deadly peace.'

'But peace none the less, Hull.'

'Acquitor, you might as well know, and so understand me clearly. I mean to shatter that gathering. I mean to incite the Edur into war with Letheras.'

Stunned, she stared at him.

Hull Beddict turned away. 'With that knowledge,' he said, 'do as you will.'

CHAPTER THREE

Face to the Light
betrayed by the Dark
Father Shadow
lies bleeding
Unseen and unseeing
lost
until his Children
take the final path
and in the solitude
of strangers
Awaken once more

Tiste Edur prayer

A hard silence that seemed at home in the dense, impenetrable fog. The Blackwood paddles had been drawn from water thick as blood, which ran in rivulets, then beads, down the polished shafts, finally drying with a patina of salt in the cool, motionless air. And now there was nothing to do but wait.

Daughter Menandore had delivered a grim omen that morning. The body of a Beneda warrior. A bloated corpse scorched by sorcery, skin peeled back by the ceaseless hungers of the sea. The whispering roar of flies stung into flight by the arrival of those Edur whose slaves had first found it.

Letherii sorcery.

The warrior wore no scabbard, no armour. He had been fishing.

Four K'orthan longboats had set out from the river mouth shortly after the discovery. In the lead craft rode Hannan Mosag and his K'risnan Cadre, along with seventy-five blooded warriors. Crews of one hundred followed in the three additional raiders.

The tide carried them out for a time. It soon became clear that no wind waited offshore, so they left the three triangular sails on each ship furled and, thirty-five warriors to a side, had begun paddling.

Until the Warlock King had signalled a halt.

The fog enclosed the four raider longboats. Nothing could be seen twenty strokes of the paddle in any direction. Trull Sengar sat on the bench behind Fear. He had set his paddle down and now gripped the new iron-sheathed spear his father had given him.

The Letherii ships were close, he knew, drifting in the same manner as the Edur longboats. But they relied solely upon sail and so could do nothing until a wind rose.

And Hannan Mosag had made certain there would be no wind.

Shadow wraiths flickered over the deck, roving restlessly, long-clawed hands reaching down as they clambered on all fours. They prowled as if eager to leave the confines of the raider. Trull had never seen so many of them, and he knew that they were present on the other longboats as well. They would not, however, be the slayers of the Letherii. For that, the Warlock King had summoned something else.

He could feel it. Waiting beneath them. A vast patience, suspended in the depths.

Near the prow, Hannan Mosag slowly raised a hand, and, looking beyond the Warlock King, Trull saw the hulk of a Letherii harvest ship slowly emerge from the fog. Sails furled, lanterns at the end of out-thrust poles, casting dull, yellow light.

113

And then a second ship, bound to the first by a thick cable.

Shark fins cut the pellucid surface of the water around them.

And then, suddenly, those fins were gone.

Whatever waited below rose.

Emerged unseen with a shivering of the water.

A moment, blurred and uncertain.

Then screams.

Trull dropped his spear and clapped both hands to his ears – and he was not alone in that response, for the screams grew louder, drawn out from helpless throats and rising to shrieks. Sorcery flashed in the fog, briefly, then ceased.

The Letherii ships were on all sides now. Yet nothing could be seen of what was happening on them. The fog had blackened around them, coiling like smoke, and from that impenetrable gloom only the screams clawed free, like shreds of horror, the writhing of souls.

The sounds were in Trull's skull, indifferent to his efforts to block them. Hundreds of voices. Hundreds upon hundreds.

Then silence. Hard and absolute.

Hannan Mosag gestured.

The white cloak of fog vanished abruptly.

The calm seas now rolled beneath a steady wind. Above, the sun glared down from a fiercely blue sky.

Gone, too, was the black emanation that had engulfed the Letherii fleet.

The ships wallowed, burned-out lanterns pitching wildly.

'Paddle.'

Hannan Mosag's voice seemed to issue from directly beside Trull. He started, then reached down, along with everyone else, for a paddle. Rose to plant his hip against the gunnel, then chopped down into the water.

The longboat surged forward.

In moments they were holding blades firm in the water,

halting their craft alongside the hull of one of the ships.

Shadow wraiths swarmed up its red-stained side.

And Trull saw that the waterline on the hull had changed. Its hold was, he realized, now empty.

'Fear,' he hissed. 'What is going on? What has happened?'

His brother turned, and Trull was shocked by Fear's pallid visage. 'It is not for us, Trull,' he said, then swung round once more.

It is not for us. What does he mean by that? What isn't?

Dead sharks rolled in the waves around them. Their carcasses were split open, as if they had exploded from within. The water was streaked with viscid froth.

'We return now,' Hannan Mosag said. 'Man the sails, my warriors. We have witnessed. Now we must leave.'

Witnessed – in the name of Father Shadow, what?

Aboard the Letherii ships, canvas snapped and billowed.

The wraiths will deliver them. By the Dusk, this is no simple show of power. This – this is a challenge. A challenge, of such profound arrogance that it far surpassed that of these Letherii hunters and their foolish, suicidal harvest of the tusked seals. At that realization, a new thought came to Trull as he watched other warriors tending to the sails. *Who among the Letherii would knowingly send the crews of nineteen ships to their deaths? And why would those crews even agree to it?*

It was said gold was all that mattered to the Letherii. But who, in their right mind, would seek wealth when it meant certain death? They had to have known there would be no escape. *Then again, what if I had not stumbled upon them? What if I had not chosen the Calach strand to look for jade?* But no, now he was the one being arrogant. If not Trull, then another. The crime would never have gone unnoticed. The crime was *never intended* to go unnoticed.

He shared the confusion of his fellow warriors. Something was awry here. With both the Letherii and with . . . *us. With Hannan Mosag. Our Warlock King.*

Our shadows are dancing. Letherii and Edur, dancing out a

ritual – but these are not steps I can recognize. Father Shadow forgive me, I am frightened.

Nineteen ships of death sailed south, while four K'orthan raiders cut eastward. Four hundred Edur warriors, once more riding a hard silence.

It fell to the slaves to attend to the preparations. The Beneda corpse was laid out on a bed of sand on the floor of a large stone outbuilding adjoining the citadel, and left to drain.

The eye sockets, ears, nostrils and gaping mouth were all cleaned and evened out with soft wax. Chewed holes in its flesh were packed with a mixture of clay and oil.

With six Edur widows overseeing, a huge iron tray was set atop a trench filled with coals that had been prepared alongside the corpse. Copper coins rested on the tray, snapping and popping as the droplets of condensation on them sizzled and hissed then vanished.

Udinaas crouched beside the trench, staying far enough back to ensure that his sweat did not drip onto the coins – a blasphemy that meant instant death for the careless slave – and watched the coins, seeing them darken, becoming smoky black. Then, as the first glowing spot emerged in each coin's centre, he used pincers to pluck it from the tray and set it down on one of a row of fired-clay plates – one plate for each widow.

The widow, kneeling before the plate, employed a finer set of pincers to pick up the coin. And then pivoted to lean over the corpse.

First placement was the left eye socket. A crackling hiss, worms of smoke rising upward as the woman pressed down with the pincers, keeping the coin firmly in place, until it melded with the flesh and would thereafter resist being dislodged. Right eye socket followed. Nose, then forehead and cheeks, every coin touching its neighbours.

When the body's front and sides, including all the limbs, were done, melted wax was poured over the coin-sheathed

116

corpse. And, when that had cooled, it was then turned over. More coins, until the entire body was covered, excepting the soles of the feet and the palms of the hands. Another layer of melted wax followed.

The task of sheathing consumed most of the day, and it was near dusk when Udinaas finally stumbled from the outbuilding and stood, head bowed, while the cool air plucked at the sweat on his skin. He spat in an effort to get the foul stench out of his mouth. Burnt, rotting flesh in the building's turgid, oven-hot confines. The reek of scorched hair. No amount of scented oil and skin-combing could defeat what had seeped into his pores. It would be days before Udinaas had rid himself of that cloying, dreadful taste.

He stared down at the ground between his feet. His shoulder still ached from the forced healing done by Uruth. Since that time, he had had no opportunity to speak with Feather Witch.

To his masters, he had explained nothing. They had, in truth, not pressed him very hard. A handful of questions, and they'd seemed content with his awkward, ineffectual answers. Udinaas wondered if Uruth had been as unmotivated in her own questioning of Feather Witch. The Tiste Edur rarely displayed much awareness of their slaves, and even less understanding of their ways. It was, of course, the privilege of the conquerors to be that way, and the universal fate of the conquered to suffer that disregard.

Yet identities persisted. On a personal level. Freedom was little more than a tattered net, draped over a host of minor, self-imposed bindings. Its stripping away changed little, except, perhaps, the comforting delusion of the ideal. *Mind bound to self, self to flesh, flesh to bone. As the Errant wills, we are a latticework of cages, and whatever flutters within knows but one freedom, and that is death.*

The conquerors always assumed that what they conquered was identity. But the truth was, identity could only be killed from within, and even that gesture was but a chimera. Isolation had many children, and dissolution was but one of them – yet its path was unique, for that path began when identity was left behind.

From the building behind him emerged the song of mourning, the Edur cadence of grief. *Hunh, hunh, hunh, hunh . . .* A sound that always chilled Udinaas. *Like emotion striking the same wall, again and again and again. The voice of the trapped, the blocked. A voice overwhelmed by the truths of the world.* For the Edur, grieving was less about loss than about being lost.

Is that what comes when you live a hundred thousand years?

The widows then emerged, surrounding the corpse that floated waist-high on thick, swirling shadows. A figure of copper coins. The Edur's singular use of money. Copper, tin, bronze, iron, silver and gold, it was the armour of the dead.

At least that's honest. Letherii use money to purchase the opposite. Well, not quite. More like the illusion of the opposite. Wealth as life's armour. Keep, fortress, citadel, eternally vigilant army. But the enemy cares nothing for all that, for the enemy knows you are defenceless.

'Hunh, hunh, hunh, hunh . . .'

This was Daughter Sheltatha Lore's hour, when all things material became uncertain. Smudged by light's retreat, when the air lost clarity and revealed its motes and grains, the imperfections both light and dark so perfectly disguised at other times. When the throne was shown to be empty.

Why not *worship money? At least its rewards are obvious and immediate.* But no, that was simplistic. Letherii worship was more subtle, its ethics bound to those traits and habits that well served the acquisition of wealth. Diligence, discipline, hard work, optimism, the personalization of glory. And the corresponding evils: sloth, despair and the anonymity of failure. The world was brutal enough to winnow one from the other and leave no room for doubt or mealy equivocation. In this way, worship could become pragmatism, and pragmatism was a cold god.

Errant make ours a cold god, so we may act without

constraint. A suitable Letherii prayer, though none would utter it in such a bold fashion. Feather Witch said that every act made was a prayer, and thus in the course of a day were served a host of gods. Wine and nectar and rustleaf and the imbibing thereof was a prayer to death, she said. Love was a prayer to life. Vengeance was a prayer to the demons of righteousness. Sealing a business pact was, she said with a faint smile, a prayer to the whisperer of illusions. Attainment for one was born of deprivation for another, after all. A game played with two hands.

'Hunh, hunh, hunh, hunh . . .'

He shook himself. His sodden tunic now wrapped him in damp chill.

A shout from the direction of the sea. The K'orthan raiders were returning. Udinaas walked across the compound, towards the Sengar household. He saw Tomad Sengar and his wife Uruth emerge, and dropped to his knees, head pressed to the ground, until they passed. Then he rose and hurried into the longhouse.

The copper-sheathed corpse would be placed within the hollowed trunk of a Blackwood, the ends sealed with discs of cedar. Six days from now, the bole would be buried in one of a dozen sacred groves in the forest. Until that moment, the dirge would continue. The widows taking turns with that blunt, terrible utterance.

He made his way to the small alcove where his sleeping pallet waited. The longboats would file into the canal, one after the other in the grainy half-light. They would not have failed. They never did. The crews of nineteen Letherii ships were now dead – no slaves taken, not this time. Standing on both sides of the canal, the noble wives and fathers greeted their warriors in silence.

In silence.

Because something terrible has happened.

He lay down on his back, staring up at the slanted ceiling, feeling a strange, unnerving constriction in his throat. And could hear, in the rush of his blood, a faint

echo behind his heart. A double beat. *Hunh hunh Huh huh.
Hunh hunh Huh huh . . .*

*Who are you? What are you waiting for? What do you want
with me?*

Trull clambered onto the landing, the cold haft of his spear
in his right hand, its iron-shod butt striking sparks on the
flagstones as he stepped away from the canal's edge and
halted beside Fear. Opposite them, but remaining five paces
away, stood Tomad and Uruth. Rhulad was nowhere to be
seen.

Nor, he realized, was Mayen.

A glance revealed that Fear was scanning the welcoming
crowd. There was no change in expression, but he strode
towards Tomad.

'Mayen is in the forest with the other maidens,' Tomad
said. 'Collecting morok. They are guarded by Theradas, and
Midik and Rhulad.'

'My son.' Uruth stepped closer, eyes searching Fear's
visage. '*What did he do?*'

Fear shook his head.

'They died without honour,' Trull said. 'We could not see
the hand that delivered that death, but it was . . .
monstrous.'

'And the harvest?' Tomad asked.

'It was taken, Father. By that same hand.'

A flash of anger in Uruth's eyes. 'This was no full unveiling. This was a *demonic* summoning.'

Trull frowned. 'I do not understand, Mother. There were
shadows—'

'And a darkness,' Fear cut in. 'From the depths . . .
darkness.'

She crossed her arms and looked away. Trull had never
seen Uruth so distressed.

And in himself, his own growing unease. Fully three-
fifths of the Tiste Edur employed sorcery. A multitude of
fragments from the riven warren of Kurald Emurlahn.

120

Shadow's power displayed myriad flavours. Among Uruth's sons, only Binadas walked the paths of sorcery. Fear's words had none the less triggered a recognition in Trull. Every Tiste Edur understood his own, after all. Caster of magic or not.

'Mother, Hannan Mosag's sorcery was not Kurald Emurlahn.' He did not need their expressions to realize that he had been the last among them to understand that truth. He grimaced. 'Forgive me my foolish words—'

'Foolish only in speaking them aloud,' Uruth said. 'Fear, take Trull and Rhulad. Go to the Stone Bowl—'

'Stop this. Now.' Tomad's voice was hard, his expression dark. 'Fear. Trull. Return to the house and await me there. Uruth, tend to the needs of the widows. A fallen warrior faces his first dusk among kin. Propitiations must be made.'

For a moment Trull thought she was going to object. Instead, lips pressed into a line, she nodded and strode away.

Fear beckoned Trull and they walked to the longhouse, leaving their father standing alone beside the canal.

'These are awkward times,' Trull said.

'Is there need,' Fear asked, 'when you stand between Rhulad and Mayen?'

Trull clamped his mouth shut. Too off-balance to deflect the question with a disarming reply.

Fear took the silence for an answer. 'And when you stand between them, who do you face?'

'I – I am sorry, Fear. Your question was unexpected. Is there need, you ask. My answer is: I don't know.'

'Ah, I see.'

'His strutting . . . irritates me.'

Fear made no response.

They came to the doorway. Trull studied his brother. 'Fear, what is this Stone Bowl? I have never heard—'

'It doesn't matter,' he replied, then walked inside.

Trull remained at the threshold. He ran a hand through his hair, turned and looked back across the compound. Those

121

who had stood in welcome were gone, as were their warrior kin. Hannan Mosag and his K'risnan Cadre were nowhere to be seen. A lone figure remained. Tomad.

Are we so different from everyone else?

Yes. For the Warlock King has asked for Tomad's sons. To pursue a vision.

He has made us his servants. Yet . . . is he the master?

In his dream, Udinaas found himself kneeling in ashes. He was cut and bleeding. His hands. His legs. The ash seemed to gnaw into the wounds with avid hunger. The tightness in his throat made him gasp for breath. He clawed at the air as he clambered onto his feet and stood, wavering – and the sky roared and raced in on all sides.

Fire. A storm of fire.

He screamed.

And found himself on his knees once more.

Beyond his ragged breathing, only silence. Udinaas lifted his head. The storm was gone.

Figures on the plain. Walking, dust roiling up behind them like wind-tossed shrouds. Weapons impaled them. Limbs hung from shreds of tendon and muscle. Sightless eyes and expressions twisted with fearful recognition – faces seeing their own deaths – blind to his own presence as they marched past.

Rising up within him, a vast sense of loss. Grief, then the bitter whisper of betrayal.

Someone will pay for this. Someone will pay.

Someone.

Someone.

The words were not his, the thoughts were another's, but the voice, there in the centre of his skull – that voice was his own.

A dead warrior walked close. Tall, black-skinned. A sword had taken most of his face. Bone gleamed, latticed with red cracks from some fierce impact.

A flash of motion.

Metal-clad hand crashed into the side of Udinaas's head. Blood sprayed. He was in a cloud of grey ash, on the ground. Blinking burning fire.

He felt gauntleted fingers close about his left ankle. His leg was viciously yanked upward.

And then the warrior began dragging him.

Where are we going?

'The Lady is harsh.'

The Lady?

'Is harsh.'

She awaits us at journey's end?

'She is not one who waits.'

He twisted as he was pulled along, found himself staring back at the furrow he'd made in the ashes. A track reaching to the horizon. And black blood was welling from that ragged gouge. *How long has he been dragging me? Whom do I wound?*

The thunder of hoofs.

'She comes.'

Udinaas turned onto his back, struggled to raise his head.

A piercing scream.

Then a sword ripped through the warrior dragging Udinaas. Cutting it in half. The hand fell away from his ankle and he rolled to one side as iron-shod hoofs thundered past.

She blazed, blinding white. A sword flickering like lightning in one hand. In the other, a double-bladed axe that dripped something molten in its wake. The horse—

Naught but bones, bound by fire.

The huge skeletal beast tossed its head as it wheeled round. The woman was masked in flat, featureless gold. A headdress of arching, gilt scales rose like hackles about her head. Weapons lifted.

And Udinaas stared into her eyes.

He flinched away, scrabbling to his feet, then running.

Hoofs pounded behind him.

Daughter Dawn. Menandore—

123

Before him were sprawled the warriors that had walked alongside the one dragging him. Flames licking along wounds, dull smoke rising from torn flesh. None moved. *They keep dying, don't they? Again and again. They keep dying—*

He ran.

Then was struck. A wall of ridged bone smashing into his right shoulder, spinning him through the air. He hit the ground, tumbled and rolled, limbs flopping.

His eyes stared up into swirling dust, the sky behind it spinning.

A shape appeared in its midst, and a hard-soled boot settled on his chest.

When she spoke, her voice was like the hissing of a thousand snakes. 'The blood of a Locqui Wyval . . . in the body of a slave. Which heart, mortal, will you ride?'

He could not draw breath. The pressure of the boot was building, crushing his chest. He clawed at it.

'Let your soul answer. Before you die.'

I ride . . . that which I have always ridden.

'A coward's answer.'

Yes.

'A moment remains. For you to reconsider.'

Blackness closed around him. He could taste blood in the grit filling his mouth. *Wyval! I ride the Wyval!*

The boot slipped to one side.

A gauntleted hand reached down to the rope he used as a belt. Fingers clenched and he was lifted from the ground, arching, head dangling. Before him, a world turned upside down. Lifted, until his hips pushed up against the inside of her thighs.

He felt his tunic pulled up onto his belly. A hand tearing his loincloth away. Cold iron fingers clamped round him.

He groaned.

And was pushed inside.

Fire in his blood. Agony in his hips and lower back as, with one hand, she drove him up again and again.

Until he spasmed.

The hand released him and he thumped back onto the ground, shuddering.

He did not hear her walk away.

He heard nothing. Nothing but the two hearts within him. Their beats drawing closer, ever closer.

After a time someone settled down beside Udinaas.

'Debtor.'

Someone will pay. He almost laughed.

A hand on his shoulder. 'Udinaas. Where is this place?'

'I don't know.' He turned his head, stared up into the frightened eyes of Feather Witch. 'What do the tiles tell you?'

'I don't have them.'

'Think of them. Cast them, in your mind.'

'What do you know of such things, Udinaas?'

He slowly sat up. The pain was gone. No bruises, not even a scratch beneath the layer of ash. He dragged his tunic down to cover his crotch. 'Nothing,' he replied.

'You do not need divination,' she said, 'to know what has just happened.'

His smile was bitter. 'I do. Dawn. The Edur's most feared Daughter. Menandore. She was here.'

'The Letherii are not visited by Tiste Edur gods—'

'I was.' He looked away. 'She, uh, made use of me.'

Feather Witch rose. 'Wyval blood has taken you. You are poisoned with visions, Debtor. Madness. Dreams that you are more than the man everyone else sees.'

'Look at the bodies around us, Feather Witch. She cut them down.'

'They are long dead.'

'Aye, yet they were *walking*. See this track – one of them dragged me and that is my trail. And there, her horse's hoofs made those.'

But she was not looking, her gaze instead fixed on Udinaas. 'This is a world of your own conjuring,' she said. 'Your mind is beset by false visions.'

'Cast your tiles.'

'No. This is a dead place.'

'The Wyval's blood is alive, Feather Witch. The Wyval's blood is what binds us to the Tiste Edur.'

'Impossible. Wyval are spawn of the Eleint. They are the mongrels of the dragons, and even the dragons do not control them. They are of the Hold, yet feral.'

'I saw a white crow. On the strand. That is what I was coming to tell you, hoping to reach you before you cast the tiles. I sought to banish it, and its answer was laughter. When you were attacked, I thought it was the White Crow. But don't you see? White, the face of Menandore, of Dawn. That is what the Fulcra were showing us.'

'I will not be devoured by your madness, Debtor.'

'You asked me to lie to Uruth and the other Edur. I did as you asked, Feather Witch.'

'But now the Wyval has taken you. And soon it will kill you, and even the Edur can do nothing. As soon as they realize that you are indeed poisoned, they will cut out your heart.'

'Do you fear that I will become a Wyval? Is that my fate?'

She shook her head. 'This is not the kiss of a Soletaken, Udinaas. It is a disease that attacks your brain. Poisons the clear blood of your thoughts.'

'Are you truly here, Feather Witch? Here, in my dream?'

With the question her form grew translucent, wavered, then scattered like windblown sand.

He was alone once more.

Will I never awaken?

Motion in the sky to his right drew him round.

Dragons. A score of the creatures, riding distant currents just above the uncertain horizon. Around them swarmed Wyval, like gnats.

And Udinaas suddenly understood something.

They are going to war.

Morok leaves covered the corpse. Over the next few days, those leaves would begin to rot, leaching into the amber wax a bluish stain, until the coin-sheathed body beneath became a blurred shape, as if encased in ice.

The shadow in the wax, enclosing the Beneda warrior for all time. A haven for wandering wraiths, there within the hollowed log.

Trull stood beside the corpse. The Blackwood bole was still being prepared in an unlit building to one side of the citadel. Living wood resisted the hands that would alter its shape. But it loved death and so could be cajoled.

Distant cries in the village as voices lifted in a final prayer to Daughter Dusk. Night was moments from arriving. The empty hours, when even faith itself must be held quiescent, lay ahead. Night belonged to the Betrayer. Who sought to murder Father Shadow at their very moment of triumph, and who very nearly succeeded.

There were prohibitions against serious discourse during this passage of time. In darkness prowled deceit, an unseen breath that any could draw in, and so become infected.

No swords were buried beneath the threshold of homes wherein maidens dwelt. To seal marriage now would be to doom its fate. A child delivered was put to death. Lovers did not touch one another. The day was dead.

Soon, however, the moon would rise and shadows would return once more. Just as Scabandari Bloodeye emerged from the darkness, so too did the world. *Failure awaits the Betrayer.* It could not be otherwise, lest the realms descend into chaos.

He stared down at the mound of leaves beneath which lay the body of the warrior. He had volunteered to stand guard this first night. No Edur corpse was ever left unattended when darkness prowled, for it cared naught whether its breath flowed into warm flesh or cold. A corpse could unleash dire events as easily as the acts of someone alive. It had no need for a voice or gestures of its own. Others were ever eager to speak for it, to draw blade or dagger.

Hannan Mosag had proclaimed this the greatest flaw among the Edur. Old men and the dead were the first whisperers of the word *vengeance*. Old men and the dead stood at the same wall, and while the dead faced it, old men held their backs to it. Beyond that wall was oblivion. They spoke from the end times, and both knew a need to lead the young onto identical paths, if only to give meaning to all they had known and all they had done.

Feuds were now forbidden. Crimes of vengeance sentenced an entire bloodline to disgraced execution.

Trull Sengar had watched, from where he stood in the gloom beneath a tree – the body before him – had watched his brother Rhulad walk out into the forest. In these, the dark hours, he had been furtive in his movement, stealing like a wraith from the village edge.

Into the forest, onto the north trail.

That led to the cemetery that had been chosen for the Beneda warrior's interment.

Where a lone woman stood vigil against the night.

It may be an attempt . . . that will fail. Or it is a repetition of meetings that have occurred before, many times. She is unknowable. As all women are unknowable. But he isn't. He was too late to the war and so his belt is bare. He would draw blood another way.

Because Rhulad must win. In everything, he must win. That is the cliff-edge of his life, the narrow strand he himself fashions, with every slight observed – whether it be real or imagined matters not – every silent moment that, to him, screams scorn upon the vast emptiness of his achievements.

Rhulad. Everything worth fighting for is gained without fighting. Every struggle is a struggle against doubt. Honour is not a thing to be chased, for it, as with all other forces of life, is in fact impelled, streaking straight for you. The moment of collision is where the truth of you is revealed.

An attempt. Which she will refuse, with outrage in her eyes.

Or their arms are now entwined, and in the darkness there is heat and sweat. And betrayal.

And he could not move, could not abandon his own vigil above this anonymous Beneda warrior.

His brother Fear had made a sword, as was the custom.

128

He had stood before Mayen with the blade resting on the backs of his hands. And she had stepped forward, witnessed by all, to take the weapon from him. Carrying it back to her home.

Betrothal.

A year from that day – less than five weeks from now – she would emerge from the doorway with that sword. Then, using it to excavate a trench before the threshold, she would set it down in the earth and bury it. Iron and soil, weapon and home. Man and woman.

Marriage.

Before that day when Fear presented the sword, Rhulad had not once looked at Mayen. Was it the uninterest of youth? No, the Edur were not like Letherii. A year among the Letherii was as a day among the Edur. There were a handful of prettier women among the maidens of noble-born households. But he had set his eyes upon her thereafter.

And that made it what it was.

He could abandon this vigil. A Beneda warrior was not a Hiroth warrior, after all. A sea-gnawed corpse clothed in copper, not gold. He could set out on that trail, padding through the darkness.

To find what? Certainty, the sharp teeth behind all that gnawed at his thoughts.

And the worth of that?

It is these dark hours—

Trull Sengar's eyes slowly widened. A figure had emerged from the forest edge opposite him. Heart thudding, he stared.

It stepped forward. Black blood in its mouth. Skin a pallid, dulled reflection of moonlight, smeared in dirt, smudged by something like mould. Twin, empty scabbards of polished wood at its hips. Fragments of armour hanging from it. Tall, yet stoop-shouldered, as if height had become its own imposition.

Eyes like dying coals.

'Ah,' it murmured, looking down on the heap of leaves, 'what have we here?' It spoke the language of night, close kin to that of the Edur.

Trembling, Trull forced himself to step forward, shifting his spear into a two-handed grip, the iron blade hovering above the corpse. 'He is not for you,' he said, his throat suddenly parched and strangely tight.

The eyes glowed brighter for a moment as the white-skinned apparition glanced up at Trull. 'Tiste Edur, do you know me?'

Trull nodded. 'The ghost of darkness. The Betrayer.'

A yellow and black grin.

Trull flinched as it drew a step closer and then settled to a crouch on the other side of the leaves. 'Begone from here, ghost,' the Edur said.

'Or you will do what?'

'Sound the alarm.'

'How? Your voice is but a whisper now. Your throat is clenched. You struggle to breathe. Is it betrayal that strangles you, Edur? Never mind. I have wandered far, and have no desire to wear this man's armour.' It straightened. 'Move back, warrior, if you wish to draw breath.'

Trull held himself where he was. The air hissed its way down his constricted throat, and he could feel his limbs weakening.

'Well, cowardice was never a flaw among the Edur. Have it your way, then.' The figure turned and walked towards the forest edge.

Blessed lungful of air, then another. Head spinning, Trull planted his spear and leaned on it. 'Wait!'

The Betrayer halted, faced him once more.

'This – this has never happened before. The vigil—'

'Contested only by hungry earth spirits.' The Betrayer nodded. 'Or, even more pathetic, by the spirits of uprooted Blackwoods, sinking into the flesh to do ... what? Nothing, just as they did in life. There are myriad forces in this world, Tiste Edur, and the majority of them are weak.'

'Father Shadow imprisoned you—'

'So he did, and there I remain.' Once again, that ghastly smile. 'Except when I dream. Mother Dark's reluctant gift, a reminder to me that She does not forget. A reminder to me that I, too, must never forget.'

'This is not a dream,' Trull said.

'They were shattered,' the Betrayer said. 'Long ago. Fragments scattered across a battlefield. Why would anyone want them? Those broken shards can never be reunited. They are, each and every one, now folded in on themselves. So, I wonder, *what did he do with them?*'

The figure walked into the forest and was gone.

'This,' Trull whispered, 'is not a dream.'

Udinaas opened his eyes. The stench of the seared corpse remained in his nose and mouth, thick in his throat. Above him, the longhouse's close slanted ceiling, rough black bark and yellowed chinking. He remained motionless beneath the blankets.

Was it near dawn?

He could hear nothing, no voices from the chambers beyond. But that told him little. The hours before the moon rose were silent ones. As were, of course, the hours when everyone slept. He had nets to repair the coming day. And rope strands to weave.

Perhaps that is the truth of madness, when a mind can do nothing but make endless lists of the mundane tasks awaiting it, as proof of its sanity. Mend those nets. Wind those strands. *See? I have not lost the meaning of my life.*

The blood of the Wyval was neither hot nor cold. It did not rage. Udinaas felt no different in his body. *But the clear blood of my thoughts, oh, they are stained indeed.* He pushed the blankets away and sat up. *This is the path, then, and I am to stay on it. Until the moment comes.*

Mend the nets. Weave the strands.

Dig the hole for that Beneda warrior, who would have just opened his eyes, had he any. And seen not the blackness of the

131

imprisoning coins. Seen not the blue wax, nor the morok leaves reacting to that wax and turning wet and black. Seen, instead, the face of . . . something else.

Wyval circled dragons in flight. He had seen that. Like hounds surrounding their master as the hunt is about to be unleashed. *I know, then, why I am where I have arrived. And when is an answer the night is yet to whisper – no, not whisper, but howl. The call to the chase by Darkness itself.*

Udinaas realized he was among the enemy. Not as a Letherii sentenced to a life of slavery. That was as nothing to the peril his new blood felt, here in this heart of Edur and Kurald Emurlahn.

Feather Witch would have been better, I suppose, but Mother Dark moves unseen even in things such as these.

He made his way into the main chamber.

And came face to face with Uruth.

'These are not the hours to wander, slave,' she said.

He saw that she was trembling.

Udinaas sank to the floor and set his forehead against the worn planks.

'Prepare the cloaks of Fear, Rhulad and Trull, for travel this night. Be ready before the moon's rise. Food and drink for a morning's repast.'

He quickly climbed to his feet to do as she bid, but was stopped by an outstretched hand.

'Udinaas,' Uruth said. 'You do this alone, telling no-one.'

He nodded.

Shadows crept out from the forest. The moon had risen, prison world to Menandore's true father, who was trapped within it. Father Shadow's ancient battles had made this world, shaped it in so many ways. Scabandari Bloodeye, stalwart defender against the fanatic servants of implacable certitude, whether that certitude blazed blinding white, or was the all-swallowing black. The defeats he had delivered – the burying of Brother Dark and the imprisonment of Brother Light there in that distant, latticed world in the sky – were both gifts, and not just to the Edur but to all who were born and lived only to one day die.

The gifts of freedom, a will unchained unless one affixed upon oneself such chains – the crowding host's uncountable, ever-rattling offers, each whispering promises of salvation against confusion – and wore them like armour.

Trull Sengar saw chains upon the Letherii. He saw the impenetrable net which bound them, the links of reasoning woven together into a chaotic mass where no beginning and no end could be found. He understood why they worshipped an empty throne. And he knew the manner in which they would justify all that they did. Progress was necessity, growth was gain. Reciprocity belonged to fools and debt was the binding force of all nature, of every people and every civilization. Debt was its own language, within which were used words like negotiation, compensation and justification, and legality was a skein of duplicity that blinded the eyes of justice.

An empty throne. Atop a mountain of gold coins.

Father Shadow had sought a world wherein uncertainty could work its insidious poison against those who chose intransigence as their weapon – with which they held wisdom at bay. Where every fortress eventually crumbled from within, from the very weight of those chains that exerted so inflexible an embrace.

In his mind he argued with that ghost – the Betrayer. The one who sought to murder Scabandari Bloodeye all those thousands of years ago. He argued that every certainty is an empty throne. That those who knew but one path would come to worship it, even as it led to a cliff's edge. He argued, and in the silence of that ghost's indifference to his words he came to realize that he himself spoke – fierce with heat – from the foot of an empty throne.

Scabandari Bloodeye had never made that world. He had vanished in this one, lost on a path no-one else could follow.

Trull Sengar stood before the corpse and its mound of

133

rotting leaves, and felt desolation in his soul. A multitude of paths waited before him, and they were all sordid, sodden with despair.

The sound of boots on the trail. He turned.

Fear and Rhulad approached. Wearing their cloaks. Fear carried Trull's own in his arms, and from the man's shoulders hung a small pack.

Rhulad's face was flushed, and Trull could not tell if it was born of anxiety or excitement.

'I greet you, Trull,' Fear said, handing him the cloak.

'Where are we going?'

'Our father passes this night in the temple. Praying for guidance.'

'The Stone Bowl,' Rhulad said, his eyes glittering. 'Mother sends us to the Stone Bowl.'

'Why?'

Rhulad shrugged.

Trull faced Fear. 'What is this Stone Bowl? I have never heard of it.'

'An old place. In the Kaschan Trench.'

'You knew of this place, Rhulad?'

His younger brother shook his head. 'Not until tonight, when Mother described it. We have all walked the edge of the Trench. Of course the darkness of its heart is impenetrable – how could we have guessed that a holy site hid within it?'

'A holy site? In absolute darkness?'

'The significance of that,' Fear said, 'will be made evident soon enough, Trull.'

They began walking, eldest brother in the lead. Into the forest, onto a trail leading northwest. 'Fear,' Trull said, 'has Uruth spoken to you of the Stone Bowl before?'

'I am Weapons Master,' Fear replied. 'There were rites to observe . . .'

Among them, Trull knew, the memorization of every battle the Edur ever fought. He then wondered why that thought had come to him, in answer to Fear's words. What hidden linkages was his own mind seeking to reveal, and why was he unable to discern them?

They continued on, avoiding pools of moonlight unbroken by shadows. 'Tomad forbade us this journey,' Trull said after a time.

'In matters of sorcery,' Fear said, 'Uruth is superior to Tomad.'

'And this is a matter of sorcery?'

Rhulad snorted behind Trull. 'You stood with us in the Warlock King's longboat.'

'I did,' agreed Trull. 'Fear, would Hannan Mosag approve of what we do, of what Uruth commands of us?'

Fear said nothing.

'You,' Rhulad said, 'are too filled with doubt, brother. It binds you in place—'

'I watched you walk the path to the chosen cemetery, Rhulad. After Dusk's departure and before the moon's rise.'

If Fear reacted to this, his back did not reveal it, nor did his steps falter on the trail.

'What of it?' Rhulad asked, his tone too loose, too casual.

'My words, brother, are not to be answered with flippancy.'

'I knew that Fear was busy overseeing the return of weapons to the armoury,' Rhulad said. 'And I sensed a malevolence prowling the darkness. And so I stood in hidden vigil over his betrothed, who was alone in the cemetery. I may be unblooded, brother, but I am not without courage. I know you believe that inexperience is the soil in which thrive the roots of false courage. But I am not false, no matter what you think. For me, inexperience is unbroken soil, not yet ready for roots. I stood in my brother's place.'

'Malevolence in the night, Rhulad? Whose?'

'I could not be certain. But I felt it.'

'Fear,' Trull said, 'have you no questions for Rhulad on this matter?'

'No,' Fear replied drily. 'There is no need for that . . .

when you are around.'

Trull clamped his mouth shut, thankful that the night obscured the flush on his face.

There was silence for some time after that.

The trail began climbing, winding among outcrops of lichen-skinned granite. They climbed over fallen trees here and there, scrambled up steep slides. The moon's light grew diffuse, and Trull sensed it was near dawn by the time they reached the highest point of the trail.

The path now took them inland – eastward – along a ridge of toppled trees and broken boulders. Water trapped in depressions in the bedrock formed impenetrable black pools that spread across the trail. The sky began to lighten overhead.

Fear then led them off the path, north, across tumbled scree and among the twisted trees. A short while later Kaschan Trench was before them.

A vast gorge, like a knife's puncturing wound in the bedrock, its sides sheer and streaming with water, it ran in a jagged line, beginning beneath Hasana Inlet half a day to the west, and finally vanishing into the bedrock more than a day's travel to the east. They were at its widest point, two hundred or so paces across, the landscape opposite slightly higher but otherwise identical – scattered boulders looking as if they had been pushed up from the gorge and mangled trees that seemed sickened by some unseen breath from the depths.

Fear unclasped his cloak, dropped his pack and walked over to a misshapen mound of stones. He cleared away dead branches and Trull saw that the stones were a cairn of some sort. Fear removed the capstone, and reached down into the hollow beneath. He lifted clear a coil of knotted rope.

'Remove your cloak and your weapons,' he said as he carried the coil to the edge.

He found one end and tied his pack, cloak, sword and spear to it. Trull and Rhulad came close with their own gear and all was bound to the rope. Fear then began lowering it over the side.

'Trull, take this other end and lead it to a place of shadow. A place where the shadow will not retreat before the sun as the day passes.'

He picked up the rope end and walked to a large, tilted boulder. When he fed the end into the shadows at its base he felt countless hands grasp it. Trull stepped back. The rope was now taut.

Returning to the edge, he saw that Fear had already begun his descent. Rhulad stood staring down.

'We're to wait until he reaches the bottom,' Rhulad said. 'He will tug thrice upon the rope. He asked that I go next.'

'Very well.'

'She has the sweetest lips,' Rhulad murmured, then looked up and met Trull's eyes. 'Is that what you want me to say? To give proof to your suspicions?'

'I have many suspicions, brother,' Trull replied. 'We have sun-scorched thoughts, we have dark-swallowed thoughts. But it is the shadow thoughts that move with stealth, creeping to the very edge of the rival realms – if only to see what there is to be seen.'

'And if they see nothing?'

'They never see nothing, Rhulad.'

'Then illusions? What if they see only what their imagination conjures? False games of light? Shapes in the darkness? Is this not how suspicion becomes a poison? But a poison like white nectar, every taste leaving you thirsting for more.'

Trull was silent for a long moment. Then he said, 'Fear spoke to me not long ago. Of how one is perceived, rather than how one truly is. How the power of the former can overwhelm that of the latter. How, indeed, perception shapes truth like waves on stone.'

'What would you ask of me, Trull?'

He faced Rhulad directly. 'Cease your strutting before Mayen.'

A strange smile, then, 'Very well, brother.'

137

Trull's eyes widened slightly.

The rope snapped three times.

'My turn,' Rhulad said. He grasped hold of the rope and was quickly gone from sight.

The knots of these words were anything but loose. Trull drew a deep breath, let it out slowly, wondering at that smile. The peculiarity of it. A smile that might have been pain, a smile born of hurt.

Then he turned upon himself and studied what he was feeling. Difficult to find, to recognize, but . . . *Father Shadow forgive me. I feel . . . sullied.*

The three tugs startled him.

Trull took the heavy rope in his hands, feeling the sheath of beeswax rubbed into the fibres to keep them from rotting. Without the knots for foot- and hand-holds, the descent would be treacherous indeed. He walked out over the edge, facing inward, then leaned back and began making his way down.

Glittering streams ran down the raw stone before him. Red-stained calcretions limned the surface here and there. Flea-like insects skipped across the surface. The scrapes left by the passage of Rhulad and Fear glistened in the fading light, ragged furrows wounding all that clung to the rock.

Knot to knot, he went down the rope, the darkness deepening around him. The air grew cool and damp, then cold. Then his feet struck mossy boulders, and hands reached out to steady him.

His eyes struggled to make out the forms of his brothers. 'We should have brought a lantern.'

'There is light from the Stone Bowl,' Fear said. 'An Elder Warren. Kaschan.'

'That warren is dead,' Trull said. 'Destroyed by Father Shadow's own hand.'

'Its children are dead, brother, but the sorcery lingers. Have your eyes adjusted? Can you see the ground before you?'

A tumble of boulders and the glitter of flowing water

138

between them. 'I can.'

'Then follow me.'

They made their way out from the wall. Footing was treacherous, forcing them to proceed slowly. Dead branches festooned with mushrooms and moss. Trull saw a pallid, hairless rodent of some kind slip into a crack between two rocks, tail slithering in its wake. 'This is the Betrayer's realm,' he said.

Fear grunted. 'More than you know, brother.'

'Something lies ahead,' Rhulad said in a whisper.

Vast, towering shapes. Standing stones, devoid of lichen or moss, the surface strangely textured, made, Trull realized as they drew closer, to resemble the bark of the Blackwood. Thick roots coiled out from the base of each obelisk, spreading out to entwine with those of the stones to each side. Beyond, the ground fell away in a broad depression, from which light leaked like mist.

Fear led them between the standing stones and they halted at the pit's edge.

The roots writhed downward, and woven in their midst were bones. Thousands upon thousands. Trull saw Kaschan, the feared ancient enemies of the Edur, reptilian snouts and gleaming fangs. And bones that clearly belonged to the Tiste. Among them, finely curved wing-bones from Wyval, and, at the very base, the massive skull of an Eleint, the broad, flat bone of its forehead crushed inward, as if by the blow of a gigantic, gauntleted fist.

Leafless scrub had grown up from the chaotic mat on the slopes, the branches and twigs grey and clenching. Then the breath hissed between Trull's teeth. The scrub was stone, growing not in the manner of crystal, but of living wood.

'Kaschan sorcery,' Fear said after a time, 'is born of sounds our ears cannot hear, formed into words that loosen the bindings that hold all matter together, that hold it to the ground. Sounds that bend and stretch light, as a tidal inflow up a river is drawn apart at the moment of turning.

139

With this sorcery, they fashioned fortresses of stone that rode the sky like clouds. With this sorcery, they turned Darkness in upon itself with a hunger none who came too close could defy, an all-devouring hunger that fed first and foremost upon itself.' His voice was strangely muted as he spoke. 'Kaschan sorcery was sent into the warren of Mother Dark, like a plague. Thus was sealed the gate from Kurald Galain to every other realm. Thus was Mother Dark driven into the very core of the Abyss, witness to an endless swirl of light surrounding her – all that she would one day devour, until the last speck of matter vanishes into her. Annihilating Mother Dark. Thus the Kaschan, who are long dead, set upon Mother Dark a ritual that will end in her murder. When all Light is gone. When there is naught to cast Shadow, and so Shadow too is doomed to die.

'When Scabandari Bloodeye discovered what they had done, it was too late. The end, the *death* of the Abyss, cannot be averted. The journey of all that exists repeats on every scale, brothers. From those realms too small for us to see, to the Abyss itself. The Kaschan locked all things into mortality, into the relentless plunge towards extinction. This was their vengeance. An act born, perhaps, of despair. Or the fiercest hatred imaginable. Witness to their own extinction, they forced all else to share that fate.'

His brothers were silent. The dull echoes of Fear's last words faded away.

Then Rhulad grunted. 'I see no signs of this final convergence, Fear.'

'A distant death, aye. More distant than one could imagine. Yet it will come.'

'And what is that to us?'

'The Tiste Invasions drove the Kaschan to their last act. Father Shadow earned the enmity of every Elder god, of every ascendant. Because of the Kaschan ritual, the eternal game among Dark, Light and Shadow would one day end. And with it, all of existence.' He faced his brothers. 'I tell you this secret knowledge so that you will better understand what happened here, what was done. And why Hannan Mosag speaks of enemies far beyond the mortal Letherii.'

The first glimmerings of realization whispered through Trull. He dragged his gaze from Fear's dark, haunted eyes, and looked down into the pit. To the very base, to the skull of that slain dragon. 'They killed him.'

'They destroyed his corporeal body, yes. And imprisoned his soul.'

'Scabandari Bloodeye,' Rhulad said, shaking his head as if to deny all that he saw. 'He cannot be dead. That skull is not—'

'It is,' Fear said. 'They killed our god.'

'Who?' Trull demanded.

'All of them. Elder gods. And Eleint. The Elder gods loosed the blood in their veins. The dragons spawned a child of indescribable terror, to seek out and hunt down Scabandari Bloodeye. Father Shadow was brought down. An Elder god named Kilmandaros shattered his skull. They then made for Bloodeye's spirit a prison of eternal pain, of agony beyond measure, to last until the Abyss itself is devoured.

'Hannan Mosag means to avenge our god.'

Trull frowned. 'The Elder gods are gone, Fear. As are the Eleint. Hannan Mosag commands six tribes of Tiste Edur and a fragmented warren.'

'Four hundred and twenty-odd thousand Edur,' Rhulad said. 'And, for all our endless explorations, we have found no kin among the fragments of Kurald Emurlahn. Fear, Hannan Mosag sees through stained thoughts. It is one thing to challenge Letherii hegemony with summoned demons and, if necessary, iron blades. Are we now to wage war against every god in this world?'

Fear slowly nodded. 'You are here,' he told them, 'and you have been told what is known. Not to see you bend to one knee and praise the Warlock King's name. He seeks power, brothers. He *needs* power, and he cares nothing for

141

its provenance, nor its taint.'

'Your words are treasonous,' Rhulad said, and Trull heard a strange delight in his brother's voice.

'Are they?' Fear asked. 'Hannan Mosag has charged us to undertake a perilous journey. To receive for him a gift. To then deliver it into his hands. A gift, brothers, from whom?'

'We cannot deny him,' Trull said. 'He will simply choose others to go in our stead. And we will face banishment, or worse.'

'Of course we shall not deny him, Trull. But we must not journey like blind old men.'

'What of Binadas?' Rhulad asked. 'What does he know of this?'

'Everything,' Fear replied. 'More, perhaps, than Uruth herself.'

Trull stared down once more at the mouldy dragon skull at the bottom of the pit. 'How are you certain that is Scabandari Bloodeye?'

'Because it was the widows who brought him here. The knowledge was passed down every generation among the women.'

'And Hannan Mosag?'

'Uruth knows he has been here, to this place. How he discovered the truth remains a mystery. Uruth would never have told me and Binadas, if not for her desperation. The Warlock King is drawing upon deadly powers. Are his thoughts stained? If not before, they are now.'

Trull's eyes remained on that skull. A blunt, brutal execution, that mailed fist. 'We had better hope,' he whispered, 'that the Elder gods are indeed gone.'

CHAPTER FOUR

There are tides beneath every tide
And the surface of water
Holds no weight

Tiste Edur saying

The Nerek believed the Tiste Edur were children of demons. There was ash in their blood, staining their skin. To look into an Edur's eyes was to see the greying of the world, the smearing of the sun and the rough skin of night itself.

As the Hiroth warrior named Binadas strode towards the group, the Nerek began keening. Fists beating their own faces and chests, they fell to their knees.

Buruk the Pale marched among them, screaming curses and shrieking demands, but they were deaf to him. The merchant finally turned to where stood Seren Pedac and Hull Beddict, and began laughing.

Hull frowned. 'This will pass, Buruk,' he said.

'Oh, will it now? And the world itself, will that too pass? Like a deathly wind, our lives swirling like dust amidst its headlong rush? Only to settle in its wake, dead and senseless – and all that frenzied cavorting empty of meaning? Hah! Would that I had hired Faraed!'

Seren Pedac's attention remained on the approaching Tiste Edur. A hunter. A killer. One who probably also possessed the trait of long silences. She could imagine this

143

Binadas, sharing a fire in the wilderness with Hull Beddict. In the course of an evening, a night and the following morning, perhaps a half-dozen words exchanged between them. And, she suspected, the forging of a vast, depthless friendship. These were the mysteries of men, so baffling to women. Where silences could become a conjoining of paths. Where a handful of inconsequential words could bind spirits in an ineffable understanding. Forces at play that she could sense, indeed witness, yet ever remaining outside them. Baffled and frustrated and half disbelieving.

Words knit the skein between and among women. And the language of gesture and expression, all merging to fashion a tapestry that, as every woman understood, could tear in but one direction, by deliberate, vicious effort. A friendship among women knew but one enemy, and that was malice.

Thus, the more words, the tighter the weave.

Seren Pedac had lived most of her life in the company of men, and now, on her rare visits to her home in Letheras, she was viewed by women who knew her with unease. As if her choice had made her loyalty uncertain, cause for suspicion. And she had found an unwelcome awkwardness in herself when in their company. They wove from different threads, on different frames, discordant with her own rhythms. She felt clumsy and coarse among them, trapped by her own silences.

To which she answered with flight, away from the city, from her past. From women.

Yet, in the briefest of moments, in a meeting of two men with their almost indifferent exchange of greetings, she was knocked a step back – almost physically – and shut out. Here, sharing this ground, this trail with its rocks and trees, yet in another world.

Too easy to conclude, with a private sneer, that men were simple. Granted, had they been strangers, they might well be circling and sniffing each other's anuses right now. Inviting conclusions that swept aside all notions of complexity, in their place a host of comforting generalizations.

144

But the meeting of two men who were friends destroyed such generalizations and challenged the contempt that went with them, invariably leading a woman to anger.

And the strange, malicious desire to step between them.

On a cobbled beach, a man looks down and sees one rock, then another and another. A woman looks down and sees . . . rocks. But perhaps even this is simplistic. Man as singular and women as plural. More likely we are bits of both, some of one in the other.

We just don't like admitting it.

He was taller than Hull, shoulders level with the Letherii's eyes. His hair was brown and bound in finger-length braids. Eyes the colour of wet sand. Skin like smeared ash. Youthful features, long and narrow barring the broad mouth.

Seren Pedac knew the Sengar name. It was likely she had seen this man's kin, among the delegations she had treated with in her three official visits to Hannan Mosag's tribe.

'Hiroth warrior,' Buruk the Pale said, shouting to be heard above the wailing Nerek, 'I welcome you as guest. I am—'

'I know who you are,' Binadas replied.

At his words the Nerek voices trailed off, leaving only the wind moaning its way up the trail, and the constant trickling flow of melt water from the higher reaches.

'I bring to the Hiroth,' Buruk was saying, 'ingots of iron—'

'And would test,' Hull Beddict interrupted, 'the thickness of the ice.'

'The season has turned,' Binadas replied to Hull. 'The ice is riven with cracks. There has been an illegal harvest of tusked seals. Hannan Mosag will have given answer.'

Seren Pedac swung to the merchant. Studied Buruk the Pale's face. Alcohol, white nectar and the bitter wind had lifted the blood vessels to just beneath the pallid skin on his nose and cheeks. The man's eyes were bleary and shot with red. He conveyed no reaction at the Edur's words.

'Regrettable. It is unfortunate that, among my merchant brethren, there are those who choose to disregard the agreements. The lure of gold. A tide none can withstand.'

'The same can be said of vengeance,' Binadas pointed out.

Buruk nodded. 'Aye, all debts must be repaid.'

Hull Beddict snorted. 'Gold and blood are not the same.'

'Aren't they?' Buruk challenged. 'Hiroth warrior, the interests I represent would adhere now and evermore to the bound agreements. Alas, Lether is a many-headed beast. The surest control of the more voracious elements will be found in an alliance – between the Edur and those Letherii who hold to the words binding our two peoples.'

Binadas turned away. 'Save your speeches for the Warlock King,' he said. 'I will escort you to the village. That is all that need be understood between us.'

Shrugging, Buruk the Pale walked back to his wagon. 'On your feet, Nerek! The trail is downhill from here on, isn't it just!'

Seren watched the merchant climb into the covered back, vanishing from sight, as the Nerek began scurrying about. A glance showed Hull and Binadas facing each other once more. The wind carried their words to her.

'I will speak against Buruk's lies,' Hull Beddict said. 'He will seek to ensnare you with smooth assurances and promises, none of which will be worth a dock.'

Binadas shrugged. 'We have seen the traps you laid out before the Nerek and the Tarthenal. Each word is a knot in an invisible net. Against it, the Nerek's swords were too blunt. The Tarthenal too slow to anger. The Faraed could only smile in their confusion. We are not as those tribes.'

'I know,' Hull said. 'Friend, my people believe in the stacking of coins. One atop another, climbing, ever climbing to glorious heights. The climb signifies progress, and progress is the natural proclivity of civilization. Progress, Binadas, is the belief from which emerge notions of destiny. The Letherii believe in destiny – their own. They are deserving of all things, born of their avowed virtues. The empty throne is ever there for the taking.'

Binadas was smiling at Hull's words, but it was a wry smile. He turned suddenly to Seren Pedac. 'Acquitor. Join us, please. Do old wounds mar Hull Beddict's view of Lether?'

'Destiny wounds us all,' she replied, 'and we Letherii wear the scars with pride. Most of us,' she added with an apologetic look at Hull.

'One of your virtues?'

'Yes, if you could call it that. We have a talent for disguising greed under the cloak of freedom. As for past acts of depravity, we prefer to ignore those. Progress, after all, means to look ever forward, and whatever we have trampled in our wake is best forgotten.'

'Progress, then,' Binadas said, still smiling, 'sees no end.'

'Our wagons ever roll down the hill, Hiroth. Faster and faster.'

'Until they strike a wall.'

'We crash through most of those.'

The smile faded, and Seren thought she detected a look of sadness in the Edur's eyes before he turned away. 'We live in different worlds.'

'And I would choose yours,' Hull Beddict said.

Binadas shot the man a glance, his expression quizzical. 'Would you, friend?'

Something in the Hiroth's tone made the hairs rise on the back of Seren Pedac's neck.

Hull frowned, suggesting that he too had detected something awry in that question.

No more words were exchanged then, and Seren Pedac permitted Hull and Binadas to take the lead on the trail, allowing them such distance that their privacy was assured. Even so, they seemed disinclined to speak. She watched them, their matching strides, the way they walked. And wondered.

Hull was so clearly lost. Seeking to make the Tiste Edur

the hand of his own vengeance. He would drive them to war, if he could. But destruction yielded only strife, and his dream of finding peace within his soul in the blood and ashes of slaughter filled her with pity for the man. She could not, however, let that blind her to the danger he presented.

Seren Pedac held no love for her own people. The Letherii's rapacious hunger and inability to shift to any perspective that did not serve them virtually assured a host of bloody clashes with every foreign power they met. And, one day, they would meet their match. *The wagons will shatter against a wall more solid than any we have seen. Will it be the Tiste Edur?* It did not seem likely. True, they possessed formidable sorcery, and the Letherii had yet to encounter fiercer fighters. But the combined tribes amounted to less than a quarter-million. King Diskanar's capital alone was home to over a hundred thousand, and there were a half-dozen cities nearly as large in Lether. With the protectorates across Dracons Sea and to the east, the hegemony could amass and field six hundred thousand soldiers, maybe more. Attached to each legion there would be a master of sorcery, trained by the Ceda, Kuru Qan himself. The Edur would be crushed. Annihilated.

And Hull Beddict . . .

She turned her thoughts from him with an effort. The choices were his to make, after all. Nor, she suspected, would he listen to her warnings.

Seren Pedac acknowledged her own uncertainty and confusion. Would she advocate peace at any price? What were the rewards of capitulation? Letherii access to the resources now claimed by the Edur. The harvest from the sea. *And the Blackwood . . .*

Of course. It's the living wood that we hunger for, the source of ships that can heal themselves, that cut the waves faster than our sleekest galleys, that resist magic unleashed upon them. That is at the heart of this game.

But King Diskanar was not a fool – he was not the one harbouring such aspirations. Kuru Qan would have seen to

148

that. No, this gambit was the queen's. Such conceit, to believe the Letherii could master the living wood. That the Edur would so easily surrender their secrets, their arcane arts in coaxing the will of the Blackwood, in binding its power to their own.

Harvesting the tusked seals was a feint. The monetary loss was part of a much larger scheme, an investment with the aim of generating political dividends, which in turn would recoup the losses a hundredfold. And only someone as wealthy as the queen or Chancellor Triban Gnol could absorb such losses. Ships crewed by the Indebted, with the provision of clearing those debts upon the event of their deaths. Lives given up for the sake of children and grand-children. They would have had no trouble manning those ships. Blood and gold, then.

She could not be certain of her suspicions, but they seemed to fit, and were as bitterly unpalatable to her as they probably were to Buruk the Pale. The Tiste Edur would not surrender the Blackwood. The conclusion was foregone. There was to be war. *And Hull Beddict will make of himself its fiercest proponent. The queen's own unwitting agent. No wonder Buruk tolerates his presence.*

And the part she would play? *I am the escort of this snarled madness. Nothing more than that. Keep your distance, Seren Pedac.* She was Acquitor. She would do as she had been charged to do. Deliver Buruk the Pale.

Nothing will be decided. Not by us. The game's end awaits the Great Meeting.

If only she could find comfort in that thought.

Twenty paces ahead, the forest swallowed Hull Beddict and Binadas Sengar. Darkness and shadows, drawing closer with every step she took.

Any criminal who could swim across the canal with a sack of docks strapped to his back won freedom. The amount of coin was dependent upon the nature of the transgression. Theft, kidnapping, failure to pay a debt, damage to property

149

and murder yielded the maximum fine of five hundred docks. Embezzlement, assault without cause, cursing in public upon the names of the Empty Throne, the king or the queen, demanded three hundred docks in reparation. The least of the fines, one hundred docks, were levied upon loitering, voiding in public and disrespect.

These were the fines for men. Women so charged were accorded half-weights.

If someone could pay the fine, he did so, thus expunging his criminal record.

The canal awaited those who could not.

The Drownings were more than public spectacle, they were the primary event among a host of activities upon which fortunes were gambled every day in Letheras. Since few criminals ever managed to make it across the canal with their burden, distance and number of strokes provided the measure for wagering bets. As did Risings, Flailings, Flounderings and Vanishings.

The criminals had ropes tied to them, allowing for retrieval of the coins once the drowning was confirmed. The corpse was dumped back into the river. *Guilty as sludge.*

Brys Beddict found Finadd Gerun Eberict on the Second Tier overlooking the canal, amidst a crowd of similarly privileged onlookers to the morning's Drownings. Bookmakers swarmed through the press, handing out payment tiles and collecting wagers. Voices rang in the air above the buzz of excited conversation. Nearby, a woman squealed, then laughed. Male voices rose in response.

'Finadd.'

The flat, scarred face known to virtually every citizen swung to Brys, thin eyebrows lifting in recognition. 'King's Champion. You're just in time. Ublala Pung is about to take a swim. I've eight hundred docks on the bastard.'

Brys Beddict leaned on the railing. He scanned the guards and officials on the launch below. 'I've heard

150

the name,' he said, 'but cannot recall his crime. Is that Ublala?' He pointed down to a cloaked figure towering above the others.

'That's him. Tarthenal half-blood. So they've added two hundred docks to his fine.'

'What did he do?'

'What didn't he do? Murder times three, destruction of property, assault, kidnapping times two, cursing, fraud, failure to pay debt and voiding in public. All in one afternoon.'

'The ruckus at Urum's Lenders?' The criminal had flung off his cloak. He was wearing naught but a loincloth. His burnished skin was lined with whip scars. The muscles beneath it were enormous.

'That's the one.'

'So what's he carrying?'

'Forty-three hundred.'

And Brys now saw the enormous double-lined sack being manhandled onto the huge man's back. 'Errant's blessing, he'll not manage a stroke.'

'That's the consensus,' Gerun said. 'Every call's on Flailing, Floundering and Vanishing. No strokes, no Risings.'

'And your call?'

'Seventy to one.'

Brys frowned. Odds like that meant but one thing. 'You believe he'll make it!'

Heads turned at his exclamation, the buzz around them grew louder.

Gerun leaned on the railing, drawing a long breath through his teeth, making that now infamous whistling sound. 'Most half-blood Tarthenal get the worst traits,' he muttered in a low voice, then grinned. 'But not Ublala Pung.'

A roar from the crowds lining the walkway and tiers, and from the opposite side. The guards were leading the criminal down the launch. Ublala walked hunched over, straining with the weight of the sack. At the water's edge he pushed the guards away and turned.

Pulling down his loincloth. And urinating in an arcing stream.

Somewhere, a woman screamed.

'They'll collect that body,' one merchant said, awed, 'down at the Eddies. I've heard there're surgeons who can—'

'And wouldn't you pay a peak for that, Inchers!' his companion cut in.

'I'm not lacking, Hulbat – watch yourself! I was just *saying*—'

'And ten thousand women are *dreaming*!'

A sudden hush, as Ublala Pung turned to face the canal. Then strode forward. Hips. Chest. Shoulders.

A moment later his head disappeared beneath the thick, foul water.

Not a flounder, not a flail. Those who had bet on Vanishing crowed. Crowds pulled apart, figures closing on bookmakers.

'Brys Beddict, what's the distance across?'

'A hundred paces.'

'Aye.'

They remained leaning on the railing. After a moment, Brys shot the Finadd a quizzical look. Gerun nodded towards the launch below. 'Look at the line, lad.'

There was some commotion around the retrieval line, and Brys saw – at about the same time as, by the rising voices, did others – that the rope was still playing out. 'He's walking the bottom!'

Brys found he could not pull his eyes from that uncoiling rope. A dozen heartbeats. Two dozen. A half-hundred. And still that rope snaked its way into the water.

The cries and shouts had risen to deafening pitch. Pigeons burst into the air from nearby rooftops, scattering in panic. Bettors were fighting with bookmakers for payment tiles. Someone fell from the Third Tier and, haplessly, missed the canal by a scant two paces. He struck flagstones and did not move, a circle of witnesses closing round his body.

'That's it,' Gerun Eberict sighed.

A figure was emerging on the far-side launch. Streaming mud.

'Four lungs, lad.'

Eight hundred docks. At seventy to one. 'You're a rich man who's just got richer, Finadd.'

'And Ublala Pung's a free one. Hey, I saw your brother earlier. Tehol. Other side of the canal. He was wearing a skirt.'

'Don't stand so close – no, closer, so you can hear me, Shand, but not too close. Not like we know each other.'

'You've lost your mind,' she replied.

'Maybe. Anyway, see that man?'

'Who?'

'That criminal, of course. The half-blood who tore apart Urum's – the extortionist deserved it by the way—'

'Tarthenal have four lungs.'

'And so does he. I take it you didn't wager?'

'I despise gambling.'

'Very droll, lass.'

'What about him?'

'Hire him.'

'With pleasure.'

'Then buy him some clothes.'

'Do I have to?'

'He's not being employed because of his physical attributes – well, not those ones, anyway. You three need a bodyguard.'

'He can guard my body any time.'

'That's it, Shand. I'm done talking with you today.'

'No you're not, Tehol. Tonight. The workshop. And bring Bugg.'

'Everything is going as planned. There's no need—'

'Be there.'

153

* * *

Four years ago, Finadd Gerun Eberict single-handedly foiled an assassination attempt on King Diskanar. Returning to the palace late one night, he came upon the bodies of two guards outside the door to the king's private chambers. A sorcerous attack had filled their lungs with sand, resulting in asphyxiation. Their flesh was still warm. The door was ajar.

The palace Finadd had drawn his sword. He burst into the king's bedchamber to find three figures leaning over Ezgara Diskanar's sleeping form. A mage and two assassins. Gerun killed the sorceror first, with a chop to the back of the man's neck, severing his spinal cord. He had then stop-thrust the nearest assassin's attack, the point of his sword burying itself in the man's chest, just beneath the left collarbone. It would prove to be a mortal wound. The second assassin thrust his dagger at the Finadd's face. Probably he had been aiming for one of Gerun's eyes, but the Finadd threw his head back and the point entered his mouth, slicing through both lips, then driving hard between his front teeth. Pushing them apart, upon which the blade jammed.

The sword in Gerun's hand chopped down, shattering the outstretched arm. Three more wild hacks killed the assassin.

This last engagement was witnessed by a wide-eyed king.

Two weeks later, Finadd Gerun Eberict, his breath whistling through the new gap in his front teeth, knelt before Ezgara Diskanar in the throne room, and before the assembled masses was granted the King's Leave. For the remainder of the soldier's life, he was immune to criminal conviction. He was, in short, free to do as he pleased, to whomever he pleased, barring the king's own line.

The identity of the person behind the assassination attempt was never discovered.

Since then, Gerun Eberict had been on a private

crusade. A lone, implacable vigilante. He was known to have personally murdered thirty-one citizens, including two wealthy, highly respected and politically powerful merchants, and at least a dozen other mysterious deaths were commonly attributed to him. He had, in short, become the most feared man in Letheras.

He had also, in that time, made himself rich.

Yet, for all that, he remained a Finadd in the King's Guard, and so was bound to the usual responsibilities. Brys Beddict suspected the decision to send Gerun Eberict with the delegation was as much to relieve the city of the pressure of his presence as it was a statement to the queen and the prince. And Brys wondered if the king had come to regret his sanction.

The two palace guards walked side by side across Soulan Bridge and into the Pursers' District. The day was hot, the sky white with thin, high clouds. They entered Rild's, an establishment known for its fish cuisine, as well as an alcoholic drink made from orange rinds, honey and Tusked Seal sperm. They sat in the inner courtyard, at Gerun's private table.

As soon as drinks and lunch were ordered, Gerun Eberict leaned back in his chair and regarded Brys with curiosity. 'Is my guest this day the King's Champion?'

'In a manner of speaking,' Brys admitted. 'My brother, Hull, is accompanying Buruk the Pale. It is believed that Buruk will remain with the Edur until the Great Meeting. There is concern about Hull.'

'What kind of concern?'

'Well, you knew him years ago.'

'I did. Rather well, in fact. He was my Finadd back then. And upon my promotion, he and I got roaring drunk at Porul's and likely sired a dozen bastards each with a visiting troupe of flower dancers from Trate. In any case, the company folded about ten months later, or so we heard.'

'Yes, well. He's not the same man, you know.'

'Isn't he?'

155

The drinks arrived, an amber wine for Brys, the Tusked Milk for Gerun.

'No,' Brys said in answer to the Finadd's question, 'I don't think so.'

'Hull believes in one thing, and that is loyalty. The only gift he feels is worth giving. Granted, it was sorely abused, and the legacy of that is a new list in your brother's head, with the names of every man and woman who betrayed him.' Gerun tossed back his drink and gestured for another one. 'The only difference between him and me is that I'm able to cross names off my list.'

'And what if,' Brys said quietly, 'the king's name is on Hull's list?'

Gerun's eyes went flat. 'As I said, I'm the only one crossing off names.'

'Then why is Hull with Buruk the Pale?'

'Buruk is not the king's man, Brys. The very opposite, in fact. I look forward to finally meeting him.'

A cold chill ran through Brys.

'In any case,' Gerun went on, 'it's your other brother who interests me.'

'Tehol? Don't tell me he's on your list.'

Gerun smiled, revealing the sideways tilt of his upper and lower teeth. 'And I'd tell you if he was? Relax, he isn't. Not yet, in any case. But he's up to something.'

'I find that hard to believe. Tehol stopped being up to anything a long time ago.'

'That's what you think.'

'I know nothing to suggest otherwise, but it seems that you do.'

Gerun's second drink arrived. 'Were you aware,' the Finadd said, dipping a finger into the thick, viscid liquid, 'that Tehol still possesses myriad interests, in property, licences, mercantile investments and transportation? He's raised pretty solid fronts, enough to be fairly sure that no-one else knows that he's remained active.'

'Not solid enough, it seems.'

156

Gerun shrugged. 'In many ways, Tehol walked the path of the King's Leave long before me, and without the actual sanction.'

'Tehol's never killed anyone—'

Gerun's smile grew feral. 'The day the Tolls collapsed, Brys, an even dozen financiers committed suicide. And that collapse was solely and exclusively by Tehol's hand. Perfectly, indeed brilliantly timed. He had his own list, only he didn't stick a knife in their throats; instead, he made them all his business partners. And took every one of them down—'

'But he went down, too.'

'He didn't kill himself over it, though, did he? Didn't that tell you something? It should have.'

'Only that he didn't care.'

'Precisely. Brys, tell me, who is Tehol's greatest admirer?'

'You?'

'No. Oh, I'm suitably impressed. Enough to be suspicious as the Errant's Pit now that he's stirring the pot once more. No. Someone else.'

Brys looked away. Trying to decide if he liked this man sitting opposite him. Liked him enough for this conversation. He knew he hated the subject matter.

Their lunches arrived.

Gerun Eberict focused his attention on the grilled fillet on the silver plate in front of him, after ordering a third Tusked Milk.

It occurred to Brys that he had never seen a woman drink that particular concoction.

'I don't speak to Tehol,' he said after a time, his gaze on his own serving as he slowly picked the white flesh apart, revealing the row of vertebrae and the dorsal spines.

'You despise what he did?'

Brys frowned, then shook his head. 'No. What he did after.'

'Which was?'

'Nothing.'

157

'The water had to clear, lad. So he could look around once more and see what remained.'

'You're suggesting diabolical genius, Gerun.'

'I am. Tehol possesses what Hull does not. Knowledge is not enough. It never is. It's the capacity to do something with that knowledge. To do it perfectly. Absolute timing. With devastating consequences. That's what Tehol has. Hull, Errant protect him, does not.'

Brys looked up and met the Finadd's pale eyes. 'Are you suggesting that Hull is Tehol's greatest admirer?'

'Hull's very own inspiration. And that is why he is with Buruk the Pale.'

'Do you intend to stand in his way at the Great Meeting?'

'It might well be too late by that time, Brys. Assuming that is my intention.'

'It isn't?'

'I haven't decided.'

'You want war?'

Gerun's gaze remained level. 'That particular tide stirs the deepest silts. Blinding everyone. A man with a goal can get a lot done in that cloud. And, eventually, it settles.'

'And lo,' Brys said, unable to hide his bitterness, 'the world has changed.'

'Possibly.'

'War as the means—'

'To a peaceful end—'

'That you will find pleasing to your eye.'

Gerun pushed his plate away and sat back once more. 'What is life without ambition, Brys?'

Brys rose, his meal pried apart into a chaotic mass on the plate before him. 'Tehol would be better at answering that than am I, Finadd.'

Gerun smiled up at him. 'Inform Nifadas and Kuru Qan that I am not unaware of the complexities wrought through the impending Great Meeting. Nor am I blind to the need to usher me out of the city for a time. I have, of course,

158

compensated for my own absence, in anticipation of my triumphant return.'

'I will convey your words, Finadd.'

'I regret your loss of appetite, Brys. The fish was excellent. Next time, we will speak of inconsequential things. I both respect and admire you, Champion.'

'Ah, so I am not on your list.'

'Not yet. A joke, Brys,' he added upon seeing the Champion's expression. 'Besides, you'd cut me to pieces. How can I not admire that? I see it this way – the history of this decade, for our dear Letheras, can be most succinctly understood by a faithful recounting of the three Beddict brothers. And, as is clear, the tale's not yet done.'

So it would seem. 'I thank you, Finadd, for the company and the invitation.'

Gerun leaned forward and picked up the Champion's plate. 'Take the back exit, if you please,' he said, offering Brys the plate. 'There's a starveling lad living in the alley. Mind, he's to return the silver – make sure he understands that. Tell him you were my guest.'

'Very well, Finadd.'

'Try these on.'

Tehol stared at the woollen trousers, then reached for them. 'Tell me, Bugg, is there any point in you continuing?'

'Do you mean these leggings, or with my sorry existence?'

'Have you hired your crew?' He stripped off his skirt and began donning the trousers.

'Twenty of the most miserable malcontents I could find.'

'Grievances?'

'Every one of them, and I'm pretty certain they are all legitimate. Granted, a few probably deserved their banishment from the trade.'

'Most de-certifications are political, Bugg. Just be sure none of them are incompetent. All we need is for them to keep a secret, and for that, spite against the guilds is the best motivation.'

'I'm not entirely convinced. Besides, we've had some warnings from the guilds.'

'In person?'

'Delivered missives. So far. Your left knee will stay warm.'

'Warm? It's hot out there, Bugg, despite what your old rheumy bones tell you.'

'Well, they're trousers for every season.'

'Really? Assure the guilds we're not out to underbid. In fact, the very opposite. Nor do we pay our crew higher rates. No benefits, either—'

'Barring a stake in the enterprise.'

'Say nothing of that, Bugg. Look at the hairs on my right thigh. They're standing on end.'

'It's the contrast they don't like.'

'The guilds?'

'No, your hairs. The guilds just want to know where by the Errant I came from. And how dare I register a company.'

'Don't worry about that, Bugg. Once they find out what you're claiming to be able to do, they'll be sure you'll fail and so ignore you thereafter. Until you succeed, that is.'

'I'm having second thoughts.'

'About what?'

'Put the skirt back on.'

'I'm inclined to agree with you. Find some more wool. Preferably the same colour, although that is not essential, I suppose. In any case, we have a meeting with the three darlings this evening.'

'Risky.'

'We must be circumspect.'

'That goes both ways. I stole that wool.'

Tehol wrapped the sheet once more about his waist. 'I'll be back down later to collect you. Clean up around here, will you?'

'If I've the time.'

Tehol climbed the ladder to the roof.

The sun's light was deepening, as it edged towards the horizon, bathing the surrounding buildings in a warm glow. Two artists had set up easels on the Third Tier, competing to immortalize Tehol and his bed. He gave them a wave that seemed to trigger a loud argument, then settled down on the sun-warmed mattress. Stared up at the darkening sky.

He had seen his brother Brys at the Drownings. On the other side of the canal, in conversation with Gerun Eberict. Rumour had it that Gerun was accompanying the delegation to the Tiste Edur. Hardly surprising. The King needed that wild man out of the city.

The problem with gold was the way it crawled. Where nothing else could. It seeped out from secrets, flowered in what should have been lifeless cracks. It strutted when it should have remained hidden, beneath notice. Brazen as any weed between the cobbles, and, if one was so inclined, one could track those roots all the way down. Sudden spending, from kin of dead hirelings, followed quickly – but not quickly enough – by sudden, inexplicable demises. A strange severing that left the king's inquisitors with no-one to question, no-one to torture to find the source of the conspiracy. Assassination attempts were no small thing, after all, especially when the king himself was the target. Extraordinary, almost unbelievable success – to have reached Diskanar's own bedchamber, to stand poised above the man, mere heartbeats from delivering death. That particular sorceror had never before shown such skill in the relevant arts. To conjure sand to fill the chests of two men was highest sorcery.

Natural curiosity and possible advantage, these had been Tehol's motives, and he'd been much quicker than the royal inquisitors. A fortune, he had discovered, had been spent on the conspiracy, a life's savings.

Clearly, only Gerun Eberict had known the full extent of the scheme. His hirelings would not have anticipated their employer's attacking them. Killing them. They'd fought back, and one had come close to succeeding. And the

161

Finadd carried the scars still, lips and crooked teeth, to show the nearness of the thing.

Immunity from conviction. So that Gerun Eberict could set out and do what he wanted to do. Judge and executioner, for crimes real and imagined, for offences both major and minor.

In a way, Tehol admired the man. For his determination, if not his methods. And for devising and gambling all on a scheme that took one's breath away with its bold ... extremity.

No doubt Brys had official business with the man. As King's Champion.

Even so, worrying. It wouldn't do to have his young brother so close to Gerun Eberict.

For if Tehol possessed a true enemy, a foe to match his own cleverness who – it would appear – surpassed Tehol himself in viciousness – it was Finadd Gerun Eberict, possessor of the King's Leave.

And he'd been sniffing around, twisting arms. Safer, then, to assume Gerun knew that Tehol was not as destitute as most would believe. Nor entirely ... inactive.

Thus, a new fold to consider in this rumpled, tangled tapestry.

Gerun was immune. But not without enemies. Granted, deadly with a sword, and known to have a dozen sworn, blood-bound bodyguards to protect him when he slept. His estate was rumoured to be impregnable, and possessed of its own armoury, apothecary with resident alchemist well versed in poisons and their antidotes, voluminous store-houses, and independent source of water. All in all, Gerun had planned for virtually every contingency.

Barring the singular focus of the mind of one Tehol Beddict.

Sometimes the only solution was also the simplest, most obvious. *See a weed between the cobbles . . . pull it out.*

'Bugg!'

A faint voice from below. 'What?'

'Who was holding Gerun's tiles on that bet this afternoon?'

His servant's grizzled head appeared in the hatch. 'You already know, since you own the bastard. Turble. Assuming he's not dead of a heart attack . . . or suicide.'

'Turble? Not a chance. My guess is, the man's packing. A sudden trip to the Outer Isles.'

'He'll never make it to the city gates.'

'Meaning Gerun is on the poor bastard.'

'Wouldn't you be? With that payoff?'

Tehol frowned. 'Suicide, I'm now thinking, might well be Turble's conclusion to his sorry state of affairs. Unexpected, true, and all the more shocking for it. He's got no kin, as I recall. So the debt dies with him.'

'And Gerun is out eight hundred docks.'

'He might wince at that, but not so much as you'd notice. The man's worth a peak, maybe more.'

'You don't know?'

'All right, so I was generalizing. Of course I know, down to the last dock. Nay, the last stripling. In any case, I was saying, or, rather, suggesting, that the loss of eight hundred docks is not what would make Gerun sting. It's the *escape*. The one trail even Gerun can't doggedly follow – not willingly, anyway. Thus, Turble has to commit suicide.'

'I doubt he'll agree to it.'

'No, probably not. But set it in motion, Bugg. Down to the Eddies. Find us a suitable corpse. Fresh, and not yet drained. Get a bottle or two of Turble's blood from him in exchange—'

'What'll it be? Fire? Who commits suicide using fire?'

'The fire will be an unfortunate consequence of an unattended oil lamp. Unattended because of the suicide. Burnt beyond recognition, alas, but the scrivers will swear by the blood's owner. That's how they work, isn't it?'

'A man's veins never lie.'

'Right. Only, they can.'

'Right, if you're insane enough to drain a corpse and pump new blood into it.'

'A ghastly exercise, Bugg. Glad you're up to it.'

The wizened face at the hatch was scowling. 'And Turble?'

'We smuggle him out the usual way. He's always wanted to take up fishing. Put someone in the tunnel, in case he bolts sooner than we expect. Gerun's watchers will be our finest witnesses. Oh, and won't the Finadd spit.'

'Is this wise?' Bugg asked.

'No choice. He's the only man who can stop me. So I'm getting him first.'

'If he catches a whiff that it's you—'

'Then I'm a dead man.'

'And I'm out of work.'

'Nonsense. The lasses will carry on. Besides, you are my beneficiary – unofficially, of course.'

'Should you have told me that?'

'Why not? I'm lying.'

Bugg's head sank back down.

Tehol settled back onto the bed. *Now, I need to find me a thief. A good one.*

Ah! I know the very one. Poor lass . . .

'Bugg!'

Shurq Elalle's fate had taken a turn for the worse. Nothing to do with her profession, for her skills in the art of thievery were legendary among the lawless class. An argument with her landlord, sadly escalating to attempted murder on his part, to which she of course – in all legality – responded by flinging him out the window. The hapless man's fall had, unfortunately, been broken by a waddling merchant on the street below. The landlord's neck broke. So did the merchant's.

Careless self-defence leading to the death of an innocent had been the charge. Four hundred docks, halved. Normally, Shurq could have paid the fine and that would have been that. Alas, her argument with the landlord had been over a certain hoard of gold that had inexplicably vanished from Shurq's cache. Without a dock to her name, she had been marched down to the canal.

Even then, she was a fit woman. Two hundred docks were probably manageable – had not the retrieval rope snagged on the spines of a forty-stone lupe-fish that had surfaced for a look at the swimmer, only to dive back down to the bottom, taking Shurq with it.

Lupe fish, while rare in the canal, ate only men. Never women. No-one knew why this was the case.

Shurq Ellale drowned.

But, as it turned out, there was dead and then there was dead. Unbeknownst to her, Shurq had been cursed by one of her past victims. A curse fully paid for and sanctified by the Empty Temple. So, though her lungs filled with foul water, though her heart stopped, as did all other discernible functions of the body and mind, there she stood when finally retrieved from the canal, sheathed in mud, eyes dull and the whites browned by burst vessels and lifeless blood, all in all most miserable and sadly bemused.

Even the lawless and the homeless shunned her thereafter. All the living, in fact. Walking past as if she was in truth a ghost, a dead memory.

Her flesh did not decay, although its pallor was noticeably unhealthy. Nor were her reactions and deft abilities in any way diminished. She could speak. See. Hear. Think. None of which improved her mood, much.

Bugg found her where Tehol had said she'd be found. In an alley behind a bordello. Listening, as she did every night, to the moans of pleasure – real and improvised – issuing from the windows above.

'Shurq Elalle.'

Listless, murky eyes fixed on him. 'I give no pleasure,' she said.

'Alas, neither do I, these days. I am here to deliver to you an indefinite contract from my master.'

'And who would that be?'

'Not yet, I'm afraid. Thieving work, Shurq.'

'What need have I for riches?'

'Well, that would depend on their substance, I'd imagine.'

She stepped out from the shadowed alcove where she'd been standing. 'And what does your master imagine I desire?'

'Negotiable.'

'Does he know I'm dead?'

'Of course. And sends his regrets.'

'Does he?'

'No, I made that up.'

'No-one hires me any more.'

'That is why he knew you would be available.'

'No-one likes my company.'

'Well, a bath wouldn't hurt, but he's prepared to make allowances.'

'I will speak to him.'

'Very good. He has anticipated your wishes. Midnight.'

'Where?'

'A rooftop. With a bed.'

'*Him?*'

'Yes.'

'In his bed?'

'Um, I'm not sure if that was in his mind—'

'Glad to hear it. I may be dead, but I'm not easy. I'll be there. Midnight, until a quarter past. No more. If he can convince me in that time, all and well. If not, too bad.'

'A quarter should be more than enough, Shurq.'

'You are foolish to be so confident of that.'

Bugg smiled. 'Am I?'

'Where's Bugg?'

'He'll be meeting us here.' Tehol walked over to the couch and settled down on it, drawing his legs up until he was in a reclining position. He eyed the three women.

166

'Now, what is so important that I must risk discovery via this reckless meeting?'

Shand ran a calloused palm over her shaved head. 'We want to know what you've been up to, Tehol.'

'That's right,' Rissarh said.

Hejun's arms were crossed, and there was a scowl on her face as she added, 'We don't need a bodyguard.'

'Oh, forgot about him. Where is he?'

'Said he had some belongings to collect,' Shand said. 'He should be here any time now. No, the others haven't met him yet.'

'Ah, so they are sceptical of your enthusiasm.'

'She's been known to exaggerate,' Rissarh said.

'Besides,' Hejun snapped, 'what's all that got to do with being a bodyguard? I don't care how big his—'

The warehouse door creaked, and everyone looked over.

Ublala Pung's round face peered timidly inside, from just under the overhang.

'Dear sir!' Tehol called out. 'Please, come in!'

The half-blood hesitated. His pale eyes flitted among Shand, Rissarh and Hejun. 'There's . . . three of them,' he said.

'Three of what?'

'Women.'

'Yes, indeed,' said Tehol. 'And . . . ?'

Ublala frowned, lips drawing together into something much resembling a pout.

'Don't worry,' Tehol invited with a wave of a hand, 'I promise to protect you from them.'

'Really?'

'Absolutely. Come in, Ublala Pung, and be welcome.'

The huge man pushed the door back further and edged inside.

Ublala's belongings did not, it was clear, include trousers or loincloth. He was as naked as he had been down at the canal. Not that clothing would have much disguised his attributes, Tehol concluded after a moment of despondent

167

reflection. *Well, never mind that.* 'Hungry? Thirsty? Relax, friend. Set your bag down ... yes, there is just fine. Sit down – no, the bench, not the chair – you'd end up wearing it, which, now that I think on it ... no, probably not. Ublala, these women require a bodyguard. I assume you accepted the offer from Shand—'

'I thought it was just her.'

'And that makes a difference?'

'Makes it harder.'

'Granted. But, most of the time you'll be here ...' Tehol's voice trailed away, as he finally noticed that Shand, Rissarh and Hejun had neither moved since Ublala's arrival, nor said a word. *Oh, now really ...*

Nisall had been the King's First Concubine for three years. No official power was accorded the title, barring what the personality of the woman in question could achieve. There had been considerable variation throughout history, often dependent upon the fortitude of the king at the time, as well as that of the queen and the chancellor.

At present, there were six concubines in all, the others young, minor daughters of powerful families. Potential investments in the future, there as much to capture the prince's attention as the king's. Like the queen's four consorts, they were housed in a private, isolated quarter of the palace. Only the First Consort, Turudal Brizad, and the First Concubine were permitted contact with anyone other than the royal personages themselves.

Brys Beddict bowed to Nisall, then saluted Preda Unnutal Hebaz. He was not surprised to find the First Concubine in the Preda's office. Nisall had decided her loyalties long ago.

'Champion,' the young woman smiled. 'Unnutal and I were just discussing you.'

'More precisely,' the Preda said, 'we were conjecturing on the content of your conversation with Finadd Gerun Eberict earlier today.'

'Preda, I regret my delay in reporting to you.'

'A well-rehearsed report by now,' Nisall said, 'given that you have already been required to provide it to the First Eunuch and Ceda Kuru Qan. Thus, we will allow you a certain lack of animation in your telling.'

Brys frowned, his eyes on his commander. 'Preda, it occurs to me that Gerun Eberict remains one of your officers, regardless of the King's Leave. I am surprised he has not already reported to you the details of today's conversation.'

'And who is to say he hasn't?' Unnutal enquired. Then she waved a hand. 'An uncharitable response on my part. I apologize, Brys. It has been a long day indeed.'

'No apology required, Preda. I spoke out of turn—'

'Brys,' Nisall interrupted. 'You are the King's Champion now. There is no place where you can speak out of turn. Even unto Ezgara himself. Forgive the Preda her brusque manner. Conversations with Gerun tend to make one exasperated.'

'He has a certain hauteur about him,' Brys said.

'Arrogance,' Unnutal snapped. 'He did not give you cause to call him out?'

'No.'

'How unfortunate,' Nisall sighed.

'Although I believe I was warned.'

Both women fixed their eyes on him.

Brys shrugged. 'I was reminded that his list is an ongoing project.'

'He considers killing Buruk the Pale.'

'I believe so. The First Eunuch has been made aware of that possibility.'

'Now,' Nisall said, beginning to pace in the room, 'should the king be informed of this development, he might be inclined to withdraw Gerun from the delegation. Which will be perceived as a victory by the queen and the Chancellor.'

'Perceptions can be made integral to strategy,' Brys said.

'Spoken as a duellist,' Nisall said. 'But the advantages to the queen granted by Gerun's absence perhaps outweigh any advantage we might fashion. Besides, we know Buruk the Pale proceeds under directions from her camp, so his loss will not hurt us.'

Brys considered this, uneasy at such a cavalier dismissal of a man's life. 'How well does Buruk sit with his burdens?'

'We have a spy close to him, of course,' the Preda said. 'The man is tortured by his conscience. He escapes with white nectar and drink, and dissolute sexual indulgences.'

'The queen . . .'

'Wants war,' Nisall finished with a sharp nod. 'The irresponsible, greedy, short-sighted sea-cow. A fine partner to the stupidest chancellor in the history of Letheras. And a thick, easily led prince waiting impatiently to take the throne.'

Brys shifted uncomfortably. 'Perhaps, if Buruk's conscience is haunting him, he can be swayed to another course.'

'Beneath the hawk gaze of Moroch Nevath? Not likely.'

The Champion's eyes narrowed on Nisall. This was all leading to something. He just wasn't sure what.

The Preda sighed. 'Gerun needs to add a name to his list.'

'Moroch Nevath?'

'And that will be difficult.'

'It will. The man is singular. In every way imaginable. Incorruptible, with a history to match.'

'And to whom is the man sworn?'

'Why, the prince, of course. But the King's Leave does not include killing royalty.'

'Yet his history is far less pure.'

Nisall added, 'Gerun would not be able to act directly against the prince. He would need to attack obliquely.'

'First Concubine, I have little understanding of Gerun Eberict's motivations. I do not comprehend the nature of his cause.'

'I do,' the Preda said. 'I know precisely what he's up to. And I believe we can see that he adds to his list.'

'The concern is,' Nisall said, 'what role will his old Finadd, Hull Beddict, have during the playing out of all this.'

Brys looked away. He was beginning to feel under siege. If not one brother, then the other. 'I will give it some thought.'

'Not too long, Finadd,' Unnutal Hebaz said.

'A day or two, perhaps.'

'Agreed. Until then, Brys.'

'Goodnight Preda, First Concubine.'

He made his way out of the office.

In the corridor, five paces from the two guards standing vigil at the door through which he had just exited, his steps slowed to a halt. Unmindful of the curious eyes on his back, the King's Champion stood motionless.

In the minds of the two guards, three titles. Master of the Sword, Finadd and King's Champion – all were cause for envy and admiration. They might have wondered at him at that moment, however. The way he stood, as if entirely alone in a large, overwhelming world. Eyes clearly fixed on some inner landscape. Weariness in his shoulders. They might have wondered, but if so it was a brief, ephemeral empathy, quickly replaced by those harder sentiments, envy and admiration. And the gruff assertion that supreme ability purchased many things, including isolation. And the man could damn well live with it.

'There's no place for sentiment here,' Tehol said, 'sad to say. Letheras is unforgiving. We can't afford to make mistakes. For Errant's sake, Ublala, relax. You're turning blue. Anyway, as I was saying, Shand, it's careless being careless. In other words, we can't keep meeting like this.'

'Do you practise?' Rissarh asked.

'At what?'

Bugg cleared his throat. 'I have a meeting tomorrow with the royal architects.'

'Finally!' Shand sighed from where she sat at the table, knuckling her eyes before continuing, 'As far as we could tell nothing was happening about anything.'

'Well,' Tehol said, 'that's precisely the impression we want.'

'Fine, but that's the *outside* impression. It's not supposed to apply to us, you idiot. If we aren't in on the scheme then no-one is.'

'Preparation, Shand. The groundwork. This can't be rushed. Now, I've got to go.'

'What?'

'It's late. My bed beckons. Fix up a room for Ublala. Get him some clothes. Maybe even a weapon he knows how to use.'

'Don't leave me here!' Ublala moaned.

'This is all business,' Tehol assured him. 'You're safe here. Isn't he, Shand?'

'Of course,' she murmured.

'Cut that out. Or I'll hire a bodyguard for our bodyguard.'

'Maybe Ublala has a brother.'

Tehol gestured for Bugg to follow as he headed for the door. 'I suppose meetings like this are useful. Every now and then.'

'No doubt,' Bugg replied.

They emerged onto the street. The night crowd was bustling. Shops stayed open late in the summer, to take advantage of the season's frenzy. Heat made for restlessness, which made for a certain insatiability. Later in the season, when the temperatures became unbearable, there would be enervation, and debt.

Tehol and Bugg left the high street fronting the canal and made their way down various alleys, gradually leaving the spending crowds behind and finding themselves among the destitute. Voices called out from shadows. Dishevelled children followed the two men, a few reaching out grubby hands to pluck at Tehol's skirt before running away laughing. Before long, they too

172

were gone, and the way ahead was empty.

'Ah, the welcoming silence of our neighbourhood,' Tehol said as they walked towards their house. 'It's the headlong rush that always troubles me. As if the present is unending.'

'Is this your contemplative moment?' Bugg asked.

'It was. Now over, thankfully.'

They entered and Tehol strode straight for the ladder. 'Clean the place up tomorrow morning.'

'Remember, you'll have a visitor tonight.'

'Not just in my dreams?'

Tehol clambered onto the roof. He closed the hatch then stood and studied the stars overhead until she emerged from the darkness to one side and spoke. 'You're late.'

'No, I'm not. Midnight. Still a quarter off.'

'Is it? Oh.'

'And how's life, Shurq? Sorry, I couldn't resist.'

'And I've never heard that particular quip before. It's a miserable existence. Day after day, night after night. One step in front of the other, on and on to nowhere in particular.'

'And being dead has changed all that?'

'Don't make me laugh, Tehol Beddict. I cough up stuff when I laugh. You want to offer me a contract. To do what?'

'Well, a retainer, actually.'

'Ongoing employment. I refused all retainers when I was alive; why should I do anything else now?'

'Job security, of course. You're not young any more.' He walked over to his bed and sat down, facing her. 'All right. Consider the challenges I offer. I have targets in mind that not a thief alive today would touch. In fact, only a high mage or someone who's dead could defeat the wards and leave no trail. I don't trust high mages, leaving only you.'

'There are others.'

'Two others, to be precise. And neither one a professional thief.'

'How did you know there were two others?'

173

'I know lots of things, Shurq. One is a woman who cheated on her husband, who in turn spent his life savings on the curse against her. The other is a child, origin of curse unknown, who dwells in the grounds of the old tower behind the palace.'

'Yes. I visit her on occasion. She doesn't know who cursed her. In fact, the child has no memory of her life at all.'

'Probably an addition to the original curse,' Tehol mused. 'But that is curious indeed.'

'It is. Half a peak was the going price. How much for sorcery to steal her memories?'

'Half as much again, I'd think. That's a lot to do to a ten-year-old child. Why not just kill her and bury her in some out of the way place, or dump her in the canal?' He sat forward. 'Tell you what, Shurq, we'll include the pursuit of that mystery – I suspect it interests you in spite of yourself.'

'I would not mind sticking a knife in the eye of whoever cursed the child. But I have no leads.'

'Ah, so you've not been entirely apathetic, then.'

'Never said I was, Tehol. But, finding no trail at all, I admit to a diminishment in motivation.'

'I'll see what I can do.'

The dead woman cocked her head and regarded him in silence for a moment. 'You were a genius once.'

'Very true.'

'Then you lost everything.'

'That's right.'

'And with that, presumably, a similar loss in confidence.'

'Oh, hardly, Shurq Elalle.'

'All part of your diabolical plan.'

'Every worthwhile plan is diabolical.'

'Don't make me laugh.'

'I'm trying not to, Shurq. Do we have a deal?'

'The secret of the curse upon the child was not your intended payment for my services, Tehol. What else?'

'I'm open to suggestions. Do you want the curse undone?

Do you long for eternal night? The final stealthy departure of your slinking soul? Do you want to be resurrected in truth? Gifted life once more? Revenge against the one who cursed you?'

'I already did that.'

'All right. I admit I'm not surprised. Who was blamed for it?'

'Gerun Eberict.'

'Oh, that's clever. Speaking of him . . .'

'Is he one of your targets?'

'Very much so.'

'I don't like assassination, in principle. Besides, he's killed more than one knave.'

'I don't want you to kill him, Shurq. Just steal his fortune.'

'Gerun Eberict has been getting more brazen, it's true.'

'An actual liability.'

'Assuming maintaining the status quo is a worthwhile endeavour.'

'Make no assumptions, Shurq. It's more a matter of who's controlling the dissolution of said status quo. The Finadd is losing control of his own appetites.'

'Are you one of his targets, Tehol?'

'Not that I'm aware of, not yet, anyway. Preferably not at all.'

'It would be quite a challenge defeating his estate's defensive measures.'

'I'm sure it would.'

'As for my retainer, I'm not interested in living again. Nor in dying with finality. No, what I want is to be granted the *semblance* of life.'

Tehol's brows rose.

'I want my skin glowing with palpable vigour. I want a certain dark allure to my eyes. My hair needs styling. New clothes, a flowery scent lingering in my wake. And I want to feel pleasure again.'

'Pleasure?'

175

'Sexual.'

'Maybe it's just the company you've been keeping.'

'Don't make me laugh.'

'You'll cough up stuff.'

'You don't want to know, Tehol Beddict. Maybe we can do something about that, too. That river water is three years old.'

'I'm curious. How do you manage to speak without breath?'

'I don't know. I can draw air into my throat. It starts drying out after a while.'

'I've noticed. All right, some of those things can be achieved easily enough, although we'll have to be circumspect. Others, for example the reawakening of pleasure, will obviously be more problematic. But I'm sure something can be managed—'

'It won't be cheap.'

'I'm sure Gerun Eberict will be happy to pay for it.'

'What if it takes all he has?'

Tehol shrugged. 'My dear, the money is not the point of the exercise. I was planning on dumping it in the river.'

She studied him in silence for a moment longer, then said, 'I could take it with me.'

'Don't make *me* laugh, Shurq. Seriously.'

'Why?'

'Because it's a very infectious laugh.'

'Ah. Point taken.'

'And the retainer?' Tehol asked.

'Taken, as well. Presumably, you don't want me hanging around you.'

'Midnight meetings like this one should suffice. Come by tomorrow night, and we'll make of you a new woman.'

'So long as I *smell* new.'

'Don't worry. I know just the people for the task at hand.'

The thief left by climbing down the outside wall of the building. Tehol stood at the roof's edge and watched her progress, then, when she had reached the alley below, he permitted himself a roll of the eyes. He turned away and approached his bed.

Only to hear voices down below. Surprised tones from Bugg, but not alarm. And loud enough to warn Tehol in case Shurq had lingered.

Tehol sighed. Life had been better – simpler – only a few weeks ago. When he'd been without plans, schemes, goals. Without, in short, purpose. A modest stir, and now everyone wanted to see him.

Creaks from the ladder, then a dark figure climbed into view.

It was a moment before Tehol recognized him, and his brows rose a moment before he stepped forward. 'Well, this is unexpected.'

'Your manservant seemed sure that you'd be awake. Why is that?'

'Dear brother, Bugg's talents are veritably preternatural.'

Brys walked over to the bed and studied it for a moment. 'What happens when it rains?'

'Alas, I am forced to retire to the room below. There to suffer Bugg's incessant snoring.'

'Is that what's driven you to sleeping on the roof?'

Tehol smiled, then realized it was not likely Brys could see that smile in the darkness. Then decided it was all for the best. 'King's Champion. I have been remiss in congratulating you. Thus, congratulations.'

Brys was motionless. 'How often do you visit the crypt? Or do you ever visit?'

Crossing his arms, Tehol swung his gaze to the canal below. A smeared gleam of reflected stars, crawling through the city. 'It's been years, Brys.'

'Since you last visited?'

'Since they died. We all have different ways of honouring their memory. The family crypt?' He shrugged. 'A stone-walled sunken room containing nothing of consequence.'

'I see. I'm curious, Tehol, how precisely do you honour their memory these days?'

'You have no idea.'

'No, I don't.'

Tehol rubbed at his eyes, only now realizing how tired he was. Thinking was proving a voracious feeder on his energies, leading him to admit he'd been out of practice. Not just thinking, of course. The brain did other things, as well, even more exhausting. The revisiting of siblings, of long-estranged relationships, saw old, burnished armour donned once more, weapons reached for, old stances once believed abandoned proving to have simply been lying dormant. 'Is this a festive holiday, Brys? Have I missed something? Had we cousins, uncles and aunts, nephews and nieces, we could gather to walk the familiar ruts. Round and round the empty chairs where our mother and father once sat. And we could make our language unspoken in a manner to mimic another truth – that the dead speak in silences and so never leave us in peace—'

'I need your help, Tehol.'

He glanced up, but could make nothing of his brother's expression in the gloom.

'It's Hull,' Brys went on. 'He's going to get himself killed.'

'Tell me,' Tehol said, 'have you ever wondered why not one of us has found a wife?'

'I was talking about—'

'It's simple, really. Blame our mother, Brys. She was too smart. Errant take us, what an understatement. It wasn't Father who managed the investments.'

'And you are her son, Tehol. More than me and Hull, by far. Every time I look at you, every time I listen to you, struggle to follow your lines of thought. But I don't see how that—'

'Our expectations reside in the clouds, Brys. Oh, we try. All of us have tried, haven't we?'

'Damn it, Tehol, what's your point?'

'Hull, of course. That's who you came here to talk about,

isn't it? Well. He met a woman. As smart as our mother, in her own way. Or, rather, she found him. Hull's greatest gift, but he didn't even recognize it for what it was, when it was right there in his hands.'

Brys stepped closer, hands lifting as if about to grasp his brother by the throat. 'You don't understand,' he said, his voice cracking with emotion. After a moment his hands fell away. 'The prince will see him killed. Or, if not the prince, then the First Eunuch – should Hull speak out against the king. But wait!' He laughed without humour. 'There's also Gerun Eberict! Who'll also be there! Have I left anyone out? I'm not sure. Does it matter? Hull will be at the parley. The only one whose motives are unknown – to anyone. You can't play your game if a stranger wades in at the last moment, can you?'

'Calm yourself, brother,' Tehol said. 'I was getting to my point.'

'Well, I can't see it!'

'Quietly, please. Hull found her, then lost her. But she's still there – that much is clear. Seren Pedac, Brys. She'll protect him—'

Brys snarled and turned away. 'Like Mother did Father?'

Tehol winced, then sighed. 'Mitigating circumstances—'

'And Hull is our father's son!'

'You asked, a moment ago, how I honour the memory of our parents. I can tell you this, Brys. When I see you. How you stand. The deadly grace – your skill, taught you by his hand – well, I have no need for memory. He stands before me, right now. More than with Hull. Far more. And, I'd hazard, I am much as you say – like *her*. Thus,' he spread his hands helplessly, 'you ask for help, but will not hear what I tell you. Need there be reminders of the fates of our parents? Need there be memory, Brys? We stand here, you and I, and play out once more the old familial tortures.'

'You describe, then,' he said hoarsely, 'our doom.'

'She could have saved him, Brys. If not for us. Her fear for us. The whole game of debt, so deftly contrived to snare

Father – she would have torn it apart, except that, like me, she could see nothing of the world that would rise from the ashes. And, seeing nothing, she *feared*.'

'Without us, then, she would have saved him – kept him from that moment of supreme cowardice?'

Brys was facing him now, his eyes glittering.

'I think so,' Tehol answered. 'And from them, we have drawn our lessons of life. You chose the protection of the King's Guard, and now the role of Champion. Where debt will never find you. As for Hull, he walked away – from gold, from its deadly traps – and sought honour in saving people. And even when that failed … do you honestly imagine Hull would ever consider killing himself? Our father's cowardice was betrayal, Brys. Of the worst sort.'

'And what of you, Tehol? What lesson are you living out right now?'

'The difference between me and our mother is that I carry no burden. No children. So, brother, I think I will end up achieving the very thing she could not do, despite her love for Father.'

'By dressing in rags and sleeping on your roof?'

'Perception enforces expectation, Brys.' And thought he saw a wry smile from his brother.

'Even so, Tehol, Gerun Eberict is not as deceived as you might believe. As, I admit, I was.'

'Until tonight?'

'I suppose so.'

'Go home, Brys,' Tehol said. 'Seren Pedac stands at Hull's back, and will continue to do so no matter how much she might disagree with whatever he seeks to do. She cannot help herself. Even genius has its flaws.'

Another grin. 'Even with you, Tehol?'

'Well, I was generalizing to put you at ease. I never include myself in my own generalizations. I am ever the exception to the rule.'

'And how do you manage that?'

'Well, I define the rules, of course. That's my particular game, brother.'

'By the Errant, I hate you sometimes, Tehol. Listen. Do not underestimate Gerun Eberict—'

'I'll take care of Gerun. Now, presumably you were followed here?'

'I hadn't thought of that. Yes, probably I was. Do you think our voices carried?'

'Not through the wards Bugg raises every night before he goes to sleep.'

'Bugg?'

Tehol clapped his brother on the shoulder and guided him towards the hatch. 'He's only mostly worthless. We ever seek out hidden talents, an exercise assuring endless amusement. For me, at least.'

'Did he not embalm our parents? The name—'

'That was Bugg. That's where I first met him, and saw immediately his lack of potential. The entrance can be viewed in secret from one place and no other, Brys. Normally, you could make no approach without being detected. And then there'd be a chase, which is messy and likely to fail on your part. You will have to kill the man – Gerun's, I suspect. And not in a duel. Outright execution, Brys. Are you up to it?'

'Of course. But you said there was no approach that could not—'

'Ah, well, I forgot to mention our tunnel.'

Brys paused at the hatch. 'You have a tunnel.'

'Keeping Bugg busy is an eternal chore.'

Still five paces from the shadowed section of the warehouse wall that offered the only hiding place with a clear line of sight to the doorway of Tehol's house, Brys Beddict halted. His eyes were well adjusted, and he could see that no-one was there.

But he could smell blood. Metallic and thick.

Sword drawn, he approached.

No man could have survived such a loss. It was a black pool on the cobbles, reluctant to seep into the cracks between the set stones. A throat opened wide, the wound left to drain before the corpse had been dragged away. And the trail was plain, twin heel tracks alongside the warehouse wall, round a corner and out of sight.

The Finadd considered following it.

Then, upon seeing a single footprint, traced in dried dust on the dust, he changed his mind.

The footprint left by a child. Bared. As it dragged the dead man away.

Every city had its darkness, its denizens who prowled only at night in their own game of predator and prey. Brys knew it was not his world, nor did he wish to hunt down its secrets. These hours belonged to the white crow, and it was welcome to them.

He turned the other way, began his walk back to the palace.

His brother's formidable mind had not been idle, it seemed. His indifference no more than a feint. Which made Tehol a very dangerous man. *Thank the Errant he's on my side . . .*

He is on my side, isn't he?

The old palace, soon to be entirely abandoned in favour of the Eternal Domicile, sat on a sunken hill, the building proper a hundred paces in from the river's seasonally uncertain banks. Sections of a high wall indicated that there had been an enclosure once, extending from the palace to the river, in which an assortment of structures had been effectively isolated from the rest of the city.

Not so much in a proprietary claim to ownership, for the structures in question predated even the founding First Empire. Perhaps, for those original builders, there had been a recognition, of sorts, of something verging on the sacred about these grounds, although, of course, not holy to the colonizers. Another possibility was that the first Letherii

182

were possessors of a more complete arcane knowledge – secrets long since lost – that inspired them to do honour to the Jaghut dwellings and the single, oddly different tower in their midst.

The truth had crumbled along with the enclosure walls, and no answers could be found sifting the dust of crumbled mortar and flakes of exfoliated schist. The area, while no longer sealed, was by habit avoided. The land itself was worthless, by virtue of a royal proclamation six centuries old that prohibited demolition of the ancient structures, and subsequent resettlement. Every legal challenge or, indeed, enquiry regarding that proclamation was summarily dismissed without even so much as recourse to the courts.

All very well. Skilled practitioners of the tiles of the Holds well knew the significance of that squat, square, leaning tower with its rumpled, overgrown grounds. And indeed of the Jaghut dwellings, representative as they were of the Ice Hold. Many held that the Azath tower was the very first true structure of the Azath on this world.

From her new perspective, Shurq Elalle was less sceptical than she might have once been. The grounds surrounding the battered grey stone tower exerted an ominous pull on the dead thief. There were kin there, but not of blood. No, this was the family of the undead, of those unable or unwilling to surrender to oblivion. In the case of those interred in the lumpy, clay-shot earth around the tower, their graves were prisons. The Azath did not give up its children.

She sensed as well that there were living creatures buried there, most of them driven mad by centuries upon centuries snared in ancient roots that held them fast. Others remained ominously silent and motionless, as if awaiting eternity's end.

The thief approached the forbidden grounds behind the palace. She could see the Azath tower, its third and upper-most storey edging above the curved walls of the Jaghut dwellings. Not one of the structures stood fully upright. All

183

were tilted in some fashion, the subsurface clay squeezing out from beneath their immense weight or lenses of sand washed away by underground runoff. Vines had climbed the sides in chaotic webs, although those that had reached out to the Azath died there, withered against the foundation stones amidst yellowed grasses.

She did not need to see the blood trail in order to follow it. The smell was heavy in the sultry night air, invisible streaks riding the currents, and she pursued its wake until she came to the low, crooked wall surrounding the Azath tower.

Just beyond, at the base of a twisted tree, sat the child Kettle. Nine or ten years old . . . for ever. Naked, her pale skin smeared, her long hair clotted with coagulating blood. The corpse before her was already half under the earth, being dragged down into the darkness.

To feed the Azath? Or some ravenous denizen? Shurq had no idea. Nor did she care. The grounds swallowed bodies, and that was useful.

Kettle looked up, black eyes dully reflecting starlight. There were moulds that, if left unattended, could blind, and the film was thick over the girl's dead eyes. She slowly rose and walked over.

'Why won't you be my mother?'

'I've already told you, Kettle. I am no-one's mother.'

'I followed you tonight.'

'You're always following me,' Shurq said.

'Just after you left that roof, another man came to the house. A soldier. And he was followed.'

'And which of the two did you kill?'

'Why, the one who followed, of course. I'm a good girl. I take care of you. Just as you take care of me—'

'I take care of no-one, Kettle. You were dead long before I was. Living here in these grounds. I used to bring you bodies.'

'Never enough.'

'I don't like killing. Only when I have no choice. Besides, I wasn't the only one employing your services.'

'Yes you were.'

Shurq stared at the girl for a long moment. 'I was?'

'Yes. And you wanted to know my story. Everyone else runs from me, just like they run from you now. Except that man on the roof. Is he another one not like everyone else?'

'I don't know, Kettle. But I am working for him now.'

'I am glad. Grown-ups should work. It helps fill their minds. Empty minds are bad. Dangerous. They fill themselves up. With bad things. Nobody's happy.'

Shurq cocked her head. 'Who's not happy?'

Kettle waved one grubby hand at the rumpled yard. 'Restless. All of them. I don't know why. The tower sweats all the time now.'

'I will bring you some salt water,' Shurq said, 'for your eyes. You need to wash them out.'

'I can see easily enough. With more than my eyes now. My skin sees. And tastes. And dreams of light.'

'What do you mean?'

Kettle pushed bloody strands of hair from her heart-shaped face. 'Five of them are trying to get out. I don't like those five – I don't like most of them, but especially those five. The roots are dying. I don't know what to do. They whisper how they'll tear me to pieces. Soon. I don't want to be torn to pieces. What should I do?'

Shurq was silent. Then she asked, 'How much do you sense of the Buried Ones, Kettle?'

'Most don't talk to me. They have lost their minds. Others hate me for not helping them. Some beg and plead. They talk through the roots.'

'Are there any who ask nothing of you?'

'Some are ever silent.'

'Talk to them. Find someone else to speak to, Kettle. Someone who might be able to help you.' *Someone else to be your mother . . . or father.* 'Ask for opinions, on any and all matters. If one remains then who does not seek to please you, who does not attempt to twist your desires so that you free it, and who holds no loyalty to the others, then

185

you will tell me of that one. All that you know. And I will advise you as best I can – not as a mother, but as a comrade.'

'All right.'

'Good. Now, I came here for another reason, Kettle. I want to know, how did you kill that spy?'

'I bit through his throat. It's the quickest, and I like the blood.'

'Why do you like the blood?'

'In my hair, to keep it from my face. And it smells alive, doesn't it? I like that smell.'

'How many do you kill?'

'Lots. The ground needs them.'

'Why does the ground need them?'

'Because it's dying.'

'Dying? And what would happen if it does die, Kettle?'

'Everything will get out.'

'Oh.'

'I like it here.'

'Kettle, from now on,' Shurq said, 'I will tell you who to kill – don't worry, there should be plenty.'

'All right. That's nice of you.'

Among the hundreds of creatures buried in the grounds of the Azath, only one was capable of listening to the conversation between the two undead on the surface above. The Azath was relinquishing its hold on this denizen, not out of weakness, but out of necessity. The Guardian was anything but ready. Indeed, might never be ready. The choice itself had been flawed, yet another sign of faltering power, of age crawling forward to claim the oldest stone structure in the realm.

The Azath tower was indeed dying. And desperation forced a straying onto unprecedented paths.

Among all the prisoners, a choice had been made. And preparations were under way, slow as the track of roots through stone, but equally inexorable. But there was so little time.

The urgency was a silent scream that squeezed blood from the Azath tower. Five kin creatures, taken and held since the time of the K'Chain Che'Malle, were almost within reach of the surface.

And this was not good, for they were Toblakai.

CHAPTER FIVE

Against the flat like thunder
Where the self dwells between the eyes,
Beneath the blow the bone shattered
And the soul was dragged forth
To writhe in the grip
Of unredeemed vengeance . . .

> *The Last Night of Bloodeye*
> Author unknown
> (compiled by Tiste Andii scholars
> of Black Coral)

The Shadow's laughter was low, a sound that promised madness to all who heard it. Udinaas let the netting fall away from his fingers and leaned back against the sun-warmed rock. He squinted up at the bright sky. He was alone on the beach, the choppy waves of the bay stretching out before him. Alone, except for the wraith that now haunted him at every waking moment.

Conjured, then forgotten. Wandering, an eternal flight from the sun, but there were always places to hide.

'Stop that,' Udinaas said, closing his eyes.

'Why ever? I smell your blood, slave. Growing colder. I once knew a world of ice. After I was killed, yes, after. Even darkness has flaws, and that's how they stole me. But I have dreams.'

'So you're always saying. Then follow them, wraith, and leave me alone.'

'I have dreams and you understand nothing, slave. Was I pleased to serve? Never. Never ever never and again, never. I'm following you.'

Udinaas opened his eyes and stared down at the sliver of shadow between two rocks, from which the voice was emerging. Sand fleas scampered and darted on the flanking stone, but of the wraith itself there was no visible sign. 'Why?'

'Why ever why? That which you cast beckons me, slave. You promise a worthy journey – do you dream of gardens, slave? I know you do – I can smell it. Half dead and overgrown, why ever not? There is no escape. So, with my dreams, it serves me to serve. Serves to serve. Was I not once a Tiste Andii? I believe I was. Murdered and flung into the mud, until the ice came. Then torn loose, after so long, to serve my slayers. My slavers, whose diligence then wavered. Shall we whisper of betrayers, slave?'

'You would bargain?'

'Hither when you call me, call me Wither. I have dreams. Give me that which you cast. Give me your shadow, and I will become yours. Your eyes behind you, whom no-one else can see or hear, unless they guess and have power but why would they guess? You are a slave. Who behaves. Be sure to behave, slave, until the moment you betray.'

'I thought Tiste Andii were supposed to be dour and miserable. And please, Wither, no more rhymes.'

'Agreed, once you give me your shadow.'

'Can other wraiths see you? Hannan Mosag's—'

'That oaf? I will hide in your natural casting. Hidden. Never found. See, no rhymes. We were bold in those days, slave. Soldiers in a war, an invasion. Soaked in the cold blood of K'Chain Che'Malle. We followed the youngest child of Mother Dark herself. And we were witness.'

'To what?'

'To Bloodeye's betrayal of our leader. To the dagger driven into our lord's back. I myself fell to a blade wielded by a Tiste Edur. Unexpected. Sudden slaughter. We stood no chance. No chance at all.'

189

Udinaas made a face, studied the tossing waves that warred with the river's outpouring current. 'The Edur claim it was the other way round, Wither.'

'*Then why am I dead and they alive? If we were the ambushers that day?*'

'How should I know? Now, if you intend to lurk in my shadow, Wither, you must learn to be silent. Unless I speak to you. Silent, and watchful, and nothing more.'

'*First, slave, you must do something for me.*'

Udinaas sighed. Most of the noble-born Edur were at the interment ceremony for the murdered fisherman, along with a half-dozen kin from the Beneda, since the Edur's identity had finally been determined. Fewer than a dozen warriors remained in the compound behind him. Shadow wraiths seemed to grow bolder at such times, emerging to flit across the ground, between longhouses and along the palisade walls.

He had often wondered at that. But now, if Wither was to be believed, he had his answer. *Those wraiths are not ancestral kin to the mortal Edur. They are Tiste Andii, the bound souls of the slain. And, I was desperate for allies . . .* 'Very well, what do you wish me to do, Wither?'

'*Before the seas rose in this place, slave, the Hasana Inlet was a lake. To the south and west, the land stretched out to join with the westernmost tip of the Reach. A vast plain, upon which the last of my people were slaughtered. Walk the shoreline before you, slave. South. There is something of mine – we must find it.*'

Udinaas rose and brushed the sand from his coarse woollen trousers. He looked about. Three slaves from the Warlock King's citadel were down by the river mouth, beating clothes against rocks. A lone fisherboat was out on the water, but distant. 'How far will I need to walk?'

'*It lies close.*'

'If I am perceived to be straying too far, I will be killed outright.'

'*Not far, slave—*'

'I am named Udinaas, and so you will address me.'

'You claim the privilege of pride?'

'I am more than a slave, Wither, as you well know.'

'But you must behave as if you were not. I call you "slave" to remind you of that. Fail in your deception, and the pain they shall inflict upon you in the search for all you would hide from them shall be without measure—'

'Enough.' He walked down to the waterline. The sun threw his shadow into his wake, pulled long and monstrous.

The rollers had built a humped sweep of sand over the stones, on which lay tangled strands of seaweed and a scattering of detritus. A pace inland of this elongated rise was a depression filled with slick pebbles and rocks. 'Where should I be looking?'

'Among the stones. A little further. Three, two paces. Yes. Here.'

Udinaas stared down, scanning the area. 'I see nothing.'

'Dig. No, to your left – those rocks, move those. That one. Now, deeper. There, pull it free.'

A misshapen lump that sat heavy in his hand. Finger-length and tapered at one end, the metal object within swallowed by thick calcifications. 'What is it?'

'An arrowhead, slave. Hundreds of millennia, crawling to this shore. The passage of ages is measured by chance. The deep roll of tides, the succession of wayward storms. This is how the world moves—'

'Hundreds of millennia? There would be nothing left—'

'A blade of simple iron without sorcerous investment would indeed have vanished. The arrowhead remains, slave, because it will not surrender. You must chip away at all that surrounds it. You must resurrect it.'

'Why?'

'I have my reasons, slave.'

There was nothing pleasing in this, but Udinaas straightened and tucked the lump in his belt pouch. He returned to his nets. 'I shall not,' he muttered, 'be the hand of your vengeance.'

Wither's laugh followed him in the crunch of stones.

* * *

There was smoke hanging above the lowlands, like clouds dragged low and now shredded by the dark treetops.

'A funeral,' Binadas said.

Seren Pedac nodded. There had been no storms, and besides, the forest was too wet to sustain a wildfire. The Edur practice of burial involved a tumulus construction, which was then covered to form a pyre. The intense heat baked the coin-sheathed corpse as if it was clay, and stained the barrow stones red. Shadow wraiths danced amidst the flames, twisted skyward with the smoke, and would linger long after the mourners were gone.

Seren drew her knife and bent to scrape mud from her boots. This side of the mountains the weather daily crept in from the sea shedding rain and mist in pernicious waves. Her clothes were soaked through. Three times since morning the heavily burdened wagons had skidded off the trail, once crushing a Nerek to death beneath the solid, iron-rimmed wheels.

Straightening, she cleaned her knife between two gloved fingers, then sheathed it at her side.

Moods were foul. Buruk the Pale had not emerged from his wagon in two days, nor had his three half-blood Nerek concubines. But the descent was finally done, and ahead was a wide, mostly level trail leading to Hannan Mosag's village.

Binadas stood and watched as the last wagon rocked clear of the slope, and Seren sensed the Edur's impatience. Someone had died in his village, after all. She glanced over at Hull Beddict, but could sense nothing from him. He had withdrawn deep into himself, as if building reserves in anticipation of what was to come. Or, equally likely, struggling to bolster crumbling resolve. She seemed to have lost her ability to read him. Pain worn without pause and for so long could itself become a mask.

'Binadas,' Seren said, 'the Nerek need to rest. The journey before us is clear. There is no need for you to remain with us as escort. Go to your people.'

His eyes narrowed on her, suspicious of her offer.

She added nothing more. He would believe what he would believe, after all, no matter how genuine her intent.

'She speaks true,' Hull said. 'We would not constrain you, Binadas.'

'Very well. I shall inform Hannan Mosag of your impending visit.'

They watched the Edur set off down the trail. In moments the trees swallowed him.

'Do you see?' Hull asked her.

'I saw only conflicting desires and obligations,' Seren replied, turning away.

'Only, then, what you chose to.'

Seren's shrug was weary. 'Oh, Hull, that is the way of us all.'

He stepped close. 'But it need not be so, Acquitor.'

Surprised, she met his gaze, and wondered at the sudden earnestness there. 'How am I supposed to respond to that?' she asked. 'We are all like soldiers, crouching behind the fortifications we have raised. You will do what you believe you must, Hull.'

'And you, Seren Pedac? What course awaits you?'

Ever the same course. 'The Tiste Edur are not yours to use. They may listen, but they are not bound to follow.'

He turned away. 'I have no expectations, Seren, only fears. We should resume the journey.'

She glanced over at the Nerek. They sat or squatted near the wagons, steam rising from their backs. Their expressions were slack, strangely indifferent to the dead kin they had left behind in his makeshift grave of rutted mud, rocks and roots. How much could be stripped from a people before they began stripping away themselves? The steep slope of dissolution began with a skid, only to become a headlong run.

The Letherii believed in cold-hearted truths. Momentum was an avalanche and no-one was privileged with the choice of stepping aside. The division between life and death was measured in incremental jostling for position amidst all-devouring progress. No-one could afford compassion. Accordingly, none expected it from others either.

We live in an inimical time. But then, they are all inimical times.

It began to rain once more.

Far to the south, beyond the mountains they had just crossed, the downfall of the Tiste Edur was being plotted. And, she suspected, Hull Beddict's life had been made forfeit. They could not afford the risk he presented, the treason he had as much as promised. The irony existed in their conjoined desires. Both sought war, after all. It was only the face of victory that was different.

But Hull possessed little of the necessary acumen to play this particular game and stay alive.

And she had begun to wonder if she would make any effort to save him.

A shout from Buruk's wagon. The Nerek climbed wearily to their feet. Seren drew her cloak tighter about her shoulders, eyes narrowed on the path ahead. She sensed Hull coming to her side, but did not look over.

'What temple was it you were schooled at?'

She snorted, then shook her head. 'Thurlas, the Shrouded Sisters of the Empty Throne.'

'Just opposite Small Canal. I remember it. What sort of child were you, Seren?'

'Clearly, you have an image in your mind.'

She caught his nod in her periphery, and he said, 'Zealous. Proper to excess. Earnest.'

'There are ledgers, recording the names of notable students. You will find mine in them, again and again. For example, I hold title to the most punishments inflicted in a year. Two hundred and seventy-one. I was more familiar with the Unlit Cell than my own room. I was also accused of seducing a visiting priest. And before you ask, yes, I was guilty. But the priest swore otherwise, to protect me. He was excommunicated. I later heard he killed himself. Had I still possessed any innocence, I would have lost it then.'

He came round to stand before her, as the first wagon was pulled past by the Nerek. She was forced to look at him. Hesitated, then offered him a wry smile. 'Have I shocked you, Hull Beddict?'

'The ice has broken beneath me.'

A flash of anger, then she realized the self-mockery in his confession. 'We are not born innocent, simply unmeasured.'

'And, presumably, immeasurable as well.'

'For a few years at least. Until the outside is inflicted upon the inside, then the brutal war begins. We are not born to compassion either – large wide eyes and sweet demeanour notwithstanding.'

'And you came to recognize your war early.'

Seren shrugged. 'My enemy was not authority, although perhaps it seemed so. It was childhood itself. The lowered expectations of adults, the eagerness to *forgive*. It sickened me—'

'Because it was unjust.'

'A child's sense of injustice is ever self-serving, Hull. I couldn't fool myself with that indignation. Why are we speaking of this?'

'Questions I forgot to ask. Back then. I think I was a child myself in those days. All inside, no outside.'

Her brows rose, but she said nothing.

Hull understood anyway. 'You might be right. In some things, that is. But not when it comes to the Edur.'

The second wagon trundled past. Seren studied the man before her. 'Are you so certain of that?' she asked. 'Because I see you driven by your own needs. The Edur are the sword but the hand is your own, Hull. Where is the compassion in that?'

'You have it wrong, Seren. I intend to be the sword.'

The chill in her bones deepened. 'In what way?'

But he shook his head. 'I cannot trust you, Seren. Like

everyone else, you shall have to wait. One thing, however. Do not stand in my way. Please.'

I cannot trust you. Words that cut to her soul. Then again, the issue of trust stood on both sides of the path, didn't it?

The third wagon halted beside them. The curtain in the door window was dragged aside and Buruk's deathly face peered out. 'And this is guidance? Who blazes the trail? Are we doomed now to wander lost? Don't tell me you have become lovers once more! Seren, you look positively *besieged*. Such is the curse of love, oh, my heart weeps for you!'

'Enough, Buruk,' Seren said. She wiped the rain from her face and, ignoring Hull, moved past onto the path. Nerek stepped to either side to let her pass.

The forest trail was flanked by Blackwood trees, planted to assert Edur possession of these lands. Rough midnight bark that had been twisted into nightmarish images and arcane script by the shadow wraiths that clung to every groove and fissure in the rugged skin. Wraiths that now rose into view to watch Seren and those following in her wake.

There seemed more than usual. Flowing restless like black mist between the huge boles. Scores, then hundreds, crowding either side of the trail. Seren's steps slowed.

She could hear the Nerek behind her, low moans, the clack of the wagons slowing, then halting.

Hull came alongside her. 'They have raised an army,' he whispered.

There was dark satisfaction in his tone.

'Are they truly the ancestors of the Edur?'

His gaze snapped to her, feverish. 'Of course. What else could they be?'

She shook herself. 'Urge the Nerek onward, Hull. They'll listen to you. Two days remaining, that's all—' And then she fell silent.

For a figure was standing upon the trail. Skin the colour

196

of bleached linen, tall as an Edur, a face obscured by dark streaks, as if blood-stained fingers had drawn down the gaunt cheeks. An apparition, the dull red eyes burning from those deep sockets dead. Mould hung in ragged sheets from rotting armour. Two scabbards, both empty.

Wraiths swarmed at the figure's feet, as if in worship.

A wagon door clattered and Buruk staggered out, wrapped in a blanket that dragged the ground behind him as he came to Seren's side.

'*Barrow and Root!*' the merchant hissed. 'The tiles did not lie!'

Seren took a step forward.

Hull reached out a hand. 'No—'

'Would you have us stand here for ever?' she snapped, pulling herself free. Despite the bravado of her words, she was terrified. Ghosts revealed themselves in childhood tales and legends, and in the occasional fevered rumour in the capital. She had believed in such apparitions in a half-hearted way, an idea made wilfully manifest. A whispery vision of history, risen as harbinger, as silent warning. A notion, then, as much symbolic as actual.

And even then, she had imagined something far more . . . ephemeral. Lacking distinction, a face comprised of forlorn hints, features blurred by the fading of their relevance. Half seen in currents of darkness, there one moment, gone the next.

But there was a palpability in the tall conjuration standing before her, an assertion of physical insistence. Etched details on the long, pallid face, the flat, filmed eyes watching her approach with fullest comprehension.

As if he has just clambered free of one of the barrows in this forest. But he is not . . . is not Edur.

'A dragon,' the apparition said in the language of the Tiste, 'once dragged itself down this trail. No forest back then. Naught but devastation. Blood in the broken earth. The dragon, mortal, *made* this trail. Do you feel this? Beneath you, the scattering of memory that pushes the

197

roots away, that bows the trees to either side. A dragon.'
The figure then turned, looked down the path behind
it. 'The Edur – he ran unseeing, unmindful. Kin of my
betrayer. Yet . . . an innocent.' He faced her once more.
'But you, mortal, are not nearly so innocent, are you?'

Taken aback, Seren said nothing.

Behind her, Hull Beddict spoke. 'Of what do you accuse
her, ghost?'

'A thousand. A thousand upon a thousand misdeeds.
Her. You. Your kind. The gods are as nothing. Demons less
than children. Every Ascendant an awkward mummer.
Compared to you. Is it ever the way, I wonder? That
depravity thrives in the folds of the flower, when its season
has come. The secret seeds of decay hidden beneath the
burgeoning glory. All of us, here in your wake, we are as
nothing.'

'What do you want?' Hull demanded.

The wraiths had slipped away, back among the trees. But
a new tide had come to swarm about the ghost's tattered
boots. Mice, a seething mass pouring up the trail. Ankle
deep, the first reached Seren's feet, scampered round them.
A grey and brown tide, mindless motion. A *multitude of tiny
selves, seized by some unknown and unknowable imperative.
From here . . . to there.*

There was something terrible, horrifying, about them.
Thousands, tens of thousands – the trail ahead, for as far as
she could see, was covered with mice.

'The land was shattered,' the apparition said. 'Not a tree
left standing. Naught but corpses. And the tiny creatures
that fed on them. Hood's own legion. Death's sordid tide,
mortals, fur-backed and rising. It seems so . . . facile.' The
undead seemed to shake himself. 'I want nothing from you.
The journeys are all begun. Do you imagine that your path
has never before known footfalls?'

'We are not so blind as to believe that,' Seren Pedac said.
She struggled against kicking away the mice swarming
around her ankles, fearing the descent into hysteria. 'If you

198

will not – or cannot – clear this trail, then we've little choice—'

The apparition's head tilted. 'You would deliver count-less small deaths? In the name of what? Convenience?'

'I see no end to these creatures of yours, ghost.'

'Mine? They are not mine, mortal. They simply belong to my time. To the age of their squalid supremacy on this land. A multitude of tyrants to rule over the ash and dust we left in our wake. They see in my spirit a promise.'

'And,' Hull growled, 'are we meant to see the same?'

The apparition had begun fading, colours bleeding away. 'If it pleases you,' came the faint, derisive reply. 'Of course, it may be that the spirit they see is yours, not mine.'

Then the ghost was gone.

The mice began flowing out to the forest on either side of the trail, as if suddenly confused, blinded once more to whatever greater force had claimed them. They bled away into the mulch, the shadows and the rotted wood of fallen trees. One moment there, the next, gone.

Seren swung to Buruk the Pale. 'What did you mean when you said the tiles didn't lie? Barrow and Root, those are tiles in the Hold of the Azath, are they not? You witnessed a casting before you began this journey. In Trate. Do you deny it?'

He would not meet her eyes. His face was pale. 'The Holds are awakening, Acquitor. *All of them.*'

'Who was he, then?' Hull Beddict asked.

'I do not know.' Abruptly Buruk scowled and turned away. 'Does it matter? The mud stirs and things clamber free, that is all. The Seventh Closure draws near – but I fear it will be nothing like what all of us have been taught. The birth of empire, oh yes, but who shall rule it? The prophecy is perniciously vague. The trail has cleared – let us proceed.'

He clambered back into his wagon.

'Are we to make sense of that?' Hull asked.

Seren shrugged. 'Prophecies are like the tiles themselves, Hull. See in them what you will.' The aftermath of her terror was sour in her throat, and her limbs felt loose and weak. Suddenly weary, she unstrapped her helm and lifted it off. The fine rain was like ice on her brow. She closed her eyes.

I can't save him. I can't save any of us.

Hull Beddict spoke to the Nerek.

Blinking her eyes open, Seren shook herself. She tied her helm to her pack.

The journey resumed. Clattering, groaning wagons, the harsh breathing of the Nerek. Motionless air and the mist falling through it like the breath of an exhausted god.

Two days. Then it is done.

Thirty paces ahead, unseen by any of them, an owl sailed across the path, silent on its broad, dark wings. There was blood on its talons, blood around its beak.

Sudden bounties were unquestioned. Extravagance unworthy of celebration. The hunter knew only hunting, and was indifferent to the fear of the prey. Indifferent, as well, to the white crow that sailed in its wake.

A random twist of the wind drew the remnants of the pyre's smoke into the village. It had burned for a day and a night, and Trull Sengar emerged from his father's longhouse the following morning to find the mist drifting across the compound bitter with its taint.

He regretted the new world he had found. Revelations could not be undone. And now he shared secrets and the truth was, he would rather have done without them. Once familiar faces had changed. What did they know? How vast and insidious this deceit? How many warriors had Hannan Mosag drawn into his ambitions? To what extent had the women organized against the Warlock King?

No words on the subject had been exchanged among the brothers, not since that conversation in the pit, the stove-in dragon skull the only witness to what most would call treason. The preparations for the impending journey were under way. There would be no slaves accompanying them, after all. Hannan Mosag had sent wraiths ahead to the villages lying between here and the ice-fields, and so provisions would await them, mitigating the need for burdensome supplies, at least until the very end.

A wagon drawn by a half-dozen slaves had trundled across the bridge, in its bed newly forged weapons. Iron-tipped spears stood upright in bound bundles. Copper sheathing protected the shafts for fully half their length. Cross-hilted swords were also visible, hand-and-a-half grips and boiled leather scabbards. Billhooks for unseating riders, sheaves of long arrows with leather fletching. Throwing axes, as favoured by the Arapay. Broad cutlasses in the Merude style.

The forges hammered the din of war once more.

Trull saw Fear and Rhulad stride up to the wagon, more slaves trailing them, and Fear began directing the storage of the weapons.

Rhulad glanced over as Trull approached. 'Have you need of more spears, brother?' he asked.

'No, Rhulad. I see Arapay and Merude weapons here – and Beneda and Den-Ratha—'

'Every tribe, yes. So it is now among all the forges, in every village. A sharing of skills.'

Trull glanced over at Fear. 'Your thoughts on this, brother? Will you now be training the Hiroth warriors in new weapons?'

'I have taught how to defend against them, Trull. It is the Warlock King's intention to create a true army, such as those of the Letherii. This will involve specialist units.' Fear studied Trull for a moment, before adding, 'I am Weapons Master for the Hiroth, and now, at the Warlock King's command, for all of the tribes.'

'You are to lead this army?'

'If war should come, yes, I will lead it into battle.'

'Thus are the Sengar honoured,' Rhulad said, his face expressionless, the tone without inflection.

Thus are we rewarded.

'Binadas returned at dawn,' Fear said. 'He will take this day in rest. Then we shall depart.'

Trull nodded.

'A Letherii trader caravan is coming,' Rhulad said. 'Binadas met them on the trail. The Acquitor is Seren Pedac. And Hull Beddict is with them.'

Hull Beddict, the Sentinel who betrayed the Nerek, the Tarthenal and the Faraed. What did he want? Not all Letherii were the same, Trull knew. Opposing views sang with the clash of swords. Betrayals abounded among the rapacious multitude in the vast cities and indeed, if rumours were true, in the palace of the king himself. The merchant was charged to deliver the words of whoever had bought him. Whilst Seren Pedac, in the profession of Acquitor, would neither speak her mind nor interfere with the aims of the others. He had not been in the village during her other visits, and so could judge no more than that. But Hull, the once Sentinel – it was said he was immune to corruption, such as only a man once betrayed could be.

Trull was silent as he watched the slaves drag the weapon bundles from the cart bed and carry them off to the armoury.

Even his brothers seemed . . . different somehow. As if shadows stretched taut between them, unseen by anyone else, and could make the wind drone with weighted trepidation. Darkness, then, in the blood of brothers. None of this served the journey about to begin. None of it.

I was ever the worrier. I do not see too much, I see only the wrong things. And so the fault is mine, within me. I need to remain mindful of that. Such as with my assumptions about Rhulad and Mayen. Wrong things, wrong thoughts, they are the ones that seem to be . . . tireless . . .

'Binadas says Buruk carries Letherii iron,' Rhulad said, breaking Trull's reverie. 'That will prove useful. Dapple knows, the Letherii are truly fools—'

'They are not,' Fear said. 'They are indifferent. They see

202

no contradiction in selling us iron at one moment and waging war with us the next.'

'Nor the harvesting of tusked seals,' Trull added, nodding. 'They are a nation of ten thousand grasping hands, and none can tell which ones are true, which ones belong to those in power.'

'King Ezgara Diskanar is not like Hannan Mosag,' Fear said. 'He does not rule his people with absolute . . .'

Trull glanced over as his brother's voice trailed off.

Fear swung away. 'Mayen is guest tonight,' he said. 'Mother may request you partake in the supper preparations.'

'And so we shall,' Rhulad said, meeting Trull's eyes a moment before fixing his attention once more on the slaves.

Absolute power . . . no, we have undone that, haven't we? And indeed, perhaps it never existed at all. The women, after all . . .

The other slaves were busy in the longhouse, scurrying back and forth across the trusses as Udinaas entered and made his way to his sleeping pallet. He was to serve this night, and so was permitted a short period of rest beforehand. He saw Uruth standing near the central hearth but was able to slip past unnoticed in the confusion, just another slave in the gloom.

Feather Witch's assertions remained with him, tightening his every breath. Should the Edur discover the truth that coursed through his veins, they would kill him. He knew he must hide, only he did not know how.

He settled onto his mat. The sounds and smells of the chambers beyond drifted over him. Lying back, he closed his eyes.

This night he would be working alongside Feather Witch. She had visited him that one time, in his dream. Apart from that, he had had no occasion to speak with her. Nor, he suspected, was she likely to invite an exchange of words. Beyond the mundane impropriety established by their respective class, she had seen in him the blood of the Wyval – or so she had claimed in the dream. *Unless that was not her at all. Nothing more than a conjuration from my own mind, a reshaping of dust.* He would, if possible, speak to her, whether invited or not.

Rugs had been dragged outside and laid across trestles. The thump of the clubs the slaves used to beat the dust from them was like distant, hollow thunder.

A flitting thought, vague wondering where the shadow wraith had gone, then sleep took him.

He was without form, an insubstantial binding of senses. In ice. A blue, murky world, smeared with streaks of green, the grit of dirt and sand, the smell of cold. Distant groaning sounds, solid rivers sliding against each other. Lenses of sunlight delivering heat into the depths, where it built until a thundering snap shook the world.

Udinaas flowed through this frozen landscape, which to all eyes in the world beyond was locked motionless, timeless. And nothing of the pressures, the heaved weights and disparate forces, was revealed, until that final explosive moment when things *broke*.

There were shapes in the ice. Bodies lifted from the ground far below and held in awkward poses. Fleshed, eyes half open. Blossoms of blood suspended in motionless clouds around wounds. Flows of bile and waste. Udinaas found himself travelling through scenes of slaughter. Tiste Edur and darker-skinned kin. Enormous reptilian beasts, some with naught but blades for hands. In multitudes beyond counting.

He came to a place where the reptilian bodies formed a near-solid mass. Flowing among them, he suddenly recoiled. A vertical stream of melt water rose through the ice before him, threading up and out from the heaped corpses. The water was pink, mud-streaked, pulsing as it climbed upward, as if driven by some deep, subterranean heart.

And that water was poison.

Udinaas found himself fleeing through the ice, clashing with corpses, rock-hard flesh. Then past, into fissure-twisted sweeps devoid of bodies. Down solid channels. Racing, ever faster, the gloom swallowing him.

Massive brown-furred creatures, trapped standing upright, green plants in their mouths. Herds held suspended above black earth. Ivory tusks and glittering eyes. Tufts of uprooted grasses. Long shapes – wolves, steep-shouldered and grey – caught in the act of leaping, running alongside an enormous horned beast. This was yet another scene of slaughter, lives stolen in an instant of catastrophic alteration – the world flung onto its side, the rush of seas, breathless cold that cut through flesh down to bone.

The world . . . the world itself betrays. Errant take us, how can this be?

Udinaas had known many for whom certainty was a god, the only god, no matter the cast of its features. And he had seen the manner in which such belief made the world simple, where all was divisible by the sharp cleaving of cold judgement, after which no mending was possible. He had seen such certainty, yet had never shared it.

But he had always believed the world itself was . . . unquestionable. Not static – never static – but capable of being understood. It was undoubtedly cruel at times, and deadly . . . *but you could almost always see it coming.* Creatures frozen in mid-leap. Frozen whilst standing, grasses hanging from their mouths. This was beyond comprehension. *Sorcery. It must have been.* Even then, the power seemed unimaginable, for it was a tenet that the world and all that lived on it possessed a natural resistance to magic. Self-evident, else mages and gods would have reshaped and probably destroyed the balance of all things long ago. Thus, the land would resist. The beasts that dwelt upon it would resist. The flow of air, the seep of water, the growing plants and the droning insects – all would resist.

Yet they failed.

Then, in the depths, a shape. Squatting on bedrock, a stone tower. A tall narrow slash suggested a doorway, and Udinaas found himself approaching it through solid ice.

Into that black portal.

Something shattered, and, suddenly corporeal, he stumbled onto his knees. The stone was cold enough to tear the skin from his knees and the palms of his hands. He staggered upright, and his shoulder struck something that tottered with the impact.

The cold made the air brutal, blinding him, shocking his lungs. Through freezing tears he saw, amidst a faint blue glow, a tall figure. Skin like bleached vellum, limbs too long and angular with too many joints. Black, frosted eyes, an expression of faint surprise on its narrow, arched features. The clothes it wore consisted of a harness of leather straps and nothing more. It was unarmed. A man, but anything but a man.

And then Udinaas saw, scattered on the floor around the figure, corpses twisted in death. Dark, greenish skin, tusked. A man, a woman, two children. Their bodies had been broken, the ends of shattered bone jutting out from flesh. The way they lay suggested that the white-skinned man had been their killer.

Udinaas was shivering uncontrollably. His hands and feet were numb. 'Wither? Shadow wraith? Are you with me?'

Silence.

His heart began hammering hard in his chest. This did not feel like a dream. It was too real. He felt no dislocation, no whispering assurance of a body lying on its sleeping pallet in an Edur longhouse.

He was here, and he was freezing to death.

Here. In the depths of ice, this world of secrets where time has ceased.

He turned and studied the doorway.

And only then noticed the footprints impressed upon

206

the frost-laden flagstones. Leading out. Bared feet, human, a child's.

There was no ice visible beyond the portal. Naught but opaque silver, as if a curtain had fallen across the entrance.

Feeling ebbing from his limbs, Udinaas backtracked the footprints. To behind the standing figure. Where he saw, after a numbed moment, that the back of the man's head had been stove in. Hair and skin still attached to the shattered plates of the skull that hung down on the neck. Something like a fist had reached into the figure's head, tearing through the grey flesh of the brain.

The break looked unaccountably recent.

Tiny tracks indicated that the child had stood behind the figure – no, had *appeared* behind it, for there were no others to be found. Had appeared . . . *to do what? Reach into a dead man's skull?* Yet the figure was as tall as an Edur. The child would have had to climb.

His thoughts were slowing. There was a pleasurable languor to his contemplation of this horrid mystery. And he was growing sleepy. Which amused him. A dream that made him sleepy. *A dream that will kill me.* Would they find a frozen corpse on the sleeping pallet? Would it be taken as an omen?

Oh well, follow the prints . . . into that silver world. What else could he do?

With a final glance back at the immobile scene of past murder and recent desecration, Udinaas staggered slowly towards the doorway.

The silver enveloped him, and sounds rushed in from all sides. Battle. Screams, the ringing hammering of weapons. But he could see nothing. Heat rolled over him from the left, carrying with it a cacophony of inhuman shrieks.

Contact with the ground beneath vanished, and the sounds dropped, swiftly dwindled to far below. Winds howled, and Udinaas realized he was flying, held aloft on leathery wings. Others of his kind sailed the tortured currents – he could see them now, emerging from the cloud.

Grey-scaled bodies the size of oxen, muscle-bunched necks, taloned hands and feet. Long, sloping heads, the jaws revealing rows of dagger-like teeth and the pale gums that held them. Eyes the colour of clay, the pupils vertical slits.

Locqui Wyval. That is our name. Spawn of Starvald Demelain, the squalid children whom none would claim as their own. We are as flies spreading across a rotting feast, one realm after another. D'isthal Wyvalla, Enkar'al, Trol, we are a plague of demons in a thousand pantheons.

Savage exultation. There were things other than love upon which to thrive.

A tide of air pushed – drove him and his kind to one side. Bestial screams from his kin as something loomed into view.

Eleint! Soletaken but oh so much draconic blood. Tiam's own.

Bone-white scales, the red of wounds smeared like misty paint, monstrously huge, the dragon the Wyval had chosen to follow loomed alongside them.

And Udinaas knew its name.

Silchas Ruin. Tiste Andii, who fed in the wake of his brother – fed on Tiam's blood, and drank deep. Deeper than Anomander Rake by far. Darkness and chaos. He would have accepted the burden of godhood . . . had he been given the chance.

Udinaas knew now what he was about to witness. The sembling on the hilltop far below. The betrayal. Shadow's murder of honour in the breaking of vows. A knife in the back and the screams of the Wyval here in the roiling skies above the battlefield. The shadow wraith had not lied. The legacy of the deed remained in the Edur's brutal enslavement of Tiste Andii spirits. Faith was proved a lie, and in ignorance was found weakness. The righteousness of the Edur stood on shifting sands.

Silchas Ruin. The weapons of those days possessed terrifying power, but his had been shattered. By a K'Chain Che'Malle matron's death-cry.

The silver light flickered. A physical wrenching, and he found himself lying on his sleeping pallet in the Sengar longhouse.

The skin had been torn from his palms, his knees. His clothes were sodden with melted frost.

A voice murmured from the shadows, '*I sought to follow, but could not. You travelled far.*'

Wither. Udinaas rolled onto his side. 'Your place of slaughter,' he whispered. 'I was there. What do you want of me?'

'*What does anyone want, slave? Escape. From the past, from their past. I will lead you onto the path. The blood of the Wyval shall protect you—*'

'Against the Edur?'

'*Leave the threat of the Edur to me. Now, ready yourself. You have tasks before you this night.*'

A sleep that had left him exhausted and battered. Grimacing, he climbed to his feet.

With two of her chosen slaves, Mayen walked across the threshold then paused two strides into the main chamber. She was willow thin, the shade of her skin darker than most. Green eyes framed by long, umber hair in which glittered beads of onyx. A traditional tunic of silver sealskin and a wide belt of pearlescent shells. Bracelets and anklets of whale ivory.

Trull Sengar could see in her eyes a supreme awareness of her own beauty, and there was darkness within that heavy-lidded regard, as if she was not averse to wielding that beauty, to achieving dominance, and with it a potentially unpleasant freedom in which to indulge her desires.

There were all kinds of pleasure, and hungers which spoke naught of virtues, only depravity. Once again, however, Trull was struck by self-doubt as he watched his mother stride to stand before Mayen to voice the household's welcome. Perhaps he once more saw through shadows of his own casting.

Leaning until his back was to the wall, he glanced over at Fear. Uncertain pride. There was also unease in his brother's expression, but it could have been born of anything – the journey they would undertake on the morrow, the very future of his people. Just beyond him, Rhulad, whose eyes devoured Mayen as if her mere presence answered his cruellest appetites.

Mayen herself held Uruth in her gaze.

She absorbs. These tumbling waves of attention, drawn in and fed upon. Dusk shield me, am I mad, to find such thoughts spilling from the dark places in my own soul?

The formal greeting was complete. Uruth stepped to one side and Mayen glided forward, towards the Blackwood table on which the first course had already been arrayed. She would take her place at the nearest end, with Tomad opposite her at the table's head. On her left, Fear, on her right, Uruth. Binadas beside Uruth and Trull beside Fear. Rhulad was to Binadas's right.

'Mayen,' Tomad said once she had seated herself, 'welcome to the hearth of the Sengar. It grieves me that this night also marks, for the next while, the last in which all my sons are present. They undertake a journey for the Warlock King, and I pray for their safe return.'

'I am led to believe the ice-fields pose no great risks for warriors of the Edur,' Mayen replied. 'Yet I see gravity and concern in your eyes, Tomad Sengar.'

'An aged father's fretting,' Tomad said with a faint smile. 'Nothing more.'

Rhulad spoke, 'The Arapay rarely venture onto the ice-fields, for fear of hauntings. More, ice can blind, and the cold can steal life like the bleeding of an unseen wound. It is said there are beasts as well—'

Fear cut in, 'My brother seeks resounding glory in the unknown, Mayen, so that you may look upon us all with awe and wonder.'

'I am afraid he has left me with naught but dread,' she said. 'And now I must worry for your fates.'

'We are equal to all that might assail us,' Rhulad said quickly.

Barring the babbling tongue of an unblooded fool.

Wine goblets were refilled, and a few moments passed, then Uruth spoke. 'When one does not know what one seeks, caution is the surest armour.' She faced Binadas. 'Among us, you alone have ventured beyond the eastern borders of Arapay land. What dangers do the ice-fields pose?'

Binadas frowned. 'Old sorcery, Mother. But it seems inclined to slumber.' He paused, thinking. 'A tribe of hunters who live on the ice – I have seen naught but tracks. The Arapay say they hunt at night.'

'Hunt what?' Trull asked.

His brother shrugged.

'There will be six of us,' Rhulad said. 'Theradas and Midik Buhn, and all can speak to Theradas's skills. Although unblooded,' he added, 'Midik is nearly my equal with the sword. Hannan Mosag chose well in choosing the warrior sons of Tomad Sengar.'

This last statement hung strange in the air, as if rife with possible meanings, each one tumbling in a different direction. Such was the poison of suspicion. The women had their beliefs, Trull well knew, and now probably looked upon the six warriors in question, wondering at Hannan Mosag's motivations, his reasons for choosing these particular men. And Fear, as well, would hold to his own thoughts, knowing what he knew – *as we Sengar all know, now.*

Trull sensed the uncertainty and began wondering for himself. Fear, after all, was Weapons Master for all the tribes, and indeed had been tasked with reshaping the Edur military structure. From Weapons Master to War Master, then. It seemed capricious to so risk Fear Sengar. And Binadas was considered by most to be among the united tribes' more formidable sorcerors. Together, Fear and Binadas had been crucial during the campaigns of

211

conquest, whilst Theradas Buhn was unequalled in leading raids from the sea. *The only expendable members of this expedition are myself, Rhulad and Midik.* Was the issue, therefore, one of trust?

What precisely *was* this gift they were to recover?

'There have been untoward events of late,' Mayen said, with a glance at Uruth.

Trull caught his father's scowl, but Mayen must have seen acquiescence in Uruth's expression, for she continued, 'Spirits walked the darkness the night of the vigil. Unwelcome of aspect, intruders upon our holy sites – the wraiths fled at their approach.'

'This is the first I have heard of such things,' Tomad said.

Uruth reached for her wine cup and held it out to be refilled by a slave. 'They are known none the less, husband. Hannan Mosag and his K'risnan have stirred deep shadows. The tide of change rises – and soon, I fear, it will sweep us away.'

'But it is we who are rising on that tide,' Tomad said, his face darkening. 'It is one thing to question defeat, but now you question victory, wife.'

'I speak only of the Great Meeting to come. Did not our own sons tell of the summoning from the depths that stole the souls of the Letherii seal-hunters? When those ships sail into the harbour at Trate, how think you the Letherii will react? We have begun the dance of war.'

'If that were so,' Tomad retorted, 'then there would be little point to treat with them.'

'Except,' Trull cut in, recalling his father's own words when he first returned from the Calach beds, 'to take their measure.'

'It was taken long ago,' Fear said. 'The Letherii will seek to do to us as they have done to the Nerek and the Tarthenal. Most among them see no error or moral flaw in their past deeds. Those who do are unable or unwilling to question the methods, only the execution, and so they are doomed to repeat the horrors, and see the result – no matter its nature – as yet one more test of firmly held principles. And even should the blood run in a river around them, they will obsess on the details. One cannot challenge the fundamental beliefs of such people, for they will not hear you.'

'Then there will be war,' Trull whispered.

'There is always war, brother,' Fear replied. 'Faiths, words and swords: history resounds with their interminable clash.'

'That, and the breaking of bones,' Rhulad said, with the smile of a man with a secret.

Foolish conceit, for Tomad could not miss it and he leaned forward. 'Rhulad Sengar, you speak like a blind elder with a sack full of wraiths. I am tempted to drag you across this table and choke the gloat from your face.'

Trull felt sweat prickle beneath his clothes. He saw the blood leave his brother's face. *Oh, Father, you deliver a wound deeper than you could ever have imagined.* He glanced over at Mayen and was startled to see something avid in her eyes, a malice, a barely constrained delight.

'I am not so young, Father,' Rhulad said in a rasp, 'nor you so old, to let such words pass—'

Tomad's fist thumped the tabletop, sending cups and plates clattering. 'Then speak like a man, Rhulad! Tell us all this dread knowledge that coils your every strut and has for the past week! Or do you seek to part tender thighs with your womanish ways? Do you imagine you are the first young warrior who seeks to walk in step with women? Sympathy, son, is a poor path to lust—'

Rhulad was on his feet, his face twisting with rage. 'And which bitch would you have me bed, Father? To whom am I promised? And in whose name? You have leashed me here in this village and then you mock when I strain.' He glared at the others, fixing at last on Trull. 'When the war begins, Hannan Mosag will announce a sacrifice. He must. A throat will be opened to spill down the bow of the lead ship. He will choose me, won't he?'

'Rhulad,' Trull said, 'I have heard no such thing—'

'He will! I am to bed three daughters! Sheltatha Lore, Sukul Ankhadu and Menandore!'

A plate skittered out from the hands of a slave and cracked onto the tabletop, spilling the shellfish it held. As the slave reached forward to contain the accident, Uruth's hands snapped out and grasped the Letherii by the wrists. A savage twist to reveal the palms.

The skin had been torn from them, raw, red, glittering wet and cracked.

'What is this, Udinaas?' Uruth demanded. She rose and yanked him close.

'I fell—' the Letherii gasped.

'To weep your wounds onto our food? Have you lost your mind?'

'Mistress!' another slave ventured, edging forward. 'I saw him come in earlier – he bore no such wounds then, I swear it!'

'He is the one who fought the Wyval!' another cried, backing away in sudden terror.

'Udinaas is possessed!' the other slave shrieked.

'Quiet!' Uruth set a hand against Udinaas's forehead and pushed back hard. He grunted in pain.

Sorcery swirled out to surround the slave. He spasmed, then went limp, collapsing at Uruth's feet.

'There is nothing within him,' she said, withdrawing a trembling hand.

Mayen spoke. 'Feather Witch, attend to Uruth's slave.'

The young Letherii woman darted forward. Another slave appeared to help her drag the unconscious man away.

'I saw no insult in the slave's actions,' Mayen continued. 'The wounds were indeed raw, but he held cloth against them.' She reached out and lifted the plate to reveal the bleached linen that Udinaas had used to cover his hands.

Uruth grunted and slowly sat. 'None the less, he should have informed me. And for that oversight he must be punished.'

214

'You just raped his mind,' Mayen replied. 'Is that not sufficient?'

Silence.

Daughters take us, the coming year should prove interesting. One year, as demanded by tradition, and then Fear and Mayen would take up residence in a house of their own.

Uruth simply glared at the younger woman, then, to Trull's surprise, she nodded. 'Very well, Mayen. You are guest this night, and so I will abide by your wishes.'

Through all of this Rhulad had remained standing, but now he slowly sat once more.

Tomad said, 'Rhulad, I know of no plans to resurrect the ancient blood sacrifice to announce a war. Hannan Mosag is not careless with the lives of his warriors, even those as yet unblooded. I cannot fathom how you came to believe such a fate awaited you. Perhaps,' he added, 'this journey you are about to undertake will provide you with the opportunity to become a blooded warrior, and so stand with pride alongside your brothers. So I shall pray.'

It was a clear overture, this wish for glory, and Rhulad displayed uncharacteristic wisdom in accepting it with a simple nod.

Neither Feather Witch nor Udinaas returned, but the remaining slaves proved sufficient in serving the rest of the meal.

And for all this, Trull still could not claim any understanding of Mayen, Fear's betrothed.

A stinging slap and he opened his eyes.

To see Feather Witch's face hovering above his own, a face filled with rage. 'You damned fool!' she hissed.

Blinking, Udinaas looked around. They were huddled in his sleeping niche. Beyond the cloth hanging, the low sounds of eating and soft conversation.

Udinaas smiled.

Feather Witch scowled. 'She—'

'I know,' he cut in. 'And she found nothing.'

215

He watched her beautiful eyes widen. 'It is true, then?'

'It must be.'

'You are lying, Udinaas. The Wyval hid. Somehow, somewhere, it hid itself from Uruth.'

'Why are you so certain of that, Feather Witch?'

She sat back suddenly. 'It doesn't matter—'

'You have had dreams, haven't you?'

She started, then looked away. 'You are a Debtor's son. You are nothing to me.'

'And you are everything to me, Feather Witch.'

'Don't be an idiot, Udinaas! I might as well wed a hold rat! Now, be quiet, I need to think.'

He slowly sat up, drawing their faces close once again. 'There is no need,' he said. 'I trust you, and so I will explain. She looked deep indeed, but the Wyval was gone. It would have been different, had Uruth sought out my shadow.'

She blinked in sudden comprehension, then: 'That cannot be,' she said, shaking her head. 'You are Letherii. The wraiths serve only the Edur—'

'The wraiths bend a knee because they must. They are as much slaves to the Edur as we are, Feather Witch. I have found an ally . . .'

'To what end, Udinaas?'

He smiled again, and this time it was a much darker smile. 'Something I well understand. The repaying of debts, Feather Witch. In full.'

BOOK TWO

PROWS OF THE DAY

We are seized in the age
of our youth
dragged over this road's stones
spent and burdened
by your desires.
And unshod hoofs clatter beneath bones
to remind us of every
fateful charge
upon the hills you have sown
with frozen seeds
in this dead earth.
Swallowing ground
and grinding bit
we climb into the sky so alone
in our fretted ways
a heaving of limbs
and the iron stars burst from your heels
baffling urgency
warning us of your savage bite.

Destriers (Sons to Fathers)
Fisher kel Tath

CHAPTER SIX

The Errant bends fate,
As unseen armour
Lifting to blunt the blade
On a field sudden
With battle, and the crowd
Jostles blind their eyes gouged out
By the strait of these affairs
Where dark fools dance on tiles
And chance rides a spear
With red bronze
To spit worlds like skulls
One upon the other
Until the seas pour down
To thicken metal-clad hands
So this then is the Errant
Who guides every fate
Unerring
Upon the breast of men.

The Casting of Tiles
Ceda Ankaran Qan (1059 Burn's Sleep)

The Tarancede tower rose from the south side of Trate's harbour. Hewn from raw basalt it was devoid of elegance or beauty, reaching like a gnarled arm seven storeys from an artificial island of jagged rocks. Waves hammered it from all sides, flinging spume into the air. There were no windows, no doors, yet a series of glossy obsidian plates ringed the uppermost level, each one as tall as a man and almost as wide.

Nine similar towers rose above the borderlands, but the Tarancede was the only one to stand above the harsh seas of the north.

The sun's light was a lurid glare against the obsidian plates, high above a harbour already swallowed by the day's end. A dozen fisherboats rode the choppy waters beyond the bay, plying the shelf of shallows to the south. They were well out of the sea-lanes and probably heedless of the three ships that appeared to the north, their full-bellied sails as they drove on down towards the harbour, the air around them crowded with squalling gulls.

They drew closer, and a ship's pilot scow set out from the main pier to meet them.

The three harvest ships were reflected in the tower's obsidian plates, sliding in strange ripples from one to the next, the gulls smudged white streaks around them.

The scow's oars suddenly backed wildly, twisting the craft away.

Shapes swarmed across the rigging of the lead ship. The steady wind that had borne the sails fell, sudden as a drawn breath, and canvas billowed down. The figures flitting above the deck, only vaguely human-shaped, seemed to drift away, like black banners, across the deepening gloom. The gulls spun from their paths with shrill cries.

From the scow an alarm bell began clanging. Not steady. Discordant, a cacophony of panic.

No sailor who had lived or would ever live discounted the sea's hungry depths. Ancient spirits rode the currents of darkness far from the sun's light, stirring silts that swallowed history beneath endless layers of indifferent silence. Their powers were immense, their appetites insatiable. All that came down from the lit world above settled into their embrace.

The surface of the seas, every sailor knew, was ephemeral. Quaint sketchings across an ever-changing slate, and lives were but sparks, so easily quenched by the demon forces that could rise from far below to shake their beast hides and so up-end the world.

Propitiation was aversion, a prayer to pass unnoticed, to escape untaken. Blood before the bow, dolphins dancing to starboard and a gob of spit to ride blessed winds. The left hand scrubs, the right hand dries. Wind widdershins on the cleats, sun-bleached rags tied to the sea-anchor's chain. A score of gestures, unquestioned and bound in tradition, all to slide the seas in peace.

None sought to call up the ravelled spirits from those water-crushed valleys that saw no light. They were not things to be bound, after all. Nor bargained with. Their hearts beat in the cycles of the moon, their voice was the heaving storm and their wings could spread from horizon to horizon, in towering white-veined sheets of water that swept all before them.

Beneath the waves of Trate Harbour, with three dead ships like fins on its back, the bound spirit clambered in a surge of cold currents towards shore. The last spears of sunlight slanted through its swirling flesh, and the easing of massive pressures made the creature grow in size, pushing onto the rocky coastlines ahead and to the sides the bay's own warmer waters, so that the fish and crustaceans of the shallows tumbled up from the waves in mangled shreds of flesh and shattered shell, granting the gulls and land crabs a sudden feast of slaughter.

The spirit lifted the ships, careering wild now, on a single wave that rose high as it swelled shoreward. The docks, which had a few moments earlier been crowded with silent onlookers, became a swarm of fleeing figures, the streets leading inland filling with stampedes that slowed to choking, crushing masses of humanity.

The wave tumbled closer, then suddenly fell away. Hulls thundered at the swift plunge, spars snapped and, on the third ship, the main mast exploded in a cloud of splintered wood. Rocking, trailing wreckage, the harvesters coasted between the piers.

Pressures drawing inward, building once more, the spirit withdrew from the bay. In its wake, devastation.

Glimmering in its obsidian world, the first ship crunched and slid against a pier, and came to a gentle rest. The white flecks of the gulls plunged down to the deck, to begin at long last their feeding. The Tarancede Tower had witnessed all, the smooth tiles near its pinnacle absorbing every flickering detail of the event, despite the failing light.

And, in a chamber beneath the old palace in the city of Letheras, far to the southeast, Ceda Kuru Qan watched. Before him lay a tile that matched those of the distant tower above Trate's harbour, and, as he stared at the enormous black shadow that had filled the bay and most of the inlet, and was now beginning its slow withdrawal, the sorceror blinked sweat from his eyes and forced his gaze back to those three harvest ships now lolling against the piers.

The gulls and the gathering darkness made it difficult to see much, barring the twisted corpses huddled on the deck, and the last few flickering wraiths.

But Kuru Qan had seen enough.

Five wings to the Eternal Domicile, of which only three were complete. Each of the latter consisted of wide hallways with arched ceilings sheathed in gold-leaf. Between elaborate flying buttresses to either side and running the entire length were doorways leading to chambers that would serve as offices and domiciles of the Royal Household's administrative and maintenance staff. Towards the centre the adjoining rooms would house guards, armouries and trapdoors leading to private passages – beneath ground level – that encircled the entire palace that was the heart of the Eternal Domicile.

At the moment, however, those passages were

chest-deep in muddy water, through which rats moved with no particular purpose barring that of, possibly, pleasure. Brys Beddict stood on a landing three steps from the silt-laden flood and watched the up-thrust heads swimming back and forth in the gloom. Beside him stood a palace engineer covered in drying mud.

'The pumps are next to useless,' the man was saying. 'We went with big hoses, we went with small ones, made no difference. Once the pull got strong enough in went a rat, or ten, plugging things up. Besides, the seep's as steady as ever. Though the Plumbs still swear we're above the table here.'

'I'm sure the Ceda will consent to attaching a mage to your crew.'

'I'd appreciate it, Finadd. All we need is to hold the flow back for a time, so's we can bucket the water out and the catchers can go down and collect the rats. We lost Ormly last night, the palace's best catcher. Likely drowned – the fool couldn't swim. If the Errant's looking away, we might be spared finding much more than bones. Rats know when it's a catcher they've found, you know.'

'These tunnels are essential to maintaining the security of the king—'

'Well, ain't nobody likely to try using them if they're flooded—'

'Not as a means of ingress for assassins,' Brys cut in. 'They are to permit the swift passage of guards to any area above that is breached.'

'Yes, yes. I was only making a joke, Finadd. Of course, you could choose fast swimmers among your guards . . . all right, never mind. Get us a mage to sniff round and tell us what's going on and then to stop the water coming in and we'll take care of the rest.'

'Presumably,' Brys said, 'this is not indicative of subsidence—'

'Like the other wings? No, nothing's slumped – we'd be able to tell. Anyway, there's rumours that those ones are going to get a fresh look at. A new construction company has been working down there, nearby. Some fool bought up the surrounding land. There's whispers they've figured out how to shore up buildings.'

'Really? I've heard nothing about it.'

'The guilds aren't happy about it, that's for sure, since these upstarts are hiring the Unwelcomes – those malcontents who made the List. Paying 'em less than the usual rate, though, which is the only thing going for them, I suppose. The guilds can't close them down so long as they do that.' The engineer shrugged, began prying pieces of hardened clay from his forearms, wincing at the pulled hairs. 'Of course, if the royal architects decide that Bugg's shoring works, then that company's roll is going sky-high.'

Brys slowly turned from his study of the rats and eyed the engineer. 'Bugg?'

'Damn, I need a bath. Look at my nails. Yeah, Bugg's Construction. There must be a Bugg, then, right? Else why name it Bugg's Construction?'

A shout from a crewman down on the lowest step, then a scream. Wild scrambling up to the landing, where the worker spun round and pointed.

A mass of rats, almost as wide as the passageway itself, had edged into view. Moving like a raft, it crept into the pool of lantern light towards the stairs. In its centre – the revelation eliciting yet another scream from the worker and a curse from the engineer – floated a human head. Yellow-tinted silver hair, a pallid, deeply lined face with a forehead high and broad above staring, narrow-set eyes.

Other rats raced away as the raft slipped to nudge against the lowest step.

The worker gasped, 'Errant take us, it's Ormly!'

The eyes flickered, then the head was rising, lifting the nearest rats in the raft with it, humped over shoulders, streaming glimmering water. 'Who in the Hold else would it be?' the apparition snapped, pausing to hawk up a mouthful of phlegm and spitting it into the swirling water. 'Like my trophies?' he asked, raising his arms beneath the vast cape of rats. 'Strings and tails. Damned heavy when wet, though.'

'We thought you were dead,' the engineer muttered, in a tone suggesting that he would rather it were true.

'You *thought*. You're always *thinking*, ain't ya, Grum? Maybe this, probably that, could be, might be, should be – hah! Think these rats scared me? Think I was just going to drown? Hold's welcoming pit, I'm a catcher and not any old catcher. They know me, all right. Every rat in this damned city knows Ormly the Catcher! Who's this?'

'Finadd Brys Beddict.' The King's Champion introduced himself. 'That is an impressive collection of trophies you've amassed there, Catcher.'

The man's eyes brightened. 'Isn't it just! Better when it's floating, though. Right now, damned heavy. Damned heavy.'

'Best climb out from under it,' Brys suggested. 'Engineer Grum, I think a fine meal, plenty of wine and a night off is due Ormly the Catcher.'

'Yes, sir.'

'I will speak with the Ceda regarding your request.'

'Thanks.'

Brys left them on the landing. It seemed increasingly unlikely that the Eternal Domicile would be ready for the birth of the Eighth Age. Among the populace, there seemed to be less than faint enthusiasm for the coming celebration. The histories might well recount prophecies about the glorious empire destined to rise once more in less than a year from now, but in truth, there was little in this particular time that supported the notion of a renaissance, neither economically nor militarily. If anything, there was a slight uneasiness, centred on the impending treaty gathering with the tribes of the Tiste Edur. Risk and opportunity; the two were synonymous for the Letherii. Even so, war was never pleasant, although thus far always satisfactory in its conclusion. Thus risk led to opportunity, with few thoughts spared for the defeated.

Granted, the Edur tribes were now united. At the same

time, other such alliances had formed in opposition to Letherii ambitions in the past, and not one had proved immune to divisive strategies. Gold bought betrayal again and again. Alliances crumbled and the enemy collapsed. What likelihood that it would be any different this time round?

Brys wondered at the implicit complacency of his own people. He was not, he was certain, misreading public sentiment. Nerves were on edge, but only slightly. Markets remained strong. And the day-in, day-out mindless yearnings of a people for whom possession was everything continued unabated.

Within the palace, however, emotions were more fraught. The Ceda's divinations promised a fundamental alteration awaiting Lether. Kuru Qan spoke, in a meandering, bemused way, of some sort of Ascension. A transformation . . . *from king to emperor*, although how such a progression would manifest itself remained to be seen. The annexation of the Tiste Edur and their rich homelands would indeed initiate a renewed vigour, a frenzy of profit. Victory would carry its own affirmation of the righteousness of Lether and its ways.

Brys emerged from the Second Wing and made his way down towards Narrow Canal. It was late morning, almost noon. Earlier that day, he had exercised and sparred with the other off-duty palace guards in the compound backing the barracks, then had breakfasted at a courtyard restaurant alongside Quillas Canal, thankful for this brief time of solitude, although his separation from the palace – permitted only because the king was visiting the chambers of the First Concubine and would not emerge until mid-afternoon – was an invisible tether that gradually tightened, until he felt compelled to resume his duties by visiting the Eternal Domicile and checking on progress there. And then back to the old palace.

To find it, upon passing through the main gate and striding into the Grand Hall, in an uproar.

Heart thudding hard in his chest, Brys approached the nearest guard. 'Corporal, what has happened?'

The soldier saluted. 'Not sure, Finadd. News from Trate, I gather. The Edur have slaughtered some Letherii sailors. With foulest sorcery.'

'The king?'

'Has called a council in two bells' time.'

'Thank you, Corporal.'

Brys continued on into the palace.

He made his way into the inner chambers. Among the retainers and messengers rushing along the central corridor he saw Chancellor Triban Gnol standing with a handful of followers, a certain animation to his whispered conversation. The man's dark eyes flicked to Brys as the Champion strode past, but his lips did not cease moving. Behind the Chancellor, Brys saw, was the Queen's Consort, Turudal Brizad, leaning insouciantly against the wall, his soft, almost feminine features displaying a faint smirk.

Brys had always found the man strangely disturbing, and it had nothing to do with his singular function as consort to Janall. He was a silent presence, often at meetings dealing with the most sensitive issues of state, ever watchful despite his studied indifference. And it was well known that he shared his bed with more than just the queen, although whether Janall herself knew of that was the subject of conjecture in the court. Among his lovers, it was rumoured, was Chancellor Triban Gnol.

An untidy nest, all in all.

The door to the First Eunuch's office was closed and guarded by two of Nifadas's own Rulith, eunuch bodyguards, tall men with nothing of the common body-fat one might expect to see. Heavy kohl lined their eyes and red paint broadened their mouths into a perpetual downturned grimace. Their only weapons were a brace of hooked daggers sheathed under their crossed arms, and if they wore any armour it was well disguised beneath long, crimson silk shirts and tan pantaloons. They were barefoot.

Both nodded and stepped aside to permit Brys to pass.

He tugged the braided tassel and could faintly hear the dull chime sound in the chamber beyond.

The door clicked open.

Nifadas was alone, standing behind his desk, the surface of which was crowded with scrolls and unfurled maps. His back was to the room, and he seemed to be staring at a wall. 'King's Champion. I have been expecting you.'

'This seemed the first in order, First Eunuch.'

'Just so.' He was silent for a few heartbeats, then: 'There are beliefs that constitute the official religion of a nation, but those beliefs and that religion are in truth little more than the thinnest gold hammered on far older bones. No nation is singular, or exclusive – rather, it should not be, for its own good. There is much danger in asserting for oneself a claim to purity, whether of blood or of origin. Few may acknowledge it, but Lether is far richer for its devouring minorities, provided that digestion remains eternally incomplete.'

'Be that as it may, Finadd, I confess to you a certain ignorance. The palace isolates those trapped within it, and its roots nurture poorly. I would know of the people's private beliefs.'

Brys thought for a moment, then asked, 'Can you be more specific, First Eunuch?'

Nifadas still did not turn to face him. 'The seas. The denizens of the deep. Demons and old gods, Brys.'

'The Tiste Edur call the dark waters the realm of Galain, which is said to belong to kin, for whom Darkness is home. The Tarthenal, I have heard, view the seas as a single beast with countless limbs – including those that reach inland as rivers and streams. The Nerek fear it as their netherworld, a place where drowning is eternal, a fate awaiting betrayers and murderers.'

'And the Letherii?'

Brys shrugged. 'Kuru Qan knows more of this than I, First Eunuch. Sailors fear but do not worship. They make

228

sacrifices in the hopes of avoiding notice. On the seas, the arrogant suffer, whilst only the meek survive, although it's said if abasement is carried too far, the hunger below grows irritated and spiteful. Tides and currents reveal the patterns one must follow, which in part explains the host of superstitions and rituals demanded of those who would travel by sea.'

'And this . . . hunger below. It has no place among the Holds?'

'Not that I know of, First Eunuch.'

Nifadas finally turned, regarded Brys with half-closed eyes. 'Does that not strike you as odd, Finadd Beddict? Lether was born of colonists who came here from the First Empire. That First Empire was then destroyed, the paradise razed to lifeless desert. Yet it was the First Empire in which the Holds were first discovered. True, the Empty Hold proved a later manifestation, at least in so far as it related to ourselves. Thus, are we to imagine that yet older beliefs survived and were carried to this new land all those millennia ago? Or, conversely, does each land – and its adjoining seas – evoke an indigenous set of beliefs? If that is the case, then the argument supporting the presence of physical, undeniable gods is greatly supported.'

'But even then,' Brys said, 'there is no evidence that such gods are remotely concerned with mortal affairs. I do not think sailors envisage the hunger I spoke of as a god. More as a demon, I think.'

'To answer the unanswerable, a need from which we all suffer.' Nifadas sighed. 'Finadd, the independent seal harvesters were all slain. Three of their ships survived the return journey to Trate, crewed up to the very piers by Edur wraiths, yet carried on seas that were more than seas. A demon, such as the sailors swear upon . . . yet, it was something far more, or so our Ceda believes. Are you familiar with Faraed beliefs? Theirs is an oral tradition, and if the listing of generations is accurate and not mere poetic pretence, then the tradition is ancient indeed. The Faraed

229

creation myths centre on Elder gods. Each named and aspected, a divisive pantheon of entirely unwholesome personalities. In any case, among them is the Elder Lord of the Seas, the Dweller Below. It is named Mael. Furthermore, the Faraed have singled out Mael in their oldest stories. It once walked this land, Finadd, as a physical manifestation, following the death of an Age.'

'An Age? What kind of Age?'

'Of the time before the Faraed, I think. There are . . . contradictions and obscurities.'

'Ceda Kuru Qan believes the demon that carried the ships was this Mael?'

'If it was, then Mael has suffered much degradation. Almost mindless, a turgid maelstrom of untethered emotions. But powerful none the less.'

'Yet the Tiste Edur have chained it?'

Nifadas's thin brows rose. 'Clear a path through a forest and every beast will use it. Is this control? Of a sort, perhaps.'

'Hannan Mosag sought to make a statement.'

'Indeed, Finadd, and so he has. Yet is it a true statement or deceptive bravado?'

Brys shook his head. He had no answer to offer.

Nifadas swung away once more. 'The king has deemed this of sufficient import. The Ceda even now prepares the . . . means. None the less, you deserve the right to be asked rather than commanded.'

'What is it I am asked to do, First Eunuch?'

A faint shrug. 'Awaken an Elder god.'

'There is great flux in the composite. Is this relevant? I think not.' Ceda Kuru Qan pushed his wire-bound lenses further up the bridge of his nose and peered at Brys. 'This is a journey of the mind, King's Champion, yet the risk to you is such that you might as well travel into the netherworld in truth. If your mind is slain, there is no return. Extreme necessity, alas; the king wills that you proceed.'

'I did not imagine that there would be no danger, Ceda. Tell me, will my martial skills be applicable?'

'Unknown. But you are young, quick-witted and resilient.' He turned away and scanned the cluttered work-top behind him. 'Great flux, alas. Leaving but one choice.' He reached out and picked up a goblet. A pause, a dubious squint at its contents, then he took a cautious sip. 'Ah! As suspected. The flux in the composite is due entirely to curdled milk. Brys Beddict, are you ready?'

The King's Champion shrugged.

Kuru Qan nodded. 'I was going to have you drink this.'

'Curdled milk will not harm me,' Brys said, taking the goblet from the Ceda. He quickly tossed it down, then set the silver cup on the table. 'How long?'

'For what?'

'Until the potion takes effect.'

'What potion? Come with me. We shall use the Cedance for this journey.'

Brys followed the old sorceror from the chamber. At the door he cast a glance back at the goblet. The mixture had tasted of citrus and sour goat's milk; he could already feel it bubbling ominously in his stomach. 'I must now assume there was no purpose to what I just drank.'

'A repast. One of my experiments. I was hoping you'd enjoy it, but judging by your pallor it would seem that that was not the case.'

'I'm afraid you are correct.'

'Ah well, if it proves inimical you will no doubt bring it back up.'

'That's comforting knowledge, Ceda.'

The remainder of the journey to the palace depths was mercifully uneventful. Ceda Kuru Qan led Brys into the vast chamber where waited the tiles of the Holds. 'We shall employ a tile of the Fulcra in this effort, King's Champion. Dolmen.'

They walked out across the narrow causeway to the

central disc. The massive tiles stretched out on all sides beneath them.

The roiling in Brys's stomach had subsided somewhat. He waited for the Ceda to speak.

'Some things are important. Others are not. Yet all would claim a mortal's attention. It falls to each of us to remain ever mindful, and thus purchase wisdom in the threading of possibilities. It is our common failing, Brys Beddict, that we are guided by our indifference to eventualities. The moment pleases, the future can await consideration.

'The old histories we brought with us from the First Empire recount similar failings. Rich ports at river mouths that were abandoned after three centuries, due to silting caused by the clearing of forests and poorly conceived irrigation methods. Ports that, were you to visit their ruins now, you would find a league or more inland of the present coast. The land crawls to the sea; it was ever thus. Even so, what we humans do can greatly accelerate the process.

'Is all that relevant? Only partly, I admit. As I must perforce admit to many things, I admit to that. There are natural progressions that, when unveiled, are profoundly exemplary of the sheer vastness of antiquity. Beyond even the age of the existence of people, this world is very, very old, Brys Beddict.' Kuru Qan gestured.

Brys looked down to where he had indicated, and saw the tile of the Dolmen. The carved and painted image depicted a single, tilted monolith half-buried in lifeless clay. The sky behind it was colourless and devoid of features.

'Even seas are born only to one day die,' Kuru Qan said. 'Yet the land clings to its memory, and all that it has endured is clawed onto its visage. Conversely, at the very depths of the deepest ocean, you will find the traces of when it stood above the waves. It is this knowledge that we shall use, Brys.'

'Nifadas was rather vague as to my task, Ceda. I am to awaken Mael, presumably to apprise the Elder god that it is being manipulated. But I am not a worshipper, nor is there a single Letherii who would claim otherwise for him or herself – why would Mael listen to me?'

'I have no idea, Brys. You shall have to improvise.'

'And if this god is truly and absolutely fallen, until it is little more than a mindless beast, then what?'

Kuru Qan blinked behind the lenses, and said nothing.

Brys shifted uneasily. 'If my mind is all that shall make the journey, how will I appear to myself? Can I carry weapons?'

'How you manifest your defences is entirely up to you, Finadd. Clearly, I anticipate you will find yourself as you are now. Armed and armoured. All conceit, of course, but that is not relevant. Shall we begin?'

'Very well.'

Kuru Qan stepped forward, one arm snapping out to grasp Brys by his weapons harness. A savage, surprisingly powerful tug pitched him forward, headlong over the edge of the disc. Shouting in alarm, he flailed about, then plummeted down towards the tile of the Dolmen.

'Even in the noblest of ventures, there's the occasional stumble.'

Bugg's eyes were flat, his lined face expressionless, as he stared steadily at Tehol without speaking.

'Besides, it's only a small failing, all things considered. As for myself, why, I am happy enough. Truly. Yours is the perfectly understandable disappointment and, dare I say it, a modest battering of confidence, that comes with an effort poorly conceived. No fault in the deed itself, I assure you.' As proof he did a slow turn in front of his manservant. 'See? The legs are indeed of matching length. I shall remain warm, no matter how cool the nights become. Granted, we don't have cool nights. Sultry is best we can manage, I'll grant you, but what's a little sweat between . . . uh . . . the legs?'

'That shade of grey and that tone of yellow are the worst

233

combination I have ever attempted, master,' Bugg said. 'I grow nauseous just looking at you.'

'But what has that to do with the trousers?'

'Very little, admittedly. My concern is with principles, of course.'

'Can't argue with that. Now, tell me of the day's doings, and hurry up, I've a midnight date with a dead woman.'

'The extent of your desperation, master, never fails to astonish me.'

'Did our favourite money-lender commit suicide as woefully anticipated?'

'With nary a hitch.'

'Barring the one by which he purportedly hung himself?'

'As you say, but that was before fire tragically swept through his premises.'

'And any word on Finadd Gerun Eberict's reaction to all this?'

'Decidedly despondent, master.'

'But not unduly suspicious?'

'Who can say? His agents have made inquiries, but more directly towards a search for a hidden cache of winnings, an attempt to recoup the loss and such. No such fortune, however, has surfaced.'

'And it had better not. Eberict needs to swallow the loss entire, not that it was in truth a loss, only a denial of increased fortune. His primary investments remain intact, after all. Now, stop blathering, Bugg. I need to do some thinking.' Tehol hitched up his trousers, wincing at Bugg's sudden frown. 'Must be losing weight,' he muttered, then began pacing.

Four steps brought him to the roof's edge. He wheeled and faced Bugg. 'What's that you're wearing?'

'It's the latest fashion among masons and such.'

'The Dusty Few.'

'Exactly.'

'A wide leather belt with plenty of loops and pouches.'

Bugg nodded.

'Presumably,' Tehol continued, 'there are supposed to be tools and assorted instruments in those loops and pouches. Things a mason might use.'

'Well, I run the company. I don't use those things.'

'But you need the belt.'

'If I'm to be taken seriously, master, yes.'

'Oh yes, that is important, isn't it? Duly noted in expenses, I presume?'

'Of course. That and the wooden hat.'

'You mean one of those red bowl-shaped things?'

'That's right.'

'So why aren't you wearing it?'

'I'm not working right now. Not as sole proprietor of Bugg's Construction, anyway.'

'Yet you've got the belt.'

'It's comforting, master. I suppose this must be what it's like wearing a sword-belt. There's something immensely reassuring about a solid weight on the hips.'

'As if you were eternally duelling with your materials.'

'Yes, master. Are you done with your thinking?'

'I am.'

'Good.' Bugg unstrapped his belt and tossed it to the rooftop. 'Makes my hips lopsided. I walk in circles.'

'How about some herbal tea?'

'I'd love some.'

'Excellent.'

They stared at one another for a moment longer, then Bugg nodded and made his way to the ladder. As soon as his back was turned, Tehol tugged the trousers higher once more. Glancing down at the belt, he hesitated, then shook his head. *That would be a presumption.*

Bugg climbed down and out of sight. Tehol strode to his bed and settled down on the creaking frame. He stared up at the murky stars. A holiday festival was approaching, this one dedicated to the Errant, that eternally mysterious purveyor of chance, fateful circumstance and ill-chosen impulses. Or some such thing. Tehol was never certain.

The Holds and their multitude of denizens were invented as dependable sources of blame for virtually anything, or so he suspected. Evading responsibility was a proclivity of the human species, it seemed.

There would be vast senseless celebration, in any case. Of something, perhaps nothing, and certainly involving everything. Frenzied wagers at the Special Drownings, in which the most notorious criminals would try to swim like swans. People who liked to be seen would make a point of being seen. Spectacle was an investment in worthy indolence, and indolence bespoke wealth. And meanwhile, housebound guards in empty estates would mutter and doze at their posts.

A scuffing sound from the gloom to his right. Tehol glanced over. 'You're early.'

Shurq Elalle stepped closer. 'You said midnight.'

'Which is at least two bells from now.'

'Is it? Oh.'

Tehol sat up. 'Well, you're here. No point in sending you away. Even so, we're not to visit Selush until a chime past midnight.'

'We could go early.'

'We could, although I'd rather not alarm her. She indicated she'd need lots of supplies, after all.'

'What makes me worse than any other corpse?'

'Other corpses don't fight back, for one thing.'

The undead woman came closer. 'Why would I feel compelled to resist? Is she not simply making me pretty?'

'Of course. I was just making conversation. And how have you been, Shurq Elalle?'

'The same.'

'The same. Which is?'

'I've been better. Still, many would call consistency a virtue. Those are extraordinary trousers.'

'I agree. Not to everyone's taste, alas—'

'I have no taste.'

'Ah. And is that a consequence of being dead, or a more generic self-admission?'

The flat, lifeless eyes, which had until now been evading direct contact, fixed on Tehol. 'I was thinking . . . the night of Errant's Festival.'

Tehol smiled. 'You anticipate me, Shurq.'

'There are sixteen guards on duty at all times, with an additional eight sleeping or gambling in the barracks, which is attached to the estate's main house via a single covered walkway that is nineteen strides in length. All outer doors are double-barred. There are four guards stationed in cubbies at each corner of the roof, and wards skeined over every window. The estate walls are twice the height of a man.'

'Sounds formidable.'

Shurq Elalle's shrug elicited a wet-leather sound, though whether from her clothes or from somewhere else could not be determined.

Bugg reappeared, climbing one-handed, the other balancing a tray made from a crate lid. Two clay cups were on the tray, their contents steaming. He slowly edged onto the roof, then, glancing up and seeing the two of them, he halted in consternation. 'My apologies. Shurq Elalle, greetings. Would you care for some tea?'

'Don't be absurd.'

'Ah, yes. Thoughtless of me. Your pardon.' Bugg walked over with the tray.

Tehol collected his cup and cautiously sniffed. Then he frowned at his manservant.

Who shrugged. 'We don't have no herbs, master. I had to improvise.'

'With what? Sheep hide?'

Bugg's brows rose. 'Very close indeed. I had some leftover wool.'

'The yellow or the grey?'

'The grey.'

'Well, that's all right, then.' He sipped. 'Smooth.'

'Yes, it would be.'

'We're not poisoning ourselves, are we?'

237

'Only mildly, master.'

'There are times,' Shurq Elalle said, 'when I regret being dead. This is not one of those times, however.'

The two men eyed her speculatively, sipping at their tea.

'Ideally,' she continued, 'I would now clear my throat to cover this moment of awkwardness. But I am incapable of feeling any more awkward than is my normal state. Secondly, clearing my throat has unpleasant consequences.'

'Ah, but Selush has devised a pump,' Tehol said. 'The operation will be, uh, not for the delicate. Even so, soon you shall exude the perfume of roses.'

'And how will she manage that?'

'With roses, I imagine.'

Shurq raised a thin brow. 'I am to be stuffed with dried flowers?'

'Well, not everywhere, of course.'

'A practical question, Tehol Beddict. How am I to be stealthy if I crackle with every step I take?'

'A good question. I suggest you bring that up with Selush.'

'Along with everything else, it would seem. Shall I resume my account of the potential victim's estate? I assume your manservant is trustworthy.'

'Exceptionally so,' Tehol replied. 'Please continue.'

'Finadd Gerun Eberict will be attending the Special Drownings, whereupon, at its conclusion, he will be a guest at an event hosted by Turudal Brizad—'

'The Queen's Consort?'

'Yes. I once robbed him.'

'Indeed! And what did you take?'

'His virginity. We were very young – well, he was, anyway. This was long before he danced at the palace and so earned the interest of the queen.'

'Now that's an interesting detail. Were you his true love, if I may ask such a personal question?'

'Turudal's only love is for himself. As I said, he was younger and I the older. Of course, he's now older than me,

238

which is a curious fact. Somewhat curious, anyway. In any case, there was no shortage of men and women pursuing him even back then. I imagine he believed the conquest was his. Perhaps he still does. The measure of the perfect theft is when the victim remains blissfully unaware that he or she has been stolen from.'

'I'd think,' observed Bugg, 'that Turudal Brizad did not regret his surrender.'

'None the less,' Shurq Elalle said. She was silent, then: 'There is nothing in this world that cannot be stolen.'

'And with that thought swirling like lanolin in our stomachs,' Tehol said, setting his cup down, 'you and I should take a walk, Shurq.'

'How far to Selush's?'

'We can stretch it out. Thank you, dear Bugg, for the delightfully unique refreshment. Clean up around here, will you?'

'If I've the time.'

Shurq hesitated. 'Should I climb down the wall then shadow you unseen?'

Tehol frowned. 'Only if you must. You could just draw that hood up and so achieve anonymity.'

'Very well. I will meet you in the street, so that I am not seen exiting a house I never entered.'

'There are still watchers spying on me?'

'Probably not, but it pays to be cautious.'

'Very good. I will see you in a moment, then.'

Tehol descended the ladder. The single room reeked of sheep sweat, and the heat from the hearth was fierce. He quickly made his way outside, turned right instead of left and came to what had once been a sort of unofficial mews, now cluttered with refuse and discarded building materials, the fronts facing onto it sealed by bricks or doors with their latches removed.

Shurq Elalle emerged from the shadows, her hood drawn about her face. 'Tell me more about this Selush.'

They began walking, threading single file down a narrow

239

lane to reach the street beyond. 'A past associate of Bugg's. Embalmers and other dealers of the dead are a kind of extended family, it seems. Constantly exchanging techniques and body parts. It's quite an art, I gather. A body's story can be unfurled from a vast host of details, to be read like a scroll.'

'What value assembling a list of flaws when the subject is already dead?'

'Morbid curiosity, I imagine. Or curious morbidity.'

'Are you trying to be funny?'

'Never, Shurq Elalle. I have taken to heart your warnings on that.'

'You, Tehol Beddict, are very dangerous to me. Yet I am drawn, as if you were intellectual white nectar. I thirst for the tension created by my struggle to avoid being too amused.'

'Well, if Selush succeeds in what she intends, the risk associated with laughter will vanish, and you may chortle fearlessly.'

'Even when I was alive, I never *chortled*. Nor do I expect to do so now that I am dead. But what you suggest invites . . . disappointment. A releasing of said tension, a dying of the sparks. I now fear getting depressed.'

'The risk of achieving what you wish for,' Tehol said, nodding as they reached Trench Canal and began to walk along its foul length. 'I empathize, Shurq Elalle. It is a sore consequence to success.'

'Tell me what you know of the old tower in the forbidden grounds behind the palace.'

'Not much, except that your undead comrade resides in the vicinity. The girl.'

'Yes, she does. I have named her Kettle.'

'We cross here.' Tehol indicated a footbridge. 'She means something to you?'

'That is difficult to answer. Perhaps. It may prove that she means something to all of us, Tehol Beddict.'

'Ah. And can I be of some help in this matter?'

'Your offer surprises me.'

'I endeavour to remain ever surprising, Shurq Elalle.'

'I am seeking to discover her . . . history. It is, I think, important. The old tower appears to be haunted in some way, and that haunting is in communication with Kettle. It poses desperate need.'

'For what?'

'Human flesh.'

'Oh my.'

'In any case, this is why Gerun Eberict is losing the spies he sets on you.'

Tehol halted. 'Excuse me?'

'Kettle kills them.'

Steeply sloped, the black wall of rock reached up into the light. The currents swept across its rippled face with unceasing ferocity, and all that clung to it to draw sustenance from that roiling stream was squat, hard-shelled and stubborn. Vast flats stretched out from the base of the trench wall, and these were scoured down to bedrock. Enormous tangled islands of detritus, crushed and bound together by unimaginable pressures, crawled across the surface, like migrating leviathans in the flow of dark water.

Brys stood on the plain, watching the nearest tumbling mass roll past. He knew he was witness to sights no mortal had ever seen, where natural eyes would see only darkness, where the pressures would have long since killed corporeal flesh descending from the surface far above. Yet here he stood, to his own senses as real, as physical, as he had been in the palace. Clothed, armoured, his sword hanging at his hip. He could feel the icy water and its wild torrent in a vague, remote fashion, but the currents could not challenge his balance, could not drag him off his feet. Nor did the cold steal the strength from his limbs.

He drew breath, and the air was cool and damp – it was, he realized, the air of the subterranean chamber of the Cedance.

241

That recognition calmed his heart, diminished his disorientation.

A god dwells in this place. It seemed well suited for such a thing. Primal, fraught with extremes, a realm of raw violence and immense, clashing forces of nature.

Another mass of wreckage shambled past, and Brys saw, amidst pale, skeletal branches and what seemed to be bundles of unravelled rope, flattened pieces of metal whose edges showed extruded white tendrils. *By the Errant, that metal is armour, and those tendrils are . . .*

The detritus tumbled away. As it did, Brys saw something beyond it. Stationary, blockish, vertical shapes rearing from the plain.

He walked towards them.

Dolmens.

This beggared comprehension. It seemed impossible that the plain before him had once known air, sunlight and dry winds.

And then he saw that the towering stones were of the same rock as the plain, and that they were indeed part of it, lifting as solid projections. As Brys drew nearer, he saw that their surfaces were carved, an unbroken skein of linked glyphs.

Six dolmens in all, forming a row that cut diagonally from the angle of the trench wall.

He halted before the nearest one.

The glyphs formed a silver latticework over the black stone, and in the uneven surface beneath the symbols he saw the hints of a figure. Multi-limbed, the head small, sloping and squat, a massive brow ridge projecting over a single eye socket. The broad mouth appeared to be a row of elongated tendrils, the end of each sporting long, thin fangs, and it was closed to form an interlocking, spiny row. Six segmented arms, two – possibly four – legs, barely suggested in the black stone's undulations.

The glyphs shrouded the figure, and Brys suspected they formed a prison of sorts, a barrier that prevented the emergence of the creature.

The silver seemed to flow in its carved grooves.

Brys circled the dolmen, and saw other shapes on every side, no two alike, a host of nightmarish, demonic beasts. After a long moment's regard, he moved on to the next standing stone. And found more.

The fourth dolmen was different. On one side the glyphs had unravelled, the silver bled away, and where a figure should have been there was a suggestive indentation, a massive, hulking creature, with snaking tentacles for limbs.

The mute absence was chilling. Something was loose, and Brys did not think it was a god.

Mael, where are you? Are these your servants?

Or your trophies?

He stared up at the indentation. The absence here was more profound than that which reared before him. His soul whispered . . . *abandonment*. Mael was gone. This world had been left to the dark, torrid currents and the herds of detritus.

'Come for another one, have you?'

Brys whirled. Ten paces away stood a huge figure sheathed in armour. Black, patinated iron studded with rivets green with verdigris. A great helm with full cheek guards vertically slatted down to the jawline, reinforced along the bridge of the nose to the chin. The thin eye slits were caged in a grille mesh that extended down beneath the guards to hang ragged and stiff on shoulders and breastplate. Barnacles crusted the joints of arms and legs, and tendrils of brightly coloured plants clinging to joins in the armour streamed in the current. Gauntlets of overlapping plates of untarnished silver held on to a two-handed sword, the blade as wide as Brys's hands were long. The sword's blunt end rested on the bedrock. From those metal-clad hands, he now saw, blood streamed.

The Letherii drew his own longsword. The roiling currents suddenly tugged at him, as if whatever had held him immune to the ravages of this deep world had vanished. The blade was turned and twisted in his hand

243

with every surge of water. To counter such a weapon as that wielded by the warrior, he would need speed, his primary tactic one of evasion. The Letherii steel of his longsword would not break clashing in hard parry, but his arms might.

And now, the currents buffeted him, battled with the sword in his hand. He had no hope of fighting this creature.

The words the warrior had spoken were in a language unknown to Brys, yet he understood it. 'Come for another one? I am not here to free these demons from their sorcerous cages—'

The apparition stepped forward. 'Demons? There are no demons here. Only gods. Forgotten gods. You think the skein of words is a prison?'

'I do not know what to think. I do not know the words written—'

'Power is remembrance. Power is evocation – a god dies when it becomes nameless. Thus did Mael offer this gift, this sanctuary. Without their names, the gods vanish. The crime committed here is beyond measure. The obliteration of the names, the binding of a new name, the making of a slave. Beyond measure, mortal. In answer I was made, to guard those that remain. It is my task.' The sword lifted and the warrior took another step closer.

Some fighters delivered an unseen wound before weapons were even drawn. In them, raised like a penumbra, was the promise of mortality. It drew blood, weakened will and strength. Brys had faced men and women with this innate talent before. And he had answered it with . . . amusement.

The guardian before him promised such mortality, with palpable force.

Another heavy step. A force to match the roiling waters. In sudden understanding, Brys smiled.

The vicious current ceased its maelstrom. Speed and agility returned in a rush.

The huge sword slashed horizontally. Brys leapt back, the point of his sword darting out and up in a stop-thrust against the only target within reach.

Letherii steel slipped in between the silver plates of the left gauntlet, sank deep.

Behind them a dolmen exploded, the concussion thundering through the bedrock underfoot. The warrior staggered, then swung his sword in a downward chop. Brys threw himself backward, rolling over one shoulder to regain his feet in a crouch.

The warrior's sword had driven into the basalt a quarter of its length. And was stuck fast.

He darted to close. Planting his left leg behind the guardian, Brys set both hands against the armoured chest and shoved.

The effort failed as the guardian held himself upright by gripping the embedded sword.

Brys spun and hammered his right elbow into the iron-sheathed face. Pain exploded in his arm as the head was snapped back, and the Letherii pitched to one side, his left hand taking the longsword from his fast-numbing right.

The warrior tugged on his own sword, but it did not budge.

Brys leapt forward once again, driving his left boot down onto the side of the guardian's nearest leg, low, a hand's width above the ankle.

Ancient iron crumpled. Bones snapped.

The warrior sank down on that side, yet remained partly upright by leaning on the jammed sword.

Brys quickly backed away. 'Enough. I have no desire to kill any more gods.'

The armoured face lifted to regard him. 'I am defeated. We have failed.'

The Letherii studied the warrior for a long moment, then spoke. 'The blood seeping from your hands – does it belong to the surviving gods here?'

'Diminished, now.'

'Can they heal you?'

'No. We have nothing left.'

'Why does the blood leak? What happens when it runs out?'

'It is power. It steals courage – against you it failed. It was expected that the blood of slain enemies would . . . it does not matter now.'

'What of Mael? Can you receive no help from him?'

'He has not visited in thousands of years.'

Brys frowned. Kuru Qan had said to follow his instincts. He did not like what had come to pass here. 'I would help. Thus, I would give you my own blood.'

The warrior was silent for a long time. Then, 'You do not know what you offer, mortal.'

'Well, I don't mean to die. I intend to survive the ordeal. Will it suffice?'

'Blood from a dying or dead foe has power. Compared to the blood from a mortal who lives, that power is minuscule. I say again, you do not know what you offer.'

'I have more in mind, Guardian. May I approach?'

'We are helpless before you.'

'Your sword isn't going anywhere, even with my help. I would give you mine. It cannot be broken, or so I am told. And indeed I have never seen Letherii steel break. Your two-handed weapon is only effective if your opponent quails and so is made slow and clumsy.'

'So it would seem.'

Brys was pleased at the wry tone in the warrior's voice. While there had been no self-pity in the admissions of failure, he had disliked hearing them. He reversed grip on his longsword and offered the pommel to the warrior. 'Here.'

'If I release my hands I will fall.'

'One will do.'

The guardian prised a hand loose and grasped the longsword. 'By the Abyss, it weighs as nothing!'

'The forging is a secret art, known only to my people. It will not fail you.'

'Do you treat all your defeated foes in this manner?'

'No, only the ones I had no wish to harm in the first place.'

246

'Tell me, mortal, are you considered a fine swordsman in your world?'

'Passing.' Brys tugged off the leather glove on his right hand, then drew his dagger. 'This arm is still mostly numb—'

'I am pleased. Although I wish I could say the same for my face.'

Brys cut his palm, watched as blood blossomed out to whip away on the current. He set the bleeding hand down on the warrior's left, which was still closed about the grip of the embedded weapon. He felt his blood being drawn between the silver plates.

The warrior's hand twisted round to grasp his own in a grip hard as stone. A clenching of muscles, and the guardian began straightening.

Brys glanced down and saw that the shattered leg was mending in painful-looking spasms, growing solid beneath the huge warrior's weight.

Sudden weakness rushed through him.

'Release my hand,' the warrior said, 'lest you die.'

Nodding, Brys pulled his hand free, and staggered back. 'Will you live?'

'I hope so,' he gasped, his head spinning. 'Now, before I go, tell me their names.'

'What?'

'I have a good memory, Guardian. There will be no more enslavement, so long as I remain alive. And beyond my life, I will ensure that those names are not forgotten—'

'We are ancient gods, mortal. You risk—'

'You have earned your peace, as far as I am concerned. Against the Tiste Edur – those who came before to chain one of your kin – you will be ready next time. My life can add to your strength, and hopefully it will be sufficient for you to resist.'

The guardian straightened to its full height. 'It shall, mortal. Your sacrifice shall not be forgotten.'

'The names! I feel – I am fading—'

Words filled his mind, a tumbling avalanche of names, each searing a brand in his memory. He screamed at the shock of the assault, of countless layers of grief, dreams, lives and deaths, of realms unimaginable, of civilizations crumbling to ruins, then dust.

Stories. *So many stories – ah, Errant—*

'Errant save us, *what have you done?*'

Brys found himself lying on his back, beneath him a hard, enamelled floor. He blinked open his eyes and saw Kuru Qan's wizened face hovering over him.

'I could not find Mael,' the King's Champion said. He felt incredibly weak, barely able to lift a hand to his face.

'You've scarcely a drop of blood left in you, Finadd. Tell me all that happened.'

The Holds forsake me, stories without end . . . 'I discovered what the Tiste Edur have done, Ceda. An ancient god, stripped of its names, bound by a new one. It now serves the Edur.'

Kuru Qan's eyes narrowed behind the thick lenses. 'Stripped of its names. Relevant? Perhaps. Can one of those names be found? Will it serve to pry it loose from Hannan Mosag's grasp?'

Brys closed his eyes. Of all the names now held within him . . . had any of the other gods known its kin's identity? 'I may have it, Ceda, but finding it will take time.'

'You return with secrets, Finadd Brys Beddict.'

'And barely a handful of answers.'

The Ceda leaned back. 'You need time to recover, my young friend. Food, and wine, and plenty of both. Can you stand?'

'I will try . . .'

The humble manservant Bugg walked through the darkness of Sherp's Last Lane, so named because poor Sherp died there a few decades past. He had been a fixture in this neighbourhood, Bugg recalled. Old, half blind and muttering endlessly about a mysterious cracked altar long lost in the clay beneath the streets. Or, more specifically, beneath this particular lane.

His body had been found curled up within a scratched circle, amidst rubbish and a half-dozen neck-wrung rats. Peculiar as that had been, there were few who cared or were curious enough to seek explanations. People died in the alleys and streets all the time, after all.

Bugg missed old Sherp, even after all these years, but some things could not be undone.

He had been awakened by a rattling of the reed mat that now served as a door to Tehol's modest residence. A dirt-smeared child delivering an urgent summons. She now scampered a few paces ahead, glancing back every now and then to make sure she was still being followed.

At the end of Sherp's Last Lane was another alley, this one running perpendicular, to the left leading down to a sinkhole known as Errant's Heel which had become a refuse pit, and to the right ceasing after fifteen paces in a ruined house with a mostly collapsed roof.

The child led Bugg to that ruin.

One section remained with sufficient headroom to stand, and in this chamber a family now resided. Nerek: six children and a grandmother who'd wandered down from the north after the children's parents died of Truce Fever – which itself was a senseless injustice, since Truce Fever was easily cured by any Letherii healer, given sufficient coin.

Bugg did not know them, but he knew *of* them, and clearly they in turn had heard of the services he was prepared to offer, in certain circumstances, free of charge.

A tiny hand reached out to close about his own and the girl led him through the doorway into a corridor where he was forced to crouch beneath the sagging, sloping ceiling. Three paces along and the lower half of another doorway was revealed and, beyond it, a crowded room.

Smelling of death.

Murmured greetings and bowed heads as Bugg entered,

249

his eyes settling on the motionless form lying on a bloody blanket in the room's centre. After a moment's study, he glanced up and sought out the gaze of the eldest of the children, a girl of about ten or eleven years of age – though possibly older and stunted by malnutrition, or younger and prematurely aged by the same. Large, hard eyes met his.

'Where did you find her?'

'She made it home,' the girl replied, her tone wooden.

Bugg looked down at the dead grandmother once more. 'From how far away?'

'Buried Round, she said.'

'She spoke, then, before life left her.' Bugg's jaw muscles bunched. Buried Round was two, three hundred paces distant. An extraordinary will, in the old woman, to have walked all that distance with two mortal sword-thrusts in her chest. 'She knew great need, I think.'

'To tell us who killed her, yes.'

And not to simply disappear, as so many of the destitute do, thus raising the spectre of abandonment – a scar these children could do without.

'Who, then?'

'She was crossing the Round, and found herself in the path of an entourage. Seven men and their master, all armed. The master was raging, something about all his spies disappearing. Our grandmother begged for coin. The master lost his mind with anger and ordered his guards to kill her. And so they did.'

'And is the identity of this master known?'

'You will find his face on newly minted docks.'

Ah.

Bugg knelt beside the old woman. He laid a hand on her cold, lined forehead, and sought the remnants of her life. 'Urusan of the Clan known as the Owl. Her strength was born of love. For her grandchildren. She is gone, but she has not gone far.' He raised his head and met the eyes of each of the six children. 'I hear the shifting of vast stones, the grinding surrender of a long closed portal. There is cold clay, but it did not embrace her.' He drew a deep breath. 'I will prepare this flesh for Nerek interment—'

'We would have your blessing,' the girl said.

Bugg's brows lifted. 'Mine? I am not Nerek, nor even a priest—'

'We would have your blessing.'

The manservant hesitated, then sighed. 'As you will. But tell me, how will you live now?'

As if in answer there was a commotion at the doorway, then a huge figure lumbered into the small room, seeming to fill it entirely. He was young, his size and features evincing Tarthenal and Nerek blood both. Small eyes fixed upon Urusan's corpse, and the whole face darkened.

'And who is this?' Bugg asked. *A shifting of vast stones – now this . . . this shoving aside of entire mountains. What begins here?*

'Our cousin,' the girl said, her eyes wide and adoring and full of pleading as she looked up at the young man. 'He works on the harbour front. Unn is his name. Unn, this is the man known as Bugg. A dresser of the dead.'

Unn's voice was so low-pitched it could barely be heard. 'Who did this?'

Oh, Finadd Gerun Eberict, to your senseless feast of blood you shall have an uninvited guest, and something tells me you will come to regret it.

Selush of the Stinking House was tall and amply proportioned, yet her most notable feature was her hair. Twenty-seven short braids of the thick black hair, projecting in all directions, each wrapped round an antler tine, which meant that the braids curved and twisted in peculiar fashion. She was somewhere between thirty-five and fifty years of age, the obscurity the product of her formidable talent as a disguiser of flaws. Violet eyes, produced by an unusual ink collected from segmented worms that lived deep in the sand of the south island beaches, and lips kept full and red by a mildly toxic snake venom that she painted on every morning.

As she stood before Tehol and Shurq Elalle at the threshold of her modest and unfortunately named abode, she was dressed in skin-tight silks, inviting Tehol against his own sense of decorum to examine her nipples beneath the gilt sheen – and so it was a long moment before he looked up to see the alarm in her eyes.

'You're early! I wasn't expecting you. Oh! Now I'm all nervous. Really, Tehol, you should know better than to do the unexpected! Is this the dead woman?'

'If not,' Shurq Elalle replied, 'then I'm in even deeper trouble, wouldn't you say?'

Selush stepped closer. 'This is the worst embalming I've ever seen.'

'I wasn't embalmed.'

'Oh! An outrage! How did you die?'

Shurq raised a lifeless brow. 'I am curious. How often is that question answered by your clients?'

Selush blinked. 'Enter, if you must. So early!'

'My dear,' Tehol said reasonably, 'it's less than a couple of hundred heartbeats from the midnight bell.'

'Precisely! See how flustered you've made me? Quickly, inside, I must close the door. There! Oh, the dark streets are so frightening. Now, sweetie, let me look more closely at you. My servant was unusually reticent, I'm afraid.' She abruptly leaned close until her nose was almost touching Shurq's lips.

Tehol flinched, but luckily neither woman noticed.

'You drowned.'

'Really.'

'In Quillas Canal. Just downstream of Windlow's Meatgrinders on the last day of a summer month. Which one? Wanderer's Month? Watcher's?'

'Betrayer's.'

'Oh! Windlow must have had unusually good business that month, then. Tell me, do people scream when they see you?'

'Sometimes.'

252

'Me too.'

'Do you,' Shurq asked, 'get compliments on your hair?'

'Never.'

'Well, that was pleasing small-talk,' Tehol said hastily. 'We haven't got all night, alas—'

'Why, yes we have, you silly man,' Selush said.

'Oh, right. Sorry. In any case. Shurq was a victim of the Drownings, and, it turned out, an abiding curse.'

'Isn't it always the way?' Selush sighed, turning to walk to the long table along the back wall of the room.

'Tehol mentioned roses,' Shurq said, following.

'Roses? Dear me, no. Cinnamon and patchouli, I would think. But first, we need to do something about all that mould, and the moss in your nostrils. And then there's the ootooloo—'

'The *what*?' Shurq and Tehol asked in unison.

'Lives in hot springs in the Bluerose Mountains.' She swung about and regarded Shurq with raised brows. 'A secret among women. I'm surprised you've never heard of them.'

'It would seem my education is lacking.'

'Well, an ootooloo is a small soft-bodied creature that feeds through a crevice, a sort of vertical slit for a mouth. Its skin is covered in cilia with the unusual quality of transmitting sensation. These cilia can take root in membranous flesh—'

'Hold on a moment,' Tehol said, aghast, 'you're not suggesting—'

'Most men can't tell the difference, but it enhances pleasure many times . . . or so I am led to believe. I have never invited one inside, since the emplacement of an ootooloo is permanent, and it needs, uhm, constant feeding.'

'How often?' Shurq demanded, and Tehol heard suitable alarm in her tone.

'Daily.'

'But Shurq's nerves are dead – how can she feel what this ottoolie thing feels?'

'Not dead, Tehol Beddict, simply unawakened. Besides, before too long, the ootooloo's cilia will have permeated her entire body, and the healthier the organism the brighter and more vigorous her glowing flesh!'

'I see. And what of my brain? Will these roots grow in it as well?'

'Well, we can't have that, can we, lest you live out the remainder of existence drooling in a hot bath. No, we shall infuse your brain with a poison – well, not a true poison, but the exudation of a small creature that shares those hot springs with the ootooloo. Said exudation is unpalatable to the ootooloo. Isn't nature wonderful?'

Grainy-eyed, Bugg staggered inside his master's home. It was less than an hour before dawn. He felt drained, more by the blessing he had given than by preparing the old woman's corpse for burial. Two strides into the single room and he halted.

Seated on the floor and leaning against the wall opposite was Shand. 'Where is the bastard, Bugg?'

'Working, although I imagine you are sceptical. I've not slept this night and so am unequal to conversation, Shand—'

'And I care? What kind of work? What's he doing that has to be done when the rest of the world's asleep?'

'Shand, I—'

'Answer me!'

Bugg walked over to the pot sitting on a grille above the now cool hearth. He dipped a cup into the tepid, stewed tea. 'Twelve lines of investment, like unseen streams beneath foundations, eating away but yet to reveal a tremor. There are essential trusses to every economy, Shand, upon which all else rests.'

'You can't do business in the middle of the night.'

'Not that kind of business, no. But there are dangers to all this, Shand. Threats. And they need to be met. Anyway, what are you doing out at night without your bodyguard?'

'Ublala? That oaf? In Rissarh's bed. Or Hejun's. Not mine, not tonight, anyway. We take it in turns.'

Bugg stared at her through the gloom. He drank the last of the tea and set the cup down.

'Is all that true?' Shand asked after a moment. 'Those investments?'

'Yes.'

'Why isn't he telling us these things?'

'Because your investments have to remain separate, disconnected. There can be no comparable pattern. Thus, follow his instructions with precision. It will all come clear eventually.'

'I hate geniuses.'

'Understandable. All he does seems to confound, it's true. One gets used to it.'

'And how is Bugg's Construction doing?'

'Well enough.'

'What's the purpose of it, anyway? Just to make money?'

'No. The intention is to acquire the contract for the Eternal Domicile.'

Shand stared. 'Why?'

Bugg smiled.

Disinfecting, bleaching, scraping, combing. Fragrant oils rubbed into clothing and skin. Preserving oils rubbed in everywhere else. Scouring flushes of eyes, nose, ears and mouth. Then it was time for the pump.

At which point Tehol staggered outside for some air.

The sky was paling to the east, the city's less sane denizens already risen and venturing out onto the streets. Clattering carts on the cobbles. Somewhere a rooster crowed, only to have its exuberant cry cut off into strangled silence. A dog barked happily.

Footsteps, halting to Tehol's right. 'You still here?'

'Ah, Selush's assistant. And how are you this grisly morning, Padderunt?'

The old man's expression was eternally sour, but at

Tehol's courteous enquiry it seemed to implode into a wrinkled mess. 'How am I? Sleepless! That's how I am, y'damned snake! They still in there? It's a lost cause, I say. A lost cause. Just like you, Tehol Beddict. I knew your mother – what would she say seeing you now?'

'You knew her corpse, you old fool. Before that we'd never met you.'

'Think she didn't tell me all about herself anyway? Think I can't see what's there to be seen? The soul inside shapes the flesh. Oh, she talked to me all right.'

Tehol's brows rose. 'The soul inside shapes the flesh?' He stared down at the wrinkled prune face glaring up at him. 'Oh my.'

'Oh, that's a cutting remark, is it? True enough, here's what happens when a decent man gets no sleep!'

A small clay pot exploded on the cobbles between them, followed by a furious shout from a window in the building opposite.

'There!' Padderunt cried, hand to his head as he staggered in circles. 'Make of our neighbours vicious enemies! You don't live here, do you?'

'Calm down,' Tehol said. 'I simply asked how you were this morning, in case you've forgotten. Your reply was supposed to be equally inane and nondescript. If I'd wanted a list of your ailments – well, I wouldn't. Who would? Innocuous civility is what was expected, Padderunt. Not foul invective.'

'Oh really? Well, how am I supposed to know that? Come on, there's a place nearby makes great grain cakes. And rustleaf tea, which can wake the dead.'

The two made their way down the street.

'Have you tried it?' Tehol asked.

'Tried what?'

'Waking the dead with rustleaf tea.'

'Should've worked.'

'But, alas, it didn't.'

'Still should've. The stuff doubles your heart rate and makes you heave everything in your stomach.'

'I can't wait.'

'Until you get used to it. Makes a fine insect killer, too. Just splash it on the floor and in cracks and such. I can't recommend it highly enough.'

'Most people smoke rustleaf, not drink it.'

'Barbarians. Here we are. You're buying, right?'

'With what?'

'Then it goes on Selush's account, meaning you just have to pay later.'

'Fine.'

Shurq Elalle stood in front of the long silver mirror. Instinct had her gauging the worth of all that silver for a moment before she finally focused on the reflected image. A healthy pallor to her skin, her cheeks glowing with vigour. Her hair was clean and had been cut for the first time in years, scented with a hint of patchouli oil. The whites of her eyes were clear, a wet gleam reflecting from her pupils.

The rotted leathers and linen of her clothing had been replaced with black silks beneath a short black calf-hide jacket. A new weapons belt, tanned leggings and high boots. Tight leather gloves. 'I look like a whore.'

'Not any old whore, though, right?' Selush said.

'True, I'll take your coin then kill you. That's how I look.'

'There are plenty of men out there who'll go for that, you know.'

'Getting killed?'

'Absolutely. In any case, I was led to believe that wasn't your profession. Although I suppose you might feel inclined to try something new – how does the ootooloo feel, by the way?'

'Hungry. Can't I feed it, uh, something else?'

Selush's eyes sparkled. 'Experimentation, that's the spirit!'

Some comments, the undead woman reflected, deserved no response.

Shurq Elalle flexed the muscles that would permit her to draw breath – they were long out of practice, and it was strange to feel the still vague and remote sense of air sliding down her throat and filling her chest. After the pump, there had been infusions. The breath she released smelled of cinnamon and myrrh. Better than river mud any day.

'Your work is acceptable,' she said.

'Well, that's a relief! It's nearly dawn, and I'm starving. Shall we test you out, dear? I imagine my assistant and Tehol are at the local establishment, breaking their fast. Let us join them.'

'I thought I wasn't supposed to eat or drink.'

'No, but you can preen and flirt, can't you?'

Shurq stared at the woman.

Selush smiled. Then her eyelids fluttered and she turned away. 'Where's my shawl?'

Kuru Qan had left and returned with two assistants who carried Brys back to the Ceda's chambers, where he was laid down on a bench and plied with various liquids and food. Even so, strength was slow to return and he was still lying supine, head propped up on a cushion, when the doors opened and First Eunuch Nifadas entered.

His small eyes glittered as he looked down on Brys. 'King's Champion, are you well enough to meet your king? He will be here in a moment.'

Brys struggled to sit straighter. 'This is unfortunate. I am, for the moment, unequal to my responsibilities—'

'Never mind that, Finadd. Your king seeks only to ensure you will recover from your ordeal. Genuine concern motivates Ezgara Diskanar in this instance. Please, remain where you are. I have never seen you so pale.'

'Something has fed on his blood,' Kuru Qan said, 'but he will not tell me what it was.'

Nifadas pursed his lips as he regarded Brys. 'I cannot imagine that a god would do such a thing.'

'Mael was not there, First Eunuch,' Brys said. 'The Tiste

258

Edur found something else, and have bound it to their service.'

'Can you tell us what this thing is?'

'A forgotten god, but that is the extent of my knowledge. I do not know its nature, nor the full breadth of its power. It is old, older than the ocean itself. Whatever worshipped it was not human.'

A voice spoke from the doorway. 'I am ever careless with my assets, although the Errant has spared me the cruellest consequence thus far, for which I am thankful.'

Kuru Qan and Nifadas both bowed low as Ezgara Diskanar entered the chamber. In his sixth decade, the king's features remained surprisingly youthful. He was of average height, slightly on the lean side, his gestures reveal-ing a nervous energy that seemed tireless. The bones beneath his features were prominent and somewhat asymmetrical, the result of a childhood incident with a bad-tempered horse. Right cheekbone and orbital arch sat flatter and higher than their counterparts on the left side of the king's face, making the eye on that side seem larger and rounder. It was a poorly functioning eye and had a tendency to wander independently when Ezgara was irritated or weary. Healers could have corrected the damage, but the king forbade it – even as a child, he had been obstinate and wilful, and not in the least concerned with outward appearance.

Further proof of that observation was evinced in his modest attire, more befitting a citizen in the markets than a king.

Brys managed a slight bow from his reclined position. 'My apologies, your highness—'

'None needed, Finadd,' Ezgara Diskanar cut in, waving a hand. 'Indeed, it is I who must apologize to you. Unpleasant tasks that take you from your official functions. I have sorely abused your loyalty, my young Champion. And you have suffered for it.'

'I shall recover, sire,' Brys said.

259

Ezgara smiled, then surveyed the others in the room. 'Well, this is a fell gathering, isn't it? We should be relieved that my dearest wife is at the moment senseless beneath an exhausted consort, so that even her most trusted spies dare not intrude to report on this meeting. Hopefully, when that finally occurs, it will be far too late.'

Nifadas spoke. 'My king, I shall be the first to take my leave, if you will permit. The hour of my departure from the city fast approaches, and my preparations are far from complete.'

Ezgara's lopsided smile broadened. 'First Eunuch, your diligence in such matters is legendary, leaving me sceptical of your claims. None the less, you have my leave, if only that you might ensure your spies are made aware of precisely when *her* spies make their report, so that they in turn may report to you and you may then report to me. Although what I am to do with such knowledge will no doubt escape me, given that the event initiating these flurries of reporting is none other than the one occurring right now in this room.'

Nifadas bowed. 'None can rest in this dance, sire, as you well know.'

The king's smile tightened. 'Well I do, indeed, First Eunuch. Be off with you, then.'

Brys watched Nifadas depart. As soon as the door was closed the king faced Kuru Qan. 'Ceda, the Chancellor continues to petition against Finadd Gerun Eberict's attachment to the delegation. His arguments are persuasive.'

'He fears for the life of your son, your highness.'

Ezgara nodded. 'And has the Finadd's restraint so weakened that he might murder my heir?'

'One would hope not, sire.'

'Do you imagine that my son understands the risk and will therefore act with constraint and decorum?'

'Prince Quillas has been advised of the dangers, sire,' Kuru Qan carefully replied. 'He has gathered about him his

260

most trusted bodyguards, under the command of Moroch Nevath.'

'Presumably, Moroch feels equal to the task of defending his prince's life.' At this Ezgara turned and fixed Brys with an inquisitive gaze.

'Moroch is supremely skilled, sire,' Brys Beddict said after a moment. 'I would hazard he will have tasters in line before the prince, and mages replete with a host of wards.'

'To the latter, your highness,' Kuru Qan said, 'I can attest. I have lost a number of skilled students to the queen's command.'

'Thus,' Ezgara Diskanar said, 'we seek balance in the threat, and rely upon the wisdom of the players. Should one party decide on pre-emptive action, however, the scenario fast unravels.'

'True, sire.'

'Finadd Brys Beddict, is Moroch Nevath capable of advising restraint?'

'I believe so, sire.'

'The question remaining, however,' Ezgara said, 'is whether my son is capable of receiving it.'

Neither the Ceda nor Brys made response to that.

Their king eyed them both for a long moment, then settled his attention on Brys. 'I look forward to your return to duties, Champion, and am relieved that you are recovering from your adventures.'

Ezgara Diskanar strode from the chamber. At the doorway's threshold he said – without turning or pausing – 'Gerun Eberict will need to reduce his own entourage, I think . . .'

The door was closed by one of Kuru Qan's servants, leaving the two men alone. The Ceda glanced over at Brys, then shrugged.

'If wherewithal was an immortal virtue . . .' Brys ventured.

'Our king would be a god,' Kuru Qan finished, nodding. 'And upon that we now stake our lives.' The lenses covering his eyes flashed with reflected light. 'Curious observation to make at this time. Profoundly prescient, I think. Brys Beddict, will you tell me more of your journey?'

'Only that I sought to right a wrong, and that, as a consequence, the Tiste Edur will be unable to bind any more forgotten gods.'

'A worthwhile deed, then.'

'Such is my hope.'

'What do the old witches in the market always say? "The end of the world is announced with a kind word."'

Brys winced.

'Of course,' the Ceda continued distractedly, 'they just use that as an excuse to be rude to inquisitive old men.'

'They have another saying, Ceda,' Brys said after a moment. '"Truth hides in colourless clothes."'

'Surely not the same witches? If so, then they're all the greatest liars known to the mortal world!'

Brys smiled at the jest. But a taste of ashes had come to his mouth, and he inwardly quailed at the first whispers of dread.

CHAPTER SEVEN

You see naught but flesh
in the wrought schemes
that stitch every dance
in patterns of rising –
the ritual of our days
our lives bedecked
with precious import
as if we stand unbolstered
before tables feast-heavy
and tapestries burdened
with simple deeds
are all that call us
and all that we call upon
as would flesh blood-swollen
by something other than need.
But my vision is not so
privileged and what I see
are the bones in ghostly motion,
the bones who are the
slaves and they weave
the solid world underfoot
with every stride you take.

Slaves Beneath
Fisher kel Tath

263

Acquitor Seren Pedac watched Edur children playing among the sacred trees. The shadows writhing in the black bark of the boles were a chaotic swirl of motion surrounding the children, to which they seemed entirely indifferent. For some ineffable reason, she found the juxtaposition horrifying.

She had, years ago, seen young Nerek playing amidst the scattered bones of their ancestors, and it had left her more shaken than any battlefield she had walked. The scene before her now resonated in the same manner. She was here, in the Warlock King's village, and in the midst of people, of figures in motion and voices ringing through the misty air, she felt lost and alone.

Encircling the holy grove was a broad walkway, the mud covered with shaggy strips of shredded bark, along which sat logs roughly carved into benches. Ten paces to Seren's left was Hull Beddict, seated with his forearms on his knees, hands anchoring his head as he stared at the ground. He had neither moved nor spoken in some time, and the mundane inconsequentiality of their exchanged greetings no longer echoed between them, barring a faint flavour of sadness in the mutual silence.

The Tiste Edur ignored the two Letherii strangers in their midst. Lodgings had been provided for them and for Buruk the Pale. The first meeting with Hannan Mosag was to be this night, but the company had already been here for five days. Normally, a wait of a day or two was to be expected. It was clear that the Warlock King was sending them a message with this unprecedented delay.

A more dire warning still was to be found in the many Edur from other tribes now resident in the village. She had seen Arapay, Merude, Beneda and Sollanta among the native Hiroth. Den-Ratha, who dwelt in the northernmost regions of Edur territory, were notoriously reluctant to venture from their own lands. Even so, the fact of the unified tribes could be made no more apparent and deliberate than it had been, and a truth she had known only in the abstract was given chilling confirmation in its actuality. The divisive weaknesses of old were no more. Everything had changed.

The Nerek had pulled the wagons close to the guest lodge and were now huddled among them, fearful of venturing into the village. The Tiste Edur had a manner of looking right through those they deemed to be lesser folk. This frightened the Nerek in some way, as if the fact of their own existence could be damaged by the Edur's indifference. Since arriving they had seemed to wither, immune to Buruk's exhortations, barely inclined to so much as feed themselves. Seren had gone in search of Hull, in the hope of convincing him to speak to the Nerek.

Upon finding him, she had begun to wonder whether he'd been inflicted with something similar to the enervating pall that had settled on the Nerek. Hull Beddict looked old, as if the journey's end had carried with it a fierce cost, and before him waited still heavier burdens.

Seren Pedac pulled her gaze from the playing children and walked back to where Hull sat on the log bench. Men were quick and stubborn with their barriers, but she'd had enough. 'Those Nerek will starve if you don't do something.'

There was no indication that he'd heard her.

'Fine,' she snapped. 'What's a few more Nerek deaths to your toll?'

She'd wanted anger. Outrage. She'd wanted to wound him with that, if only to confirm that there was still blood to flow. But at her vicious words, he slowly looked up and met her eyes with a soft smile. 'Seren Pedac. The Nerek await acceptance by the Tiste Edur, just as we do – although we Letherii are far less sensitive to the spiritual damage the Edur want us to suffer. Our skin is thick, after all——'

'Born of our fixation on our so-called infallible destiny,' she replied. 'What of it?'

'I used to think,' he said, smile fading, 'that the thickness of our . . . armour was naught but an illusion. Bluster and

265

self-righteous arrogance disguising deep-seated insecurities. That we lived in perpetual crisis, since self-avowed destinies wear a thousand masks and not one of them truly fits—'

'How can they, Hull Beddict, when they're modelled on perfection?'

He shrugged, looked down and seemed to study his hands. 'But in most ways our armour is indeed thick. Impervious to nuances, blind to subtlety. Which is why we're always so suspicious of subtle things, especially when exhibited by strangers, by outsiders.'

'We Letherii know our own games of deceit,' Seren said. 'You paint us as blundering fools—'

'Which we are, in so many ways,' he replied. 'Oh, we visualize our goals clearly enough. But we ignore the fact that every step we take towards them crushes someone, somewhere.'

'Even our own.'

'Yes, there is that.' He rose, and Seren Pedac was struck once more by his bulk. A huge, broken man. 'I will endeavour to ease the plight of the Nerek. But the answer rests with the Tiste Edur.'

'Very well.' She stepped back and turned round. The children played on, amidst the lost shadows. She listened to Hull walk away, the soft crackle of his moccasined feet on the wood chips fading.

Very well.

She made her way into the village, onto the main avenue, across the bridge that led through open gates into the inner ward, where the noble-born Hiroth had their residences. Just beyond them was Hannan Mosag's longhouse. Seren Pedac paused in the broad clearing just within the palisade wall. No children in sight, only slaves busy with their menial chores and a half-dozen Edur warriors sparring with a wide assortment of weapons. None spared the Acquitor any notice, at least not outwardly, though she was certain that her arrival had been surreptitiously observed and that her movements would be tracked.

Two Letherii slaves were walking nearby, carrying between them a net-sling bulging with mussels. Seren approached.

'I would speak with an Edur matron.'

'She comes,' one of them replied, not glancing over.

Seren turned.

The Edur woman who strode towards her was flanked by attendants. She looked young, but there was in truth no way of knowing. Attractive, but that in itself was not unusual. She wore a long robe, the wool dyed midnight blue, with gold-threaded patterns adorning cuffs and brocade. Her long, straight brown hair was unbound.

'Acquitor,' she said in Edur, 'are you lost?'

'No, milady. I would speak with you on behalf of the Nerek.'

Thin brows arched above the heart-shaped face. 'With me?'

'With an Edur,' Seren replied.

'Ah. And what is it you wish to say?'

'Until such time that the Tiste Edur offer an official welcome to the Nerek, they starve and suffer spiritual torment. I would ask that you show them mercy.'

'I am sure that this is but an oversight, Acquitor. Is it not true that your audience with the Warlock King occurs this very night?'

'Yes. But that is no guarantee that we will be proclaimed guests at that time, is it?'

'You would demand special treatment?'

'Not for ourselves. For the Nerek.'

The woman studied her for a time, then, 'Tell me, if you will, who or what are these Nerek?'

A half-dozen heartbeats passed, as Seren struggled to adjust to this unexpected ignorance. Unexpected, she told herself, but not altogether surprising – she had but fallen to her own assumptions. It seemed the Letherii were not

267

unique in their self-obsessions. Or, for that matter, their arrogance. 'Your pardon, milady—'

'I am named Mayen.'

'Your pardon, Mayen. The Nerek are the servants of Buruk the Pale. Similar in status to your slaves. They are of a tribe that was assimilated by Lether some time back, and now work to pay against their debt.'

'Joining the Letherii entails debt?'

Seren's gaze narrowed. 'Not direc— not as such, Mayen. There were . . . unique circumstances.'

'Yes, of course. Those do arise, don't they?' The Edur woman pressed a fingertip to her lips, then seemed to reach a decision. 'Take me, then, to these Nerek, Acquitor.'

'I'm sorry? Now?'

'Yes, the sooner their spirits are eased the better. Or have I misunderstood you?'

'No.'

'Presumably, the blessing of any Edur will suffice for these pitiful tribespeople of yours. Nor can I see how it will affect the Warlock King's dealings with you. Indeed, I am sure it won't.' She turned to one of her Letherii slaves. 'Feather Witch, please inform Uruth Sengar that I will be somewhat delayed, but assure her it will not be for long.'

The young woman named Feather Witch bowed and rushed off towards a longhouse. Seren stared after her for a moment. 'Mayen, if I may ask, who gave her that name?'

'Feather Witch? It is Letherii, is it not? Those Letherii born as slaves among us are named by their mothers. Or grandmothers, whatever the practice among your kind may be. I have not given it much thought. Why?'

Seren shrugged. 'It is an old name, that is all. I've not heard it used in a long time, and then only in the histories.'

'Shall we walk, Acquitor?'

Udinaas sat on a low stool near the entrance, stripping scales from a basketful of dried fish. His hands were wet, red and cracked by the salt paste the fish had been packed in.

268

He had watched the Acquitor's arrival, followed Mayen's detour, and now Feather Witch was approaching, a troubled expression on her face.

'Indebted,' she snapped, 'is Uruth within?'

'She is, but you must wait.'

'Why?'

'She speaks with the highborn widows. They have been in there some time, and no, I do not know what concerns them.'

'And you imagine I would have asked you?'

'How are your dreams, Feather Witch?'

She paled, and looked round as if seeking somewhere else to wait. But a light rain had begun to fall, and beneath the projecting roof of the longhouse they were dry. 'You know nothing of my dreams, Indebted.'

'How can I not? You come to me in them every night. We talk, you and I. We argue. You demand answers from me. You curse the look in my eyes. And, eventually, you flee.'

She would not meet his gaze. 'You cannot be there. In my mind,' she said. 'You are nothing to me.'

'We are just the fallen, Feather Witch. You, me, the ghosts. All of us. We're the dust swirling around the ankles of the conquerors as they stride on into glory. In time, we may rise in their ceaseless scuffling, and so choke them, but it is a paltry vengeance, don't you think?'

'You do not speak as you used to, Udinaas. I no longer know who speaks through you.'

He looked down at his scale-smeared hands. 'And how do I answer that? Am I unchanged? Hardly. But does that mean the changes are not mine? I fought the White Crow for you, Feather Witch. I wrested you from its grasp, and now all you do is curse me.'

'Do you think I appreciate owing you my life?'

He winced, then managed a smile as he lifted his gaze once more, catching her studying him – though once more she glanced away. 'Ah, I see now. You have found yourself . . . indebted. To me.'

'Wrong,' she hissed. 'Uruth would have saved me. You did nothing, except make a fool of yourself.'

'She was too late, Feather Witch. And you insist on calling me Indebted, as if saying it often enough will take away—'

'Be quiet! I want nothing to do with you!'

'You have no choice, although if you speak any louder both our heads will top a pike outside the walls. What did the Acquitor want with Mayen?'

She shifted nervously, hesitated, then said, 'A welcome for the Nerek. They're dying.'

Udinaas shook his head. 'That gift is for the Warlock King to make.'

'So you would think, yet Mayen offered herself in his stead.'

His eyes widened. 'She did? Has she lost her mind?'

'Quiet, you fool!' Feather Witch crouched down across from him. 'The impending marriage has filled her head. She fashions herself as a queen and so has become insufferable. And now she would bless the Nerek—'

'*Bless?*'

'Her word, yes. I think even the Acquitor was taken aback.'

'That was Seren Pedac, wasn't it?'

Feather Witch nodded.

Both were silent for a few moments, then Udinaas said, 'What would such a blessing do, do you think?'

'Probably nothing. The Nerek are a broken people. Their gods are dead, the spirits of their ancestors scattered. Oh, a ghost or two might be drawn to the newly sanctified ground—'

'An Edur's blessing could do that? Sanctify the ground?'

'Maybe. I don't know. But there could be a binding. Of destinies, depending on the purity of Mayen's bloodline, on all that awaits her in her life, on whether she's—' Feather Witch gestured angrily and clamped her mouth shut.

On whether she's a virgin. But how could that be in question?

270

She's not yet married, and Edur do not break those rules. 'We did not speak of this, you and I,' Udinaas said. 'I told you that you had to wait, because that is expected of me. You had no reason to think your message from Mayen was urgent. We are slaves, Feather Witch. We do not think for ourselves, and of the Edur and their ways we know next to nothing.'

Her eyes finally locked with his. 'Yes.' A moment, then, 'Hannan Mosag meets with the Letherii tonight.'

'I know.'

'Buruk the Pale. Seren Pedac. Hull Beddict.'

Udinaas smiled, but the smile held no humour. 'If you will, at whose feet shall the tiles be cast, Feather Witch?'

'Among those three? Errant knows, Udinaas.' As if sensing her own softening towards him, she scowled and straightened. 'I will stand over there. Waiting.'

'You do intend to cast the tiles tonight, don't you?'

She admitted it with a terse nod, then walked to the corner of the longhouse front, to the very edge of the thickening rain.

Udinaas resumed stripping scales. He thought back to his own words earlier. *Fallen. Who tracks our footsteps, I wonder? We who are the forgotten, the discounted and the ignored. When the path is failure, it is never willingly taken. The fallen. Why does my heart weep for them? Not them but us, for most assuredly I am counted among them. Slaves, serfs, nameless peasants and labourers, the blurred faces in the crowd – just a smear on memory, a scuffing of feet down the side passages of history.*

Can one stop, can one turn and force one's eyes to pierce the gloom? And see the fallen? Can one ever see the fallen? And if so, what emotion is born in that moment?

There were tears on his cheeks, dripping down onto his chafed hands. He knew the answer to that question, knife-sharp and driven deep, and the answer was . . . recognition.

Hull Beddict moved to stand beside Seren Pedac as Mayen walked away. Behind them, the Nerek were speaking in their native tongue, harsh and fast words, taut with dis-belief. Rain hissed in the cookfires.

'She should not have done that,' Hull said.

'No,' Seren agreed, 'she should not have. Still, I am not quite certain what has just happened. They were just words, after all. Weren't they?'

'She didn't proclaim them guests, Seren. She blessed their arrival.'

The Acquitor glanced back at the Nerek, frowned at their flushed, nervous expressions. 'What are they talking about?'

'It's the old dialect – there are trader words in it that I understand, but many others that I don't.'

'I didn't know the Nerek had two languages.'

'Their name is mentioned in the annals of the First Landings,' Hull said. 'They are the indigenous people whose territory spanned the entire south. There were Nerek watching the first ships approach. Nerek who came to greet the first Letherii to set foot on this continent. Nerek who traded, taught the colonizers how to live in this land, gave them the medicines against the heat fevers. They have been here a long, long time. Two languages? I'm surprised there aren't a thousand.'

'Well,' Seren Pedac said after a moment, 'at least they're animated once more. They'll eat, do as Buruk commands—'

'Yes. But I sense a new fear among them – not one to incapacitate, but the source of troubled thoughts. It seems that even they do not comprehend the full significance of that blessing.'

'This was never their land, was it?'

'I don't know. The Edur certainly claim to have always been here, from the time when the ice first retreated from the world.'

'Oh yes, I'd forgotten. Their strange creation myths. Lizards and dragons and ice, a god-king betrayed.'

After a moment she glanced over, and saw him staring at her.

272

'What is it, Hull?'

'How do you know such things? It was years before Binadas Sengar relinquished such information to me, and that as a solemn gift following our binding.'

Seren blinked. 'I heard it . . . somewhere. I suppose.' She shrugged, wiping rainwater from her face. 'Everyone has some sort of creation myth. Nonsense, typically. Or actual memories all jumbled up and infused with magic and miracles.'

'You are being surprisingly dismissive, Acquitor.'

'And what do the Nerek believe?'

'That they were all born of a single mother, countless generations past, who was the thief of fire and walked through time, seeking that which might answer a need that consumed her – although she could never discover the nature of that need. One time, in her journey, she took within her a sacred seed, and so gave birth to a girl-child. To all outward appearances,' he continued, 'that child was little different from her mother, for the sacredness was hidden, and so it remains hidden to this day. Within the Nerek, who are the offspring of that child.'

'And by this, the Nerek justify their strange patriarchy.'

'Perhaps,' Hull conceded, 'although it is the female line that is taken as purest.'

'And does this first mother's mother have a name?'

'Ah, you noted the confused blending of the two, as if they were roles rather than distinct individuals. Maiden, mother and grandmother, a progression through time—'

'Discounting the drudgery spent as wife. Wisdom unfurls like a flower in a pile of dung.'

His gaze sharpened on her. 'In any case, she is known by a number of related names, also suggesting variations of a single person. Eres, N'eres, Eres'al.'

'And this is what lies at the heart of the Nerek ancestor worship?'

'Was, Seren Pedac. You forget, their culture is destroyed.'

273

'Cultures can die, Hull, but the people live on, and what they carry within them are the seeds of rebirth—'

'A delusion, Seren Pedac,' he replied. 'Whatever might be born of that is twisted, weak, a self-mockery.'

'Even stone changes. Nothing can stand still—'

'Yet we would. Wouldn't we? Oh, we talk of progress, but what we really desire is the perpetuation of the present. With its seemingly endless excesses, its ravenous appetites. Ever the same rules, ever the same game.'

Seren Pedac shrugged. 'We were discussing the Nerek. A noble-born woman of the Hiroth Tiste Edur has blessed them—'

'Before even our own formal welcome has been voiced.'

Her brows rose. 'You think this is yet another veiled insult to the Letherii? Instigated by Hannan Mosag himself? Hull, I think your imagination has the better of you this time.'

'Think what you like.'

She turned away. 'I'm going for a walk.'

Uruth had intercepted Mayen at the bridge. Whatever was exchanged between them was brief and without drama, at least none that Udinaas could determine from where he sat in front of the longhouse. Feather Witch had trailed Uruth after delivering the message from her mistress, and waited a half-dozen paces distant from the two Edur women, though not so far as to be out of earshot. Uruth and Mayen then approached side by side, the slaves trailing.

Hearing low laughter, Udinaas stiffened and hunched lower on the stool. 'Be quiet, Wither!' he hissed.

'There are realms, dead slave,' the wraith whispered, *'where memories shape oblivion, and so make of ages long past a world as real as this one. In this way, time is defeated. Death is defied. And sometimes, Udinaas the Indebted, such a realm drifts close. Very close.'*

'No more, I beg you. I'm not interested in your stupid riddles—'

'*Would you see what I see? Right now? Shall I send Shadow's veil to slip over your eyes and so reveal to you unseen pasts?*'

'Not now—'

'*Too late.*'

Layers unfolded before the slave's eyes, cobweb-thin, and the surrounding village seemed to shrink back, blurred and colourless, beneath the onslaught. Udinaas struggled to focus. The clearing had vanished, replaced by towering trees and a forest floor of rumpled moss, where the rain fell in sheets. The sea to his left was much closer, fiercely toppling grey, foaming waves against the shoreline's jagged black rock, spume exploding skyward.

Udinaas flinched away from the violence of those waves – and all at once they faded into darkness, and another scene rose before the slave's eyes. The sea had retreated, beyond the western horizon, leaving behind trench-scarred bedrock ringed in sheer ice cliffs. The chill air carried the stench of decay.

Figures scurried past Udinaas, wearing furs or perhaps bearing their own thick coat, mottled brown, tan and black. They were surprisingly tall, their bodies disproportionately large below small-skulled, heavy-jawed heads. One sported a reed-woven belt from which dead otters hung, and all carried coils of rope made from twisted grasses.

They were silent, yet Udinaas sensed their terror as they stared at something in the northern sky.

The slave squinted, then saw what had captured their attention.

A mountain of black stone, hanging suspended in the air above low slopes crowded with shattered ice. It was drifting closer, and Udinaas sensed a malevolence emanating from the enormous, impossible conjuration – an emotion the tall, pelted creatures clearly sensed as well.

They stared for a moment longer, then broke. Fled past Udinaas—

—and the scene changed.

Battered bedrock, pulverized stone, roiling mists. Two tall figures appeared, dragging between them a third one – a woman, unconscious or dead, long dark brown hair unbound and trailing on the ground. Udinaas flinched upon recognizing one of the walking figures – that blinding armour, the iron-clad boots and silver cloak, the helmed face. *Menandore. Sister Dawn.* He sought to flee – she could not avoid seeing him – but found himself frozen in place.

He recognized the other woman as well, from fearfully carved statues left half buried in loam in the forest surrounding the Hiroth village. Piebald skin, grey and black, making her hard face resemble a war-mask. A cuirass of dulled, patchy iron. Chain and leather vambraces and greaves, a full-length cape of sealskin billowing out behind her. *Dapple, the fickle sister. Sukul Ankhadu.*

And he knew, then, the woman they dragged between them. Dusk, Sheltatha Lore. Scabandari's most cherished daughter, the Protectress of the Tiste Edur.

The two women halted, releasing the limp arms of the one between them, who dropped to the gritty bedrock as if dead. Two sets of wide, epicanthic Tiste eyes seemed to fix on Udinaas.

Menandore was the first to speak. 'I didn't expect to find you here.'

As Udinaas struggled to find a response to that, a man's voice at his side said, 'What have you done to her?'

The slave turned to see another Tiste, standing within an arm's reach from where Udinaas sat on the stool. Taller than the women facing him, he was wearing white enamelled armour, blood-spattered, smudged and scarred by sword-cuts. A broken helm was strapped to his right hip. His skin was white as ivory. Dried blood marked the left side of his face with a pattern like branched lightning. Fire had burned most of his hair away, and the skin of his pate was cracked, red and oozing.

Twin scabbarded longswords were slung on his back, the grips and pommels jutting up behind his broad shoulders.

'Nothing she didn't deserve,' Menandore replied in answer to the Tiste man's question.

The other woman bared her teeth. 'Our dear uncle had ambitions for this precious cousin of ours. Yet did he come when she screamed her need?'

The battle-scarred man stepped past the slave's position, his attention on the body of Sheltatha Lore. 'This is a dread mess. I would wash my hands of it – all of it.'

'But you can't,' Menandore said with strange glee. 'We're all poisoned by the mother's blood, after all—'

Sukul Ankhadu swung to her sister with the words, 'Her daughters have fared worse than poison! There is nothing balanced to this shattering of selves. Look at us! Spiteful bitches – Tiam's squalling heads rearing up again and again, generation after generation!' She stabbed a finger at the Tiste man. 'And what of you, Father? That she-nightmare sails out on feathered wings from the dark of another realm, legs spread oh so wide and inviting, and were you not first in line? Pure Osserc, First Son of Dark and Light, so precious! Yet there you were, weaving your blood with that whore – tell us, did you proclaim her your sister before or after you fucked her?'

If the venom of her words had any effect, there was no outward sign. The one named Osserc simply smiled and looked away. 'You shouldn't speak of your mother that way, Sukul. She died giving birth to you, after all—'

'She died giving birth to us all!' Sukul Ankhadu's raised hand closed into a fist that seemed to twist the air. 'Dies, and is reborn. Tiam and her children. Tiam and her lovers. Her thousand deaths, and yet *nothing changes*!'

Menandore spoke in a calm tone. 'And who have you been arguing with, Osserc?'

Osserc scowled. 'Anomander. He got the better of me this time. Upon consideration,' he continued after a moment, 'not surprising. The weapon of anger often proves stronger than cold reason's armour.' Then he shrugged. 'Even so, I delayed him long enough—'

'To permit Scabandari's escape?' Menandore asked. 'Why? Your kin or not, he's shown himself for what he truly is – a treacherous murderer.'

Osserc's brows rose mockingly and he regarded the unconscious woman lying on the ground between his daughters. 'Presumably, your cousin who's clearly suffered at your hands is not dead, then. Accordingly, I might point out that Scabandari did not murder Silchas Ruin—'

'True,' Sukul snapped, 'something far worse. Unless you think eating mud for eternity is a preferable fate.'

'Spare me the outrage,' Osserc sighed. 'As you so often note, dear child, treachery and betrayal is our extended family's most precious trait, or, if not precious, certainly its most popular one. In any case, I am done here. What do you intend doing with her?'

'We think Silchas might enjoy the company.'

Osserc stiffened. 'Two draconean Ascendants in the same grounds? You sorely test that Azath House, daughters.'

'Will Scabandari seek to free her?' Menandore asked.

'Scabandari is in no condition to free anyone,' Osserc replied, 'including himself.'

The two women were clearly startled by this. After a moment, Menandore asked, 'Who managed that?'

The man shrugged. 'Does it matter? It was Scabandari's conceit to think this world's gods had not the power to oppose him.' He paused then to eye his daughters speculatively, and said, 'Heed that as a warning, my dears. Mother Dark's *first* children were spawned without need of any sire. And, despite what Anomander might claim, they were *not* Tiste Andii.'

'We did not know this,' Menandore said.

'Well, now you do. Tread softly, children.'

Udinaas watched the tall figure walk away, then the slave gasped as Osserc's form blurred, shifted, unfolded to find a new shape. Huge, glittering gold and silver scales rippling as wings spread wide. A surge of power, and the enormous dragon was in the air.

Sukul Ankhadu and Menandore stared after him, until the dragon dwindled to a gleaming ember in the heavy sky, winked out and was gone.

Sukul grunted, then said, 'I'm surprised Anomander didn't kill him.'

'Something binds them, sister, of which not we nor anyone else knows a thing about. I am certain of it.'

'Perhaps. Or it might be something far simpler.'

'Such as?'

'They would the game continue,' Sukul said with a tight smile. 'And the pleasure would pale indeed were one to kill the other outright.'

Menandore's eyes fell to the motionless form of Sheltatha Lore. 'This one. She took a lover from among this world's gods, did she not?'

'For a time. Begetting two horrid little children.'

'Horrid? Daughters, then.'

Sukul nodded. 'And their father saw that clearly enough from the very start, for he named them appropriately.'

'Oh? And what were those names, sister?'

'Envy and Spite.'

Menandore smiled. 'This god – I think I would enjoy meeting him one day.'

'It is possible he would object to what we plan to do with Sheltatha Lore. Indeed, it is possible that even now he seeks our trail, so that he might prevent our revenge. Accordingly, as Osserc is wont to say, we should make haste.'

Udinaas watched as the two women moved apart, leaving their unconscious cousin where she lay.

Menandore faced her sister across the distance. 'Sheltatha's lover. That god – what is his name?'

Sukul's reply seemed to come from a vast distance, 'Draconus.'

Then the two women veered into dragons, of a size almost to match that of Osserc. One dappled, one blindingly bright.

The dappled creature lifted into the air, slid in a banking motion until she hovered over Sheltatha Lore's body. A taloned claw reached down and gathered her in its grasp.

Then the dragon rose higher to join her sister. And away they wheeled. Southward.

The scene quickly faded before the slave's eyes.

And, once more, Udinaas was sitting outside the Sengar longhouse, a half-scaled fish in his red, cracked hands, its facing eye staring up at him with that ever-disturbing look of witless surprise – an eye that he had seen, with the barest of variations, all morning and all afternoon, and now, as dusk closed round him, it stared yet again, mute and emptied of life. As if what he held was not a fish at all.

Just eyes. Dead, senseless eyes . . . Yet even the dead accuse.

'You have done enough, slave.'

Udinaas looked up.

Uruth and Mayen stood before him. Two Tiste women, neither dappled, neither blindingly bright. Just shades in faint, desultory variation.

Between them and a step behind, Feather Witch stood foremost among the attending slaves. Large eyes filled with feverish warnings, fixed on his own.

Udinaas bowed his head to Uruth. 'Yes, mistress.'

'Find a salve for those hands,' Uruth said.

'Thank you, mistress.'

The procession filed past, into the longhouse.

Udinaas stared down at the fish. Studied that eye a moment longer, then dug it out with his thumb.

Seren Pedac stood on the beach in the rain, watching the water in its ceaseless motion, the way the pelting rain transformed the surface into a muricated skin, grey and spider-haired as it swelled shoreward to break hissing, thin and sullen on the smooth stones.

Night had arrived, crawling out from the precious shadows. The dark hours were upon them all, a shawl of silence settling on the village behind her. She was thinking of the Letherii slaves.

Her people seemed particularly well suited to surrender. Freedom was an altar supplicants struggled to reach all their lives, clawing the smooth floor until blood spattered the gleaming, flawless stone, yet the truth was it remained for ever beyond the grasp of mortals. Even as any sacrifice was justified in its gloried name. For all that, she knew that blasphemy was a hollow crime. Freedom was no god, and if it was, and if it had a face turned upon its worshippers, its expression was mocking. A slave's chains stole something he or she had never owned.

The Letherii slaves in this village owed no debt. They served recognizable needs, and were paid in food and shelter. They could marry. Produce children who would not inherit the debts of their parents. The portions of their day allotted their tasks did not progress, did not devour ever more time from their lives. In all, the loss of freedom was shown to be almost meaningless to these kin of hers.

A child named Feather Witch. As if a witch from the distant past, awkwardly dressed, stiff and mannered as all outdated things appear to be, had stepped out from the histories. Womb-chosen caster of the tiles, who practised her arts of divination for the service of her community, rather than for the coins in a leather pouch. Perhaps the name had lost its meaning among these slaves. Perhaps there were no old tiles to be found, no solemn nights when fates gathered into a smudged, crack-laced path, the dread mosaic of destiny set out before one and all – with a hood-eyed woman-child overseeing the frightful ritual.

She heard the crunch of stones from near the river mouth and turned to see a male slave crouching down at the waterline. He thrust his hands into the cold, fresh water as if seeking absolution, or ice-numbing escape.

Curious, Seren Pedac walked over.

The glance he cast at her was guarded, diffident.

'Acquitor,' he said, 'these are fraught hours among the Edur. Words are best left unspoken.'

'We are not Edur, however,' she replied, 'are we?'

He withdrew his hands, and she saw that they were red and swollen. 'Emurlahn bleeds from the ground in these lands, Acquitor.'

'None the less, we are Letherii.'

His grin was wry. 'Acquitor, I am a slave.'

'I have been thinking on that. Slavery. And freedom from debt. How do you weigh the exchange?'

He settled back on his haunches, water dripping from his hands, and seemed to study the clear water swirling past. The rain had fallen off and mist was edging out from the forest. 'The debt remains, Acquitor. It governs every Letherii slave among the Edur, yet it is a debt that can never be repaid.'

She stared down at him, shocked. 'But that is madness!'

He smiled once more. 'By such things we are all measured. Why did you imagine that mere slavery would change it?'

Seren was silent for a time, studying the man crouched at the edge of the flowing water. Not at all unhandsome, yet, now that she knew, she could see his indebtedness, the sure burden upon him, and the truth that, for him, for every child he might sire, there would be no absolving the stigma. It was brutal. It was . . . Letherii. 'There is a slave,' she said, 'who is named Feather Witch.'

He seemed to wince. 'Yes, our resident caster of the tiles.'

'Ah. I had wondered. How many generations has that woman's family dwelt as a slave among the Edur?'

'A score, perhaps.'

'Yet the talent persisted? Within this world of Kurald Emurlahn? That is extraordinary.'

'Is it?' He shrugged and rose. 'When you and your companions are guest to Hannan Mosag this night, Feather Witch will cast.'

Sudden chill rippled through Seren Pedac. She drew a

deep breath and released it slow and heavy. 'There is . . . risk, doing such a thing.'

'That is known, Acquitor.'

'Yes, I see now that it would be.'

'I must return to my tasks,' he said, not meeting her eyes.

'Of course. I hope my delaying you does not yield grief.'

He smiled yet again, but said nothing.

She watched him walk up the strand.

Buruk the Pale stood wrapped in his rain cape before the Nerek fire. Hull Beddict was nearby, positioned slightly behind the merchant, hooded and withdrawn.

Seren walked to Buruk's side, studied the struggling flames from which smoke rose to hang smeared, stretched and motionless above them. The night's chill had seeped into the Acquitor's bones and the muscles of her neck had tightened in response. A headache was building behind her eyes.

'Seren Pedac,' Buruk sighed. 'I am unwell.'

She heard as much in his weak, shaky voice. 'You ran long and far,' she said.

'Only to find myself standing still, here before a sickly fire. I am not so foolish as to be unaware of my crimes.'

Hull grunted behind them. 'Would those be crimes already committed, or those to come, Buruk the Pale?'

'The distinction is without meaning,' the merchant replied. 'Tonight,' he said, straightening himself, 'we shall be made guests of Hannan Mosag. Are you both ready?'

'The formality,' Seren said, 'is the least of what this meeting portends, Buruk. The Warlock King intends to make his position unambiguous. We will hear a warning, which we are expected to deliver to the delegation when it arrives.'

'Intentions are similarly without relevance, Acquitor. I am without expectations, whereas one of us three is consumed by nothing else. Rehearsed statements, dire pronouncements, all await this fell visit.' Buruk swung his head

283

to regard Hull Beddict. 'You still think like a child, don't you? Clay figurines sunk to their ankles in the sand, one here, one there, standing just so. One says this, the other says that, then you reach down and rearrange them accordingly. Scenes, vistas, stark with certainty. Poor Hull Beddict, who took a knife to his heart so long ago that he twists daily to confirm it's still there.'

'If you would see me as a child,' the huge man said in growl, 'that is your error, not mine, Buruk.'

'A gentle warning,' the merchant replied, 'that you are not among children.'

Buruk then gestured them to follow and made his way towards the citadel.

Falling in step beside Hull – with the merchant a half-dozen paces ahead, barely visible in the dark – Seren asked, 'Have you met this Hannan Mosag?'

'I have been guest here before, Seren.'

'Of the Warlock King's?'

'No, of the Sengar household. Close to the royal blood, the eldest son, Fear Sengar, is Hannan Mosag's Marshal of War – not his actual title, but it serves well as translation.'

Seren considered this for a moment, then frowned and said, 'You anticipate, then, that friends will be present tonight.'

'I had, but it is not to be. None of the Sengar barring the patriarch, Tomad, and his wife are in the village. The sons have left.'

'Left? Where?'

Hull shook his head. 'I don't know. It is . . . odd. I have to assume Fear and his brothers will be back in time for the treaty meeting.'

'Is the Warlock King aware of the blood-ties you have bound with Binadas Sengar?'

'Of course.'

Buruk the Pale had reached the bridge leading to the inner ward. The mists had thickened into fog, obscuring the world surrounding the three Letherii. There was no-one else in sight, nor any sound beyond the crunch of their feet on the pebbled path. The massive bulk of the citadel rose before them.

The broad, arched entranceway was lurid with firelight.

'He has no guards,' Seren murmured.

'None that can be seen,' Hull Beddict replied.

Buruk climbed the two shallow steps to the landing, paused to release the clasps of his cape, then strode inside. A moment later Seren and Hull followed.

The long hall was virtually empty. The feast table was a much smaller version than what normally occupied the centre axis of the room, as evinced by the wear patterns on the vast rug covering the wood-slatted floor. And off to the right, Seren saw, stood that table, pushed flush against the tapestry-lined wall.

Near the far end of the chamber, the modest feast table had been positioned crossways, with three high-backed chairs awaiting the Letherii on this side. Opposite them sat the Warlock King, already well into his meal. Five Edur warriors stood in shadows behind Hannan Mosag, motionless.

They must be the K'risnan. Sorcerors . . . they look young.

The Warlock King waited until they had divested themselves of their outer clothing, then gestured them forward, and said in passable Letherii, 'Join me, please. I dislike cold food, so here you see me, rudely filling my belly.'

Buruk the Pale bowed from the waist, then said, 'I did not think we were late, sire—'

'You're not, but I am not one for formality. Indeed, I am often tried by mere courtesy. Forgive, if you will, this king's impatience.'

'Appetites care little for demands of decorum, sire,' Buruk said, approaching.

'I was confident a Letherii would understand. Now,' he suddenly rose, the gesture halting the three in their tracks, 'I proclaim as my guests Buruk the Pale, Acquitor Seren Pedac and Sentinel Hull Beddict. Seat yourselves, please. I only devour what my cooks prepare for me.'

His was a voice one could listen to, hours passing without notice, discomforts forgotten. Hannan Mosag was, Seren realized, a very dangerous king.

Buruk the Pale took the central seat, Seren moving to the one on the merchant's left, Hull to the right. As they settled into the Blackwood chairs, the Warlock King sat down once more and reached for a goblet. 'Wine from Trate,' he said, 'to honour my guests.'

'Acquired through peaceful trade, one hopes,' Buruk said.

'Alas, I am afraid not,' Hannan Mosag replied, glancing up almost diffidently into the merchant's eyes, then away once more. 'But we are all hardy folk here at this table, I'm sure.'

Buruk collected his goblet and sipped. He seemed to consider, then sighed, 'Only slightly soured by provenance, sire.'

The Warlock King frowned. 'I had assumed it was supposed to taste that way.'

'Not surprising, sire, once one becomes used to it.'

'The comfort that is familiarity, Buruk the Pale, proves a powerful arbiter once again.'

'The Letherii often grow restless with familiarity, alas, and as a consequence often see it as a diminishment in quality.'

'That is too complicated a notion, Buruk,' Hannan Mosag said. 'We've not yet drunk enough to dance with words, unless of course you eased your thirst back in your lodging, in which case I find myself at a disadvantage.'

Buruk reached for a sliver of smoked fish. 'Horribly sober, I'm afraid. If disadvantage exists, then it belongs to us.'

'How so?'

'Well, sire, you honour us with blood-tainted wine, a most unbalancing gesture. More, we have received word of the slaughter of Letherii seal hunters. The blood has grown deep enough to drown us.'

It seemed Buruk the Pale was not interested in veiled

exchanges. A curious tactic, Seren reflected, and one that, she suspected, King Ezgara Diskanar would not appreciate in the circumstances.

'I am sure the few remaining kin of the butchered tusked seals would concur, tugged as they are in that fell tide,' the Warlock King said in a musing sort of way.

'Word has also reached us,' Buruk continued, 'of the ships' return to Trate's harbour. The holds that should have held the costly harvest were inexplicably empty.'

'Empty? That was careless.'

Buruk leaned back in his chair, closing both hands about the goblet as he studied the dark contents.

Hull Beddict suddenly spoke. 'Warlock King, I for one feel no displeasure in the resolution of that treacherous event. Those hunters defied long-established agreements, and so deserved their fate.'

'Sentinel,' Hannan Mosag said, a new seriousness to his tone, 'I doubt their grieving kin would agree. Your words are cold. I am given to understand that the notion of debt is a pervasive force among your people. These hapless harvesters were likely *Indebted*, were they not? Their desperation preyed upon by masters as heartless in their sentiments as you have just been.' He scanned the three Letherii before him. 'Am I alone in my grief?'

'The potential consequences of that slaughter promise yet more grief, sire,' Buruk the Pale said.

'And is that inevitable, merchant?'

Buruk blinked.

'It is,' Hull Beddict answered, leaning forward in his chair. 'Warlock King, is there any doubt upon whom that grief should be visited? You spoke of cold masters, and yes, it is their blood that should have been spilled in this instance. Even so, they are masters only because the Indebted accept them as such. This is the poison of gold as the only measure of worth. Those harvesters are no less guilty for their desperation, sire. They are all participants in the same game.'

'Hull Beddict,' Buruk said, 'speaks only for himself.'

'Are we not all speaking only for ourselves?' Hannan Mosag asked.

'As desirable as that would be, sire, it would be a lie to make such claims – for myself, for you.'

The Warlock King pushed his plate away and leaned back. 'And what of the Acquitor, then? She does not speak at all.' Calm, soft eyes fixed on her. 'You have escorted these men, Acquitor Seren Pedac.'

'I have, sire,' she replied, 'and so my task is done.'

'And in your silence you seek to absolve yourself of all to come of this meeting.'

'Such is the role of Acquitor, sire.'

'Unlike that of, say, Sentinel.'

Hull Beddict flinched, then said, 'I ceased being Sentinel long ago, sire.'

'Indeed? Then why, may I ask, are you here?'

'He volunteered himself,' Buruk answered. 'It was not for me to turn him away.'

'True. That responsibility, as I understand the matter, belonged to the Acquitor.' Hannan Mosag studied her, waiting.

'I did not feel compelled to deny Hull Beddict's decision to accompany us, sire.'

'Yes,' the Warlock King replied. 'Isn't that curious?'

Sweat prickled beneath her damp clothes. 'Permit me to correct myself, sire. I did not believe I would succeed, had I attempted to deny Hull Beddict. And so I decided to maintain the illusion of my authority.'

Hannan Mosag's sudden smile was profoundly disarming. 'An honest reply. Well done, Acquitor. You may now go.'

She rose shakily, bowed. 'It was a pleasure meeting you, Warlock King.'

'I reciprocate the sentiment, Acquitor. I would we speak later, you and I.'

'I am at your call, sire.'

Not meeting the eyes of her fellow Letherii, Seren stepped round the chair, then made her way outside.

The Warlock King had denied her the burden of witnessing all that followed this night between himself, Hull and Buruk. On a personal level, it stung, but she knew that he might very well have just saved her life.

In any case, all that had needed to be said had been said. She wondered if Hull Beddict had understood that. There was no doubt that Buruk had.

We are sorely unbalanced, indeed. Hannan Mosag, the Warlock King, wants peace.

The rain had returned. She drew her cloak tighter about her shoulders.

Poor Hull.

Someone edged to his side. Udinaas glanced over to see Hulad, the familiar lined face drawn, troubled and wan. 'Are you all right?'

Hulad shrugged. 'I was remembering the last time she cast, Udinaas. My nerves are ruined this night.'

Udinaas said nothing. It was with some measure of surprise that he himself was not feeling something similar. Changes had come to him, that much was clear. Feather Witch, he'd heard, had felt the brunt of Mayen's displeasure. It seemed Uruth's fury with the Nerek blessing, while delivered with quiet brevity, had been harsh in its content. Subsequently, Mayen had taken a switch to her slave's back.

Of course, when it came to dealing with slaves, justice was without meaning.

He watched her move to stand in the centre of the cleared area. There were more slaves crowding the vast barn than there had been the last time. Enticed by the fraught tales of the past casting, no doubt. *Almost as good as the Drownings.*

Feather Witch sat down on the hard-packed floor and everyone else quickly followed suit, moving with an

289

alacrity that she herself was not able to match, bruised and battered as she was. Udinaas saw the strain in her movements, and wondered to what extent she blamed him for her suffering. Mayen was no harder a mistress than any other Edur. Beatings were mercifully uncommon – most egregious crimes committed by slaves were punished with swift death. If one was not going to kill a slave, what value incapacitating them?

The last casting had not proceeded so far as to the actual scattering of the tiles. The Wyval's sudden arrival had torn Feather Witch from the realm of the manifest Holds. Udinaas felt the first tremors of anticipation in his chest.

Sudden silence as Feather Witch closed her eyes and lowered her head, her yellow hair closing over her face like twin curtains. She shuddered, then drew a deep, ragged breath, and looked up with empty eyes, in which the black smear of a starless night sky slowly grew, as from behind thinning fog, followed by spirals of luminous light.

The Beginnings swept upon her with its mask of terror, twisting her features into something primal and chilling. She was, Udinaas knew, gazing upon the Abyss, suspended in the vast oblivion of all that lay between the stars. There were no Makers yet, nor the worlds they would fashion.

And now the Fulcra. Fire, Dolmen and the Errant. The Errant, who gives shape to the Holds—

'*Walk with me to the Holds.*'

The Letherii slaves loosed long-held breaths.

'*We stand upon Dolmen, and all is as it should be.*' Yet there was a strain to her voice. '*To live is to wage war against the Abyss. In our growth we find conquest, in our stagnation we find ourselves under siege, and in our dying our last defences are assailed. These are the truths of the Beast Hold. Blade and Knuckles, the war we cannot escape. Age has clawed the face and gouged the eyes of the Elder. He is scarred and battle-ravaged. Crone cackles with bitter spit, and twitches with dreams of flight. Seer's mouth moves yet there are none to hear. Shaman wails the weft of the dead in fields of bones, yet believes none of the patterns*

290

he fashions from those scattered remains. Tracker walks his steps assured and purposeful, to belie that he wanders lost.'

She fell silent.

Muttered voices from the crowd. This was a cold invitation into the Holds.

Errant guard us, we are in trouble. Dread trouble.

Hulad plucked at his arm, gestured to the far wall where shadows lay thick as muddy water. A figure stood there, back to the dirt-spattered plaster wall. The Acquitor. Seren Pedac.

Feather Witch remained silent, and unease grew.

Udinaas climbed to his feet and threaded his way through the crowd, ignoring the glares from the slaves he edged past. He reached the back wall and made his way along it until he reached the Acquitor's side.

'What has gone wrong?' she asked.

'I don't know—'

Feather Witch began speaking once more. *'Bone Perch now stands as a throne that none shall occupy, for its shape has become inimical to taming. The throne's back is now hunched, the ribs drawn downward, the shoulder blades steep and narrow. The arms, upon which a ruler's arms would rest, are risen now, each in the visage of a wolf, and in their eyes burns savage life.'* She paused, then intoned, *'The Hold of the Beast has found Twin Rulers.'*

'That is impossible,' Seren Pedac murmured.

'And before us now . . . the Hold of the Azath. Its stones bleed. The earth heaves and steams. A silent, unceasing scream shakes the branches of the ancient trees. The Azath stands besieged.'

Voices rose in denial, the slaves shifting about.

'Ice Hold!' Feather Witch shouted, head tilted back, teeth bared.

Silence once more, all eyes fixing on her.

'Riven tomb! Corpses lie scattered before the sundered threshold. Urquall Jaghuthan taezmalas. They are not here to mend the damage. They are forgotten, and the ice itself cannot recall the weight of their passage.'

291

'What language was that?' Seren Pedac asked.

'Jaghut,' Udinaas replied, then snapped his mouth shut.

'What is Jaghut?'

He shrugged. 'Forgers of the Ice, Acquitor. It is of no matter. They are gone.'

She gripped his arm and swung him round. 'How do you know this?'

'*The Hold of the Dragon*,' Feather Witch said, her skin glistening with sweat. '*Eleint Tiam purake setoram n'brael buras—*'

'Draconean words,' Udinaas said, suddenly revelling in his secret knowledge. ' "Children of the Mother Tiam lost in all that they surrendered." More or less. The poetry suffers in translation—'

'*The Eleint would destroy all in their paths to achieve vengeance,*' Feather Witch said in a grating voice. '*As we all shall see in the long night to come. The Queen lies dead and may never again rise. The Consort writhes upon a tree and whispers with madness of the time of his release. The Liege is lost, dragging chains in a world where to walk is to endure, and where to halt is to be devoured. The Knight strides his own doomed path, soon to cross blades with his own vengeance. Gate rages with wild fire. Wyval—*'

Her head snapped back as if struck by an invisible hand, and blood sprayed from her mouth and nose. She gasped, then smiled a red smile. '*Locqui Wyval waits. The Lady and the Sister dance round each other, each on her own side of the world. Blood-Drinker waits as well, waits to be found. Path-Shaper knows fever in his fell blood and staggers on the edge of the precipice.*

'*Thus! The Holds, save one.*'

'Someone stop her,' Seren Pedac hissed, releasing Udinaas's arm.

And now it was his turn to grasp her, hold her back. She snapped a glare at him and twisted to escape his grip.

He pulled her close. 'This is *not your world*, Acquitor.

292

No-one invited you. Now, stand here and say nothing . . . *or leave!'*

'*The Empty Hold has become . . .*' Feather Witch's smile broadened, '*very crowded indeed. 'Ware the brothers! Listen! Blood weaves a web that will trap the entire world! None shall escape, none shall find refuge!*' Her right hand snapped out, spraying the ancient tiles onto the floor. From the rafters far above pigeons burst out of the gloom, a wild, chaotic beat of wings. They circled in a frenzy, feathers skirling down.

'*The Watchers stand in place as if made of stone! Their faces are masks of horror. The Mistresses dance with thwarted desire.*' Her eyes were closed, yet she pointed to one tile after another, proclaiming their identity in a harsh, rasping voice. '*The Wanderers have broken through the ice and cold darkness comes with its deathly embrace. The Walkers cannot halt in the growing torrent that pulls them ever onward. The Saviours—*'

'What is she saying?' Seren Pedac demanded. 'She has made them all plural – the players within the Hold of the Empty Throne – this makes no sense—'

'*—face one another, and both are doomed, and in broken reflection so stand the Betrayers, and this is what lies before us, before us all.*' Her voice trailed away with her last words, and once more her chin settled, head tilting forward, long hair sweeping down to cover her face.

The pigeons overhead whipped round and round, the only sound in the massive barn.

'Contestants to the Empty Throne,' Feather Witch whispered in a tone heavy with sorrow. '*Blood and madness . . .*'

Udinaas slowly released his grip on Seren Pedac.

She made no move, as frozen in place as everyone else present.

Udinaas grunted, amused, and said to the Acquitor, 'She's not slept well lately, you see.'

* * *

Seren Pedac staggered outside, into a solid sheet of cold rain. A hissing deluge on the path's pebbles, tiny rivers cutting through the sands, the forest beyond seeming pulled down by streaming threads and ropes. An angry susurration from the direction of the river and the sea. As if the world was collapsing in melt water.

She blinked against the cold tears.

And recalled the play of Edur children, the oblivious chatter of a thousand moments ago, so far back in her mind now as to echo like someone else's reminiscence. Of times weathered slick and shapeless.

Memories rushing, rushing down to the sea.

Like children in flight.

CHAPTER EIGHT

Where are the days we once held
So loose in our sure hands?
When did these racing streams
Carve depthless caves beneath our feet?
And how did this scene stagger
And shift to make fraught our deft lies
In the places where youth will meet,
In the lands of our proud dreams?
Where, among all you before me,
Are the faces I once knew?

Words etched into the wall,
K'rul Belfry, Darujhistan

I n the battle that saw Theradas Buhn blooded, a Merude
cutlass had laid open his right cheek, snapping the bone
beneath the eye and cutting through maxilla and the
upper half of his mandible. The savage wound had been
slow to heal, and the thread that had been used to seal the
gaping hole into his mouth had festered the flesh before his
comrades could return the warrior to a nearby Hiroth
encampment, where a healer had done what she could –
driving out the infection, knitting the bones. The result
was a long, crooked scar within a seamed concave depression
on that side of his face, and a certain flat look to his eyes
that hinted of unseen wounds that would never heal.

Trull Sengar sat with the others five paces from the edge

of the ice-field, watching Theradas as he paced back and forth along the crusted line of ice and snow, the red-tipped fox fur of his cloak flashing in the gusting wind. The Arapay lands were behind them now, and with them the grudging hospitality of that subjugated Edur tribe. The Hiroth warriors were alone, and before them stretched a white, shattered landscape.

It looked lifeless, but the Arapay had spoken of night hunters, strange, fur-shrouded killers who came out of the darkness wielding jagged blades of black iron. They took body parts as trophies, to the point of leaving limbless, headless torsos in their wake. None had ever been captured, and the bodies of those who fell were never left where they lay.

Even so, they tended to prey only upon paired Edur hunters. More formidable groups were generally left alone. The Arapay called them *Jheck*, which meant, roughly, *standing wolves*.

'There are eyes upon us,' Theradas pronounced in his thick, blunted voice.

Fear Sengar shrugged. 'The ice wastes are not as lifeless as they appear. Hares, foxes, ground owls, white wolves, bears, aranag—'

'The Arapay spoke of huge beasts,' Rhulad cut in. 'Brown-furred and tusked – we saw the ivory—'

'Old ivory, Rhulad,' Fear said. 'Found in the ice. It is likely such beasts are no more.'

'The Arapay say otherwise.'

Theradas grunted. 'And they live in fear of the ice wastes, Rhulad, and so have filled them with nightmare beasts and demons. It is this: we will see what we see. Are you done your repasts? We are losing daylight.'

'Yes,' Fear said, rising, 'we should go on.'

Rhulad and Midik Buhn moved out to the flanks. Both wore bear furs, black and silver-collared. Their hands, within fur-lined gauntlets – Arapay gifts – were wrapped round the long spears they used as walking sticks, testing the packed snow before them with each step. Theradas moved to point, fifteen paces ahead, leaving Trull, Fear and Binadas travelling as the core group, pulling the two sleds packed with leather satchels filled with supplies.

It was said that, further out in the wastes, there was water beneath the ice, salt-laden remnants from an inland sea, and cavernous pockets hidden beneath thin-skin mantles of snow. Treachery waited underfoot, forcing them to travel slowly.

The wind swept down upon them, biting at exposed skin, and they were forced to lean forward against its gusting, frigid blasts.

Despite the furs enshrouding him, Trull felt the shock of that sudden cold, a force mindless and indifferent, yet eager to steal. Flooding his air passages in a numbing assault. And within that current, a faint smell of death.

The Edur wrapped swaths of wool about their faces, leaving the barest of slits for their eyes. Conversations were quickly abandoned, and they walked in silence, the crunch of their fur-lined moccasins muffled and distant.

The sun's warmth and turn of season could not win the war in this place. The snow and ice rose on the wind to glitter overhead, mocking the sun itself with twin mirror images, leading Trull to suspect that the wind held close to the ground, whilst high overhead the suspended ice crystals hovered unmoving, inured to the passing of seasons, of years.

He tilted his head to stare upward for a moment, wondering if that glistening, near-opaque canopy above them held the frozen memories of the past, minute images locked in each crystal, bearing witness to all that had occurred below. A multitude of fates, perhaps reaching back to when there was sea, in place of the ice. Did unknown creatures ply the waters in arcane, dugout canoes all those thousands of years ago? Would they one day become these Jheck?

The Letherii spoke of Holds, that strange pantheon of

elements, and among them there was the Hold of Ice. As if winter was born of sorcery, as if ice and snow were instruments of wilful destruction. Something of that notion was present in Edur legends as well. Ice plunging down to steal the land that was soaked in Tiste blood, the brutal theft of hard-won territories committed as an act of vengeance, perhaps the gelid flowering of some curse uttered in a last breath, a final defiance.

The sentiment, then – if one such existed – was of old enmity. Ice was a thief, of life, land and righteous reward. Bound in death and blood, an eternal prison. From all this, it could earn hatred.

They continued through the day, moving slowly but steadily, through jumbled fields of broken, upthrust shards of ice that in the distance seemed simply white, but when neared was revealed to possess countless shades of greens, blues and browns. They crossed flats of wind-sculpted, hard-packed snow that formed rippled patterns as smooth as sand. Strange fault lines where unseen forces had sheered the ice, pushing one side up against the other, grinding opposing paths as if the solid world beneath them jostled in wayward migration.

Towards late afternoon, a muted shout from Theradas halted them. Trull, who had been walking with his eyes on the ground before him, looked up at the muffled sound and saw that Theradas was standing before something, gesturing them forward with a fur-wrapped hand. A few moments later they reached his side.

A broad crevasse cut across their path, the span at least fifteen paces. The sheer walls of ice swept down into darkness, and from its depths rose a strange smell.

'Salt,' Binadas said after pulling away his face-covering. 'Tidal pools.'

Rhulad and Midik joined them from the flanks. 'It seems to stretch to the very horizon,' Rhulad said.

'The break looks recent,' Binadas observed, crouching at the edge. 'As if the surface is shrinking.'

'Perhaps summer has managed a modest alteration to these wastes,' Fear mused. 'We have passed sealed faults that might be the remnant scars from similar wounds in the past.'

'How will we cross?' Midik asked.

'I could draw shadows from below,' Binadas said, then shook his head, 'but the notion makes me uneasy. If there are spirits within, they might well prove unruly. There are layers of sorcery here, woven in the snow and ice, and they do not welcome Emurlahn.'

'Get out the ropes,' Fear said.

'Dusk approaches.'

'If necessary we will camp below.'

Trull shot Fear a look. 'What if it closes whilst we are down there?'

'I do not think that likely,' Fear said. 'Besides, we will remain unseen this night, hidden as we will be in the depths. If there are indeed beasts in this land – though we've seen no true sign as yet – then I would rather we took every opportunity to avoid them.'

Wet pebbles skidded under his moccasins as Trull alighted, stepping clear of the ropes. He looked around, surprised at the faint green glow suffusing the scene. They were indeed on a seabed. Salt had rotted the ice at the edges, creating vast caverns crowded with glittering pillars. The air was cold, turgid and rank.

Off to one side Midik and Rhulad had drawn bundles of wood out from a pack and were preparing a cookfire. Binadas and Fear were reloading the sleds to keep the food satchels off the wet ground, and Theradas had set off to scout the caverns.

Trull strode to a shallow pool and crouched down at its edge. The saline water swarmed with tiny grey shrimps. Barnacles crowded the waterline.

'The ice is dying.'

At Fear's words behind him, Trull rose and faced his brother. 'Why do you say that?'

299

'The salt gnaws its flesh. We are at the lowest region of the ancient seabed, I believe. Where the last of the water gathered, then slowly evaporated. Those columns of salt are all that remains. If the entire basin was like this place, then the canopy of ice would have collapsed—'

'Perhaps it does just that,' Binadas suggested, joining them. 'In cycles over thousands of years. Collapse, then the salt begins its work once again.'

Trull stared into the gloomy reaches. 'I cannot believe those pillars can hold up all this ice. There must be a cycle of collapse, as Binadas has said.' His eyes caught movement, then Theradas emerged, and Trull saw that the warrior had his sword out.

'There is a path,' Theradas said. 'And a place of gathering. We are not the first to have come down here.'

Rhulad and Midik joined them. No-one spoke for a time.

Then Fear nodded and asked, 'How recent are the signs, Theradas?'

'Days.'

'Binadas and Trull, go with Theradas to this place of gathering. I will remain here with the Unblooded.'

The path began twenty paces in from the crevasse, a trail cleared of cobbles and detritus that wound between the rough, crystalline columns of salt. Melt water dripped from the rotting ceiling in a steady downpour. Theradas led them onward another thirty paces, where the path ended at the edge of a vast roughly domed expanse devoid of pillars.

Near the centre squatted a low, misshapen altar stone. Votive offerings surrounded it – shells, mostly, among which the odd piece of carved ivory was visible. Yet Trull spared it but a momentary glance, for his gaze had been drawn to the far wall.

A sheer plane of ice a hundred paces or more across, rising in a tilted overhang – a wall in which countless beasts had been caught in mid-stampede, frozen in full flight. Antlers projected from the ice, heads and shoulders

– still solid and immobile – and forelegs lifted or stretched forward. Frost-rimed eyes dully reflected the muted blue-green light. Deeper within, the blurred shapes of hundreds more.

Stunned by the vista, Trull slowly walked closer, round the altar, half expecting at any moment to see the charging beasts burst into sudden motion, onrushing, to crush them all beneath countless hoofs.

As he neared, he saw heaped bodies near the base, beasts that had fallen out from the retreating ice, had thawed, eventually collapsing into viscid pools.

Tiny black flies rose in clouds from the decaying flesh and hide, swarmed towards Trull as if determined to defend their feast. He halted, waved his hands until they dispersed and began winging back to the rotting carcasses. The beasts – caribou – had been running on snow, a packed layer knee-deep above the seabed. He could still see the panic in their eyes – and there, smeared behind an arm's length of ice, the head and shoulders of an enormous wolf, silver-haired and amber-eyed, running alongside a caribou, shoulder to shoulder. The wolf's head was raised, jaws open, close to the victim's neck. Canines as long as Trull's thumb gleamed beneath peeled-back lips.

Nature's drama, life unheeding of the cataclysm that rushed upon it from behind – or above. The brutal hand of a god as indifferent as the beasts themselves.

Binadas came to his side. 'This was born of a warren,' he said.

Trull nodded. Sorcery. Nothing else made sense. 'A god.'

'Perhaps, but not necessarily so, brother. Some forces need only be unleashed. A natural momentum then burgeons.'

'The Hold of Ice,' Trull said. 'Such as the Letherii describe in their faith.'

'The Hand of the Watcher,' Binadas said, 'who waited until the war was done before striding forward to unleash his power.'

301

Trull had thought himself more knowledgeable than most Edur warriors regarding the old legends of their people. With Binadas's words echoing in his head, however, he felt woefully ignorant. 'Where have they gone?' he asked. 'Those powers of old? Why do we dwell as if . . . as if *alone*?'

His brother shrugged, ever reluctant to surrender his reserve, his mindful silence. 'We remain alone,' he finally said, 'to preserve the sanctity of our past.'

Trull considered this, his gaze travelling over the tableau before him, those dark, murky lives that could not outrun their doom, then said, 'Our cherished truths are vulnerable.'

'To challenge, yes.'

'And the salt gnaws at the ice beneath us, until our world grows perilously thin beneath our feet.'

'Until what was frozen . . . thaws.'

Trull took a step closer to the one of the charging caribou. 'What thaws in turn collapses and falls to the ground. And rots, Binadas. The past is covered in flies.'

His brother walked towards the altar, and said, 'The ones who kneel before this shrine were here only a few days ago.'

'They did not come the way we did.'

'No doubt there are other paths into this underworld.'

Trull glanced over at Theradas, only now recalling his presence. The warrior stood at the threshold, his breath pluming in the air.

'We should return to the others,' Binadas said. 'We have far to walk tomorrow.'

The night passed, damp, cold, the melt water ceaselessly whispering. Each Edur stood watch in turn, wrapped in furs and weapons at the ready. But there was nothing to see in the dull, faintly luminescent light. Ice, water and stone, death, hungry motion and impermeable bones, a blind triumvirate ruling a gelid realm.

Just before dawn the company rose, ate a quick meal,

then Rhulad clambered up the ropes, trusting to the spikes driven into the ice far overhead, about two-thirds of the way, where the fissure narrowed in one place sufficient to permit a cross-over to the north wall. Beyond that point, Rhulad began hammering new spikes into the ice. Splinters and shards rained down on the waiters below for a time, then there came a distant shout from Rhulad. Midik went to the ropes and began climbing, while Trull and Fear bound the food packs to braided leather lines. The sleds would be pulled up last.

'Today,' Binadas said, 'we will have to be careful. They will know we were here, that we found their shrine.'

Trull glanced over. 'But we did not desecrate it.'

'Perhaps our presence alone was sufficient outrage, brother.'

The sun was above the horizon by the time the Edur warriors were assembled on the other side of the crevasse, the sleds loaded and ready. The sky was clear and there was no wind, yet the air was bitter cold. The sun's fiery ball was flanked on either side by smaller versions – sharper and brighter than last time, as if in the course of the night just past the world above them had completed its transformation from the one they knew to something strange and forbidding, inimical to life.

Theradas in the lead once more, they set out.

Ice crunching underfoot, the hiss and clatter of the antler-rimmed sled runners, and a hissing sound both close and distant, as if silence had itself grown audible, a sound that Trull finally understood was the rush of his own blood, woven in and around the rhythm of his breath, the drum of his heart. The glare burned his eyes. His lungs stung with every rush of air.

The Edur did not belong in this landscape. *The Hold of Ice. Feared by the Letherii. Stealer of life – why has Hannan Mosag sent us here?*

Theradas halted and turned about. 'Wolf tracks,' he said, 'heavy enough to break through the crust of snow.'

303

They reached him, stopped the sleds. Trull drew the harness from his aching shoulders.

The tracks cut across their route, heading west. They were huge.

'These belong to a creature such as the one we saw in the ice last night,' Binadas said. 'What do they hunt? We've seen nothing.'

Fear grunted, then said, 'That does not mean much, brother. We are not quiet travellers, with these sleds.'

'Even so,' Binadas replied, 'herds leave sign. We should have come upon something, by now.'

They resumed the journey.

Shortly past midday Fear called a halt for another meal. The plain of ice stretched out flat and featureless on all sides.

'There's nothing to worry about out here,' Rhulad said, sitting on one of the sleds. 'We can see anyone coming . . . or any*thing*, for that matter. Tell us, Fear, how much farther will we go? Where is this gift that Hannan Mosag wants us to find?'

'Another day to the north,' Fear replied.

'If it is indeed a gift,' Trull asked, 'who is offering it?'

'I do not know.'

No-one spoke for a time.

Trull studied the hard-packed snow at his feet, his unease deepening. Something ominous hung in the still, frigid air. Their solitude suddenly seemed threatening, absence a promise of unknown danger. Yet he was among blood kin, among Hiroth warriors. *Thus.*

Still, why does this gift stink of death?

Another night. The tents were raised, a meal cooked, then the watches were set. Trull's was first. He walked the perimeter of their camp, spear in hand, in a continuous circuit in order to keep awake. The food in his stomach made him drowsy, and the sheer emptiness of the ice wastes seemed to project a force that dulled concentration.

Overhead the sky was alive with strange, shifting hues that rose and fell in disconnected patterns. He had seen such things before, in the deepest winter in Hiroth lands, but never as sharp, never as flush, voicing a strange hissing song as of broken glass crunching underfoot.

When it was time, he awoke Theradas. The warrior emerged from his tent and rose, adjusting his fur cloak until it wrapped him tightly, then drawing his sword. He glared at the lively night sky, but said nothing.

Trull crawled into the tent. The air within was damp. Ice had formed on the tent walls, etching maps of unknown worlds on the stretched, waxy fabric. From outside came the steady footsteps of Theradas as he walked his rounds. The sound followed Trull into sleep.

Disjointed dreams followed. He saw Mayen, naked in the forest, settling down atop a man, then writhing with hungry lust. He stumbled closer, ever seeking to see that man's face, to discover who it was – and instead he found himself lost, the forest unreadable, unrecognizable, a sensation he had never experienced before, and it left him terrified. Trembling on his knees in the wet loam, while from somewhere beyond he could hear her cries of pleasure, bestial and rhythmic.

And desire rose within him. Not for Mayen, but for what she had found, in her wild release, closing down into the moment, into the present, future and past without meaning. A moment unmindful of consequences. His hunger became a pain within him, lodged like a broken knife-tip in his chest, cutting with each ragged breath, and in his dream he cried out, as if answering Mayen's own voice, and he heard her laugh with recognition. A laugh inviting him to join her world.

Mayen, his brother's betrothed. A detached part of his mind remained cool and objective, almost sardonic in its self-regard. Understanding the nature of this web, this sideways envy and his own burgeoning appetites.

Edur males were slow to such things. It was the reason

305

betrothal and marriage followed at least a decade – often two – of full adulthood. Edur women arrived at their womanly hungers far earlier in their lives. It was whispered, among the men, that they often made use of the Letherii slaves, but Trull doubted the truth of that. It seemed . . . inconceivable.

The detached self was amused by that, as if derisive of Trull's own naivety.

He awoke chilled, weak with doubts and confusion, and lay for a time in the pale half-light that preceded dawn, watching his breath plume in the close air of the tent.

Something gnawed at him, but it was a long time before he realized what it was. No footsteps.

Trull scrambled from the tent, stumbling on the snow and ice, and straightened.

It was Rhulad's watch. Near the dead fire, the hunched, bundled form of his brother, seated with hooded head bowed.

Trull strode up to stand behind Rhulad. Sudden rage took him with the realization that his brother slept. He lifted his spear into both hands, then swung the butt end in a snapping motion that connected with the side of Rhulad's head.

A muffled crack that sent his brother pitching to one side. Rhulad loosed a piercing shriek as he sprawled on the hard-packed snow, then rolled onto his back, scrabbling for his sword.

Trull's spear-point was at his brother's neck. 'You slept on your watch!' he hissed.

'I did not!'

'I saw you sleeping! I walked right up to you!'

'I did not!' Rhulad scrambled to his feet, one hand held against the side of his head.

The others were emerging now from their tents. Fear stared at Trull and Rhulad for a moment, then turned to the packs.

Trull was trembling, drawing deep, frigid breaths. For a

306

moment, it struck him how disproportionate his anger was, then the magnitude of the risk flooded through him yet again.

'We have had visitors,' Fear announced, rising and scanning the frozen ground. 'They left no tracks—'

'How do you know, then?' Rhulad demanded.

'Because all our food is gone, Rhulad. It seems we shall grow hungry for a time.'

Theradas swore and began a wider circuit, seeking a trail.

They were among us. The Jheck. They could have killed us all where we slept. All because Rhulad will not grasp what it is to be a warrior. There was nothing more to be said, and all knew it.

Except for Rhulad. 'I wasn't sleeping! I swear it! Fear, you have to believe me! I simply sat down for a moment to rest my legs. I saw no-one!'

'Behind closed lids,' Theradas growled, 'that's not surprising.'

'You think I'm lying, but I'm not! I'm telling the truth, I swear it!'

'Never mind,' Fear said. 'It is done. From now on, we will double the watch.'

Rhulad walked towards Midik. 'You believe me, don't you?'

Midik Buhn turned away. 'It was a battle just waking you for your watch, Rhulad,' he said, his tone both sad and weary.

Rhulad stood as if in shock, the pain of what he saw as betrayal clear and deep-struck on his face. His lips thinned, jaw muscles bunching, and he slowly turned away.

The bastards were in our camp. Hannan Mosag's faith in us . . .

'Let us strike the tents,' Fear said, 'and be on our way.'

Trull found himself scanning the horizon in an endless sweep, his sense of vulnerability at times near overwhelming. They were being watched, tracked. The

307

emptiness of the landscape was a lie, somehow. Possibly there was sorcery at work, although this did not – could not – excuse Rhulad's failing.

Trust was gone, and Trull well knew that Rhulad's future would now be dominated by the effort to regain it. A lapse, and the young man's future path awaited him, deep-rutted and inevitable. A private journey beset by battle, each step resisted by a host of doubts, real and imagined – the distinction made no difference any more. Rhulad would see in his brothers and friends an unbroken succession of recriminations. Every gesture, every word, every glance. And, the tragedy was, he would not be far from the truth.

This would not be kept from the village. Sengar shame or not, the tale would come out, sung with quiet glee among rivals and the spiteful – and, given the opportunity, there were plenty of those to be found. A stain that claimed them all, the entire Sengar line.

They moved on. Northward, through the empty day.

Late in the afternoon, Theradas caught sight of something ahead, and moments later the others saw it as well. A glimmer of reflected sunlight, tall and narrow and angular, rising from the flat waste. Difficult to judge its size, but Trull sensed that the projection was substantial, and unnatural.

'That is the place,' Fear said. 'Hannan Mosag's dreams were true. We shall find the gift there.'

'Then let us be about it,' Theradas said, setting off.

The spar grew steadily before them. Cracks appeared in the snow and ice underfoot, the surface sloping upward the closer they approached. The shard had risen up from the deep, cataclysmically, a sudden upthrust that had sent wagon-sized chunks of ice into the air, to crash and tumble down the sides. Angular boulders of mud, now frozen and rimed, had rolled across the snow and ringed the area in a rough circle.

Prismatic planes caught and split the sunlight within the spar. The ice in that towering shard was pure and clear.

At the base of the fissured up-welling – still thirty or more paces from the spar – the group halted. Trull slipped out from the sled harness, Binadas following suit.

'Theradas, Midik, stay here and guard the sleds,' Fear said. 'Trull, draw your spear from its sling. Binadas, Rhulad, to our flanks. Let's go.'

They climbed the slope, winding their way between masses of ice and mud.

A foul smell filled the air, of old rot and brine.

Binadas hissed warningly, then said, 'The spirit Hannan Mosag called up from the ocean deep has been here, beneath the ice. This is its handiwork, and the sorcery lingers.'

'Emurlahn?' Trull asked.

'No.'

They came to the base of the spar. Its girth surpassed that of thousand-year-old Blackwood trees. Countless planes rose in twisted confusion, a mass of sharp, sheered surfaces in which the setting sun's red light flowed thick as blood.

Fear pointed. 'There. The gift.'

And now Trull saw it. Faint and murky, the smudged form of a two-handed sword, bell-hilted, its blade strangely fractured and mottled – although perhaps that effect was created by the intervening thickness of ice.

'Binadas, weave Emurlahn into Trull's spear. As much as you can – this will take many, many shadows.'

Their brother frowned. 'Take? In what way?'

'Shattering the ice will destroy them. Annihilation is demanded, to free the gift. And remember, do not close your unguarded hand about the grip, once the weapon comes free. And keep the wraiths from attempting the same, for attempt it they will. With desperate resolve.'

'What manner of sword is this?' Trull whispered.

Fear did not answer.

'If we are to shatter this spar,' Binadas said after a moment, 'all of you should stand well clear of myself and Trull.'

'We shall not be harmed,' Fear said. 'Hannan Mosag's vision was clear on this.'

'And how far did that vision go, brother?' Trull asked. 'Did he see our return journey?'

Fear shook his head. 'To the shattering, to the fall of the last fragment of ice. No further.'

'I wonder why?'

'This is not a time for doubt, Trull,' Fear said.

'Isn't it? It would seem that this is precisely the time for doubt.'

His brothers faced him.

Trull looked away. 'This feels wrong.'

'Have you lost your courage?' Rhulad snapped. 'We have walked all this way, and now you voice your doubts?'

'What sort of weapon is this gift? Who fashioned it? We know nothing of what we are about to release.'

'Our Warlock King has commanded us,' Fear said, his expression darkening. 'What would you have us do, Trull?'

'I don't know.' He turned to Binadas. 'Is there no means of prying the secrets loose?'

'I will know more, I think, when we have freed the sword.'

Fear grunted. 'Then begin, Binadas.'

They were interrupted by a shout from Theradas. 'A wolf!' he cried, pointing to the south.

The beast was barely visible, white-furred against the snow, standing motionless a thousand or more paces distant, watching them.

'Waste no more time,' Fear said to Binadas.

Shadows spun from where Binadas was standing, blue stains crawling out across the snow, coiling up the shaft of the Blackwood spear in Trull's hands, where they seemed to sink into the glossy wood. The weapon felt no different through the thick fur of his gauntlets, but Trull thought he could hear something new, a keening sound that seemed to reverberate in his bones. It felt like terror.

'No more,' Binadas gasped.

Trull glanced at his brother, saw the pallor of his face, the glistening sweat on his brow. 'They are resisting this?'

Binadas nodded. 'They know they are about to die.'

'How can wraiths die?' Rhulad demanded. 'Are they not already ghosts? The spirits of our ancestors?'

'Not ours,' Binadas replied, but did not elaborate, gesturing instead towards Trull. 'Strike at the ice, brother.'

Trull hesitated. He looked round over his left shoulder, searched until he found the distant wolf. It had lowered its head, legs gathering under it. 'Daughter Dusk,' he whispered, 'it's about to charge.' Below, Theradas and Midik were readying their spears.

'Now, Trull!'

Fear's bellow startled him, so that he almost dropped the spear. Jaw clenching, he faced the spar once more, then slashed the iron spear-head against the ice.

Even as the weapon whipped forward, Trull's peripheral vision caught motion on all sides, as figures seemed to rise from the very snow itself.

Then the spar exploded into blinding, white mist.

Sudden shouts.

Trull felt a savage wrench on the spear in his hands, the Blackwood ringing like iron as countless wraiths were torn free. Their death-cries filled his skull. Stumbling, he tightened his grip, striving to see through the cloud.

Weapons clashed.

An antler clawed for his face, each tine carved into a barbed point tipped with quartzite. Trull reeled back, flinging the spear shaft into the antler's path. Trapping it. He twisted the spear round, reversing grip, and succeeded in forcing the attacker into releasing the antler. It spun away to one side. An upward slash with the spear, and Trull felt the iron blade tear through hide and flesh, clattering along ribs before momentarily springing free, to connect hard against the underside of a jaw.

The scene around him was becoming more visible. They were beset by savages, small and bestial, wearing

311

white-skinned hides, faces hidden behind flat white masks. Wielding claw-like antler weapons and short stabbing spears with glittering stone points, the Jheck swarmed on all sides.

Fear was holding three at bay, and behind him stood the sword, upright and freed from the ice, its point jammed into the frozen ground. It seemed the Jheck were desperate to claim it.

Trull struck at the closest of Fear's opponents, iron tip punching deep into the savage's neck. Blood sprayed, jetted down the spear-shaft. He tore the weapon loose, in time to see the last of the Jheck in front of Fear wheel away, mortally wounded by a sword-thrust.

Spinning round, Trull saw Binadas go down beneath a mass of Jheck. Shadows then enveloped the writhing figures.

Rhulad was nowhere to be seen.

Down below, Theradas and Midik had met the wolf's charge, and the huge beast was on its side, skewered by spears, legs kicking even as Theradas stepped in with his broad-bladed cutlass. Two more wolves were closing in, alongside them a half-dozen Jheck.

Another score of the savages were ascending the slope.

Trull readied his weapon.

Nearby, Binadas was climbing free of a mound of corpses. He was sheathed in blood, favouring his right side.

'Behind us, Binadas,' Fear commanded. 'Trull, get on my left. Quickly.'

'Where is Rhulad?'

Fear shook his head.

As Trull moved to his brother's left he scanned the bodies sprawled on the snow. But they were all Jheck. Even so, the belief struck him hard as a blow to his chest. They were going to die here. They were going to fail.

The savages on the slope charged.

Antlers flew from their hands, dagger-sharp tines flashing as the deadly weapons spun end over end.

Trull shouted, warding with his spear as he ducked beneath the whirling onslaught. One flew past his guard, a tine clipping his left knee. He gasped at the pain and felt the sudden spurt of blood beneath his leggings, but his leg held his weight and he remained upright.

Behind the flung weapons, the Jheck arrived in a rush.

A dozen heartbeats on the defensive, then the Edur warriors found openings for counter-attacks almost simultaneously. Sword and spear bit flesh, and two of the Jheck were down.

A shriek from behind Trull and Fear, and the savages recoiled, then in unison darted to their right—

—as Rhulad leapt into their midst, the long, bell-hilted sword in his hands.

A wild slash, and a Jheck head pitched away from shoulders to bounce and roll down the slope.

Another chop, a gush of blood.

Both Fear and Trull rushed to close with the combatants—

—even as stabbing spears found their way into Rhulad from all sides. He shrieked, blood-slick blade wavering over his head. Then he sagged. A shove toppled him onto his back, the sword still in his hands.

The surrounding Jheck darted away, then ran down the slope, weapons dropping or flung aside in sudden panic.

Trull arrived, skidding on the blood-slick ice, the wound in his leg forgotten as he knelt at Rhulad's side.

'They're withdrawing,' Fear said between harshly drawn breaths, moving to stand guard before Trull and Rhulad.

Numbed, Trull tore off a gauntlet and set his hand against Rhulad's neck, seeking a pulse.

Binadas staggered over, settling down opposite Trull. 'How does he fare, brother?'

Trull looked up, stared until Binadas glanced up and locked gazes.

'Rhulad is dead,' Trull said, dropping his eyes and seeing now, for the first time, the massive impaling wounds

313

punched into his brother's torso, the smear of already freezing blood on the furs, smelling bitter urine and pungent faeces.

'Theradas and Midik are coming,' Fear said. 'The Jheck have fled.' He then set off, round towards the back of the rise.

But that makes no sense. They had us. There were too many of them. None of this makes sense. Rhulad. He's dead. Our brother is dead.

A short time later, Fear returned, crouched down beside him, and tenderly reached out . . . to take the sword. Trull watched Fear's hands close about Rhulad's where they still clutched the leather-wrapped grip. Watched, as Fear sought to pry those dead fingers loose.

And could not.

Trull studied that fell weapon. The blade was indeed mottled, seemingly forged of polished iron and black shards of some harder, glassier material, the surface of both cracked and uneven. Splashes of blood were freezing black here and there, like a fast-spreading rot.

Fear sought to wrench the sword free.

But Rhulad would not release it.

'Hannan Mosag warned us,' Binadas said, 'did he not? Do not allow your flesh to touch the gift.'

'But he's dead,' Trull whispered.

Dusk was swiftly closing round them, the chill in the air deepening.

Theradas and Midik arrived. Both were wounded, but neither seriously so. They were silent as they stared down on Rhulad.

Fear leaned back, having reached some sort of decision. He was silent a moment longer, slowly pulling on his gauntlets. Then he straightened. 'Carry him – sword and all – down to the sleds. We will wrap body and blade together. Releasing the gift from our brother's hands is for Hannan Mosag to manage, now.'

No-one else spoke.

Fear studied each of them in turn, then said, 'We travel through this night. I want us out of these wastes as soon as possible.' He looked down on Rhulad once more. 'Our brother is blooded. He died a warrior of the Hiroth. His shall be a hero's funeral, one that all the Hiroth shall remember.'

In the wake of numbness came ... other things. Questions. But what was the point of those? Any answers that could be found were no better than suppositions, born of uncertainties vulnerable to countless poisons – that host of doubts even now besieging Trull's thoughts. Where had Rhulad disappeared to? What had he sought to achieve by charging into that knot of Jheck savages? And he had well understood the prohibition against taking up the gift, yet he had done so none the less.

So much of what happened seemed ... senseless.

Even in his final act of extremity, Rhulad answers not the loss of trust under which he laboured. No clean gesture, this messy end. Fear called him a hero, but Trull suspected the motivation behind that claim. A son of Tomad Sengar had failed in his duties on night watch. And now was dead, the sacrifice itself marred with incomprehensible intentions.

The questions led Trull nowhere, and faded to a new wave, one that sickened him, clenching at his gut with spasms of anguish. There had been bravery in that last act. If nothing else. Surprising bravery, when Trull had, of his brother Rhulad, begun to suspect ... otherwise. *I doubted him. In every way, I doubted him.*

Into his heart whispered ... guilt, a ghost and a ghost's voice, growing monstrous with taloned hands tightening, ever tightening, until his soul began to scream. A piercing cry only Trull could hear, yet a sound that threatened to drive him mad.

And through it all, a more pervasive sense, a hollowness deep within him. The loss of a brother. The face that would never again smile, the voice that Trull would never again

315

hear. There seemed no end to the layers of loss settling dire and heavy upon him.

He helped Fear wrap Rhulad and the sword in a waxed canvas groundsheet, hearing Midik's weeping as if from a great distance, listening to Binadas talk as he bound wounds and drew upon Emurlahn to quicken healing. As the stiff folds closed over Rhulad's face, Trull's breath caught in a ragged gasp, and he flinched back as Fear tightened the covering with leather straps.

'It is done,' Fear murmured. 'Death cannot be struggled against, brother. It ever arrives, defiant of every hiding place, of every frantic attempt to escape. Death is every mortal's shadow, his true shadow, and time is its servant, spinning that shadow slowly round, until what stretched behind one now stretches before him.'

'You called him a hero.'

'I did, and it was not an empty claim. He went to the other side of the rise, which is why we did not see him, and discovered Jheck seeking the sword by subterfuge.'

Trull looked up.

'I needed answers of my own, brother. He killed two on that side of the hill, yet lost his weapon doing so. Others were coming, I imagine, and so Rhulad must have concluded he had no choice. The Jheck wanted the sword. They would have to kill him to get it. Trull, it is done. He died, blooded and brave. I myself came upon the corpses beyond the rise, before I came back to you and Binadas.'

All my doubts . . . the poisons of suspicion, in all their foul flavours – Daughter Dusk take me – but I have drunk deep.

'Trull, we need you and your skills with that spear in our wake,' Fear said. 'Both Binadas and Rhulad here will have to be pulled on the sleds, and for this Theradas and I will be needed. Midik takes point.'

Trull blinked confusedly. 'Binadas cannot walk?'

'His hip is broken, and he has not the strength left to heal it.'

Trull straightened. 'Do you think they will pursue?'

'Yes,' Fear said.

Their flight began. Darkness swept down upon them, and a wind began blowing, lifting high the fine-grained snow until the sky itself was grey-white and lowering. The temperature dropped still further, as if with vicious intent, until even the furs they wore began to fail them.

Favouring his wounded leg, Trull jogged twenty paces behind the sleds – they were barely visible through the wind-whipped snow. The blood-frosted spear was in his grip, a detail he confirmed every few moments since his fingers had gone numb, but this did little to encourage him. The enemy might well be all around him, just beyond the range of his vision, padding through the darkness, only moments from rushing in.

He would have no time to react, and whatever shout of warning he managed would be torn away by the wind, and his companions would hear nothing. Nor would they return for his body. The gift must be delivered.

Trull ran on, constantly scanning to either side, occasionally twisting round to look behind, seeing nothing but faint white. The rhythmic stab of pain in his knee cut through a growing, deadly lassitude, the seep of exhaustion slowing his shivering beneath the furs, dragging at his limbs.

Dawn's arrival was announced by a dull, reluctant surrender of the pervasive gloom – there was no break in the blizzard's onslaught, no rise in temperature. Trull had given up his vigil. He simply ran on, one foot in front of the other, his ice-clad moccasins the entire extent of his vision. His hands had grown strangely warm beneath the gauntlets, a remote warmth, pooled somewhere beyond his wrists. Something about that vaguely disturbed him.

Hunger had faded, as had the pain in his knee.

A tingling unease, and Trull looked up.

The sleds were nowhere in sight. He gasped bitter air,

slowed his steps, blinking in an effort to see through the ice crystals on his lashes. The muted daylight was fading. He had run through the day, mindless as a millstone, and another night was fast approaching. And he was lost.

Trull dropped the spear. He cried out in pain as he wheeled his arms, seeking to pump more blood into his cold, stiff muscles. He drew his fingers into fists within the gauntlets, and was horrified by nearly failing at so simple a task. The warmth grew warmer, then hot, then searing as if his fingers were on fire. He fought through the agony, pounding his fists on his thighs, flexing against the waves of burning pain.

He was surrounded in white, as if the physical world had been scrubbed away, eroded into oblivion by the snow and wind. Terror whispered into his mind, for he sensed that he was not alone.

Trull retrieved the spear. He studied the blowing snow on all sides. One direction seemed slightly darker than any other – the east – and he determined that he had been running due west. Following the unseen sun. And now, he needed to turn southerly.

Until his pursuers tired of their game.

He set out.

A hundred paces, and he glanced behind him, to see two wolves emerge from the blowing snow. Trull halted and spun round. The beasts vanished once more.

Heart thundering, Trull drew out his longsword and jammed it point-first into the hard-packed snow. Then he strode six paces back along his trail and readied his spear.

They came again, this time at a charge.

He had time to plant his spear and drop to one knee before the first beast was upon him. The spear shaft bowed as the iron point slammed dead-centre into the wolf's sternum. Bone and Blackwood shattered simultaneously, then it was as if a boulder hammered into Trull, throwing him back in the air. He landed on his left shoulder, to skid and roll in a spray of snow. As he tumbled, he caught sight of his left forearm, blood whipping out from the black splinters jutting from it. Then he came to a stop, up against the longsword.

Trull tugged it loose and half rose as he turned about.

A mass of white fur, black-gummed jaws stretched wide.

Bellowing, Trull slashed horizontally with the sword, falling in the wake of the desperate swing.

Iron edge sheared through bones, one set, then another.

The wolf fell onto him, its forelimbs severed halfway down and spraying blood.

Teeth closed down on the blade of his sword in a snapping frenzy.

Trull kicked himself clear, tearing his sword free of the wolf's jaws. Tumbling blood, a mass of tongue slapping onto the crusty ice in front of his face, the muscle twitching like a thing still alive. He scrambled into a crouch, then lunged towards the thrashing beast. Thrusting the swordpoint into its neck.

The wolf coughed, kicking as if seeking to escape, then slumped motionless on the red snow.

Trull reeled back. He saw the first beast, lying where the spear had stolen its life before breaking. Beyond it stood three Jheck hunters – who melted back into the whiteness.

Blood was streaming down Trull's left forearm, gathering in his gauntlet. He lifted the arm and tucked it close against his stomach. Pulling the splinters would have to wait. Gasping, he set his sword down and worked his left forearm through his spear harness. Then, retrieving the sword, he set out once more.

Oblivion on all sides. In which nightmares could flower, sudden and unimpeded, rushing upon him, as fast as his terror-filled mind could conjure them into being, one after another, the succession endless, until death took him – until the whiteness slipped behind his eyes.

He stumbled on, wondering if the fight had actually occurred, unwilling to look down to confirm the wounds on his arm – fearing that he would see nothing. He could not

319

have killed two wolves. He could not have simply chosen to face in one direction and not another, to find himself meeting that charge head-on. He could not have thrust his sword into the ground the precise number of paces behind him, as if knowing how far he would be thrown by the impact. No, he had conjured the entire battle from his own imagination. No other explanation made sense.

And so he looked down.

A mass of splinters rising like crooked spines from his forearm. A blackening sword in his right hand, tufts of white fur caught in the clotted blood near the hilt. His spear was gone.

I am fevered. The will of my thoughts has seeped out from my eyes, twisting the truth of all that I see. Even the ache in my shoulder is but an illusion.

A rush of footsteps behind him.

With a roar, Trull whipped around, sword hissing.

Blade chopping into the side of a savage's head, just above the ear. Bone buckling, blood spurting from eye and ear on that side. Figure toppling.

Another, darting in low from his right. Trull leapt back, stop-thrusting. He watched, the motion seeming appallingly slow, as the Jheck turned his stabbing spear to parry. Watched as the sword dipped under the block, then extended once more, to slide point-first beneath the man's left collarbone.

A third attacker on his left, slashing a spear-point at Trull's eyes. He leaned back, then spun full circle, pivoting on his right foot, and brought his sword's edge smoothly across the savage's throat. A red flood down the Jheck's chest.

Trull completed his spin and resumed his jog, the snow stinging his eyes.

Nothing but nightmares.

He was lying motionless, the snow slowly covering him, whilst his mind ran on and on, fleeing this lie, this empty world that was not empty, this thick whiteness that exploded into motion and colour again and again.

Attackers, appearing out of the darkness and blowing snow. Moments of frenzied fighting, sparks and the hiss of iron and the bite of wood and stone. A succession of ambushes that seemed without end, convincing Trull that he was indeed within a nightmare, ever folding in on itself. Each time, the Jheck appeared in threes, never more, and the Hiroth warrior began to believe that they were the same three, dying only to rise once again – and so it would continue, until they finally succeeded, until they killed him.

Yet he fought on, leaving blood and bodies in his wake.

Running, snow crunching underfoot.

And then the wind fell off, sudden like a spent breath.

Patches of dark ground ahead. An unseen barrier burst across, the lurid glare of a setting sun to his right, the languid flow of cool, damp air, the smell of mud.

And shouts. Figures off to his left, half a thousand paces distant. Brothers of the hearth, the dead welcoming his arrival.

Gladness welling in his heart, Trull staggered towards them. He was not to be a ghost wandering for ever alone, then. There would be kin at his side. Fear, and Binadas. And Rhulad.

Midik Buhn, and Theradas, rushing towards him.

Brothers, all of them. My brothers—

The sun's light wavered, rippled like water, then darkness rose up in a devouring flood.

The sleds were off to one side, their runners buried in mud. On one was a wrapped figure, around which jagged slabs of ice had been packed and strapped in place. Binadas was propped up on the other sled, his eyes closed, his face deeply lined with pain.

Trull slowly sat up, feeling light-headed and strangely awkward. Furs tumbled from him as he clambered to his feet and stood, wavering, and dazedly looked around. To the west shimmered a lake, flat grey beneath the overcast sky. The faint wind was warm and humid.

321

A fire had been lit, and over it was spit a scrawny hare, tended to by Midik Buhn. Off to one side stood Fear and Theradas, facing the distant ice-fields to the east as they spoke in quiet tones.

The smell of the roasting meat drew Trull to the fire. Midik Buhn glanced up at him, then looked quickly away, as if shamed by something.

Trull's fingers were fiercely itching, and he lifted them into view. Red, the skin peeling, but at least he had not lost them to the cold. Indeed, he seemed intact, although his leather armour was split and cut all across his chest and shoulders, and he could see that the quilted under-padding bore slices, here and there stained dark red, and beneath them was the sting of shallow wounds on his body.

Not a nightmare, then, those countless attacks. He checked for his sword and found he was not wearing the belted scabbard. A moment later he spied his weapon, leaning against a pack. It was barely recognizable. The blade was twisted, the edge so battered as to make the sword little more than a club.

Footsteps, and Trull turned.

Fear laid a hand upon his shoulder. 'Trull Sengar, we did not expect to see you again. Leading the Jheck away from our path was a bold tactic, and it saved our lives.' He nodded towards the sword. 'Your weapon tells the tale. Do you know how many you defeated?'

Trull shook his head. 'No. Fear, I did not intentionally lead them away from you. I became lost in the storm.'

His brother smiled and said nothing.

Trull glanced over at Theradas. 'I became lost, Theradas Buhn.'

'It matters not,' Theradas replied in a growl.

'I believed I was dead.' Trull looked away, rubbed at his face. 'I saw you, and thought I was joining you in death. I'd expected . . .' He shook his head. 'Rhulad . . .'

'He was a true warrior, Trull,' Fear said. 'It is done, and now we must move on. There are Arapay on the way –

322

Binadas managed to awaken their shamans to our plight. They will hasten our journey home.'

Trull nodded distractedly. He stared at the distant field of ice. Remembering the feel and sound beneath his moccasins, the blast of the wind, the enervating cold. The horrifying Jheck, silent hunters who claimed a frozen world as their own. They had wanted the sword. Why?

How many Jheck could those ice-fields sustain? How many had they killed? How many wives and children were left to grieve? To starve?

There should have been five hundred of us. Then they would have left us alone.

'Over there!'

At Midik's shout Trull swung round, then faced in the direction Midik was pointing. Northward, where a dozen huge beasts strode, coming down from the ice, four-legged and brown-furred, each bearing long, curved tusks to either side of a thick, sinuous snout.

Ponderous, majestic, the enormous creatures walked towards the lake.

This is not our world.

A sword waited in the unyielding grip of a corpse, sheathed in waxed cloth, bound with ice. A weapon familiar with cold's implacable embrace. It did not belong in Hannan Mosag's hands.

Unless the Warlock King had changed.

And perhaps he has.

'Come and eat, Trull Sengar,' his brother called behind him.

Sisters have mercy on us, in the way we simply go on, and on. Would that we had all died, back there on the ice. Would that we had failed.

CHAPTER NINE

You may be written this way
Spun in strands sewn in thread
Blood woven to the child you once were
Huddled in the fold of night
And the demons beyond the corner
Of your eye stream down
A flurry of arachnid limbs
Twisting and tumbling you tight
To feed upon later.
You may be written this way
Stung senseless at the side of the road
Waylaid on the dark trail
And the recollections beyond the corner
Of your eye suckle in the mud
Dreadful fluids seeping
From improbable pasts
And all that might have been.
You would be written this way
Could you crack the carcass
And unfurl once more
The child you once were

Waylaid
Wrathen Urut

Rolled onto the beach, naked and grey, the young man lay motionless in the sand. His long brown hair was tangled, snarled with twigs and strands of seaweed. Scaled birds pranced around the body, serrated beaks gaping in the morning heat.

They scattered at Withal's arrival, flapping into the air. Then, as three black Nachts bounded down from the verge, the birds screamed and whirled out over the waves.

Withal crouched down at the figure's side, studied it for a moment, then reached out and rolled the body onto its back.

'Wake up, lad.'

Eyes snapped open, filled with sudden terror and pain. Mouth gaped, neck stretched, and piercing screams rose into the air. The young man convulsed, legs scissoring the sand, and clawed at his scalp.

Withal leaned back on his haunches and waited.

The screams grew hoarse, were replaced by weeping. The convulsions diminished to waves of shuddering as the young man slowly curled up in the sand.

'It gets easier, one hopes,' Withal murmured.

Head twisted round, large, wet eyes fixing on Withal's own. 'What . . . where . . .'

'The two questions I am least able to answer, lad. Let's try the easier ones. I'm named Withal, once of the Third Meckros city. You are here – wherever here is – because my master wills it.' He rose with a grunt. 'Can you stand? He awaits you inland – not far.'

The eyes shifted away, focused on the three Nachts at the edge of the verge. 'What are those things? What's that one doing?'

'Bhoka'ral. Nachts. Name them as you will. As I have. The one making the nest is Pule, a young male. This particular nest has taken almost a week – see how he obsesses over it, adjusting twigs just so, weaving the seaweed, going round and round with a critical eye. The older male, over there and watching Pule, is Rind. He's moments from

325

hilarity, as you'll see. The female preening on the rock is Mape. You've arrived at a propitious time, lad. Watch.'

The nest-builder, Pule, had begun backing away from the intricate construct on the verge, black tail flicking from side to side, head bobbing. Fifteen paces from the nest, it suddenly sat, arms folded, and seemed to study the colourless sky.

The female, Mape, ceased preening, paused a moment, then ambled casually towards the nest.

Pule tensed, even as it visibly struggled to keep its gaze on the sky.

Reaching the nest, Mape hesitated, then attacked. Driftwood, grasses and twigs flew in all directions. Within moments, the nest had been destroyed in a wild frenzy, and Mape was squatting in the wreckage, urinating.

Nearby, Rind was rolling about in helpless mirth.

Pule slumped in obvious dejection.

'This has happened more times than I'd care to count,' Withal said, sighing.

'How is it you speak my language?'

'I'd a smattering, from traders. My master has, it seems, improved upon it. A gift, you might say, one of a number of gifts, none of which I asked for. I suspect,' he continued, 'you will come to similar sentiments, lad. We should get going.'

Withal watched the young man struggle to his feet. 'Tall,' he observed, 'but I've seen taller.'

Pain flooded the youth's features once more and he doubled over. Withal stepped close and supported him before he toppled.

'It's ghost pain, lad. Ghost pain and ghost fear. Fight through it.'

'No! It's real! It's *real*, you bastard!'

Withal strained as the youth's full weight settled in his arms. 'Enough of that. Stand up!'

'It's no good! I'm *dying*!'

'On your feet, dammit!'

A rough shake, then Withal pushed him away.

He staggered, then slowly straightened, drawing in deep, ragged breaths. He began shivering. 'It's so cold . . .'

'Hood's breath, lad, it's blistering hot. And getting hotter with every day.'

Arms wrapped about himself, the young man regarded Withal. 'How long have you lived . . . lived here?'

'Longer than I'd like. Some choices aren't for you to make. Not for you, not for me. Now, our master's losing patience. Follow me.'

The youth stumbled along behind him. 'You said "our".'

'Did I?'

'Where are my clothes? Where are my – no, never mind – it hurts to remember. Never mind.'

They reached the verge, withered grasses pulling at their legs as they made their way inland. The Nachts joined them, clambering and hopping, hooting and snorting as they kept pace.

Two hundred paces ahead squatted a ragged tent, the canvas sun-bleached and stained. Wafts of grey-brown smoke drifted from the wide entrance, where most of one side had been drawn back to reveal the interior.

Where sat a hooded figure.

'That's him?' the youth asked. 'That's your master? Are you a slave, then?'

'I serve,' Withal replied, 'but I am not *owned*.'

'Who is he?'

Withal glanced back. 'He is a god.' He noted the disbelief writ on the lad's face, and smiled wryly. 'Who's seen better days.'

The Nachts halted and huddled together in a threesome.

A last few strides across withered ground, then Withal stepped to one side. 'I found him on the strand,' he said to the seated figure, 'moments before the lizard gulls did.'

Darkness hid the Crippled God's features, as was ever the case when Withal had been summoned to an attendance. The smoke from the brazier filled the tent, seeping out to

327

stream along the mild breeze. A gnarled, thin hand emerged from the folds of a sleeve as the god gestured. 'Closer,' he rasped. 'Sit.'

'You are not my god,' the youth said.

'Sit. I am neither petty nor overly sensitive, young warrior.'

Withal watched the lad hesitate, then slowly settle onto the ground, cross-legged, arms wrapped about his shivering frame. 'It's cold.'

'Some furs for our guest, Withal.'

'Furs? We don't have any—' He stopped when he noticed the bundled bearskin heaped beside him. He gathered it up and pushed it into the lad's hands.

The Crippled God scattered some seeds onto the brazier's coals. Popping sounds, then more smoke. '*Peace.* Warm yourself, warrior, while I tell you of peace. History is unerring, and even the least observant mortal can be made to understand, through innumerable repetition. Do you see peace as little more than the absence of war? Perhaps, on a surface level, it is just that. But let me describe the characteristics of peace, my young friend. A pervasive dulling of the senses, a decadence afflicting the culture, evinced by a growing obsession with low entertainment. The virtues of extremity – honour, loyalty, sacrifice – are lifted high as shoddy icons, currency for the cheapest of labours. The longer peace lasts, the more those words are used, and the weaker they become. Sentimentality pervades daily life. All becomes a mockery of itself, and the spirit grows . . . restless.'

The Crippled God paused, breath rasping. 'Is this a singular pessimism? Allow me to continue with a description of what follows a period of peace. Old warriors sit in taverns, telling tales of vigorous youth, their pasts when all things were simpler, clearer cut. They are not blind to the decay all around them, are not immune to the loss of respect for themselves, for all that they gave for their king, their land, their fellow citizens.

'The young must not be abandoned to forgetfulness. There are always enemies beyond the borders, and if none exist in truth, then one must be fashioned. Old crimes dug out of the indifferent earth. Slights and open insults, or the rumours thereof. A suddenly perceived threat where none existed before. The reasons matter not – what matters is that war is fashioned from peace, and once the journey is begun, an irresistible momentum is born.

'The old warriors are satisfied. The young are on fire with zeal. The king fears yet is relieved of domestic pressures. The army draws its oil and whetstone. Forges blast with molten iron, the anvils ring like temple bells. Grain-sellers and armourers and clothiers and horse-sellers and countless other suppliers smile with the pleasure of impending wealth. A new energy has gripped the kingdom, and those few voices raised in objection are quickly silenced. Charges of treason and summary execution soon persuade the doubters.'

The Crippled God spread his hands. 'Peace, my young warrior, is born of relief, endured in exhaustion, and dies with false remembrance. False? Ah, perhaps I am too cynical. Too old, witness to far too much. Do honour, loyalty and sacrifice truly exist? Are such virtues born only from extremity? What transforms them into empty words, words devalued by their overuse? What are the rules of the economy of the spirit, that civilization repeatedly twists and mocks?'

He shifted slightly and Withal sensed the god's regard. 'Withal of the Third City. You have fought wars. You have forged weapons. You have seen loyalty, and honour. You have seen courage and sacrifice. What say you to all this?'

'Nothing,' Withal replied.

Hacking laughter. 'You fear angering me, yes? No need. I give you leave to speak your mind.'

'I have sat in my share of taverns,' Withal said, 'in the company of fellow veterans. A select company, perhaps, not grown so blind with sentimentality as to fashion

329

nostalgia from times of horror and terror. Did we spin out those days of our youth? No. Did we speak of war? Not if we could avoid it, and we worked hard at avoiding it.'

'Why?'

'Why? Because the faces come back. So young, one after another. A flash of life, an eternity of death, there in our minds. Because loyalty is not to be spoken of, and honour is to be endured. Whilst courage is to be survived. Those virtues, Chained One, belong to silence.'

'Indeed,' the god rasped, leaning forward. 'Yet how they proliferate in peace! Crowed again and again, as if solemn pronouncement bestows those very qualities upon the speaker. Do they not make you wince, every time you hear them? Do they not twist in your gut, grip hard your throat? Do you not feel a building rage—'

'Aye,' Withal growled, 'when I hear them used to raise a people once more to war.'

The Crippled God was silent a moment, then he leaned back and dismissed Withal's words with a careless wave of one hand. He fixed his attention on the young warrior. 'I spoke of peace as anathema. A poison that weakens the spirit. Tell me, warrior, have you spilled blood?'

The youth flinched beneath his furs. Tremors of pain crossed his face. Then fear. 'Spilled blood? Spilled, down, so much of it – everywhere. I don't – I can't – oh, Daughters take me—'

'Oh no,' the Crippled God hissed, 'not the Daughters. *I have taken you.* Chosen you. Because your king betrayed me! Your king hungered for the power I offered, but not for conquest. No, he simply sought to make himself and his people unassailable.' Misshapen fingers curled into fists. '*Not good enough!*'

The Crippled God seemed to spasm beneath his ragged blankets, then coughed wretchedly.

Some time later the hacking abated. More seeds on the coals, roiling smoke, then, 'I have chosen you, Rhulad Sengar, for my gift. Do you remember?'

Shivering, his lips strangely blue, the young warrior's face underwent a series of fraught expressions, ending on dread. He nodded. 'I died.'

'Well,' the Crippled God murmured, 'every gift has a price. There are powers buried in that sword, Rhulad Sengar. Powers unimagined. But they are reluctant to yield. You must pay for them. In combat. With death. No, I should be precise in this. With *your* death, Rhulad Sengar.'

A gesture, and the mottled sword was in the Crippled God's hand. He tossed it down in front of the young warrior. 'Your first death is done, and as a consequence your skills – your powers – have burgeoned. But it is just the beginning. Take your weapon, Rhulad Sengar. Will your next death prove easier for you to bear? Probably not. In time, perhaps . . .'

Withal studied the horror on the young warrior's face, and saw beneath it the glimmer of . . . *ambition.*

Hood, do not turn away.

A long, frozen moment, during which Withal saw the ambition grow like flames behind the Tiste Edur's eyes.

Ah. The Crippled God's chosen well. And deny it not, Withal, your hand is in this, plunged deep. So very deep.

The smoke gusted, then spun, momentarily blinding Withal even as Rhulad Sengar reached for the sword.

A god's mercy? He was unconvinced.

In four days, the Letherii delegation would arrive. Two nights had passed since the Warlock King had called Seren, Hull and Buruk the Pale into his audience at the feast table. Buruk's spirits were high, a development that had not surprised Seren Pedac. Merchants whose interests were tempered by wisdom ever preferred the long term over speculative endeavours. There were always vultures of commerce who hungered for strife, and often profited by such discord, but Buruk the Pale was not one of them.

Contrary to the desires of those back in Letheras who

331

had conscripted Buruk, the merchant did not want a war. And so, with Hannan Mosag's intimation that the Edur would seek peace, the tumult in Buruk's soul had eased. The issue had been taken from his hands.

If the Warlock King wanted peace, he was in for a fight. But Seren Pedac's confidence in Hannan Mosag had grown. The Edur leader possessed cunning and resilience. There would be no manipulation at the treaty, no treachery sewn into the fabric of generous pronouncements.

A weight had been lifted from her, mitigated only by Hull Beddict. He had come to understand that his desires would not be met. At least, not by Hannan Mosag. If he would have his war, it would of necessity have to come from the Letherii. And so, if he would follow that path, he would need to reverse his outward allegiances. No longer on the side of the Tiste Edur, but accreted to at least one element of the Letherii delegation – a faction characterized by betrayal and unrelenting greed.

Hull had left the village and was now somewhere out in the forest. She knew he would return for the treaty gathering, but probably not before. She did not envy him his dilemma.

With renewed energy, Buruk the Pale decided to set about selling his iron, and for this he was required to have an Acquitor accompanying him. Three Nerek trailed them as they walked up towards the forges, each carrying an ingot.

It had been raining steadily since the feast in the Warlock King's longhouse. Water flowed in turgid streams down the stony streets. Acrid clouds hung low in the vicinity of the forges, coating the wood and stone walls in oily soot. Slaves swathed in heavy rain cloaks moved to and fro along the narrow passages between compound walls.

Seren led Buruk and his servants towards a squat stone building with high, slitted windows, the entranceway three steps from ground level and flanked by Blackwood columns carved to mimic hammered bronze, complete with rivets and dents. The door was Blackwood inlaid with silver and black iron, the patterns an archaic, stylized script that Seren suspected contained shadow-wrought wards.

She turned to Buruk. 'I have to enter alone to begin with—'

The door was flung open, startling her, and three Edur rushed out, pushing past her. She stared after them, wondering at their tense expressions. A flutter of fear ran through her. 'Send the Nerek back,' she said to Buruk. 'Something's happened.'

The merchant did not argue. He gestured and the three Nerek hurried away.

Instead of entering the guild house, Seren and Buruk made their way to the centre street, seeing more Edur emerging from buildings and side alleys to line the approach to the noble quarter. No-one spoke.

'What is going on, Acquitor?'

She shook her head. 'Here is fine.' They had a clear enough view up the street, two hundred or more paces, and in the distance a procession had appeared. She counted five Edur warriors, one employing a staff as he limped along. Two others were pulling a pair of sleds across the slick stones of the street. A fourth walked slightly ahead of the others.

'Isn't that Binadas Sengar?' Buruk asked. 'The one with the stick, I mean.'

Seren nodded. He looked to be in pain, exhausted by successive layers of sorcerous healing. The warrior who walked ahead was clearly kin to Binadas. This, then, was the return of the group Hannan Mosag had sent away.

And now she saw, strapped to one of the sleds, a wrapped form – hides over pieces of ice that wept steadily down the sides. A shape more than ominous. Unmistakable.

'They carry a body,' Buruk whispered.

Where did they go? Those bundled furs – north, then. But there's nothing up there, nothing but ice. What did the Warlock King ask of them?

333

The memory of Feather Witch's divinations returned to her suddenly, inexplicably, and the chill in her bones deepened. 'Come on,' she said in a quiet tone. 'To the inner ward. I want to witness this.' She edged back from the crowd and set off.

'If they'll let us,' Buruk muttered, hurrying to catch up.

'We stay in the background and say nothing,' she instructed. 'It's likely they'll all be too preoccupied to pay us much attention.'

'I don't like this, Acquitor. Not any of it.'

She shared his dread, but said nothing.

They crossed the bridge well ahead of the procession, although it was evident that word had preceded them. The noble families were all out in the compound, motionless in the rain. Foremost among them were Tomad and Uruth, a respectful space around the two Edur and their slaves.

'It's one of the Sengar brothers,' Seren Pedac said under her breath.

Buruk heard her. 'Tomad Sengar was once a rival of Hannan Mosag's for the throne,' he muttered. 'How will he take this, I wonder?'

She glanced over at him. 'How do you know that?'

'I was briefed, Acquitor. That shouldn't surprise you, all things considered.'

The procession had reached the bridge.

'Ah.' Buruk sighed. 'The Warlock King and his K'risnan have emerged from the citadel.'

Udinaas stood a pace behind Uruth on her right, the rain running down his face.

Rhulad Sengar was dead.

He was indifferent to that fact. A young Edur eager for violence – there were plenty of those, and one fewer made little difference. That he was a Sengar virtually guaranteed that Udinaas would be tasked with dressing the corpse. He was not looking forward to that.

334

Three days for the ritual, including the vigil and the staining of the flesh. In his mind, he ran through possibilities in a detached sort of way, as the rain seeped down behind his collar and no doubt gathered in the hood he had not bothered to draw up over his head. If Rhulad had remained unblooded, the coins would be copper, with stone discs to cover the eyes. If blooded and killed in battle, it was probable that gold coins would be used. Letherii coins, mostly. Enough of them to ransom a prince. An extravagant waste that he found strangely delicious to contemplate.

Even so, he could already smell the stench of burning flesh.

He watched the group cross the bridge, Fear pulling the sled on which Rhulad's wrapped body had been laid. Binadas was limping badly – there must have been considerable damage, to resist the sorcerous healing that must already have been cast upon him. Theradas and Midik Buhn. And Trull Sengar, in the lead. Without the ever-present spear. *So, a battle indeed.*

'Udinaas, do you have your supplies?' Uruth asked in a dull voice.

'Yes, mistress, I have,' he replied, settling a hand on the leather pack slung from his left shoulder.

'Good. We will waste no time in this. You are to dress the body. No other.'

'Yes, mistress. The coals have been fired.'

'You are a diligent slave, Udinaas,' she said. 'I am pleased you are in my household.'

He barely resisted looking at her at that, confused and alarmed as he was by the admission. *And had you found the Wyval blood within me, you would have snapped my neck without a second thought.* 'Thank you, mistress.'

'He died a blooded warrior,' Tomad said. 'I see it in Fear's pride.'

The Warlock King and his five apprentice sorcerors strode to intercept the party as they arrived on this side

335

of the bridge, and Udinaas heard Uruth's gasp of outrage.

Tomad reached out to still her with one hand. 'There must be a reason for this,' he said. 'Come, we will join them.'

There was no command to remain behind, and so Udinaas and the other slaves followed Tomad and Uruth as they strode towards their sons.

Hannan Mosag and his K'risnan met the procession first. Quiet words were exchanged between the Warlock King and Fear Sengar. A question, an answer, and Hannan Mosag seemed to stagger. As one, the five sorcerors closed on him, but their eyes were on Rhulad's swathed form, and Udinaas saw a mixture of consternation, dread and alarm on their young faces.

Fear's gaze swung from the Warlock King to his father as Tomad's group arrived. 'I have failed you, Father,' he said. 'Your youngest son is dead.'

'He holds the gift,' Hannan Mosag snapped, shockingly accusatory in his tone. 'I need it, but he holds it. Was I not clear enough in my instructions, Fear Sengar?'

The warrior's face darkened. 'We were attacked, Warlock King, by the Jheck. I believe you know who and what they are—'

Tomad growled, 'I do not.'

Binadas spoke. 'They are Soletaken, Father. Able to assume the guise of wolves. It was their intention to claim the sword—'

'What sword?' Uruth asked. 'What—'

'Enough of this!' Hannan Mosag shouted.

'Warlock King,' Tomad Sengar said, stepping closer, 'Rhulad is dead. You can retrieve this gift of yours—'

'It is not so simple,' Fear cut in. 'Rhulad holds the sword still – I cannot pry his fingers from the grip.'

'It must be cut off,' Hannan Mosag said.

Uruth hissed, then shook her head. 'No, Warlock King. You are forbidden to mutilate our son. Fear, did Rhulad die as a blooded warrior?'

'He did.'

'Then the prohibitions are all the greater,' she said to Hannan Mosag, crossing her arms.

'I *need* that sword!'

In the fraught silence that followed that outburst, Trull Sengar spoke for the first time. 'Warlock King. Rhulad's body is still frozen. It may be, upon thawing, that his grip on the sword loosens. In any case, it seems clear the matter demands calm, reasoned discussion. It may in the end prove that our conflicting desires can be resolved by some form of compromise.' He faced his father and mother. 'It was our task, given us by the Warlock King, to retrieve a gift, and that gift is the sword Rhulad now holds. Mother, we must complete the task demanded of us. The sword must be placed in Hannan Mosag's hands.'

There was shock and horror in her voice as Uruth replied, 'You would cut off your dead brother's hands? Are you my son? I would—'

Her husband stopped her with a fierce gesture. 'Trull, I understand the difficulty of this situation, and I concur with your counsel that decisions be withheld for the time being. Warlock King, Rhulad's body must be prepared. This can be conducted without attention being accorded the hands. We have some time, then, do you agree?'

Hannan Mosag answered with a curt nod.

Trull approached Udinaas, and the slave could see the warrior's exhaustion, the old blood of countless wounds in his tattered armour. 'Take charge of the body,' he said in a quiet tone. 'To the House of the Dead, as you would any other. Do not, however, expect the widows to attend the ritual – we must needs postpone that until certain matters are resolved.'

'Yes, master,' Udinaas replied. He swung round and selected Hulad and one more of his fellow slaves. 'Help me with the sled's tethers. With solemn accord, as always.'

Both men he addressed were clearly frightened. This kind of open conflict among the Hiroth Edur was

337

unprecedented. They seemed on the verge of panic, although Udinaas's words calmed them somewhat. There were values in ritual, and self-control was foremost among them.

Stepping past the Edur, Udinaas led his two fellow slaves to the sled.

The waxed canvas sheathing the ice had slowed the melt, although the slabs beneath it were much diminished, the edges softened and milky white.

Fear passed the harness over to Udinaas. The two other slaves helping, they began dragging it towards the large wooden structure where Edur corpses were prepared for burial. No-one stopped them.

Seren Pedac gripped Buruk's arm and began pulling him back towards the bridge. He swung her a wild look, but wisely said nothing.

They could not manage the passage unseen, and Seren felt sweat prickling on her neck and in the small of her back as she guided the merchant back towards the guest camp. They were not accosted, but their presence had without doubt been marked. The consequences of that would remain undetermined, until such time as the conflict they had witnessed was resolved.

The Nerek had extended a tarp from one of the wagons to shield the hearth they kept continually burning. They scurried from the smoky flames as soon as Buruk and Seren arrived, quickly disappearing into their tents.

'That looks,' Buruk muttered as he edged closer to the hearth and held out his hands, 'to be serious trouble. The Warlock King was badly shaken, and I like not this talk of a gift. A sword? Some kind of sword, yes? A gift from whom? Surely not an alliance with the Jheck—'

'No,' agreed Seren, 'given that it was the Jheck with whom they fought. There's nothing else out there, Buruk. Nothing at all.'

She thought back to that scene on the other side of the

338

bridge. Fear's brother, not Binadas, but the other one, who'd counselled reason, he . . . interested her. Physically attractive, of course. Most Edur were. But there was more. There was . . . intelligence. And pain. Seren scowled. She was always drawn to the hurting ones.

'A sword,' Buruk mused, staring into the flames, 'of such value that Hannan Mosag contemplates mutilating a blooded warrior's corpse.'

'Doesn't that strike you as odd?' Seren asked. 'A corpse, holding on to a sword so tight even Fear Sengar cannot pull it loose?'

'Perhaps frozen?'

'From the moment of death?'

He grunted. 'I suppose not, unless it took his brothers a while to get to him.'

'A day or longer, at least. Granted, we don't know the circumstances, but that does seem unlikely, doesn't it?'

'It does.' Buruk shrugged. 'A damned Edur funeral. That won't put the Warlock King in a good mood. The delegation will arrive at precisely the wrong time.'

'I think not,' Seren said. 'The Edur have been un-balanced by this. Hannan Mosag especially. Unless there's quick resolution, we will be among a divided people.'

A quick, bitter smile. 'We?'

'Letherii, Buruk. I am not part of the delegation. Nor, strictly speaking, are you.'

'Nor Hull Beddict,' he added. 'Yet something tells me we are irredeemably bound in that net, whether it sees the light of day or sinks to the deep.'

She said nothing, because he was right.

The sled glided easily along the wet straw and Udinaas raised a boot to halt its progress alongside the stone platform. Unspeaking, the three slaves began unclasping the straps, pulling them free from beneath the body. The tarp was then lifted clear. The slabs of ice were resting on a cloth-wrapped shape clearly formed by the body it contained, and all three saw at the same time that Rhulad's jaw had opened in death, as if voicing a silent, endless scream.

Hulad stepped back. 'Errant preserve us,' he hissed.

'It's common enough, Hulad,' Udinaas said. 'You two can go, but first drag that chest over here, the one resting on the rollers.'

'Gold coins, then?'

'I am assuming so,' Udinaas replied. 'Rhulad died a blooded warrior. He was noble-born. Thus, it must be gold.'

'What a waste,' said Hulad.

The other slave, Irim, grinned and said, 'When the Edur are conquered, we should form a company, the three of us, to loot the barrows.' He and Hulad pulled the chest along the runners.

The coals were red, the sheet of iron black with heat.

Udinaas smiled. 'There are wards in those barrows, Irim. And shadow wraiths guarding them.'

'Then we hire a mage who can dispel them. The wraiths will be gone, along with every damned Edur. Nothing but rotting bones. I dream of that day.'

Udinaas glanced over at the old man. 'And how badly Indebted are you, Irim?'

The grin faded. 'That's just it. I'd be able to pay it off. For my grandchildren, who are still in Trate. Pay it off, Udinaas. Don't you dream the same for yourself?'

'Some debts can't be paid off with gold, Irim. My dreams are not of wealth.'

'No.' Irim's grin returned. 'You just want the heart of a lass so far above you, you've not the Errant's hope of owning it. Poor Udinaas, we all shake our heads at the sadness of it.'

'Less sadness than pity, I suspect,' Udinaas said, shrugging. 'Close enough. You can go.'

'The stench lingers even now,' Hulad said. 'How can you stand it, Udinaas?'

'Inform Uruth that I have begun.'

* * *

It was not the time to be alone, yet Trull Sengar found himself just that. The realization was sudden, and he blinked, slowly making sense of his surroundings. He was in the longhouse, the place of his birth, standing before the centre post with its jutting sword-blade. The heat from the hearth seemed incapable of reaching through to his bones. His clothes were sodden.

He'd left the others outside, locked in their quiet clash of wills. The Warlock King and his need against Tomad and Uruth and their insistence on proper observance of a dead blooded warrior, a warrior who was their son. With this conflict, Hannan Mosag could lose his authority among the Tiste Edur.

The Warlock King should have shown constraint. This could have been dealt with quietly, unknown to anyone else. How hard can it be to wrest a sword loose from a dead man's hands? And if sorcery was involved – and it certainly seemed to be – then Hannan Mosag was in his element. He had his K'risnan as well. They could have done something. And if not . . . *then cut his fingers off.* A corpse no longer housed the spirit. Death had severed the binding. Trull could feel nothing for the cold flesh beneath the ice. It was not Rhulad any more, not any longer.

But now there could be no chance of secrecy. The quarrel had been witnessed, and, in accordance with tradition, so too must be the resolution.

And . . . does any of it matter?

I did not trust Rhulad Sengar. Long before his failure on night watch. That is the truth of it. I knew . . . doubts.

His thoughts could take him no further. Anguish rose in a flood, burning like acid. As if he had raised his own demon, hulking and hungry, and could only watch as it fed on his soul. Gnawing regret and avid guilt, remorse an unending feast.

We are doomed, now, to give answer to his death, again and again. Countless answers, to crowd the solitary question of his

341

life. Is it our fate, then, to suffer beneath the siege of all that can never be known?

There had been strangers witnessing the scene. The realization was sudden, shocking. A merchant and his Acquitor. Letherii visitors. Advance spies of the treaty delegation.

Hannan Mosag's confrontation was a dreadful error in so many ways. Trull's high regard for the Warlock King had been damaged, sullied, and he longed for the world of a month past. Before the revelation of flaws and frailties.

Padding through the forest, mind filled with the urgency of dire news. A spear left in his wake, iron point buried deep in the chest of a Letherii. Leaden legs taking him through shadows, moccasins thudding on the dappled trail. The sense of having just missed something, an omen unwitnessed. Like entering a chamber someone else has just walked from, although in his case the chamber had been a forest cathedral, Hiroth sanctified land, and he had seen no signs of passage to give substance to his suspicion.

And it was this sense that had returned to him. They had passed through fraught events, all unmindful of significance, of hidden truths. The exigencies of survival had forced upon them a kind of carelessness.

A gelid wave of conviction rose within Trull Sengar, and he knew, solid as a knife in his heart, that something terrible was about to happen.

He stood, alone in the longhouse.

Facing the centre post and its crooked sword.

And he could not move.

Rhulad Sengar's body was frozen. A pallid grey, stiff-limbed figure lying on the stone platform. Head thrown back, eyes squeezed shut, mouth stretched long as if striving for a breath never found. The warrior's hands were closed about the grip of a strange, mottled, straight-bladed sword, frost-rimed and black-flecked with dried blood.

Udinaas had filled the nose and ear holes with wax.

He held the pincers, waiting for the first gold coin to reach optimum heat on the iron plate suspended above the coals. He had placed one on the sheet, then, twenty heart-beats later, another. The order of placement for noble-born blooded warriors was precise, as was the allotted time for the entire ritual. Awaiting Udinaas was a period of mind-numbing repetition and exhaustion.

But a slave could be bent to any task. There were hard truths found only in the denigration of one's own spirit, if one was inclined to look for them. *Should, for example, a man require self-justification. Prior to, say, murder, or some other atrocity.*

Take this body. A young man whose flesh is now a proclamation of death. The Edur use coins. Letherii use linen, lead and stone. In both, the need to cover, to disguise, to hide away the horrible absence writ there in that motionless face.

Open, or closed, it began with the eyes.

Udinaas gripped the edge of the Letherii coin with the pincers. These first two had to be slightly cooler than the others, lest the eyes behind the lids burst. He had witnessed that once, when he was apprenticed to an elder slave who had begun losing his sense of time. Sizzling, then an explosive spurt of lifeless fluid, foul-smelling and murky with decay, the coin settling far too deep in the socket, the hissing evaporation and crinkling, blackening skin.

He swung round on the stool, careful not to drop the coin, then leaned over Rhulad Sengar's face. Lowered the hot gold disc.

A soft sizzle, as the skin of the lid melted, all moisture drawn from it so that it tightened round the coin. Holding it fast.

He repeated the task with the second coin.

The heat in the chamber was thawing the corpse, and, as Udinaas worked setting coins on the torso, he was continually startled by movement. Arched back settling, an elbow voicing a soft thud, rivulets of melt water crawling

343

across the stone to drip from the sides, as if the body now wept.

The stench of burnt skin was thick in the hot, humid air. Rhulad Sengar's corpse was undergoing a transformation, acquiring gleaming armour, becoming something other than Tiste Edur. In the mind of Udinaas he ceased to exist as a thing once living, the work before the slave little different from mending nets.

Chest, to abdomen. Each spear-wound packed with clay and oil, encircled with coins then sealed. Pelvis, thighs, knees, shins, ankles, the tops of the feet. Shoulders, upper arms, elbows, forearms.

One hundred and sixty-three coins.

Udinaas wiped sweat from his eyes then rose and walked, limbs aching, over to the cauldron containing the melted wax. He had no idea how much time had passed. The stench kept his appetite at bay, but he had filled the hollow in his stomach a half-dozen times with cool water. Outside, the rain had continued, battering on the roof, swirling over the ground beyond the walls. A village in mourning – none would disturb him until he emerged.

He would have preferred a half-dozen Edur widows conducting the laying of coins, with him at his usual station tending to the fire. The last time he had done this in solitude had been with Uruth's father, killed in battle by the Arapay. He had been younger then, awed by the spectacle and his role in its making.

Attaching the handle to the cauldron, Udinaas lifted it from the hearth and carefully carried it back to the corpse. A thick coating over the front and sides of the corpse. A short time for the wax to cool – not too much, so that it cracked when he turned over the body – then he would return to the gold coins.

Udinaas paused for a moment, standing over the dead Tiste Edur. 'Ah, Rhulad,' he sighed. 'You could surely strut before the women now, couldn't you?'

* * *

'The mourning has begun.'

Trull started, then turned to find Fear standing at his shoulder. 'What? Oh. Then what has been decided?'

'Nothing.' His brother swung away and walked to the hearth. His face twisted as he regarded the low flames. 'The Warlock King proclaims our efforts a failure. Worse, he believes we betrayed him. He would hide that suspicion, but I see it none the less.'

Trull was silent a moment, then he murmured, 'I wonder when the betrayal began. And with whom.'

'You doubted this "gift", from the very first.'

'I doubt it even more now. A sword that will not relinquish its grip on a dead warrior. What sort of weapon is this, Fear? What sorcery rages on within it?' He faced his brother. 'Did you look closely at that blade? Oh, skilfully done, but there are . . . shards, trapped in the iron. Of some other metal, which resisted the forging. Any apprentice swordsmith could tell you that such a blade will shatter at first blow.'

'No doubt the sorcery invested would have prevented that,' Fear replied.

'So,' Trull sighed, 'Rhulad's body is being prepared.'

'Yes, it has begun. The Warlock King has drawn our parents into the privacy of his longhouse. All others are forbidden to enter. There will be . . . negotiations.'

'The severing of their youngest son's hands, in exchange for what?'

'I don't know. The decision will be publicly announced, of course. In the meantime, we are left to our own.'

'Where is Binadas?'

Fear shrugged. 'The healers have taken him. It will be days before we see him again. Mages are difficult to heal, especially when it's broken bone. The Arapay who tended to him said there were over twenty pieces loose in the flesh of his hip. All need to be drawn back into place and mended. Muscle and tendons to knit, vessels to be sealed and dead blood expunged.'

Trull walked over to a bench alongside a wall and sat down, settling his head in his hands. The whole journey seemed unreal now, barring the battle-scars on flesh and armour, and the brutal evidence of a wrapped corpse now being dressed for burial.

The Jheck had been Soletaken. He had not realized. Those wolves . . .

To be Soletaken was a gift belonging to Father Shadow and his kin. It belonged to the skies, to creatures of immense power. That primitive, ignorant barbarians should possess a gift of such prodigious, holy power made no sense.

Soletaken. It now seemed . . . sordid. A weapon as savage and as mundane as a raw-edged axe. He did not understand how such a thing could be.

'A grave test awaits us, brother.'

Trull blinked up at Fear. 'You sense it as well. Something's coming, isn't it?'

'I am unused to this . . . to this feeling. Of helplessness. Of . . . not knowing.' He rubbed at his face, as if seeking to awaken the right words from muscle, blood and bone. As if all that waited within him ever struggled, futile and frustrated, to find a voice that others could hear.

A pang of sympathy struck Trull, and he dropped his gaze, no longer wanting to witness his brother's discomfort. 'It is the same with me,' he said, although the admission was not entirely true. He was not unused to helplessness; some feelings one learned to live with. He had none of Fear's natural, physical talents, none of his brother's ease. It seemed his only true skill was that of relentless observation, fettered to a dark imagination. 'We should get some sleep,' he added. 'Exhaustion ill fits these moments. Nothing will be announced without us.'

'True enough, brother.' Fear hesitated, then reached out and settled a hand on Trull's shoulder. 'I would you stand at my side always, if only to keep me from stumbling.' The hand withdrew and Fear walked towards the sleeping chambers at the back of the longhouse.

Trull stared after him, stunned by the admission, half disbelieving. *As I gave words to comfort him, has he just done the same for me?*

Theradas had told him they could hear the sounds of battle, again and again, cutting through the wind and the blowing snow. They'd heard bestial screams of pain, wolf-howls crying in mortal despair. They'd heard him leading the Jheck from their path. Heard, until distance stole from them all knowledge of his fate. And then, they had awaited the arrival of the enemy – who never came.

Trull had already forgotten most of those clashes, the numbers melding into one, a chaotic nightmare unstepped from time, swathed in the gauze of snow stretched and torn by the circling wind, wrapping ever tighter. Bound and carried as if made disparate, disconnected from the world. *Is this how the direst moments of the past are preserved? Does this pain-ridden separation occur to each and every one of us – us . . . survivors?* The mind's own barrow field, the trail winding between the mounded earth hiding the heavy stones and the caverns of darkness with their blood-painted walls and fire-scorched capstones – a life's wake, forlorn beneath a grey sky. Once walked, that trail could never be walked again. One could only look back, and know horror at the vastness and the riotous accumulation of yet more barrows. More, and more.

He rose and made his way to his sleeping mat. Wearied by the thought of those whom the Edur worshipped, who had lived tens upon tens of thousands of years, and the interminable horror of all that lay behind them, the endless road of deed and regret, the bones and lives now dust bedding corroded remnants of metal – nothing more, because the burden life could carry was so very limited, because life could only walk onward, ever onward, the passage achieving little more than a stirring of dust in its wake.

Sorrow grown bitter with despair, Trull sank down onto the thinly padded mattress, lay back and closed his eyes.

The gesture served only to unleash his imagination, image after image sobbing to life with silent but inconsolable cries that filled his head.

He reeled before the onslaught, and, like a warrior staggering senseless before relentless battering, he fell backward in his mind, into oblivion.

Like a bed of gold in a mountain stream, a blurred gleam swimming before his eyes. Udinaas leaned back, only now fully feeling the leaden weight of his exhausted muscles, slung like chains from his bones. The stench of burnt flesh had painted his lungs, coating the inside of his chest and seeping its insipid poison into his veins. His flesh felt mired in dross.

He stared down at the gold-studded back of Rhulad Sengar. The wax coating the form had cooled, growing more opaque with every passing moment.

Wealth belongs to the dead, or so it must be for one such as me. Beyond my reach. He considered those notions, the way they drifted through the fog in his mind. Indebtedness and poverty. The defining limits of most lives. Only a small proportion of the Letherii population knew riches, could indulge in excesses. Theirs was a distinct world, an invisible paradise framed by interests and concerns unknown to everyone else.

Udinaas frowned, curious at his own feelings. There was no envy. Only sorrow, a sense of all that lay beyond his grasp, and would ever remain so. In a strange way, the wealthy Letherii had become as remote and alien to him as the Edur. He was disconnected, the division as sharp and absolute as the one before him now – his own worn self and the gold-sheathed corpse before him. The living and the dead, the dark motion of his body and the perfect immobility of Rhulad Sengar.

He prepared for his final task before leaving the chamber. The wax had solidified sufficiently to permit the turning over of the body. Upon entering this house,

Rhulad's parents would expect to find their dead son lying on his back, made virtually unrecognizable by the coins and the wax. Made, in fact, into a sarcophagus, already remote, with the journey to the shadow world begun.

Errant take me, have I the strength for this?

The corpse had been rolled onto wooden paddles with curved handles that were both attached to a single lever. A four-legged ridge pole was set crossways beneath the lever, providing the fulcrum. Udinaas straightened and positioned himself at the lever, taking the Blackwood in both hands and settling on it the weight of his upper body. He hesitated, lowering his head until his brow rested on his forearms.

The shadow wraith was silent, not a single whisper in his ear for days now. The blood of the Wyval slept. He was alone.

He had been expecting an interruption through the entire procedure. Hannan Mosag and his K'risnan, thundering into the chamber. To cut off Rhulad's fingers, or the entire hands. Having no instructions to the contrary, Udinaas had sheathed the sword in wax, angled slightly as it reached down along the body's thighs.

He drew a deep breath, then pushed down on the lever. Lifting the body a fraction. Cracks in the wax, a crazed web of lines, but that was to be expected. Easily repaired. Udinaas pushed harder, watching as the body began turning, edging onto its side. The sword's weight defeated the wax sheathing the blade, and the point clunked down on the stone platform, drawing the arms with it. Udinaas swore under his breath, blinking the sweat from his eyes. Plate-sized sheets of wax had fallen away. The coins, at least – he saw with relief – remained firmly affixed.

He slipped a restraining strap over the lever to hold it in place, then moved to the corpse. Repositioning the sword, he nudged the massive weight further over in increments, until the balance shifted and the body thumped onto its back.

Udinaas waited until he regained his breath. Another coating of wax was needed, to repair the damage. Then he could stumble out of this nightmare.

A slave needn't think. There were tasks to be done. Too many thoughts were crawling through him, interfering with his concentration.

He stumbled back to the hearth to retrieve the cauldron of wax.

A strange snapping sound behind him. Udinaas turned. He studied the corpse, seeking the place where the wax had broken loose. There, along the jaw, splitting wide over the mouth. He recalled the facial contortion that had been revealed when the bindings had been removed. It was possible he would have to sew the lips together.

He picked up the cauldron and made his way back to the corpse.

He saw the head jerk back.

A shuddering breath.

And then the corpse screamed.

From nothingness a scene slowly came into resolution, and Trull Sengar found himself standing, once more amidst gusting wind and swirling snow. He was surrounded, a ring of dark, vague shapes. The smeared gleam of amber eyes was fixed on him, and Trull reached for his sword, only to find the scabbard empty.

The Jheck had found him at last, and this time there would be no escape. Trull spun round, and again, as the huge wolves edged closer. The wind's howl filled his ears.

He searched for a dagger – anything – but could find nothing. His hands were numb with cold, the blowing snow stinging his eyes.

Closer, now, on all sides. Trull's heart pounded. He was filled with terror, filled as a drowning man is filled by the inrush of deadly water, the shock of denial, the sudden loss of all strength, and with it, all will.

The wolves charged.

Jaws closed on his limbs, fangs punching through skin. He was dragged down beneath the weight of onslaught. A wolf closed its mouth round the back of his neck. Dreadful grinding motions chewed through muscle. Bones snapped. His mouth gushed full and hot with blood and bile. He sagged, unable even to curl tight as the beasts tore at his arms and legs, ripped into his belly.

He could hear nothing but the wind's shriek, ever climbing.

Trull opened his eyes. He was sprawled on his sleeping mat, pain throbbing in his muscles with the ghost memory of those savage teeth.

And heard screaming.

Fear appeared in the entranceway, his eyes strangely red-rimmed, blinking in bewilderment. 'Trull?'

'It's coming from outside,' he replied, climbing stiffly to his feet.

They emerged to see figures running, converging on the House of the Dead.

'What is happening?'

Trull shook his head at his brother's question. 'Perhaps Udinaas . . .'

They set off.

Two slaves stumbled from the building's entrance, then fled in panic, one of them shouting incoherently.

The brothers picked up their pace.

Trull saw the Letherii Acquitor and her merchant on the bridge, figures rushing past them as they made a slow, hesitant approach.

The screams had not abated. There was pain in those cries, and horror. The sound, renewed breath after breath, made the blood gelid in Trull's veins. He could almost . . .

Mayen was in the doorway, which was ajar. Behind her stood the slave Feather Witch.

Neither moved.

Fear and Trull reached them.

351

Feather Witch's head snapped round, the eyes half mad as they stared up at first Trull, then Fear.

Fear came to the side of his betrothed in the doorway. He stared inward, face flinching with every scream. 'Mayen,' he said, 'keep everyone else out. Except for Tomad and Uruth and the Warlock King, when they arrive. Trull—' The name was spoken like a plea.

Mayen stepped back and Trull edged forward.

Side by side, they entered the House of the Dead.

A mass, a hunched shape, covered in wax like peeling skin, revealing the glitter of gold coins, slouched down at the foot of the stone platform, face lowered, forehead on knees, arms wrapped tight about shins but still holding the sword. A mass, a hunched shape, voicing endless shrieks.

The slave Udinaas stood nearby. He had been carrying a cauldron of wax. It lay on its side two paces to the Letherii's left, the wax spilled out amidst twigs and straw.

Udinaas was murmuring. Soothing words cutting beneath the screams. He was moving closer to the shape, step by careful step.

Fear made to start forward but Trull gripped his upper arm and held him back. He'd heard something in those shrieks. They had come to answer the slave's low soothings, defiant at first, but now thinning, the voice filling with pleading. Strangled again and again into shudders of raw despair. And through it all Udinaas continued to speak.

Sister bless us, that is Rhulad. My brother.

Who was dead.

The slave slowly crouched before the horrid figure, and Trull could make out his words as he said, 'There are coins before your eyes, Rhulad Sengar. That is why you can see nothing. I would remove them. Your brothers are here. Fear and Trull. They are here.'

The shrieks broke then, replaced by helpless weeping.

Trull stared as Udinaas then did something he did not think possible. The slave reached out and took Rhulad's head in his hands, as a mother might an inconsolable child.

Tender, yet firm, the hands slowly lifted it clear of the knees.

A sobbing sound came from Fear, quickly silenced, but Trull felt his brother tremble.

The face – oh, Father Shadow, the face.

A crazed mask of wax, cracked and scarred. And beneath it, gold coins, melded onto the flesh – not one had dislodged – angled like the scales of armour around the stretched jaw, the gasping mouth.

Udinaas leaned closer still, spoke low beside Rhulad's left ear.

Words, answered with a shudder, a spasm that made coins click – the sound audible but muted beneath wax. A foot scraped across the stone flagstones surrounding the platform, drew in tighter.

Fear jolted in Trull's grip, but he held on, held his brother back as Udinaas reached down to his belt and drew out a work knife.

Whispering; rhythmic, almost musical. The slave brought the knife up. Carefully set the edge near the tip alongside the coin covering Rhulad's left eye.

The face flinched, but Udinaas drew his right arm round into a kind of embrace, leaned closer, not pausing in his murmuring. Pressure with the edge, minute motion, then the coin flashed as it came loose along the bottom. A moment later it fell away.

The eye was closed, a mangled, red welt. Rhulad must have sought to open it because Udinaas laid two fingers against the lid and Trull saw him shake his head as he said something, then repeated it.

A strange tic from Rhulad's head, and Trull realized it had been a nod.

Udinaas then reversed the position of his arms, and set the knife edge to Rhulad's right eye.

Outside was the sound of a mass of people, but Trull did not turn about. He could not pull his gaze from the Letherii, from his brother.

He was dead. There was no doubt. None.

The slave, who had worked on Rhulad for a day and a night, filling mortal wounds with wax, burning coins into the cold flesh, who had then seen his charge return to life, now knelt before the Edur, his voice holding insanity at bay, his voice – and his hands – guiding Rhulad back to the living.

A Letherii slave.

Father Shadow, who are we to have done this?

The coin was prised loose.

Trull pulled Fear along as he stepped closer. He did not speak. Not yet.

Udinaas returned the knife to its sheath. He leaned back, one hand withdrawing to settle on Rhulad's left shoulder. Then the slave pivoted and looked up at Trull. 'He's not ready to speak. The screaming has exhausted him, given the weight of the coins encasing his chest.' Udinaas half rose, intending to move away, but Rhulad's left arm rustled, hand sobbing away from the sword's grip, coins clicking as the fingers groped, then found the slave's arm. And held on.

Udinaas almost smiled – and Trull saw for the first time the exhaustion of the man, the extremity of all that he had gone through – and settled down once more. 'Your brothers, Rhulad,' he said. 'Trull, and Fear. They are here to take care of you now. I am but a slave—'

Two coins fell away as Rhulad's grip tightened.

'You will stay, Udinaas,' Trull said. 'Our brother needs you. We need you.'

The Letherii nodded. 'As you wish, master. Only . . . I am tired. I – I keep blacking out, only to awaken at the sound of my own voice.' He shook his head helplessly. 'I don't even know what I have said to your brother—'

'It matters not,' Fear cut in. 'What you have done . . .' His words trailed away, and for a moment it seemed his face would crumple. Trull saw the muscles of his brother's neck tauten, then Fear's eyes closed tight, he drew a deep breath and was himself once more. He shook his head, unable to speak.

Trull crouched beside Udinaas and Rhulad. 'Udinaas, I understand. You need rest. But stay for a few moments longer, if you can.'

The slave nodded.

Trull shifted his gaze, studied Rhulad's ravaged face, the eyes still shut – but there was movement behind them. 'Rhulad. It is Trull. Listen to me, my brother. Keep your eyes closed, for now. We must get this – this armour – off you—'

At that Rhulad shook his head.

'They are funereal coins, Rhulad—'

'Y-yes. I . . . know.'

Words raw and heavy, the breath pushed out from a constricted chest.

Trull hesitated, then said, 'Udinaas has been with you, alone, preparing you—'

'Yes.'

'He is used up, brother.'

'Yes. Tell Mother. I want. I want him.'

'Of course. But let him go now, please—'

The hand dropped away from the slave's arm, clunking hard and seemingly insensate on the floor. The other hand, still holding the sword, suddenly twitched.

And a ghastly smile emerged on Rhulad's face. 'Yes. I hold it still. This. This is what he meant.'

Trull edged back slightly.

Udinaas crawled off a short distance, leaned up against the chest of coins. He drew himself up into a shape echoing that of Rhulad, and, in the moment before he turned his face away, Trull saw the visage fill with anguish.

Exhaustion or no, for Udinaas peace and rest was ten thousand paces away – Trull could see that, could understand that brutal truth. Rhulad had had the slave, but whom did Udinaas have?

Not a typical Edur thought.

But nothing – *nothing* – was as it was. Trull rose and moved close to Fear. He thought for a moment, then swung round to the entranceway. Mayen was still standing there, at her side the Letherii, Feather Witch. Trull gestured at the slave, then pointed to where Udinaas crouched.

He saw her face stretch in horror. Saw her shake her head.

Then she ran from the building.

Trull grimaced.

A commotion at the entrance, and Mayen withdrew from sight.

Tomad and Uruth appeared.

And behind them, as they slowly edged forward, came Hannan Mosag.

Oh. Oh no. The sword. The damned sword—

CHAPTER TEN

White petals spin and curl on their way
down to the depthless sea.
The woman and her basket, her hand flashing red
in quick soft motion scattering these
pure wings, to ride a moment on the wind.
She stands, a forlorn goddess birthing flight
that fails and falls on the river's broad breast.
A basket of birds destined to drown.
See her weep in the city's drawn shadow
her hand a thing disembodied,
carrion-clawed and ceaseless in repetition,
she delivers death and in her eyes
is seen the horror of living.

Lady Elassara of Trate
Cormor Fural

The roll of thunder, the heavy trammelling of rain on the roof. The storm was following the course of the river, drawn northward and dragging one edge of its heaving clouds across Letheras. Unseasonal, unwelcome, making the single room of Tehol's abode close and steamy. There were two more stools than there had been, retrieved by Bugg from a rubbish heap. On one of them, in the far corner, sat Ublala Pung, weeping.

As he had been without pause for over a bell, his huge frame racked with a shuddering that made the stool creak alarmingly.

In the centre of the small room, Tehol paced.

A splashing of feet outside, then the curtain in the doorway was tugged to one side and Bugg stamped in, water streaming from him. He coughed. 'What's burning in the hearth?'

Tehol shrugged. 'Whatever was piled up beside it, of course.'

'But that was your rain hat. I wove it myself, with my own two hands.'

'A rain hat? Those reeds had wrapped rotting fish—'

'That's the stink, all right.' Bugg nodded, wiping at his eyes. 'Anyway, rotting is a relative term, master.'

'It is?'

'The Faraed consider it a delicacy.'

'You just wanted me to smell like fish.'

'Better you than the whole house,' Bugg said, glancing over at Ublala. 'What's wrong with him?'

'I haven't a clue,' Tehol said. 'So, what's the news?'

'I found her.'

'Great.'

'But we'll have to go and get her.'

'Go outside?'

'Yes.'

'Into the rain?'

'Yes.'

'Well,' Tehol said, resuming his pacing, 'I don't like that at all. Too risky.'

'Risky?'

'Why, yes. Risky. I might get wet. Especially now that I don't have a rain hat.'

'And whose fault is that, I wonder?'

'It was already smouldering, sitting so close to the hearth. I barely nudged it with my toe and up it went.'

'I was drying it out.'

Tehol paused in mid-step, studied Bugg for a moment, then resumed pacing. 'It's a storm,' he said after a moment. 'Storms pass. I need a reason to procrastinate.'

'Yes, master.'

Tehol swung round and approached Ublala Pung. 'Most beloved bodyguard, whatever is wrong?'

Red-rimmed eyes stared up at him. 'You're not interested. Not really. Nobody is.'

'Of course I'm interested. Bugg, I'm interested, aren't I? It's my nature, isn't it?'

'Absolutely, master. Most of the time.'

'It's the women, isn't it, Ublala? I can tell.'

The huge man nodded miserably.

'Are they fighting over you?'

He shook his head.

'Have you fallen for one of them?'

'That's just it. I haven't had a chance to.'

Tehol glanced over at Bugg, then back to Ublala. 'You haven't had a chance to. What a strange statement. Can you elaborate?'

'It's not fair, that's what it is. Not fair. You won't understand. It's not a problem you have. I mean, what am I? Am I to be nothing but a toy? Just because I have a big—'

'Hold on a moment,' Tehol cut in. 'Let's see if I fully understand you, Ublala. You feel they're just using you. Interested only in your, uh, attributes. All they want from you is sex. No commitment, no loyalty even. They're happy taking turns with you, taking no account of your feelings, your sensitive nature. They probably don't even want to cuddle afterwards or make small talk, right?'

Ublala nodded.

'And all that is making you miserable?'

He nodded again, snuffling, his lower lip protruding, his broad mouth downturned at the corners, a muscle twitching in his right cheek.

Tehol stared for a moment longer, then he tossed up his hands. 'Ublala! Don't you understand? You're in a man's paradise! What all the rest of us can only dream about!'

'But I want something more!'

359

'No! You don't! Trust me! Bugg, don't you agree? Tell him!'

Bugg frowned, then said, 'It is as Tehol says, Ublala. Granted, a tragic truth, and granted, Master's nature is to revel in tragic truths, which to many might seem unusual, unhealthy even—'

'Thanks for the affirmation, Bugg,' Tehol interrupted with a scowl. 'Go clean up, will you?' He faced Ublala again. 'You are at the pinnacle of male achievement, my friend – wait! Did you say it's not a problem I have? What did you mean by that?'

Ublala blinked. 'What? Uh, are you at that pinnacle, or whatever you called it – are you at it too?'

Bugg snorted. 'He hasn't been at it in months.'

'Well, that's it!' Tehol stormed to the hearth and plucked out what was left of the matted reeds. He stamped out the flames, then picked the charred object up and set it on his head. 'All right, Bugg, let's go and get her. As for this brainless giant here, he can mope around all alone in here, for all I care. How many insults can a sensitive man like me endure, anyway?'

Wisps of smoke drifted from the reeds on Tehol's head.

'That's about to take flame again, master.'

'Well, that's what's good about rain, then, isn't it? Let's go.'

Outside in the narrow aisle, water streamed ankle-deep towards the clogged drain at the far end, where a small lake was forming. Bugg a half-step in the lead, they sloshed their way across its swirling, rain-pocked expanse.

'You should be more sympathetic to Ublala, master,' Bugg said over a shoulder. 'He's a very unhappy man.'

'Sympathy belongs to the small-membered, Bugg. Ublala has three women drooling all over him, or have you forgotten?'

'That's a rather disgusting image.'

'You've been too old too long, dear servant. There's nothing inherently disgusting about drool.' He paused, then said, 'All right, maybe there is. However, do we have to talk about sex? That subject makes me nostalgic.'

'Errant forbid.'

'So, where is she?'

'In a brothel.'

'Oh, now that's really pathetic.'

'More like a newly acquired raging addiction, master. The more she feeds it, the hungrier it gets.'

They crossed Turol Avenue and made their way into the Prostitutes' District. The downpour was diminishing, the tail ends of the storm front streaming overhead. 'Well,' Tehol commented, 'that is not a desirable condition for one of my most valued employees. Especially since her addiction doesn't include her handsome, elegant boss. Something tells me it should have been me weeping in a corner back there, not Ublala.'

'It may simply be a case of Shurq not wanting to mix business with pleasure.'

'Bugg, you told me she's in a brothel.'

'Oh. Right. Sorry.'

'Now I'm truly miserable. I wasn't miserable this morning. If the trend continues, by dusk I'll be swimming the canal with bags of coins around my neck.'

'Here we are.'

They stood before a narrow, three-storey tenement, set slightly in from the adjoining buildings and looking a few centuries older than anything else on the street. The front facing held a carved façade around two square, inset columns of dusty blue marble. Decidedly female demons in bas-relief, contorted and writhing in a mass orgy, crowded the panels, and atop the columns crouched stone gargoyles with enormous breasts held high and inviting.

Tehol turned to Bugg. 'This is the Temple. She's in the Temple?'

'Does that surprise you?'

'I can't even afford to step across the threshold. Even Queen Janall frequents this place but a few times a year.

361

Annual membership dues are ten thousand docks . . . I've heard . . . it rumoured. From someone, once.'

'Matron Delisp is probably very pleased with her newest property.'

'I'd wager she is at that. So, how do we extract Shurq Elalle, especially since it's obvious she is where she wants to be, and the Matron has at least thirty thugs in her employ who're likely to try and stop us? Should we simply consider this a lost cause and be on our way?'

Bugg shrugged. 'That is up to you to decide, master.'

'Well.' He considered. 'I'd like at least a word with her.'

'Probably all you can afford.'

'Don't be absurd, Bugg. She doesn't charge by the word . . . does she?'

'She might well charge by the glance, master. Our dear dead thief has blossomed—'

'Thanks to me! Who arranged for her overhaul? Her dry-dock repairs, the new coat of paint? We had a deal—'

'Tell it to her, master, not me. I am well aware of the lengths you go to in appeasing your own peculiar appetites.'

'I'm not even going to ask what you mean by that, Bugg. It sounds sordid, and my sordid self is my own affair.'

'So it is, master, so it is. Good thing you're not the nostalgic type.'

Tehol glared at Bugg for a moment, then swung his attention once more to the Temple. The oldest brothel in all the land. Some said it was standing here long before the city rose up around it, and indeed the city rose up around it because of the brothel itself. That didn't make much sense, but then few things did when it came to love and its many false but alluring shades. He tilted his head back to study the gargoyles, and the scorched reed hat slid off to splash on the cobbles behind him. 'Well, that settles it. Either I stand here getting my hair wet, or I go inside.'

'As far as I can tell, master, my rain hat was a tragic failure in any case.'

'It's your over-critical nature, Bugg, what's done you in. Follow me!'

Tehol ascended the steps with proprietary determination. As he reached the landing the front door swung open and the frame was filled by a huge, hooded man wearing a black surcoat, a massive double-bladed axe in his gauntleted hands.

Appalled, Tehol halted, Bugg stumbling into him from behind on the lower step.

'Excuse me,' Tehol managed, stepping to one side and pulling Bugg along with him. 'Off to a beheading, then?' He gestured for the man to pass.

Small eyes glittered from the hood's shadows. 'Thank you, sir,' he said in a raspy voice. 'You are most courteous.' He strode forward onto the landing, then paused. 'It's raining.'

'Indeed, almost finished, I'd wager. See the blue overhead?'

The axe-carrying giant faced Tehol. 'If anyone asks, sir, you never saw me here.'

'You have my word.'

'Most kind.' He faced the street again, then cautiously descended the steps.

'Ooh,' he said as he set off, 'it's wet! Ooh!'

Tehol and Bugg watched him scurry away, hunched over and weaving to avoid the deeper puddles.

Bugg sighed. 'I admit to being greatly affrighted by his sudden appearance.'

Brows raised, Tehol regarded his servant. 'Really? Poor Bugg, you need to do something about those nerves of yours. Come on, then, and fear nothing whilst you are with me.'

They entered the Temple.

And Tehol halted once more, as suddenly as the first time, as the point of a knife settled on his cheek beneath his right eye, which blinked rapidly. Bugg managed to draw up in time to avoid bumping into his master, for which Tehol's gratitude was sufficient to weaken his knees.

A sweet feminine voice murmured close to his ear, 'You're not in disguise, sir. Which means, well, we both know what that means, don't we?'

'I've come for my daughter—'

'Now that's in very poor taste. We can't abide such twisted, sick desires in here—'

'You misunderstand – understandably, of course, that is. I meant to say, I've come to retrieve her, before it's too late.'

'Her name?'

'Shurq Elalle.'

'Well, it's too late.'

'You mean she being dead? I'm aware of that. It's her ancestors, you see, they want her to come home to the crypt. They miss her terribly, and a few of them are getting alarmingly angry. Ghosts can be a lot of trouble – not just for you and this establishment, but for me as well. You see my predicament?'

The knife point withdrew, and a short, lithe woman stepped round to stand before him. Close-fitting silks in rusty hues, a broad silk belt wrapped about her tiny waist, upturned slippers on her minuscule feet. A sweet, heart-shaped face, strangely overlarge eyes, now narrowing. 'Are you done?'

Tehol smiled sheepishly. 'You must get that a lot. Sorry. Are you, perchance, Matron Delisp?'

She spun about. 'Follow me. I hate this room.'

He glanced about for the first time. Two paces wide, four deep, a door at the far end, the walls hidden behind lush tapestries depicting countless couplings of all sorts. 'Seems inviting enough,' he said, following the woman to the door.

'It's the spent smell.'

'Spent? Oh, yes.'

'Smells of . . . regret. I hate that smell. I hate everything about it.' She opened the door and slipped through.

Tehol and Bugg hastened to follow.

The chamber beyond was dominated by a steep staircase,

which began a single pace beyond the doorway. The woman led them round it to a plush waiting room, thick-padded sofas along the side walls, a single high-backed chair occupying the far wall. She walked directly to that chair and sat down. 'Sit. Now, what's all this about ghosts? Oh, never mind that. You were, what, ten years old when you fathered Shurq Elalle? No wonder she never mentioned you. Even when she was alive. Tell me, were you disappointed when she decided on a career of thievery?'

'From your tone,' Tehol said, 'I gather you are challenging the veracity of my claims.'

'Which question gave me away?'

'But, you see, I am not so ignorant as you think. Hence my disguise.'

She blinked. 'Your disguise is to appear as a man in his early thirties, wearing sodden, badly made wool—'

Bugg sat straighter. 'Badly made? Now, hold on—'

Tehol nudged his servant with an elbow, hard in the ribs. Bugg grunted, then subsided.

'That is correct,' Tehol said.

'A vast investment in sorcery, then. How old are you in truth?'

'Sixty-nine . . . my dear.'

'I'm impressed. Now, you mentioned ghosts?'

'Afraid so, Matron. Terrible ones. Vengeful, disinclined to discourse. Thus far I have managed to keep them penned up in the family crypt, but they'll get out sooner or later. And proceed on a rampage through the streets – a night of terror for all Letheras's citizens, I fear – until they arrive here. And then, well, I shudder at the thought.'

'As I am shuddering right now, although for entirely different reasons. But yes, we certainly have a dilemma. My particular dilemma, however, is one I admit to having been struggling with for some time now.'

'Oh?'

'Fortunately, you appear to have provided me with a solution.'

'I am pleased.'

The woman leaned forward. 'Top floor – there's only one room. Talk that damned demoness out of here! Before my other lasses flay me alive!'

The stairs were steep but well padded, the wooden railing beneath their hands an unbroken undulation of lovingly carved breasts polished and oiled by countless sweaty palms. They met no-one on the way and reached the top floor breathless – due to the ascent, of course, Tehol told himself as he paused at the door and wiped his hands on his soaked leggings.

Head lowered and panting, Bugg was at his side. 'Errant take me, what have they rubbed into that wood?'

'I'm not sure,' Tehol admitted, 'but I can barely walk.'

'Perhaps we should take a moment,' Bugg suggested, wiping the sweat from his face.

'Good idea. Let's.'

A short time later Tehol straightened, with a wince, and nodded at Bugg, who grimaced in reply. Tehol raised a hand and thumped on the heavy wooden door.

'Enter,' came the muffled command.

Tehol opened the door and stepped into the room. Behind him, Bugg hissed, 'Errant take me, look at all the breasts!'

The wall panels and ceiling continued the theme begun on the wooden railing, a riotous proliferation of mammary excess. Even the floor beneath the thick rugs was lumpy.

'A singular obsession—' Tehol began, and was interrupted.

'Oh,' said a voice from the huge bed before them, 'it's you.'

Tehol cleared his throat. 'Shurq Elalle.'

'If you've come for services,' she said, 'you might be relieved to know the executioner's big axe was pathetic compensation.'

'He got wet in the rain,' Bugg said.

366

Tehol glanced back at him. 'What is the relevance of that?'

'I don't know, but I thought you might.'

'I'm not leaving,' Shurq said, 'if that's why you're here.'

'You have to,' Tehol countered. 'The Matron insists.'

She sat straighter in the bed. 'It's those damned cows downstairs, isn't it? I've stolen all their clients and they want me out!'

'I imagine so.' Tehol shrugged. 'But that's hardly surprising, is it? Listen, Shurq, we had a deal, didn't we?'

Her expression darkened. 'So I should do the honourable thing? All right, but I have a problem regarding certain appetites . . .'

'I wish I could help.'

Her brows rose.

'Uh, I meant – I mean – oh, I don't know what I mean.' He paused, then brightened. 'But I'll introduce you to Ublala, an unhappy bodyguard longing for commitment.'

Her brows rose higher.

'Well, why not? You don't have to tell him you're dead! He'll never notice, of that I'm certain! And as for your appetites, I doubt there'll be a problem there, although there's a trio of women who might be very upset, but I'll handle that. Look, it's a brilliant solution, Shurq.'

'I'll give it a try, I suppose, but I'm not making any promises. Now, step outside, please, so I can get dressed.'

Tehol and Bugg exchanged glances and then complied, softly shutting the door behind them.

Bugg studied his master. 'I am very impressed,' he said after a moment. 'I'd thought this a situation without a solution. Master, my admiration for you grows like a—'

'Stop staring at that railing, Bugg.'

'Uh, yes. You're right.'

Matron Delisp was waiting at the bottom of the stairs. Seeing Shurq Elalle following a step behind Bugg, her face twisted with distaste. 'Errant bless you, Tehol Beddict. I owe you one.'

Tehol sighed. 'I had a feeling you were sceptical of my story.'

'The woollen leggings,' she replied. 'I hear virtually everyone's put in orders for them.'

Tehol shot Bugg a look, but the servant's brows rose and he said, 'Not with me, master. That would be disloyal. Rest assured that everyone else's version will prove but pathetic imitations.'

'Perhaps, Matron Delisp,' Tehol said, 'I am merely disguised as Tehol Beddict. That would be clever, wouldn't it?'

'Too clever for you.'

'Well, you have a point there.'

'Anyway, do you want me in your debt or not?'

Shurq Elalle pushed past Bugg. 'I don't like being ignored. You're all ignoring me as if I was—'

'Dead?' Delisp asked.

'I just wanted to point out my reason for vacating this house, which is that I, too, owe Tehol Beddict. I may be dead, but I am not without honour. In any case, Delisp, I believe you owe me a rather substantial payment right now. Sixty per cent, I seem to recall—'

'What do you need all that money for?' the Matron demanded. 'How many variations of sex-assassin attire exist out there? How many bundles of raw spices do you need to keep fresh? No, wait, I don't want to know the answer. Sixty per cent. Fine, but it'll take me a day or two – I don't keep that kind of coin around here. Where should I have it delivered?'

'Tehol Beddict's residence will suffice.'

'Hold on,' Tehol objected. 'I can't secure—'

'I intend,' Shurq cut in, 'to spend it quickly.'

'Oh. All right, but I'm not happy. Too many comings and goings there. Suspicions will be insatiably aroused—'

'Stop staring at the railing, master.'

'Errant's dreams! Let's get out of here.'

* * *

The storm had passed. Rainwater still flowed down the streets, but people were venturing out once more. It was late afternoon. Shurq Elalle halted at the foot of the Temple's steps. 'I will rejoin you tonight, on your roof, Tehol Beddict. Midnight.'

'What about Ublala Pung?'

'I admit to having second thoughts.'

'Shurq Elalle. Ublala Pung survived a Drowning. He walked across the bottom of the canal. You two have a lot in common, if you think about it.'

'He's also massively endowed,' Bugg added.

Tehol made a face at him. 'You are being crude—'

'Bring him to the roof tonight,' Shurq said.

'This is a conspiracy to make me miserable, isn't it? Both of you, leave me. I'm going for a walk. Bugg, when you get back home, give it a tidy. No doubt Shand will be storming in before too long. Tell her I'll drop by tomorrow on some important business—'

'What important business?'

'I don't know. I'll invent something. You have other things to worry about – how's the foundation work coming along, anyway?'

'It's piling up.'

'Then sort it out.'

'You misunderstand, master. We're on schedule.'

'I didn't misunderstand. I was being obdurate. Now, I'm off to find a more reasonable conversation, somewhere.' He swung round for a final word with Shurq, but she was gone. 'Damned thief. Go on, Bugg. Wait, what's for supper?'

'Banana leaves.'

'Not fishy ones, I trust.'

'Of course not, master.'

'Then what?'

'The material they were wrapped around was unidentifiable, which, if you think about it, is probably a good thing.'

'How do we live on this stuff?'

369

'A good question, master. It is indeed baffling.'

Tehol studied his servant for a long moment, then he gestured the man away.

Bugg turned right, so Tehol went left. The air was warming, yet still fresh after the rain. Wet dogs nosed the rubbish in the settling puddles. Cats chased the cockroaches that had swarmed up from the drains. A beggar had found a sliver of soap and stood naked beneath a stream of water coming from a cracked eaves trough, working up a murky lather while he sang a lament that had been popular a hundred years ago. Residents had taken advantage of the unexpected downpour, emptying chamber pots from their windows rather than carrying them a few dozen paces to the nearest communal dump-hole. As a result, some of the pools held floating things and the streams in the gutters carried small flyblown islands that collected here and there in buzzing rafts that bled yellowy brown slime.

It was a fine evening in the city of Letheras, Tehol reflected, testing the air a moment before taking a deep breath and releasing it in a contented sigh. He went on down the street until he reached Quillas Canal, then walked along it towards the river. To his right rose a forest of masts from fisherboats moored to wait out the storm. Tarps were being pulled aside, water splashing as the crews bailed feverishly so they could make for open water before the day's light failed. Near one jetty a half-dozen city guardsmen were fishing a corpse from the murky water, a crowd of onlookers shouting advice as the squad struggled with hook-poles. Above them flapped seagulls.

Tehol came within sight of the old palace, then took a side street away from the canal, proceeding on a winding, confused route until he came to the grounds of the towers. Gathering dusk made the air grainy as Tehol reached the low crumbling wall and stared across the short expanse of broken, uneven yard to the one, battered tower that was clearly different in construction from all the others, being square instead of round.

The strange triangular windows were dark, crowded with dead vines. The inset, black-stained wooden door was shrouded in shadow. Tehol wondered how such a door could have survived – normal wood would have rotted to dust centuries ago.

He could see no-one in the yard. 'Kettle! Child, are you in there?'

A small bedraggled figure stepped out from behind a tree. Startled, Tehol said, 'That was a good trick, lass.'

She approached. 'There's an artist. A painter. He comes to paint the tower. He wants to paint me too, but I stay behind trees. It makes him very angry. You are the man who sleeps on the roof of your house. Lots of people try spying on you.'

'Yes, I know. Shurq tells me you, uh, take care of them.'

'She said maybe you could help find out who I was.'

He studied her. 'Have you seen Shurq lately?'

'Only once. She was all fixed. I barely recognized her.'

'Well, lass, we could see the same done for you, if you like.'

The grubby, mould-patched face wrinkled into a frown. 'Why?'

'Why? To make you less noticeable, I suppose. Wouldn't you enjoy looking the way Shurq does now?'

'Enjoy?'

'Think about it at least?'

'All right. You look friendly. You look like I could like you. I don't like many people, but I could like you. Can I call you Father? Shurq is my mother. She isn't, really, but that's what I call her. I'm looking for brothers and sisters, too.' She paused, then asked, 'Can you help me?'

'I'll try, Kettle. Shurq tells me the tower talks to you.'

'Not words. Just thoughts. Feelings. It's afraid. There's someone in the ground who is going to help. Once he gets free, he'll help us. He's my uncle. But the bad ones scare me.'

'The bad ones? Who are they? Are they in the ground, too?'

371

She nodded.

'Is there a chance they will get out of the ground before your uncle does?'

'If they do, they'll destroy us all. Me, Uncle and the tower. They've said so. And that will free all the others.'

'And are the others bad, too?'

She shrugged. 'They don't talk much. Except one. She says she'll make me an empress. I'd like to be an empress.'

'Well, I wouldn't trust that one. Just my opinion, Kettle, but promises like that are suspect.'

'That's what Shurq says, too. But she sounds very nice. She wants to give me lots of treats and stuff.'

'Be careful, lass.'

'Do you ever dream of dragons, Father?'

'Dragons?'

Shrugging again, she turned away. 'It's getting dark,' she said over her shoulder. 'I need to kill someone . . . maybe that artist . . .'

Turudal Brizad, the consort to Queen Janall, stood leaning against the wall whilst Brys Beddict led his students through the last of the counter-attack exercises.

Audiences were not uncommon during his training regime with the king's own guard, although Brys had been mildly surprised that Turudal was among the various onlookers, most of whom were practitioners with the weapons he used in his instruction. The consort was well known for his indolent ways, a privilege that, in the days of Brys's grandfather, would not have been tolerated in a young, fit Letherii. Four years of military service beginning in the seventeenth year had been mandatory. In those days there had been external threats aplenty. Bluerose to the north, the independent, unruly city-states of the archipelago in Dracons Sea, and the various tribes on the eastern plain had been pressuring Lether, driven against the outposts by one of the cyclical expansionist regimes of far Kolanse.

Bluerose now paid tribute to King Ezgara Diskanar, the city-states had been crushed, leaving little more than a handful of goat-herders and fisherfolk on the islands, and Kolanse had subsided into isolation following some sort of civil war a few decades past.

It was difficult for Brys to imagine a life possessing virtually no ability to defend itself, at least upon the attainment of adulthood, but Turudal Brizad was such a creature. Indeed, the consort had expressed the opinion that he was but a forerunner, a pioneer of a state of human life wherein soldiering was left to the Indebted and the mentally inadequate. Although Brys had initially scoffed at hearing a recounting of Brizad's words, his disbelief had begun to waver. The Letherii military was still strong, yet increasingly it was bound to economics. Every campaign was an opportunity for wealth. And, among the civilian population of traders, merchants and all those who served the innumerable needs of civilization, few were bothering with martial training any more. An undercurrent of contempt now coloured their regard of soldiers.

Until they need us, of course. Or they discover a means to profit by our actions.

He completed the exercise, then lingered to see who left the chamber and who remained to practise on their own. Most remained, and Brys was pleased. The two who had left were, he knew, the queen's spies in the bodyguard. Ironically, everyone else knew that detail as well.

Brys sheathed his sword and strode over to Turudal Brizad. 'Consort?'

A casual tilt of the head. 'Finadd.'

'Have you found yourself at a loose end? I don't recall ever seeing you here before.'

'The palace seems strangely empty, don't you think?'

'Well,' Brys ventured, 'there's certainly less shouting.'

Turudal Brizad smiled. 'The prince is young, Finadd. Some exuberance is to be expected. The Chancellor would have a word with you, at your convenience. I understand you are fully recovered from your mysterious ordeal?'

'The King's healers were their usual proficient selves, Consort. Thank you for asking. Why does the Chancellor wish to speak with me?'

The man shrugged. 'I am not the one to ask. I am but a messenger in this, Finadd.'

Brys studied him for a moment, then simply nodded. 'I accept Triban Gnol's invitation. A bell from now?'

'That should suffice. Let us hope for all our sakes that this will not mark an expansion of the present feud between the Chancellor and the Ceda.'

Brys was surprised. 'There is a feud? I hadn't heard. I mean, apart from the, well, the usual clash of opinions.' He considered, then said, 'I share your concern, Consort.'

'Does it ever strike you, Finadd, that peace leads to an indulgence in strife?'

'No, since your statement is nonsensical. The opposite of peace is war, while war is an extreme expression of strife. By your argument, life is characterized as an oscillation between strife during peace and strife during war.'

'Not entirely nonsensical, then,' Turudal Brizad said. 'We exist in a state of perpetual stress. Both within ourselves and in the world beyond.' He shrugged. 'We may speak of a longing for balance, but in our soul burns a lust for discord.'

'If your soul is troubled, Consort,' Brys said, 'you hide it well.'

'None of us here lack that skill, Finadd.'

Brys cocked his head. 'I have no inclination to indulge in strife. I find I still disagree with your premise. In any case, I must take my leave of you now, Consort.'

On his way back to his chambers, Brys reflected on Turudal Brizad's words. There might well have been a warn-ing hidden in there, but apart from the obvious suggestion that all was not as it seemed – and in the palace this was taken as given – he could not pierce the subtlety of the consort's intentions.

Stress lay in the cast of the mind, as far as Brys was

concerned. Born of perspective and the hue through which one saw the world, and such things were shaped by both nature and nurture. Perhaps on some most basic level the struggle to live yielded a certain stress, but that was not the same as the strife conjured by an active mind, its myriad storms of desires, emotions, worries and terrors, its relentless dialogue with death.

Brys had realized long ago what had drawn him into the arts of fighting. The martial world, from duelling to warfare, was inherently reductionist, the dialogue made simple and straightforward. Threats, bargains and compromises were proscribed by the length of Letherii steel. Self-discipline imposed a measure of control over one's own fate, which in turn served to diminish the damaging effects of stress, more so when it became clear to the practitioner that death fought using blind chance when all else failed, and so one had no choice but to accept the consequences, however brutal they may be. Simple notions that one could reflect upon at leisure, should one choose – but never when face to face with an enemy with blades unsheathed and dancing.

Physical laws imposed specific limitations, and Brys was satisfied with that clear imposition of predictability – sufficient to provide the structure around which he built his life.

Turudal Brizad's life was far less certain. His physicality and its attractiveness to others was his singular quality, and no amount of diligence could hold back the years that threatened it. Granted, there were alchemies and sorceries that could be mustered to stand in the breach, but the dark tide was reluctant to bargain, for it abided by its own laws and those laws were immutable. Worse yet, Brizad's efficacy was defined by the whims of others. As professional as he might be, his every partner was, potentially, a fathomless well of raw emotions, yearning to grasp hold of Brizad and ensnare him. Outwardly, of course, there were rules in place. He was a consort, after all. The queen already had a husband. The Chancellor was bound to ancient laws denying him formal relationships with man or woman. Turudal Brizad possessed virtually no rights; the children he might sire would be without name or political power – indeed, the queen was required to ensure such pregnancies did not occur, and thus far she had held to that prohibition.

But it was rumoured that Janall had given her heart to Brizad. And that Triban Gnol might well have done the very same, with the potential consequence of tearing apart the old alliance between queen and Chancellor. If so, then Turudal Brizad had become the unhappy fulcrum. No wonder the man was plagued with stress.

Yet what were the consort's own ambitions? Had he too surrendered his heart, and if so, to which lover?

Brys entered his room. He divested himself of his belt and armour, then drew off his sweat-damp undergarments. He layered himself in scented oil which he then scraped off with a wooden comb. Dressing in clean clothes, he set to donning his formal armour. He replaced the heavier practice sword with his regular longsword in the scabbard at his waist. A final moment scanning the contents of his modest residence, noticing the misplaced brace of knives on the shelf above his bed, indicating that yet another spy had gone through his room. Not one careless enough to leave the knives in the wrong position – that had been done by whoever had been spying on the spy, to let Brys know that yet another search for who knew what had taken place, a weekly occurrence of late.

He moved the knives back into their usual position, then left.

'Enter.'

Brys stepped inside, then paused to search through the crowded, cluttered chamber.

'Over here, King's Champion.'

He followed the sound of the voice and finally caught sight of the Ceda, who was suspended in a leather-strap harness depending from the ceiling. Face-down and close to a man's height above the floor, Kuru Qan was wearing a strange metal helmet with multiple lenses fixed in a slotted frame in front of his eyes. On the floor was an archaic, yellowed map.

'I have little time, Ceda,' Brys said. 'The Chancellor has requested that I attend him in a short while. What are you doing?'

'Is it important, lad?'

'That I know? I suppose not. I was just curious.'

'No, the Chancellor's summons.'

'I'm not sure. It seems I am to be increasingly viewed as some kind of pivotal player in a game of which I have no comprehension. After all, the king rarely asks for my advice on matters of state, for which I am eternally grateful, since I make it a point not to involve myself with such considerations. Thus, I have no opportunity to influence our Sire's opinion, nor would I wish to.'

'By this means,' Kuru Qan said, 'I am proving that the world is round.'

'Indeed? Did not the early colonizers from the First Empire make that evident? They circumnavigated the globe, after all.'

'Ah, but that was physical proof rather than theoretical. I wished to determine the same truth via hypothesis and theory.'

'In order to test the veracity of the methods?'

'Oh, no. Said veracity is already a given. No, lad, I seek to prove the veracity of physical evidence. Who can trust what the eyes witness, after all? Now, if mathematical evidence supports such practical observation, then we're getting somewhere.'

Brys looked round. 'Where are your helpers?'

'I sent them to the Royal Lens-maker for more lenses.'

'When was that?'

'Sometime this morning, I believe. Yes, just after breakfast.'

'You have therefore been hanging there all day.'

'And turning this way and that, without my own volition. There are forces, lad, unseen forces, that pull upon us every moment of our existence. Forces, I now believe, in conflict.'

'Conflict? In what way?'

'The ground beneath us exerts an imperative, evidenced by the blood settling in my face, the lightness in the back of my skull, the unseen hands seeking to drag me down – I have had the most exquisite hallucinations. Yet there is a contrary, weaker force seeking to drag me – another world, one which travels the sky around this one—'

'The moon?'

'There are actually at least four moons, lad, but the others are not only distant, but perpetually occluded from reflecting the sun's light. Very difficult to see, although early texts suggest that this was not always so. Reasons for their fading as yet unknown, although I suspect our world's own bulk has something to do with it. Then again, it may be that they are not farther away at all, but indeed closer, only very small. Relatively speaking.'

Brys studied the map on the floor. 'That's the original, isn't it? What new perspective have you achieved with all those lenses?'

'An important question? Probably, but in an indirect fashion. I had the map in my hands, lad, but then it fell. None the less, I have been rewarded with an insight. The continents were once all joined. What forces, one must therefore ask, have pulled them apart? Who forwarded the Chancellor's request?'

'What? Oh, Turudal Brizad.'

'Ah, yes. Such an errant, troubled lad. One sees such sorrow in his eyes, or at least in his demeanour.'

'One does?'

'And he said?'

'He spoke of a feud between you and the Chancellor. A, uh, new one.'

'There is? First I've heard of it.'

'Oh. So there isn't one.'

'No, no, lad, I'm sure there is. Be good enough to find out about it for me, will you?'

Brys nodded. 'Of course, Ceda. If I can. Is that the extent of your advice?'

'So it is.'

'Well, can I at least help you down?'

'Not at all, lad. Who knows how many more insights I will experience?'

'You may also lose your limbs, or pass out.'

'I still have my limbs?'

Brys moved directly beneath the Ceda, positioning his left shoulder below Kuru Qan's hips. 'I'm unstrapping you.'

'Be assured I will take your word for it, lad.'

'And I intend to have a word or two with your assistants once I'm done with the Chancellor.'

'Go easy on them, please. They're woefully forgetful.'

'Well, they won't forget me after today.'

Hands clasped behind his back, Triban Gnol paced. 'What is the readiness of the military, Finadd?'

Brys frowned. 'Preda Unnutal Hebaz would be better equipped to give you answer to that, Chancellor.'

'She is presently indisposed, and so I would ask you.'

They were alone in the Chancellor's office. Two guards waited outside. Votive candles exuded a scent of rare Kolanse spices, giving the chamber an atmosphere vaguely religious. *A temple of gold coins, and this man is the high priest* . . . 'It is a mandate that the army and navy be maintained at a level of preparedness, Chancellor. Supplies and stores sufficient for a full season's campaign. As you know, contracts with suppliers stipulate that, in times of conflict, the needs of the military are to take precedence over all other clients. These contracts are of course maintained and will be rigorously enforced.'

'Yes yes, Finadd. But I am seeking a soldier's opinion. Are

the king's soldiers ready and capable of war?'

'I believe so, Chancellor.'

Triban Gnol halted and fixed Brys with his glittering eyes. 'I will hold you to that, Finadd.'

'I would not have ventured an opinion were I not prepared to stand by it, Chancellor.'

A sudden smile. 'Excellent. Tell me, have you taken a wife yet? I thought not, although I doubt there's a maiden among the nobility who would hesitate in such a coup. There are many legacies one must live with, Finadd, and the means in which they are answered are the defining features of a man's or a woman's life.'

'I'm sorry, Chancellor. What are you getting at?'

'Your family history is well known, Finadd, and I hold deep sympathy for you and indeed, for your hapless brothers. In particular Hull, for whom I feel sincere worry, given his predilection for involving himself in crucial matters which are, strictly, not of his concern. I admit to fretting on his behalf, for I would not wish sorrow upon you and your kin.'

'It strikes me, Chancellor, that you are too generous in assembling your list of concerns. As for legacies, well, they are my own affair, as you no doubt appreciate. For what it is worth, I suggest that you are according Hull too much power in these matters—'

'Do you imagine I am here delivering a veiled warning?' Gnol waved a hand dismissively and resumed pacing. 'It insults me that you believe I am as crass as that. Does a seal-hunter warn the seal of the net closing round it? Hardly. No, Finadd, I am done with you. Rest assured I will waste no more sympathy upon you and your brothers.'

'I am relieved to hear that,' Brys said.

A venomous look. 'Please close the door on your way out, Finadd.'

'Of course, Chancellor.'

* * *

Outside, walking alone down the corridor, Brys sighed. He

380

had failed to learn anything of the purported feud between Gnol and Kuru Qan. It seemed he had achieved little more than adding himself to the Chancellor's list of enemies.

A second, deeper sigh.

He had nothing of Hull's stolid determination. Nothing of Tehol's cunning. He had but some skill with a sword. And what value that, when his attackers employed insinuation and threat in some verbal knife-game? Seeking to deliver wounds that time did not heal?

Reluctantly, he realized he needed advice.

Which meant another duel, this time with his own brother.

At least Tehol had no desire to wound. *Errant bless him, he seems to have no desires at all.*

'What I desire,' Tehol said, scowling, 'is a meal that actually began with real food. Sort of a founding premise that what one is to eat is actually sustaining at its most basic level.' He lifted one of the dark, limp leaves, studied it for a moment, then forced it into his mouth. Chewing, he glowered at Bugg.

'There are apes, master, for whom banana leaves constitute an essential source of nutrition.'

'Indeed? And are they extinct yet?'

'I don't know. I am only recounting a sailor's story I heard once at a bar.'

'He was a drunkard and a liar.'

'Oh, you know him, then.'

Tehol looked round. 'Where's Ublala? I need him here, so Shurq Elalle can gauge his . . .'

'Length?'

'Worth. Where is he?'

'On the roof. Pining.'

'Oh. The roof is good. Pining is not. Does he need yet another talking to, do you think?'

'From you, master? No.'

'Some more leaves, please. Don't skimp on the sauce or

381

whatever it is.'

'Right the second time.'

'Whatever it is? You don't know?'

'No, master. It just leaked out. Maybe from the leaves, maybe from something else. It reminds one of—'

'Tanneries?'

'Yes, that's it exactly. Well done.'

Tehol paled and slowly set down his bowl. 'I just had a thought.'

Bugg's eyes widened and he too put his bowl down. 'Please, master, do not pursue that thought.'

'It keeps coming back.'

'The thought?'

'No, the supper.' He rose suddenly. 'Time for some air.'

'Mind if I join you?'

'Not at all, Bugg. Clearly, during the course of preparing this meal, you worked hard at ignoring whatever impressions you may have had. I understand that you might well be exhausted by that effort. And if not, you should be.'

They turned at a sound from the alley, then the curtain across the entrance was swept aside.

'Ah, Shand, we were wondering when you would arrive!'

'You're a liar and a thief, Tehol Beddict.'

'It's the company I keep,' Bugg muttered.

Rissarh and Hejun followed behind Shand as she stormed into the small room.

Tehol backed to the far wall, which wasn't nearly far enough. 'Needless to say,' he said, 'I'm impressed.'

Shand halted. 'With what?'

He saw that her fists were clenched. 'Well, your vigour, of course. At the same time, I realize I have been remiss in directing your admirable energies, Shand. It's now clear to me that you – all three of you, in fact – require a more direct involvement in our nefarious undertaking.'

'He's doing it again,' Rissarh growled.

'We're supposed to be beating him up right now,' Hejun added. 'Look what he's done. Shand, less than a bell ago you were saying—'

'Be quiet about what I was saying,' Shand cut in. 'Direct involvement, you said, Tehol. Finally. It's about time, and no games, you slippery bastard. Talk to save your life.'

'Of course,' Tehol said, smiling. 'Please, make yourselves comfortable—'

'We're comfortable enough. Talk.'

'Well, you don't look comfortable—'

'Tehol.'

'As you like. Now, I'm going to give you a list of names, which you will have to memorize. Horul Esterrict, of Cargo Olives. Mirrik the Blunt, eldest of the Blunts, owner of Blunt's Letherii Steel and Blunt Weaponry. Stoople Rott, the grain magnate of Fort Shake. His brother, Puryst, the ale brewer. Erudinaas, queen of the rustleaf plantations at Dissent. The financiers, Bruck Stiffen, Horul Rinnesict, Grate Chizev of Letheras, Hepar the Pleaser, of Trate. Debt-holders Druz Thennict, Pralit Peff, Barrakta Ilk, Uster Taran, Lystry Maullict, all of Letheras. Tharav the Hidden, of room eleven, Chobor's Manse on Seal Street, Trate. Got those?'

Shand was glassy-eyed. 'There's more?'

'A dozen or so.'

'You want them killed?' Hejun asked.

'Errant no! I want you to begin purchasing shares in their enterprises. Under a variety of names, of course. Strive for forty-nine per cent. Once there, we'll be poised to force a coup. The goal, of course, is controlling interest, but to gain that will only be achieved with sudden ambush, and for that the timing has to be perfect. In any case, once you have done all that – the purchasing, that is – make no further move, just get back to me.'

'And how are we going to afford all that?' Shand demanded.

'Oh,' Tehol waved a hand, 'we're flush. The coin I invested for you is making a sizeable return. Time's come to make use of it.'

'How much of a return?'

383

'More than enough—'

'How much?'

'Well, I haven't actually counted it—'

Bugg spoke. 'About a peak.'

'Errant's blessing!' Shand stared at Tehol. 'But I haven't seen you do a thing!'

'If you had, Shand, then I wouldn't have been careful enough. Now, best we start with just the names I've given you. The next list can come later. Now, I have meetings scheduled this night—'

'What kind of meetings?'

'Oh, this and that. Now, please, I beg you – no more charging in through my front door. It's bound to get noticed sooner or later, and that could be bad.'

'What have you two been eating?' Rissarh suddenly asked, her nose wrinkling.

'This and that,' Bugg replied.

'Come on,' Shand said to her companions, 'let's go home. Maybe Ublala will turn up.'

'I'm sure he will,' Tehol said, smiling as he escorted the three women to the doorway. 'Now, get some sleep. You've busy times ahead.'

Hejun half turned. 'Cargo Olives – Horul who?'

Shand reached out and dragged Hejun into the alley.

Still smiling, Tehol adjusted the curtain until it once more covered the entrance. Then he spun round. 'That went well.'

'Rissarh had a knife,' Bugg said, 'tucked up along her wrist.'

'She did? Tucked up?'

'Yes, master.'

Tehol walked to the ladder. 'I trust you had your own knives close to hand.'

'I don't have any knives.'

Tehol paused, one hand on the nearest rung. 'What? Well, where are all our weapons?'

'We don't have any weapons, master.'

'None? Did we ever?'

'No. Some wooden spoons . . . .'

'And are you adept with them?'

'Very.'

'Well, that's all right, then. You coming?'

'In a moment, master.'

'Right, and be sure to clean up. This place is a dreadful mess.'

'If I find the time.'

Ublala Pung was lying face-down on the roof, near the bed.

'Ublala,' Tehol said, approaching, 'is something wrong?'

'No.' The word was muffled.

'What are you doing down there?'

'Nothing.'

'Well, we're about to have a guest who wants to meet you.'

'That's fine.'

'It might be worth your while to endeavour to make a good impression,' Tehol said.

'All right.'

'That might prove a little difficult, Ublala, with you lying there like that. When I first came up, I admit to thinking that you were dead.' He paused, then, considering, and brightened. 'Mind you, that might be a good thing—'

A scuff of boots to one side, then Shurq Elalle stepped from the shadows. 'Is this him?'

'You're early,' Tehol said.

'I am? Oh. Well, are you waiting for a necromancer to animate him or something?'

'I would be, were he dead. Ublala, if you will, stand up. I would like to introduce you to Shurq Elalle—'

'Is she the dead one?' he asked, not yet moving. 'The thief who drowned?'

'Already you're holding something against me,' Shurq

385

replied, her tone despondent.

'We haven't got to that yet,' Tehol said. 'Ublala, get up. Shurq has needs. You can meet them, and in return you get Shand, Rissarh and Hejun to leave off—'

'Why would they?' Ublala demanded.

'Because Shurq will tell them to.'

'I will?'

'Look,' Tehol said, exasperated, 'neither of you are co-operating here. On your feet, Ublala.'

'That won't be necessary,' Shurq cut in. 'Just roll him over.'

'Oh, fine, that's very nice. Crass, but nice.' Tehol crouched down alongside Ublala, pushed his hands beneath the huge man, then lifted. Tehol's feet skidded. He grunted, gasped, heaved again and again, to little effect.

'Stop it,' Shurq said in a strange voice. 'You're going to make me laugh. And laughing right now would be expensive.'

Sprawled across Ublala, Tehol stared up at her. 'Expensive?'

'All those spices, of course. Tell me, Ublala, what did you see when you walked across the bottom of the canal?'

'Mud.'

'What else?'

'Junk.'

'What else? What were you walking on?'

'Bodies. Bones. Crayfish, crabs. Old nets. Broken pots, furniture—'

'Furniture?' Tehol asked. 'Serviceable furniture?'

'Well, there was a chair. But I didn't sit in it.'

'Bodies,' Shurq said. 'Yes. Lots of bodies. How deep was the canal originally?'

Bugg had arrived, and with this question Tehol looked over at his manservant. 'Well? You must know, being an engineer and all that.'

'But I'm only pretending to be an engineer,' Bugg

386

pointed out.

'So pretend to know the answer to Shurq's question!'

'It was said seven tall men could stand, foot to shoulder, and the last would be able to reach up with his hands and find the surface. Used to be big trader ships could make their way the entire length.'

'I wasn't far from the surface,' Ublala said, rolling over, unmindful of Tehol who yelped as he was tumbled to one side with a thump. 'I could almost reach,' he added as he stood, brushing himself off.

'That's a lot of rubbish,' Bugg commented.

'I'm not lying,' Ublala said.

'I didn't say you were,' Bugg said.

'So,' Shurq asked, 'who is killing all those people?'

'Never mind all that,' Tehol said as he clambered to his feet. 'Shurq Elalle, permit me to introduce Ublala Pung. The canal walk is very lovely at night, yes? Not in it, I mean. Alongside it, just for a change. Perfect for a promenade—'

'I intend to rob Gerun Eberict's estate,' Shurq said to Ublala. 'But there are outlying watchers that need taking care of. Can you create a diversion, Ublala Pung?'

The huge man scratched his jaw. 'I don't know. I got nothing against them—'

'They don't like you.'

'They don't? Why?'

'No reason. They just don't.'

'Then I don't like them either.'

'So you say, but I haven't seen any proof.'

'You want proof? Good. Let's go.'

Shurq hooked one arm in Ublala's and led him towards the far edge of the roof. 'We have to jump to that other roof,' she said. 'I don't think you can do it, Ublala. Not quietly, anyway.'

'Yes I can. I'll show you I can.'

'We'll see . . .'

Tehol stared after them, then he swung to Bugg.

The manservant shrugged. 'It's the complexities of the male mind, master.'

The rain earlier that day had made the night air blessedly cool. Brys Beddict left the palace by a side postern and proceeded on a circuitous route towards his brother's residence. Although it was close to midnight, there were plenty of people on the streets.

He had never felt entirely comfortable in the crowded, sordid maze that was Letheras. The face of wealth stayed mostly hidden, leaving only the ravaged mien of poverty, and that was at times almost overwhelming. Beyond the Indebted were the lost, those who had given up entirely, and among them could be seen not just refugees from annexed tribes, but Letherii as well – more than he would have imagined. For all the explosive growth driving the kingdom, it seemed an ever greater proportion of the population was being left behind, and that was troubling.

At what point in the history of Letheras, he wondered, did rampant greed become a virtue? The level of self-justification required was staggering in its tautological complexity, and it seemed language itself was its greatest armour against common sense.

You can't leave all these people behind. They're outside the endless excitement and lust, the frenzied accumulation. They're outside and can only look on with growing despair and envy. What happens when rage supplants helplessness?

Increasingly, the ranks of the military were filling with the lowest classes. Training, acceptable income and a full belly provided the incentives, yet these soldiers were not enamoured of the civilization they were sworn to defend. True, many of them joined with dreams of booty, of wealth stolen and glory gained. But such riches came only with aggression, and successful aggression at that. What would happen if the military found itself on the defensive? *They'll fight to defend their homes, their loved ones. Of course they will. There's no cause for worry, is there?*

388

He swung into the alley leading to Tehol's home, and heard, somewhere beyond the squalid tenement, the sounds of a fierce argument. Things came crashing down in a cacophony that ended with a shriek.

Brys hesitated. He could not reach the source of the sounds from this alley, but Tehol's rooftop might permit him a view down on the opposite street. He went on.

With the pommel of his knife Brys tapped on the door-frame. There was no reply. He pulled aside the curtain and peered in. A single wavering oil lamp, the faint glow from the hearth, and voices coming down from above.

Brys entered and climbed the rickety ladder.

He emerged onto the roof to see Tehol and his man-servant standing at the far edge, looking down – presumably on the argument that was still under way.

'Tehol,' Brys called, approaching. 'Is this a matter for the city guard?'

His brother swung about, then shook his head. 'I don't think so, brother. A resolution is but moments away. Wouldn't you agree, Bugg?'

'I think so, since he's almost out and that old woman's run out of things to throw.'

Brys came alongside and looked down. A huge man was busy extricating himself from a pile of dusty rubble, ducking when objects were flung at him by a old woman in the tenement doorway.

'What happened?' Brys asked.

'An associate of mine,' Tehol said, 'jumped onto the roof over there from this one. He landed quietly enough, I suppose. Then the roof gave out, alas. As you can see, he's a big man.'

The hapless associate had climbed free at last. It appeared that he had taken most of the wall with him in his descent. It was a miracle that he seemed uninjured. 'Why was he jumping from your roof, Tehol?'

'It was a dare.'

'Yours?'

389

'Oh no, I'd never do that.'

'Then who? Surely not your manservant?'

Bugg sputtered, 'Me? Most assuredly not, Finadd!'

'Another guest,' Tehol explained. 'Who has since gone, although not far, I imagine. Somewhere in the shadows, waiting for dear Ublala.'

'Ublala? Ublala Pung? Oh, yes, I recognize him now. An associate? Tehol, the man's a criminal—'

'Who proved his innocence in the canal—'

'That's not innocence,' Brys retorted, 'that's stubborn will.'

'A will that the Errant would surely have weakened were Ublala truly guilty of the crimes of which he had been accused.'

'Tehol, really—'

His brother faced him, brows raised. 'Are you, a soldier of the king, casting aspersions on our justice system?'

'Tehol, the *king* casts aspersions on the justice system!'

'None the less, Brys – oh, what are you doing here, by the way?'

'I have come seeking your advice.'

'Oh. Well, shall we retire to a more private section of my rooftop? Here, follow me – that far corner is ideal.'

'Wouldn't down below be better?'

'Well, it would, if Bugg had bothered cleaning up. As it is, my abode is an unacceptable mess. I can't concentrate down there, not for a moment. My stomach turns at the thought—'

'That would be supper,' Bugg said behind them.

The brothers turned to look back at him.

Bugg gave a sheepish wave. 'I'll be down below, then.'

They watched him leave.

Brys cleared his throat. 'There are factions in the palace. Intrigues. And it seems certain people would force me into involvement, when all I wish is to remain loyal to my king.'

'Ah, and some of those factions are less than loyal to the king?'

'Not in any manner that could be proved. Rather, it's

simply a matter of reinterpretation of what would best serve the king and the kingdom's interests.'

'Ah, but those are two entirely different things. The king's interests versus the kingdom's interests. At least, I assume that's how they see it, and who knows, they might be right.'

'They might, Tehol, but I have doubts.'

Tehol folded his arms and stared out on the city. 'So,' he said, 'there's the queen's faction, which includes Prince Quillas, Chancellor Triban Gnol, and the First Consort, Turudal Brizad. Have I missed anyone?'

Brys was staring at his brother. He shook his head. 'Officers and guards, various spies.'

'And the king's own faction. Ceda Kuru Qan, First Eunuch Nifadas, Preda Unnutal Hebaz and perhaps First Concubine Nisall. And, of course, you.'

'But I have no desire to be in any faction—'

'You're the King's Champion, brother. As I see it, you have little choice.'

'Tehol, I am hopeless at such games of intrigue.'

'So say nothing. Ever.'

'What good will that do?'

'You'll convince them you're smarter than they are. Even scarier, that you know everything. You can see through all their façades—'

'But I can't see through all that, Tehol. Therefore, I'm not smarter.'

'Of course you are. You just need to treat it like a duel. In fact, treat everything like a duel. Feint, parry, disengage, all that complicated stuff.'

'Easy for you to say,' Brys muttered.

They fell silent, staring out over the dark city. Oil lamps lit the canal walks, but the water itself was black as ink, winding like ribbons of oblivion between the squat, hulking buildings. Other lights swung in motion down the streets, carried by people going about their tasks. For all that, darkness dominated the scene.

Brys stared up at the nearest tier, watched a few lanterns

391

slide along the span like minuscule moons. 'I have been thinking about Hull,' he said after a time.

'I would hold out little hope,' Tehol said. 'Our brother's desires have nothing to do with self-preservation. It is in his mind, I believe, that he is going to die soon.'

Brys nodded.

'And,' Tehol continued, 'if he can, in so doing he will also take down as much of Lether as possible. For that reason alone, someone will stop him. With finality.'

'And vengeance against those murderers will be expected of me,' Brys said.

'Not necessarily,' Tehol said. 'After all, your foremost loyalty is to your king.'

'Superseding even that to my family?'

'Well, yes.'

'To do nothing would be seen as cowardice. Worse yet, I do not think I could face Hull's killers without reaching for my sword.'

'You may have to, Brys. Of course,' Tehol added, 'I am not so bound by such prohibitions.'

Brys studied his brother for a long moment. 'You would avenge Hull?'

'Count on it.'

Eventually, Brys smiled.

Tehol glanced over and nodded. 'That's perfect, brother. When you come face to face with them, show that smile. It will put terror in their hearts.'

Brys sighed and returned his gaze to the city. 'Outwardly, we seem so different, the three of us.'

'And so we are,' Tehol replied. 'It comes down to methods, and we each walk unique paths. At the same time, alas, we must all live with an identical legacy, a particularly unpleasant inheritance.' He shrugged, then pulled up his sagging trousers. 'Three stones in a stream. All subjected to the same rushing water, yet each shaped differently, depending upon its nature.'

'And which of us is sandstone?'

'Hull. He's been worn down the most, brother, by far. You, you're basalt.'

'And you, Tehol?'

'Maybe a mix of the two, yielding a sadly misshapen result. But I can live with it.'

'Perhaps you can,' Brys observed, 'but what about the rest of us?'

'There's a matter on which you can help me, brother.'

'Oh?'

'Presumably, there are recorders of obscure information in the palace. People who tally various events, trends and such.'

'A veritable army of them, Tehol.'

'Indeed. Now, might you make some discreet inquiries for me?'

'Regarding what?'

'People going missing in Letheras. Annual numbers, that sort of thing.'

'If you like. Why?'

'At the moment, I'm just curious.'

'What are you up to, Tehol?'

'This and that.'

Brys grimaced. 'Be careful.'

'I shall. Do you smell that? Bugg is brewing tea.'

'That doesn't smell like tea.'

'Yes, he's full of surprises. Let's go down. I for one am very thirsty.'

Shurq Elalle watched Ublala Pung close in on the pair of guards who had just come round the corner of the estate's outer wall. They had time to look up in alarm before he threw his punch. Crunching into one jaw, then following through to crack against the other man's temple. Both collapsed. Ublala paused, looking down on them, then headed off in search of more.

Shurq stepped from the shadows and approached the wall. Wards had been etched into the ochre stone, but she

393

knew they were linked to intrusions by someone living. The heat of a body, the moist breaths, the thump of a heart. Those relating to motion were far more expensive to maintain, and would be reserved for the main house.

She reached the wall, paused to take a final look round, then quickly scaled it.

The top was studded with shards of razor-sharp iron that cut deep into the reinforced padding on her gloves. As she drew herself up, the shards cut through the layers of leather and sank into her palms, improving her grip. She would get the lacerations sewn up later, to keep out lint and insects and other creatures that might seek to take up residence in the punctures.

Her upper body perched above her arms, she studied the compound below. Seeing no-one, she lifted herself over, pivoting on her hands, then edged down onto the other side. She pried her left hand loose of the spikes and gripped the ledge with her fingers, then tugged her right hand loose as well. Freed of the shards, she quickly descended to crouch in the shadows beneath the wall.

Dozens of guards somewhere ahead, between her and her goal. Men – but no, she couldn't think about that, not right now. Later, with Ublala. Unfortunately, the mindless guest within her understood nothing of the value of anticipation. It knew hunger, and hunger must be appeased. The nature of things alive, she mused, as opposed to things dead. Urgency, dissatisfaction, the burden of appetites. She'd forgotten.

Four guards standing at the estate entrance, one to either side of the double doors, the remaining two flanking the broad steps. They looked bored. There were windows on the main floor, but these were shuttered. Balconies on the next level – the small doors there would be warded. The uppermost floor consisted of three A-frame rooms facing front, their peaked roofs steep and tiled in slate. Inward of these projections, the estate roof was flat and low-walled, a veritable forest of potted plants and stunted trees. And hidden watchers.

All in all, seemingly impregnable.

Just the kind she liked.

She set out towards the nearest outbuilding, a maintenance shed with a sloped roof that faced onto the compound. Careful, silent steps, then settling alongside the nearest wall of the shed. Where she waited.

A loud thumping on the front gates.

The four guards at the estate entrance straightened, exchanged glances. There were at least eight of their comrades patrolling the street and alley beyond the wall. It was too late for a guest, and besides, Master Gerun Eberict was not at home. Alternatively, perhaps he had sent a messenger. But then there would have been a signal from the patrol. No, she could see them conclude, this was unusual.

The two guards at the base of the steps set off towards the gate, hands on the grips of their swords.

The thumping stopped when the two men were halfway to the gate. They slowed, drawing weapons.

Two steps from the gate.

The twin massive portals exploded inward, taking both guards down beneath the battered wood and bronze. Ublala's forward momentum carried him over the flattened doors and the men trapped beneath them.

At the top of the stairs, shouts of alarm, and the last two guards were rushing towards the giant.

'I never done nothing to any of you!' Ublala bellowed, or at least that is what Shurq thought he said – the words were made indistinct by his bristling indignation as he charged the two guards.

A brief moment of concern for Shurq, since her man was unarmed.

Swords slashed out. Ublala seemed to slap at them along the flat, and one of the swords cartwheeled through the air. The other ploughed into the pavestones at the giant's feet. A backhand slap spun the nearest man round and off his feet. The remaining guard was screaming, stumbling back. Ublala reached out, caught him by the right arm, and tugged him close.

'I'm not meat I'm a new body!'

Or 'I'm not mean to nobody!'

The guard was dragged off his feet and shaken about in a clatter of armour to accompany the incoherent assertion. The hapless man went limp, his limbs flailing about. Ublala dropped him and looked up.

Guards were streaming towards him from either side of the estate.

He grunted in alarm, turned about and ran back through the gaping gateway.

Shurq glanced up at the roof. Four figures up there, looking down at the fleeing giant, two of them readying javelins.

But he was already through the archway.

Shurq slipped round the back of the shed and darted across the narrow gap to come alongside the estate wall. She padded towards the stairs, onto the platform and through the unwarded entrance. Outside, she heard someone shout orders for a rearguard to hold the compound, but clearly no-one had turned round to keep an eye on the front doors.

Shurq found herself in a reception hall, the walls covered in frescos illustrating Gerun's desperate defence of King Ezgara Diskanar. She paused, drew out a knife to scratch a moustache on Gerun's manly, grimacing, triumphant face, then continued on through an archway leading to a large chamber modelled in the fashion of a throne room, although the throne – an ornate, high-backed monstrosity – was simply positioned at the head of a long table instead of surmounting a raised dais.

Doors at every corner of the chamber, each one elaborately framed. A fifth one, narrow and inset at the back, probably with a servants' passage beyond.

No doubt the inhabitants were awake by now. Yet, being

servants – Indebted one and all – they'd be hiding under their cots during this terrifying tumult.

She set off towards that last door. The passageway beyond was narrow and poorly lit. Curtained cells lined it, the pathetic residences of the staff. No light showed from beneath any of the hangings, but Shurq caught the sound of scuffing from one room halfway down, and a stifled gasp from one closer, on her left.

She closed her gloved hand on the grip of the fighting knife strapped beneath her left arm, and ran the back of the blade hard against the scabbard edge as she drew it forth. More gasps. A terrified squeal.

Slow steps down the narrow passage, pausing every now and then, but never long enough to elicit a scream from anyone, until she came to a T-intersection. To the right the aisle opened out onto the kitchen. To the left, a staircase leading both up and to cellars below ground. Shurq swung round and faced the passageway she had just quitted. Pitching her voice low, she hissed, 'Go to sleep. Was jus' doin' a circuit. No-one here, sweeties. Relax.'

'Who's that?' a voice asked.

'Who cares?' another replied. 'Like he said, Prist, go back t'sleep.'

But Prist continued, 'It's jus' that I don' recognize 'im—'

'Yeah,' the other countered, 'an' you ain't a gardener but a real live hero, right, Prist?'

'All I'm sayin' is—'

Shurq walked back to halt in front of Prist's curtain.

She heard movement beyond, but the man was silent.

She drew the dirty linen to one side and slipped into the cramped room. It stank of mud and manure. In the darkness she could just make out a large, crouching figure at the back wall, a blanket drawn up under its chin.

'Ah, Prist,' Shurq murmured in a voice little more than a whisper and taking another step closer, 'are you any good at keeping quiet? I hope so, because I intend to spend some time with you. Don't worry,' she added as she unbuckled her belt, 'it'll be fun.'

Two bells later, Shurq lifted her head from the gardener's muscled arm, concentrating to listen beyond his loud snores. Poor bastard had been worn right out – she hoped Ublala could manage better – and all his subsequent whimpering and mewling was disgusting. As the bell's low echoes faded, a solid silence replaced it.

The guards had returned shortly after Shurq had slipped into Prist's cubicle. Loud with speculation and bitter argument, indicating that Ublala had made good his escape, although a call for the services of the house healer suggested there'd been a clash or two. Since that time, things had settled down. There had been a cursory search of the estate, but not the servants' quarters, suggesting that no suspicion of diversion and infiltration had occurred to the house guards. Careless. Indicative of a sad lack of imagination. All in all, as she had expected. An overbearing master had that effect. Initiative was dangerous, lest it clash with Gerun's formidable ego.

Shurq pulled herself loose from Prist's exhausted, childlike embrace, and rose silently to don her clothes and gear. Gerun would have an office, adjoining his private rooms. Men like Gerun always had offices. It served their need for legitimacy.

Its defences would be elaborate, the magic expensive and thorough. But not so complicated as to leave a Finadd confused. Accordingly, the mechanisms of deactivation would be straightforward. Another thing to consider, of course, was the fact that Gerun was absent. It was likely there were additional wards in place that could not be negated. She suspected they would be life-aspected, since other kinds could more easily be accidentally triggered.

She quietly stepped back into the passageway. Sounds of sleep and naught else. Satisfied, Shurq returned to the T-intersection and turned left. Ascending the staircase, she was careful to place each foot along alternating edges where the joins reduced the likelihood of a telltale creak.

Reaching the first landing, Shurq stepped close to the door, then paused. Motionless. A tripwire was set along the seam of the door, locked in place by the last servant to use the passage. Sometimes the simplest alarms succeeded where more elaborate ones failed, if only because the thief was over-anticipating the complication. She released the mechanism and turned the latch.

Into another servants' passage, running parallel to the formal hallway, assuming a typical layout for Gerun's estate. She found the lone door where she expected, on the right at the far end. Another tripwire to release, then she stepped through. The hallway was unlit, which was clever. Three doors along the opposite wall, the rooms beyond showing no light.

She was fairly certain she had found Gerun Eberict's private quarters. Barely detectable in the gloom were a host of arcane sigils painted on the nearest door.

Shurq edged closer to study those symbols.

And froze as a dull voice spoke from down the corridor. 'It was incompetence. Or so he says. And now I'm supposed to make it up to him.'

She slowly turned. A seated figure, sprawled back with legs stretched out, head tilted to one side.

'You're dead,' the man said.

'Is that a promise or an observation?'

'Just something we have in common,' he answered. 'That doesn't happen to me much, any more.'

'I know just how you feel. So, Gerun has you here guarding his rooms.'

'It's my penance.'

'For incompetence.'

'Yes. Gerun doesn't fire people, you know. He kills them and then, depending on how angry he is, either buries them or keeps them on for a time. I suppose he'll bury me eventually.'

'Without releasing your soul?'

'He often forgets about that part.'

'I'm here to steal everything he has.'

'If you were living I would of course kill you in some monstrous, terrifying way. I would get up from this chair, feet dragging, arms out with my hands clawing the air. I'd make bestial sounds and moans and hisses as if I was hungry to sink my teeth into your throat.'

'That would certainly prove sufficient to deter a thief. A living one, that is.'

'It would, and I'd probably enjoy it, too.'

'But I'm not living, am I?'

'No. But I have one question for you and it's an important one.'

'All right. Ask it.'

'Why, since you're dead, do you look so good? Who cut your hair? Why aren't you rotting away like me? Are you stuffed with herbs or something? Are you wearing make-up? Why are the whites of your eyes so white? Your lips so glossy?'

Shurq was silent a moment, then asked, 'Is that your one question?'

'Yes.'

'If you like, I can introduce you to the people responsible for the new me. I am sure they can do the same for you.'

'Really? Including a manicure?'

'Absolutely.'

'What about filing my teeth? You know, to make them sharp and scary.'

'Well, I don't know how scary you will be with styled hair, make-up, perfect nails and glossy lips.'

'But sharp teeth? Don't you think the sharp teeth will terrify people?'

'Why not just settle for those? Most people are frightened of rotting things, of things crawling with vermin and stinking like a freshly turned grave. Fangs and finger-nails clipped into talons.'

'I like it. I like how you think.'

'My pleasure. Now, do I have to worry about these

400

wards?'

'No. In fact, I can show you where all the mechanisms are for the alarms.'

'Won't that give you away?'

'Give me away? Why, I am coming with you, of course. Assuming you can get us both out of here.'

'Oh, I see. I'm sure we'll manage. What is your name, by the way?'

'Harlest Eberict.'

Shurq cocked her head, then said, 'Oh. But you died ten years ago, according to your brother.'

'Ten years? Is that all?'

'He said you fell down the stairs, I believe. Or something like that.'

'Stairs. Or pitched off the balcony. Maybe both.'

'And what did you do or fail to do that earned such punishment?'

'I don't remember. Only that I was incompetent.'

'That was long before Gerun saved the king's life. How could he have afforded the sorcery needed to bind your soul to your body?'

'I believe he called in a favour.'

Shurq swung back to the door. 'Does this lead to his office?'

'No, that one goes to his love-making room. You want the one over here.'

'Any chance of anyone hearing us talking right now, Harlest?'

'No, the walls are thick.'

'One last thing,' Shurq said, eyeing Harlest. 'Why didn't Gerun bind your loyalty with magic?'

The pale, patchy face displayed surprise. 'Well, we're brothers!'

Alarms negated, the two undead stood in Finadd Gerun Eberict's office.

'He doesn't keep much actual coin here,' Harlest said.

401

'Mostly writs of holding. He spreads his wealth around to protect it.'

'Very wise. Where is his seal?'

'On the desk.'

'Very unwise. Do me a favour and start collecting those writs.' She walked over to the desk and gathered up the heavy, ornate seal and the thick sheets of wax piled beside it. 'This wax is an exclusive colour?'

'Oh yes. He paid plenty for that.' Harlest had gone to a wall and was removing a large tapestry behind which was an inset cabinet. He disengaged a number of tripwires, then swung open the small door. Within were stacks of scrolls and a small jewelled box.

'What's in the box?' Shurq asked.

Harlest lifted it out and tossed it to Shurq. 'His cash. Like I said, he never keeps much around.'

She examined the clasp. Satisfied that it wasn't booby-trapped, she slid it to one side and tipped back the lid. 'Not much? Harlest, this is full of diamonds.'

The man, his arms loaded with scrolls, walked over. 'It is?'

'He's called in a few of his holdings, I think.'

'He must have. I wonder why?'

'To use it,' she replied, 'for something very expensive. Oh well, he'll just have to go without.'

'Gerun will be so angry,' Harlest said, shaking his head. 'He will go mad. He'll start hunting us down, and he won't stop until he finds us.'

'And then what? Torture? We don't feel pain. Kill us? We're already dead—'

'He'll take his money back—'

'He can't if it doesn't exist any more.'

Harlest frowned.

Smiling, Shurq closed the box and reset the clasp. 'It's not like you and I have any use for it, is it? No, this is the equivalent of tossing Gerun off the balcony or down the stairs, only financially rather than physically.'

'Well, he is my brother.'

'Who murdered you and wouldn't even leave it at that.'

'That's true.'

'So, we're heading out via the balcony. I have a companion who is about to begin another diversion. Are you with me, Harlest?'

'Can I still get the fangs?'

'I promise.'

'Okay, let's go.'

It was nearing dawn, and the ground steamed. Kettle sat on a humped root and watched a single trailing leg slowly edge its way into the mulch. The man had lost a boot in the struggle, and she watched his toes twitch a moment before they were swallowed up in the dark earth.

He'd fought hard, but with his lower jaw torn off and his throat filling with blood, it hadn't lasted long. Kettle licked her fingers.

It was good that the tree was still hungry.

The bad ones had begun a hunt beneath the ground, clawing and slithering and killing whatever was weak. Soon there would be a handful left, but these would be the worst ones. And then they would come out.

She was not looking forward to that. And this night, she'd had a hard time finding a victim in the streets, some-one with unpleasant thoughts who was where he didn't belong for reasons that weren't nice.

It *had* been getting harder, she realized. She leaned back and pushed her stained fingers through her filthy hair, wondering where all the criminals and spies had disappeared to. It was strange, and troubling.

And her friend, the one buried beneath the oldest tree, he'd told her he was trapped. He couldn't go any further, even with her assistance. But help was on the way, although he wasn't certain it would arrive in time.

She thought about that man, Tehol, who had come by last night to talk. He seemed nice enough. She hoped he would visit again. Maybe he'd know what to do – she swung round on the root and stared up at the square tower – yes, maybe he'd know what to do, now that the tower was dead.

CHAPTER ELEVEN

Faded sails ride the horizon
So far and far away to dwindle
The dire script
Writ on that proven canvas.

I know the words belong to me
They belong to me
These tracks left by the beast
Of my presence

Then, before and now, later
And all the moments between
Those distant sails driven
Hard on senseless winds

That even now circle
My stone-hearted self
The grit of tears I never shed
Biting my eyes.

Faded sails hovering as if lifted
Above the world's curved line
And I am lost and lost to answer
If they approach or flee

Approach or flee unbidden times
In that belly swollen
With unheard screams so far
And far and so far and away.

This Blind Longing
Isbarath (of the Shore)

Drawn to the shoreline, as if among the host of unwritten truths in a mortal soul could be found a recognition of what it meant to stand on land's edge, staring out into the depthless unknown that was the sea. The yielding sand and stones beneath one's feet whispered uncertainty, rasped promises of dissolution and erosion of all that was once solid.

In the world could be assembled all the manifest symbols to reflect the human spirit, and in the subsequent dialogue was found all meaning, every hue and every flavour, rising in legion before the eyes. Leaving to the witness the decision of choosing recognition or choosing denial.

Udinaas sat on a half-buried tree trunk with the sweeping surf clawing at his moccasins. He was not blind and there was no hope for denial. He saw the sea for what it was, the dissolved memories of the past witnessed in the present and fertile fuel for the future, the very face of time. He saw the tides in their immutable susurration, the vast swish like blood from the cold heart moon, a beat of time measured and therefore measurable. Tides one could not hope to hold back.

Every year a Letherii slave, chest-deep in the water and casting nets, was grasped by an undertow and swept out to sea. With some, the waves later carried them back, lifeless and swollen and crab-eaten. At other times the tides delivered corpses and carcasses from unknown calamities, and the wreckage of ships. From living to death, the vast wilderness of water beyond the shore delivered the same message again and again.

He sat huddled in his exhaustion, gaze focused on the distant breakers of the reef, the rolling white ribbon that came again and again in heartbeat rhythm, and from all sides rushed in waves of meaning. In the grey, heavy sky. In the clarion cries of the gulls. In the misty rain carried by the moaning wind. The uncertain sands trickling away beneath his soaked moccasins. Endings and beginnings, the edge of the knowable world.

She'd run from the House of the Dead. The young woman at whose feet he'd tossed his heart. In the hope that she might glance at it – Errant take him, even pick it up and devour it like some grinning beast. Anything, anything but . . . *running away.*

He had fallen unconscious in the House of the Dead – *ah, is there meaning in that?* – and had been carried out, presumably, back to the cot in the Sengar longhouse. He had awoken later – how long he did not know, for he'd found himself alone. Not even a single slave present in the building. No food had been prepared, no dishes or other signs of a meal left behind. The hearth was a mound of white ash covering a few lingering embers. Outside, beyond the faint voice of the wind and the nearer dripping of rainwater, was silence.

Head filled with fog, his movements slow and awkward, he'd rebuilt the fire. Found a rain cape, and had then walked outside. Seeing no-one nearby, he had made his way down to the shoreline. To stare at the empty, filled sea, and the empty, filled sky. Battered by the silence and its roar of wind and gull screams and spitting rain. Alone on the beach in the midst of this clamouring legion.

The dead warrior who was alive.

The Letherii priestess who had fled in the face of a request for help, to give solace and to comfort a fellow Letherii.

In the citadel of the Warlock King, Udinaas suspected, the Edur were gathered. Wills locked in a dreadful war, and, like an island around which the storm raged in endless cycles, the monstrous form of Rhulad Sengar, who had risen from the House of the Dead. Armoured in gold, clothed in wax, probably unable to walk beneath all that weight – until, of course, those coins were removed.

The art of Udinaas . . . undone.

There would be pain in that. Excruciating pain, but it had to be done, and quickly. Before the flesh and skin grew to embrace those coins.

Rhulad was not a corpse, nor was he undead, for an undead would not scream. He lived once more. His nerves awake, his mind afire. Trapped in a prison of gold.

As was I, once. As every Letherii is trapped. Oh, he is poetry animate, is Rhulad Sengar, but his words are for the Letherii, not for the Edur.

Just one meaning culled from that dire legion, and one that would not leave him alone. Rhulad was going to go mad. There was no doubt about that in the mind of Udinaas. Dying, only to return to a body that was no longer his, a body that belonged to the forest and the leaves and barrow earth. What kind of journey had that been? Who had opened the path, and why?

It's the sword. It has to be. The sword that would not release his hands. Because it was not finished with Rhulad Sengar. Death means nothing to it. It's not finished.

A gift meant, it seemed, for Hannan Mosag. Offered by whom?

But Hannan Mosag will not have that sword. It has claimed Rhulad instead. And that sword with its power now hangs over the Warlock King.

This could tear the confederacy apart. Could topple Hannan Mosag and his K'risnan. Unless, of course, Rhulad Sengar submitted to the Warlock King's authority.

A less problematic issue had it been Fear, or Trull. Perhaps even Binadas. But no, the sword had chosen Rhulad, the unblooded who had been eager for war, a youth with secret eyes and rebellion in his soul. It might be that he was broken, but Udinaas suspected otherwise. *I was able to bring him back, to quell those screams. A respite from the madness, in which he could gather himself and recall all that he had been.*

It occurred to Udinaas that he might have made a mistake. A greater mercy might have been to not impede that swift plummet into madness.

And now he would have me as his slave.

Foam swirled around his ankles. The tide was coming in.

'We might as well be in a village abandoned to the ghosts,' Buruk the Pale said, using the toe of one boot to edge a log closer to the fire, grimacing at the steam that rose from its sodden bark.

Seren Pedac stared at him a moment longer, then shrugged and reached for the battered kettle that sat on a flat stone near the flames. She could feel the handle's heat through her leather gloves as she refilled her cup. The tea was stewed, but she didn't much care as she swallowed a mouthful of the bitter liquid. At least it was warm.

'How much longer is this going to go on?'

'Curb your impatience, Buruk,' Seren advised. 'There will be no satisfaction in the resolution of all this, assuming a resolution is even possible. We saw him with our own eyes. A dead man risen, but risen too late.'

'Then Hannan Mosag should simply lop off the lad's head and be done with it.'

She made no reply to that. In some ways, Buruk was right. Prohibitions and traditions only went so far, and there was – there could be – no precedent for what had happened. They had watched the two Sengar brothers drag their sibling out through the doorway, the limbed mass of wax and gold that was Rhulad. Red welts for eyes, melted shut, the head lifting itself up to stare blindly at the grey sky for a moment before falling back down. Braided hair sealed in wax, hanging like strips from a tattered sail. Threads of spit slinging down from his gaping mouth as they carried him towards the citadel.

Edur gathered on the bridge. On the far bank, the village side, and emerging from the other noble longhouses surrounding the citadel. Hundreds of Edur, and even more Letherii slaves, drawn to witness, silent and numbed and filled with horror. She had watched most of the Edur then file into the citadel. The slaves seemed to have simply disappeared.

Seren suspected that Feather Witch was casting the tiles,

in some place less public than the huge barn where she had last conducted the ritual. At least, there had been no-one there when she had looked.

And now, time crawled. Buruk's camp and the Nerek huddled in their tents had become an island in the mist, surrounded by the unknown.

She wondered where Hull had gone. There were ruins in the forest, and rumours of strange artefacts, some massive and sprawling, many days' travel to the northeast. Ancient as this forest was, it had found soil fertile with history. Destruction and dissolution concluded every passing of the cycle, and the breaking down delivered to the exhausted world the manifold parts to assemble a new whole.

But healing belonged to the land. It was not guaranteed to that which lived upon it. Breeds ended; the last of a particular beast, the last of a particular race, each walked alone for a time. Before the final closing of those singular eyes, and the vision behind them.

Seren longed to hold on to that long view. She desperately sought out the calm wisdom it promised, the peace that belonged to an extended perspective. With sufficient distance, even a range of mountains could look flat, the valleys between each peak unseen. In the same manner, lives and deaths, mortality's peaks and valleys, could be levelled. Thinking in this way, she felt less inclined to panic.

And that was becoming increasingly important.

'And where in the Errant's name is that delegation?' Buruk asked.

'From Trate,' Seren said, 'they'll be tacking all the way. They're coming.'

'Would that they had done so before all this.'

'Do you fear that Rhulad poses a threat to the treaty?'

Buruk's gaze remained fixed on the flames. 'It was the sword that raised him,' he said in a low voice. 'Or whoever made it and sent it to the Edur. Did you catch a glimpse of the blade? It's mottled. Made me think of one of the

410

Daughters they worship, the dappled one, what was her name?'

'Sukul Ankhadu.'

'Maybe she exists in truth. An Edur goddess—'

'A dubious gift, then, for the Edur view Sukul Ankhadu as a fickle creature. She is feared. They worship Father Shadow and Daughter Dusk, Sheltatha Lore. And, on a day to day basis, more of the latter than the former.' Seren finished the tea then refilled the tin cup. 'Sukul Ankhadu. I suppose that is possible, although I can't recall any stories about those gods and goddesses of the Edur ever manifesting themselves in such a direct manner. It seemed more like ancestor worship, the founders of the tribes elevated into holy figures, that sort of thing.' She sipped and grimaced.

'That will burn holes in your gut, Acquitor.'

'Too late for that, Buruk.'

'Well, if not Ankhadu, then who? That sword came from somewhere.'

'I don't know.'

'Nor does it sound as if you even care. This listlessness ill suits you, Acquitor.'

'It's not listlessness, Buruk, it's wisdom. I'm surprised you can't tell the difference.'

'Is it wisdom taking the life from your eyes, the sharpness from your thoughts? Is it wisdom that makes you indifferent to the nightmare miracle we witnessed yesterday?'

'Absolutely. What else could it be?'

'Despair?'

'And what have I that's worthy of despair?'

'I'm hardly the one to answer that.'

'True—'

'But I'll try anyway.' He drew out a flask and pulled out the stopper, then tilted it back. Two quick swallows, after which he sighed and leaned back. 'It strikes me you're a sensitive type, Acquitor, which probably is a quality for someone in your profession. But you're not able to separate business from everything else. Sensitivity is a pervasive

411

kind of vulnerability, after all. Makes you easy to hurt, makes the scars you carry liable to open and weep at the slightest prod.' He took another drink, his face growing slack with the effects of the potent liquor and nectar, a looseness coming to his words as he continued, 'Hull Beddict. He's pushed you away, but you know him too well. He is rushing headlong. Into a fate of his own choosing, and it will either kill him or destroy him. You want to do something about it, maybe even stop him, but you can't. You don't know how, and you feel that as your own failure. Your own flaw. A weakness. Thus, for the fate that will befall him, you choose not to blame him, but yourself. And why not? It's easier.'

She had chosen to stare at the bitter dregs in the cup embraced by her hands, sometime during the course of Buruk's pronouncements. Eyes tracking the battered rim, then out to the fingers and thumbs, swathed in stained, scarred leather. Flattened pads polished and dark, seams fraying, the knuckles stretched and gnarled. Somewhere within was skin, flesh, muscle, tendon and callus. And bone. Hands were such extraordinary tools, she mused. Tools, weapons, clumsy and deft, numb and tactile. Among tribal hunters, they could speak, a flurry of gestures eloquent in silence. But they could not taste. Could not hear. Could not weep. For all that, they killed so easily.

While from the mouth sounds issued forth, recognizably shaped into meanings of passion, of beauty, of blinding clarity. Or muddied or quietly cutting, murderous and evil. Sometimes all at once. Language was war, vaster than any host of swords, spears and sorcery. The self waging battle against everyone else. Borders enacted, defended, sallies and breaches, fields of corpses rotting like tumbled fruit. Words ever seeking allies, ever seeking iconic verisimilitude in the heaving press.

And, she realized, she was tired. Tired of it all. Peace reigned in silence, inside and out, in isolation and exhaustion.

'Why do you say nothing, Acquitor?'

He sat alone, unspeaking, a cloak of bear fur draped over his hunched shoulders, sword held point-down between his gold-clad feet, the long banded blade and broad bell-hilt in front of him. Somehow, he had managed to open his eyes, and the glitter was visible within the hooded shadows beneath his brow, framed in waxed braids. His breath came in a low rasp, the only sound in the massive chamber in the wake of the long, stilted exchange between Tomad Sengar and Hannan Mosag.

The last words had fallen away, leaving a sense of profound helplessness. None among the hundreds of Edur present moved or spoke.

Tomad could say no more on behalf of his son. Some subtle force had stolen his authority, and it came, Trull realized with dread, from the seated figure of black fur and glittering gold, from the eyes shining out from their dark holes. From the motionless sword.

Standing in the centre dais, the Warlock King's hard eyes had slowly shifted from Tomad to Rhulad, and they held there now, calculating and cold.

The sword needed to be surrendered. Hannan Mosag had sent them to retrieve it, and that task could not be called complete until Rhulad placed it in the hands of the Warlock King. Until that happened, Fear, Binadas, Trull, Theradas and Midik Buhn all stood in dishonour.

It fell now, finally, to Rhulad. To make the gesture, to heal this ragged wound.

Yet he made no move.

Trull was not even sure his brother was capable of speaking, given the terrible weight encasing his chest. Breathing sounded difficult, excruciatingly laboured. It was extraordinary that Rhulad was able to keep his arms up, the hands on the grip of the sword. From a lithe, supple youth, he had become something hulking, bestial.

The air in the hall was humid and rank. The smell of fear

413

and barely restrained panic swirled amidst the smoke from the torches and the hearth. The rain outside was unceasing, the wind creaking the thick planks of the walls.

The rasping breath caught, then a thin, broken voice spoke. 'The sword is mine.'

A glitter of fear from Hannan Mosag's eyes. 'This must not be, Rhulad Sengar.'

'Mine. He gave it to me. He said I was the one, not you. Because you were weak.'

The Warlock King recoiled as if he had been struck in the face.

Who? Trull shot the question with a sharp glance at Fear. Their eyes met, and Fear shook his head.

Their father was facing Rhulad now. Emotions worked across his face for a moment and it seemed he was ageing centuries before their very eyes. Then he asked, 'Who gave you this sword, Rhulad?'

Something like a smile. 'The one who rules us now, Father. The one Hannan Mosag made pact with. No, not one of our lost ancestors. A new . . . ally.'

'This is not for you to speak of,' the Warlock King said, his voice trembling with rage. 'The pact was—'

'Was something you intended to betray, Hannan Mosag,' Rhulad cut in savagely, leaning forward to glare past his hands where they were folded about the sword's grip. 'But that is not the Edur way, is it? You, who would lead us, cannot be trusted. The time has come, Warlock King, for a change.'

Trull watched as Rhulad surged to his feet. And stood, balanced and assured, back straight and head held high. The bear cloak was swept back, revealing the rippling coins. The gold mask of Rhulad's face twisted. 'The sword is mine, Hannan Mosag! I am equal to it. You are not. Speak, then, if you would reveal to all here the secret of this weapon. Reveal the most ancient of lies! Speak, Warlock King!'

'I shall not.'

A rustling step forward. 'Then . . . *kneel.*'

'Rhulad!'

'Silence, Father! Kneel before me, Hannan Mosag, and pledge your *brotherhood*. Think not I will simply cast you aside, for I have need of you. We all have need of you. And your K'risnan.'

'Need?' Hannan Mosag's face was ravaged, as if gripped by a physical pain.

Rhulad swung about, glittering eyes fixing on his three brothers, one by one. 'Come forward, brothers, and pledge your service to me. I am the future of the Edur. Theradas Buhn. Midik Buhn. Come forward and call me your brother. Bind yourselves to me. Power awaits us all, power you cannot yet imagine. Come. I am Rhulad, youngest son of Tomad Sengar. Blooded in battle, and *I have known death!*'

Abruptly, he turned about, sword-point scraping along the floor. 'Death,' he muttered, as if to himself. 'Faith is an illusion. The world is not as it seems. We are fools, all of us. Such . . . stupidity.' In the same low tone he continued, 'Kneel before me, Hannan Mosag. It is not so much to surrender, is it? We shall know power. We shall be as we once were, as we were meant to be. Kneel, Warlock King, and receive my blessing.'

The head lifted once more, a flash of gold in the gloom. 'Binadas. You know pain, a wound resisting mending. Come forward, and I will release you from that pain. I will heal the damage.'

Binadas frowned. 'You know nothing of sorcery, Rhulad—'

'*Come here!*' The shriek echoed in the vast chamber.

Binadas flinched, then limped closer.

Rhulad's golden hand snapped out, fingers slashing across his brother's chest. The faintest of touches, and Binadas reeled back. Fear rushed close to hold him upright. Eyes wide, Binadas righted himself. He said nothing, but it was clear as he straightened that the pain in his hip was gone. Tremors shook him.

415

'Thus,' Rhulad said in a whisper. 'Come, my brothers. It is time.'

Trull cleared his throat. He had to speak. He had to ask his questions, to say what no-one else would say. 'We saw you dead.'

'And I have returned.'

'By the power of the sword you hold, Rhulad? Why would this ally give the Edur such a thing? What does that ally hope to gain? Brother, the tribes have been unified. We have won our peace—'

'You are the weakest of us, Trull. Your words betray you. We are Tiste Edur. Have you forgotten what that means? I think you have.' He looked round. 'I think you all have. Six pathetic tribes, six pathetic kings. Hannan Mosag knew a greater ambition. Sufficient to conquer. He was necessary, but he cannot achieve what must come now.'

Trull could hear the brother he knew in Rhulad's words, but something new was threaded through them. Strange, poisonous roots – was this the voice of power?

Dull clicking of coin edges, as Rhulad faced the silent crowd beyond the inner circle. 'The Edur have lost sight of their destiny. The Warlock King would twist you away from what must be. My brothers and sisters – all of you here are that to me, and more. I shall be your voice. Your will. The Tiste Edur have journeyed beyond kings and warlock kings. What awaits us is what we once possessed, yet lost long ago. Of what am I speaking, brothers and sisters? I shall give answer. *Empire*.'

Trull stared at Rhulad. Empire. And for every empire . . . there is an emperor.

Kneel, Rhulad had commanded. Of Hannan Mosag. Of everyone here. Tiste Edur do not kneel before mere kings . . .

Fear spoke. 'You would be emperor, Rhulad?'

His brother swung to face him and spread his arms in a deprecating gesture. 'Do I make you want to turn away in horror, Fear? In revulsion? Oh, but did not that slave fashion well? Am I not a thing of beauty?'

416

There was an edge of hysteria in the tone.

Fear made no reply.

Rhulad smiled and continued, 'I should tell you, the weight no longer drags at me. I feel . . . unburdened. Yes, my brother, I find myself pleased. Oh, does that shock you? Why? Can you not see my wealth? My armour? Am I not a bold vision of an Edur warrior?'

'I am not sure,' Fear replied, 'what I am seeing. Is it truly Rhulad who dwells within that body?'

'Die, Fear, and claw your way back. Then ask yourself if the journey has not changed you.'

'Did you find yourself among our ancestors?' Fear asked.

Rhulad's answering laugh was brutal. He swung the sword into the air, twisting the blade into a wild salute, revealing a grace with the weapon that Trull had never before seen in his brother. 'Our ancestors! Proud ghosts. They stood in ranks ten thousand deep! Roaring their welcome! Blooded kin was I, worthy to join them in their stalwart defence of precious memories. Against that vast host of ignorance. Oh yes, Fear, it was a time of such *glory.*'

'Then, by your tone, Rhulad, you would challenge all that we hold dear. You would deny our beliefs—'

'And who among you can gainsay me?'

'The shadow wraiths—'

'Are Tiste Andii, brother. Slaves to our will. And I will tell you this: those who serve us died by our hands.'

'Then where are our ancestors?'

'Where?' Rhulad's voice was a rasp. 'Where? Nowhere, brother. They are nowhere. Our souls flee our bodies, flee this world, for we do not belong here. We have never belonged here.'

'And shall you lead us home, then, Rhulad?'

The eyes flashed. 'Wise brother. I knew you would find the path first.'

'Why do you demand that we kneel?'

The head tilted to one side. 'I would you pledge yourself

417

to our new destiny. A destiny into which I will lead the Tiste Edur.'

'You would take us home.'

'I would.'

Fear stepped forward, then sank to one knee, head bowing. 'Lead us home, Emperor.'

In Trull's mind, he heard a sound.

Like a spine breaking.

And he turned, as did so many others, to face Hannan Mosag and his cadre of sorcerors, to witness the Warlock King descending from the dais. To watch him kneel before Rhulad, before the emperor of the Tiste Edur.

Like a spine breaking.

The water tugging at his shins, swirling around numbed flesh, Udinaas struggled to stand. The waves rocked him, made him totter. Out on the bay, ships. Four in all, pushing through the mist, their dark hulks crouching on the grey water like migratory leviathans, sweeps crabbing the swells. He could hear the chorus of dull creaks and the slap of wooden blades in the water. Hooded, cloaked figures small on the distant decks. The delegation had arrived.

He felt as if he was standing on pegs of ice, the jagged points driven up through his knees. He did not think he was able to walk. In fact, he was moments from falling over, down into the foaming water. So easy, pulled out by the undertow, the cold flooding his lungs, washing black through his mind. Until, in perfect accord with the acceptance of surrender, it was over.

Claws stabbed into his shoulders and lifted him thrashing from the waves. Talons punching through the rain cloak, biting into flesh. Too stunned to scream, he felt himself whipped through the air, legs scissoring in a spray of water.

Flung down onto a bed of wet stones fifteen paces up from the tideline.

Whatever had dragged him was gone, although fire

burned in his chest and back where the talons had been. Floundering in a strange helplessness, Udinaas eventually pulled himself round so that he lay on his back, staring up at the colourless clouds, the rain on his face.

Locqui Wyval. Didn't want me dead, I suppose.

He lifted an arm and felt the fabric of the rain cloak. No punctures. Good. He'd have trouble explaining had it been otherwise.

Feeling was returning to his lower legs. He pushed himself onto his hands and knees. Wet, shivering. There could be no answer for Rhulad, it was as simple as that. The Warlock King would have to kill him. *Assuming that works.*

Kill him, or surrender. And what could make Hannan Mosag surrender? To a barely blooded whelp? No, chop off his hands, sever his head and crush it flat. Burn the rest into dusty ashes. Destroy the monstrosity, for Rhulad Sengar was truly a monster.

Footsteps on the stones behind him. Udinaas sat back on his haunches, blinking rain from his eyes. He looked up as Hulad stepped into view.

'Udinaas, what are you doing here?'

'Did she cast the tiles, Hulad? Did she?'

'She tried.'

'Tried?'

'It failed, Udinaas. The Holds were closed; she was blind to them. She was frightened. I've never seen her so frightened.'

'What else has happened?'

'I don't know. The Edur are still in the citadel.'

'They can't all be there.'

'No, only the nobility. The others are in their homes. They have banished their slaves for now. Most of them had nowhere to go. They're just huddled in the forest. Soaked through. There seems no end in sight.' He reached down and helped Udinaas to stand. 'Let's go to the longhouse. Get dry and warm.'

He let Hulad guide him back to the Sengar longhouse.

419

'Did you see the ships, Hulad?' he asked as they walked. 'Did you see them?'

'Yes. They're lowering boats, but no welcome seems forthcoming.'

'I wonder what they'll think of that?'

Hulad did not reply.

They entered. Sudden warmth, the crackle of flames the only sound. Hulad helped him remove the rain cloak. As he did so, he gasped and pulled at Udinaas's shirt.

'Where did you get those?'

Udinaas frowned down at the almost-black bruises where the Wyval's talons had been. 'I don't know.'

'They remind me of Feather Witch's wounds, from that demon. Just the same. Udinaas, what is happening to you?'

'Nothing. I'm going to sleep.'

Hulad said nothing more as Udinaas walked down the length of the main chamber towards his sleeping pallet.

Fighting the outflow, the three scows edged closer to the bank on the south side of the river. Each craft held about a dozen Letherii, most of them bodyguards in full armour, the visors closed on their helms.

Four steps behind Buruk the Pale, Seren followed the merchant down to the strand. It seemed they would be the sole welcoming committee, at least to begin with. 'What do you intend to tell them?' she asked.

Buruk glanced back at her, rain dripping from the rim of his hood. 'I was hoping you would say something.'

She did not believe him, but appreciated the effort. 'I'm not even certain of the protocol. Nifadas is leading the delegation, but the prince is here as well. Who do I acknowledge first?'

Buruk shrugged. 'The one most likely to be offended if you bow to other one first.'

'Assuming,' she replied, 'I do not intend a calculated insult.'

420

'Well, there is that. Mind you, Acquitor, you are supposed to be neutral.'

'Perhaps I should direct my bow to a space directly between them.'

'Whereupon they will both conclude that you have lost your mind.'

'Which is at least even-handed.'

'Ah, humour. That is much better, Acquitor. Despair gives way to anticipation.'

They reached the strand and stood side by side, watching the scows approach. The rain elected that moment to fall harder, a growing downpour prattling on the stones and hissing on the current- and tide-twisted water. The scows blurred behind a grey wall, almost vanished entirely, then reappeared suddenly, the first one crunching and lurching as it grounded. Sweeps rose and then descended as the crew stored them. Guards splashed down and clambered onto the strand. One made his way to Buruk and Seren. His expression below the visor and nose-bar was grim.

'I am Finadd Moroch Nevath, of the Prince's Guard. Where are the Edur?'

Moroch seemed to be facing Seren, so she spoke in reply, 'In the citadel, Finadd. There has been an . . . event.'

'What in the Errant's name does that mean?'

Behind the Finadd and his guards, Prince Quillas Diskanar was being carried by servants over the waves. The First Eunuch Nifadas had eschewed any such assistance and was wading onto the strand.

'It's rather complicated,' Seren said. 'Buruk's guest camp is just on the other side of the bridge. We can get under cover from the rain—'

'Never mind the rain,' Moroch snapped. Then he swung about and saluted as Quillas Diskanar, sheltered beneath a four-point umbrella held aloft by two servants, strode to halt before Buruk and Seren. 'My prince,' the Finadd said in a growl, 'it would appear the Tiste Edur have chosen this moment to be preoccupied.'

'Hardly an auspicious beginning,' Quillas snapped, turning a sneer on Seren Pedac. 'Acquitor. Has Hull Beddict elected the wise course and departed this village?'

She blinked, struggling to disguise her alarm at the preeminence the question of Hull had assumed. *Do they fear him that much?* 'He is nearby, my prince.'

'I intend to forbid his attendance, Acquitor.'

'I believe an invitation has been extended to him,' she said slowly, 'by the Warlock King.'

'Oh? And will Hull speak for the Edur now?'

Buruk spoke for the first time. 'My prince, that is a question we would all like answered.'

Quillas shifted his attention. 'You are the merchant from Trate.'

'Buruk the Pale.' With a deep bow from which Buruk had difficulty recovering.

'A drunk merchant at that.'

Seren cleared her throat. 'Your arrival was sudden, my prince. The Edur have been sequestered in the citadel for a day and a half. We've had little to do but wait.'

The First Eunuch was standing a pace back, seemingly uninterested in the conversation, his small, glittering eyes fixed on the citadel. He appeared equally indifferent to the rain pummelling his hood and cape-clad shoulders. It occurred to Seren that here was a different kind of power, and in silence the weight was being stolen from Prince Quillas Diskanar.

Proof of that was sudden, as the prince swung round to Nifadas and said, 'What do you make of all this, then, First Eunuch?'

Expressionless eyes settled on Quillas. 'My prince, we have arrived at a moment of crisis. The Acquitor and the merchant know something of it, and so we must needs await their explanation.'

'Indeed,' Quillas said. 'Acquitor, inform us of this crisis.'

Whilst you stand beneath that umbrella and we get soaked and chilled to the bone. 'Of course, my prince. The Warlock

King despatched a party of warriors into the ice wastes to retrieve what turned out to be a sword. They were, however, set upon by Jheck Soletaken. One of the warriors, who was wielding that sword, was slain. The others brought his body back for burial, but the corpse would not release its grip upon the sword. The Warlock King was greatly animated by this detail, and made his demand for the weapon plain and unequivocal. There was a public clash between him and the dead warrior's father.'

'Why not just cut off the body's fingers?' Quillas Diskanar demanded, his brows lifted in contemptuous disbelief.

'Because,' Nifadas replied, laconic and overly patient, 'there is traditional sanctity accorded a fallen warrior among the Edur. Please, Acquitor, go on. It is hard to believe this impasse is yet to be resolved.'

She nodded. 'It was but the beginning, and indeed it became something of a moot point. For the corpse returned to life.'

Quillas snorted. 'What manner of jest is this, woman?'

'No jest,' Buruk the Pale answered. 'My prince, we saw him with our own eyes. He was alive. The truth was announced by his screams, such terrible screams, for he had been dressed—'

'Dressed?' the prince asked, looking around.

The First Eunuch's eyes had widened. 'How far along, Merchant Buruk?'

'The coins, First Eunuch. And the wax.'

'Errant defend,' Nifadas whispered. 'And this sword – he will not yield it?'

Seren shook her head. 'We don't know, First Eunuch.'

'Describe the weapon, if you would, Acquitor.'

'Two-handed grip, but a thin blade. Some kind of alloy, yet reluctant to fuse. There is iron, and some sort of black metal that appears in elongated shards.'

'Origin? Can you discern anything from the style?'

'Not much, First Eunuch. The bell-hilt bears some

resemblance to the drawn twist technique used by the Meckros—'

'The Meckros?' Quillas asked. 'Those traders from the floating cities?'

'Yes, although the pattern on that bell-hilt has been shaped to resemble links of chain.'

Buruk faced her with a wry expression. 'You've sharp eyes, Acquitor. All I saw was a sword.'

'I suggest,' Nifadas said, 'we retire to the merchant's camp.'

Quillas hissed, 'You will swallow this insult, First Eunuch?'

'There is no insult,' Nifadas replied easily, striding past the prince to hook arms with a surprised Seren Pedac. 'Escort me, please, Acquitor.'

'Of course, First Eunuch.'

The others had no choice but to trail after them.

Nifadas walked quickly. After a dozen or so paces, he asked in a quiet, conversational tone, 'Was Hull Beddict witness to all this?'

'No. At least I don't think so. He's been gone for some time.'

'But he will return.'

'Yes.'

'I have left the majority of my guard aboard the *Risen Pale*, including Finadd Gerun Eberict.'

'Gerun – oh.'

'Indeed. Would it be, do you think, propitious that I send for him?'

'I – I am not sure, First Eunuch. It depends, I imagine, on what you would have him do.'

'Perhaps a word or two with Hull, upon his return?'

'Is the Finadd a persuasive man?'

'Not by way of personality, no . . .'

She nodded, struggled to repress a shiver – unsuccessfully, it turned out.

'Chilled, Acquitor?'

'The rain.'

'Of course. I trust Buruk's servants are feeding a fire of some sort?'

'Rather too eagerly.'

'Well, I doubt if anyone will complain. You and Buruk have waited here some time, I take it.'

'Yes. Some time. There was an audience with the Warlock King, but in keeping with my role I departed before anything of substance was discussed. And as to what was said, neither Hull nor Buruk has revealed anything.'

'Hull was there for that, was he?' He swung a faint smile on her. 'Nothing of substance was revealed to you, Acquitor? I admit to having trouble quite believing that assertion.'

Seren Pedac hesitated.

'Acquitor,' Nifadas said in a low voice, 'the privilege of neutrality no longer exists in this matter. Make your choice.'

'It is not that, First Eunuch,' she said, knowing her claim was untrue. 'I have a fear that whatever position the Warlock King may have chosen back then is no longer relevant.' She glanced over at him. 'I do not think Rhulad will relinquish that sword.'

'Rhulad. What can you tell me of this Rhulad?'

'Youngest son of a noble family, the Sengar.'

'The Sengar? Eldest son is Fear, yes? Commander of the Edur warriors. Prestigious blood, then.'

'Yes. Another brother is Binadas, who is blood-sworn with Hull Beddict.'

'Interesting. I begin to grasp the complexity awaiting us, Acquitor.'

And so, it seems, do I. For I appear to have made my choice.

As if Nifadas gave me any other option, as I walk here arm in arm with the First Eunuch . . .

'Wake up, Udinaas.'

Lids slid back from stinging, burning eyes. Udinaas

425

stared up at the angled wall above him. 'No. I need to sleep—'

'*Not so loud. What you need, fool, is to walk to the citadel.*'

'Why? They'll cut my throat for intruding—'

'*No, they won't. Rhulad won't let them, for you are his slave now, and no-one else's. They must be informed. The Letherii delegation awaits.*'

'Leave me be, Wither.'

'*The Tiste Edur emperor wants you. Now.*'

'Right. And does he know it?'

'*Not yet.*'

'As I thought.' He closed his eyes once more. 'Go away, wraith.'

'*The Wyval and I are in agreement in this, Udinaas. You must step to the forefront. You must make yourself invaluable to Rhulad. Tell me, do you want Feather Witch for your own or not?*'

Udinaas blinked, then sat up. 'What?'

'*Go now, and you will see.*'

'Not until you explain that, Wither.'

'*I shall not, slave. Go to the citadel. Serve the Edur emperor.*'

Udinaas pulled aside his blankets and reached for his sodden moccasins. 'Why don't you all leave me alone.'

'*She raped you, Udinaas. She took your seed. Why did she do that?*'

He went still, one moccasin on, the other cold in his hands. 'Menandore.'

'*The bitch has designs, she does. No love for Edur or Andii, no, not her.*'

'What has that to do with anything?'

The wraith made no reply.

Udinaas rubbed at his face, then pulled on the second moccasin and tugged at the soaked leather ties. 'I am a slave, Wither. Slaves are not given slaves, and that is the only way I could win Feather Witch. Unless you plan on invading her mind and twisting her will. In which case, it won't be Feather Witch, will it?'

'*You accord me powers I do not possess.*'

'Only to emphasize the absurdity of your promises, Wither. Now, be quiet. I'm going.' He rose and stumbled from the cell. Hulad was crouched by the hearth, heating soup or stew.

'You were talking to yourself, Udinaas. You shouldn't do that.'

'That's what I keep telling myself,' he replied, making his way to the doors, collecting a rain cape on the way.

Outside, the rain was a deluge. He could barely make out the anchored ships in the bay. There were figures on the strand. Soldiers.

He pulled up the hood then headed for the citadel that had once belonged to the Warlock King.

Serve the Edur emperor. And where will you take your people, Rhulad Sengar?

The shadow wraiths guarding the entrance made no move to oppose the Letherii slave as he ascended the steps. Both hands on the doors, pushing them aside, striding in on a gust of pelting rain. *Come, you damned Edur. Slide a blade across my throat. Through my chest.* There were no guards within the reception chamber, and the curtain beyond was drawn closed.

He shook the rain from his cape, then continued forward.

To the curtains. He pulled them aside.

To see the Edur kneeling. All of them, kneeling before the glimmering form of Rhulad Sengar, who stood on the dais, the sword raised in one hand above his head. Bear fur on his shoulders, face a rippling mask of gold surrounding the deep holes of his eye sockets.

Not blind, then. Nor crippled. And if this was madness, then it was a poison riding the chamber's thick currents.

Udinaas felt the emperor's eyes fix on him, as palpable as talons digging into his mind. 'Approach, slave,' he said, his voice ragged.

Heads lifted and turned as Udinaas threaded through the

427

crowd, making his way down the tiers. The Letherii did not glance at any faces, his gaze focused solely on Rhulad Sengar. In his peripheral vision he saw Hannan Mosag, kneeling with head bowed, and behind him his K'risnan in identical positions of subservience.

'Speak, Udinaas.'

'The delegation has arrived, Emperor.'

'We are bound, are we not, Udinaas? Slave and master. You heard my summons.'

'I did, master.' Lies, he realized, were getting easier.

'The delegation waits in the merchant's camp. Bring them to us, Udinaas.'

'As you command.' He bowed, then began the laborious effort of backing out.

'There is no need for that, Udinaas. I am not offended by a man's back. Go, and tell them that the ruler of the Edur will greet them now.'

Udinaas swung about and made his way from the chamber.

Beneath the rain once more, across the bridge. Solitude might invite thought, but Udinaas refused the invitation. The fog of the world beyond was mirrored in his own mind. He was a slave. Slaves did what was commanded of them.

Woodsmoke drifting out from under a broad canopy near the trader wagons. Figures standing beneath it. Acquitor Seren Pedac turned and saw him first. *Yes. There is more in her than she realizes. The ghosts like her, hovering like moths around a candle flame. She doesn't even see them.* He watched her say something, then the others swung to face him.

Udinaas halted just outside the tarp, keeping his gaze averted. 'The ruler of the Edur bids you come to the citadel.'

A soldier growled, then said, 'You stand before your prince, Letherii. Drop to your knees or I'll cut your head from your shoulders.'

'Then draw your sword,' Udinaas replied. 'My master is Tiste Edur.'

'He is nothing,' said the young, expensively dressed man at the soldier's side. A flutter of one hand. 'We are invited, finally. First Eunuch, will you lead us?'

The large, heavy man with a face as sombre as his clothes stepped out to stand beside Udinaas. 'Acquitor, please accompany us.'

Seren Pedac nodded, drawing her cloak's hood over her head and joining the First Eunuch.

Udinaas led them back across the bridge. A wind had begun whipping the rain in biting sheets that ripped across their path. Among the longhouses of the nobility, then towards the steps.

Shadow wraiths swirled before the door.

Udinaas faced Quillas Diskanar. 'Prince, your bodyguards are not welcome.'

The young man scowled. 'Wait here with your men, Finadd.'

Moroch Nevath grunted, then directed his guards to fan out to either side of the citadel's entrance.

The wraiths edged back to provide a corridor to the double doors.

Udinaas strode forward and pushed them open, moved inside then turned about. A step behind him were Nifadas and the Acquitor, the prince, his expression dark, trailing.

The First Eunuch frowned at the curtain at the far end. 'The throne room is filled with Edur nobles? Then why do I hear nothing?'

'They await your arrival,' Udinaas said. 'The ruler of the Tiste Edur stands on the centre dais. His appearance will startle you—'

'Slave,' Quillas said, making the word contemptuous, 'we are not anticipating that the negotiations will commence immediately. We are but to be proclaimed guests—'

'I am not the one to guarantee that,' Udinaas cut in, unperturbed. 'I would advise that you be ready for anything.'

'But this is absurd—'

'Let us be about it, then,' the First Eunuch said.

The prince was not used to these constant interruptions, his face flushing.

Acquitor Seren Pedac spoke. 'Udinaas, by your words I conclude that Hannan Mosag has been usurped.'

'Yes.'

'And Rhulad Sengar has proclaimed himself the new king of the Tiste Edur.'

'No, Acquitor. Emperor.'

There was silence for a half-dozen heartbeats, then the prince snorted in disbelief. 'What empire? Six tribes of seal-hunters? This fool has gone mad.'

'It is one thing,' Nifadas said slowly, 'to proclaim oneself an emperor. It is another to force the Edur nobility to bend knee to such a claim. Udinaas, have they done so?'

'They have, First Eunuch.'

'That is . . . astonishing.'

'Hannan Mosag?' Seren asked.

'He too has knelt and pledged allegiance, Acquitor.'

Once again no-one spoke for a time.

Then the First Eunuch nodded to Udinaas and said, 'Thank you. I am ready to meet the emperor now.'

Udinaas nodded and approached the curtain. Pulling it aside, he stepped through into the chamber beyond. The nobles had moved to form an avenue leading down to the centre dais. Everyone was standing. On the dais, Rhulad Sengar leaned on his sword. His motions had dislodged a few coins, leaving mottled patches of burnt skin. Humidity, heat and oil lamps made the air mist-laden and lurid. Udinaas sought to look upon the scene as if he was a stranger, and was shocked at its raw barbarity. *These are a fallen people.*

Who would rise anew.

The First Eunuch and the Acquitor appeared on the threshold, and Nifadas moved to his left to give space for Prince Quillas Diskanar.

Udinaas raised his voice. 'Emperor. First Eunuch

Nifadas and Prince Quillas Diskanar. The Letherii treaty delegation.'

'Come forward,' came the rasping invitation from the emperor. 'I am Rhulad Sengar, and I proclaim you guests of the Tiste Edur Empire.'

Nifadas bowed his head. 'We thank your highness for his welcome.'

'It is the desire of the Letherii king to establish a formal treaty with us,' Rhulad said, then shrugged. 'I was under the impression we already had one. And, while we honour it, your people do not. Thus, what value a new agreement?'

As the First Eunuch was about to speak, Quillas stepped forward. 'You confiscated a harvest of tusked seals. So be it. Such things cannot be reversed, can they? None the less, there is the matter of debt.'

Udinaas smiled, not needing to look up to see the shocked expressions from the gathered nobility.

'Hannan Mosag,' Rhulad said after a moment, 'will speak for the Edur in this matter.'

Udinaas glanced up to see the once-Warlock King stepping forward to stand in front of the dais. He was without expression. 'Prince, you will need to explain how you Letherii have arrived at the notion of debt. The harvest was illegal – do you deny it?'

'We do not – no, Nifadas, I am speaking. As I was saying to you, Hannan Mosag, we do not dispute the illegality of the harvest. But its illegality does not in turn refute the reality that it took place. And that harvest, conducted by Letherii, is now in Edur hands. The present treaty, you may recall, has an agreed market value for tusked seals, and it is this price we expect to be honoured.'

'Extraordinary logic, Prince,' Hannan Mosag said, his voice a smooth rumble.

'We are, fortunately,' Quillas continued, 'prepared for a compromise.'

'Indeed?'

Udinaas wondered why Nifadas was remaining silent.

431

His lack of interruption could only be interpreted as tacit allegiance to the prince and the position he was advocating.

'A compromise, yes. The debt shall be forgiven, in exchange for land. Specifically, the remainder of Trate Reach, which, as we both know, serves only as seasonal fishing camps for your people. Such camps would not be prohibited, of course. They shall remain available to you, for a modest percentage of your catch.'

'As it now stands, then,' Hannan Mosag said, 'we begin this treaty in your debt.'

'Yes.'

'Based upon the presumption that we possess the stolen harvest.'

'Well, of course—'

'But we do not possess it, Prince Quillas Diskanar.'

'What? But you must!'

'You are welcome to visit our store houses for yourself,' Hannan Mosag went on reasonably. 'We punished the harvesters, as was our right. But we did not retrieve the harvest.'

'The ships arrived in Trate with their holds empty!'

'Perhaps, in fleeing our wrath, they discharged their burden, so as to quicken their pace. Without success, as it turned out.' As the prince simply stared, Hannan Mosag went on, 'Thus, we are not in your debt. You, however, are in ours. To the market value of the harvested tusked seals. We are undecided, at the moment, on the nature of recompense we will demand of you. After all, we have no need of coin.'

'We have brought gifts!' Quillas shouted.

'For which you will then charge us, with interest. We are familiar with your pattern of cultural conquest among neighbouring tribes, Prince. That the situation is now reversed earns our sympathy, but as you are wont to say, business is business.'

Nifadas finally spoke. 'It seems we have much to

consider, the two of us, Emperor. Alas, our journey has been long and wearying. Perhaps you could permit us to retire for a time, to reconvene this meeting on the morrow?'

'Excellent idea,' Rhulad said, the coins on his face twisting as he smiled. 'Udinaas, escort the delegation to the guest longhouse. Then return here. A long night awaits us.'

The prince stood like a puppet with its strings cut. The faces of the Acquitor and the First Eunuch, however, remained composed.

Even so, it seems we are all puppets here . . .

Trull Sengar watched the slave lead the Acquitor and the delegation out of the chamber. The world had not crumbled, it had shattered, and before his eyes he saw the jagged pieces, a chamber fissured and latticed, a thousand shards bearing countless reflected images. Edur faces, broken crowds, the smear of smoke. Disjointed motion, a fevered murmur of sound, the liquid glint of gold and a sword as patched and fragmented as everything else in sight.

Like a crazed mosaic, slowly being reassembled by a madman's hand. He did not know where he belonged, where he fit. *Brother to an emperor. It is Rhulad, yet it is not. I don't know him. And I know him all too well and, Daughter take me, I am frightened most by that.*

Hannan Mosag had been speaking quietly with Rhulad, conveying an ease with his new role that Trull knew was intended to calm the witnesses gathered here. Trull wondered what it was costing the Warlock King.

A nod and a wave of the hand dismissed Hannan Mosag, who retreated to stand near his K'risnan. At Rhulad's instructions a large chair was carried to the dais, and the emperor sat, revealing to Trull's knowing gaze his brother's exhaustion. It would take time to acquire the strength necessary to sustain that vast, terrible weight for any length of time. The emperor settled his head back and looked out upon the nobles. His attention quickly silenced the crowd.

'I have known death,' Rhulad said, his voice rough. 'I have returned, and I am not the same, not the unblooded warrior you saw before we began our journey to the ice wastes. I have returned, to bring to you the memory of our destiny. To lead you.' He was silent then, as if needing to recover from his short speech. A dozen heartbeats, before he continued, 'Fear Sengar. Brother, step forward.'

Fear did as commanded, halting on the inner ring in front of the dais.

Rhulad stared down at him, and Trull saw a sudden hunger in those brittle eyes.

'Second only to Hannan Mosag's, your loyalty, Fear, is my greatest need.'

Fear looked rattled, as if such a matter did not need to be questioned.

The slave Udinaas returned then, but held back, his red-rimmed eyes scanning the scene. And Trull wondered at the sudden narrowing of that Letherii's gaze.

'What, Emperor,' Fear said, 'do you ask of me?'

'A gift, brother.'

'All I have is yours—'

'Are you true to that claim, Fear?' Rhulad demanded, leaning forward.

'I would not make it otherwise.'

Oh. No, Rhulad – no—

'The emperor,' Rhulad said, settling back, 'requires an empress.'

Comprehension cast a pall on Fear's face.

'A wife. Fear Sengar, will you gift me a wife?'

You grotesque bastard— Trull stepped forward.

Rhulad's hand snapped out to stay him. 'Be careful, Trull. This is not your concern.' He bared stained teeth. '*It never was.*'

'Must you break those who would follow you?' Trull asked.

'Another word!' Rhulad shrieked. 'One more word, Trull, and I will have you flayed alive!'

434

Trull recoiled at the vehemence, stunned into silence.

A coin clattered onto the dais as Rhulad lifted a hand to his face and clawed at some extremity of emotion, then he snatched his hand away and held it before him, watching it curl into a fist. 'Kill me. That is all you need do. For your proof. Yes, kill me. Again.' The glittering eyes fixed on Trull. 'You knew I was alone, guarding the rear slope. You knew it, Trull, and left me to my fate.'

'What? I knew no such thing, Rhulad—'

'No more lies, brother. Fear, gift me your betrothed. Give me Mayen. Would you stand between her and the title of empress? Tell me, are you that selfish?'

As ugly as driving knives into Fear, one after another. As rendering his flesh into ruin. This, Trull realized, this was Rhulad. The child and his brutal hungers, his vicious appetites. *Tell us, are you that selfish?*

'She is yours, Emperor.'

Words bled of all life, words that were themselves a gift to one who had known death. Though Rhulad lacked the subtle mind to comprehend that.

Instead, his face twisted beneath the coins into a broad smile, filled with glee and triumph. His eyes lifted to a place in the crowd where the unwedded maidens stood. 'Mayen,' he called. 'It is done. Come forward. Join your emperor.'

Tall, regal, the young woman strode forward as if this moment had been rehearsed a thousand times.

But that is not possible.

She walked past Fear without a glance, and came to stand, facing outward, on the left side of the chair. Rhulad's hand reached out with a gesture of smug familiarity and she clasped it.

That final act struck Fear as would a physical blow to his chest. He took a step back.

'Thank you, Fear,' Rhulad said, 'for your gift. I am assured of your loyalty, and proud to call you my brother. You, Binadas, Midik Buhn, Theradas Buhn, Hannan Mosag . . .

435

and,' the gaze shifted, 'Trull, of course. My closest brothers. We are bound by the blood of our ancestors . . .'

He continued, but Trull had ceased listening. His eyes were on Mayen's face. On the horror writ there that she could not disguise. In his mind, Trull cried out to Fear. *Look, brother! She did not seek this betrayal! Look!*

With an effort he pulled his gaze from Mayen, and saw that Fear had seen. Seen what everyone present could see, everyone but Rhulad.

It saved them all. Salvation to the desperate. She showed them that some truths could not be broken, that even this insane *thing* on its throne could not crush the visceral honour remaining to the Tiste Edur. And in her face was yet another promise. She would withstand his crimes, because there was no choice. A promise that was also a lesson to everyone present. *Withstand. Suffer. Live as you must now live. There will, one day, be answer to this.*

Yet Trull wondered. Who could give answer? What waited in the world beyond the borders of their knowledge, sufficiently formidable to challenge this monstrosity? And how long would they have to wait? *We were fallen, and the emperor proclaims that we shall rise again. He is insane, for we are not rising. We are falling, and I fear there will be no end to that descent.*

Until someone gave answer.

Rhulad had stopped speaking, as if growing aware that something was happening among his followers, something that had nothing to do with him and his newfound power. He rose suddenly from the chair. 'This gathering is done. Hannan Mosag, you and your K'risnan will remain here with me and the Empress, for we have much to discuss. Udinaas, bring to Mayen her slaves, so that they may attend her needs. The rest, leave me now. Spread the word of the rise of the new empire of the Edur. And, brothers and sisters, see to your weapons . . .'

Please, someone, give answer to this.

* * *

A dozen paces from the citadel a figure emerged from the rain to stand in front of Udinaas.

The Acquitor.

'What has he done?'

Udinaas studied her for a moment, then shrugged. 'He stole his brother's betrothed. We have an empress, and she does poorly at a brave face.'

'The Edur are usurped,' Seren Pedac said. 'And a tyrant sits on the throne.'

Udinaas hesitated, then said, 'Tell the First Eunuch. You must prepare for war.'

She revealed no surprise at his words; rather, a heavy weariness dulled her eyes. She turned away, walked into the rain and was gone.

I am a bearer of good tidings indeed. And now, it's Feather Witch's turn . . .

Rain rushed down from the sky, blinding and blind, indifferent and mindless, but it held no meaning beyond that. How could it? It was just rain, descending from the sky's massed legion of grieving clouds. And the crying wind was the breath of natural laws, born high in the mountains or out at sea. Its voice promised nothing.

There was no meaning to be found in lifeless weather, in the pulsing of tides and in the wake of turning seasons.

No meaning to living and dying, either.

The tyrant was clothed in gold, and the future smelled of blood.

It meant nothing.

BOOK THREE

ALL THAT LIES UNSEEN

The man who never smiles
Drags his nets through the deep
And we are gathered
To gape in the drowning air
Beneath the buffeting sound
Of his dreaded voice
Speaking of salvation
In the repast of justice done
And fed well on the laden table
Heaped with noble desires
He tells us all this to hone the edge
Of his eternal mercy
Slicing our bellies open
One by one.

In the Kingdom of Meaning Well
Fisher kel Tath

CHAPTER TWELVE

The frog atop the stack of coins dares not jump.

Poor Umur's Sayings
Anonymous

'Five wings will buy you a grovel. I admit, master, the meaning of that saying escapes me.'

Tehol ran both hands through his hair, pulling at the tangles. 'Ouch. It's the Eternal Domicile, Bugg. Wings numbering five, a grovel at the feet of the Errant, at the feet of destiny. The empire is risen. Lether awakens to a new day of glory.'

They stood side by side on the roof.

'But the fifth wing is sinking. What about four wings?'

'Gulls in collision, Bugg. My, it's going to be hot, a veritable furnace. What are the tasks awaiting you today?'

'My first meeting with Royal Engineer Grum. The shoring up we've done with the warehouses impressed him, it seems.'

'Good.' Tehol continued staring out over the city for another moment, then he faced his servant. 'Should it have?'

'Impressed him? Well, the floors aren't sagging and they're bone dry. The new plaster isn't showing any cracks. The owners are delighted—'

'I thought I owned those warehouses.'

'Aren't you delighted?'

'Well, you're right, I am. Every one of me.'

'That's what I told the Royal Engineer when I responded to his first missive.'

'What about the people fronting me on those investments?'

'They're delighted, too.'

'Well,' Tehol sighed, 'it's just that kind of day, isn't it?'

Bugg nodded. 'Must be, master.'

'And is that all you have planned? For the whole day?'

'No. I need to scrounge some food. Then I need to visit Shand and her partners to give them that list of yours again. It was too long.'

'Do you recall it in its entirety?'

'I do. Puryst Rott Ale, I liked that one.'

'Thank you.'

'But they weren't all fake, were they?'

'No, that would give it away too quickly. All the local ones were real. In any case, it'll keep them busy for a while. I hope. What else?'

'Another meeting with the guilds. I may need bribe money for that.'

'Nonsense. Stand fast – they're about to be hit from another quarter.'

'Strike? I hadn't heard—'

'Of course not. The incident that triggers it hasn't happened yet. You know the Royal Engineer's obliged to hire guild members only. We have to see that conflict eliminated before it gives us trouble.'

'All right. I also need to check on that safe-house for Shurq and her newfound friend.'

'Harlest Eberict. That was quite a surprise. Just how many undead people are prowling around in this city anyway?'

'Obviously more than we're aware of, master.'

'For all we know, half the population might be undead – those people on the bridge there, there, those ones with all those shopping baskets in tow, maybe they're undead.'

'Possibly, master,' Bugg conceded. 'Do you mean undead literally or figuratively?'

'Oh, yes, there is a difference, isn't there? Sorry, I got carried away. Speaking of which, how are Shurq and Ublala getting along?'

'Swimmingly.'

'Impressively droll, Bugg. So, you want to check on their hidden abode. Is that all you're up to today?'

'That's just the morning. In the afternoon—'

'Can you manage a short visit?'

'Where?'

'Rat Catchers' Guild.'

'Scale House?'

Tehol nodded. 'I have a contract for them. I want a meeting – clandestine – with the Guild Master. Tomorrow night, if possible.'

Bugg looked troubled. 'That guild—'

'I know.'

'I can drop by on my way to the gravel quarry.'

'Excellent. Why are you going to the gravel quarry?'

'Curiosity. They opened up a new hill to fill my last order, and found something.'

'What?'

'Not sure. Only that they hired a necromancer to deal with it. And the poor fool disappeared, apart from some hair and toe nails.'

'Hmm, that *is* interesting. Keep me informed.'

'As always, master. And what have you planned for today?'

'I thought I'd go back to bed.'

Brys lifted his gaze from the meticulous scroll and studied the scribe seated across from him. 'There must be some mistake,' he said.

'No, sir. Never, sir.'

'Well, if these are just the reported disappearances, what about those that haven't been reported?'

'Between thirty and fifty per cent, I would say, sir. Added on to what we have. But those would be the blue-edged scrolls. They're stored on the Projected Shelf.'

'The what?'

'Projected. That one, the one sticking out from the wall over there.'

'And what is the significance of the blue edges?'

'Posited realities, sir, that which exists beyond the statistics. We use the statistics for formal, public statements and pronouncements, but we operate on the posited realities or, if possible, the measurable realities.'

'Different sets of data?'

'Yes, sir. It's the only way to operate an effective government. The alternative would lead to anarchy. Riots, that sort of thing. We have posited realities for those projections, of course, and they're not pretty.'

'But' – Brys looked back down at the scroll – 'seven thousand disappearances in Letheras last year?'

'Six thousand nine hundred and twenty-one, sir.'

'With a possible additional thirty-five hundred?'

'Three thousand four hundred and sixty and a half, sir.'

'And is anyone assigned to conduct investigations on these?'

'That has been contracted out, sir.'

'Clearly a waste of coin, then—'

'Oh no, the coin is well spent.'

'How so?'

'A respectable amount, sir, which we can use in our formal and public pronouncements.'

'Well, who holds this contract?'

'Wrong office, sir. That information is housed in the Chamber of Contracts and Royal Charters.'

'I've never heard of it. Where is it?'

The scribe rose and walked to a small door squeezed between scroll-cases. 'In here. Follow me, sir.'

The room beyond was not much larger than a walk-in closet. Blue-edged scrolls filled cubby-holes from floor to ceiling on all sides. Rummaging in one cubby-hole at the far wall, the scribe removed a scroll and unfurled it. 'Here we are. It's a relatively new contract. Three years so far. Ongoing investigations, biannual reports delivered precisely on the due dates, yielding no queries, each one approved without prejudice.'

'With whom?'

'The Rat Catchers' Guild.'

Brys frowned. 'Now I am well and truly confused.'

The scribe shrugged and rolled up the scroll to put it away. Over his shoulder he said, 'No need to be, sir. The guild is profoundly competent in a whole host of endeavours—'

'Competence doesn't seem a relevant notion in this matter,' Brys observed.

'I disagree. Punctual reports. No queries. Two renewals without challenge. Highly competent, I would say, sir.'

'Nor is there any shortage of rats in the city, as one would readily see with even a short walk down any street.'

'Population management, sir. I dread to think what the situation would be like without the guild.'

Brys said nothing.

A defensiveness came to the scribe's expression as he studied the Finadd for a long moment. 'We have nothing but praise for the Rat Catchers' Guild, sir.'

'Thank you for your efforts,' Brys said. 'I will find my own way out. Good day.'

'And to you, sir. Pleased to have been of some service.'

Out in the corridor, Brys paused, rubbing at his eyes. Archival chambers were thick with dust. He needed to get outside, into what passed for fresh air in Letheras.

Seven thousand disappearances every year. He was appalled.

So what, I wonder, has Tehol stumbled onto? His brother remained a mystery to Brys. Clearly, Tehol was up to something, contrary to outward appearances. And he had somehow held on to a formidable level of efficacy behind –

or beneath – the scenes. That all too public fall, so shocking and traumatic to the financial tolls, now struck Brys as just another feint in his brother's grander scheme – whatever that was.

The mere thought that such a scheme might exist worried Brys. His brother had revealed, on occasion, frightening competence and ruthlessness. Tehol possessed few loyalties. He was capable of anything.

All things considered, the less Brys knew of Tehol's activities, the better. He did not want his own loyalties challenged, and his brother might well challenge them. As with Hull. *Oh, Mother, it is the Errant's blessing that you are not alive to see your sons now. Then again, how much of what we are now is what you made us into?*

Questions without answers. There seemed to be too many of those these days.

He made his way into the more familiar passages of the palace. Weapons training awaited him, and he found himself anticipating that period of blissful exhaustion. If only to silence the cacophony of his thoughts.

There were clear advantages to being dead, Bugg reflected, as he lifted the flagstone from the warehouse office floor, revealing a black gaping hole and the top rung of a pitted bronze ladder. Dead fugitives, after all, needed no food, no water. No air, come to that. Made hiding them almost effortless.

He descended the ladder, twenty-three rungs, to arrive at a tunnel roughly cut from the heavy clay and then fired to form a hard shell. Ten paces forward to a crooked stone arch beneath which was a cracked stone door crowded with hieroglyphs. Old tombs like this were rare. Most had long since collapsed beneath the weight of the city overhead or had simply sunk so far down in the mud as to be unreachable. Scholars had sought to decipher the strange sigils on the doors of the tombs, while common folk had long wondered why tombs should have doors at all. The language had only been partially deciphered, sufficient to reveal that the glyphs were curse-laden and aspected to the Errant in some mysterious way. All in all, cause enough to avoid them, especially since, after a few had been broken into, it became known that the tombs contained nothing of value, and were peculiar in that the featureless plain stone sarcophagus each tomb housed was empty. There was the added unsubstantiated rumour that those tomb-robbers had subsequently suffered horrid fates.

The door to this particular tomb had surrendered its seal to the uneven heaving descent of the entire structure. Modest effort could push it to one side.

In the tunnel, Bugg lit a lantern using a small ember box, and set it down on the threshold to the tomb. He then applied his shoulder to the door.

'Is that you?' came Shurq's voice from the darkness within.

'Why yes,' Bugg said, 'it is.'

'Liar. You're not you, you're Bugg. Where's Tehol? I need to talk to Tehol.'

'He is indisposed,' Bugg said. Having pushed the door open to allow himself passage into the tomb, he collected the lantern and edged inside.

'Where's Harlest?'

'In the sarcophagus.'

There was no lid to the huge stone coffin. Bugg walked over and peered in. 'What are you doing, Harlest?' He set the lantern down on the edge.

'The previous occupant was tall. Very tall. Hello, Bugg. What am I doing? I am lying here.'

'Yes, I see that. But why?'

'There are no chairs.'

Bugg turned to Shurq Elalle. 'Where are these diamonds?'

'Here. Have you found what I was looking for?'

'I have. A decent price, leaving you the majority of your wealth intact.'

447

'Tehol can have what's left in the box there. My earnings from the whorehouse I'll keep.'

'Are you sure you don't want a percentage from this, Shurq? Tehol would be happy with fifty per cent. After all, the risk was yours.'

'No. I'm a thief. I can always get more.'

Bugg glanced around. 'Will this do for the next little while?'

'I don't see why not. It's dry, at least. Quiet, most of the time. But I need Ublala Pung.'

Harlest's voice came from the sarcophagus. 'And I want sharp teeth and talons. Shurq said you could do that for me.'

'Work's already begun on that, Harlest.'

'I want to be scary. It's important that I be scary. I've been practising hissing and snarling.'

'No need for concern there,' Bugg replied. 'You'll be truly terrifying. In any case, I should be going—'

'Not so fast,' Shurq cut in. 'Has there been any word on the robbery at Gerun Eberict's estate?'

'No. Not surprising, if you think about it. Gerun's undead brother disappears, the same night as some half-giant beats up most of the guards. Barring that, what else is certain? Will anyone actually attempt to enter Gerun's warded office?'

'If I eat human flesh,' Harlest said, 'it will rot in my stomach, won't it? That means I will stink. I like that. I like thinking about things like that. The smell of doom.'

'The what? Shurq, probably they don't know they've been robbed. And even if they did, they wouldn't make a move until their master returns.'

'I expect you're right. Anyway, be sure to send me Ublala Pung. Tell him I miss him. Him and his—'

'I will, Shurq. I promise. Anything else?'

'I don't know,' she replied. 'Let me think.'

Bugg waited.

'Oh, yes,' she said after a time, 'what do you know about

these tombs? There was a corpse here, once, in that sarcophagus.'

'How can you be certain?'

Her lifeless eyes fixed on his. 'We can tell.'

'Oh. All right.'

'So, what do you know?'

'Not much. The language on the door belongs to an extinct people known as Forkrul Assail, who are collectively personified in our Fulcra by the personage we call the Errant. The tombs were built for another extinct people, called the Jaghut, whom we acknowledge in the Hold we call the Hold of Ice. The wards were intended to block the efforts of another people, the T'lan Imass, who were the avowed enemies of the Jaghut. The T'lan Imass pursued the Jaghut in a most relentless manner, including those Jaghut who elected to surrender their place in the world – said individuals choosing something closely resembling death. Their souls would travel to their Hold, leaving their flesh behind, the flesh being stored in tombs like this one. That wasn't good enough for the T'lan Imass. Anyway, the Forkrul Assail considered themselves impartial arbiters in the conflict, and that was, most of the time, the extent of their involvement. Apart from that,' Bugg said with a shrug, 'I really can't say.'

Harlest Eberict had slowly sat up during Bugg's monologue and was now staring at the manservant. Shurq Elalle was motionless, as the dead often were. Then she said, 'I have another question.'

'Go ahead.'

'Is this common knowledge among serving staff?'

'Not that I am aware of, Shurq. I just pick up things here and there, over time.'

'Things no scholar in Letheras picks up? Or are you just inventing as you go along?'

'I try to avoid complete fabrication.'

'And do you succeed?'

'Not always.'

'You'd better go now, Bugg.'

'Yes, I'd better. I'll have Ublala visit you tonight.'

'Do you have to?' Harlest asked. 'I'm not the voyeuristic type—'

'Liar,' Shurq said. 'Of course you are.'

'Okay, so I'm lying. It's a useful lie, and I want to keep it.'

'That position is indefensible—'

'That's a rich statement, coming from you and given what you'll be up to tonight—'

Bugg collected the lantern and slowly backed out as the argument continued. He pushed the door back in place, slapped the dust from his hands, then returned to the ladder.

Once back in the warehouse office, he replaced the flag-stone, then, collecting his drawings, he made his way to the latest construction site. Bugg's Construction's most recent acquisition had once been a school, stately and reserved for children of only the wealthiest citizens of Letheras. Residences were provided, creating the typical and highly popular prison-style educational institution. Whatever host of traumas were taught within its confines came to an end when, during one particularly wet spring, the cellar walls collapsed in a sluice of mud and small human bones. The floor of the main assembly hall promptly slumped during the next gathering of students, burying children and instructors alike in a vast pit of black, rotting mud, in which fully a third drowned, and of these the bodies of more than half were never recovered. Shoddy construction was blamed, leading to a scandal.

Since that event, fifteen years past, the derelict building had remained empty, reputedly haunted by the ghosts of outraged proctors and bewildered hall monitors.

The purchase price had been suitably modest.

The upper levels directly above the main assembly hall were structurally compromised, and Bugg's first task had been to oversee the installation of bracing, before the crews could re-excavate the pit down to the cellar floor. Once that floor was exposed – and the jumble of bones dispatched to the cemetery – shafts were extended straight down, through lenses of clay and sand, to a thick bed of gravel. Cement was poured in and a ring of vertical iron rods put in place, followed by alternating packed gravel and cement for half the depth of the shaft. Limestone pillars, their bases drilled to take the projecting rods, were then lowered. From there on upwards, normal construction practices followed. Columns, buttresses and false arches, all the usual techniques in which Bugg had little interest.

The old school was being transformed into a palatial mansion. Which they would then sell to some rich merchant or noble devoid of taste. Since there were plenty of those, the investment was a sure one.

Bugg spent a short time at the site, surrounded by foremen thrusting scrolls in his face describing countless alterations and specifications requiring approval. A bell passed before he finally managed to file his drawings and escape.

The street that became the road that led to the gravel quarry was a main thoroughfare wending parallel with the canal. It was also one of the oldest tracks in the city. Built along the path of a submerged beach ridge of pebbles and cobbles sealed in clay, the buildings lining it had resisted the sagging decay common to other sections of the city. Two hundred years old, many of them, in a style so far forgotten as to seem foreign.

Scale House was tall and narrow, squeezed between two massive stone edifices, one a temple archive and the other the monolithic heart of the Guild of Street Inspectors. A few generations past, a particularly skilled stone carver had dressed the limestone façade and formal, column-flanked entrance with lovingly rendered rats. In multitudes almost beyond counting. Cavorting rats, dancing rats, fornicating rats. Rats at war, at rest, rats feasting on corpses, swarming feast-laden tabletops amidst sleeping mongrels and drunk servants. Scaly tails formed intricate borders to the scenes,

451

and in some strange way it seemed to Bugg as he climbed the steps that the rats were in motion, at the corner of his vision, moving, writhing, grinning.

He shook off his unease, paused a moment on the landing, then opened the door and strode inside.

'How many, how bad, how long?'

The desk, solid grey Bluerose marble, almost blocked the entrance to the reception hall, spanning the width of the room barring a narrow space at the far right. The secretary seated behind it had yet to look up from his ledgers. He continued speaking after a moment. 'Answer those questions, then tell us where and what you're willing to pay and is this a one-off or are you interested in regular monthly visits? And be advised we're not accepting contracts at the moment.'

'No.'

The secretary set down his quill and looked up. Dark, small eyes glittered with suspicion from beneath a single wiry brow. Ink-stained fingers plucked at his nose, which had begun twitching as if the man was about to sneeze. 'We're not responsible.'

'For what?'

'For anything.' More tugging at his nose. 'And we're not accepting any more petitions, so if you're here to deliver one you might as well just turn round and leave.'

'What sort of petition might I want to hand to you?' Bugg asked.

'Any sort. Belligerent tenement associations have to wait in line just like everyone else.'

'I have no petition.'

'Then we didn't do it, we were never there, you heard wrong, it was someone else.'

'I am here on behalf of my master, who wishes to meet with your guild to discuss a contract.'

'We're backed up. Not taking any more contracts—'

'Price is not a consideration,' Bugg cut in, then smiled, 'within reasonable limits.'

452

'Ah, but then it is a consideration. We may well have unreasonable limits in mind. We often have, you know.'

'I do not believe my master is interested in rats.'

'Then he's insane . . . but interesting. The board will be in attendance tonight on another matter. Your master will be allotted a short period at the meeting's end, which I will note in the agenda. Anything else?'

'No. What time tonight?'

'Ninth bell, no later. Come late and he will be barred outside the chamber door. Be sure he understands that.'

'My master is always punctual.'

The secretary made a face. 'Oh, he's like that, is he? Poor you. Now, begone. I'm busy.'

Bugg abruptly leaned forward and stabbed two fingers into the secretary's eyes. There was no resistance. The secretary tilted his head back and scowled.

'Cute,' Bugg smiled, stepping back. 'My compliments to the guild sorceror.'

'What gave me away?' the secretary asked as Bugg opened the door.

The manservant glanced back. 'You are far too rat-like, betraying your creator's obsession. Even so, the illusion is superb.'

'I haven't been found out in decades. Who in the Errant's name are you?'

'For that answer,' Bugg said as he turned away, 'you'll need a petition.'

'Wait! Who's your master?'

Bugg gave a final wave then shut the door. He descended the steps and swung right. A long walk to the quarries was before him, and, as Tehol had predicted, the day was hot, and growing hotter.

Summoned to join the Ceda in the Cedance, the chamber of the tiles, Brys descended the last few steps to the landing and made his way onto the raised walkway. Kuru Qan was circling the far platform in a distracted manner, muttering under his breath.

'Ceda,' Brys called as he approached. 'You wished to see me?'

'Unpleasant, Finadd, all very unpleasant. Defying comprehension. I need a clearer mind. In other words, not mine. Perhaps yours. Come here. Listen.'

Brys had never heard the Ceda speak with such fraught dismay. 'What has happened?'

'Every Hold, Finadd. Chaos. I have witnessed a transformation. Here, see for yourself. The tile of the Fulcra, the Dolmen. Do you see? A figure huddled at its base. Bound to the menhir with chains. All obscured by smoke, a smoke that numbs my mind. The Dolmen has been *usurped*.'

Brys stared down at the tile. The figure was ghostly, and his vision blurred the longer he stared at it. 'By whom?'

'A stranger. An outsider.'

'A god?'

Kuru Qan massaged his lined brow with his fingers as he continued pacing. 'Yes. No. We hold no value in the notion of gods. Upstarts who are as nothing compared to the Holds. Most of them aren't even real, simply projections of a people's desires, hopes. Fears. Of course,' he added, 'sometimes that's all that's needed.'

'What do you mean?'

Kuru Qan shook his head. 'And the Azath Hold, this troubles me greatly. The centre tile, the Heartstone, can you sense it? The Azath Heartstone, my friend, has died. The other tiles clustered together around it, at the end, drawing tight as blood gathers in a wounded body. The Tomb is breached. Portal stands unguarded. You must make a journey for me to the square tower, Finadd. And go armed.'

'What am I to look for?'

'Anything untoward. Broken ground. But be careful – the dwellers within those tombs are not dead.'

'Very well.' Brys scanned the nearest tiles. 'Is there more?'

Kuru Qan halted, brows lifting. 'More? Dragon Hold has awakened. Wyval. Blood-Drinker. Gate. Consort. Among the Fulcra, the Errant is now positioned in the centre of things. The Pack draws nearer, and Shapefinder has become a chimera. Ice Hold's Huntress walks frozen paths. Child and Seed stir to life. The Empty Hold – you can well see – has become obscured. Every tile. A shadow stands behind the Empty Throne. And look, Saviour and Betrayer, they have coalesced. They are one and the same. How is this possible? Wanderer, Mistress, Watcher and Walker, all hidden, blurred by mysterious motion. I am frightened, Finadd.'

'Ceda, have you heard from the delegation?'

'The delegation? No. From the moment of their arrival in the Warlock King's village, all contact with them has been lost. Blocked by Edur sorcery, of a sort we've not experienced before. There is much that is troubling. Much.'

'I should leave now, Ceda, while there's still daylight.'

'Agreed. Then return here with what you have discovered.'

'Very well.'

The track leading to the quarries climbed in zigzag fashion to a notch in the hillside. The stands of coppiced trees on the flanks were sheathed in white dust. Goats coughed in the shade.

Bugg paused to wipe sweaty grit from his forehead, then went on.

Two wagons filled with stonecutters had passed him a short while earlier, and from the frustrated foreman came the unwelcome news that the crew had refused to work the quarry any longer, at least until the situation was resolved.

A cavity had been inadvertently breached, within which a creature of some sort had been imprisoned for what must have been a long, long time. Three 'cutters had been dragged inside, their shrieks short-lived. The hired necromancer hadn't fared any better.

Bugg reached the notch and stood looking down at the quarry pit with its geometric limestone sides cut deep into the surrounding land. The mouth of the cavity was barely visible near an area that had seen recent work.

He made his way down, coming to within twenty paces of the cave before he stopped.

The air was suddenly bitter cold. Frowning, Bugg stepped to one side and sat down on a block of limestone. He watched frost form on the ground to the left of the cave, reaching in a point towards the dark opening, the opposite end spreading ever wider in a swirl of fog. The sound of ice crunching underfoot, then a figure appeared from the widening end, as if striding out from nowhere. Tall, naked from the hips upward, grey-green skin. Long, streaked blonde hair hanging loose over the shoulders and down the back. Light grey eyes, the pupils vertical slits. Silver-capped tusks. Female, heavy-breasted. She was wearing a short skirt, her only clothing barring the leather-strapped moccasins, and a wide belt holding a half-dozen scabbards in which stabbing knives resided.

Her attention was on the cave. She anchored her hands on her hips and visibly sighed.

'He's not coming out,' Bugg said.

She glanced over. 'Of course he isn't, now that I'm here.'

'What kind of demon is he?'

'Hungry and insane, but a coward.'

'Did you put him there?'

She nodded. 'Damned humans. Can't leave things well enough alone.'

'I doubt they knew, Jaghut.'

'No excuse. They're always digging. Digging here, digging there. They never stop.'

Bugg nodded, then asked, 'So now what?'

She sighed again.

The frost at her feet burgeoned into angular ice, which then crawled into the cave mouth. The ice grew swiftly, filling the hole. The surrounding stone groaned, creaked,

456

then split apart, revealing solid ice beneath it. Sandy earth and limestone chunks tumbled away.

Bugg's gaze narrowed on the strange shape trapped in the centre of the steaming ice. 'A Khalibaral? Errant take us, Huntress, I'm glad you decided to return.'

'Now I need to find for him somewhere else. Any suggestions?'

Bugg considered for a time, then he smiled.

Brys made his approach between two of the ruined round towers, stepping carefully around tumbled blocks of stone half hidden in the wiry yellow grasses. The air was hot and still, the sunlight molten gold on the tower walls. Grasshoppers rose from his path in clattering panic and, at the faint sensation of crunching underfoot, Brys looked down to see that the ground was crawling with life. Insects, many of them unrecognizable to his eyes, oversized, awkward, in dull hues, scrambling to either side as he walked.

Since they were all fleeing, he was not unduly concerned.

He came within sight of the square tower. The Azath. Apart from its primitive style of architecture, there seemed to be little else to set it apart. Brys was baffled by the Ceda's assertion that a structure of stone and wood could be sentient, could breathe with a life of its own. A building presupposed a builder, yet Kuru Qan claimed that the Azath simply rose into being, drawn together of its own accord. Inviting suspicion on every law of causality generations of scholars had posited as irrefutable truth.

The surrounding grounds were less mysterious, if profoundly more dangerous. The humped barrows in the overgrown yard were unmistakable. Gnarled and stunted, dead trees rose here and there, sometimes from the highest point of the mound, but more often from the flanks. A winding flagstone pathway began opposite the front door, the gate marked by rough pillars of unmortared stone wrapped in vines and runners. The remnants of a low wall enclosed the grounds.

Brys reached the edge of the yard along one side, the gate to his right, the tower to the left. And saw immediately that many of the barrows within sight had slumped on at least one of their sides, as if gutted from within. The weeds covering the mounds were dead, blackened as if by rot.

He studied the scene for a moment longer, then made his way round the perimeter towards the gateway. Striding between the pillars, onto the first flagstone – which pitched down to one side with a grinding clunk. Brys tottered, flinging his arms out for balance, and managed to recover without falling.

High-pitched laughter from near the tower's entrance.

He looked up.

The girl emerged from the shadow cast by the tower. 'I know you. I followed the ones following you. And killed them.'

'What has happened here?'

'Bad things.' She came closer, mould-patched and dishevelled. 'Are you my friend? I was supposed to help it stay alive. But it died anyway, and things are busy killing each other. Except for the one the tower chose. He wants to talk to you.'

'To me?'

'To one of my grown-up friends.'

'Who,' Brys asked, 'are your other grown-up friends?'

'Mother Shurq, Father Tehol, Uncle Ublala, Uncle Bugg.'

Brys was silent. Then, 'What is your name?'

'Kettle.'

'Kettle, how many people have you killed in the past year?'

She cocked her head. 'I can't count past eight and two.'

'Ah.'

'Lots of eight and twos.'

'And where do the bodies go?'

'I bring them back here and push them into the ground.'

'All of them?'

458

She nodded.

'Where is this friend of yours? The one who wants to talk to me?'

'I don't know if he's a friend. Follow me. Step where I step.'

She took him by the hand and Brys fought to repress a shiver at that clammy grip. Off the flagstoned path, between barrows, the ground shifting uncertainly beneath each cautious step. There were more insects, but of fewer varieties, as if some kind of attrition had occurred on the grounds of the Azath. 'I have never seen insects like these before,' Brys said. 'They're . . . big.'

'Old, from the times when the tower was born,' Kettle said. 'Eggs in the broken ground. Those stick-like brown ones with the heads at both ends are the meanest. They eat at my toes when I sit still too long. And they're hard to crush.'

'What about those yellow, spiky ones?'

'They don't bother me. They eat only birds and mice. Here.'

She had stopped before a crumpled mound on which sat one of the larger trees in the yard, the wood strangely streaked grey and black, the twigs and branches projecting in curves rather than sharp angles. Roots spread out across the entire barrow, the remaining bark oddly scaled, like snake skin.

Brys frowned. 'And how are we to converse, with him in there and me up here?'

'He's trapped. He says you have to close your eyes and think about nothing. Like you do when you fight, he says.'

Brys was startled. 'He's speaking to you now?'

'Yes, but he says that isn't good enough, because I don't know enough . . . words. Words and things. He has to show you. He says you've done this before.'

'It seems I am to possess no secrets,' Brys said.

'Not many, no, so he says he'll do the same in return. So you can trust each other. Somewhat.'

'Somewhat. His word?'

She nodded.

Brys smiled. 'Well, I appreciate his honesty. All right, I will give this a try.' He closed his eyes. Kettle's cold hand remained in his, small, the flesh strangely loose on the bones. He pulled his thoughts from that detail. A fighter's mind was not in truth emptied during a fight. It was, instead, both coolly detached and mindful. Concentration defined by a structure which was in turn assembled under strict laws of pragmatic necessity. Thus, observational, calculating, and entirely devoid of emotion, even as every sense was awakened.

He felt himself lock into that familiar, reassuring structure.

And was stunned by the strength of the will that tugged him away. He fought against a rising panic, knowing he was helpless before such power. Then relented.

Above him, a sky transformed. Sickly, swirling green light surrounding a ragged black wound large enough to swallow a moon. Clouds twisted, tortured and shorn through by the descent of innumerable objects, each object seeming to fight the air as it fell, as if this world was actively resisting the intrusion. Objects pouring from that wound, tunnelling through layers of the sky.

On the landscape before him was a vast city, rising up from a level plain with tiered gardens and raised walkways. A cluster of towers rose from the far side, reaching to extraordinary heights. Farmland reached out from the city's outskirts in every direction for as far as Brys could see, strange shadows flowing over it as he watched.

He pulled his gaze from the scene and looked down, to find that he stood on a platform of red-stained limestone. Before him steep steps ran downward, row upon row, hundreds, to a paved expanse flanked by blue-painted columns. A glance to his right revealed a sharply angled descent. He was on a flat-topped pyramid-shaped structure,

460

and, he realized with a start, someone was standing beside him, on his left. A figure barely visible, ghostly, defying detail. It was tall, and seemed to be staring up at the sky, focused on the terrible dark wound.

Objects were striking the ground now, landing hard but with nowhere near the velocity they should have possessed. A loud crack reverberated from the concourse between the columns below, and Brys saw that a massive stone carving had come to rest there. A bizarre beast-like human, squatting with thickly muscled arms reaching down the front, converging with a two-handed grip on the penis. Shoulders and head were fashioned in the likeness of a bull. A second set of legs, feminine, were wrapped round the beast-man's hips, the platform on which he crouched cut, Brys now saw, into a woman's form, lying on her back beneath him. From nearby rose the clatter of scores of clay tablets – too distant for Brys to see if there was writing on them, though he suspected there might be – skidding as if on cushions of air before coming to a rest in a scattered swath.

Fragments of buildings – cut limestone blocks, cornerstones, walls of adobe, wattle and daub. Then severed limbs, blood-drained sections of cattle and horses, a herd of something that might have been goats, each one turned inside out, intestines flopping. Dark-skinned humans – or at least their arms, legs and torsos.

Above, the sky was filling with large pallid fragments, floating down like snow.

And something huge was coming through the wound. Wreathed in lightning that seemed to scream with pain, shrieks unending, deafening.

Soft words spoke in Brys's mind. 'My ghost, let loose to wander, perhaps, to witness. They warred against Kallor; it was a worthy cause. But . . . what they have done here . . .'

Brys could not pull his eyes from that howling sphere of lightning. He could see limbs within it, the burning arcs entwined about them like chains. 'What – what is it?'

'A god, Brys Beddict. In its own realm, it was locked

461

in a war. For there were rival gods. Temptations . . .'

'Is this a vision of the past?' Brys asked.

'The past lives on,' the figure replied. 'There is no way of knowing . . . standing here. How do we measure the beginning, the end – for all of us, yesterday was as today, and as it will be tomorrow. We are not aware. Or perhaps we are, yet choose – for convenience, for peace of mind – not to see. Not to think.' A vague gesture with one hand. 'Some say twelve mages, some say seven. It does not matter, for they are about to become dust.'

The massive sphere was roaring now, burgeoning with frightening speed as it plunged earthward. It would, Brys realized, strike the city.

'Thus, in their effort to enforce a change upon the scheme, they annihilate themselves, and their own civilization.'

'So they failed.'

The figure said nothing for a time.

And the descending god struck; a blinding flash, a detonation that shook the pyramid beneath them and sent fissures through the concourse below. Smoke, rising in a column that then billowed outward, swallowing the world in shadow. Wind rushed outward in a shock, flattening trees in the farmland, toppling the columns lining the concourse. The trees then burst into flame.

'In answer to a perceived desperation, fuelled by seething rage, they called down a god. And died with the effort. Does that mean that they failed in their gambit? No, I do not speak of Kallor. I speak of their helplessness which gave rise to their desire for *change*. Brys Beddict, were their ghosts standing with us now, here in the future world where our flesh resides, thus able to see what their deed has wrought, they would recognize that all that they sought has come to pass.

'That which was chained to the earth has twisted the walls of its prison. Beyond recognition. Its poison has spread out and infected the world and all who dwell upon it.'

'You leave me without hope,' Brys said.

462

'I am sorry for that. Do not seek to find hope among your leaders. They are the repositories of poison. Their interest in you extends only so far as their ability to control you. From you, they seek duty and obedience, and they will ply you with the language of stirring faith. They seek followers, and woe to those who question, or voice challenge.

'Civilization after civilization, it is the same. The world falls to tyranny with a whisper. The frightened are ever keen to bow to a perceived necessity, in the belief that necessity forces conformity, and conformity a certain stability. In a world shaped into conformity, dissidents stand out, are easily branded and dealt with. There is no multitude of perspectives, no dialogue. The victim assumes the face of the tyrant, self-righteous and intransigent, and wars breed like vermin. And people die.'

Brys studied the firestorm engulfing what was once a city of great beauty. He did not know its name, nor the civilization that had birthed it, and, it now struck him, it did not matter.

'In your world,' the figure said, 'the prophecy approaches its azimuth. An emperor shall arise. You are from a civilization that sees war as an extension of economics. Stacked bones become the foundation for your roads of commerce, and you see nothing untoward in that—'

'Some of us do.'

'Irrelevant. Your legacy of crushed cultures speaks its own truth. You intend to conquer the Tiste Edur. You claim that each circumstance is different, unique, but it is neither different nor unique. It is all the same. Your military might proves the virtue of your cause. But I tell you this, Brys Beddict, there is no such thing as destiny. Victory is not inevitable. Your enemy lies in waiting, in your midst. Your enemy hides without need for disguise, when belligerence and implied threat are sufficient to cause your gaze to shy away. It speaks your language, takes your words and uses them against you. It mocks your belief in truths, for it has made itself the arbiter of those truths.'

'Lether is not a tyranny—'

'You assume the spirit of your civilization is personified in your benign king. It is not. Your king exists because it is deemed permissible that he exist. You are ruled by greed, a monstrous tyrant lit gold with glory. It cannot be defeated, only annihilated.' Another gesture towards the fiery chaos below. 'That is your only hope of salvation, Brys Beddict. For greed kills itself, when there is nothing left to hoard, when the countless legions of labourers are naught but bones, when the grisly face of starvation is revealed in the mirror.

'The god is fallen. He crouches now, seeding devastation. Rise and fall, rise and fall, and with each renewal the guiding spirit is less, weaker, more tightly chained to a vision bereft of hope.'

'Why does this god do this to us?'

'Because he knows naught but pain, and yearns only to share it, to visit it upon all that lives, all that exists.'

'Why have you shown me this?'

'I make you witness, Brys Beddict, to the symbol of your demise.'

'Why?'

The figure was silent for a moment, then said, 'I advised you to not look for hope from your leaders, for they shall feed you naught but lies. Yet hope exists. Seek for it, Brys Beddict, in the one who stands at your side, from the stranger upon the other side of the street. Be brave enough to endeavour to cross that street. Look neither skyward nor upon the ground. Hope persists, and its voice is compassion, and honest doubt.'

The scene began to fade.

The figure at his side spoke one last time. 'That is all I would tell you. All I can tell you.'

He opened his eyes, and found himself once more standing before the barrow, the day dying around him. Kettle still held his hand in her cold clasp.

'You will help me now?' she asked.

'The dweller within the tomb spoke nothing of that.'

'He never does.'

'He showed me virtually nothing of himself. I don't even know who, or what, he is.'

'Yes.'

'He made no effort to convince me . . . of anything. Yet I saw . . .' Brys shook his head.

'He needs help escaping his tomb. Other things are trying to get out. And they will. Not long now, I think. They want to hurt me, and everyone else.'

'And the one we're to help will stop them?'

'Yes.'

'What can I do?'

'He needs two swords. The best iron there is. Straight blades, two-edged, pointed. Thin but strong. Narrow hilts, heavy pommels.'

Brys considered. 'I should be able to find something in the armoury. He wants me to bring them here?'

Kettle nodded.

He needed help. But he did not ask for it. 'Very well. I will do this. But I will speak to the Ceda regarding this.'

'Do you trust him? He wants to know, do you trust this Ceda?'

Brys opened his mouth to reply, to say *yes*, then he stopped. The dweller within the barrow was a powerful creature, probably too powerful to be controlled. There was nothing here that would please Kuru Qan. Yet did Brys have a choice? The Ceda had sent him here to discover what had befallen the Azath . . . He looked over at the tower. 'The Azath, it is dead?'

'Yes. It was too old, too weak. It fought for so long.'

'Kettle, are you still killing people in the city?'

'Not many. Only bad people. One or two a night. Some of the trees are still alive, but they can't feed on the tower's blood any more. So I give them other blood, so they can fight to hold the bad monsters down. But the trees are dying too.'

Brys sighed. 'All right. I will visit again, Kettle. With the swords.'

'I knew I could like you. I knew you would be nice. Because of your brother.'

That comment elicited a frown, then another sigh. He gently disengaged his hand from the dead child's grip. 'Be careful, Kettle.'

'It was a perfectly good sleep,' Tehol said as he walked alongside Bugg.

'I am sure it was, master. But you did ask for this meeting.'

'I didn't expect such a quick response. Did you do or say something to make them unduly interested?'

'Of course I did, else we would not have achieved this audience.'

'Oh, that's bad, Bugg. You gave them my name?'

'No.'

'You revealed something of my grand scheme?'

'No.'

'Well, what did you say, then?'

'I said money was not a consideration.'

'Not a consideration?' Tehol slowed his pace, drawing Bugg round. 'What do you think I'm willing to pay them?'

'I don't know,' the manservant replied. 'I have no idea of the nature of this contract you want to enter into with the Rat Catchers' Guild.'

'That's because I hadn't decided yet!'

'Well, have you decided now, master?'

'I'm thinking on it. I hope to come up with something by the time we arrive.'

'So, it *could* be expensive . . .'

Tehol's expression brightened. 'You're right, it could be indeed. Therefore, money is not a consideration.'

'Exactly.'

'I'm glad we're in agreement. You are a wonderful manservant, Bugg.'

'Thank you, master.'

They resumed walking.

Before long they halted in front of Scale House. Tehol stared up at the riotous rodent façade for a time. 'They're all looking at me,' he said.

'They do convey that impression, don't they?'

'I don't like being the singular focus of the attention of thousands of rats. What do they know that I don't?'

'Given the size of their brains, not much.'

Tehol stared for a moment longer, then he slowly blinked and regarded Bugg. Five heartbeats. Ten.

The manservant remained expressionless, then he coughed, cleared his throat, and said, 'Well, we should head inside, shouldn't we?'

The secretary sat as he had earlier that day, working on what seemed to Bugg to be the same ledger. Once again, he did not bother looking up. 'You're early. I was expecting punctual.'

'We're not early,' Tehol said.

'You're not?'

'No, but since the bell is already sounding, any more from you and we'll be late.'

'I'm not to blame. Never was at any point in this ridiculous conversation. Up the stairs. To the top. There's only one door. Knock once then enter, and Errant help you. Oh, and the manservant can stay here, provided he doesn't poke me in the eyes again.'

'He's not staying here.'

'He's not?'

'No.'

'Fine, then. Get out of my sight, the both of you.'

Tehol led the way past the desk and they began their ascent.

'You poked him in the eyes?' Tehol asked.

'I judged it useful in getting his attention.'

'I'm pleased, although somewhat alarmed.'

'The circumstances warranted extreme action on my part.'

467

'Does that happen often?'

'I'm afraid it does.'

They reached the landing. Tehol stepped forward and thumped on the door. A final glance back at Bugg, suspicious and gauging, then he swung open the door. They strode into the chamber beyond.

In which rats swarmed. Covering the floor. The tabletop. On the shelves, clambering on the crystal chandelier. Crouched on the shoulders and peering from folds in the clothes of the six board members seated on the other side of the table.

Thousands of beady eyes fixed on Tehol and Bugg, including those of the three men and three women who were the heart of the Rat Catchers' Guild.

Tehol hitched up his trousers. 'Thank you one and all—'

'You're Tehol Beddict,' cut in the woman seated on the far left. She was mostly a collection of spherical shapes, face, head, torso, breasts, her eyes tiny, dark and glittering like hardened tar. There were at least three rats in her mass of upright, billowed black hair.

'And I'm curious,' Tehol said, smiling. 'What are all these rats doing here?'

'Insane question,' snapped the man beside the roundish woman. 'We're the Rat Catchers' Guild. Where else are we supposed to put the ones we capture?'

'I thought you killed them.'

'Only if they refuse avowal,' the man said, punctuating his words with a sneer for some unexplainable reason.

'Avowal? How do rats make vows?'

'None of your business,' the woman said. 'I am Onyx. Beside me sits Scint. In order proceeding accordingly, before you sits Champion Ormly, Glisten, Bubyrd and Ruby. Tehol Beddict, we suffered losses on our investments thanks to you.'

'From which you have no doubt recovered.'

'That's not the point!' said the woman called Glisten. She was blonde, and so slight and small that only her shoulders and head were above the level of the tabletop. Heaps of squirming rats passed in front of her every now and then, forcing her to bob her head up to maintain eye contact.

'By my recollection,' Tehol said reasonably, 'you lost a little less than half a peak.'

'How do you know that?' Scint demanded. 'Nobody else but us knows that!'

'A guess, I assure you. In any case, the contract I offer will be for an identical amount.'

'Half a peak!'

Tehol's smile broadened. 'Ah, I have your fullest attention now. Excellent.'

'That's an absurd amount,' spoke Ormly for the first time. 'What would you have us do, conquer Kolanse?'

'Could you?'

Ormly scowled. 'Why would you want us to, Tehol Beddict?'

'It'd be difficult,' Glisten said worriedly. 'The strain on our human resources—'

'Difficult,' cut in Scint, 'but not impossible. We'd need to recruit from our island cells—'

'Wait!' Tehol said. 'I'm not interested in conquering Kolanse!'

'You're the type who's always changing his mind,' Onyx said. She leaned back and with a squeak a rat plummeted from her hair to thump on the floor somewhere behind her. 'I can't stand working with people like that.'

'I haven't changed my mind. It wasn't me who brought up the whole Kolanse thing. In fact, it was Champion Ormly—'

'Well, he can't make up his mind neither. You two are made for each other.'

Tehol swung to Bugg. 'I'm not indecisive, am I? Tell them, Bugg. When have you ever seen me indecisive?'

Bugg frowned.

'Bugg!'

469

'I'm thinking!'

Glisten's voice came from behind a particularly large heap of rats. 'I can't see the point of any of this.'

'That's quite understandable,' Tehol said evenly.

'Describe your contract offer,' Ormly demanded. 'But be advised, we don't do private functions.'

'What does that mean?'

'I won't waste my breath on explaining . . . unless it turns out to be relevant. Is it?'

'I don't know. How can I tell?'

'Well, that's my point exactly. Now, about the contract?'

'All right,' Tehol said, 'but be warned, it's complicated.'

Glisten's plaintive voice: 'Oh, I don't like the sound of that!'

Tehol made an effort to see her, then gave up. The mound of rats on the tabletop in front of her was milling. 'You surprise me, Glisten,' he said. 'It strikes me that the Rat Catchers' Guild thrives on complications. After all, you do much more than, uh, harvest rats, don't you? In fact, your primary function is as the unofficial assassins' guild – unofficial because, of course, it's an outlawed activity and unpleasant besides. You're also something of a thieves' guild, too, although you've yet to achieve full compliance among the more independent-minded thieves. You also provide an unusually noble function in your unofficial underground escape route for impoverished refugees from assimilated border tribes. And then there's the—'

'Stop!' Onyx shrieked. In a slightly less shrill tone she said, 'Bubyrd, get our Chief Investigator in here. Errant knows, if anyone needs investigating, it's this Tehol Beddict.'

Tehol's brows rose. 'Will that be painful?'

Onyx leered and whispered, 'Restrain your impatience, Tehol Beddict. You'll get an answer to that soon enough.'

'Is it wise to threaten a potential employer?'

'I don't see why not,' Onyx replied.

470

'Your knowledge of our operations is alarming,' Ormly said. 'We don't like it.'

'I assure you, I have only admiration for your endeavours. In fact, my contract offer is dependent upon the fullest range of the guild's activities. I could not make it without prior knowledge, could I?'

'How do we know?' Ormly asked. 'We've yet to hear it.'

'I'm getting there.'

The door behind them opened and the woman who was in all likelihood the Chief Investigator strode in past Tehol and Bugg. Stepping carefully, she took position on the far right of the table, arms crossing as she leaned against the wall.

Onyx spoke. 'Chief Investigator Rucket, we have in our presence a dangerous liability.'

The woman, tall, lithe, her reddish hair cut short, was dressed in pale leathers, the clothing South Nerek in style, as if she had just come from the steppes. Although, of course, the nearest steppes were a hundred or more leagues to the east. She appeared to be unarmed. Her eyes, a startling tawny shade that looked more feline than human, slowly fixed on Tehol. 'Him?'

'Who else?' Onyx snapped. 'Not his manservant, surely!'

'Why not?' Rucket drawled. 'He looks to be the more dangerous one.'

'I'd agree,' Bubyrd said in a hiss. 'He poked my secretary in the eyes.'

Scint started. 'Really? Just like that?' He held up a hand and stretched out the first two fingers, then jabbed the air. 'Like that? Poke! Like that?'

'Yes,' Bubyrd replied, glaring at Bugg. 'He revealed the illusion! What's the point of creating illusions when he just ups and pokes holes in them!'

Tehol swung to his manservant. 'Bugg, are we going to get out of here alive?'

'Hard to say, master.'

'All because you poked that secretary in the eyes?'

Bugg shrugged.

'Touchy, aren't they?'

'So it seems, master. Best get on with the offer, don't you think?'

'Good idea. Diversion, yes indeed.'

'You idiots,' Onyx said. 'We can hear you!'

'Excellent!' Tehol stepped forward, carefully, so as to avoid crushing the seething carpet of rats. Gentle nudging aside with the toe of his moccasin seemed to suffice. 'To wit. I need every tribal refugee in the city ushered out. Destination? The islands. Particular islands, details forthcoming. I need full resources shipped ahead of them, said supplies to be purchased by myself. You will work with Bugg here on the logistics. Second, I understand you are conducting an investigation into disappearances for the Crown. No doubt you're telling them nothing of your findings. I, on the other hand, want to know those findings. Third, I want my back protected. In a short while, there will be people who will want to kill me. You are to stop them. Thus, my contract offer. Half a peak and a list of safe investments, and as to that last point, I suggest you follow my financial advice to the letter and swallow the expense—'

'You want to be our financial adviser?' Onyx asked in clear disbelief. 'Those losses—'

'Could have been avoided, had we been engaged in a closer relationship back then, such as the one we are about to enter into.'

'What about those refugees who are Indebted?' Ormly asked. 'Having them all disappear could cause another crash in the Tolls.'

'It won't, because the trickle is to be so slow that no-one notices—'

'How could they not notice?'

'They will be . . . distracted.'

'You've got something ugly planned, haven't you, Tehol Beddict?' Ormly's small eyes glittered. 'Meaning what happened the first time wasn't no accident. Wasn't

472

incompetence neither. You just found yourself with a string in your hand, which you then tugged to see how much would unravel. You know what you're telling us? You're telling us you're the most dangerous man in Lether. Why would we ever let you walk out of this chamber?'

'Simple. This time I'm taking my friends with me. So the question is, are you my friends?'

'And what if our Chief Investigator investigates you right here and right now?'

'My scheme is already under way, Champion Ormly, whether I stay alive or not. It's going to happen. Of course, if I die, then nobody escapes what's coming.'

'Hold on,' Onyx said. 'You said something about expense. You becoming our financial adviser is going to cost us?'

'Well, naturally.'

'How much?'

'A quarter of a peak or thereabouts.'

'So you pay us half and we pay you back a quarter.'

'And so you come out ahead.'

'He's got a point,' Scint said, snatching a rat from the table and biting its head off.

Everyone stared, including a roomful of rats.

Scint noticed, chewed for a moment, making crunching sounds, then said around a mouthful of rat head, 'Sorry. Got carried away.' He looked down at the headless corpse in his hand, then tucked it into his shirt and out of sight.

From where Glisten sat came a plaintive sound, then, 'What did that rat ever do to you, Scinty?'

Scint swallowed. 'I said sorry!'

Tehol leaned close to Bugg and whispered, 'If you could poke any of them in the eyes . . .'

'Three of 'em would likely complain, master.'

'Can I guess?'

'Go ahead.'

'Ormly, Bubyrd and Rucket.'

'I'm impressed.'

473

'What are you two whispering about?' Onyx demanded.

Tehol smiled at her. 'Do you accept my offer?'

Brys found the Ceda in his work room, hunched over an upended crab lying on the table. He had removed the flat carapace covering the underside and was prodding organs with a pair of copper probes. The crab appeared to be dead.

Burners had been lit beneath a cauldron behind Kuru Qan, and the lid was rocking to gusts of steam.

'Finadd, this array of organs is fascinating. But I'm distracting myself. Shouldn't do that, not at this critical juncture.' He set the instruments down and picked up the crab. 'What have you to tell me?'

Brys watched the Ceda nudge the cauldron's lid aside then drop the crab in. 'The Azath tower is dead.'

Kuru Qan pushed the lid back into place then walked back to sit in his chair. He rubbed at his eyes. 'What physical evidence is there?'

'Little, admittedly. But a child is resident there, on the grounds,' Brys replied. 'The tower was in some sort of communication with her.'

'The role of Keeper? Odd that the Hold should choose a child. Unless the original Keeper had died. And even then . . . odd.'

'There is more,' Brys said. 'A resident within one of the barrows was accorded the role of protector. The child, Kettle, believes that person is capable of destroying the others – all of whom are close to escaping their prisons.'

'The Hold, in its desperation, made a bargain, then. What else does this Kettle know of that resident?'

'He speaks to her constantly. He speaks through her, as well. At the moment, he is trapped. He can go no further, and no, I don't know how that situation will be resolved. Ceda, I also spoke to that stranger.'

Kuru Qan looked up. 'He reached into your mind? And showed you what?'

Brys shook his head. 'He made no effort to convince me

of anything, Ceda. Voiced no arguments in his own defence. Instead, I was made witness to an event, from long ago, I believe.'

'What kind of event?'

'The bringing down of a god. By a cadre of sorcerors, none of whom survived the ritual.'

Kuru Qan's eyes widened at these words. 'Relevant? Errant bless me, I hope not.'

'You have knowledge of this, Ceda?'

'Not enough, Finadd, I'm afraid. And this stranger was witness to that dire scene?'

'He was. Inadvertently, he said.'

'Then he has lived a very long time.'

'Is he a threat?'

'Of course he is. None here could match his power, I would think. And, assuming he is successful in destroying the other residents of the yard, the question one must face is, what then?'

'It strikes me as a huge assumption, Ceda. Killing the others. Why would he hold to his bargain with a now-dead Azath?'

'One must believe that the Hold chose wisely, Finadd. Do you have doubts?'

'I'm not sure. He has asked for weapons. Two swords. I am inclined to accede to his request.'

The Ceda slowly nodded. 'Agreed. No doubt you were thinking of finding something in the armoury. But for an individual such as this, a normal weapon won't do, even one of Letherii steel. No, we must go to my private hoard.'

'I wasn't aware you had one.'

'Naturally. Now, a moment.' Kuru Qan rose and walked back to the cauldron. Using large tongs, he retrieved the crab, the shell now a fiery red. 'Ah, perfect. Of course, it can cool down some. So, follow me.'

Brys had thought he knew virtually every area of the old palace, but the series of subterranean chambers the Ceda led him into were completely unfamiliar to him, although not a single hidden door was passed through on the way. By the Finadd's internal map, they were now under the river.

They entered a low-ceilinged chamber with rack-lined walls on which were hundreds of weapons. Brys had collected a lantern along the way and he now hung it from a hook in a crossbeam. He walked to a rack crowded with swords. 'Why a private collection, Ceda?'

'Curios, most of them. Some antiques. I am fascinated with forging techniques, particularly those used by foreign peoples. Also, there is sorcery invested in these weapons.'

'All of them?' Brys lifted one particular weapon from its hooks, a close match to the description relayed to him by Kettle.

'Yes. No, put that one back, Finadd. It's cursed.'

Brys replaced it.

'In fact,' Kuru Qan went on in a troubled voice, 'they're all cursed. Well, this could prove a problem.'

'Perhaps I should go to the regular armoury—'

'Patience, Finadd. It's the nature of curses that allows us to possibly find a reasonable solution. Two swords, you said?'

'Why would sorcerors curse a weapon?'

'Oh, most often not an intentional act on their parts. Often it's simply a matter of incompetence. In many cases, the sorcerous investment refuses to function. The iron resists the imposition, and the better the forging technique the more resistant the weapon is. Sorcery thrives on flaws, whether structural in the physical sense, or metaphorical in the thematic sense. Ah, I see your eyes glazing over, Finadd. Never mind. Let's peruse the antiques, shall we?'

The Ceda led him to the far wall, and Brys immediately saw a perfect weapon, long and narrow of blade, pointed and double-edged, modest hilt. 'Letherii steel,' he said, reaching for it.

'Yes, in the Blue Style, which, as you well know, is the very earliest technique for Letherii steel. In some ways, the

476

Blue Style produces finer steel than our present methods. The drawbacks lie in other areas.'

Brys tested the weight of the weapon. 'The pommel needs to be replaced, but otherwise . . .' Then he looked up. 'But it's cursed?'

'Only in so far as all Blue Style weapons are cursed. As you know, the blade's core is twisted wire, five braids of sixty strands each. Five bars are fused to that core to produce the breadth and edge. Blue Style is very flexible, almost unbreakable, with one drawback. Finadd, touch the blade to any other here. Lightly, please. Go ahead.'

Brys did so, and a strange sound reverberated from the Blue Style sword. A cry, that went on, and on.

'Depending on where on the blade you strike, the note is unique, although each will eventually descend or ascend to the core's own voice. The effect is cumulative, and persistent.'

'Sounds like a dying goat.'

'There is a name etched into the base of the blade, Finadd. Arcane script. Can you read it?'

Brys squinted, struggled a moment with the awkward lettering, then smiled. '*Glory Goat*. Well, it seems a mostly harmless curse. Is there any other sorcery invested in it?'

'The edges self-sharpen, I believe. Nicks and notches heal, although some material is always lost. Some laws cannot be cheated.' The Ceda drew out another sword. 'This one is somewhat oversized, I'll grant you—'

'No, that's good. The stranger was very tall.'

'He was now, was he?'

Brys nodded, shifting the first sword to his left hand and taking the one Kuru Qan held in his right. 'Errant, this would be hard to wield. For me, that is.'

'*Sarat Wept*,' the Ceda said. 'About four generations old. One of the last in the Blue Style. It belonged to the King's Champion of that time.'

Brys frowned. 'Urudat?'

'Very good.'

477

'I've seen images of him in frescos and tapestries. A big man—'

'Oh, yes, but reputedly very quick.'

'Remarkable, given the weight of this sword.' He held it out. 'The blade pulls. The line is a hair's breadth outward. This is a left-handed weapon.'

'Yes.'

'Well,' Brys considered, 'the stranger fights with both hands, and he specified two full swords, suggesting—'

'A certain measure of ambidexterity. Yes.'

'Investment?'

'To make it shatter upon its wielder's death.'

'But—'

'Yes, another incompetent effort. Thus, two formidable weapons in the Blue Style of Letherii steel. Acceptable?'

Brys studied both weapons, the play of aquamarine in the lantern-light. 'Both beautiful and exquisitely crafted. Yes, I think these will do.'

'When will you deliver them?'

'Tomorrow. I have no desire to enter those grounds at night.' He thought of Kettle, and felt once more the clasp of her cold hand. It did not occur to him then that he had not informed the Ceda of one particular detail from his encounter at the tower. It was a matter that, outwardly at least, seemed of little relevance.

Kettle was more than just a child.

She was also dead.

Thanks to this careless omission, the Ceda's measure of fear was not as great as it should have been. Indeed, as it needed to be. Thanks to this omission, and in the last moments before the Finadd parted company with Kuru Qan, a crossroads was reached, and then, inexorably, a path was taken.

The night air was pleasant, a warm wind stirring the rubbish in the gutters as Tehol and Bugg paused at the foot of the steps to Scale House.

'That was exhausting,' Tehol said. 'I think I'll go to bed.'

'Don't you want to eat first, master?'

'You scrounged something?'

'No.'

'So we have nothing to eat.'

'That's right.'

'Then why did you ask me if I wanted to eat?'

'I was curious.'

Tehol anchored his fists on his hips and glared at his manservant. 'Look, it wasn't me who nearly got us investigated in there!'

'It wasn't?'

'Well, not *all* me. It was you, too. Poking eyes and all that.'

'Master, it was you who sent me there. You who had the idea of offering a contract.'

'Poking eyes!'

'All right, all right. Believe me, master, I regret my actions deeply!'

'You regret deeply?'

'Fine, deeply regret.'

'That's it, I'm going to bed. Look at this street. It's a mess!'

'I'll get around to it, master, if I find the time.'

'Well, that should be no problem, Bugg. After all, what have you done today?'

'Scant little, it's true.'

'As I thought.' Tehol cinched up his trousers. 'Never mind. Let's go, before something terrible happens.'

CHAPTER THIRTEEN

Out of the white
Out of the sun's brittle dismay
We are the grim shapes
Who haunt all fate

Out of the white
Out of the wind's hoarse bray
We are the dark ghosts
Who haunt all fate

Out of the white
Out of the snow's worldly fray
We are the sword's wolves
Who haunt all fate

Jheck Marching Chant

Fifteen paces, no more than that. Between emperor and slave. A stretch of Letherii rugs, booty from some raid a century or more past, on which paths were worn deep, a pattern of stolen colour mapping stunted roads across heroic scenes. Kings crowned. Champions triumphant. Images of history the Edur had walked on, indifferent and intent on their small journeys in this chamber.

Udinaas wasn't prepared to ascribe any significance to these details. He had come to his own pattern, a gaze unwavering and precise, the mind behind it disconnected, its surface devoid of ripples and its depths motionless.

It was safer that way. He could stand here, equidistant between two torch sconces and so bathed by the light of neither, and in this indeterminate centre he looked on, silently watching as Rhulad discarded his bearskin, to stand naked before his new wife.

Udinaas might have been amused, had he permitted the emotion, to see the coins burned into the emperor's penis pop off, one, two, two more, then four, as Rhulad's desire became apparent. Coins thumping to the rug-strewn floor, a few bouncing and managing modest rolls before settling. He might have been horrified at the look in the emperor's red-rimmed eyes as he reached out, beckoning Mayen closer. Waves of sympathy for the hapless young woman were possible, but only in the abstract.

Witnessing this macabre, strangely comic moment, the slave remained motionless, without and within, and the bizarre reality of this world played itself out without comment.

Her self-control was, at first, absolute. He took her hand and drew it down, pulling her closer. 'Mayen,' the emperor said in a rasp, in a voice that reached for tenderness and achieved little more than rough lust. 'Should I reveal to you that I have dreamed of this moment?' A harsh laugh. 'Not quite. Not like this. Not . . . in so much . . . detail.'

'You made your desires known, Rhulad. Before . . . this.'

'Yes, call me Rhulad. As you did before. Between us, nothing need change.'

'Yet I am your empress.'

'My wife.'

'We cannot speak as if nothing has changed.'

'I will teach you, Mayen. I am still Rhulad.'

He embraced her then, an awkward, child-like encirclement in gold. 'You need not think of Fear,' he said. 'Mayen, you are his gift to me. His proof of loyalty. He did as a brother should.'

481

'I was betrothed—'

'And I am emperor! I can break the rules that would bind the Edur. The past is dead, Mayen, and it is I who shall forge the future! With you at my side. I saw you looking upon me, day after day, and I could see the desire in your eyes. Oh, we both knew that Fear would have you in the end. What could we do? Nothing. But I have changed all that.' He drew back a step, although she still held him with one hand. 'Mayen, my wife.' He began undressing her.

Realities. Moments one by one, stumbling forward. Clumsy necessities. Rhulad's dreams of this scene, whatever they had been in detail, were translated into a series of mundane impracticalities. Clothes were not easily discarded, unless designed with that in mind, and these were not. Her passivity under his ministrations added to the faltering, until this became an event bereft of romance.

Udinaas could see his lust fading. Of course it would revive. Rhulad was young, after all. The feelings of the object of his hunger were irrelevant, for an object Mayen had become. His trophy.

That the emperor sensed the slipping away of any chance of interlocking desires became evident as he began speaking once more. 'I saw in your eyes how you wanted me. Now, Mayen, no-one stands between us.'

But he does, Rhulad. Moreover, your monstrosity has become something you now wear on your flesh. And now what had to arrive. Letherii gold yields to its natural inclination. Now, Letherii gold rapes this Tiste Edur. Ha.

The emperor's lust had returned. His own statements had convinced him.

He pulled her towards the bed at the far wall. It had belonged to Hannan Mosag, and so was crafted for a single occupant. There was no room for lying side by side, which proved no obstacle for Rhulad's intentions. He pushed her onto her back. Looked down at her for a moment, then said, 'No, I would crush you. Get up, my love. You will descend upon me. I will give you children. I promise. Many children, whom you will adore. There will be heirs. Many heirs.'

An appeal, Udinaas could well hear, to sure instincts, the promise of eventual redemption. Reason to survive the ordeal of the present.

Rhulad settled down on the bed. Arms out to the sides.

She stared down at him.

Then moved to straddle this cruciform-shaped body of gold. Descending over him.

A game of mortality, the act of sex. Reduced so that decades became moments. Awakening, revelling in overwrought sensation, a brief spurt meant to procreate, spent exhaustion, then death. Rhulad was young. He did not last long enough to assuage his ego.

Even so, at the moment before he spasmed beneath her, before his heavy groan that thinned into a whimper, Udinaas saw Mayen's control begin to crumble. As if she had found a spark within her that she could flame into proper desire, perhaps even pleasure. Then, as he released, that spark flickered, died.

None of which Rhulad witnessed, for his eyes were closed and he was fully inside himself.

He would improve, of course. Or so it was reasonable to expect. She might even gain a measure of control over this act, and so revive and fan into life that spark.

At that moment, Udinaas believed Mayen became the empress, wife to the emperor. At that moment, his faith in her spirit withered – if faith was the right word, that singular war between expectation and hope. Had he compassion to feel, he might have understood, and so softened with empathy. But compassion was engagement, a mindfulness beyond that of mere witness, and he felt none of that.

He heard soft weeping coming from another place of darkness in the chamber, and slowly turned his head to look upon the fourth and last person present. As he had been, a witness to the rape with its hidden, metaphorical violence. But a witness trapped in the horror of feeling.

483

Among the crisscrossing worn paths of faded colour, one led to her.

Feather Witch huddled, pressed up against the wall, hands covering her face, racked with shudders.

Much more of this and she might end up killed. Rhulad was a man growing ever more intimate with dying. He did not need reminding of what it cost him and everyone around him. Even worse, he was without constraints.

Udinaas considered walking over to her, if only to tell her to be quiet. But his eyes fell on the intervening expanse of rugs and their images, and he realized that the distance was too great.

Mayen had remained straddling Rhulad, her head hanging down.

'Again,' the emperor said.

She straightened, began her motions, and Udinaas watched her search for that spark of pleasure. And then find it.

Wanting good, yearning for bad. As simple as that? Was this contradictory, confused map universally impressed upon the minds of men and women? That did not seem a question worth answering, Udinaas decided. He had lost enough already.

'Shut that bitch up!'

The slave started at the emperor's hoarse shout.

The weeping had grown louder, probably in answer to Mayen's audible panting.

Udinaas pushed himself forward, across the rugs to where Feather Witch crouched in the gloom.

'Get her out of here! Both of you, get out!'

She did not resist as he lifted her to her feet. Udinaas leaned close. 'Listen, Feather Witch,' he said under his breath. 'What did you expect?'

Her head snapped up and he saw hatred in her eyes. 'From you,' she said in a snarl, 'nothing.'

'From her. Don't answer – we must leave.'

He guided her to the side door, then through into the

servants' corridor beyond. He closed the door behind them, then pulled her another half-dozen steps down the passage. 'There's no cause for crying,' Udinaas said. 'Mayen is trapped, just like us, Feather Witch. It is not for you to grieve that she has sought and found pleasure.'

'I know what you're getting at, Indebted,' she said, twisting her arm out of his grip. 'Is that what you want? My surrender? My finding pleasure when you make use of me?'

'I am as you say, Feather Witch. Indebted. What I want? My wants mean nothing. They have fallen silent in my mind. You think I still pursue you? I still yearn for your love?' He shook his head as he studied her face. 'You were right. What is the point?'

'I want nothing to do with you, Udinaas.'

'Yes, I know. But you are Mayen's handmaiden. And I, it appears, am to be Rhulad's own slave. Emperor and empress. That is the reality we must face. You and I, we are a conceit. Or we were. Not any more, as far as I am concerned.'

'Good. Then we need only deal with each other as necessity demands.'

He nodded.

Her eyes narrowed. 'I do not trust you.'

'I do not care.'

Uncertainty. Unease. 'What game are you playing at, Udinaas? Who speaks through your mouth?' She stepped back. 'I should tell her. About what hides within you.'

'If you do that, Feather Witch, you will destroy your only chance.'

'My only chance? What chance?'

'Freedom.'

Her face twisted. 'And with that you would purchase my silence? You are foolish, Indebted. I was born a slave. I have none of your memories to haunt me—'

'My memories? Feather Witch, my memory of freedom is as an Indebted trapped in a kingdom where even death offers no absolution. My memory is my father's memory,

485

and would have been my children's memory. But you misunderstood. I did not speak of my freedom. I spoke only of yours. Not something to be recaptured, but found anew.'

'And how do you plan on freeing me, Udinaas?'

'We are going to war, Feather Witch. The Tiste Edur will wage war against Lether.'

She scowled. 'What of it? There have been wars before—'

'Not like this one. Rhulad isn't interested in raids. This will be a war of conquest.'

'Conquer Lether? They will fail—'

'Yes, they might. The point is, when the Edur march south, we will be going with them.'

'Why are you so certain of all this? This war? This conquest?'

'Because the Emperor has summoned the shadow wraiths. All of them.'

'You cannot know such a thing.'

He said nothing.

'You cannot,' Feather Witch insisted.

Then she spun round and hurried down the passage.

Udinaas returned to the door. To await the summons he knew would come, eventually.

Emperor and slave. A score of paces, a thousand leagues. In the span of intractable command and obedience, the mind did not count distance. For the path was well worn, as it always had been and as it would ever be.

The wraiths gathered, in desultory legions, in the surrounding forest, among them massive demons bound in chains that formed a most poignant armour. Creatures heaving up from the sea to hold the four hundred or more K'orthan raider ships now being readied, eager to carry them south. Among the tribes, in every village, the sorcerors awakening to the new emperor's demand.

A summons to war.

Across a worn rug.

Heroes triumphant.

From beyond the wooden portal came Mayen's cry.

He emerged from the forest, his face pallid, his expression haunted, and halted in surprise at seeing the readied wagons, Buruk swearing at the Nerek as they scurried about. Seren Pedac had completed donning her leather armour and was strapping on her sword-belt.

She watched him approach.

'Dire events, Hull Beddict.'

'You are leaving?'

'Buruk has so commanded.'

'What of the iron he sought to sell?'

'It goes back with us.' She looked about, then said, 'Come, walk with me. I need to speak one last time with the First Eunuch.'

Hull slowly nodded. 'Good. There is much that I must tell you.'

Her answering smile was wry. 'It was my intent to accord the same to you.'

They set off for the guest house near the citadel. Once more through the ringed divisions of the Edur city. This time, however, the citizens they passed were silent, sombre. Seren and Hull moved among them like ghosts.

'I visited the old sites,' Hull said. 'And found signs of activity.'

'What old sites?' Seren asked.

'North of the crevasse, the forest cloaks what was once a vast city, stretching on for leagues. It was entirely flag-stoned, the stone of a type I've never seen before. It does not break, and only the action of roots has succeeded in shifting the slabs about.'

'Why should there be any activity at such places? Beyond that of the usual ghosts and wraiths?'

Hull glanced at her momentarily, then looked away. 'There are . . . kill sites. Piles of bones that have long since turned to stone. Skeletal remains of Tiste. Along with the bones of some kind of reptilian beast—'

'Yes, I have seen those,' Seren said. 'They are collected and ground into medicinal powder by the Nerek.'

'Just so. Acquitor, these sites have been disturbed, and the tracks I found were most disconcerting. They are, I believe, draconic.'

She stared at him in disbelief. 'The Hold of the Dragon has remained inactive, according to the casters of the tiles, for thousands of years.'

'When did you last speak to a caster?'

Seren hesitated, thinking back on Feather Witch's efforts. When, it was hinted, all was in flux. 'Very well. Draconic.' The thought of dragons, manifest in this world, was terrifying. 'But I cannot see how this relates to the Tiste Edur—'

'Seren Pedac, you must have realized by now that the Tiste Edur worship dragons. Father Shadow, the three Daughters, they are all draconic. Or Soletaken. In the depths of the crevasse a short distance from here can be found the shattered skull of a dragon. I believe that dragon is Father Shadow, the one the Edur call Scabandari Bloodeye. Perhaps this is the source of the betrayal that seems to be the heart of Edur religion. I found tracks there as well. Edur footprints.'

'And what significance have you drawn from all this, Hull?'

'There will be war. A fated war, born of a renewed sense of destiny. I fear for Hannan Mosag, for I think he has grasped a dragon's tail – perhaps more than figuratively. This could prove too much, even for him and his K'risnan.'

'Hull, the Warlock King no longer rules the Edur.'

Shock; then his expression darkened. 'Did the delegation arrive with assassins in its company?'

'He was deposed before the delegation's arrival,' she replied. 'Oh, I don't know where to begin. Binadas's brother, Rhulad. He died, then rose again, within his possession a sword – the gift that Hannan Mosag sought. Rhulad has proclaimed himself emperor. And Hannan Mosag knelt before him.'

Hull's eyes shone. 'As I said, then. Destiny.'

'Is that what you choose to call it?'

'I hear anger in your voice, Acquitor.'

'Destiny is a lie. Destiny is justification for atrocity. It is the means by which murderers armour themselves against reprimand. It is a word intended to stand in place of ethics, denying all moral context. Hull, you are embracing that lie, and not in ignorance.'

They had reached the bridge. Hull Beddict halted and rounded on her. 'You knew me once, Seren Pedac. Enough to give me back my life. I am not blind to this truth, nor to the truth of who you are. You are honourable, in a world that devours honour. And would that I had been able to take more from you than I did, to become like you. Even to join my life to yours. But I haven't your strength. I could not refashion myself.' He studied her for a moment, then continued before she could respond. 'You are right, I am not blind. I understand what it means to embrace destiny. What am I trying to tell you is, *it is the best I can do.*'

She stepped back, as if buffeted by consecutive blows. Her eyes locked with his, and she saw in them the veracity of his confession. She wanted to scream, to loose her anguish, a sound to ring through the city as if to answer, finally and irrefutably, all that had happened.

But no. I am a fool to think that others feel as I do. This tide is rising, and there are scant few who would stand before it.

With heartbreaking gentleness, Hull Beddict reached out and took her arm. 'Come, let us pay a visit to the First Eunuch.'

'At the very least,' Seren tried as they crossed the bridge, 'your own position has become less relevant, making you in less danger than you might otherwise have been.'

'Do you think so?'

'You don't?'

'That depends. Rhulad may not accept my offer of alliance. He might not trust me.'

'What would you do then, Hull?'

'I don't know.'

The guest house was crowded. Finadd Gerun Eberict had arrived, along with the First Eunuch's own bodyguard, the Rulith, and a dozen other guards and officials. As Seren and Hull entered, they found themselves in the midst of a fierce exhortation from Prince Quillas Diskanar.

'—sorcerors in both our camps. If we strike now, we might well succeed in cutting out the heart of this treacherous tyranny!' He swung round. 'Finadd Moroch Nevath, are our mages present?'

'Three of the four, my prince,' the warrior replied. 'Laerdas remains with the ships.'

'Very good. Well, First Eunuch?'

Nifadas was studying the prince, expressionless. He made no reply to Quillas, turning instead to regard Hull and Seren. 'Acquitor, does the rain continue to fall?'

'No, First Eunuch.'

'And is Buruk the Pale ready to depart?'

She nodded.

'I asked you a question, Nifadas!' Quillas said, his face darkening.

'Answering it,' the First Eunuch said slowly, fixing his small eyes on the prince, 'makes implicit the matter is worth considering. It is not. We are facing more than Hannan Mosag the warlock and his K'risnan. The emperor and his sword. Together, they are something . . . other. Those accompanying me are here under my guidance, and at present we shall remain in good faith. Tell me, Prince, how many assassins have you brought along with your sorcerors?'

Quillas said nothing.

Nifadas addressed Gerun Eberict. 'Finadd?'

'There are two,' the man replied. 'Both present in this chamber.'

The First Eunuch nodded, then seemed to dismiss the issue. 'Hull Beddict, I am hesitant to offer you welcome.'

'I am not offended by that admission, First Eunuch.'

'Has the Acquitor apprised you of the situation?'

'She has.'

'And?'

'For what it is worth, I advise you to leave. As soon as possible.'

'And what will you do?'

Hull frowned. 'I see no reason to answer that.'

'You are a traitor!' Quillas said in a hiss. 'Finadd Moroch, arrest him!'

There was dismay on the First Eunuch's features as Moroch Nevath drew his sword and stepped close to Hull Beddict.

'You cannot do that,' Seren Pedac said, her heart thundering in her chest.

All eyes fixed on her.

'I am sorry, my prince,' she continued, struggling to keep her voice even. 'Hull Beddict is under the protection of the Tiste Edur. He was granted guest status by Binadas Sengar, brother to the emperor.'

'He is Letherii!'

'The Edur will be indifferent to that detail,' Seren replied.

'We are done here,' Nifadas said. 'There will be no arrests. Prince Quillas, it is time.'

'Do we scurry at this emperor's command, First Eunuch?' Quillas was shaking with rage. 'He asks for us, well enough. Let the bastard wait.' He wheeled on Hull Beddict. 'Know that I intend to proclaim you an outlaw and traitor of Lether. Your life is forfeit.'

A weary smile was Hull's only reply.

Nifadas spoke to Seren. 'Acquitor, will you accompany us to our audience with the emperor?'

She was surprised by the offer, and more than a little alarmed. 'First Eunuch?'

'Assuming Buruk is prepared to wait, of course. I am certain he will be, and I will send someone to inform him.' He gestured and one of his servants hurried off. 'Hull

491

Beddict, I presume you are on your way to speak with Emperor Rhulad? At the very least, accompany us to the citadel. I doubt there will be any confusion of purposes once we enter.'

Seren could not determine the motives underlying the First Eunuch's invitations. She felt rattled, off balance.

'As you wish,' Hull said, shrugging.

Nifadas in the lead, the four Letherii left the guest house and made their way towards the citadel. Seren drew Hull a pace behind the First Eunuch and Prince Quillas. 'I'm not sure I like this,' she said under her breath.

Hull grunted, and it was a moment before Seren realized it had been a laugh.

'What is funny about that?'

'Your capacity for understatement, Acquitor. I have always admired your ability to stay level.'

'Indecisiveness is generally held to be a flaw, Hull.'

'If it is certainty you want, Seren, then join me.'

The offer was uttered low, barely audible. She sighed. 'I do not want certainty,' she replied. 'In fact, certainty is the one thing I fear the most.'

'I expected that sort of answer.'

Two K'risnan met the party at the entrance and escorted them into the throne chamber.

Emperor Rhulad was seated once more, his new wife standing at his side, on the left. Apart from the two K'risnan, no-one else was present. Although Mayen's face was fixed and without expression, something about it, ineffable in the way of the secret language among women, told Seren that a consummation had occurred, a binding that was reflected in Rhulad's dark eyes, a light of triumph and supreme confidence. 'Hull Beddict,' he said in his rough voice, 'blood brother to Binadas, you arrive in questionable company.'

'Emperor,' Hull said, 'your brother's faith in me is not misplaced.'

'I see. And how does your prince feel about that?'

492

'He is no longer my prince. His feelings mean nothing to me.'

Rhulad smiled. 'Then I suggest you step to one side. I would now speak to the official delegation from Lether, such as it is.'

Hull bowed and walked three paces to the right.

'Acquitor?'

'Emperor, I come to inform you that I am about to leave, as escort to Buruk the Pale.'

'We appreciate the courtesy, Acquitor. If that is all that brings you into our presence, best you join Hull.'

She bowed in acquiescence and moved away. *Now why did Nifadas want this?*

'Emperor Rhulad,' Nifadas said, 'may I speak?'

The Edur regarded the First Eunuch with half-closed lids. 'We permit it.'

'The kingdom of Lether is prepared to enter negotiations regarding the debts incurred as a result of the illegal harvest of tusked seals.'

Like a snake whose tail had just been stepped on, Quillas hissed and spat in indignation.

'The issue of debt,' Rhulad responded, ignoring the prince, 'is no longer relevant. We care nothing for your gold, First Eunuch. Indeed, we care nothing for you at all.'

'If isolation is your desire—'

'We did not say that, First Eunuch.'

Prince Quillas suddenly smiled, under control once more. 'An opening of outright hostility between our peoples, Emperor? I would warn you against such a tactic, which is not to say I would not welcome it.'

'How so, Prince Quillas?'

'We covet the resources you possess, to put it bluntly. And now you give us the opportunity to acquire them. A peaceful solution could have been found in your acknowledgement of indebtedness to Lether. Instead, you voice the absurd lie that is it we who owe you!'

Rhulad was silent a moment, then he nodded and said,

'Letherii economics seems founded on peculiar notions, Prince.'

'Peculiar? I think not. Natural and undeniable laws guide our endeavours. The results of which you will soon discover, to your regret.'

'First Eunuch, does the prince speak for Lether?'

Nifadas shrugged. 'Does it matter, Emperor?'

'Ah, you are clever indeed. Certainly more worthy of conversation with ourselves than this strutting fool whose nobility resides only in the fact of his crawling out from between a queen's legs. You are quite right, First Eunuch. It no longer matters. We were simply curious.'

'I feel no obligation to assuage that curiosity, Emperor.'

'And now you show your spine, at last, Nifadas. We are delighted. Deliver these words to your king, then. The Tiste Edur no longer bow in deference to your people. Nor are we interested in participating in your endless games of misdirection and the poisonous words you would have us swallow.' A sudden, strange pause, the ghost of some kind of spasm flitting across the emperor's face. Then he shook himself, settled back. But the look in his eyes was momentarily lost. He blinked, frowned, then the gleam of awareness returned. 'Moreover,' he resumed, 'we choose now to speak for the tribes you have subjugated, for the hapless peoples you have destroyed. It is time you answered for your crimes.'

Nifadas slowly tilted his head. 'Is this a declaration of war?' he asked in a soft voice.

'We shall announce our intention with deeds, not words, First Eunuch. We have spoken. Your delegation is dismissed. We regret that you travelled so far for what has turned out to be a short visit. Perhaps we will speak again in the future, although, we suspect, in very different circumstances.'

Nifadas bowed. 'Then, if you will excuse us, Emperor, we must make ready to depart.'

'You may go. Hull Beddict, Acquitor, remain a moment.'

Seren watched Quillas and Nifadas walk stiffly from the throne chamber. She was still thinking about that display from Rhulad. *A crack, a fissure. I think I saw him then, young Rhulad, there inside.*

'Acquitor,' Rhulad said as soon as the curtains fell back into place, drawing her attention round, 'inform Buruk the Pale that he has right of passage for his flight. However, the duration of the privilege is short, so he best make haste.'

'Emperor, the wagons perforce—'

'We fear he will not have sufficient time to take his wagons with him.'

She blinked. 'You expect him to abandon the iron in his possession?'

'There are always risks in business, Acquitor, as you Letherii are quick to point out when it is to your advantage. Alas, the same applies when the situation is reversed.'

'How many days do you permit us?'

'Three. One more detail. The Nerek remain here.'

'The Nerek?'

'Are Indebted to Buruk, yes, we understand that. Yet another vagary of economics, alas, under which the poor man must suffer. He has our sympathy.'

'Buruk is a merchant, Emperor. He is used to travelling by wagon. Three days for the return journey may well be beyond his physical abilities.'

'That would be unfortunate, for him.' The dead, cold gaze shifted. 'Hull Beddict, what have you to offer us?'

Hull dropped to one knee. 'I swear myself to your cause, Emperor.'

Rhulad smiled. 'You do not yet know that cause, Hull Beddict.'

'I believe I comprehend more than you might think, sire.'

'Indeed . . .'

'And I would stand with you.'

The emperor swung his attention back to Seren. 'Best

take your leave now, Acquitor. This discussion is not for you.'

Seren looked across at Hull, and their eyes met. Although neither moved, it seemed to her that he was retreating before her, growing ever more distant, ever further from her reach. The intervening space had become a vast gulf, a distance that could not be bridged.

And so I lose you.

To this . . . creature.

Her thoughts ended there. As blank as the future now breached, the space beyond naught but oblivion, *and so we plunge forward* . . . 'Goodbye, Hull Beddict.'

'Fare you well, Seren Pedac.'

Her legs felt wobbly beneath her as she walked to the curtained exit.

Gerun Eberict was waiting for her ten paces from the citadel doors. There was smug amusement in his expression. 'He remains inside, does he? For how long?'

Seren struggled to compose herself. 'What do you want, Finadd?'

'That is a difficult question to answer, Acquitor. I was asked by Brys Beddict to speak to his brother. But the opportunity seems increasingly remote.'

And if I tell him that Hull is lost to us, what would he do then?

Gerun Eberict smiled, as if he had read the thoughts in her mind.

She looked away. 'Hull Beddict is under the emperor's protection.'

'I am pleased for him.'

She glared. 'You do not understand. Look around, Finadd. This village is filled with shadows, and in those shadows are wraiths – servants to the Edur.'

His brows rose. 'You believe I desire to kill him? Where has that suspicion come from, Acquitor? I did say "speak", did I not? I was not being euphemistic.'

496

'Your reputation gives cause for alarm, Finadd.'

'I have no reason to proclaim Hull my enemy, regardless of his political allegiance. After all, if he proves to be a traitor, then the kingdom possesses its own means of dealing with him. I have no interest in interceding in such a matter. I was but endeavouring to consummate my promise to Brys.'

'What did Brys hope to achieve?'

'I'm not sure. Perhaps I was, once, but clearly everything has changed.'

Seren studied him.

'And what of you, Acquitor?' he asked. 'You will escort the merchant back to Trate. Then what?'

She shrugged. There seemed little reason to dissemble. 'I am going home, Finadd.'

'Letheras? That residence has seen little of you.'

'Clearly that is about to change.'

He nodded. 'There will be no demand for Acquitors in the foreseeable future, Seren Pedac. I would be honoured if you would consider working for me.'

'Work?'

'My estate. I am involved in . . . extensive enterprises, You have integrity, Acquitor. You are someone I could trust.' He hesitated, then added, 'Do not feel you need to answer here and now. I ask that you think on it. I shall call upon you in Letheras.'

'I think, Finadd,' Seren said, 'that you will find yourself rather preoccupied with your military duties, given what is about to happen.'

'My position is in the palace. I do not command armies.' He looked round, and his gap-toothed smile returned. 'These savages won't reach Letheras. They'll be lucky to make it across the frontier. You forget, Acquitor, we've faced similar enemies before. The Nerek had their spirit goddess – what was it called?'

'The Eres'al.'

'Yes, that's it. The Eres'al. And the Tarthenal their five

Seregahl, the Wrath Wielders. Warlocks and witches, curses and demons, we obliterated them one and all. And the Ceda and his cadre barely broke a sweat.'

'I fear this time it will be different, Finadd.'

He cocked his head. 'Acquitor, when you think of the Merchant Tolls, what do you imagine it to be?'

'I don't understand—'

'The commercial core, the heart of the financial system which drives all of Lether, its every citizen, its very way of looking at the world. The Tolls are not simply coins stacked high in some secret vault. Not just traders howling their numbers before the day's close. The Tolls are the roots of our civilization, the fibres reaching out to infest everything. *Everything*.'

'What is your point, Finadd?'

'You are cleverer than that, Acquitor. You understand full well. That heart feeds on the best and the worst in human nature. Exaltation and achievement, ambition and greed, all acting in self-serving concert. Thus, four facets of our nature, and not one sits well with constraints on its behaviour, on its expression. We win not just with armies, Seren Pedac. We win because our system appeals to the best and worst within all people, not just humans.'

'Destiny.'

He shrugged. 'Call it what you will. But we have made it inevitable and all-devouring—'

'I see little of exaltation and achievement in what we do, Finadd. It would seem there is a growing imbalance—'

His laugh cut her off. 'And that is the truth of freedom, Seren Pedac.'

She could feel her anger rising. 'I always believed freedom concerned the granted right to be different, without fear of repression.'

'A lofty notion, but you won't find it in the real world. We have hammered freedom into a sword. And if you won't be *like* us we will use that sword to kill you one by one, until your spirit is broken.'

'What if the Tiste Edur surprise you, Finadd? Will you in turn choose to die in defence of your great cause?'

'Some can die. Some will. Indeed, unlikely as it is, we may all die. But, unless the victors leave naught but ashes in their wake, the heart will beat on. Its roots will find new flesh. The emperor may have his demons of the seas, but we possess a monster unimaginably vast, and it devours. And what it cannot devour, it will smother, or starve. Win or lose, the Tiste Edur still *lose*.'

She stepped back. 'Finadd Gerun Eberict, I want nothing to do with your world. And so you need not wait for my answer, for I have just given it.'

'As you like, but know that I will think no less of you when you change your mind.'

'I won't.'

He turned away. 'Everyone has to work to eat, lass. See you in Letheras.'

Udinaas had stood quietly in the gloom during the audience with the delegation. His fellow Letherii had not marked his presence. And, had they done so, it would not have mattered, for it was the emperor who commanded the exchange. After the dismissal of the delegation and the Acquitor's departure, Rhulad had beckoned Hull Beddict closer.

'You swear your fealty to us,' the emperor said in a murmur, as if tasting each word before it escaped his mangled lips.

'I know the details you need, Emperor, the location and complement of every garrison, every frontier encampment. I know their tactics, the manner in which armies are arrayed for battle. The way sorcery is employed. I know where the food and water caches are hidden – these are the military repositories, and they are massive.'

Rhulad leaned forward. 'You would betray your own people. Why?'

'Vengeance,' Hull Beddict replied.

The word chilled Udinaas.

'Sire,' Hull continued, 'my people betrayed me. Long ago. I have long awaited an opportunity such as this one.'

'And so, vengeance. A worthy sentiment?'

'Emperor, there is nothing else left for me.'

'Tell us, Hull Beddict, will the mighty Letherii fleet take to the waves to challenge us?'

'No, I don't think so. Not at first, anyway.'

'And their armies?'

'The doctrine is one of an initial phase of rolling, mobile defence, drawing your forces ever forward. Then counter-attack. Deep strikes to cut your supply lines. Attack and withdraw, attack and withdraw. By the third phase, they will encircle your armies to complete the annihilation. Their fleets will avoid any sea engagement, for they know that to conquer Lether you must make landing. Instead, I suspect they will send their ships well beyond sight of the coastline, then attack your homeland. The villages here, which they will burn to the ground. And every Tiste Edur they find here, old or young, will be butchered.'

Rhulad grunted, then said, 'They think we are fools.'

'The Letherii military is malleable, Emperor. Its soldiers are trained to quick adaptation, should the circumstances warrant it. A formidable, deadly force, exquisitely trained and, employing the raised roads constructed exclusively for it, frighteningly mobile. Worse, they have numerical superiority—'

'Hardly,' Rhulad cut in, smiling. 'The Edur possess new allies, Hull Beddict, as you shall soon discover. Very well, we are satisfied, and we conclude that you shall prove useful to us. Go now to our father's house, and make greeting with Binadas, who will be pleased to see you.'

The Letherii bowed and strode from the chamber.

'Hannan Mosag,' Rhulad called in a low voice.

A side curtain was drawn aside and Udinaas watched the once-Warlock King enter.

'It would seem,' Rhulad said, 'your studies of the Letherii

500

military have yielded you an accurate assessment. His description of their tactics and strategies matches yours exactly.'

'How soon, Emperor?'

'Are the tribes readying themselves?'

'With alacrity.'

'Then very soon indeed. Tell us your thoughts on Nifadas and the prince.'

'Nifadas understood quickly that all was lost, but the prince sees that loss as a victory. At the same time, both remain confident in their kingdom's military prowess. Nifadas mourns for us, Emperor.'

'Poor man. Perhaps he has earned our mercy for that misguided sentiment.'

'Given the course you have chosen for our people, Emperor, mercy is a notion dangerous to entertain. You can be certain that none will be accorded us.'

Another spasm afflicted Rhulad, such as the one Udinaas had witnessed earlier. He thought he understood its source. A thousand bindings held together Rhulad's sanity, but madness was assailing that sanity, and the defences were buckling. Not long ago, no more than the youngest son of a noble family, strutting the village but not yet blooded. In his mind, panoramic visions of glory swinging in a slow turn round the place where he stood. The visions of a youth, crowded with imagined scenarios wherein Rhulad could freely exercise his own certainty, and so prove the righteousness of his will.

And now that boy sat on the Edur throne.

He just had to die to get there.

The sudden manifestation of glory still fed him, enough to shape his words and thoughts and feed his imperial comportment, as if the royal 'we' was something to which he had been born. But this was at the barest edge of control. An imperfect façade, bolstered by elaborately constructed speech patterns, a kind of awkward articulation that suited Rhulad's childlike notions of how an emperor should speak. These were games of persuasion, as much to himself as to his audience.

But, Udinaas was certain, other thoughts remained in Rhulad's mind, gnawing at the roots and crawling like pallid worms through his necrotic soul. For all the glittering gold, the flesh beneath was twisted and scarred. To fashion the façade, all that lay beneath it had been malformed.

The slave registered all this in the span of Rhulad's momentary spasm, and was unmoved. His gaze drifted to Mayen, but she gave nothing away, not even an awareness of her husband's sudden extremity.

Across Hannan Mosag's face, however, Udinaas saw a flash of fear, quickly buried beneath a bland regard.

A moment's consideration and Udinaas thought he understood that reaction. Hannan Mosag needed his emperor to be sane and in control. Even power unveiled could not have forced him to kneel before a madman. Probably, the once-Warlock King also comprehended that a struggle was under way within Rhulad, and had resolved to give what aid he could to the emperor's rational side.

And should the battle be lost, should Rhulad descend completely into insanity, what would Hannan Mosag do then?

The Letherii slave's eyes shifted to the sword the emperor held like a sceptre in his right hand, the point anchored on the dais near the throne's ornate foot. *The answer hides in that sword, and Hannan Mosag knows far more about that weapon – and its maker – than he has revealed.*

Then again, I do as well. Wither, the shadow wraith that had adopted Udinaas, had whispered some truths. The sword's power had given Rhulad command of the wraiths. *The Tiste Andii spirits.*

Wither had somehow avoided the summons, announcing its victory with a melodramatic chuckle rolling through the slave's head, and the wraith's presence now danced with exaggerated glee in the Letherii's mind. Witness to all through his eyes.

'Emperor,' Hannan Mosag said as soon as Rhulad had visibly regained himself, 'the warlocks among the Arapay—'

'Yes. They are not to resist. They are to give welcome.'

'And the Nerek you have claimed from the merchant?'

'A different consideration.' Momentary unease in Rhulad's dark eyes. 'They are not to be disturbed. They are to be respected.'

'Their hearth and the surrounding area has seen sanctification,' Hannan Mosag said, nodding. 'Of course that must be respected. But I have sensed little power from that blessing.'

'Do not let that deceive you. The spirits they worship are the oldest this world has known. Those spirits do not manifest in ways we might easily recognize.'

'Ah. Emperor, you have been gifted with knowledge I do not possess.'

'Yes, Hannan Mosag, I have. We must exercise all caution with the Nerek. I have no desire to see the rising of those spirits.'

The once-Warlock King was frowning. 'The Letherii sorcerors had little difficulty negating – even eradicating – the power of those spirits. Else the Nerek would not have crumbled so quickly.'

'The weakness the Letherii exploited was found in the mortal Nerek, not in the spirits they worshipped. It is our belief now, Hannan Mosag, that the Eres'al was not truly awakened. She did not rise to defend those who worshipped her.'

'Yet something has changed.'

Rhulad nodded. 'Something has.' He glanced up at Mayen. 'Begun with the blessing of the Edur woman who is now my wife.'

She flinched and would meet neither Rhulad's nor Hannan Mosag's eyes.

The emperor shrugged. 'It is done. Need we be concerned? No. Not yet. Perhaps never. None the less, we had best remain cautious.'

503

Udinaas resisted the impulse to laugh. Caution, born of fear. It was pleasing to know that the emperor of the Tiste Edur could still be afflicted with that emotion. *Then again, perhaps I have read Rhulad wrongly. Perhaps fear is at the core of the monster he has become.* Did it matter? Only if Udinaas endeavoured to entertain the game of prediction.

Was it worth the effort?

'The Den-Ratha are west of Breed Bay,' Hannan Mosag said. 'The Merude can see the smoke of their villages.'

'How many are coming by sea?'

'About eight thousand. Every ship. Most of them are warriors, of course. The rest travel overland and the first groups have already reached the Sollanta border.'

'Supplies?' the emperor asked.

'Sufficient for the journey.'

'And nothing is being left behind?'

'Naught but ashes, sire.'

'Good.'

Udinaas watched Hannan Mosag hesitate, then say, 'It is already begun. There is no going back now.'

'You have no reason to fret,' Rhulad replied. 'I have already sent wraiths to the borderlands. They watch. Soon, they will cross over, into Lether.'

'The Ceda's frontier sorcerors will find them.'

'Eventually, but the wraiths will not engage. Merely flee. I have no wish to show their power yet. I mean to encourage overconfidence.'

The two Edur continued discussing strategies. Udinaas listened, just one more wraith in the gloom.

Trull Sengar watched his father rebuilding, with meticulous determination, a kind of faith. Stringing together words spoken aloud yet clearly meant for himself, whilst his wife looked on with the face of an old, broken woman. Death had arrived, only to be shattered by a ghastly reprise, a revivification that offered nothing worth rejoicing in. A king had been cast down, an emperor risen in his place.

504

The world was knocked askew, and Trull found himself detached, numb, witness to these painful, tortured scenes in which the innumerable facets of reconciliation were being attempted, resulting in exhausted silences in which tensions slowly returned, whispering of failure.

They had one and all knelt before their new emperor. Brother and son, the kin who had died and now sat bedecked in gold coins. A voice ravaged yet recognizable. Eyes that belonged to one they had all once known, yet now looked out fevered with power and glazed with the unhealed wounds of horror.

Fear had given up his betrothed.

A terrible thing to have done.

Rhulad had demanded her. *And that was . . . obscene.*

Trull had never felt so helpless as he did now. He pulled his gaze from his father and looked over to where Binadas stood in quiet conversation with Hull Beddict. The Letherii, who had sworn his allegiance to Rhulad, who would betray his own people in the war that Trull knew was now inevitable. *What has brought us all to this? How can we stop this inexorable march?*

'Do not fight this, brother.'

Trull looked over at Fear, seated on the bench beside him. 'Fight what?'

His brother's expression was hard, almost angry. 'He carries the sword, Trull.'

'That weapon has nothing to do with the Tiste Edur. It is foreign, and it seeks to make its wielder into our god. Father Shadow and his Daughters, they are to be cast aside?'

'The sword is naught but a tool. It falls to us, to those around Rhulad, to hold to the sanctity of our beliefs, to maintain that structure and so guide Rhulad.'

Trull stared at Fear. 'He stole your betrothed.'

'Speak of that again, brother, and I will kill you.'

His eyes flinched away, and he could feel the thud of his heart, rapid in his chest. 'Rhulad will accept no guidance,

505

not from us, Fear, not from anyone. That sword and the one who made it guide him now. That, and madness.'

'Madness is what you have decided to see.'

Trull grunted. 'Perhaps you are right. Tell me, then, what you see.'

'Pain.'

And that is something you share. Trull rubbed at his face, slowly sighed. 'Fight this, Fear? There was never a chance.' He looked over again. 'But do you not wonder? Who has been manipulating us, and for how long? You called that sword a tool – are we any different?'

'We are Tiste Edur. We ruled an entire realm, once. We crossed swords with the gods of this world—'

'And lost.'

'Were betrayed.'

'I seem to recall you shared our mother's doubts—'

'I was mistaken. Lured into weakness. We all were. But we must now cast that aside, Trull. Binadas understands. So does our father. Theradas and Midik Buhn as well, and those whom the emperor has proclaimed his brothers of blood. Choram Irard, Kholb Harat and Matra Brith—'

'His unblooded friends of old,' Trull cut in, with a wry smile. 'The three he always defeated in contests with sword and spear. Them and Midik.'

'What of it?'

'They have earned nothing, Fear. And no amount of proclaiming can change that. Yet Rhulad would have us take orders from those—'

'Not us. We too are brothers of blood, you forget. And I still command the warriors of the six tribes.'

'And how do you think the other noble warriors feel? They have all followed the time-honoured path of blooding and worthy deeds in battle. They now find themselves usurped—'

'The first warrior under my command who complains will know the edge of my sword.'

'That edge may grow dull and notched.'

'No. There will be no rebellion.'

After a moment, Trull nodded. 'You are probably right, and that is perhaps the most depressing truth yet spoken this day.'

Fear stood. 'You are my brother, Trull, and a man I admire. But you walk close to treason with your words. Were you anyone else I would have silenced you by now. With finality. No more, Trull. We are an empire now. An empire reborn. And war awaits us. And so I must know – will you fight at the sides of your brothers?'

Trull leaned his back against the rough wall. He studied Fear for a moment, then asked, 'Have I ever done otherwise?'

His brother's expression softened. 'No, you have not. You saved us all when we returned from the ice wastes, and that is a deed all now know, and so they look upon you with admiration and awe. By the same token, Trull, they look to you for guidance. There are many who will find their decisions by observing your reaction to what has happened. If they see doubt in your eyes . . .'

'They will see nothing, Fear. Not in my eyes. Nor will they find cause for doubt in my actions.'

'I am relieved. The emperor shall be calling upon us soon. His brothers of blood.'

Trull also rose. 'Very well. But for now, brother, I feel in need of solitude.'

'Will that prove dangerous company?'

If it does, then I am as good as dead. 'It hasn't thus far, Fear.'

'Leave me now, Hannan Mosag,' the emperor said, his voice revealing sudden exhaustion. 'And take the K'risnan with you. Everyone, go – not you, slave. Mayen, you too, wife. Please go.'

The sudden dismissal caused a moment of confusion, but moments later the chamber was vacated barring Rhulad and Udinaas. To the slave's eyes, Mayen's departure looked

507

more like flight, her gait stilted as if driven by near hysteria.

There would be more moments like this, Udinaas suspected. Sudden breaks in the normal proceedings. And so he was not surprised when Rhulad beckoned him closer, and Udinaas saw in the emperor's eyes a welling of anguish and terror.

'Stand close by me, slave,' Rhulad gasped, fierce trembling sweeping over him. 'Remind me! Please! Udinaas—'

The slave thought for a moment, then said, 'You died. Your body was dressed for honourable burial as a blooded warrior of the Hiroth. Then you returned. By the sword now in your hand, you returned and are alive once more.'

'Yes, that is it. Yes.' A laugh that rose to a piercing shriek, stopping abruptly as a spasm ripped through Rhulad. He gaped, as if in pain, then muttered, 'The wounds . . .'

'Emperor?'

'No matter. Just the memory. Cold iron pushing into my body. Cold fire. I tried. I tried to curl up around those wounds. Up tight, to protect what I had already lost. I remember . . .'

Udinaas was silent. Since the emperor would not look at him, he was free to observe. And arrive at conclusions.

The young should not die. That final moment belonged to the aged. Some rules should never be broken, and whether the motivation was compassionate or coldly calculated hardly mattered. Rhulad had been dead too long, too long to escape some kind of spiritual damage. If the emperor was to be a tool, then he was a flawed one.

And what value that?

'We are imperfect.'

Udinaas started, said nothing.

'Do you understand that, Udinaas?'

'Yes, Emperor.'

'How? How do you understand?'

'I am a slave.'

Rhulad nodded. His left hand, gauntleted in gold, lifted

to join his right where it gripped the handle of the sword. 'Yes, of course. Yes. Imperfect. We can never match the ideals set before us. That is the burden of mortality.' A twisted grimace. 'Not just mortals.' A flicker of the eyes, momentarily fixing on the slave's own, then away again. 'He whispers in my mind. He tells me what to say. He makes me cleverer than I am. What does that make me, Udinaas? What does that make me?'

'A slave.'

'But I am Tiste Edur.'

'Yes, Emperor.'

A scowl. 'The gift of a life returned.'

'You are Indebted.'

Rhulad flinched back in his chair, his eyes flashing with sudden rage. 'We are not the same, slave! Do you understand? I am not one of your *Indebted*. I am not a Letherii.' Then he sagged in a rustle of coins. 'Daughter take me, the weight of this . . .'

'I am sorry, Emperor. It is true. You are not an Indebted. Nor, perhaps, are you a slave. Although perhaps it feels that way, at times. When exhaustion assails you.'

'Yes, that is it. I am tired. That's all. Tired.'

Udinaas hesitated, then asked, 'Emperor, does he speak through you now?'

A fragile shake of the head. 'No. But he does not speak through me. He only whispers advice, helps me choose my words. Orders my thoughts – but the thoughts are mine. They must be. I am not a fool. I possess my own cleverness. Yes, that is it. He but whispers *confidence*.'

'You have not eaten,' Udinaas said. 'Nor drunk anything. Do you know hunger and thirst, Emperor? Can I get you something to replenish your strength?'

'Yes, I would eat. And . . . some wine. Find a servant.'

'At once, master.'

Udinaas walked to the small curtain covering the entrance to the passage that led to the kitchens. He found a servant huddled in the corridor a dozen paces from the door. Terrified eyes glistened up at him as he approached. 'On your feet, Virrick. The emperor wants wine. And food.'

'The god would eat?'

'He's not a god. Food and drink, Virrick. Fit for an emperor, and be quick about it.'

The servant scrambled up, seemed about to bolt.

'You know how to do this,' Udinaas said in a calm voice. 'It's what you have been trained to do.'

'I am frightened—'

'Listen to me. I will tell you a secret. You always like secrets, don't you, Virrick?'

A tentative nod.

'It is this,' Udinaas said. 'We slaves have no reason to fear. It is the Edur who have reason, and that gives us leave to continue laughing behind their backs. Remember doing that, Virrick? It's your favourite game.'

'I – I remember, Udinaas.'

'Good. Now go into the kitchens and show the others. You know the secret, now. Show them, and they will follow. Food, and wine. When you are ready, bring it to the curtain and give the low whistle, as you would do normally. Virrick, we need things to return to normal, do you understand? And that task falls to us, the slaves.'

'Feather Witch ran—'

'Feather Witch is young, and what she did was wrong. I have spoken to her and shall do so again.'

'Yes, Udinaas. You are the emperor's slave. You have the right of it; there is much wisdom in your words. I think we will listen to you, Indebted though you are. You have been . . . elevated.' He nodded. 'Feather Witch failed us—'

'Do not be so harsh on her, Virrick. Now, go.'

He watched the servant hurry off down the corridor, then Udinaas swung about and returned to the throne chamber.

'What took you so long?' Rhulad demanded in near panic. 'I heard voices.'

'I was informing Virrick of your requirements, Emperor.'

510

'You are too slow. You must be quicker, slave.'

'I shall, master.'

'Everyone must be told what to do. No-one seems capable of thinking for themselves.'

Udinaas said nothing, and did not dare smile even as the obvious observation drifted through his mind.

'You are useful to us, slave. We will need . . . reminding . . . again. At unexpected times. And that is what shall you do for us. That, and food and drink at proper times.'

'Yes, master.'

'Now, stand in attendance, whilst we rest our eyes for a time.'

'Of course, master.'

He stood, waiting, watching, a dozen paces away.

The distance between emperor and slave.

As he made his way onto the bridge, Trull Sengar saw the Acquitor. She was standing midway across the bridge, motionless as a frightened deer, her gaze fixed on the main road leading through the village. Trull could not see what had snared her attention.

He hesitated. Then her head turned and he met her eyes.

There were no words for what passed between them at that instant. A gaze that began searchingly, then swiftly and ineffably transformed into something else. That locked contact was mutually broken in the next moment, instinctive reactions from them both.

In the awkward wake, nothing was said for a half-dozen heartbeats. Trull found himself struggling against a sense of vast emptiness deep in his chest.

Seren Pedac spoke first. 'Is there no room left, Trull Sengar?'

And he understood. 'No, Acquitor. No room left.'

'I think you would have it otherwise, wouldn't you?'

The question brushed too close to the wordless recognition they had shared only a few moments earlier, and he saw once again in her eyes a flicker of . . . something. He

511

mentally recoiled from an honest reply. 'I serve my emperor.'

The flicker vanished, replaced by a cool regard that slipped effortlessly through his defences, driving like a knife into his chest. 'Of course. Forgive me. It is too late for questions like that. I must be leaving now, to escort Buruk the Pale back to Trate.'

Each word a twist of that knife, despite their being seemingly innocuous. He did not understand how they – and the look in her eyes – could hurt him so deeply, and he wanted to cry out. Denials. Confessions. Instead he punctuated the break of that empathy with a damning shrug. 'Journey well, Acquitor.' Nothing more, and he knew himself for a coward.

He watched her walk away. Thinking on his life's journey as much as the Acquitor's, on the stumbles that occurred, with no awareness of their potential for profundity. Balance reacquired, but the path had changed.

So many choices proved irrevocable. Trull wondered if this one would as well.

CHAPTER FOURTEEN

> Where is the darkness
> In the days gone past
> When the sun bathed everything
> In godling light
> And we were burnished bright
> In our youthful ascendancy
> Delighted shrieks and
> Distant laughter
> Carried on the gilden stream
> Of days that did not pause
> For night with every shadow
> Burned through
> By immortal fire
> Where then is the darkness
> Arrived at sun's death
> Arrived creeping and low
> To growl revelations
> Of the torrid descent
> That drags us down
> Onto this moment.

> *Immortal fire*
> Fisher kel Tath

A voice spoke from the darkness. 'I wouldn't go down that street, old man.'

Bugg glanced over. 'I thank you for the warning,'

he replied, walking on.

Ten paces into the narrow alley he could smell spilled blood. Footsteps behind him told him the look-out had moved into his wake, presumably to block his avenue of retreat.

'I warned you.'

'I'm the one you sent for,' Bugg said.

Four more figures appeared from the gloom in front of him, cut-throats one and all. They looked frightened.

The look-out came round and stepped close to peer at Bugg's face. 'You're the Waiting Man? You ain't what I 'spected.'

'What has happened here? Who's dead and who killed him?'

'Not "who" killed 'im,' one of the four standing before Bugg muttered. 'More like "what". An' we don't know. Only it was big, skin black as canal water, with spikes on its arms. Eyes like a snake's, glowing grey.'

Bugg sniffed the air, seeking something beyond the blood.

'It ripped Strong Rall to pieces, it did, then went into that building.'

The manservant swung his gaze to where the man pointed. A derelict temple, sunken down at one corner, the peaked roof tilted sharply on that side. Bugg grunted. 'That was the last temple of the Fulcra, wasn't it?'

'Don't ask us.'

'That cult's been dead a hundred years at least,' the manservant continued, scowling at the dilapidated structure. The entranceway, wide and gaping, capped in a solid lintel stone, was once three steps higher than street level. Back when this alley had been a street. He could just make out the right corner of the top step. There seemed to be a heap of rubbish piled up just within, recently disturbed. Bugg glanced back at the five thugs. 'What were you doing skulking around here, anyway?'

An exchange of looks, then the look-out shrugged. 'We was hiding.'

514

'Hiding?'

'This little girl . . . well, uh . . .'

'Ah. Right.' Bugg faced the entrance once again.

'Hold on, old man,' the man said. 'You ain't goin' in there, are you?'

'Well, why else did you call for me?'

'We expected you to, uh, to get the city guards or something. Maybe a mage or three.'

'I might well do that. But first, better to know what we're dealing with.' Bugg then clambered into the ruined temple. Thick, damp air and profound darkness. A smell of freshly turned earth, and then, faintly, the sound of breathing. Slow and deep. The manservant fixed his gaze on the source of that sound. 'All right,' he said in a murmur, 'it's been some time since you last breathed the night air. But that doesn't give you the right to kill a hapless mortal, does it?'

A massive shape shuffled to one side near the far wall. 'Don't hurt me. I'm not going back. They're killing everyone.'

Bugg sighed. 'You'll have to do better than that.'

The shape seemed to break apart, and the manservant saw motion, fanning out. At least six new, smaller forms, each low and long. The gleam of reptilian eyes fixed on him from all along the back wall.

'So that is why you chose this temple,' Bugg said. 'Alas, your worshippers are long gone.'

'You may think so.' A half-dozen voices now, a whispered chorus. 'But you are wrong.'

'Why did you kill that mortal?'

'He was blocking the doorway.'

'So, now that you're here . . .'

'I will wait.'

Bugg considered this, and the implications inherent in that statement. He slowly frowned. 'Very well. But no more killing. Stay in here.'

'I will agree to that. For now.'

515

'Until what you're waiting for . . . arrives.'

'Yes. Then we shall hunt.'

Bugg turned away. 'That's what you think,' he said under his breath.

He reappeared outside the temple. Studied the five terrified faces in the gloom. 'Spread the word that no-one is to enter that temple.'

'That's it? What about the guards? The mages? What about Strong Rall?'

'Well, if you're interested in vengeance, I suggest you find a few thousand friends first. There will be a reckoning, eventually.'

The look-out snorted. 'The Waiting Man wants us to wait.'

Bugg shrugged. 'The best I can do. To oust this beast, the Ceda himself would have to come down here.'

'So send for him!'

'I'm afraid I don't possess that sort of clout. Go home, all of you.'

Bugg moved past them and made his way down the alley. Things were getting decidedly complicated. And that was never good. He wondered how many more creatures were escaping the barrows. From the Pack's words, not many. Which was a relief.

Even so, he decided, he'd better see for himself. The rendezvous awaiting him would have to wait a little longer. That would likely earn him an earful, but it couldn't be helped. The Seventh Closure was shaping up to be eventful. He wondered if that prophecy, of empire reborn, was in some way linked to the death of the Azath tower. He hoped not.

The night was surprisingly quiet. The usual crowds that appeared once the day's heat was past were virtually absent as Bugg made his way down the length of Quillas Canal. He came within sight of the Eternal Domicile. Well, he reminded himself, at least that had been a success. The Royal Engineer, aptly named Grum, had been a reluctant, envious deliverer of a royal contract, specifying Bugg's

516

Construction to assume control of shoring up the compromised wings of the new palace. He had been even less pleased when Bugg ordered the old crews to vacate, taking their equipment with them. Bugg had then spent most of the following day wading flooded tunnels, just to get a feel of the magnitude of the task ahead.

True to Tehol's prediction, Bugg's modest company was climbing in the Tolls, frighteningly fast. Since the list of shares was sealed, Bugg had managed to sell four thousand and twenty-two per cent of shares, and still hold a controlling interest. Of course, he'd be headlining the Drownings if the deceit was ever discovered. 'But I'm prepared to take that risk,' Tehol had said with a broad smile. Funny man, his master.

Nearing the old palace, then into the wending alleyways and forgotten streets behind it. This part of the city seemed virtually lifeless, no-one venturing outside. Stray dogs paused in their scavenging to watch him pass. Rats scurried from his path.

He reached the wall of the square tower, walked along it until he was at the gateway. A pause, during which he wilfully suppressed his nervousness at entering the grounds. The Azath was dead, after all. Taking a deep breath and letting it out slowly, he strode forward.

The barrows to either side were strangely crumpled, but he could see no gaping holes. Yet. He left the path. Insects crunched or squirmed underfoot. The tufts of grass looked macerated and were crawling with life.

Bugg arrived at one barrow where the near side was gone, in its place a black pit across which was the toppled bole of a dead tree. There was the sound of scrabbling from within.

Then Kettle clambered into view. Clumps of white worms writhed in her straggly, matted hair, rode seething on her shoulders. She pulled herself up using a branch of the tree, then paused to brush the worms off, the gesture dainty and oddly affecting. 'It's gone,' she said. 'Uncle Bugg, this one's gone.'

'I know.'

'I didn't see it. I should have seen it.'

He shook his head. 'It is very stealthy, Kettle. And fast. All it needed was a moment when your back was turned. A single moment, no more. In any case, I've met it, and, for now at least, it won't be bothering anyone.'

'Nothing's working, Uncle Bugg. I need the one below. I need to get him out.'

'What is impeding him, do you know?'

She shook her head, the motion shedding more worms. 'At least he's got swords now. Uncle Brys brought them. I pushed them into the barrow.'

'Brys Beddict? Lass, you are finding worthy allies. Has the Ceda visited?'

'I don't know any Ceda.'

'I am surprised by that. He should come soon, once he finds out about you.'

'Me?'

'Well, more specifically, your heart.'

She cocked her head. 'I hear thumps. In my chest. Is that my heart?'

'Yes. How often are the thumps coming?'

'Maybe eight a day. Now. Before, maybe four. To start, once. Loud, hurting my head.'

'Hurting? You are feeling pain, lass?'

'Not so much any more. Aches. Twinges. That's how I know something's wrong with me. Used to be I didn't feel anything.'

Bugg ran a hand through his thinning hair. He looked up, studied the night sky. Cloud-covered, but the clouds were high, flat and unwrinkled, a worn blanket through which stars could be seen here and there. He sighed. 'All right, lass, show me where you buried the swords.'

He followed her to a barrow closer to the tower.

'He's in this one.'

But the manservant's gaze was drawn to an identical

barrow beside the one she indicated. 'Now, who does that one belong to, I wonder.'

'She's always promising me things. Rewards. The five who are killing all the others won't go near her. Sometimes, her anger burns in my head like fire. She's very angry, but not at me, she says. *Those bitches*, she says, and that tells me she's sleeping, because she only says that when she's sleeping. When she's awake, she whispers nice things to me.'

Bugg was slowly nodding. 'It sounds absurd,' he said, mostly to himself. 'Absurd and mundane.'

'What does, Uncle?'

'She's got him by the ankles. I know. It's ridiculous, but that's why he's having trouble getting out. She's got him by the ankles.'

'To keep him where he is?'

'No. To make sure she follows him out.'

'She's cheating!'

Despite his unease, Bugg smiled. 'So she is, lass. Of course, she may only end up keeping both of them trapped.'

'Oh no, he's got the swords now. He just has to work them down. That's what he said. I didn't understand before, but I do now. He said he was going to do some sawing.'

Bugg winced.

Then he frowned. 'The five, how close are they to escaping?'

Kettle shrugged. 'They've killed most everything else. I don't know. Soon, I guess. They are going to do terrible things to me, they say.'

'Be sure to call for help before they get out.'

'I will.'

'I have to be going now.'

'Okay. Goodbye, Uncle.'

Awakened by one of the Preda's corporals, Brys quickly dressed and followed the young soldier to the Campaigns Room, where he found King Ezgara Diskanar, the Ceda, Unnutal Hebaz and the First Concubine Nisall. The king

519

and his mistress stood at one side of a map table, opposite the Preda. Kuru Qan paced a circle around the entire ensemble, removing his strange eye-lenses for a polish every now and then.

'Finadd,' Unnutal Hebaz said, 'join us, please.'

'What has happened?' Brys asked.

'We are, it seems, at war,' the Preda replied. 'I am about to inform the king of the disposition of our forces at present.'

'I apologize for interrupting, Preda.'

Ezgara Diskanar waved a hand. 'I wanted you here, Brys. Now, Unnutal, proceed.'

'Divisions, battalions and brigades,' she said. 'And garrisons. Our land forces. I will speak of the fleets later. Thus, from west to east along the frontier. On the Reach, First Maiden Fort, its defences still under construction and nowhere near complete. I have judged it indefensible and so am sending the garrison to reinforce Fent Reach. Second Maiden Fort has a garrison of six hundred indicted soldiers, presently being retrained. The island is a penal fortress, as you know. The willingness of the prisoners to fight is of course problematic. None the less, I would suggest we leave them there. Third Maiden Fort will remain active, but with a nominal presence, there to act as forward observers should an Edur fleet round the island and make for the city of Awl.'

'Where we have an army,' the king said.

'Yes, sire. The Snakebelt Battalion, stationed in the city. The Crimson Rampant Brigade is in Tulamesh down the coast. Now, eastward from the Reach, the port of Trate. Cold Clay Battalion and the Trate Legion, with the Riven Brigade and the Katter Legion down in Old Katter. High Fort has, in addition to its rotating garrison forces, the Grass Jackets Brigade. Normally, we would have the Whitefinder Battalion there as well, but they are presently conducting exercises outside First Reach. They will of course be moving north immediately.

'Further east, the situation is more satisfactory. At Fort Shake is the Harridict Brigade, with the Artisan Battalion encamped outside the Manse – more exercises.'

'How long will it take the Whitefinders to reach High Fort?' the king asked.

'Reach and Thetil Roads are in good repair, sire. Five days. They leave tomorrow. I would emphasize again, the Ceda's mages are a major tactical advantage. Our communications are instantaneous.'

'But I want something more,' Ezgara said in a growl. 'I want something pre-emptive, Preda. I want them to change their minds on this damned war.'

Unnutal slowly turned to catch Kuru Qan with her gaze. 'Ceda?'

'Relevant? Less than we would hope. You want their villages struck? Those just beyond the mountains? Very well.'

'How soon can you arrange it?' the king asked.

'The cadre in Trate is assembling, sire. Dawn, three days from now.'

'Pray to the Errant that it dissuades them.' The king managed a wry grin as he watched the Ceda resume his pacing. 'But you are not confident that it will, are you, Kuru Qan?'

'I am not, sire. Fortunately, I do not believe even Hull would suspect that we would attack the Edur villages.'

Brys felt his blood grow cold. 'Ceda? Has my brother . . . ?'

A sorrowful nod. 'This is a path Hull Beddict has been walking on for a long time. No-one here is surprised, Finadd.'

Brys swallowed, then struggled to speak. 'I would have . . . thought . . . given that knowledge—'

'That he would have been assassinated?' Ezgara asked. 'No, Brys. His presence is to *our* tactical advantage, not this damned upstart emperor's. We are well aware he is advising the Edur on our manner of waging war, and we mean to make use of that.' The king paused, looked up. 'Hull's actions in no way impugn you in our eyes, Brys. Be assured of that.'

'Thank you, sire.' *And to prove your word, you invite me to this meeting.* 'It is unfortunate that Nifadas failed in his mission. What do we know of this new "upstart" emperor you mentioned?'

'He has vast magic at his command,' Kuru Qan replied distractedly. 'We can discern little more than that.'

The First Concubine moved from the king's side, seemingly distracted.

'The most relevant detail for us,' Unnutal Hebaz added, 'is that he is in possession of absolute loyalty among the Edur tribes. And, although Hannan Mosag has been usurped, the Warlock King now stands at the emperor's side as his principal adviser.'

Brys was startled by that. 'The Warlock King simply stepped aside? That is . . . extraordinary.'

The Preda nodded. 'Sufficient to give us pause. Our forward posts have reported sightings along the frontier. Shadows moving at night.'

'The wraiths,' the Ceda said, his expression souring. 'We have dealt with them before, of course, and effectively so. None the less, they are an irritant.'

'Do the Tiste Edur have sacred sites?' Nisall asked from where she now stood, close to the far wall. Faces turned towards her. Arms crossed, she shrugged. 'Sorcery that annihilates those sites might well weaken their hold on these wraiths. Wasn't something similar done to the Nerek and the Tarthenal?'

The Ceda seemed saddened by the suggestion, but he nodded and said, 'An interesting notion, First Concubine. The Edur are very secretive regarding their sacred sites. Although it does appear to be the case that the very ground beneath their villages is sanctified. Thus, when we destroy those villages, the result may well prove more profound than we imagine. This is a relevant consideration. As for the hidden groves and such, we should make use of the various Acquitors who are familiar with that territory.'

'How soon will the delegation reach the Mouth at Gedry?' Brys asked the Preda.

She nodded towards Kuru Qan. 'The return journey is being hastened. A week, no more.'

Then three days up the river to arrive here. The war would be well under way by then. 'Sire, may I ask a question of you?'

'Of course, Brys.'

'Where is the Queen's Battalion?'

A momentary silence, then the Preda cleared her throat. 'If I may, sire . . .'

Thin-lipped, the king nodded.

'Finadd, the queen has taken personal command of her forces, along with the Quillas Brigade. She insists on independence in this matter. Accordingly, we are not factoring those assets into our discussion.'

'My dear wife has always held them to be her own, private army,' Ezgara Diskanar said. 'So be it. Better to have them pursuing her ambitions in the field than here in Letheras.'

'That being said,' Unnutal Hebaz added, 'we believe they are less than a league south of High Fort, marching northward to meet the Edur in the pass. Her doctrine seems to be one of striking first and striking hard. She will set her mages to clearing the wraiths from her path, which will no doubt be telling enough to eliminate the element of surprise.'

'Is she leading them in person?'

'She and her retinue departed four days ago,' the king said.

Brys thought back to that time. 'The royal visit to her keep at Dissent?'

'That was the pretext.'

'Then will Prince Quillas make an effort to join her?'

'My son has separated his ship from the delegation and now makes for Trate.'

'To what extent,' Brys asked, 'has her battalion made use of the caches in the region?'

'Knowing her,' the king snapped, 'she's damn near emptied them.'

'We are hastening to replace the depleted stocks,' Unnutal Hebaz said. 'Obviously, we are forced to adjust our tactics as a consequence. We will fight defensively, in keeping with our doctrine, and, yes, the Edur will be expecting that. But we will not roll back. We will not retreat. Once engaged, we intend to maintain that contact. This will be, I believe, a brutal war – perhaps the most vicious war we have fought since conquering Bluerose's League of Duchies.'

'Now,' the king said, 'I would hear details on the defence of our frontier cities and the Sea of Katter. As well, the disposition of the fleets . . .'

Brys found the words that followed drifting into a formless murmur somewhere in the background. He was thinking of his brother, marching with the Tiste Edur to wage war on his homeland. On the kingdom that had so cruelly betrayed him. The queen and the prince would want him, desperately . . . or, at the very least, his head. And through Hull's crimes, they would seek to strike at Brys, at his position as the king's protector. They might well send soldiers to round up Tehol as well, on some fabricated pretext. The added pleasure of avenging financial losses incurred as a result of Tehol's brilliant chaos. They would, in fact, waste little time.

Brys needed to warn Tehol.

The Rat Catchers' Guild Chief Investigator sat at a courtyard table beneath torchlight. A small heap of delicate bones sat in the centre of the large plate before her. Within reach was a crystal carafe of white wine. An extra goblet waited in front of the empty chair opposite her.

'You're not Tehol,' she said as Bugg arrived and sat down. 'Where's Tehol and his immodest trousers?'

'Not here, alas, Chief Investigator, but you can be certain that, wherever they are, they are together.'

'Ah, so he has meetings with people more important than me? After all, were he sleeping, he would not be wearing the trousers, would he?'

'I wouldn't know, Rucket. Now, you requested this meeting?'

'With Tehol.'

'Ah, so this was to be romantic?'

She sniffed and took a moment to glare at the only other occupants of this midnight restaurant, a husband and wife clearly not married to each other who were casting suspicious glances their way, punctuated with close leaning heads and heated whispers. 'This place serves a specific clientele, damn you. What's your name again?'

'Bugg.'

'Oh yes. I recall being unsurprised the first time it was mentioned. Well, you kept me waiting, you little worm, and what's that smell?'

Bugg withdrew a blackened, wrinkled strip, flat and slightly longer than his hand. 'I found an eel in the fish market. Thought I'd make soup for myself and the master.'

'Our financial adviser eats discarded eels?'

'Frugality is a virtue among financiers, Chief Investigator.' He tucked the dried strip back into his shirt. 'How is the wine? May I?'

'Well, why not? Here, care to pick the bones?'

'Possibly. What was it originally?'

'Cat, of course.'

'Cat. Oh yes, of course. Well, I never liked cats anyway. All those hair balls.' He drew the plate over and perused it to see what was left.

'You have a fascination for feline genitalia? That's disgusting, although I've heard worse. One of our minor catchers once tried to marry a rat. I myself possess peculiar interests, I freely admit.'

525

'That's nice,' Bugg said, popping a vertebra into his mouth to suck out the marrow.

'Well, aren't you curious?'

'No,' he said around the bone. 'Should I be?'

Rucket slowly leaned forward, as if seeing Bugg for the first time. 'You . . . interest me now. I freely admit it. Do you want to know why?'

'Why you freely admit it? All right.'

'I'm a very open person, all things considered.'

'Well, I am considering those things, and so consequently admit to being somewhat surprised.'

'That doesn't surprise me in the least, Bugg. What are you doing later tonight, and what's that insect? There, on your shoulder?'

He pulled the vertebra out and reached for another. 'It's of the two-headed variety. Very rare, for what I imagine are obvious reasons. I thought my master would like to see it.'

'So you permit it to crawl all over you?'

'That would take days. It's managed to climb from halfway up my arm to my shoulder and that's taken over a bell.'

'What a pathetic creature.'

'I suspect it has difficulty making up its minds.'

'You're being funny, aren't you? I have a thing for funny people. Why don't you come home with me after you've finished here.'

'Are you sure you don't have any business to discuss with me? Perhaps some news for Tehol?'

'Well, there's a murderous little girl who's undead, and she's been killing lots of people, although less so lately. And Gerun Eberict has been far busier than it would outwardly seem.'

'Indeed? But why would he hide that fact?'

'Because the killings do not appear to be politically motivated.'

'Oh? Then what are his motivations?'

'Hard to tell. We think he just likes killing people.'

'Well, how many has he killed this past year?'

'Somewhere between two and three thousand, we think.'

Bugg reached with haste for his goblet. He drank the wine down, then coughed. 'Errant take us!'

'So, are you coming home with me or not? I have this cat-fur rug—'

'Alas, my dear, I have taken a vow of celibacy.'

'Since when?'

'Oh, thousands of years . . . it seems.'

'I am not surprised. But even more intrigued.'

'Ah, it's the lure of the unattainable.'

'Are you truly unattainable?'

'Extraordinary, but yes, I am.'

'What a terrible loss for womanhood.'

'Now you are being funny.'

'No, I am being serious, Bugg. I think you are probably a wonderful lover.'

'Aye,' he drawled, 'the very oceans heaved. Can we move on to some other subject? You want any more wine? No? Great.' He collected the carafe, then drew a flask from under his shirt and began the delicate task of pouring the wine into it.

'Is that for your eel soup?'

'Indeed.'

'What happens now that I've decided to like you? Not just *like* you, I freely admit, but lust after you, Bugg.'

'I have no idea, Rucket. May I take the rest of these bones?'

'You certainly may. Would you like me to regurgitate my meal for you as well? I will, you know, for the thought that you will take into you what was previously in me—'

Bugg was waving both hands in the negative. 'Please, don't put yourself out for me.'

'No need to look so alarmed. Bodily functions are a wonderful, indeed sensual, thing. Why, the mere blowing clear of a nose is a potential source of ecstasy, once you grasp its phlegmatic allure.'

527

'I'd best be going, Rucket.' He quickly rose. 'Have a nice night, Chief Investigator.' And was gone.

Alone once more, Rucket sighed and leaned back in her chair. 'Well,' she sighed contentedly, 'it's always been a sure-fire way of getting rid of unwanted company.' She raised her voice. 'Servant! More wine, please!' That bit about clearing the nose was especially good, she decided. She was proud of that one, especially the way she disguised the sudden nausea generated by her own suggestion.

Any man who'd cook that . . . *eel* had surely earned eternal celibacy.

Outside the restaurant, Bugg paused to check the contents of his shirt's many hidden pockets. Flask, eel, cat bones. A successful meeting, after all. Moreover, he was appreciative of her performance. *Tehol might well and truly like this one, I think.* It was worth considering.

He stood for a moment longer, then allowed himself a soft laugh.

In any case, time to head home.

Tehol Beddict studied the three sad, pathetic women positioned variously in the chamber before him: Shand slumped behind the desk, her shaved pate looking dull and smudged; Rissarh lying down on a hard bench as if meditating on discomfort, her red hair spilled out and hanging almost to the floor; and Hejun, sprawled in a padded chair, refilling her pipe's bowl, her face looking sickly and wan. 'My,' Tehol said with a sigh, his hands on his hips, 'this is a tragic scene indeed.'

Shand looked up, bleary-eyed. 'Oh, it's you.'

'Hardly the greeting I was anticipating.' He strode into the room.

'He's gone,' Hejun said, face twisting as she jabbed a taper into the coals of the three-legged brazier at her side. 'And it's Shand's fault.'

'As much yours as mine,' Shand retorted. 'And don't

528

forget Rissarh! *"Oh, Ublala! Carry me around! Carry me around!"* Talk about excess!'

'Ublala's departure is the cause for all this despond?' Tehol shook his head. 'My dears, you did indeed drive him away.' He paused, then added with great pleasure, 'Because none of you was willing to make a *commitment*. A disgusting display of self-serving objectification. Atrocious behaviour by each and every one of you.'

'All right, all right, Tehol,' Shand muttered. 'We could have been more . . . compassionate.'

'Respectful,' Rissarh said.

'Yes,' Hejun said. 'How could one not respect Ublala's—'

'See?' Tehol demanded, then flung up his hands. 'I am led to despair!'

'You'll have company here,' Shand said.

'He was to have been your bodyguard. That was the intent. Instead, you abused him—'

'No we didn't!' Hejun snapped. 'Well, only a little. All in good fun, anyway.'

'And now I have to find you a new bodyguard.'

'Oh no you don't,' Shand said, sitting straighter. 'Don't even think it. We've been corrupted enough—'

Tehol's brows rose. 'In any case,' he said, 'Ublala has now found someone who cares deeply for him—'

'You idiot. She's dead. She's incapable of caring.'

'Not true. Or, rather, there's something inside her that does care. A lot. My point is, it's time to get over it. There's work to be done.'

'We tried following up on that list you gave us. Half those companies don't even exist. You tricked us, Tehol. In fact, we think this whole thing is a lie.'

'What an absurd accusation. Granted, I padded the list somewhat, but only because you seemed to need to stay busy. Besides which, you're now rich, right? Wealthy beyond your wildest dreams. My investment advice has been perfect thus far. How many money-lending institutions do you now hold interest in?'

'All the big ones,' Shand admitted. 'But not controlling interest—'

'Wrong. Forty per cent is sufficient and you've acquired that.'

'How is forty per cent enough?'

'Because I hold twenty. Or, if not me, then my agents, Bugg included. We are poised, dear ladies, to loose chaos upon the Tolls.'

He had their attention now, he saw. Even Rissarh sat up. Eyes fixed upon him, eyes in which the gleam of comprehension was dawning. 'When?' Hejun asked.

'Ah, well. That is entirely another matter. There is news on the wind, which, had any of you been in a proper state, would already be known to you. It seems, my sweet friends, that Lether is at war.'

'The Tiste Edur?'

'Indeed.'

'Perfect!' Shand barked, thumping the desktop with a fist. 'We strike now and it'll all come down!'

'Likely,' Tehol said. 'And also, disastrous. Do you want the Edur to march in and burn everything to the ground?'

'Why not? It's all corrupt anyway!'

'Because, Shand, bad as it is – and we're all agreed it's bad – matters can get a whole lot worse. If, for example, the Tiste Edur win this war.'

'Hold on, Tehol! The plan was to bring about a collapse! But now you're going back on it. You must be a fool to think the Edur would win this war without our help. No-one wins against Lether. Never have, never will. But if we strike now . . .'

'All very well, Shand. For myself, however, I am not convinced the Edur will prove ideal conquerors. As I said, what is to stop them from putting every Letherii to the sword, or enslaving everyone? What's to stop them from razing every city, every town, every village? It's one thing to bring down an economy, and so trigger a reformation of sorts, a reconfiguring of values and all that. It's entirely another to act in a way that exposes the Letherii to genocide.'

'Why?' Rissarh demanded. 'They've not hesitated at committing genocide of their own, have they? How many Tarthenal villages were burned to the ground? How many children of the Nerek and the Faraed were spitted on spears, how many dragged into slavery?'

'Then you would descend to their level, Rissarh? Why emulate the worst behaviours of a culture, when it is those very behaviours that fill you with horror? Revulsion at babes spitted on spears, so you would do the same in return?' He looked at each of them in turn, but they made no reply. Tehol ran a hand through his hair. 'Consider the opposite. A hypothetical situation, if you will. Letheras declares a war in the name of liberty and would therefore assert the right of the moral high ground. How would you respond?'

'With disgust,' Hejun said, relighting her pipe, face disappearing behind blue clouds.

'Why?'

'Because it's not liberty they want, not the kind of liberty that serves the people in question. Instead, it's the freedom of Letherii business interests to profit from those people.'

'And if they act to prevent genocide and tyranny, Hejun?'

'Then no moral high ground at all, for they have committed their own acts of genocide. As for tyranny, tyrannies are only reprehensible to the Letherii when they do not operate in collusion with Letherii business interests. And, by that definition, they make their claims of honour suspect to everyone else.'

'All very well. Now, I have considered each and every one of those arguments. And could only conclude one thing: the Letherii, in that situation, are damned if they do and damned if they don't. In other words, the issue is one of trust. In the past lies the evidence leading one to mistrust. In the present may be seen efforts to reacquire trust, whilst in the future awaits the proof of either one or the other.'

531

'This is a hypothetical situation, Tehol,' Shand said wearily. 'What is your point?'

'My point is, nothing is as simple as it might at first seem. And paradigms rarely shift through an act of will. They change as a consequence of chaos, in stumbling over a threshold, and all that is most reprehensible in our nature waits in the wings, eager to invade and so give shape to the reforging of order. It falls to every one of us to be mindful.'

'What in the Errant's name are you talking about?' Shand demanded.

'What I am saying, Shand, is that we cannot in good conscience trigger a collapse of the Letherii economy right now. Not until we determine how this war is going to play out.'

'Good conscience? Who cares about that? Our motive was *revenge*. The Letherii are poised to annihilate yet another people. And I want to *get them*!'

'Do not dismiss the Tiste Edur just yet, Shand. Our priority right now must be the secret evacuation of destitute and Indebted Nerek, Faraed and Tarthenal. Out to the islands. To my islands. The rest can wait, should wait, and will wait. Until I say otherwise.'

'You're betraying us.'

'No, I'm not. Nor am I having second thoughts. I am not blind to the underlying motives of greed upon which my civilization is founded, for all its claims of righteous destiny and unassailable integrity.'

'What makes you think,' Hejun asked, 'the Tiste Edur might succeed where everyone else has failed?'

'Succeed? That word makes me uneasy. Might they prove a difficult and at times devastating enemy? I think they will. Their civilization is old, Hejun. Far older than ours. Their golden age was long, long ago. They exist now in a state of fear, seeing the influence and material imposition of Letheras as a threat, as a kind of ongoing unofficial war of cultures. To the Edur, Lether is a poison, a corrupting influence, and in reaction to that the Edur have become a people entrenched and belligerent. In disgust at what they see ahead of them, they have turned their backs and dream only of what lay behind them. They dream of a return to past glories. Even could the Letherii offer a helping hand, they would view it as an invitation to surrender, and their pride will not permit that. Or, conversely, that hand represents an attack on all they hold dear, and so they will cut it and dance in the blood. The worst scenario I can imagine, for the Edur, is if they win this war. If they somehow conquer us and become occupiers.'

'Won't happen, and what if it did? They couldn't be worse.'

Tehol studied Hejun briefly, then he shrugged. 'All of this awaits resolution. In the meantime, remain vigilant. There are still things that need doing. What happened to that Nerek mother and her children I sent you?'

'We shipped them to the islands,' Shand said. 'They ate more than she cooked. Started getting fat. It was all very sad.'

'Well, it's late and I'm hungry, so I will take my leave now.'

'What about Ublala?' Rissarh demanded.

'What about him?'

'We want him back.'

'Too late, I'm afraid. That's what happens when you won't commit.'

Tehol quickly made his way out.

Walking the quiet streets back to his abode, Tehol considered his earlier words. He had to admit to himself that he was troubled. There was sufficient mystery in some of the rumours to suggest that the impending war would not be like all the others Letherii had waged. A collision of wills and desires, and beneath it a host of dubious assumptions and suspect sentiments. In that alone, no different from any other war. But in this case, the outcome was far from certain, and even the notion of victory seemed confused and elusive.

533

He passed through Burl Square and came to the entrance to the warehouse storage area, beyond which was the alley leading to his home. Pausing to push up his lopsided sleeves and cinch tight his trousers, he frowned. Was he losing weight? Hard to know. Wool stretched, after all.

A figure stepped from the nearby shadows of an alley mouth. 'You're late.'

Tehol started, then said, 'For what?'

Shurq Elalle came to within two paces of him. 'I've been waiting. Bugg made soup. Where have you been?'

'What are you doing out?' Tehol asked. 'You're supposed to be holed up right now. This is dangerous—'

'I needed to talk to you,' she cut in. 'It's about Harlest.'

'What about him?'

'He wants his sharp teeth and talons. It's all we ever hear. Fangs and talons, fangs and talons. We're sick of it. Where's Selush? Why haven't you made arrangements? You're treating us like corpses, but even the dead have needs, you know.'

'Well, no, I didn't know that. In any case, tell Harlest that Selush is working on this, probably right now in fact. Sharp solutions are forthcoming.'

'Don't make me laugh.'

'Sorry. Are you in need of a refill?'

'A what?'

'Well, uh, more herbs and stuff, I mean.'

'I don't know. Am I? Do I smell or something?'

'No. Only of sweet things, Shurq. I assure you.'

'I am less inspired by your assurances as time goes on, Tehol Beddict.'

'What a terrible thing to say! Have we stumbled yet?'

'When is Gerun Eberict returning?'

'Soon, it turns out. Things should get exciting then.'

'I am capable of excitement regarding one thing and one thing only, and that has nothing to do with Gerun Eberict. However, I want to steal again. Anything, from whomever. Point me in a direction. Any direction.'

'Well, there is of course the Tolls Repository. But that's impregnable, obviously. Or, let's see, the royal vaults, but again, impossible.'

'The Tolls. Yes, that sounds challenging.'

'You won't succeed, Shurq. No-one ever has, and that includes Green Pig who was a sorceror nearly to rival the Ceda himself—'

'I knew Green Pig. He suffered from overconfidence.'

'And was torn limb from limb as a result.'

'What do you want stolen from the Tolls Repository?'

'Shurq—'

'What?'

Tehol glanced round. 'All right. I want to find out which lender holds the largest royal debt. The king has been borrowing prodigiously, and not just to finance the Eternal Domicile. So, who and how much. Same for Queen Janall. And whatever she's done in her son's name.'

'Is that all? No gold? No diamonds?'

'That's right. No gold, no diamonds, and no evidence left behind that anyone was ever in there.'

'I can do that.'

'No you can't. You'll get caught. And dismembered.'

'Oh, that will hurt.'

'Maybe not, but it'll prove inconvenient.'

'I won't get caught, Tehol Beddict. Now, what did you want from the royal vaults?'

'A tally.'

'You want to know the present state of the treasury.'

'Yes.'

'I can do that.'

'No you can't.'

'Why not?'

'Because you'll have been dismembered by then.'

'Thus permitting me to slip into places where I otherwise wouldn't fit.'

'Shurq, they take your head off too, you know. It's the last thing they do.'

535

'Really? That's barbaric.'

'Like I said, you would be greatly inconvenienced.'

'I would at that. Well, I shall endeavour to be careful. Mind you, even a head can count.'

'What would you have me do, break in and lob your head into the vaults? Tied to a rope so I can pull you out again when you're done?'

'That sounds somewhat problematic.'

'It does, doesn't it?'

'Can't you plan any better than that, Tehol Beddict? My faith in you is fast diminishing.'

'Can't be helped, I suppose. What's this I hear about you purchasing a seagoing vessel?'

'That was supposed to be a secret. Bugg said he wouldn't tell—'

'He didn't. I have my own sources of intelligence, especially when the owner of the vessel just sold happens to be me. Indirectly, of course.'

'All right. Me and Ublala and Harlest, we want to be pirates.'

'Don't make me laugh, Shurq.'

'Now you're being cruel.'

'Sorry. Pirates, you say. Well, all three of you are notoriously hard to drown. Might work at that.'

'Your confidence and well-wishing overwhelms me.'

'And when do you plan on embarking on this new venture?'

'When you're done with us, of course.'

Tehol tugged up his trousers again. 'Yet another edifying conversation with you, Shurq. Now, I smell something that might well be soup, and you need to go back to your crypt.'

'Sometimes I really hate you.'

He led her by the hand down the shallow, crumbling steps. She liked these journeys, even though the places he took her were strange and often . . . disturbing. This time, they descended an inverted stepped pyramid – at least that was what he called it. Four sides to the vast, funnelled pit, and at the base there was a small square of darkness.

The air was humid enough to leave droplets on her bare arms. Far overhead, the sky was white and formless. She did not know if it was hot – memories of such sensations had begun to fade, along with so many other things.

They reached the base of the pit and she looked up at the tall, pale figure at her side. His face was becoming more visible, less blurred. It looked handsome, but hard. 'I'm sorry,' she said after a moment, 'that she's got you by the ankles.'

'We all have our burdens, Kettle.'

'Where are we?'

'You have no recognition of this place?'

'No. Maybe.'

'Let us continue down, then.'

Into the darkness, three rungs to a landing, then a spiral staircase of black stone.

'Round and round,' Kettle said, giggling.

A short while later they came to the end, the stairs opening out onto a sprawling, high-ceilinged chamber. The gloom was no obstacle to Kettle, nor, she suspected, to her companion. She could see a ragged mound heaped against the far wall to their right, and made to move towards it, but his hand drew her back.

'No, lass. Not there.'

He led her instead directly ahead. Three doorways, each one elaborately arched and framed with reverse impressions of columns. Between them, the walls displayed deeply carved images.

'As you can see,' he said, 'there is a reversal of perspective. That which is closest is carved deepest. There is significance to all this.'

'Where are we?'

'To achieve peace, destruction is delivered. To give the gift of freedom, one promises eternal imprisonment. Adjudication obviates the need for justice. This is a

537

studied, deliberate embrace of diametric opposition. It is a belief in balance, a belief asserted with the conviction of religion. But in this case, the proof of a god's power lies not in the cause but in the effect. Accordingly, in this world and in all others, proof is achieved by action, and therefore all action – including the act of choosing inaction – is inherently moral. No deed stands outside the moral context. At the same time, the most morally perfect act is the one taken in opposition to what has occurred before.'

'What do the rooms look like through those openings?'

'In this civilization,' he continued, 'its citizens were bound to acts of utmost savagery. Vast cities were constructed beneath the world's surface. Each chamber, every building, assembled as the physical expression of the quality of absence. Solid rock matched by empty space. From these places, where they did not dwell, but simply gathered, they set out to achieve balance.'

It seemed he would not lead her through any of the doorways, so she fixed her attention instead on the images. 'There are no faces.'

'The opposite of identity, yes, Kettle.'

'The bodies look strange.'

'Physically unique. In some ways more primitive, but as a consequence less . . . specialized, and so less constrained. Profoundly long-lived, more so than any other species. Very difficult to kill, and, it must be said, they *needed* to be killed. Or so was the conclusion reached after any initial encounter with them. Most of the time. They did fashion the occasional alliance. With the Jaghut, for example. But that was yet another tactic aimed at reasserting balance, and it ultimately failed. As did this entire civilization.'

Kettle swung round to study that distant heap of . . . something. 'Those are bodies, aren't they?'

'Bones. Scraps of clothing, the harnesses they wore.'

'Who killed them?'

'You had to understand, Kettle. The one within you must understand. My refutation of the Forkrul Assail belief in balance is absolute. It is not that I am blind to the way in which force is ever countered, the way in which the natural world strains towards balance. But in that striving I see no proof of a god's power; I see no guiding hand behind such forces. And, even if one such existed, I see no obvious connection with the actions of a self-chosen people for whom chaos is the only rational response to order. Chaos needs no allies, for it dwells like a poison in every one of us. The only relevant struggle for balance I acknowledge is that within ourselves. Externalizing it presumes inner perfection, that the internal struggle is over, victory achieved.'

'You killed them.'

'These ones here, yes. As for the rest, no. I was too late arriving and my freedom too brief for that. In any case, but a few enclaves were left by that time. My draconic kin took care of that task, since no other entity possessed the necessary power. As I said, they were damned hard to kill.'

Kettle shrugged, and she heard him sigh.

'There are places, lass, where Forkrul Assail remain. Imprisoned for the most part, but ever restless. Even more disturbing, in many of those places they are worshipped by misguided mortals.' He hesitated, then said, 'You have no idea, Kettle, of the extremity the Azath tower found itself in. To have chosen a soul such as yours . . . it was like reaching into the heart of the enemy camp. I wonder if, in its last moments, it knew regret. Misgivings. Mother knows, I do.'

'What is this soul you are talking about?'

'Perhaps it sought to use the soul's power without fully awakening it. We will never know. But you are loose upon the world now. Shaped to fight as a soldier in the war against chaos. Can that fundamental conflict within you be reconciled? Your soul, lass? It is Forkrul Assail.'

'So you have brought me home?'

His hand betrayed his sudden flinch. 'You were also a mortal human child, once. And there is a mystery in that. Who birthed you? Who took away your life, and why? Was

539

all this in preparation for your corpse to house the Assail soul? If that is the case, then the Azath tower was either deceived by someone capable of communicating with it, or it had in truth nothing at all to do with the creation of you as you now are. But that makes no sense – why would the Azath lie to me?'

'It said you were dangerous.'

He was silent for some time. Then, 'Ah, you are to kill me once I have vanquished the other entombed creatures.'

'The tower is dead,' Kettle said. 'I don't have to do anything it told me. Do I?' She looked up and found him studying her.

'What path will you choose, child?'

She smiled. 'Your path. Unless you're bad. I'll be very angry if you're bad.'

'I am pleased, Kettle. Best that you stay close to me, assuming we succeed in what we must do.'

'I understand. You may have to destroy me.'

'Yes. If I can.'

She gestured with her free hand at the heap of bones. 'I don't think you'll have much trouble.'

'Let us hope it doesn't come to that. Let us hope the soul within you does not entirely awaken.'

'It won't. That's why none of this matters.'

'What makes you so certain, Kettle?'

'The tower told me.'

'It did? What did it say to you? Try to recall its exact words.'

'It never spoke with words. It just showed me things. My body, all wrapped up. People were crying. But I could see through the gauze. I'd woken up. I was seeing everything with two sets of eyes. It was very strange. One set behind the wrappings, the other standing nearby.'

'What else did the Azath show you?'

'Those eyes from the outside. There were five others. We were just standing in the street, watching the family carrying the body. My body. Six of us. We'd walked a long way, because of the dreams. We'd been in the city for weeks, waiting for the Azath to choose someone. But I wasn't the same as the five others, though we were here for the same reason, and we'd travelled together. They were Nerek witches, and they'd prepared me. The me on the outside, not the me all wrapped up.'

'The you on the outside, Kettle, were you a child?'

'Oh no. I was tall. Not as tall as you. And I had to wear my hood up, so no-one could see how different I was. I'd come from very far away. I'd walked, when I was young, hot sands – the sands that covered the First Empire. Whatever that is.'

'What did the Nerek witches call you? Had you a name?'

'No.'

'A title?'

She shrugged. 'I'd forgotten all this. They called me the Nameless One. Is this important?'

'I think it is, Kettle. Although I am not sure in what way. Much of this realm remains unknown to me. It was very young when I was imprisoned. You are certain this "Nameless One" was an actual title? Not just something the Nerek used because they didn't know your true name?'

'It was a title. They said I'd been prepared from birth. That I was a true child of Eres. And that I was the answer to the Seventh Closure, because I had the blood of kin. "The blood of kin". What did they mean by that?'

'When I am finally free,' he said in a voice revealing strain, 'I will be able to physically touch you, Kettle. My fingers upon your brow. And then I will have your answer.'

'I guess this Eres was my real mother.'

'Yes.'

'And soon you will know who my father is.'

'I will know his blood, yes. At the very least.'

'I wonder if he's still alive.'

'Knowing how Eres plays the game, lass, he might not even be your father yet. She wanders time, Kettle, in a manner no-one else can even understand, much less emulate. And this is very much her world. She is the fire that never dies.' He paused, then said, 'She will choose – or has chosen – with great deliberation. Your father was, is, or will be someone of great importance.'

'So how many souls are in me?'

'Two, sharing the flesh and bone of a child corpse. Lass, we shall have to find a way to get you out of that body, eventually.'

'Why?'

'Because you deserve something better.'

'I want to go back. Will you take me back now?'

'I've given up on the eel itself,' Bugg said, ladling out the soup. 'It's still too tough.'

'None the less, my dear manservant, it smells wonderful.'

'That would be the wine. Courtesy of Chief Investigator Rucket, whose request for a meeting with you was for purposes not entirely professional.'

'And how did you fare on my behalf?'

'I ensured that her interest in you only deepened, master.'

'By way of contrast?'

'Indeed.'

'Well, is that a good thing? I mean, she's rather frightening.'

'You don't know the half of it. Even so, she is exceptionally clever.'

'Oh, I don't like that at all, Bugg. You know, I am tasting something fishy. A hint, anyway. Just how dried up was this eel you found?'

The manservant probed with his ladle and lifted the mentioned object into view. Black, wrinkled and not nearly as limp as it should have been.

Tehol leaned closer and studied it for a moment. 'Bugg . . .'

'Yes, master?'

'That's the sole of a sandal.'

'It is? Oh. I was wondering why it was flatter at one end than the other.'

Tehol settled back and took another sip. 'Still fishy, though. One might assume the wearer, being in the fish market, stepped on an eel, before the loss of his or her sole.'

'I am mildly disturbed by the thought of what else he or she might have stepped in.'

'There are indeed complexities on the palate, suggesting a varied and lengthy history. Now, how was your day and the subsequent evening?'

'Uneventful. Rucket informs me that Gerun Eberict has killed about three thousand citizens this year.'

'Three thousand? That seems somewhat excessive.'

'I thought so, too, master. More soup?'

'Yes, thank you. So, what is his problem, do you think?'

'Gerun's? A taste for blood, I'd wager.'

'As simple as that? How egregious. We'll have to do something about it, I think.'

'And how was your day and evening, master?'

'Busy. Exhausting, even.'

'You were on the roof?'

'Yes, mostly. Although, as I recall, I came down here once. Can't remember why. Or, rather, I couldn't at the time, so I went back up.'

Bugg tilted his head. 'Someone's approaching our door.'

The sound of boots in the alley, the faint whisper of armour.

'My brother, I'd hazard,' Tehol said, then, turning to face the curtained doorway, he raised his voice. 'Brys, do come in.'

The hanging was pulled aside and Brys entered. 'Well, that is an interesting smell,' he said.

'Sole soup,' Tehol said. 'Would you like some?'

'No, thank you. I have already eaten, it being well after the second bell. I trust you have heard the rumours.'

'The war?'

'Yes.'

543

'I've heard hardly a thing,' Tehol said.

Brys hesitated, glancing at Bugg, then he sighed. 'A new emperor has emerged to lead the Tiste Edur. Tehol, Hull has sworn his allegiance to him.'

'Now, that is indeed unfortunate.'

'Accordingly, you are at risk.'

'Arrest?'

'No, more likely assassination. All in the name of patriotism.'

Tehol set his bowl down. 'It occurs to me, Brys, that you are more at risk than I am.'

'I am well guarded, brother, whilst you are not.'

'Nonsense! I have Bugg!'

The manservant looked up at Brys with a bland smile.

'Tehol, this is not time for jokes—'

'Bugg resents that!'

'I do?'

'Well, don't you? I would, if I were you—'

'It seems you just were.'

'My apologies for making you speak out of turn, then.'

'Speaking on your behalf, master, I accept.'

'You are filled with relief—'

'Will you two stop it!' Brys shouted, throwing up his hands. He began pacing the small confines of the room. 'The threat is very real. Agents of the queen will not hesitate. You are both in very grave danger.'

'But how will killing me change the fact of Hull forsaking our homeland?'

'It won't, of course. But your history, Tehol, makes you a hated man. The queen's investments suffered thanks to you, and she's not the type to forgive and forget.'

'Well, what do you suggest, Brys?'

'Stop sleeping on your roof, for one. Let me hire a few bodyguards—'

'A few? How many are you thinking?'

'Four, at least.'

'One.'

544

'One?'

'One. No more than that. You know how I dislike crowds, Brys.'

'Crowds? You've never disliked crowds, Tehol.'

'I do now.'

Brys glowered, then sighed. 'All right. One.'

'And that will make you happy, then? Excellent—'

'No more sleeping on your roof.'

'I'm afraid, brother, that won't be possible.'

'Why not?'

Tehol gestured. 'Look at this place! It's a mess! Besides, Bugg snores. And we're not talking mild snoring, either. Imagine being chained to the floor of a cave, with the tide crashing in, louder, louder, louder—'

'I have in mind three guards, all brothers,' Brys said, 'who can spell each other. One will therefore always be with you, even when you're sleeping on your roof.'

'So long as they don't snore—'

'They won't be asleep, Tehol! They'll be standing guard!'

'All right. Calm down. I am accepting, aren't I? Now, how about some soup, just to tide you over until you break your fast?'

Brys glanced at the pot. 'There's wine in it, isn't there?'

'Indeed. Only the best, at that.'

'Fine. Half a bowl.'

Tehol and Bugg exchanged pleased smiles.

CHAPTER FIFTEEN

Black glass stands between us
The thin face of otherness
Risen into difference
These sibling worlds
You cannot reach through
Or pierce this shade so distinct
As to make us unrecognizable
Even in reflection
The black glass stands
And that is more than all
And the between us
Gropes but never finds
Focus or even meaning
The between us is ever lost
In that barrier of darkness
When backs are turned
And we do little more than refuse
Facing ourselves.

Preface to *The Nerek Absolution*
Myrkas Preadict

Light and heat rose in waves from the rock, swirled remorselessly along the narrow track. The wraiths had fled to cracks and fissures and huddled there now, like bats awaiting dusk. Seren Pedac paused to await Buruk. She set her pack down, then tugged at the sweat-sodden, quilted padding beneath her armour, feeling it peel away from her back like skin. She was wearing less than half her kit, the rest strapped onto the pack, yet it still dragged at her after the long climb to the summit of the pass.

She could hear nothing from beyond the crest twenty paces behind her, and considered going back to check on her charge. Then, faintly, came a curse, then scrabbling sounds.

The poor man.

They had been hounded by the wraiths the entire way. The ghostly creatures made the very air agitated and restless. Sleep was difficult, and the constant motion flitting in their peripheral vision, the whispered rustling through their camps, left their nerves raw and exhausted.

She glared a moment at the midday sun, then wiped the gritty sweat from her brow and walked a few paces ahead on the trail. They were almost out of Edur territory. Another thousand paces. After that, another day's worth of descent to the river. Without the wagons, they would then be able to hire a river boat to take them the rest of the way down to Trate. Another day for that.

And then? Will he still hold me to the contract? It seemed pointless, and so she had assumed he would simply release her, at least for the duration of the war, and she would be free to journey back to Letheras. But Buruk the Pale had said nothing of that. In fact, he had not said much of anything since leaving the Hiroth village.

She turned as he clambered onto the summit's flat stretch. Clothed in dust and streaks of sweat, beneath them a deeply flushed face and neck. Seren walked back towards him. 'We will rest here for a time.'

He coughed, then asked, 'Why?' The word was a vicious growl.

'Because we need it, Buruk.'

'You don't. And why speak for me? I am fine, Acquitor. Just get us to the river.'

Her pack held both their possessions and supplies. She

547

had cut down a sapling and trimmed it to serve as a walking stick for him, and this was all he carried. His once fine clothes were ragged, the leggings torn by sharp rocks. He stood before her, wheezing, bent over and leaning heavily on the stick. 'I mean to rest, Buruk,' she said after a moment. 'You can do as you please.'

'I can't stand being watched!' the merchant suddenly shrieked. 'Always watching! Those damned shades! No more!' With that he stumbled past her on the trail.

Seren returned to her pack and slung it once more over her shoulders. One sentiment she could share with Buruk: the sooner this trip was over, the better. She set out in his wake.

A dozen paces along and she reached his side. Then was past.

By the time Seren arrived at the clearing where the borders had been agreed over a century ago, Buruk the Pale was once more out of sight somewhere back on the trail. She halted, flung down her pack, and walked over to the sheer wall of polished black stone, recalling when she had last touched that strange – and strangely welcoming – surface.

Some mysteries would not unravel, whilst others were peeled back by fraught circumstance or deadly design, to reveal mostly sordid truths.

She set her hands against the warm, glassy stone, and felt something like healing steal into her. Beyond, figures in ceaseless motion, paying no attention to her whatsoever. *Preferable to the endless spying of wraiths.* And this was as it had always been. Seren settled her forehead against the wall, closing her eyes.

And heard whispering.

A language kin to Tiste Edur. She struggled to translate. Then meaning was found.

'—*when he who commands cannot be assailed. Cannot be defeated.*'

'*And now he feeds on our rage. Our anguish.*'

'Of the three, one shall return. Our salvation—'

'Fool. From each death power burgeons anew. Victory is impossible.'

'There is no place for us. We but serve. We but bleed out terror and the annihilation begins—'

'Ours as well.'

'Yes, ours as well.'

'Do you think she will come again? Does anyone think she will come again? She will, I am certain of it. With her bright sword. She is the rising sun and the rising sun ever comes, sending us scurrying, cutting us to pieces with that sharp, deadly light—'

'—annihilation well serves us. Make of us dead shards. To bring an end to this—'

'Someone is with us.'

'Who?'

'A mortal is here with us. Two Mistresses to the same Hold. She is one, and she is here. She is here now and she listens to our words.'

'Steal her mind!'

'Take her soul!'

'Let us out!'

Seren reeled away from the black wall. Staggered, hands to her ears, shaking her head. 'Enough,' she moaned. 'No more, please. No more.' She sank to her knees, was motionless as the voices faded, their screams dwindling. 'Mistress?' she whispered. *I am no-one's mistress. Just one more reluctant . . . lover of solitude. No place for voices, no place for hard purposes . . . fierce fires.*

Like Hull, only ashes. The smudged remnants of possibilities. But, unlike the man she had once thought to love, she had not knelt before a new icon to certainty. No choices to measure out like the soporific illusion of some drug, the consigning invitation to addiction. She wanted no new masters over her life. Nor the burden of friendships.

A croaking voice behind her. 'What's wrong with you?'

She shook her head. 'Nothing, Buruk.' She climbed wearily to her feet. 'We have reached the border.'

'I'm not blind, Acquitor.'

'We can move on a way, then make camp.'

'You think me weak, don't you?'

She glanced over at him. 'You are sick with exhaustion, Buruk. So am I. What point all this bravado?'

Sudden pain in his expression, then he turned away. 'I'll show you soon enough.'

'What of my contract?'

He did not face her. 'Done. Once we reach Trate. I absolve you of further responsibility.'

'So be it,' she said, walking to her pack.

They built a small fire with the last of their wood. The wraiths, it seemed, cared nothing for borders, flitting along the edges of the flickering light. A renewed interest, and Seren thought she knew why. The spirits within the stone wall. She was now marked.

Mistress of the Hold. Mistresses. There are two, and they think I am one of those two. A lie, a mistake.

Which Hold?

'You were young,' Buruk suddenly said, his eyes on the fire. 'When I first saw you.'

'And you were happy, Buruk. What of it?'

'Happiness. Ah, now that is a familiar mask. True, I wore it often, back then. Joyful in my spying, my unceasing betrayals, my deceits and the blood that appeared again and again on my hands.'

'What are you talking about?'

'My debts, Acquitor. Oh yes, outwardly I stand as a respected merchant . . . of middling wealth.'

'And what are you in truth?'

'It is where dreams fall away, Seren Pedac. That crumbling edifice where totters self-worth. You stand, too afraid to move, and watch your hands in motion, mangling every dream, every visage of the face you would desire, the true face of yourself, behind that mask. It is not helpful, speaking of truths.'

She thought for a time, then her eyes narrowed. 'You are being blackmailed.' He voiced no denial, so she continued, 'You are Indebted, aren't you?'

'Debts start small. Barely noticeable. Temporary. And so, in repayment, you are asked to do something. Something vile, a betrayal. And then, they have you. And you are indebted anew, in the maintenance of the secret, in your gratitude for not being exposed in your crime, which has since grown larger. As it always does, if you are in possession of a conscience.' He was silent a moment, then he sighed and said, 'I do envy those who have no conscience.'

'Can you not get out, Buruk?'

He would not look up from the flames. 'Of course I can,' he said easily.

That tone, so at odds with all else he had said, frightened her. 'Make yourself . . . un-useful, Buruk.'

'Indeed, that seems the way of it, Acquitor. And I am in a hurry to do just that.' He rose. 'Time to sleep. Downhill to the river, then we can trail our sore feet in the cool water, all the way to Trate.'

She remained awake for a while longer, too tired to think, too numb to feel fear.

Above the fire, sparks and stars swam without distinction.

Dusk the following day, the two travellers reached Kraig's Landing, to find its three ramshackle buildings surrounded by the tents of an encamped regiment. Soldiers were everywhere, and at the dock was tethered an ornate, luxuriously appointed barge above which drifted in the dull wind the king's banner, and directly beneath it on the spar the crest of the Ceda.

'There's a cadre here,' Buruk said as they strode down the trail towards the camp, which they would have to pass through to reach the hostel and dock.

She nodded. 'And the soldiers are here as escort. There can't have been engagements already, can there?'

He shrugged. 'At sea, maybe. The war is begun, I think.'

Seren reached out and halted Buruk. 'There, those three.'

The merchant grunted.

The three figures in question had emerged from the rows of tents, the soldiers nearby keeping their distance but fixing their attention on them as they gathered for a moment, about halfway between the two travellers and the camp.

'The one in blue – do you recognize her, Acquitor?'

She nodded. Nekal Bara, Trate's resident sorceress, whose power was a near rival to the Ceda's own. 'The man on her left, in the black furs, that's Arahathan, commander of the cadre in the Cold Clay Battalion. I don't know the third one.'

'Enedictal,' Buruk said. 'Arahathan's counterpart in the Snakebelt Battalion. We see before us the three most powerful mages of the north. They intend a ritual.'

She set off towards them.

'Acquitor! Don't!'

Ignoring Buruk, Seren unslung her pack and dropped it to the ground. She had caught the attention of the three mages. Visible in the gloom, Nekal Bara's mocking lift of the eyebrows.

'Acquitor Seren Pedac. The Errant smiles upon you indeed.'

'You're going to launch an attack,' Seren said. 'You mustn't.'

'We do not take orders from you,' Enedictal said in a growl.

'You're going to strike the villages, aren't you?'

'Only the ones closest to the borders,' Nekal Bara said, 'and those are far enough away to permit us a full unveiling – beyond those mountains, yes? If the Errant wills it, that's where the Edur armies will have already gathered.'

'We shall obliterate the smug bastards,' Enedictal said. 'And end this stupid war before it's begun.'

'There are children—'

'Too bad.'

Without another word the three mages moved to take positions, twenty paces distant from one another. They faced the slope of the trail, the rearing mountains before them.

'No!' Seren shouted.

Soldiers appeared, surrounding her, expressions dark and angry beneath the rim of their helms. One spoke. 'It's this, woman, or the fields of battle. Where people die. Make no move. Say nothing.'

Buruk the Pale arrived to stand nearby. 'Leave it be, Acquitor.'

She glared at him. 'You don't think he'll retaliate? He'll disperse the attack, Buruk. You know he will.'

'He may not have the time,' the merchant replied. 'Oh, perhaps his own village, but what of the others?'

A flash of light caught her attention and she turned to see that but one mage remained, Nekal Bara. Then Seren saw, two hundred paces distant, the figure of Enedictal. Twisting round, she could make out Arahathan, two hundred paces in the opposite direction. More flashes, and the two sorcerors reappeared again, double the distance from Nekal Bara.

'They're spreading out,' Buruk observed. 'This is going to be a big ritual.'

A soldier said, 'The Ceda himself is working tonight. Through these three here, and the rest of the cadre strung out another league in both directions. Four villages will soon be nothing but ashes.'

'This is a mistake,' Seren said.

Something was building between the motionless sorcerors. Blue and green light, ravelled taut, like lightning wound round an invisible rope linking the mages. The glow building like sea foam, a froth that began crackling, spitting drawn-out sparks that whipped like tendrils.

The sound became a hissing roar. The light grew blinding, the tendrils writhing out from the glowing foam. The twisting rope bucked and snapped between the stationary mages, reaching out past the three who were still visible, out beyond the hills to either side.

She watched the power burgeoning, the bucking frenzied, the tendrils whipping like the limbs of some giant, wave-thrashed anemone.

Darkness had been peeled back by the bristling energy, the shadows dancing wild.

A sudden shout.

The heaving chain sprang loose, the roar of its escape thundering in the ground beneath Seren's feet. Figures staggered as the wave launched skyward, obliterating the night. It crest was blinding green fire, the curving wall in its wake a luminescent ochre, webbed with foam in a stretching latticework.

The wall swallowed the north sky, and still the crest rose, power streaming upward. The grasses near the mages blackened, then spun into white ash on swirling winds.

Beneath the roar, a shriek, then screams. Seren saw a soldier stumbling forward, against the glowing wall at the base of the wave. It took him, stripped armour, clothes, then hair and skin, then, in a gush of blood, it devoured his flesh. Before the hapless figure could even crumple, the bones were plucked away, leaving naught but a single upright boot on the blistered ground in front of the foaming wall. The crimson blush shot upward, paling as it went. Until it was gone.

Air hissed past her, buffeting and bitter cold.

She sank down, the only response possible to fight that savage tugging, and dug her fingers into the stony ground. Others did the same around her, clawing in panic. Another soldier was dragged away, pulled shrieking into the wave.

The roaring snapped suddenly, like a breath caught in a throat, and Seren saw the base lift away, roll upward like a vast curtain, rising to reveal, once again, the battered slopes leading to the pass, then the pallid mountains and their blunt, ancient summits.

The wave swiftly dwindled as it soared northward, its wild light reflected momentarily in a patchwork cascade across reflective surfaces far below, sweeps of snow near the peaks and ice-polished stone blossoming sickly green and gold, as if awakened to an unexpected sunset.

Then the mountains were black silhouettes once more.

Beyond them, the wave, from horizon to horizon, was descending. Vanishing behind the range.

In the corner of her vision, Seren saw Nekal Bara slump to her knees.

Sudden light, across the rim of the world to the north, billowing like storm seas exploding against rock. The glow shot back into the night sky, this time in fiery arms and enormous, whipping tentacles.

She saw a strange ripple of grey against black on the facing mountainside, swiftly plunging.

Then comprehension struck her. 'Lie flat! Everyone! Down!'

The ripple struck the base of the slope. The few scraggly trees clinging to a nearby hillside toppled in unison, as if pushed over by a giant invisible hand.

The sound struck.

And broke around them, strangely muted.

Dazed, Seren lifted her head. Watched the shale tiles of an outlying building's roof dance away into the darkness. Watched as the north-facing wall tilted, then collapsed, taking the rest of the structure with it. She slowly climbed to her hands and knees.

Nekal Bara stood nearby, her hair and clothes untouched by the wind that raged on all sides.

Muddy rain sifted down through the strangely thick air. The stench of charred wood and the raw smell of cracked stone.

Beyond, the wind had died, and the rain pummelled the

ground. Darkness returned, and if fires still burned beyond the mountains, no sign was visible from this distance.

Buruk the Pale staggered to her side, his face splashed with mud. 'He did not block it, Acquitor!' he gasped. 'It is as I said: no time to prepare.'

A soldier shouted, 'Errant take us! Such power!'

There was good reason why Lether had never lost a war. Even the Onyx Wizards of Bluerose had been crushed by the cadres of the Ceda. Archpriests, shamans, witches and rogue sorcerors, none had ever managed to stand for long against such ferocity.

Seren felt sick inside. Sick, and bereft.

This is not war. This is . . . what? Errant save us, I have no answer, no way to describe the magnitude of this slaughter. It is mindless. Blasphemous. As if we have forgotten dignity. Theirs, our own. The word itself. No distinction between innocence and guilt, condemned by mere existence. People transformed against their will into nothing more than symbols, sketchy represent- ations, repositories of all ills, of all frustrations.

Is this what must be done? Take the enemy's flesh and fill it with diseases, corrupting and deadly to the touch, breath of poison? And that which is sick must be exterminated, lest it spread its contamination.

'I doubt,' Buruk said in an empty voice, 'there was time to suffer.'

True. Leave that to us.

There had been no defence. Hannan Mosag, Rhulad, the slave Udinaas and Feather Witch. Hull Beddict. The names skittered away in her mind, and she saw – with a sudden twisting of her insides that left her shocked – the face of Trull Sengar. *No. It was Hull I was thinking of. No. Why him?* 'But they're dead.'

'They're all dead,' Buruk said beside her. 'I need a drink.'

His hand plucked at her arm.

She did not move. 'There's nowhere to go.'

'Acquitor. The tavern beneath the hostel's built solid enough to withstand a siege. I'd imagine that's where those soldiers just went, to toast their lost comrades. Poor fools. The dead ones, I mean. Come on, Seren. I'm in the mood to spend coin.'

Blinking, she looked round. The mages were gone.

'It's raining, Acquitor. Let's go.'

His hand closed on her arm. She allowed him to drag her away.

'What's happened?'

'You're in shock, Acquitor. No surprise. Here, I've some tea for you, the captain's own. Enjoy the sunshine – it's been rare enough lately.'

The river's swift current pulled the barge along. Ahead, the sun was faintly copper, but the breeze sidling across the water's spinning surface was warm.

She took the cup from his hands.

'We'll be there by dusk,' Buruk said. 'Soon, we should be able to make out its skyline. Or at least the smoke.'

'The smoke,' she said. 'Yes, there will be that.'

'Think on it this way, Seren. You'll soon be free of me.'

'Not if there's not to be a war.'

'No. I intend to release you from your contract in any case.'

She looked over at him, struggled to focus. There had been a night. After the sorcerous assault. In the tavern. Boisterous soldiers. Scouting parties were to head north the next day – today. She was starting to recall details, the gleam of some strange excitement as lurid as the tavern's oil lamps. 'Why would you do that?'

'My need for you is ended, Acquitor.'

'Presumably, the Edur will sue for peace. If anything, Buruk, you will find yourself far busier than ever.' She sipped the tea.

He nodded, slowly, and she sensed from him a kind of resignation.

'Oh,' she said, 'I'd forgotten. You must needs make yourself of no use.'

'Indeed. My days as a spy are over, Acquitor.'

'You will be the better for it, Buruk.'

'Assuredly.'

'Will you stay in Trate?'

'Oh yes. It is my home, after all. I intend never to leave Trate.'

Seren drank her tea. Mint, and something else that thickened her tongue. Flowed turgid and cloying through her thoughts. 'You have poisoned this tea, Buruk.' The words slurred.

'Had to, Seren Pedac. Since last night. I can't have you thinking clearly. Not right now. You'll sleep again. One of the dockhands will waken you tonight – I will make sure of that, and that you're safe.'

'Is this another . . . another betrayal?' She felt herself sagging on the bench.

'My last, dear. Remember this, if you can: I didn't want your help.'

'My . . . help.'

'Although,' he added from a great distance, 'you have always held my heart.'

Fierce pain behind her eyes. She blinked them open. It was night. A robe covered her, tucked up round her chin. The slow rise and fall beneath her and the faint creaks told her she was still aboard the barge, which was now tied up alongside a stone pier. Groaning, she sat up.

Scuffling sounds beside her, then a tankard was hovering before her face. 'Drink this, lass.'

She did not recognize the voice, but pushed the tankard away.

'No, it's all right,' the man insisted. 'Just ale. Clean, cool ale. To take the ache from your head. He said you'd be hurting, you see. And ale's always done it for me, when I done and drunk too much.'

'I wasn't drunk—'

'No matter, you wasn't sleeping a natural sleep. It ain't

558

no different, you see? Come now, lass, I need to get you up and around. It's my wife, you see, she's poorly. We're past the third bell an' I don't like leaving her too long alone. But he paid me good. Errant knows, more than an honest man makes in a year. Jus' to sit with you, you see. See you're safe an' up and walking.'

She struggled to her feet, clutching at and missing the cloak as it slipped down to her feet.

The dockhand, a bent, wizened old man, set the tankard down and collected it. 'Turn now, lass. I got the clasps. There's a chill this night – you're shivering. Turn now, yes, good, that's it.'

'Thank you.' The weight of the cloak pulled at her neck muscles and shoulders, making the pain in her head throb.

'I had a daughter, once. A noble took her. Debts, you see. Maybe she's alive, maybe she isn't. He went through lasses, that one. Back in Letheras. We couldn't stay there, you see, not after that. Chance t'see her, or a body turning up, like they do. Anyway, she was tall like you, that's all. Here, have some ale.'

She accepted the tankard, drank down three quick mouthfuls.

'There, better now.'

'I have to go. So do you, to your wife.'

'Well enough, lass. Can you walk?'

'Where's my pack?'

'He took it with him, said you could collect it. In the shed behind his house. He was specific 'bout that. The shed. Don't go in the house, he said. Very specific—'

She swung to the ladder. 'Help me.'

Rough hands under her arms, moving down to her behind as she climbed, then her thighs. 'Best I can do, lass,' came a gasp below her as she moved beyond his reach. She clambered onto the pier.

'Thank you, sir,' she said.

The city was quiet, barring a pair of dogs scrapping some-where behind a warehouse. Seren stumbled on occasion as she hurried down the streets. But, true to the dockhand's word, the ale dulled the pain behind her eyes. Made her thoughts all too clear.

She reached Buruk the Pale's home, an old but well-maintained house halfway down a row on the street just in from the riverside warehouses.

No lights showed behind the shuttered windows.

Seren climbed the steps and drove her boot against the door.

Four kicks and the locks broke. By this time, neighbours had awakened. There were shouts, calls for the guard. Somewhere down the row a bell began ringing.

She followed the collapsing door into the cloakroom beyond. No servants, no sound from within. Into the dark hallway, ascending the stairs to the next level. Another hallway, step by step closing in on the door to Buruk's bedroom. Through the doorway. Inside.

Where he hung beneath a crossbeam, face bloated in the shadows. A toppled chair off to one side, up against the narrow bed.

A scream, filled with rage, tore loose from Seren's throat.

Below, boots on the stairs.

She screamed again, the sound falling away to a hoarse sob.

You have always held my heart.

Smoke rising in broad plumes, only to fall back and unfold like a grey cloak over the lands to the north. Obscuring all, hiding nothing.

Hanradi Khalag's weathered face was set, expressionless, as he stared at the distant devastation. Beside the chief of the Merude, Trull Sengar remained silent, wondering why Hanradi had joined him at this moment, when the mass of warriors were in the midst of breaking camp on the forested slopes all around them.

'Hull Beddict spoke true,' the chief said in his raspy voice. 'They would strike pre-emptively. Beneda, Hiroth and Arapay villages.'

A night of red fires filling the north. At least four villages, and among them Trull's own. Destroyed.

He swung round to study the slopes. Seething with warriors, Edur women and their slaves, elders and children. *No going back, now. The Letherii sorcery has obliterated our homes . . . but those homes were empty, the villages left to the crows.*

And a handful of hapless Nerek.

Nothing but ashes, now.

'Trull Sengar,' Hanradi Khalag said, 'our allies arrived last night. Three thousand. You were seen. It seems they know you well, if only by reputation. The sons of Tomad Sengar, but you especially. The one who leads them is called the Dominant. A hulk of a man, even for one of his kind. More grey than black in his mane. He is named B'nagga—'

'This does not interest me, Chief,' Trull cut in. 'They have been as sorely used as we have, and that use is far from over. I do not know this B'nagga.'

'As I said, he knows you, and would speak with you.'

Trull turned away.

'You had best accept the truth of things, Trull Sengar—'

'One day I will know your mind, Hanradi Khalag. The self you hide so well. Hannan Mosag bent you to his will. And now you kneel before my brother, the emperor. The usurper. Is this what the unification of the tribes was intended to mean? Is this the future you desired?'

'Usurper. Words like that will see you killed or cast out.'

Trull grunted. 'Rhulad is with the western army—'

'But the wraiths now serve him.'

'Ah, and we are to have spies among us now? An emperor who fears his own. An emperor who would be immune to criticism. Someone must speak in the name of reason.'

'Speak no more of this. Not to me. I reject all you say. You are being foolish, Trull Sengar. Foolish. Your anger is born of envy. No more.' He turned and walked back down

561

the narrow track, leaving Trull alone once again on the precipice rising above the valleys of the pass. It did not occur to him to see if Hanradi had indeed lost his shadow.

A precipice. Where he could look down and watch the thousands swarm among the trees.

Three land armies and four fleets held, divided among them, the entire population of the Tiste Edur. This camp before him was a league wide and two leagues deep. Trull had never seen so many Edur gathered in one place. Hiroth, Arapay, Sollanta, Beneda.

He caught movement below, on the edge of Fear's command area, squat, fur-clad figures, and felt himself grow cold. *Our . . . allies.*

Jheck.

Summoned by the Edur they had killed. Worshippers of the sword.

The night just past, beginning at dusk, had vanished behind a nightmarish display of sorcery. Unimaginable powers unveiled by the Letherii mages, an expression of appalling brutality in its intent. This was clearly going to be a war where no quarter was given, where conquest and annihilation were, for the Letherii, synonymous. Trull wondered if Rhulad would answer in like manner.

Except we have no homes to return to. We are committed to occupation of the south. Of Lether. We cannot raze the cities . . . can we? He drew a deep breath. He needed to talk to Fear again. But his brother had plunged into his role as commander of this army. His lead elements, half a day ahead, would come within sight of High Fort. The army would cross the Katter River at the Narrow Chute, which was spanned by a stone bridge centuries old, then swing down to join those lead elements.

And there would be a battle.

For Fear, the time for questions was past.

But why can I not manage the same for myself? Certainty, even fatality, eluded Trull. His mind would not rest from its tortured thoughts, his worries of what awaited them.

He made his way down the track. The Jheck were there, a contingent present in Fear's command area. He was not required, he told himself, to speak to them.

Edur warriors readying armour and weapons on all sides. Women chanting protective wards to weave a net of invisibility about the entire encampment. Wraiths darting among the trees, most of them streaming southward, through the pass and into the southlands. Here and there, demonic conjurations towered, hulking and motionless along the many newly worn trails leading to the summit. They were in full armour of bronze scales, green with verdigris, with heavy helms, the cheek guards battered plates that reached down past the jawlines, their faces hidden. Polearms, glaives, double-edged axes and maces, an array of mêlée weapons. Once, not so long ago, such summoned demons had been rare, the ritual – conducted by women – one of cajoling, false promises and final deception. The creatures were bound, now doomed to fight a war not of their making, where the only release was annihilation. They numbered in the high hundreds in this, Fear's army. The truth of that sickened him.

Helping with the striking of tents, children. Torn from their familiar world, subject to a new shaping. If this gambit failed . . .

Fear was standing near the remnants of a hearth from which smoke rose in a low wreath about his legs. Flanked by the two K'risnan the emperor had attached to this force. Hanradi Khalag stood off to one side.

A Jheck was approaching, probably the one the Merude chief had spoken of, given the wild iron-streaked, tangled head of hair, the flattened, seamed face displaying countless battle-scars. Various shells dangled from knotted strips hanging on his sleeveless sealskin shirt. Other small trophies depended from a narrow belt beneath the man's round paunch – pieces of Edur armour, jewellery. A bold reminder of past enmity.

What had Hanradi called him? The Dominant. B'nagga.

The Jheck's eyes were yellow, the whites dull grey and embryonic with blue vessels. They looked half mad.

Filed teeth flashed in a fierce smile. 'See who comes, Fear Sengar!' The accent was awkward behind the Arapay intonations. 'The one we could not defeat!'

Trull scowled as his brother turned to watch him approach. To the Dominant, he said, 'You'll find no fields of ice to the south, Jheck.'

'Mange and moult, Slayer. No other enemy gives us such terror.' His broadening smile underscored the irony of his words. 'Fear Sengar, your brother is worthy of much pride. Again and again, my hunters sought to best this warrior in individual combat. Veered or sembled, it mattered not. He defeated them all. Never before have we witnessed such skill, such ferocity.'

'Among all who I trained, B'nagga,' Fear said, 'Trull was and remains the finest.'

Trull started, then his scowl deepened with disbelief. 'Enough of this. Fear, has our emperor spoken to us through the wraiths? Does he voice his satisfaction at the failed attempt by the Letherii? Does he spit with rage?'

One of the K'risnan spoke. 'Not a single Edur was lost, Trull Sengar. For that, we have Hull Beddict to thank.'

'Ah yes, the traitor. And what of the Nerek camped in our village?'

The warlock shrugged. 'We could not command them.'

'Relinquish your anger, brother,' Fear said. 'The devastation was wrought by the Letherii, not us.'

'True. And now it is our turn.'

'Yes. The wraiths have reported an army ascending to the pass.'

Ah, no. So soon.

B'nagga laughed. 'Do we ambush them? Shall I send my wolves forward?'

'They are not yet at the bridge,' Fear replied. 'I expect they will seek to contest that crossing should we fail to reach it before them. For the moment, however, they are in a slow-march, and, it seems, not expecting much opposition.'

'That much is clear,' Hanradi said. 'What commander would seek an engagement against an enemy upslope? This is a probe. At first contact they will withdraw. Back to High Fort. Fear, we should bloody them all the way.'

'B'nagga, send half your force forward. Observe the enemy, but remain unseen.'

The K'risnan who had spoken earlier said, 'Fear, there will be a mage cadre attached to the army.'

Fear nodded. 'Withdraw the wraiths barring a dozen or so. I would convey the belief that those few are but residents of the area. The enemy must remain unsuspecting. Hanradi Khalag, our warriors must be made ready to march. You will lead them.'

'We shall be under way before mid-morning.'

Trull watched the Merude chief walk away, then said, 'Those Letherii mages will prove troublesome.'

The K'risnan grunted. 'Trull Sengar, we are their match.'

He looked at the two warlocks. Chiefs' sons. Of Rhulad's age.

The K'risnan's smile was knowing. 'We are linked to Hannan Mosag, and through him to the emperor himself. Trull Sengar, the power we now call upon is more vast, and deadlier, than any the Edur have known before.'

'And that does not concern you? What is the aspect of this power? Do you even know? Does Hannan Mosag know? Rhulad?'

'The power comes to the emperor through the sword,' the K'risnan said.

'That is no answer—'

'Trull!' Fear snapped. 'No more. I have asked that you assemble a unit from our village. Have you done so?'

'Yes, brother. Fifty warriors, half of them unblooded, as you commanded.'

'And have you created squads and chosen your officers?'

Trull nodded.

'Lead them to the bridge. Take advance positions on the other side and wait until Hanradi's forces reach you – it should not be a long wait.'

'And if the Letherii have sent scouts ahead and they arrive first?'

'Gauge their strength and act accordingly. But Trull, no last stands. A skirmish will suffice to hold up the enemy's advance, particularly if they are uncertain as to your strength. Now, gather your warriors and be off.'

'Very well.'

There was no point in arguing any further, he told himself as he made his way to where his company waited. No-one wanted to listen. Independent thought had been relinquished, with appalling eagerness, it seemed to him, and in its place had risen a stolid resolve to question nothing. Worse, Trull found he could not help himself. Even as he saw the anger grow in the faces of those around him – anger that he dare challenge, that he dare think in ways contrary to theirs, and so threaten their certainty – he was unable to stay silent.

Momentum was building all around him, and the stronger it grew, the more he resisted it. In a way, he suspected, he was becoming as reactionary as they were, driven into extreme opposition, and though he struggled against this dogmatic obstinacy it was a battle he sensed he was losing.

There was nothing of value in such opposed positions of thought. And no possible conclusion but his own isolation and, eventually, the loss of trust.

His warriors were waiting, gear packed, armour donned. Trull knew them all by name, and had endeavoured to achieve a balanced force, not just in skill but in attitude. Accordingly, he knew many of them resented being under his command, for his dissatisfaction with this war was well known. None the less, he knew they would follow him.

There were no nobles among them.

Trull joined the warrior he had chosen as his captain.

566

Ahlrada Ahn had trained alongside Trull, specializing in the Merude cutlass as his preferred weapon. He was left-handed, rare among the Edur, yet used his other hand to wield a short, wide-bladed knife for close fighting. The bell-hilt of his cutlass sprouted a profusion of quillons designed to trap opposing sword-blades and spear-shafts, and his ceaseless exercises concentrating on that tactic had made his left wrist almost twice the bulk of its opposite. Trull had seen more than one of his practice spears snap at a shoulder-wrenching twist from Ahlrada's sword-arm.

The warrior also hated him, for reasons Trull had yet to fathom. Although now, he amended, Ahlrada had probably found a new reason.

'Captain.'

The dark eyes would not meet his. They never did. Ahlrada's skin was darker than any other Edur Trull had seen. There were colourless streaks in his long, unbound hair. Shadow wraiths swarmed round him – another strange detail unique to the warrior. 'Leader,' he replied.

'Inform the sergeants, we're heading out. Minimum kits – we need to travel quickly.'

'Already done. We were waiting for you.'

Trull walked over to his own gear, shouldered the small leather pack, then selected four spears from his cache. Whatever was left behind would be collected by the Letherii slaves and carried with the main body as it made its cautious way south in the wake of Trull's company and Hanradi's forces.

When he turned, he saw that the company were on their feet, all eyes fixed on him. 'We must needs run, warriors. The south end of the bridge. Once through the pass, each squad sends out a point and makes its own way off-trail down to the bridge. Thus, you must be both swift and silent.'

A sergeant spoke. 'Leader, if we leave the trail we are slowed.'

'Then we had best get moving.'

'Leader,' the sergeant persisted, 'we will lose speed—'

'I do not trust the trail beyond the pass, Canarth. Now, move out.' In his head he cursed himself. A leader need not give reasons. The command was sufficient. Nor, he silently added, was a sergeant expected to voice public challenge. This was not beginning well.

One squad in the lead, followed by Trull, then the remaining squads with Ahlrada taking up the rear, the company set out for the pass at a steady run. They quickly left the camp behind. Then, through an avenue provided them, they swept past Hanradi Khalag's forces.

Trull found pleasure, and relief, in the pace they set. The mind could vanish in the steady rhythm, and the forest slid past with each stride, the trees growing more stunted and thinner on the ground the closer they approached the summit, while overhead the sun climbed a cloudless sky.

Shortly before mid-morning they halted on the south end of the pass. Trull was pleased to see that none of his warriors was short of breath, instead drawing long, deep lungfuls to slow their hearts. The exertion and the heat left them, one and all, sheathed in sweat. They drank a little water, then ate a small meal of dried salmon and thin bread wrapped round pine nut paste.

Rested and fed, the warriors formed up into their squads, then, without another word, headed into the sparse forest to either side of the trail.

Trull elected to accompany the squad led by Canarth. They headed into the forest on the trail's west side, then began the slow, silent descent, staying thirty or so paces from the main path. Another squad was further west, fifteen paces distant, whilst the third trailed midway between them and thirty paces back. An identical pattern had been formed on the eastern side.

Sergeant Canarth made his disapproval plain, constantly edging ahead until he was almost on the heels of the warrior at point. Trull thought to gesture him back but Canarth was ignoring him as if he was not there.

Then, halfway down the slope, the point halted and crouched low, one hand reaching back to stop Canarth.

Trull and the others also ceased moving. The forest had thickened during the descent, an army of blackened pine boles blocking line of sight beyond fifteen paces. There was little undergrowth, but the slope was uneven and treacherous with moss-coated boulders and rotting tree-falls. A glance to his right showed the nearest warrior of the flanking squad a half-dozen paces further down, but now also halted, one hand raised, his gaze fixed on Trull.

Ahead, the point was whispering to Canarth. After a moment, the sergeant reversed direction and made his way cautiously back to where Trull and the others waited.

'There is a scout on the edge of the main trail. Faraed, likely serving with the Letherii army. He has a good line of sight on the trail itself, maybe seventy-five or more paces.'

Trull looked back at the rest of the squad. He singled one warrior out and beckoned him closer. 'Badar, go back to the third squad. They are to choose a warrior to head upslope a hundred and twenty paces, then cut in to the main path. He is then to make his way down, as if on point. Once you have delivered the message, return to us.'

Badar nodded and slipped away.

'What of us?' Canarth asked.

'We wait, then join the squad to our west. Make our way down below the scout's position, and lay our own trap.'

'What of the squads to the east of the trail?'

A good question. He had split his forces with no way of communicating with half his company. A mistake. 'We had best hope they too have seen the scout. And will have rightly judged that a Faraed is virtually impossible to sneak up on.'

The sergeant simply nodded. He did not need to point out Trull's error. Nor, it was evident, his own.

We even out. Fair enough.

A short time later Badar returned and gave them a perfunctory nod. Trull gestured the squad to follow and struck out westward to join the outlying warriors.

Once there, he quickly related his plan and the fifteen warriors set off downslope.

They descended sixty paces before Trull waved them towards the main path. The position they reached was directly below a crook in the trail. He had his warriors draw and ready weapons.

Canarth gestured. 'Across from us, Leader. Rethal's squad. They have anticipated you.'

Trull nodded. 'Into position. We'll take him when he comes opposite us.'

Heartbeats. The sun's heat bouncing from the gravel and dust of the trail. Insects buzzing past.

Then, light thumping, the sound swiftly growing. Suddenly upon them.

The Faraed was a blur, plunging round the bend in the trail then flashing past.

Spears darted out shin-high to trip him up.

The scout leapt them.

A curse, then a shaft raced past Trull, the iron head crunching into the Faraed's back, between the shoulder blades. Snapping through the spine. The scout sprawled, then tumbled, limbs flopping, and came to a rest ten paces down the path.

Settling dust. Silence.

Trull made his way down to where the body lay in a twisted heap. The scout, he saw, was a boy. Fourteen, fifteen years of age. His smeared face held an expression of surprise, filling the eyes. The mouth was a grimace of terror. 'We killed a child.'

'An enemy,' Canarth said beside him. 'It is the Letherii you must look to, Leader. They throw children into this war.' He turned to face uptrail. 'Well thrown, Badar. You are now blooded.'

Badar scrambled down and retrieved his spear.

The third squad appeared at the crook. One of them spoke. 'I never even saw him.'

'Our first kill, Leader,' Ahlrada Ahn said.

Trull felt sick. 'Drag the body from the trail, Sergeant Canarth. Cover this blood with dust. We must move on.'

The bridge was not a bridge at all. Trull had visited it once before, and left with naught but questions. Constructed, it seemed, from a single massive disc, notched in rows across its rim, which was broad enough to permit eight warriors to stride across it without shoulders touching. The disc was on end, filling the gap of the deep gorge below which roared the Katter River. The base of the wheel was lost in the chute's darkness and the mist rising ceaselessly from the rushing water. To cross to the other side, one had to walk that curved, slick rim. The hub of the enormous wheel was visible, at least three man-lengths down. Thigh-thick rods of polished stone, spear-shaft straight, angled out from a projection on the hub on both sides, appearing to plunge into the rock wall of the gorge's south side.

The squads gathered on the north edge, scanning the treeline opposite. Two of the Edur had already crossed, one returning to report back. No signs of scouts, no evidence of recent camps. The lone Faraed they had killed seemed to have been sent far in advance of the main forces, or had taken upon himself the task of a deep mission. His courage and his intelligence had cost him his life.

Trull approached the very edge of the wheel, where the angle of the stone first emerged from the surrounding rock. As before, he saw a thin, milky film between that carved perfection and the rough rock of the precipice. As he had done once before, long ago, he wiped that foam away with a finger, to reveal the straight line, too narrow to slip a dagger blade into, that separated the construct from the raw stone. A disc in truth, somehow set into the notch of the gorge.

And, even stranger, the disc moved. Incrementally turning in place. At the moment, it was midway along one of the shallow grooves carved in parallel rows across the rim.

He knew he could set his feet on that first notch, and halt. And, had he the patience, he would eventually – days, maybe a week, maybe more – find himself stepping off onto the south side of the gorge.

A mystery without an answer. Trull suspected it was never intended as a bridge. Rather, it had been built for some other purpose. It did not make sense to him that it functioned solely as what had immediately occurred to him the first time he had visited. There were, after all, easier ways to measure the passage of time.

Trull straightened, then waved his warriors across.

Ahlrada took the lead.

They reached the other side and fanned out, seeking cover. The ground resumed its downward slope, amidst boulders, pines and straggly oaks. They would cautiously move down in a few moments, to search for defensible positions that permitted a line of sight down the trail.

Trull crouched near Ahlrada, scanning the area ahead, when he heard the warrior grunt, then step away, swearing under his breath.

'What's wrong, Captain?'

'I felt it . . . move. Here.'

Trull edged over, and saw that Ahlrada's original position had been on a slightly curved panel of stone, set lower than the surrounding rock. It was covered in dust and gravel, but looked too smooth to be natural. He reached down and brushed the panel clear.

And saw arcane symbols carved into the stone, row upon row, the language unknown to him. Deeply delineated grooves formed an incomplete box around the writing, the base and side lines visible. Beneath the base a new row of lettering was just beginning to show.

Trull glanced back at the bridge, then back at the recessed panel. 'It moved?'

'Yes, I am certain of it,' Ahlrada said. 'Not much, but yes.'

'Was there a sound?'

'More felt than heard, Leader. As if something huge and buried was . . . shifting.'

Trull stared down at the panel, running his fingers along the lettering. 'Do you recognize the language?'

Ahlrada shrugged and looked away. 'We should head down, Leader.'

'You have seen such writing before.'

'Not in . . . stone. In ice. It doesn't matter.'

'Ice?'

'I once lived and hunted with the Den-Ratha, on the north coast. North and east, deep into the ice seas. Before the unification. There was a wall, covered in such writing, a berg that blocked our way. Twenty man-heights high, half a league wide. But it sank into the sea – it was gone the next season.'

Trull knew that Ahlrada had, like Binadas, journeyed far and wide, had fashioned blood-bound kinships with many Edur from rival tribes. And, like Trull himself, had opposed the wars of subjugation conducted by Hannan Mosag. By all counts, he realized, they should be friends. 'What did your Den-Ratha comrades say about it?'

'The Tusked Man wrote them, they said.' He shrugged again. 'It is nothing. A myth.'

'A man with tusks?'

'He has been . . . seen. Over generations, sightings every now and then. Skin of green or grey. Tusks white as whale-bone. Always to the north, standing on snow or ice. Leader, this is not the time.'

Trull sighed, then said, 'Send the squads down.'

A short time later Canarth reported that he smelled rotting meat.

But it was only a dead owl, lying beside the trail.

There were dark times for the Letherii, so long ago now. The First Empire, from which vast fleets had sailed forth to map the world. The coasts of all six continents had been charted, eight hundred and eleven islands scattered in the vast oceans, ruins and riches discovered, ancient sorceries and fierce, ignorant tribes encountered. Other peoples, not human, all of whom bled easily enough. Barghast, Trell, Tartheno, Fenn, Mare, Jhag, Krinn, Jheck . . . Colonies had been established on foreign coasts. Wars and conquests, always conquests. Until . . . all was brought down, all was destroyed. The First Empire collapsed in upon itself. Beasts rose in the midst of its cities, a nightmare burgeoning like plague.

The Emperor who was One was now Seven, and the Seven were scattered, lost in madness. The great cities burned. And people died in the millions.

The nightmare had a name, and that name was T'lan Imass.

Two words, inspiring hatred and terror. But, beyond those two words, there was nothing. All memory of who or what the T'lan Imass had been was lost in the chaos that followed.

Few Letherii remained who were aware of even that much. True, they knew the name 'First Empire'. And they knew of the fall of that glorious civilization of so long ago, a civilization that was their legacy. And little else, barring the prophecy of rebirth.

Udinaas could no longer make that claim of blissful ignorance for himself. Within the world of ghosts and shades, the past lived on, breathed like a thing alive and ever restive. And voices haunted him, long dead voices. The Tiste Andii shade, Wither, was indifferent to the Letherii slave's own desires, his pleading for silence, for an end to the grisly cacophony of regrets which seemed to be all that held ghosts together.

Udinaas knew enough horror, here among the living. And the distilling of old truths was, as far as he was concerned, not worth it.

T'lan Imass.

T'lan Imass . . .

What did he care about some ancient nemesis?

Because the dust of over four thousand of them was beneath their feet at this moment. A truth riding Wither's raspy laughter.

'And that dust has eyes, slave. Should you fear? Probably

574

not. *They're not interested. Much. Not enough to rise up and slaughter you all, which they might not succeed in doing anyway. But, I tell you this, Udinaas, they would give it a good try.'*

'If they are dust,' Udinaas muttered, 'they cannot slaughter anyone.'

It was night. He sat with his back to a sloping rock face, on a ledge perched above the massive Edur encampment. The emperor had sent him off a short while ago. The hulking, gold-smeared bastard was in a foul mood. Wearied from dragging his bulk around, arguments with Hannan Mosag, the endless logistics of moving an army tens of thousands strong, families in tow. Not all was glory.

'The dust can rise, Udinaas. Can take shape. Warriors of bone and withered flesh, with swords of stone. Where are these ones from? Which warleader sent them here? They do not answer our questions. They never do. There are no bonecasters among them. They are, like us, lost.'

Udinaas was tired of listening. The wraith was worse than a burrowing tick, buried deep in his brain. He had begun to doubt its existence. More likely the product of madness, a persona invented in his own mind. An inventor of secrets, seeding armies of ghosts to explain the countless voices whispering in his skull. Of course, it would insist otherwise. It might even flit across his vision, creeping disembodied, the sourceless, inexplicably moving shadow where none belonged. But the slave knew his eyes could be deceived. All part of the same corrupted perception.

The wraith hides in the blood of the Wyval. The Wyval hides in the shadow of the wraith. A game of mutual negation. The emperor sensed nothing. Hannan Mosag and his K'risnan sensed nothing. Feather Witch, Mayen, Uruth, the host of bound wraiths, the hunting dogs, the birds and the buzzing insects – all sensed nothing.

And that was absurd.

As far as Udinaas was concerned, in any case – the judgement conjured by some rational, sceptical part of his brain, that knot of consciousness the wraith endlessly sought to unravel – Wither was not real.

Wyval blood. Sister of Dawn, the sword-wielding mistress known to the Edur as Menandore – her and the hungry place between her legs. Infection and something like rape. He thought he understood the connection now. He was indeed infected, and true to Feather Witch's prediction, that un-human blood was driving him mad. There had been no blazing white bitch who stole his seed. Fevered delusions, visions of self-aggrandizement, followed by the paranoid suspicion that the promised glory had been stolen from him.

Thus explaining his sordid state right now, slave to an insane Tiste Edur. A slave, huddled beneath every conceivable heel. Cowering and useless once all the internal posturing and self-justifications were cast away.

Feather Witch. He had loved her and he would never have her and that was that. The underscored truth laid bare, grisly exposure from which he withheld any direct, honest examination.

Madmen built houses of solid stone. Then circled looking for a way inside. Inside, where cosy perfection waited. People and schemes and outright lies barred his every effort, and that was the heart of the conspiracy. From outside, after all, the house looked real. Therefore it was real. Just a little more clawing at the stone door, a little more battering, one more pounding collision will burst that barrier.

And on and on and round and round. The worn ruts of madness.

He heard scrabbling on the stone below, and a moment later Feather Witch clambered into view. She pulled herself up beside him, her motions jerky, as if fevered.

'Is it my turn to run?' he asked.

'Take me there, Indebted. That dream realm. Where I found you before.'

'You were right all along,' Udinaas said. 'It doesn't exist.'

'I need to go there. I need to see for myself.'

'No. I don't know how.'

'Idiot. I can open the path. I'm good at opening paths.'

'Then what?'

'Then you choose. Udinaas, take me to the ghosts.'

'This is not a good place to do that—'

She had one hand clenched around something, and she now reached out and clutched his arm with that hand, and he felt the impression of a tile pressed between them.

And there was fire.

Blinding, raging on all sides.

Udinaas felt a weight push him from behind and he stumbled forward. Through the flames. In the world he had just left, he would now be falling down the cliffside, briefly, then striking the rocky slope and tumbling towards the treeline. But his moccasins skidded across flat, dusty ground.

Twisting, down onto one knee. Feather Witch staggered into view, like him passing unharmed through the wall of fire. He wheeled on her. *'What have you done?'*

A hand closed round the back of his neck, lifted him clear of the ground, then flung him down onto his back. The cold, ragged edge of a stone blade pressed against the side of his neck. He heard Feather Witch scream.

Blinking, in a cloud of dust.

A man stood above him. Short but a mass of muscles. Broad shoulders and overlong arms, the honey-coloured skin almost hairless. Long black hair hanging loose, surrounding a wide, heavily featured face. Dark eyes glittered from beneath a shelf-like brow. Furs hung in a roughly sewn cloak, a patchwork of tones and textures, the visible underside pale and wrinkled.

'Peth tol ool havra d ara.' The words were thick, the vocal range oddly truncated, as if the throat from which those sounds issued lacked the flexibility of a normal man's.

'I don't understand you,' Udinaas said. He sensed others

577

gathered round, and could hear Feather Witch cursing as she too was thrown to the ground.

'Arad havra'd ara. En'aralack havra d'drah.'

Countless scars. Evidence of a broken forearm, the bone unevenly mended and now knotted beneath muscle and skin. The man's left cheekbone was dimpled inward, his broad nose flattened and pressed to one side. None of the damage looked recent. 'I do not speak your language.'

The sword-edge lifted away from the slave's neck. The warrior stepped back and gestured.

Udinaas climbed to his feet.

More fur-clad figures.

A natural basin, steeply walled on three sides. Vertical cracks in the stone walls, some large enough to provide shelter. Where these people lived.

On the final side of the basin, to the Letherii's left, the land opened out. And in the distance – the slave's eyes widened – a shattered city. As if it had been pulled from the ground, roots and all, then broken into pieces. Timber framework beneath tilted, heaved cobble streets. Squat buildings pitched at random angles. Toppled columns, buildings torn in half with the rooms and floors inside revealed, many of those rooms still furnished. Vast chunks of rotting ice were visible in the midst of the broken cityscape.

'What place is this?' Feather Witch asked.

He turned to see her following his gaze from a few paces away.

'Udinaas, where have you brought us? Who are these savages?'

'Vis vol'raele absi'arad.'

He glanced at the warrior who'd spoken, then shrugged and returned his attention to the distant city. 'I want to go and look.'

'They won't let you.'

There was only one way to find out. Udinaas set out for the plain.

The warriors simply watched.

After a moment, Feather Witch followed, and came to his side. 'It looks as if it has just been ... left here. Dropped.'

'It is a Meckros city,' he said. 'The wood at the bases, it is the kind that never grows waterlogged. Never rots. And see there' – he pointed – 'those are the remnants of docks. Landings. That's a ship's rail, dangling from those lines. I've never seen a Meckros city, but I've heard enough descriptions, and this is one. Plucked from the sea. That ice came with it.'

'There are mounds, freshly raised,' she said. 'Do you see them?'

Raw, dark earth rising from the flats around the ruins, each barrow ringed in boulders. 'The savages buried the Meckros dead,' he said.

'There are hundreds ...'

'And every one big enough to hold hundreds of corpses.'

'They feared disease,' she said.

'Or, despite their appearance, they are a compassionate people.'

'Don't be a fool, Indebted. The task would have taken months.'

He hesitated, then said, 'That was but one clan, Feather Witch, back there. There are almost four thousand living in this region.'

She halted, grasped his arm and pulled him round. 'Explain this to me!' she hissed.

He twisted his arm loose and continued walking. 'These ghosts hold strong memories. Of their lives, of their flesh. Strong enough to manifest as real, physical creatures. They're called T'lan Imass—'

Her breath caught. 'The Beast Hold.'

He glanced at her. 'What?'

'The Bone Perch. Elder, Crone, Seer, Shaman, Hunter and Tracker. The Stealers of Fire. Stolen from the Eres'al.'

'Eres'al. That's the Nerek goddess. The false goddess, or

so claimed our scholars and mages, as justification for conquering the Nerek. I am shocked to discover the lie. In any case, aren't the images on the tiles those of beasts? For the Beast Hold, I mean.'

'Only among the poorer versions. The *skins* of beasts, draped round dark, squat savages. That is what you will see on the oldest, purest tiles. Do not pretend at ignorance, Udinaas. You brought us here, after all.'

They were approaching the nearest barrows, and could see, studding the raw earth, countless objects. Broken pottery, jewellery, iron weapons, gold, silver, small wooden idols, scraps of cloth. The remnant possessions of the people buried beneath.

Feather Witch made a sound that might have been a laugh. 'They left the treasure on the surfaces, instead of burying it with the bodies. What a strange thing to do.'

'Maybe so looters won't bother digging and disturbing the corpses.'

'Oh, plenty of looters around here.'

'I don't know this realm well enough to say either way,' Udinaas said, shrugging.

The look she cast him was uneasy.

Closer now, the destroyed city loomed before them. Crusted barnacles clinging to the bases of massive upright wooden pillars. Black, withered strips of seaweed. Above, the cross-sectioned profiles of framework and platforms supporting streets and buildings. And, in the massive chunks of grey, porous ice, swaths of rotting flesh – not human. Oversized limbs, clad in dull scales. A long, reptilian head, dangling from a twisted, torn neck. Entrails spilled from a split belly. Taloned, three-toed feet. Serrated tails. Misshapen armour and harnesses of leather, stretches of brightly coloured cloth, shiny as silk.

'What are those things?'

Udinaas shook his head. 'This city was struck by ice, even as it was torn from our world. Clearly, that ice held its own ancient secrets.'

'Why did you bring us here?'

He rounded on her, struggled to contain his anger, and managed to release it in a long sigh. Then he said, 'Feather Witch, what was the tile you held in your hand?'

'One of the Fulcra. Fire.' She faltered, then resumed. 'When I saw you, that first time, I lied when I said I saw nothing else. No-one.'

'You saw her, didn't you?'

'Sister Dawn . . . the flames—'

'And you saw what she did to me.'

'Yes.' A whisper.

Udinaas turned away. 'Not imagined, then,' he muttered. 'Not conjured by my imagination. Not . . . madness . . .'

'It is not fair. You, you're nothing. An Indebted. A slave. That Wyval was meant for me. Me, Udinaas!'

He flinched from her rage, even as understanding struck him. Forcing a bitter laugh. 'You summoned it, didn't you? The Wyval. You wanted its blood, and it had you, and so its poison should have infected you. But it didn't. Instead, it chose me. If I could, Feather Witch, I'd give it to you. With pleasure – no, that is not true, much as I'd like it to be. Be thankful that blood does not flow in your veins. It is in truth the curse you said it was.'

'Better to be cursed than—' She stopped, looked away.

He studied her pale face, and around it the blonde, crinkled hair shivering in the vague, near-lifeless wind. 'Than what, Feather Witch? A slave born of slaves. Doomed to listen to endless dreams of freedom – a word you do not understand, probably will never understand. The tiles were to be your way out, weren't they? Not taken in service to your fellow Letherii. But for yourself. You caught a whisper of freedom, didn't you, deep within those tiles? Or, something you *thought* was freedom. For what it is worth, Feather Witch, a curse is not freedom. Every path is a trap, a snare, to entangle you in the games of forces beyond all understanding. Those forces probably prefer

581

slaves when they use mortals, since slaves understand intrinsically the nature of the relationship imposed.'

She glared at him. 'Then why you?'

'And not you?' He looked away. 'Because I wasn't dreaming of freedom. Perhaps. Before I was a slave, I was Indebted – as you remind me at every opportunity. Debt fashions its own kind of slavery, Feather Witch, within a system designed to ensure few ever escape once those chains have closed round them.'

She lifted her hands and stared at them. 'Are we truly here? It all seems so real.'

'I doubt it,' Udinaas replied.

'We can't stay?'

'In the world of the tiles? You tell me, Feather Witch.'

'This isn't the realm of your dreaming, is it?'

He grimaced to hide his amusement at the unintended meaning behind her question. 'No. I did warn you.'

'I have been waiting for you to say that. Only not in such a tone of regret.'

'Expecting anger?'

She nodded.

'I had plenty of that,' he admitted. 'But it went away.'

'How? How do you make it go away?'

He met her eyes, then simply shook his head. A casual turning away, gaze once more upon the ruins. 'This destruction, this slaughter. A terrible thing to do.'

'Maybe they deserved it. Maybe they did something—'

'Feather Witch, the question of what is deserved should rarely, if ever, be asked. Asking it leads to deadly judgement, and acts of unmitigated evil. Atrocity revisited in the name of justice breeds its own atrocity. We Letherii are cursed enough with righteousness, without inviting yet more.'

'You live soft, Udinaas, in a very hard world.'

'I told you I was not without anger.'

'Which you bleed away, somehow, before it can hurt anyone else.'

'So I do all the bleeding, do I?'

582

She nodded. 'I'm afraid you do, Udinaas.'

He sighed and turned. 'Let's go back.'

Side by side, they made their way towards the waiting savages and their village of caves.

'Would that we could understand them,' Feather Witch said.

'Their shaman is dead.'

'Damn you, Udinaas!'

Into the basin, where something had changed. Four women had appeared, and with them was a young boy. Who was human.

The warrior who had spoken earlier now addressed the boy, and he replied in the same language, then looked over at Udinaas and Feather Witch. He pointed, then, with a frown, said, 'Letherii.'

'Do you understand me?' Udinaas asked.

'Some.'

'You are Meckros?'

'Some. Letherii Indebted. Indebted. Mother and father. They fled to live with Meckros. Live free, freedom. In freedom.'

Udinaas gestured towards the ruined city. 'Your home?'

'Some.' He took the hand of one of the women attending him. 'Here.'

'What is your name?'

'Rud Elalle.'

Udinaas glanced at Feather Witch. *Rud* meant *found* in the Meckros trade tongue. But, of course, he realized, she would not know that. 'Found Elalle,' he said in the traders' language, 'can you understand me better?'

The boy's face brightened. 'Yes! Good, yes! You are a sailor, like my father was. Yes.'

'These people rescued you from the city?'

'Yes. They are Bentract. Or were, whatever that means – do you know?'

He shook his head. 'Found, were there any other survivors?'

'No. All dead. Or dying, then dead.'

'And how did you survive?'

'I was playing. Then there were terrible noises, and screams, and the street lifted then broke, and my house was gone. I slid towards a big crack that was full of ice fangs. I was going to die. Like everyone else. Then I hit two legs. Standing, she was standing, as if the street was still level.'

'She?'

'This is traders' tongue, isn't it?' Feather Witch said. 'I'm starting to understand it – it's what you and Hulad use when together.'

'She was white fire,' the boy said. 'Tall, very very tall, and she reached down and picked me up.' He made a gesture to mime a hand gripping the collar of his weathered shirt. 'And she said: *Oh no he won't*. Then we were walking. In the air. Floating above everything until we all arrived here. And she was swearing. Swearing and swearing.'

'Did she say anything else, apart from swearing?'

'She said she worked hard on this beget, and that damned legless bastard wasn't going to ruin her plans. Not a chance, no, not a chance, and he'll pay for this. What's beget mean?'

'I thought so,' Feather Witch muttered in Letherii.

No.

'Remarkable eyes,' Feather Witch continued. 'Must be hers. Yours are much darker. Duller. But that mouth . . .'

No. 'Found,' Udinaas managed, 'how old are you?'

'I forget.'

'How old were you before the ice broke the city?'

'Seven.'

Triumphant, Udinaas spun to face Feather Witch.

'Seven,' the boy said again. 'Seven weeks. Mother kept saying I was growing too fast, so I must be tall for my age.'

Feather Witch's smile was strangely broken.

The Bentract warrior spoke again.

The boy nodded, and said, 'Ulshun Pral says he has a question he wants to ask you.'

A numbed reply. 'Go ahead.'

'Rae'd. Veb entara tog'rudd n'lan n'vis thal? List vah olar n'lan? Ste shabyn?'

'The women want to know if I will eat them when I get older. They want to know what dragons eat. They want to know if they should be afraid. I don't know what all that means.'

'How can they be eaten? They're—' Udinaas stopped. *Errant take me, they don't know they're dead!* 'Tell them not to worry, Found.'

'Ki'bri arasteshabyn bri por'tol tun logdara kul absi.'

'Ulshun Pral says they promised her to take care of me until she returns.'

'Entara tog'rudd av?'

The boy shook his head and replied in the warrior's language.

'What did he ask?' Udinaas demanded.

'Ulshun Pral wanted to know if you're my father. I told him my father's dead. I told him, no, you aren't. My father was Araq Elalle. He died.'

In Letherii, Feather Witch said, 'Tell him, Udinaas.'

'No. There's nothing to tell.'

'You would leave him to that . . . *woman?*'

He spun to face her. 'And what would you have me do? Take him with us? *We're not even here!* '

'T'un havra'ad eventara. T'un veb vol'raele bri rea han d En'ev?'

The boy said, 'Ulshun Pral is understanding you now. Some. He says there are holes and would you like to go there?'

'Holes?' Udinaas asked.

Feather Witch snorted. 'Gates. He means gates. I have been sensing them. There are gates, Udinaas. Powerful ones.'

'All right,' Udinaas said to Found.

'I don't like that place,' the boy said. 'But I will come with you. It's not far.'

They strode towards the mouth of one of the larger caves. Passed into the cool darkness, the rough floor sloping upward for twenty or so paces, then beginning to dip again. Into caverns with the walls crowded with painted images in red and yellow ochre, black outlines portraying ancient beasts standing or running, some falling with spears protruding from them. Further in, a smaller cavern with black stick-like efforts on the walls and ceiling, a struggling attempt by the T'lan Imass to paint their own forms. Blooms of red paint outlining ghostly hand-prints. Then the path narrowed and began a gradual ascent once more. Ahead, a vertical fissure from which light spilled inward, a light filled with flowing colours, as if some unearthly flame burned beyond.

They emerged onto an uneven but mostly level sweep of blackened bedrock. Small boulders set end to end formed an avenue of approach from the cave mouth that led them on an inward spiral towards the centre of the clearing. Beyond, the sky shimmered with swirling colours, like shattered rainbows. A cairn of flat stones dominated the centre of the spiral, in the rough, awkward form of a figure standing on two legs made of stacked stones, a single broad one forming the hips, the torso made of three more, the arms each a single projecting, rectangular stone out to the side, the head a single, oblong rock sheathed in lichen. The crude figure stood before a squat tower-like structure with at least twelve sides. The facings were smooth, burnished like the facets of natural crystal. Yet light in countless colours flared beneath each of those surfaces, each plane spiralling inward to a dark hole.

Udinaas could feel a pressure in the air, as of taut forces held in balance. The scene seemed perilously fragile.

'Vi han onralmashalle. S'ril k'ul havra En'ev. N'vist'. Lan'te.'

'Ulshun says his people came here with a bonecaster. It was a realm of storms. And beasts, countless beasts coming from those holes. They did not know what they were, but there was much fighting.'

The T'lan Imass warrior spoke again, at length.

'Their bonecaster realized that the breaches must be sealed, and so she drew upon the power of stone and earth, then rose into her new, eternal body to stand before the wounds. And hold all with stillness. She stands there now and she shall stand there for all time.'

'Yet her sacrifice has stranded the T'lan Imass here, hasn't it?' Udinaas asked.

'Yes. But Ulshun and his people are content.'

'Vi truh larpahal. Ranag, bhed, tenag tollarpahal. Kul havra thelar. Kul.'

'This land is a path, what we would call a road,' Found said, frowning as he struggled to make sense of Ulshun's words. 'Herds migrate, back and forth. They seem to come from nowhere, but they always come.'

Because, like the T'lan Imass themselves, they are ghost memories.

'The road leads here?' Feather Witch asked in halting traders' tongue.

'Yes,' Found said.

'And comes from where?'

'Epal en. Vol'sav, thelan.'

The boy sighed, crossed his arms in frustration. 'Ulshun says we are in an . . . overflow? Where the road comes from has bled out to claim the road itself. And surround this place. Beyond, there is . . . nothing. Oblivion. Unrealized.'

'So we are within a realm?' Feather Witch asked. 'Which Hold claims this place?'

'A evbrox'l list Tev. Starvald Demelain Tev.'

'Ulshun is pleased you understand Holds. He is bright-gem-eye. Pleased, and surprised. He calls this Hold Starvald Demelain.'

'I do not know that name,' she said, scowling.

The T'lan Imass spoke again, and in the words Udinaas

587

sensed a list. Then more lists, and in hearing the second list, he began to recognize names.

The boy shrugged. 'T'iam, Kalse, Silannah, Ampelas, Okaros, Karosis, Sorrit, Atrahal, Eloth, Anthras, Kessobahn, Alkend, Karatallid, Korbas . . . Olar. Eleint. Draconean. Dragons. The Pure Dragons. The place where the road comes from is closed. By the mixed bloods who gathered long ago. Draconus, K'rul, Anomandaris, Osserc, Silchas Ruin, Scabandari, Sheltatha Lore, Sukul Ankhadu and Menandore. It was, he says, Menandore who saved me.' The boy's eyes suddenly widened. 'She didn't look like a dragon!'

Ulshun spoke.

Found nodded. 'All right. He says you should be able to pass through from here. He looks forward to seeing you again. They will prepare a feast for you. Tenag calf. You are coming back, aren't you?'

'If we can,' Feather Witch said, then switched to Letherii. 'Aren't we, Udinaas?'

He scowled. 'How would I know?'

'Be gracious.'

'To you or them?'

'Both. But especially to your son.'

He didn't want to hear any of this, and chose to study the faceted tower instead. Not a single path, then, but multiple doorways. At least twelve. Twelve other worlds, then? What would they be like? What kind of creatures populated them? Demons. And perhaps that was all the word 'demon' meant. Some creature torn from its own realm. Bound like a slave by a new master who cared nothing for its life, its well-being, who would simply use it like any other tool. Until made useless, whereupon it would be discarded.

But I am tired of sympathy. Of feeling it, at least. I'd welcome receiving it, if only to salve all this self-pity. Be gracious, she said. A little rich, coming from her. He looked back down at the boy. My son. No, just my seed. She took nothing else, needed nothing else. It was the Wyval blood that drew her, it must have been. Nothing else. Not my son. My seed.

Growing too fast. Was that the trait of dragons? No wonder the T'lan Imass women were frightened. He sighed, then said, 'Found, thank you. And our thanks as well to Ulshun Pral. We look forward to a feast of Tenag calf.' He faced Feather Witch. 'Can you choose the proper path?'

'Our flesh will draw us back,' she replied. 'Come, we have no idea how much time has passed in our world.' She took him by the hand and led him past the stone figure. 'Dream worlds. Imagine what we might see, were we able to choose . . .'

'They're not dream worlds, Feather Witch. They're real. In those places, we are the ghosts.'

She snorted, but said nothing.

Udinaas turned for a final glance back. The boy, Found, get of a slave and a draconic-blooded woman, raised by neither. And at his side this rudely fashioned savage who believed he still lived. Believed he was flesh and blood, a hunter and leader with appetites, desires, a future to stride into. Udinaas could not decide which of the two was the more pathetic. Seeing them, as he did now, they both broke his heart, and there seemed no way to distinguish between the two. *As if grief had flavours.*

He swung round. 'All right, take us back.'

Her hand tightened on his, and she drew him forward. He watched her stride into the wall of flaring light. Then followed.

Atri-Preda Yan Tovis, called Twilight by those soldiers under her command who possessed in their ancestry the blood of the long-vanished indigenous fishers of Fent Reach – for that was what her name meant – stood on the massive wall skirting the North Coast Tower, and looked out upon the waters of Nepah Sea. Behind her, a broad, raised road exited from the base of the watchtower and cut a straight path south through two leagues of old forest, then a third of a league of farmland, to end at the crossroads directly before the Inland Gate of the fortified city of Fent Reach.

That was a road she was about to take. In haste.

Beside her, the local Finadd, a willow-thin, haunted man whose skin seemed almost bloodless, cleared his throat for the third time in the last dozen heartbeats.

'All right, Finadd,' Twilight said.

The man sighed, a sound of unabashed relief. 'I will assemble the squads, Atri-Preda.'

'In a moment. You've still a choice to make.'

'Atri-Preda?'

'By your estimate, how many Edur ships are we looking at?'

The Finadd squinted northward. 'Eight, nine hundred of their raiders, I would judge. Merude, Den-Ratha, Beneda. Those oversized transports – I've not seen those before. Five hundred?'

'Those transports are modelled on our own,' Twilight said. 'And ours hold five hundred soldiers each, one full supply ship in every five. Assuming the same ratio here. Four hundred transports packed with Edur warriors. That's two hundred thousand. Those raiders carry eighty to a hundred. Assume a hundred. Thus, ninety thousand. The force about to land on the strand below is, therefore, almost three hundred thousand.'

'Yes, Atri-Preda.'

'Five thousand Edur landed outside First Maiden Fort this morning. The skeleton garrison saddled every horse they had left and are riding hard for Fent Reach. Where I have my garrison.'

'We can conclude,' the Finadd said, 'that this represents the main force of the Edur fleet, the main force, indeed, of the entire people and their suicidal invasion.'

She glanced at him. 'No, we cannot conclude any such thing. We have never known the population of Edur lands.'

'Atri-Preda, we can hold Fent Reach for weeks. In that

time, a relieving army will have arrived and we can crush the grey-skinned bastards.'

'My mage cadre in the city,' she said after a moment, 'amounts to three dubious sorcerors, one of them never sober and the other two seemingly intent on killing each other over some past slight. Finadd, do you see the darkness of the sea beneath those ships? The residents of Trate know well that dark water, and what it holds.'

'What are you saying, Atri-Preda?'

'By all means ride back with us with your soldiers, Finadd. Or stay and arrange your official surrender with the first elements to land.'

The man's mouth slowly opened.

Twilight turned away and walked to the stairs leading down to the courtyard. 'I am surrendering Fent Reach, Finadd.'

'But Atri-Preda! We could withdraw back to Trate! All of us!'

She stopped three steps down. 'A third fleet has appeared, Finadd. In Katter Sea. We have already been cut off.'

'Errant take us!'

Twilight resumed her descent. Under her breath, she muttered, 'If only he could . . .'

All the questions were over. The invasion had begun.

My city is about to be conquered. Again.

CHAPTER SIXTEEN

The old drainage trench had once been a stream, long
before the huts were knocked down and the overlords
began building their houses of stone. Rubble and foul
silts formed the banks, crawling with vermin. But there
in my chest some dark fire flamed in quiet rage as I
walked the track seeking the lost voice, the voice of that
freed watery flow, the pebbles beneath the streaming tongue.
Oh I knew so well those smooth stones, the child's treasure
of comforting form and the way, when dried, a single
drop of tear or rain could make the colour blossom
once more the found recollection of its home – this
child's treasure and the child was me and the treasure
was mine, and mine own child this very morning I
discovered, kneeling smeared on the rotting bank
playing with shards of broken pots that knew only
shades of grey no matter how deep and how streaming
these tears.

Before Trate
Nameless Fent

Dreams could pass between the blinks of a man's eyes,
answered by wild casting about, disorientation, and
an unstoppered flood of discordant emotions.
Udinaas found he had slid down, was perched precariously
on the ledge, his limbs stiff and aching. The sun had fallen
lower, but not by much. Behind him, rising from a

crumpled heap, was Feather Witch, the two halves of a broken tile falling from one hand to clatter on the stone a moment before sliding off into the brush and rocks below. Her hair disguised her face, hid the emotions writ there.

Udinaas wanted to scream, let loose his grief, and the sourceless anger beneath it. But what was new in being used? What was new in having nothing to reach for, nothing to strive towards? He pulled himself up from the edge of crumbling stone, and looked about.

The army was on the move. Something had changed. He saw haste below. 'We must return,' he said.

'To what?' Harsh, bitter.

'To what we were before.'

'Slaves, Udinaas.'

'Yes.'

'I've tasted it now. I've tasted it!'

He glanced over at her, watched as she sat straighter, dragging the hair from her eyes, and fixed him with a fierce glare. 'You cannot live like this.'

'I can't?'

She looked away. Not wanting to see, he guessed. Not wanting to understand.

'We're marching to Trate, Feather Witch.'

'To conquer. To . . . enslave.'

'Details,' he muttered, climbing cautiously to his feet. He offered her a hand. 'Mayen wants you.'

'She beats me, now.'

'I know. You've failed to hide the bruises.'

'She tears my clothes off. Uses me. In ways that hurt. I hurt all the time.'

'Well,' Udinaas said, 'he doesn't do that to her. Not that there's much . . . tenderness. He's too young for that, I suppose. Nor has she the power to take charge. Teach him. She's . . . frustrated.'

'Enough of your understanding this, understanding that. Enough, Indebted! I don't care about her point of view, I'm not interested in stepping into her shadow, in trying to see the world how she sees it. None of that matters, when she twists, when she bites, when she pushes . . . just stop talking, Udinaas. Stop. No more.'

'Take my hand, Feather Witch. It's time.'

'I'd rather bite it off.'

I know. He said nothing.

'So he doesn't hurt her, does he?'

'Not physically,' he replied.

'Yes. What he does to her . . .' she looked up, searching his eyes, 'I do to you.'

'And you'd rather bite.'

She made no reply. Something flickered in her gaze, then she turned away even as she took his hand.

He drew her onto her feet.

She would not look at him. 'I'll go down first. Wait a bit.'

'All right.'

An army kicked awake, swarming the forest floor. To the north, the ashes of home. To the south, Trate. There would be . . . vengeance.

Details.

A flicker of movement downslope, then . . . nothing.

Trull Sengar continued scanning for a moment longer, then he settled back down behind the tree-fall. 'We have been discovered,' he said.

Ahlrada Ahn grunted. 'Now what?'

Trull looked to the left and the right. He could barely make out the nearest warriors, motionless and under cover. 'That depends,' he muttered. 'If they now come in force.'

They waited, as the afternoon waned.

Somewhere in the forest below was a Letherii brigade, and within it a mage cadre that had detected the presence of Tiste Edur positioned to defend the bridge. Among the officers, surprise, perhaps consternation. The mages would be at work attempting to discern precise numbers, but that would prove difficult. Something in Edur blood defied them, remained elusive to their sorcerous efforts. A decision would have to be made, and much depended on the personality of the commander. Proceed in a cautious and measured way until direct contact was established, whereupon a succession of probes would determine the strength of the enemy. There were risks, however, to that. Drawing close enough to gauge the sharpness of the enemy's fangs invited a bite that might not let go, leading to a pitched engagement where all the advantage lay with the Tiste Edur. Uphill battles were always costly. And often withdrawal proved bloody and difficult. Worse, there was a good chance of an all-out rout, which would lead to slaughter.

Or the commander could order the mage cadre to unleash a sorcerous attack and so lay waste the forest reaches above them. Such an attack, of course, served to expose the mages' position to those Edur warlocks who might be present. And to the wraiths and demons attending them. If the attack was blunted, the cadre was in trouble.

Finally, the commander could choose to pull back. Yield the bridge, and return to the solid defences of High Fort, inviting a more traditional battle – the kind the Letherii had fought for centuries, against enemy forces of all sorts, and almost invariably with great success.

Was the commander overconfident and precipitous? If so, then Trull Sengar and his fifty warriors would either be slaughtered or forced back to the other side of the bridge, either result proving tactically disastrous for Hanradi Khalag and his advancing warriors. A contested crossing of the bridge would force Fear and Hanradi into unveiling the full extent of the sorcerous power accompanying the army – power intended to shatter the defenders of High Fort. Conversely, a cautious or timid commander would elect to retreat, and that would ensure an Edur success.

Trull edged his way back up to peer over the tree-fall. No movement below. The air seemed preternaturally still.

'If they don't close soon,' Ahlrada said in a low voice, 'they will have lost the advantage.'

Trull nodded. Sufficient concerns to occupy his mind, to steal his fullest attention. He did not have the luxury of thinking of other things. This, he decided, was preferable. A relief. *And I can stay here, in this tense cast of my mind's thoughts, from now on. It will take me through this war. It has to. Please, take me through this war.*

The shadows were long on the slope below, cutting crossways, the shafts of dusty sunlight ebbing into golden mist through which insects flitted.

A whisper of sound – behind them, then on all sides.

Wraiths, streaming down, slipping past into the spreading gloom below.

'They've arrived,' Ahlrada said.

Trull slid back down and rolled onto his back. Padding between brush and trees upslope, silver-backed wolves. A half-dozen, then a score, lambent eyes flashing from lowered heads.

One beast approached Trull. It suddenly blurred, the air filling with a pungent, spicy scent, and a moment later Trull found himself looking into the amber eyes of B'nagga.

The Jheck grinned. 'A thousand paces below, Trull Sengar. They are in full retreat.'

'You made good time,' Ahlrada said.

The grin widened. 'The warriors are but two thousand paces from the bridge. My brothers found a body, hidden in the brush. Your work?'

'An advance scout,' Trull said.

'The mages had tied a thread to him. They knew you were coming. No doubt that slowed them even more.'

'So,' Ahlrada said, 'are we to contest their retreat?'

'It was a thought. But no, the wraiths will do naught but hound them. Keep them on edge and moving at doublemarch. By the time they reach High Fort they will be footsore and bleary-eyed. We won't be giving them much time to rest.' He settled into a crouch. 'I have news. First Maiden Fort has fallen. No battle – the garrison had already fled back to Fent Reach.'

'As anticipated,' Trull said.

'Yes. If the Letherii choose to make a stand at Fent Reach, it will be a short siege. Even now, our ships have made landing and the warriors march on the city.'

'No contact with any Letherii fleets?' Trull was surprised. Those transports were vulnerable.

'None. The emperor's forces are poised above Trate, undetected as yet. Within the next few days, my friends, there will be four major battles. And, sword willing, the northern frontier shall fall.'

At the very least, we'll have their fullest attention.

Blind drunk. A description Seren Pedac sought to explore, with all the fumbling murky intent of a mind poisoned into stupidity. But, somehow, she was failing. Instead of blind, she was painfully aware of the figures on all sides of her small table, the seething press and the loose rubble sound of countless voices. Stupidity had yet to arrive and possibly never would, as stolid sobriety held on, dogged and immovable and indifferent to the seemingly endless cups of wine she drank down.

Fevered excitement, scores of voices uttering their I-told-you-so variations to herds of nodding heads. Proclamations and predictions, the gleaming words of greed eager to be unleashed on the booty of battlefields crowded with dead Edur. *Give 'em First Maiden Fort, aye. Why not? Pull the bastards in and in. You saw what the cadre did that night? They'll do it again, this time against the ash-faced bastards themselves. I've got a perch halfway up the lighthouse, paid a fortune for it, I'll see it all.*

It'll all be over at Fent Reach. They'll get their noses bloodied and that's when the cadre will hit the fleet in Katter Sea. I got an interest in a stretch on Bight Coast, salvage rights. Heading up there as soon as it's over.

They let themselves get surrounded, I tell you. Twilight's just waiting for the siege to settle in. What's that? You saying she surrendered? Errant take us, man, what kind of lies you

597

throwing about in here? You a damned traitor, you a damned Hull Beddict? Shut that mouth of yours or I'll do it for you—

I'll help, Cribal, that's a promise. Sewing lips tight is easy as mending sails an' I been doing that for years—

Where'd he go?

Ah, never mind him, Cribal—

Traitors need to be taught a lesson, Feluda. Come on, I see 'im making for the door—

Sittin' alone don't do no woman no good, sweetheart. Let a decent man take you away from all this . . .

Seren Pedac frowned, looked up at the figure looming over her table. Her mind replied, *All right*, even as she scowled and turned away.

'Nothing worth its spit is being said here, lass. You want to drink. Fine, jus' sit and drink. All I was offerin' was a quieter place to do it, is all.'

'Go away.'

Instead, the man sat down. 'Been watchin' you all evening. Jus' another Letherii? Asked myself that once and once only. No, I think, not this one. So I ask, and someone says, "That's the Acquitor, Seren Pedac. Was up at the treaty that went sour. Was under contract with Buruk the Pale, the one that hung himself and damned if it wasn't her that found him all fish-eyed and fouled." And I think, that ain't an easy thing. No wonder she's sittin' there tryin' t'get drunk an' it's not working.'

She fixed her gaze on him, seeing him clearly for the first time. Seamed face, clean-shaven, hair shoulder-length and the hue of polished iron. His voice sounded again in her head, confirming what she saw. 'You're no Letherii.'

A broad smile, even, white teeth. 'You got that right, and, no offence, but glad of it.'

'You're not Faraed. Nerek. Tarthenal. Not Fent, either, not even Meckros—'

'What I am you never heard of, believe me, lass. A long way from home.'

'What do you want?'

'Was making an offer, but it needed to be done in quiet. Private—'

'I'm sure—'

'Not like that, though I'd consider my fortunes on the upswing if it was to happen the way you think I meant. No.' He leaned forward, gesturing her closer as well.

Her smile ironic, she tilted over the table until their noses were almost touching. 'I can't wait.'

He withdrew a fraction. 'Lass, you're a breathin' vineyard. All right, then, listen. We got ourselves a boat—'

'We?'

'A boat, and we're leaving this pock-on-Hood's-ass of a kingdom.'

'Where to? Korshenn? Pilott, Truce? Kolanse?'

'What would be the point of that? The first three you named are all paying tribute to Lether, and Kolanse is a mess from all we hear. Acquitor, the world's a lot bigger than you might think—'

'Is it? Actually, it's *smaller* than I think.'

'Same rubbish, different hole, eh? Maybe you're right. But maybe not.'

'Who are you?'

'Just someone a long way from home, like I said. We clawed our way out of Assail, only to find ourselves here, and just by arriving in our damned sieve of a boat, we owed money. Just by steppin' onto the dock, we owed more. It's been seven months, and we're so far in debt Prince K'azz himself couldn't clear our way back out. Livin' off scraps and doin' ugly work and it's rotting us all—'

'You were a soldier.'

'Still am, lass.'

'So join a brigade—'

He rubbed at his face, closed his eyes for a moment, then seemed to reach a decision. He fixed her with his cool, blue eyes. 'It's shouting to the Abyss, lass, and not one Letherii's listening. You people are in trouble. Serious trouble. Fent Reach surrendered. Now, Twilight's a smart, able commander, so what made her do that? Think, Acquitor.'

'She saw it was hopeless. She saw she couldn't hold the city, and there was no way to retreat.'

He nodded. 'You weren't here when the harvest ships returned. You didn't see what delivered 'em. We did. Lass, if dhenrabi worship a god then that was it, right there in the harbour.'

'Who are dhenrabi?'

He shook his head. 'We got room for people worth their salt. And you won't be the only woman, so it's not like that.'

'So why me at all, then?'

'Because you ain't blind, Seren Pedac.'

Smiling, she leaned back, then looked away. *Not drunk, either.* 'Who are you?'

'It won't mean a thing—'

'Tell me anyway.'

'Iron Bars, Second Blade, Fourth Company, Crimson Guard. Was in the service of Commander Cal-Brinn before we was all scattered between here and Hood's gates.'

'Meaningless *and* long. I'm impressed, Iron Bars.'

'Lass, you got more sharp teeth than an enkar'al with a mouthful of rhizan. Probably why I like you so much.'

All right. 'I'm not interested in your offer, Iron Bars.'

'Try thinking on it. There's time for that, provided you get out of Trate as soon as you can.'

She looked at him. 'That doesn't make any sense.'

'You'd be right, if our boat was in the harbour here. But it isn't. It's in Letheras. We signed on as crew, through an agent.' He shrugged. 'As soon as we get out to sea . . .'

'You'll kill the captain and mates and turn pirate.'

'We won't kill anybody if there's a way round it, and we're not pirates. We just want to get home. We *need* to get home.' He studied her for a moment, then rose. 'If it works out right, we'll look you up in Letheras.'

All right. 'You'd be wasting your time.'

He shrugged. 'Between here and then, Acquitor, a whole

lot is going to change. Get out of this city, lass. As soon as you sober up, go. Just go.'

Then he was gone.

They caught him, dragged him into the alley and they're sewing up his mouth – c'mon, let's watch—

Just his mouth? He's a damned traitor. No reason to go easy on the bastard. Sew him up everywhere, see how he likes that—

Wish it was Hull Beddict, that's what I wish—

They'll do a lot worse on 'im, mark my words. You just wait and see . . .

Her blue silks snapping in the wind, Nekal Bara stood atop the lighthouse tower and faced out to sea. Nothing was going as planned. Their pre-emptive attack had destroyed empty villages; the entire Tiste Edur people were on the move. *And they're about to arrive on our very doorstep.*

The fleet that had appeared in Katter Sea, poised to interpose its forces to prevent the retreat of Twilight's garrison at Fent Reach, had, upon the city's surrender, simply moved on. Preternaturally swift, the blood-red sails of five hundred raiders now approached Trate Bay. And in the waters beneath those sleek hulls . . . *a thing.* Ancient, terrible, eager with hunger. It knew this path. It had been here before.

Since that time, and at the Ceda's command, she had delved deep in her search to discover the nature of the creature the Tiste Edur had bound to their service. The harbour and the bay beyond had once been dry land, a massive limestone shelf beneath which raced vast underground rivers. Erosion had collapsed the shelf in places, creating roughly circular, deep wells. Sometimes the water below continued to flow as part of the rivers. But in some, the percolating effect of the limestone was blocked by concretions over time, and the water was black and still.

One such well had become, long ago, a place of worship. Treasures were flung into its depths. Gold, jade, silver and living sacrifices. Drowning voices had screamed in the chill water, cold flesh and bone had settled on the pale floor.

And a spirit was fashioned. Fed on blood and despair, beseeching propitiation, the unwilling surrender of mortal lives. There were mysteries to this, she well knew. Had the spirit existed before the worship began, and was simply drawn to the gifts offered? Or was it conjured into existence by the very will of those ancient worshippers? Either way, the result was the same. A creature came into being, and was taught the nature of hunger, of desire. Made into an addict of blood and grief and terror.

The worshippers vanished. Died out or departed, or driven to such extreme sacrifices as to destroy themselves. There was no telling how deep the bed of bones at the bottom of that well, but, by the end, it must have been appalling in its vastness.

The spirit was doomed, and should have eventually died. Had not the seas risen to swallow the land, had not its world's walls suddenly vanished, releasing it to all that lay beyond.

Shorelines were places of worship the world over. The earliest records surviving from the First Empire made note of that again and again among peoples encountered during the explorations. The verge between sea and land marked the manifestation of the symbolic transition between the known and the unknown. Between life and death, spirit and mind, between an unlimited host of elements and forces contrary yet locked together. Lives were given to the seas, treasures were flung into their depths. And, upon the waters themselves, ships and their crews were dragged into the deep time and again.

For all that, the spirit had known . . . competition. And, Nekal Bara suspected, had fared poorly. Weakened, suffering, it had returned to its hole, there beneath the deluge. Returned to die.

There was no way of knowing how the Tiste Edur warlocks had found it, or came to understand its nature and the potential within it. But they had bound it, fed it blood until its strength returned, and it had grown, and with that growth, a burgeoning hunger.

And now, I must find a way to kill it.

She could sense its approach, drawing ever nearer beneath the Edur raiders. Along the harbour front below, soldiers were crowding the fortifications. Crews readied at the trebuchets and ballistae. Fires were stoked and racks of hull-breaching quarrels were wheeled out.

Arahathan in his black furs had positioned himself at the far end of the main pier and, like her, stood facing the fast-approaching Edur fleet. He would seek to block the spirit's attack, engage it fully for as long as it took for Nekal Bara to magically draw close to the entity and strike at its heart.

She wished Enedictal had remained in the city, rather than returning to his battalion at Awl. Indeed, she wished the Snakebelts had marched to join them here. Once the spirit was engaged, Enedictal could have then shattered the Edur fleet. She had no idea how much damage she and Arahathan would sustain while killing the spirit – it was possible they would have nothing left with which to destroy the fleet. It might come down to hand to hand fighting along the harbour front.

And that is the absurdity of magic in war – we do little more than negate each other. Unless one cadre finds itself outnumbered . . .

She had six minor sorcerors under her command, interspersed among the companies of the Cold Clay Battalion arrayed below. They would have to be sufficient against the Edur warlocks accompanying the fleet.

Nekal Bara was worried, but not unduly so.

The red sails fluttered. She could just make out the crews, scampering on the foredecks and in the rigging. The fleet was heaving to. Beneath the lead ships, a dark tide surged forward, spreading its midnight bruise into the harbour.

She felt a sudden fear. It was . . . *huge.*

603

A glance down. To the lone, black-swathed figure at the very end of the main pier. The arms spreading wide.

The spirit heaved up in a swelling wave, gaining speed as it rushed towards the harbour front. On the docks, soldiers behind shields, a wavering of spear-heads. Someone loosed a ball of flaming pitch from one of the trebuchets. Fascinated, Nekal Bara watched its arcing flight, its smoke-trailing descent, down towards the rising wave.

It vanished in a smear of steam.

She heard Arahathan's roar, saw a line of water shiver, then boil just beyond the docks, lifting skyward a wall of steam even as the spirit's bulk seemed to lunge a moment before striking it.

The concussion sent the lighthouse wavering beneath her feet and she threw her arms out for balance. Two-thirds of the way down, along a narrow iron balcony, onlookers were flung into the air, to pitch screaming down to the rocks below. The balcony twisted like thin wire in the hands of a blacksmith, the fittings exploding in puffs of dust. A terrible groaning rose up through the tower as it rocked back and forth.

Steam and dark water raged in battle, clambering ever higher directly before Arahathan. The sorceror was swallowed by shadow.

The lighthouse was toppling.

Nekal Bara faced the harbour, held her arms out, then flung herself from the edge.

Vanishing within a tumbling shaft of magic. Slanting downward in coruscating threads of blue fire that swarmed around a blinding, white core.

Like a god's spear, the shaft pierced the flank of the spirit. Tore a path of incandescence into the dark, surging water.

Errant – he's failing! Falling! She sensed, then saw, Arahathan. Red flesh curling away from his bones, blackening, snatched away as if by a fierce whirling wind. She saw his teeth, the lips gone, the grimace suddenly a maddening smile. Eyes wrinkled, then darkening, then collapsing inward.

She sensed, in that last moment, his surprise, his disbelief—

Into the spirit's flesh, down through layer upon layer of thick, coagulated blood, matted hair, slivered pieces of bone. Encrusted jewellery, mangled coins. Layers of withered newborn corpses, each one wrapped in leather, each one with its forehead stove in, above a face twisted with pain and baffled suffering. *Layers. Oh, Mistress, what have we mortals done? Done, and done, and done?*

Stone tools, pearls, bits of shell—

Through—

To find that she had been wrong. Terribly wrong.

The spirit – naught but a shell, held together by the memory within bone, teeth and hair, by that memory and nothing more.

Within—

Nekal Bara saw that she was about to die. Against all that rose to greet her, she had no defence. None. Could not – could never – *Ceda! Kuru Qan! Hear me! See—*

Seren Pedac staggered out into the street. Pushed, spun round, knocked to her knees by fleeing figures.

She had woken in a dark cellar, surrounded by empty, broken kegs. She had been robbed, most of her armour stripped away. Sword and knife gone. The ache between her legs told her that worse had happened. Lips puffed and cut by kisses she had never felt, her hair tangled and matted with blood, she crawled across greasy cobbles to curl up against a stained brick wall. Stared out numbly on the panicked scene.

Smoke had stolen the sky. Brown, murky light, the distant sound of battle – at the harbour front to her left, and along the north and east walls ahead and to her right. In the street before her, citizens raced in seemingly random directions. Across from her, two men were locked in mortal combat, and she watched as one managed to pin the other, then began pounding the man's head against the cobbles. The hard impacts gave way to soft crunches, and the victor rolled away from the spasming victim, scrambled upright, then limped away.

Doors were being kicked down. Women screamed as their hiding places were discovered.

There were no Tiste Edur in sight.

From her right, three men shambling like marauders. One carried a bloodstained club, another a single-handed sickle. The third man was dragging a dead or unconscious girl-child by one foot.

They saw her. The one with the club smiled. 'We was coming to c'llect you, *Acquitor*. Woke up wanting more, did ya?'

She did not recognize any of them, but there was terrible familiarity in their eyes as they looked upon her.

'The city's fallen,' the man continued, drawing closer. 'But we got a way out, an' we're taking you with us.'

The one with the sickle laughed. 'We've decided to keep you to ourselves, lass. Don't worry, we'll keep you safe.'

Seren curled tighter against the wall.

'Hold there!'

A new voice. The three men looked up.

Iron-haired, blue-eyed – she recognized the newcomer. Maybe. She wasn't sure. She'd never seen armour like that before: she would have remembered the blood-red surcoat. A plain sword at the stranger's left hip, which he was not reaching towards.

'It's that foreign bastard,' the man with the club said. 'Find your own.'

'I just have,' he replied. 'Been looking for her the last two days—'

'She's ours,' said the sickle-wielder.

'No closer,' the third man growled, raising the child in one hand as if he meant to use the body for a weapon.

Which, Seren now saw, he had done already. *Oh, please be dead, child. Please have been dead all along . . .*

606

'You know us, foreigner,' the man with the club said.

'Oh yes, you're the terrors of the shanty town. I've heard all about your exploits. Which puts me at an advantage.'

'How so?'

The stranger continued walking closer. She saw something in his eyes, as he said, 'Because you haven't heard a thing about mine.'

Club swung. Sickle flashed. Body whipped through the air.

And the girl-child was caught by the stranger, who then reached one hand over, palm up, and seemed to push his fingertips under the man's chin.

She didn't understand.

The man with the club was on the ground. The other had his own sickle sticking from his chest and he stood staring down at it. Then he toppled.

A snap. Flood and spray of blood.

The stranger stepped back, tucking the girl-child's body under his right arm, the hand of his left holding, like a leather-wrapped handle from a pail, the third man's lower jaw.

Horrible grunting sounds from the staggering figure to her right. Bulging eyes, a spattered gust of breath.

The stranger tossed the mandible away with its attendant lower palate and tongue. He set the child down, then stepped closer to the last man. 'I don't like what you did. I don't like anything you've done, but most of all, I don't like what you did to this woman here, and that child. So, I am going to make you hurt. A lot.'

The man spun as if to flee. Then he slammed onto the cobbles, landing on his chest, his feet taken out from under him – but Seren didn't see how it had happened.

With serene patience, the stranger crouched over him. Two blurred punches to either side of the man's spine, almost at neck level, and she heard breastbones snap. Blood was pooling around the man's head.

The stranger shifted to reach down between the man's legs.

'Stop.'

He looked over, brows lifting.

'Stop. Kill him. Clean. Kill him clean, Iron Bars.'

'Are you sure?'

From the buildings opposite, faces framed by windows. Eyes fixed, staring down.

'Enough,' she said, the word a croak.

'All right.'

He leaned back. One punch to the back of the man's head. It folded inward. And all was still.

Iron Bars straightened. 'All right?'

All right, yes.

The Crimson Guardsman came closer. 'My fault,' he said. 'I had to sleep, thought you'd be safe for a bit. I was wrong. I'm sorry.'

'The child?'

A pained look. 'Run down by horses, I think. Some time past.'

'What's happening?'

'Trate's falling. The Edur fleet held off. Until Nekal Bara and Arahathan were finished. Then closed. The defences were swarmed by shadow wraiths. Then the warriors landed. It was bad, Acquitor.' He glanced over a shoulder, said, 'At about that time, an army came down from inland. Swept the undermanned fortifications and, not a hundred heartbeats ago, finally succeeded in knocking down the North Gate. The Edur are taking their time, killing every soldier they find. No quarter. So far, they've not touched non-combatants. But that's no guarantee of anything, is it?'

He helped her to stand, and she flinched at the touch of his hands – those weapons, stained with murder.

If he noticed he gave nothing away. 'My Blade's waiting. Corlo's managed to find a warren in this damned Hood-pit – first time in the two years we been stuck here. What the Edur brought, he says. That's why.'

She realized they were walking now. Taking winding alleys and avoiding the main thoroughfares. The sound of slaughter was on all sides. Iron Bars suddenly hesitated, cocked his head. 'Damn, we've been cut off.'

Dragged into the slaughter. Bemused witness to the killing of hapless, disorganized soldiers. Wondering if the money-lenders would be next. Udinaas was left staggering in the wake of the emperor of the Tiste Edur and twelve frenzied warriors as they waded through flesh, cutting lives down as if clearing a path through reeds.

Rhulad was displaying skill that did not belong to him. His arms were a blur, his every move heedless and fearless. And he was gibbering, the manic sound punctuated every now and then by a scream that was as much terror as it was rage. Not a warrior triumphant. Neither berserk nor swathed in drenched glory. A killer . . . killing.

An Edur warrior near him fell to a Letherii soldier's desperate sword-thrust, and the emperor shrieked, lunged forward. The mottled sword swung, and blood splashed like water. His laughter pulled at his breath, making him gasp. Edur faces flashed furtively towards their savage ruler.

Down the street, carving through a rearguard of some sort. Udinaas stumbled over corpses, writhing, weeping figures. Blind with dying, men called for their mothers, and to these the slave reached down and touched a shoulder, or laid fingertips to slick foreheads, and murmured, 'I'm here, my boy. It's all right. You can go now.'

The apologetic priest, chain-snapped forward step by step, whispering hollow blessings, soft lies, forgiving even as he prayed for someone – something – to forgive him in turn. But no-one touched him, no fingertips brushed his brow.

For the burned villages. Retribution. Where were the moneylenders? This war belonged to them, after all.

Another hundred paces. Three more Edur were down. Rhulad and eight brethren. Fighting on. Where was the rest of the army?

Somewhere else.

If one could always choose the right questions, then every answer could be as obvious. A clever revelation, he was on to something here . . .

Another Edur screamed, skidded and fell over, face smacking the street.

Rhulad killed two more soldiers, and suddenly no-one stood in their path.

Halting in strange consternation, trapped in the centre of an intersection, drifts of smoke sliding past.

From the right, a sudden arrival.

Two Edur reeled back, mortally wounded.

The attacker reached out with his left hand, and a third Edur warrior's head snapped round with a loud crack.

Clash of blades, more blood, another Edur toppling, then the attacker was through and wheeling about.

Rhulad leapt to meet him. Swords – one heavy and mottled, the other modest, plain – collided, and somehow were bound together with a twist and pronation of the stranger's wrist, whilst his free hand blurred out and over the weapons, palm connecting with Rhulad's forehead.

Breaking the emperor's neck with a loud snap.

Mottled sword slid down the attacker's blade and he was already stepping past, his weapon's point already sliding out from the chest of another Edur.

Another heartbeat, and the last two Tiste Edur warriors were down, their bodies eagerly dispensing blood like payment onto the cobbles.

The stranger looked about, saw Udinaas, nodded, then waved to an alley-mouth, from which a woman emerged.

She took a half-dozen strides before Udinaas recognized her.

Badly used.

But no more of that. Not while this man lives.

Seren Pedac took no notice of him, nor of the dead Edur. The stranger grasped her hand.

Udinaas watched them head off down the street, disappear round a corner.

Somewhere behind him, the shouts of Edur warriors, the sound of running feet.

The slave found he was standing beside Rhulad's body, staring down at it, the bizarre angle of the head on its twisted neck, the hands closed tight about the sword.

Waiting for the mouth to open with mad laughter.

'Damned strangest armour I've ever seen.'

Seren blinked. 'What?'

'But he was good, with that sword. Fast. In another five years he'd have had the experience to have made him deadly. Enough to give anyone trouble. Shimmer, Blues, maybe even Skinner. But that armour! A damned fortune, right there for the taking. If we'd the time.'

'What?'

'That Tiste Edur, lass.'

'Tiste Edur?'

'Never mind. There they are.'

Ahead, crouched at the dead end of an alley, six figures. Two women, four men. All in crimson surcoats. Weapons out. Blood on the blades. One, more lightly armoured than the others and holding what looked to be some sort of diadem in his left hand, stepped forward.

And said something in a language Seren had never heard before.

Iron Bars replied in an impatient growl. He drew Seren closer as the man who'd spoken began gesturing. The air seemed to shimmer all round them.

'Corlo's opening the warren, lass. We're going through, and if we're lucky we won't run into anything in there. No telling how far we can get. Far enough, I hope.'

'Where?' she asked. 'Where are we going?'

A murky wall of blackness yawned where the alley's blank wall had been.

'Letheras, Acquitor. We got a ship awaiting us, remember?'

Strangest armour I've ever seen.

611

A damned fortune.

'Is he dead?'

'Who?'

'Is he dead? Did you kill him? That Tiste Edur!'

'No choice, lass. He was slowing us up and more were coming.'

Oh, no.

Vomit spilling out onto the sand.

At least, Withal mused, the shrieks had stopped. He waited, seated on grass just above the beach, while the young Edur, on his hands and knees, head hanging down, shuddered and convulsed, coughed and spat.

Off to one side, two of the Nachts, Rind and Pule, were fighting over a piece of driftwood that was falling apart with their efforts. Their games of destruction had become obsessive of late, leading the Meckros weaponsmith to wonder if they were in fact miming a truth on his behalf. Or the isolation was driving them insane.

Another kind of truth, that one.

He despised religion. Set no gods in his path. Ascendants were worse than rabid beasts. It was enough that mortals were capable of appalling evil; he wanted nothing to do with their immortal, immeasurably more powerful counterparts.

And this broken god in his squalid tent, his eternal pain and the numbing smoke of the seeds he scattered onto the brazier before him, it was all of a piece to Withal. Suffering made manifest, consumed by the desire to spread the misery of its own existence into the world, into all the worlds. Misery and false escape, pain and mindless surrender. *All of a piece.*

On this small island, amidst this empty sea, Withal was lost. Within himself, among a host of faces that were all his own, he was losing the capacity to recognize any of them. Thought and self was reduced, formless and untethered. Wandering amidst a stranger's memories, whilst the world beyond unravelled.

612

Nest building.

Frenzied destruction.

Fanged mouth agape in silent, convulsive laughter.

Three jesters repeating the same performance again and again. What did it mean? What obvious lesson was being shown him that he was too blind, too thick, to understand?

The Edur lad was done, nothing left in his stomach. He lifted his head, eyes stripped naked to the bones of pain and horror. 'No,' he whispered.

Withal looked away, squinted along the strand.

'No more . . . please.'

'Never much in the way of sunsets here,' Withal mused. 'Or sunrises, for that matter.'

'You don't know what it's like!'

The Edur's scream trailed away. 'The nests are getting more elaborate,' Withal said. 'I think he's striving for a particular shape. Sloped walls, a triangular entrance. Then Mape wrecks it. What am I to take from all that?'

'He can keep his damned sword. I'm not going. Over there. I'm not going over there and don't try to make me.'

'I have nothing to do. Nothing.'

Rhulad crawled towards him. 'You made that sword!' he said in an accusatory rasp.

'Fire, hammer, anvil and quenching. I've made more swords than I can count. Just iron and sweat. They were broken blades, I think. Those black shards. From some kind of narrow-bladed, overlong knife. Two of them, black and brittle. Just pieces, really. I wonder where he collected them from?'

'Everything breaks,' Rhulad said.

Withal glanced over. 'Aye, lad. Everything breaks.'

'You could do it.'

'Do what?'

'Break that sword.'

'No. I can't.'

'Everything breaks!'

'Including people, lad.'

613

'That's not good enough.'

Withal shrugged. 'I don't remember much of anything any more. I think he's stealing my mind. He says he's my god. All I need to do is worship him, he says. And everything will come clear. So tell me, Rhulad Sengar, is it all clear to you?'

'This evil – it's of your making!'

'Is it? Maybe you're right. I accepted his bargain. But he lied, you see. He said he'd set me free, once I made the sword. He lies, Rhulad. That much I know. I know that now. This god *lies*.'

'I have power. I am emperor. I've taken a wife. We are at war and Lether shall fall.'

Withal gestured inland. 'And he's waiting for you.'

'They're frightened of me.'

'Fear breeds its own loyalty, lad. They'll follow. They're waiting too, right now.'

Rhulad clawed at his face, shuddered. 'He killed me. That man – not a Letherii, not a Letherii at all. He killed us. Seven of my brothers. And me. He was so . . . *fast*. It seemed he barely moved, and my kin were falling, dying.'

'Next time will be harder. You'll be harder. It won't be as easy to find someone to kill you, next time. And the time after that. Do you understand that, lad? It's the essence of that mangled god who's waiting for you.'

'*Who is he?*'

'The god? A miserable little shit, Rhulad. Who has your soul in his hands.'

'Father Shadow has abandoned us.'

'Father Shadow is dead. Or as good as.'

'How do you know?'

'Because if he wasn't, he'd have never let the Crippled God steal you. You and your people. He'd have come marching ashore . . .' Withal fell silent.

And that, he realized, was what he was coming to. A blood-soaked truth.

He hated religion, hated the gods. And he was alone.

'I will kill him. With the sword.'

'Fool. There's nothing on this island that he doesn't hear, doesn't see, doesn't know.'

Except, maybe, what's in my mind now. And, even if he knew, how could he stop me? No, he doesn't know. I must believe that. After all, if he did, he'd kill me. Right now, he'd kill me.

Rhulad climbed to his feet. 'I'm ready for him.'

'Are you?'

'Yes.'

Withal sighed. He glanced over at the two Nachts. Their contested driftwood was a scattering of splinters lying between them. Both creatures were staring down at it, bemused, poking fingers through the mess. The Meckros rose. 'All right then, lad, let's go.'

She was behind the black glass, within a tunnel of translucent obsidian, and there were no ghosts.

'Kurald Galain,' Corlo said in a whisper, casting a glance back at them over one shoulder. 'Unexpected. It's a rotten conquest. That, or the Edur don't even know it, don't even know what they're using.'

The air stank of death. Withered flesh, the breath of a crypt. The black stone beneath their feet was greasy and uncertain. Overhead, the ceiling was uneven, barely a hand's width higher than Iron Bars, who was the tallest among the group.

'It's a damned rats' maze,' the mage continued, pausing at a branching.

'Just take us south,' Iron Bars said in a low growl.

'Fine, but which way is that?'

The soldiers crowded round, muttering and cursing in their strange language.

Corlo faced Seren, his expression strangely taut. 'Any suggestions, Acquitor?'

'What?'

The mage said something in their native tongue to Iron

Bars, who scowled and replied, 'That's enough, all of you. In Letherii. Since when was rudeness in the creed of the Crimson Guard? Acquitor, this is the Hold of Darkness—'

'There is no Hold of Darkness.'

'Well, I'm trying to say it in a way that makes sense to you.'

'All right.'

Corlo said, 'But, you see, Acquitor, it shouldn't be.'

She simply looked at him in the gloom.

The mage rubbed the back of his neck, and she saw the hand come away glistening with sweat. 'These are Tiste Edur, right? Not Tiste Andii. The Hold of Darkness, that's Tiste Andii. The Edur, they were from the, uh, Hold of Shadow. So, it was natural, you see, to expect that the warren would be Kurald Emurlahn. But it isn't. It's Kurald Galain, only it's breached. Over-run. Thick with spirits – Tiste Andii spirits—'

'They're not here,' she said. 'I've seen them. Those spirits. They're not here.'

'They are, Acquitor. I'm just keeping them away. For now . . .'

'But it's proving difficult.'

The mage nodded reluctantly.

'And you're lost.'

Another nod.

She tried to think, cut through the numbness – which seemed to be the only thing keeping away the pain of her battered flesh. 'You said the spirits are not Edur.'

'That's right. Tiste Andii.'

'What is the relationship between the two? Are they allied?'

Corlo's eyes narrowed. 'Allied?'

'Those wraiths,' Iron Bars said.

The mage's gaze darted to his commander, then back again to Seren Pedac. 'Those wraiths are bound. Compelled to fight alongside the Edur. Are they Andii spirits? Hood's breath, this is starting to make sense. What

616

else would they be? Not Edur spirits, since no binding magic would be needed, would it?'

Iron Bars stepped in front of Seren. 'What are you suggesting?'

She remembered back to her only contact with the spirits, their hunger. 'Mage Corlo, you say you're keeping them away. Are they trying to attack us?'

'I'm not sure.'

'Let one through. Maybe we can talk to it, maybe we can get help.'

'Why would it be interested in helping us?'

'Make a bargain.'

'With what?'

She shrugged. 'Think of something.'

He muttered a string of foreign words that she guessed were curses.

'Let one through,' Iron Bars said.

More curses, then Corlo walked a few steps ahead to clear some space. 'Ready weapons,' he said. 'In case it ain't interested in talking.'

A moment later, the gloom in front of the mage wavered, and something black spread outward like spilled ink. A figure emerged, halting, uncertain.

A woman, tall as an Edur but midnight-skinned, a reddish glint to her long, unbound hair. Green eyes, tilted and large, a face softer and rounder than Seren would have expected given her height and long limbs. She was wearing a leather harness and leggings, and on her shoulders rode the skin of some white-furred beast. She was unarmed.

Her eyes hardened. She spoke, and in her words Seren heard a resemblance to Edur.

'I hate it when that happens,' Corlo said.

Seren tried Edur. 'Hello. We apologize for intruding on your world. We do not intend to stay long.'

The woman's expression did not change. 'The Betrayers never do.'

'I may speak in the language of the Edur, but they

617

are no allies of ours. Perhaps in that, we share something.'

'I was among the first to die in the war,' the woman said, 'and so not at the hands of an Edur. They cannot take me, cannot force me to fight for them. I and those like me are beyond their grasp.'

'Yet your spirit remains trapped,' Seren said. 'Here, in this place.'

'What do you want?'

Seren turned to Iron Bars. 'She asks what we want of her.'

'Corlo?'

The mage shrugged, then said, 'We need to escape the influence of the Edur. We need to get beyond their reach. Then to return to our world.'

Seren relayed Corlo's statements to the woman.

'You are mortal,' she replied. 'You can pass through when we cannot.'

'Can you guide us?'

'And what is to be my reward for this service?'

'What do you seek?'

She considered, then shook her head. 'No. An unfair bargain. My service is not worth the payment I would ask. You require a guide to lead you to the border's edge. I will not deceive. It is not far. You would find it yourselves before too long.'

Seren translated the exchange for the Crimson Guardsmen, then added, 'This is odd . . .'

Iron Bars smiled. 'An honest broker?'

She nodded wryly. 'I am Letherii, after all. Honesty makes me suspicious.'

'Ask her what she would have us do for her,' Iron Bars said.

Seren Pedac did, and the woman held up her right hand, and in it was a small object, encrusted and corroded and unrecognizable. 'The K'Chain Che'Malle counter-attack drove a number of us down to the shoreline, then into the waves. I am a poor fighter. I died on that sea's foaming edge, and my corpse rolled out, drawn by the tide, along the muddy sands, where the mud swallowed it.' She looked down at the object in her palm. 'This was a ring I wore. Returned to me by a wraith – many wraiths have done this for those of us beyond the reach of the Edur. I would ask that you return me to my bones, to what little of me remains. So that I can find oblivion. But this is too vast a gift, for offering you so little—'

'How would we go about doing as you ask?'

'I would join with the substance of this ring. You would see me no more. And you would need to travel to the shoreline, then cast this into the sea.'

'That does not seem difficult.'

'Perhaps it isn't. The inequity lies in the exchange of values.'

Seren shook her head. 'We see no inequity. Our desire is of equal value as far as we are concerned. We accept your bargain.'

'How do I know you will not betray me?'

The Letherii turned to Iron Bars. 'She doesn't trust us.'

The man strode to halt directly before the Tiste Andii woman. 'Acquitor, tell her I am an Avowed, of the Crimson Guard. If she would, she can seek the meaning of that. By laying her hand on my chest. Tell her I shall honour our pact.'

'I've not told you what it is yet. She wants us to throw the thing she's holding into the sea.'

'That's it?'

'Doing so will end her existence. Which seems to be what she wants.'

'Tell her to seek the cast of my soul.'

'Very well.'

The suspicious look in the woman's eyes grew more pronounced, but she stepped forward and set her left hand on the man's chest.

The hand flinched away and the woman staggered back a step, shock, then horror, writ on her face. 'How – how could you do – *why?*'

619

Seren said, 'Not the response you sought, I think, Iron Bars. She is . . . appalled.'

'That is of no concern,' the man replied. 'Does she accept my word?'

The woman straightened, then, to Seren's question, she nodded and said, 'I cannot do otherwise. But . . . I had forgotten . . . this feeling.'

'What feeling?'

'Sorrow.'

'Iron Bars,' Seren said, 'whatever this "Avowed" means, she is overwhelmed with . . . pity.'

'Yes well,' he said, turning away, 'we all make mistakes.'

The woman said, 'I will lead you now.'

'What is your name?'

'Sandalath Drukorlat.'

'Thank you, Sandalath. It grieves me to know that our gift to you is oblivion.'

She shrugged. 'Those who I once loved and who loved me believe I am gone in truth. There is no need for grief.'

No need for grief. Where, then, does the pity lie?

'Stand up, lads,' Iron Bars said, 'she's making ready to go.'

Mape lay on the knoll like something dead, but the Nacht's head slowly turned as Withal and Rhulad strode into view. She had stolen a hammer from the smithy some time back, to better facilitate her destruction of Pule's nests, and now carried it with her everywhere. Withal watched askance as the gnarled, black-skinned creature lifted the hammer into view, eyes still fixed on him and the Tiste Edur, as if contemplating murder.

Of the three Nachts, Mape made him the most nervous. Too much intelligence glittered in her small black eyes, too often she watched with something like a smile on her apish face. And the strength the creatures had displayed was sufficient to make any man worried. He knew Mape could tear his arms from his shoulders, were she so inclined.

Perhaps the Crippled God had bound them, as demons

could be bound, and it was this and this alone that kept the beasts from Withal's throat. An unpleasant notion.

'What's to stop me,' Rhulad asked in a growl, 'from driving the sword right through his scrawny chest?'

'Do not ask that question of me, Edur. Only the Crippled God can answer it. But I don't think it could ever be that easy. He's a clever bastard, and there in that tent his power is probably absolute.'

'The vastness of his realm,' Rhulad said, sneering.

Yes. Now why do those words, said in that way, interest me?

The ragged canvas shelter was directly ahead, smoke drifting from the side that had been drawn open. As they approached, the air grew hotter, drier, the grasses withered and bleached underfoot. The earth seemed strangely blighted.

They came opposite the entrance. Within, the god's huddled form in the gloom. Tendrils of smoke rising from the brazier.

A cough, then, 'Such anger. Unreasonable, I think, given the efficacy of my gift.'

'I don't want to go back,' Rhulad said. 'Leave me here. Choose someone else.'

'Unwitting servants to our cause appear ... from unexpected sources. Imagine, an Avowed of the Crimson Guard. Be glad it was not Skinner, or indeed Cowl. They would have taken more notice of you, and that would not have been a good thing. We're not yet ready for that.' A hacking cough. 'Not yet ready.'

'I'm not going back.'

'You detest the flesh given you. I understand. But, Rhulad Sengar, the gold is your payment. For the power you seek.'

'I want nothing more of that power.'

'But you do,' the Crippled God said, clearly amused. 'Consider the rewards already reaped. The throne of the Tiste Edur, the woman after whom you lusted for years – now in your possession, to do with as you please. Your brothers, bowing one and all before you. And a burgeoning prowess with the sword—'

'It's not *mine*, though, is it? It is all I can do to hold on! The skill does not belong to me – and all can see that! I have *earned nothing*!'

'And what value is all that pride you seek, Rhulad Sengar? You mortals baffle me. It is a fool's curse, to measure oneself in endless dissatisfaction. It is not for me to guide you in the rule of your empire. That task belongs to you and you alone. There, make that your place of pride. Besides, has not your strength grown? You have muscles now surpassing your brother Fear's. Cease your whimpering, Edur.'

'You are using me!'

The Crippled God laughed. 'And Scabandari Bloodeye did not? Oh, I know the tale now. All of it. The seas whisper old truths, Rhulad Sengar. Revered Father Shadow, oh, such an absurd conceit. Murderer, knife-wielder, betrayer—'

'Lies!'

'—who then led you into your own betrayal. Of your once-allies, the Tiste Andii. You fell upon them at Scabandari's command. You killed those who had fought alongside you. That is the legacy of the Tiste Edur, Rhulad Sengar. Ask Hannan Mosag. He knows. Ask your brother, Fear. Your mother – the women know. Their memory has been far less . . . selective.'

'No more of this,' the Edur pleaded, clawing at his face. 'You would poison me with dishonour. That is your purpose . . . for all you say.'

'Perhaps what I offer,' the Crippled God murmured, 'is absolution. The opportunity to make amends. It is within you, Rhulad Sengar. The power is yours to shape as you will. The empire shall cast your reflection, no-one else's. Will you flee from that? If that is your choice, then indeed I shall be forced to choose another. One who will prove, perhaps, less honourable.'

The sword clattered at Rhulad's feet.

'*Choose.*'

Withal watched, saw the Edur's expression change.

With a scream, Rhulad snatched up the weapon and lunged—

—and was gone.

Rasping laughter. 'There is so little, Withal, that surprises me any more.'

Disgusted, the Meckros turned away.

'A moment, Withal. I see your weariness, your displeasure. What is it that plagues you so? That is what I ask myself.'

'The lad doesn't deserve it—'

'Oh, but he does. They all do.'

'Aye,' Withal said, eyes level as he stared at the Crippled God, 'that does seem to be the sole judgement you possess. But it's hardly clean, is it?'

'Careful. My gratitude for what you have done for me wears thin.'

'Gratitude?' Withal's laugh was harsh. 'You are thankful after compelling me into doing your bidding. That's a good one. May you be as generous of thought after I force you into killing me.' He studied the hooded figure. 'I see your problem, you know. I see it now, and curse myself for having missed it before. You have no realm to command, as do other gods. So you sit there, alone, in your tent, and that is the extent of your realm, isn't it? Broken flesh and foul, stifling air. Skin-thin walls and the heat the old and lame desire. Your world, and you alone in it, and the irony is, you cannot even command your own body.'

A wretched cough, then, 'Spare me your sympathy, Meckros. I have given the problem of you considerable thought, and have found a solution, as you shall soon discover. When you do, think on what you have said to me. Now, go.'

'You still don't understand, do you? The more pain you deliver to others, god, the more shall be visited upon

623

you. You sow your own misery, and because of that whatever sympathy you might rightly receive is swept away.'

'I said go, Withal. Build yourself a nest. Mape's waiting.'

They emerged onto a windswept sward with the crashing waves of the sea on their right and before them the delta of a broad river. On the river's other side stood a walled city.

Seren Pedac studied the distant buildings, the tall, thin towers that seemed to lean seaward. 'Old Katter,' she said. 'We're thirty leagues south of Trate. How is that possible?'

'Warrens,' Corlo muttered, sagging until he sat on the ground. 'Rotted. Septic, but still, a warren.'

The Acquitor made her way down to the beach. The sun was high and hot overhead. *I must wash. Get clean. The sea . . .*

Iron Bars followed, in one hand the encrusted object where the spirit of a Tiste Andii woman now resided.

She strode into the water, the foaming waves thrashing round her shins.

The Avowed flung the object past her – a small splash not far ahead.

Thighs, then hips.

Clean. Get clean.

To her chest. A wave rolled, lifted her from the bottom, spun and flung her towards the shore. She clawed herself round until she could push forward once again. Cold salty water rising over her face. Bright, sunlit, silty water, washing sight from her eyes. Water biting at scabbed wounds, stinging her broken lips, water filling her mouth and begging to be drawn inside.

Like this.

Hands grasped her, pulled her back. She fought, but could not break loose.

Clean!

Her face swept by cold wind, eyes blinking in painful light. Coughing, weeping, she struggled, but the hands dragged her remorselessly onto the beach, flung her onto the sand. Then, as she tried to claw free, arms wrapped tight about her, pinning her own arms, and a voice gasped close to her ear, 'I know, lass. I know what it's about. But it ain't the way.'

Heaving, helpless sobs, now.

And he held her still.

'Heal her, Corlo.'

'I'm damn near done—'

'Now. And sleep. Make her sleep—'

No, you can't die. Not again. I have need of you.

So many layers, pressing down upon these indurative remnants, a moment of vast pressure, the thick, so thick skin tracing innumerable small deaths. And life was voice, not words, but sound, motion. Where all else was still, silent. Oblivion waited when the last echo faded.

Dying the first time should have been enough. This world was foreign, after all. The gate sealed, swept away. Her husband – if he still lived – was long past his grief. Her daughter, perhaps a mother herself by now, a grandmother. She had fed on draconic blood, there in the wake of Anomander. Somewhere, she persisted, and lived free of sorrow.

It had been important to think that way. Her only weapon against insanity.

No gifts in death but one.

But something held her back.

Something with a voice. *These are restless seas indeed. I had not thought my questing would prove so . . . easy. True, you are not human, but you will do. You will do.*

These remnants, suddenly in motion, grating motion. Fragments, particles too small to see, drawing together. As if remembering to what they had once belonged. And, within the sea, within the silts, waited all that was needed. For flesh, for bone and blood. All these echoes, resurrected, finding shape. She looked on in horror.

Watched, as the body – so familiar, so strange – clawed

its way upward through the silts. Silts that lightened, thinned, then burst into a plume that swirled in the currents. Arms reaching upward, a body heaving into view.

She hovered near, compelled to close, to enter, but knowing it was too soon.

Her body, which she had left so long ago. It was not right. Not fair.

Scrambling mindlessly along the sea bottom. Finned creatures darting in and out of sight, drawn to the stirred-up sediments, frightened away by the flailing figure. Multi-legged shapes scrabbling from its path.

A strange blurring, passed through, and then sunlight glittered close overhead. Hands broke the surface, firm sand underfoot, sloping upward.

Face in the air.

And she swept forward, plunged into the body, raced like fire within muscle and bone.

Sensations. Cold, a wind, the smell of salt and a shore-line's decay.

Mother Dark, I am . . . alive.

The voice of return came not in laughter, but in screams.

All had gathered as word of the emperor's death spread. The city was taken, but Rhulad Sengar had been killed. Neck snapped like a sapling. His body lay where it fell, with the slave Udinaas standing guard, a macabre sentinel who did not acknowledge anyone, but simply stared down at the coin-clad corpse.

Hannan Mosag. Mayen with Feather Witch trailing. Midik Buhn, now blooded and a warrior in truth. Hundreds of Edur warriors, blood-spattered with glory and slaughter. Silent, pale citizens, terrified of the taut expectancy in the smoky air.

All witness to the body's sudden convulsions, its piercing screams. For a ghastly moment, Rhulad's neck remained broken, rocking his head in impossible angles as he staggered to his feet. Then the bone mended, and the

626

head righted itself, sudden light in the hooded eyes.

More screams, from Letherii now. Figures fleeing.

Rhulad's ragged shrieks died and he stood, wavering, the sword trembling in his hands.

Udinaas spoke. 'Emperor, Trate is yours.'

A sudden spasm, then Rhulad seemed to see the others for the first time. 'Hannan Mosag, settle the garrison. The rest of the army shall camp outside the city. Send word to your K'risnan with the fleet: they are to make for Old Katter.'

The Warlock King stepped close and said in a low voice, 'It is true, then. You cannot die.'

Rhulad flinched. 'I die, Hannan Mosag. It is all I know, dying. Leave me now. Udinaas.'

'Emperor.'

'I need – find – I am . . .'

'Your tent awaits you and Mayen,' the slave said.

'Yes.'

Midik Buhn spoke, 'Emperor, I shall lead your escort.'

His expression confused, Rhulad looked down at his body, the smeared, crusted coins, the spattered furs. 'Yes, brother Midik. An escort.'

'And we shall find the one who . . . did this, sire . . . to you.'

Rhulad's eyes flashed. 'He cannot be defeated. We are helpless before him. He lies . . .'

Midik was frowning. He glanced at Udinaas.

'Emperor,' the slave said, 'he meant the one who killed you and your kin. Here in this street.'

Clawing at his face, Rhulad turned away. 'Of course. He wore . . . crimson.'

Udinaas said to Midik, 'I will give you a detailed description.'

A sharp nod. 'Yes. The city will be searched.'

But he's gone, you fool. No, I don't know how I know. Still, the man's gone. With Seren Pedac. 'Of course.'

'Udinaas!' A desperate gasp.

627

'I am here, Emperor.'

'Take me out of this place!'

It was known, now, and soon the Ceda would learn of it. But would he understand? How could he? It was impossible, insane.

He can do nothing. Will he realize this?

The warrior in gold trailed the slave, step by step, through the fallen city, Mayen and Feather Witch in their wake. Midik Buhn and a dozen warriors flanked them all, weapons at the ready. The passage was uncontested.

Withal sat on a bench in his smithy. Plain walls, stone and plaster, the forge cold and filled with ash. Paved floor, the small workshop three-walled, the open side facing onto a fenced compound where stood a cut-stone-rimmed well, a quenching trough, firewood and a heap of tailings and slag. A hut on the opposite side housed his cot and nothing else.

The extent of his world. Mocking reminder of his profession, the purpose behind living.

The Crippled God's voice whispered in his mind, *Withal. My gift. I am not without sympathy, no matter what you might think. I understood. Nachts are poor company for a man. Go, Withal, down to the beach. Take possession of my gift.*

He slowly rose, bemused. *A boat? A raft? A damned log I could ride out with the tide?* He made his way outside.

And heard the Nachts, chattering excitedly down on the strand.

Withal walked to the verge, and stood, looking down.

A woman was staggering from the water. Tall, black-skinned, naked, long red hair.

And the Meckros turned round, strode away.

'You bastard—'

The Crippled God replied in mock consternation, *Is this not what you want? Is she too tall for you? Her eyes too strange? Withal, I do not understand . . .*

'How could you have done this? Take possession, you

628

said. It's all you know, isn't it? Possession. Things to be used. People. Lives.'

She needs your help, Withal. She is lost, alarmed by the Nachts. Slow to recall her flesh.

'Later. Leave me alone, now. Leave us both alone.'

A soft laugh, then a cough. *As you wish. Disappointing, this lack of gratitude.*

'Go to the Abyss.'

No reply.

Withal entered the hut, stood facing the cot for a time, until he was certain that the Crippled God was not lurking somewhere in his skull. Then he lowered himself to his knees and bowed his head.

He hated religion. Detested gods. But the nest was empty. The nest needed tearing apart. Rebuilding.

The Meckros had a host of gods for the choosing. But one was older than all the others, and that one belonged to the sea.

Withal began to pray.

In Mael's name.

CHAPTER SEVENTEEN

None had seen the like. Chorum's Mill was a
Marvel of invention. Wheels upon wheels,
Granite and interlocking gears, axles and
Spokes and rims of iron, a machine that climbed
From that fast river three full levels and ground
The finest flour Lether had ever seen –
Some say it was the rain, the deluge that filled
The water's course through the mill's stony toes.
Some say it was the sheer complexity that was
The cause of it all, the conceit of a mortal man's
Vision. Some say it was the Errant's nudge, fickle
And wayward that voiced the sudden roar that dawn,
The explosions of stone and the shrieks of iron,
And the vast wheels breaking free and bursting
Through the thick walls, and the washing women
Downstream the foam at their thighs looked up
To see their granite doom rolling down –
Not a wrinkle left, not a stain survived, and old
Misker, perched on Ribble the Mule, well the mule
Knew its place as it bolted and leapt head-first
Down the well, but poor old Misker hugged the
Draw pail on its rope and so swung clear, to
Skin his knees on the round's cobbles and swear
Loud, the boisterous breath preceding the fateful
Descent of toothy death the gear wheel, tall as any
Man but far taller than Misker (even perched on
His mule) and that would not be hard once it was

Done with him, why the rat – oh, did I forget to
Mention the rat?

Excerpt from *The Rat's Tail (the cause of it all)*
Chant Prip

S tumbling in the gloom, the drunk had fallen into the
canal. Tehol had mostly lost sight of him from his
position at the edge of the roof, but he could hear
splashing and curses, and the scrabbling against the rings
set in the stone wall.

Sighing, Tehol glanced over at the nameless guard Brys
had sent. Or one of them, at least. The three brothers
looked pretty much identical, and none had given their
names. Nothing outward or obvious to impress or inspire
fear. And, by the unwavering cast of their lipless, eye-
slitted expressions, sadly unqualified as welcome company.

'Can your friends tell you apart?' Tehol enquired, then
frowned. 'What a strange question to ask of a man. But you
must be used to strange questions, since people will assume
you were somewhere when you weren't, or, rather, not you,
but the other yous, each of whom could be anywhere. It
now occurs to me that saying nothing is a fine method for
dealing with such confusion, to which each of you have
agreed to as the proper response, unless you are the same
amongst yourselves, in which case it was a silent agreement. Always the best kind.'

The drunk, far below, was climbing from the canal, swearing in more languages than Tehol believed existed. 'Will you
listen to that? Atrocious. To hear such no doubt foul words
uttered with such vehemence – hold on, that's no drunk,
that's my manservant!' Tehol waved and shouted, 'Bugg!
What are you doing down there? Is this what I pay you for?'

The sodden manservant was looking upward, and he
yelled something back that Tehol could not make out.
'What? What did you say?'

'You – don't – pay – me!'

'Oh, tell everyone, why don't you!'

Tehol watched as Bugg made his way to the bridge and crossed, then disappeared from view behind the nearby buildings. 'How embarrassing. Time's come for a serious talk with dear old Bugg.'

Sounds from below, more cursing. Then creaking from the ladder.

Bugg's mud-smeared head and face rose into view.

'Now,' Tehol said, hands on hips, 'I'm sure I sent you off to do something important, and what do you do? Go falling into the canal. Was that on the list of tasks? I think not.'

'Are you berating me, master?'

'Yes. What did you think?'

'More effective, I believe, had you indeed sent me off to do something important. As it was, I was on a stroll, mesmerized by moonlight—'

'Don't step there! Back! Back!'

Alarmed, Bugg froze, then edged away.

'You nearly crushed Ezgara! And could he have got out of the way? I think not!' Tehol moved closer and knelt beside the insect making its slow way across the roof's uneven surface. 'Oh, look, you startled it!'

'How can you tell?' Bugg asked.

'Well, it's reversed direction, hasn't it? That must be startling, I would imagine.'

'You know, master, it was a curio – I didn't think you would make it a pet.'

'That's because you're devoid of sentiment, Bugg. Whereas Ezgara here is doubly—'

'Ovoid?'

'Charmingly so.' Tehol glanced over at the guard, who was staring back at him as was his wont. 'And this man agrees. Or, if not him, then his brothers. Why, one let Ezgara crawl all over his face, and he didn't even blink!'

'How did Ezgara manage to get onto his face, master?'

'And down the other's jerkin, not a flinch. These are warm-hearted men, Bugg, look well upon them and learn.'

632

'I shall, master.'

'Now, did you enjoy your swim?'

'Not particularly.'

'A misstep, you say?'

'I thought I heard someone whisper my name—'

'Shurq Elalle?'

'No.'

'Harlest Eberict? Kettle? Chief Investigator Rucket? Champion Ormly?'

'No.'

'Might you have been imagining things?'

'Quite possibly. For example, I believe I am being followed by rats.'

'You probably are, Bugg. Maybe one of them whispered your name.'

'An unpleasant notion, master.'

'Yes it is. Do you think it pleases me that my manservant consorts with rats?'

'Would you rather go hungry?' Bugg reached under his shirt.

'You haven't!'

'No, it's cat,' he said, withdrawing a small, skinned, headless and pawless carcass. 'Canal flavoured, alas.'

'Another gift from Rucket?'

'No, oddly enough. The canal.'

'Ugh.'

'Smells fresh enough—'

'What's that wire trailing from it?'

The manservant lifted the carcass higher, then took the dangling wire between two fingers and followed it back until it vanished in the flesh. He tugged, then grunted.

'What?' Tehol asked.

'The wire leads to a large, barbed hook.'

'Oh.'

'And the wire's snapped at this end – I thought something broke my fall.' He tore a small sliver of meat from one of the cat's legs, broke it in two, then placed one piece at each end of the insect named Ezgara. It settled to feed. 'Anyway, a quick rinse and we're ahead by two, if not three meals. Quite a run of fortune, master, of late.'

'Yes,' Tehol mused. 'Now I'm nervous. So, have you any news to tell me?'

'Do you realize, master, that Gerun Eberict would have had to kill on average between ten and fifteen people a day in order to achieve his annual dividend? How does he find the time to do anything else?'

'Perhaps he's recruited thugs sharing his insane appetites.'

'Indeed. Anyway, Shurq has disappeared – both Harlest and Ublala are distraught—'

'Why Harlest?'

'He had only Ublala to whom he could show off his new fangs and talons, and Ublala was less than impressed, so much so that he pushed Harlest into the sarcophagus and sealed him in.'

'Poor Harlest.'

'He adjusted quickly enough,' said Bugg, 'and now contemplates his dramatic resurrection – whenever it occurs.'

'Disturbing news about Shurq Elalle.'

'Why?'

'It means she didn't change her mind. It means she's going to break into the Tolls Repository. Perhaps even this very night.'

Bugg glanced over at the guard. 'Master . . .'

'Oops, that was careless, wasn't it?' He rose and walked over. 'He hears all, it's true. My friend, we can at least agree on one thing, can't we?'

The eyes flickered as the man stared at Tehol.

'Any thief attempting the Repository is as good as dead, right?' He smiled, then swung back to face his manservant.

Bugg began removing his wet clothes. 'I believe I've caught a chill.'

'The canal is notoriously noxious—'

'No, from earlier, master. The Fifth Wing. I've managed to successfully shore up the foundations—'

'Already? Why, that's extraordinary.'

'It is, isn't it? In any case, it's chilly in those tunnels . . . now.'

'Dare I ask?'

Bugg stood naked, eyes on the faint stars overhead. 'Best not, master.'

'And what of the Fourth Wing?'

'Well, that's where my crews are working at the moment. A week, perhaps ten days. There's an old drainage course beneath it. Rather than fight it, we're installing a fired-clay conduit—'

'A sewage pipe.'

'In the trade, it's a fired-clay conduit.'

'Sorry.'

'Which we'll then pack with gravel. I don't know why Grum didn't do that in the first place, but it's his loss and our gain.'

'Are you dry yet, Bugg? Please say you're dry. Look at our guard here, he's horrified. Speechless.'

'I can tell, and I apologize.'

'I don't think I've ever seen so many scars on one person,' Tehol said. 'What do you do in your spare time, Bugg, wrestle angry cacti?'

'I don't understand. Why would they have to be angry?'

'Wouldn't you be if you attacked you for no reason? Hey, that's a question I could ask our guard here, isn't it?'

'Only if he – or they – were similarly afflicted, master.'

'Good point. And he'd have to take his clothes off for us to find out.'

'Not likely.'

'No. Now, Bugg, here's my shirt. Put it on, and be thankful for the sacrifices I make on your behalf.'

'Thank you, master.'

'Good. Ready? It's time to go.'

'Where?'

635

'Familiar territory for you, or so I was surprised to discover. You are a man of many mysteries, Bugg. Occasional priest, healer, the Waiting Man, consorter with demons and worse. Were I not so self-centred, I'd be intrigued.'

'I am ever grateful for your self-centredness, master.'

'That's only right, Bugg. Now, presumably, our silent bodyguard will be accompanying us. Thus, we three. Marching purposefully off into the night. Shall we?'

Into the maze of shanties on the east side of Letheras. The night air was hot, redolent and turgid. Things skittered through the heaps of rotting rubbish, wild dogs slunk through shadows in ill-tempered packs looking for trouble – threatening enough to cause the bodyguard to draw his sword. Sight of the bared blade was enough to send the beasts scampering.

Those few homeless indigents brave or desperate enough to risk the dangers of the alleys and streets had used rubbish to build barricades and hovels. Others had begged for space on the sagging roofs of creaky huts and slept fitfully or not at all. Tehol could feel countless pairs of eyes looking down upon them, tracking their passage deeper into the heart of the ghetto.

As they walked, Tehol spoke. '. . . the assumption is the foundation stone of Letherii society, perhaps all societies the world over. The notion of inequity, my friends. For from inequity derives the concept of value, whether measured by money or the countless other means of gauging human worth. Simply put, there resides in all of us the unchallenged belief that the poor and the starving are in some way deserving of their fate. In other words, there will always be poor people. A truism to grant structure to the continual task of comparison, the establishment through observation of not our mutual similarities, but our essential differences.

'I know what you're thinking, to which I have no choice but to challenge you both. Like this. Imagine walking down

636

this street, doling out coins by the thousands. Until everyone here is in possession of vast wealth. A solution? No, you say, because among these suddenly rich folk there will be perhaps a majority who will prove wasteful, profligate and foolish, and before long they will be poor once again. Besides, if wealth were distributed in such a fashion, the coins themselves would lose all value – they would cease being useful. And without such utility, the entire social structure we love so dearly would collapse.

'Ah, but to that I say, so what? There are other ways of measuring self-worth. To which you both heatedly reply: with no value applicable to labour, all sense of worth vanishes! And in answer to that I simply smile and shake my head. Labour and its product become the negotiable commodities. But wait, you object, then value sneaks in after all! Because a man who makes bricks cannot be equated with, say, a man who paints portraits. Material is inherently value-laden, on the basis of our need to assert comparison – but ah, was I not challenging the very assumption that one must proceed with such intricate structures of value?

'And so you ask, what's your point, Tehol? To which I reply with a shrug. Did I say my discourse was a valuable means of using this time? I did not. No, you *assumed* it was. Thus proving my point!'

'I'm sorry, master,' Bugg said, 'but what was that point again?'

'I forget. But we've arrived. Behold, gentlemen, the poor.'

They stood at the edge of an old market round, now a mass of squalid shelters seething with humanity. A few communal hearths smouldered. The area was ringed in rubbish – mostly dog and cat bones – which was crawling with rats. Children wandered in the dazed, lost fashion of the malnourished. Newborns lay swaddled and virtually unattended. Voices rose in arguments and somewhere on the opposite side was a fight of some sort. Mixed-bloods, Nerek,

Faraed, Tarthenal, even the odd Fent. A few Letherii as well, escapees from Indebtedness.

Bugg looked on in silence for a half-dozen heartbeats, then said, 'Master, transporting them out to the Isles won't solve anything.'

'No?'

'These are broken spirits.'

'Beyond hope of recovery?'

'Well, that depends on how paternalistic you intend to be, master. The rigours of past lifestyles are beyond these people. We're a generation or more too late. They've not old skills to fall back on, and as a community this one is intrinsically flawed. It breeds violence and neglect and little else.'

'I know what you're saying, Bugg. You're saying you've had better nights and the timing wasn't good, not good at all. You're miserable, you've got a chill, you should be in bed.'

'Thank you, master. I was wondering myself.'

'Your issue of paternalism has some merit, I admit,' Tehol said, hands on hips as he studied the grubby shanty-town. 'That is to say, you have a point. In any case, doom is about to sweep through this sad place. Lether is at war, Bugg. There will be . . . recruitment drives.'

'Press-ganging,' the manservant said, nodding morosely.

'Yes, all that malignant violence put to good use. Of course, such poor soldiers will be employed as fodder. A harsh solution to this perennial problem, admittedly, but one with long precedent.'

'So, what have you planned, master?'

'The challenge facing myself and the sharp minds of the Rat Catchers' Guild, was, as you have observed, how does one reshape an entire society? How does one convert this impressive example of the instinct to survive into a communally positive force? Clearly, we needed to follow a well-established, highly successful social structure as our inspiration—'

'Rats.'

'Well done, Bugg. I knew I could count on you. Thus, we began with recognizing the need for a leader. Powerful, dynamic, charismatic, dangerous.'

'A criminal mastermind with plenty of thugs to enforce his or her will.'

Tehol frowned. 'Your choice of words disappoints me, Bugg.'

'You?'

'Me? Of course not. Well, not directly, that is. A truly successful leader is a reluctant leader. Not one whose every word is greeted with frenzied cheering either – after all, what happens to the mind of such a leader, after such scenes are repeated again and again? A growing certainty, a belief in one's own infallibility, and onward goes the march into disaster. No, Bugg, I won't have anyone kissing my feet—'

'I'm relieved to hear that, master, since those feet have not known soap in a long, long time.'

'The body eventually resumes its own natural cleansing mechanisms, Bugg.'

'Like shedding?'

'Exactly. In any case, I was speaking of leadership in a general sort of way—'

'Who, master?'

'Why, the Waiting Man, of course. Occasional priest, healer, consorter with demons . . .'

'That's probably not such a good idea, master,' Bugg said, rubbing his bristled jaw. 'I am rather . . . busy at the moment.'

'A leader should be busy. Distracted. Preoccupied. Prepared to delegate.'

'Master, I really don't think this is a good idea. Really.'

'Perfectly reluctant, perfect! And look! You've been noticed! See those hopeful faces—'

'That's hunger, master.'

639

'For salvation! Word's gone out, you see. They're ready for you, Bugg. They've been waiting . . .'

'This is very bad, master.'

'Your expression is perfect, Bugg. Sickly and wan with dismay, deeply troubled and nervous, yes indeed. I couldn't have managed better myself.'

'Master—'

'Go out among your flock, Bugg. Tell them – they're leaving. Tomorrow night. All of them. A better place, a better life awaits them. Go on, Bugg.'

'As long as no-one worships me,' the manservant replied. 'I don't like being worshipped.'

'Just stay fallible,' Tehol said.

Bugg cast him a strange look, then he walked into the shanty-town.

'Thank you for coming, Brys.'

Kuru Qan was sitting in the thickly padded chair near the wall opposite the library's entrance. Polished lenses and cloth in his hands, cleaning one lens then the other, then repeating the gesture, again and again. His eyes were fixed on nothing visible to Brys.

'More news from Trate, Ceda?'

'Something, yes, but we will discuss that later. In any case, we must consider the city lost.'

'Occupied.'

'Yes. Another battle is imminent, at High Fort.'

'The queen and the prince have withdrawn their forces, then? I understood they were seeking the pass.'

'Too late. The Edur had already made crossing.'

'Will you contribute to the defence?' Brys asked, striding into the small room and settling down on the bench to the Ceda's left.

'No.'

Surprised, Brys said nothing. He had been in the company of the king and Unnutal Hebaz for most of the evening, studying the detected movements of the enemy armies, immersed in the painful exercise of trying to predict the nature of his brother Hull's advice to the Edur emperor. Clearly, Hull had anticipated the pre-emptive attack on the villages. To Brys's mind, the rabid display of greed from the camps of the queen and the prince had tipped their hand. Janall, Quillas and their investors had already begun dividing up the potential spoils, which made clear their desire for a quick war, one that devastated the Tiste Edur, and that meant catching them unawares. Janall's march for the pass had indicated no change in her thinking. Yet now she had retreated.

The Tiste Edur had stolen the initiative. The appearance above High Fort, the surrender of Fent Reach and the fall of Trate indicated at least two enemy armies, as well as two fleets, all moving fast.

'Ceda, have you learned anything more of the demon that entered Trate harbour?'

'The danger is not singular, but plural,' Kuru Qan said. 'I see before me the Cedance, and have learned, to my horror, that it is . . . incomplete.'

'Incomplete? What do you mean?'

The Ceda continued cleaning the lenses in his hands. 'I must needs conserve my power, until the appropriate time. The seas must be freed. It is as simple as that.'

Brys waited, then, when Kuru Qan said no more, he ventured, 'Do you have a task for me, Ceda?'

'I would counsel a withdrawal from High Fort, but the king would not agree to that, would he?'

Brys shook his head. 'Your assessment is accurate. Even a disaster would be seen to have . . . benefits.'

'The elimination of his wife and son, yes. A tragic state of affairs, wouldn't you say, my young friend? The heart of the Cedance, I have come to realize, can be found in a systemic denial. And from that heart, all else is derived. Our very way of life and of seeing the world. We send soldiers to their deaths and how do we see those deaths? As glorious sacrifices. The enemy dead? As the victims of our

641

honourable righteousness. Whilst in our cities, in the narrow, foul alleys, a life that ends is but tragic failure. What, then, is the denial whereof I speak?'

'Death.'

Kuru Qan placed the lenses once more before his eyes and peered at Brys. 'You see, then. I knew you would. Brys, *there is no Hold of Death.* Your task? Naught but keeping an old man company on this night.'

The King's Champion rubbed at his face. His eyes felt full of grit, and he was unaccountably chilled. He was, he realized, exhausted.

'Our manic accumulation of wealth,' Kuru Qan went on. 'Our headlong progress, as if motion was purpose and purpose inherently virtuous. Our lack of compassion, which we called being realistic. The extremity of our judgements, our self-righteousness – all a flight from death, Brys. All a vast denial smothered in semantics and euphemisms. Bravery and sacrifice, pathos and failure, as if life is a contest to be won or lost. As if death is the arbiter of meaning, the moment of final judgement, and above all else judgement is a thing to be delivered, not delivered unto.'

'Would you rather we worship death, Ceda?'

'Equally pointless. One needs no faith to die, one dies none the less. I spoke of systemic denial, and it is indeed and in every way systemic. The very fabric of our world, here in Lether and perhaps elsewhere, has been twisted round that . . . absence. *There should be* a Hold of Death, do you understand? Relevant? The only relevance. It must have existed, once. Perhaps even a god, some ghastly skeleton on a throne of bones, a spin and dance of cold-legged flies for a crown. Yet here we are, and we have given it no face, no shape, no position in our elaborate scheme of existence.'

'Perhaps because it is the very opposite of existence—'

'But it isn't, Brys, it isn't. Errant take us, death is all around us. We stride over it, we breathe it, we soak its essence into our lungs, our blood. We feed upon it daily. We thrive in the midst of decay and dissolution.'

Brys studied the Ceda. 'It occurs to me,' he said slowly, 'that life itself is a celebration of denial. The denial of which you speak, Kuru Qan. Our flight – well, to flee is to lift oneself clear of the bones, the ashes, the fallen away.'

'Flee – to where?'

'Granted. Nowhere but elsewhere. I wonder if what you've said is being manifested, in creatures such as Kettle and that thief, Shurq Elalle—'

The Ceda's head snapped up, eyes suddenly alert behind the thick lenses. 'I'm sorry? What did you say?'

'Well, I was speaking of those who are denied death in truth, Ceda. The child, Kettle—'

'The guardian of the Azath? She is undead?'

'Yes. I'm sure I mentioned—'

Kuru Qan was on his feet. 'Are you certain of this? Brys Beddict, she is an undead?'

'She is. But I don't understand—'

'Stand up, Brys. We're going. Now.'

'It's all the fallen people,' Kettle said. 'They want answers. They won't go until they get answers.'

Shurq Elalle kicked away an insect that had crawled onto her boot. 'Answers about what?'

'Why they died.'

'There are no answers,' Shurq replied. 'It's what people do. Die. They die. They always die.'

'We didn't.'

'Yes we did.'

'Well, we didn't go away.'

'From the sound of it, Kettle, neither did they.'

'That's true. I wonder why I didn't think of that.'

'Because you were about ten years old when you died.'

'Well, what do I do now?'

Shurq studied the overgrown, ground-heaved yard. 'You gave me the idea, and that's why I am here. You said the dead were gathering. Gathering round this place, hovering just outside the walls. Can you talk to them?'

643

'Why would I want to? They never say anything interesting.'

'But you could if you had to.'

Kettle shrugged. 'I guess.'

'Good. Ask for volunteers.'

'For what?'

'I want them to come with me. On an outing. Tonight and again tomorrow night.'

'Why would they want to, Mother?'

'Tell them they will see more gold than they can imagine. They will learn secrets few in this kingdom possess. Tell them I am going to lead them on a tour of the Tolls Repository and the royal vaults. Tell them, the time's come to have fun. Terrifying the living.'

'Why would ghosts want to scare the living?'

'I know, it's a strange notion, but I predict they will discover they're very good at it. Further, I predict they will enjoy the endeavour.'

'But, how will they do that? They're ghosts. The living can't even see them.'

Shurq Elalle swung about and stared out on the milling crowds. 'Kettle, they look pretty solid to us, don't they?'

'But we're dead—'

'Then why couldn't we see them a week ago? They were just flits, on the edge of our vision back then, weren't they? If that, even. So what has changed? Where has their power come from? Why is it growing?'

'I don't know.'

Shurq smiled. 'I do.'

Kettle walked over to one of the low walls.

The thief watched her speaking to the ghosts. *I wonder if she realizes. I wonder if she knows she's more alive now than dead. I wonder if she knows she's coming back to life.*

After a moment the child returned, pulling her fingers through her hair to loosen the snarls. 'You are smart, Mother,' she said. 'I'm glad you're my mother and that's why.'

'I have some volunteers?'

'They'll all go. They want to see the gold. They want to scare people.'

'I need some who can read and some who can count.'

'That's okay. So tell me, Mother, why are they growing more powerful? What's changed?'

Shurq looked back at the square, squalid tower of stone. 'That, Kettle.'

'The Azath?'

'Yes.'

'Oh,' the child said. 'I understand now. It died.'

'Yes,' Shurq said, nodding. 'It died.'

After Mother had left, thousands of ghosts following, Kettle walked to the tower's entrance. She studied the flagstones set before the door, then selected one and knelt before it. Her fingernails broke prying it loose, and she was surprised at the sting of pain and the welling of blood.

She had not told Shurq how hard it had been speaking to those ghosts. Their endless voices had been fading the last day or two, as if she was becoming deaf. Although other sounds – the wind, the dead leaves scurrying about, the crunch and munch of the insects in the yard, and the sounds of the city itself – all were as clear as ever. Something was happening to her. That beating vibration in her chest had quickened. Five, six eights a day, now. The places where her skin had broken long ago were closing up with new, pink skin, and earlier today she had been thirsty. It had taken some time to realize – to remember, perhaps – what thirst was, what it signified, but the stagnant water she had found at the base of one of the pits in the yard had tasted wonderful. So many things were changing, it seemed, confusing her.

She dragged the flagstone to one side, then sat beside it. She wiped the dust from its blank, polished surface. There were funny patterns in it. Shells, the imprint of plants – reeds with their onion-like root-balls – and the pebbled impressions of coral. Tiny bones. Someone had done a lot of carving to make such a pretty scene of dead things.

She looked down the path, through the gate and onto the street. Strange, to see it so empty now. But, she knew, it wouldn't be for long.

And so she waited.

The bleeding from her fingertips had stopped by the time she heard the footfalls approaching. She looked up, then smiled upon seeing Uncle Brys and the old man with the glass eyes – the one she had never seen before yet knew anyway.

They saw her, and Brys strode through the gate, the old man following behind with nervous, tentative steps.

'Hello, Uncle,' Kettle said.

'Kettle. You are looking . . . better. I have brought a guest, Ceda Kuru Qan.'

'Yes, the one who's always looking at me but not seeing me, but looking anyway.'

'I wasn't aware of that,' the Ceda said.

'Not like you're doing now,' Kettle said. 'Not when you have those things in front of your eyes.'

'You mean, when I look upon the Cedance? Is that when I see you without seeing you?'

She nodded.

'The Hold of the Azath is gone, child, yet here you remain. You were its guardian when it was alive – when you were not. And now, you are its guardian still? When it is dead and you are not?'

'I'm not dead?'

'Not quite. The heart placed within you. Once frozen . . . now . . . thawing. I do not understand its power, and, I admit, it frightens me.'

'I have a friend who said he'll destroy me if he has to,' Kettle said, smiling. 'But he says he probably won't have to.'

'Why not?'

'He says the heart won't wake up. Not completely. That's why the Nameless One took my body.'

She watched the old man's mouth moving, but no words came forth. At his side, Uncle Brys stepped closer, concern on his face.

'Ceda? Are you all right?'

'Nameless One?' The old man was shivering. 'This place – this is the Hold of Death, isn't it? It's become the Hold of Death.'

Kettle reached over and picked up the flagstone. It was as heavy as a corpse, so she was used to the weight. 'This is for your Cedance, for where you look when you don't see me.'

'A tile.' Kuru Qan looked away as she set it down in front of him.

'Ceda,' Uncle Brys said, 'I do not understand. What has happened here?'

'Our history ... so much is proving untrue. The Nameless Ones were of the First Empire. A cult. It was expunged. Eliminated. It cannot have survived, but it seems to have done just that. It seems to have outlived the First Empire itself.'

'Are they some sort of death cult?'

'No. They were servants of the Azath.'

'Then why,' Brys asked, 'do they appear to have been overseeing the death of this Azath tower?'

Kuru Qan shook his head. 'Unless they saw it as inevitable. And so they acted in order to counter those within the barrows who would escape once the tower died. The manifestation of a Hold of Death may turn out to have nothing to do with them.'

'Then why is she still the guardian?'

'She may not be, Brys. She waits in order to deal with those who are about to escape the grounds.' The Ceda's gaze returned to Kettle. 'Child, is that why you remain?'

She shrugged. 'It won't be long now.'

'And the one the Azath chose to help you, Kettle, will he emerge in time?'

'I don't know. I hope so.'

'So do I,' Kuru Qan said. 'Thank you, child, for the tile. Still, I wonder at your knowledge of this new Hold.'

Kettle pulled an insect from her hair and tossed it aside. 'The pretty man told me all about it,' she said.

'Another visitor?'

'Only once. Mostly he just stands in the shadows, across the street. Sometimes he followed me when I went hunting, but he never said anything. Not until today, when he came over and we talked.'

'Did he tell you his name?' the Ceda asked.

'No. But he was very handsome. Only he said he had a girlfriend. Lots. Boyfriends, too. Besides, I shouldn't give my heart away. That's what he said. He never does. Never ever.'

'And this man told you all about the Hold of Death?'

'Yes, Grandfather. He knew all about it. He said it doesn't need a new guardian, because the throne is already occupied, at least everywhere else. Here too, soon. I'm tired of talking now.'

'Of course, Kettle,' Kuru Qan said. 'We shall take our leave of you, then.'

'Goodbye. Oh, don't forget the tile!'

'We will send some people to collect it, child.'

'All right.'

She watched them walk away. When they were gone from sight she headed over to her friend's barrow, and felt him close. 'Where are you taking me this time?'

Her hand in his, she found herself standing on a low hill, and before them was a vast, shallow valley, filled with corpses.

It was dusk, a layer of smoke hanging over the vista. Just above the horizon opposite, a suspended mountain of black stone was burning, columns of smoke billowing from its gashed flanks. Below, the bodies were mostly of some kind of huge, reptilian creature wearing strange armour. Grey-skinned and long-snouted, their forms were contorted and ribboned with slashes, lying in tangled heaps. Here and there in their midst lay other figures. Tall, some with grey skins, some with black.

Standing beside her, he spoke. 'Over four hundred thousand, Kettle. Here in this valley alone. There are other . . . valleys. Like this one.'

A score of leathery-winged beasts were crossing the valley at one end, far to their right.

'Ooh, are those dragons?'

'Spawn. Locqui Wyval, searching for their master. But he is gone. Once they realize that, they will know to wait. It will prove a long wait.'

'Are they waiting still?'

'Yes.'

'When did this battle happen?'

'Many thousands of years ago, Kettle. But the damage remains. In a short while, the ice will arrive, sealing all you see. Holding all in stasis, a sorcery of impressive power, so powerful it will prove a barrier to the dead themselves – to the path their spirits would take. I wonder if that was what the Jaghut had intended. In any case, the land was twisted by the magic. The dead . . . lingered. Here, in the north, and far to the south, as far as Letheras itself. To my mind, an Elder god meddled. But none could have foreseen the consequences, not even an Elder god.'

'Is that why the tower has become the Hold of Death?'

'It has? I was not aware of that. This, then, is what comes, when the sorcery finally dies and the world thaws. Balance is reasserted.'

'Shurq Elalle says we are at war. The Tiste Edur, she says, are invading Lether.'

'Let us hope they do not arrive before I am free.'

'Why?'

'Because they will endeavour to kill me, Kettle.'

'Why?'

'For fear that I will seek to kill them.'

'Will you?'

'On many levels,' he replied, 'there is no reason why I

shouldn't. But no, not unless they get in my way. You and I know, after all, that the true threat waits in the barrows of the Azath grounds.'

'I don't think the Edur will win the war,' she said.

'Yes, failure on their part would be ideal.'

'So what else did you want to show me?'

A pale white hand gestured towards the valley. 'There is something odd to all this. Do you see? Or, rather, what don't you see?'

'I don't see any ghosts.'

'Yes. The spirits are gone. The question is, where are they?'

Terrified screams echoed as Shurq Elalle walked down the wide, high-ceilinged corridor to the Master Chamber of the Tolls Repository. Guards, servants, clerks and cleaning staff had one and all succumbed to perfectly understandable panic. There was nothing worse, she reflected, than the unexpected visitations of dead relatives.

Ahead, the double doors were wide open, and the lanterns in the huge room beyond were swinging wildly to immanent gusts of spirited haste.

The thief strode into the chamber.

A squalid ghost rushed up to her, rotted face grinning wildly. 'I touched it! My last coin! I found it in the stacks! And touched it!'

'I am happy for you,' Shurq said. 'Now, where are the counters and readers?'

'Eh?'

Shurq moved past the ghost. The chamber was seething, spirits hurrying this way and that, others hunched over tumbled scrolls, still others squirming along the shelves. Chests of coins had been knocked over, the glittering gold coins stirring about on the marble floor as gibbering wraiths pawed them.

'I worked here!'

Shurq eyed the ghost drifting her way. 'You did?'

'Oh yes. They put in more shelves, and look at those lantern nooks – what idiot decided on those dust-traps? Dust is a fire hazard. Terrible fire hazard. Why, I was always telling them that. And now I could prove my point – a nudge, a simple nudge of that lantern there, yes . . .'

'Come back here! Nothing burns. Understand?'

'If you say so. Fine. I was just kidding, anyway.'

'Have you looked at the ledgers?'

'Yes, yes, and counted. And memorized. I was always good at memorizing; that's why they hired me. I could count and count and never lose my place. But the dust! Those nooks! Everything might burn, burn terribly—'

'Enough of that. We have what we need. Time for everyone to leave.'

A chorus of wavering voices answered her. 'We don't want to!'

'There'll be priests coming. Probably already on their way. And mages, eager to collect wraiths to enslave as their servants for eternity.'

'We're leaving!'

'You,' said Shurq to the ghost before her, 'come with me. Talk. Give me details.'

'Yes, yes. Of course.'

'Leave that lantern alone, damn you!'

'Sorry. Terrible fire hazard, oh, the flames there'd be. Such flames, all those inks, the colours!'

'Everyone!' the thief shouted. 'We're going now! And you, stop rolling that coin – it stays here!'

'The Seventh Closure,' Kuru Qan muttered as they made their way back to the palace. 'It is all spiralling inward. Troubling, this concatenation of details. The Azath dies, a Hold of Death comes into being. A Nameless One appears and somehow possesses the corpse of a child, then fashions an alliance with a denizen of a barrow. A usurper proclaims himself emperor of the Tiste Edur, and now leads an invasion. Among his allies, a demon from the sea, one of

651

sufficient power to destroy two of my best mages. And now, if other rumours are true, it may be the emperor is himself a man of many lives . . .'

Brys glanced over. 'What rumours?'

'Citizens witnessed his death in Trate. The Edur emperor was cut down in battle. Yet he . . . *returned*. Probably an exaggeration, but I am nervous none the less at my own assumptions in this matter, Brys. Still, the Tiste Edur have superb healers. Perhaps a binding spell of some sort, cleaving the soul to the flesh until they can arrive . . . I must give this more thought.'

'And you believe, Ceda, that all this is somehow linked to the Seventh Closure?'

'The rebirth of our empire. That is my fear, Champion. That we have in some fatal way misread our ancient prophecy. Perhaps the empire has already appeared.'

'The Tiste Edur? Why would a Letherii prophecy have anything to do with them?'

Kuru Qan shook his head. 'It is a prophecy that arose in the last days of the First Empire. Brys, there is so much we have lost. Knowledge, the world of that time. Sorcery gone awry, birthing horrific beasts, the armies of undead who delivered such slaughter among our people, then simply left. Mysterious tales of a strange realm of magic that was torn apart. Could the role of an entire people fit in any of the gaps in our knowing? Yes. And what of other people who are named, yet nothing more than the names survives – no descriptions? Barghast, Jhag, Trell. Neighbouring tribes? We'll never know.'

They came to the gates. Sleepy guards identified them and opened the lesser postern door. The palace grounds were empty, silent. The Ceda paused and stared up at the hazy stars overhead.

Brys said nothing. He waited, standing at the old man's side, seeing the night sky reflected in the twin lenses in front of Kuru Qan's eyes. Wondering what the Ceda was thinking.

Tehol Beddict smiled as she threaded her way through the crowd towards him. 'Chief Investigator Rucket, I am delighted to see you again.'

'No you're not,' she replied. 'You're just trying to put me on the defensive.'

'How does my delight make you defensive?'

'Because I get suspicious, that's why. You're not fooling me, with those absurd trousers and that idiotic insect on your shoulder.'

Tehol looked down in surprise. 'Ezgara! I thought I left you on the roof.'

'You've named him Ezgara? He doesn't look a thing like our king. Oh, maybe if our king had two heads, then I might see the resemblance, but as it stands, that's a stupid name.'

'The three of us are deeply offended, as is my bodyguard here and, one must assume, his two brothers wherever they are. Thus, the six of us. Deeply offended.'

'Where is Bugg?'

'Somewhere in that crowd behind you, I suppose.'

'Well, no. They're all looking.'

'Oh, he was there a moment ago.'

'But he isn't any longer, and the people are clamouring.'

'No they aren't, Rucket. They're milling.'

'Now you're challenging my assessment. Concluding, no doubt, that contrariness is sexually attractive. Maybe for some women it is, the kind you prefer, I'd wager. But I take exception to your taking exception to everything I say.'

'Now who's being contrary?'

She scowled. 'I was intending to invite you to a late night bite. There is a courtyard restaurant not far from here—'

'The Trampled Peacock.'

'Why, yes. I am dismayed that you are familiar with it. Suggesting to me, for obvious reasons, that clandestine trysts are common with you, further suggesting a certain cheapness and slatternly behaviour on your part. I don't know why I am surprised that you're so loose, actually. I should have expected it. Accordingly, I want nothing to do with you.'

'I've never been there.'

'You haven't? Then how do you know of it?'

I own it. 'Reputation, I imagine. I wish I could be more precise. Who said what and when and all that, but it's late and even if it wasn't I'd probably not recall such details.'

'So, are you hungry?'

'Always. Oh, here's my manservant. Did you hear, Bugg? Chief Investigator Rucket has invited us to supper.'

'Well, the cat can wait.'

Rucket glared at Tehol. 'Who said anything about him?'

'I go everywhere with my manservant, Rucket. And my bodyguard.'

'Everywhere? Even on dates?'

'Bugg,' Tehol said, 'have you done all you can here? Is it time to let these poor people sleep?'

'Well past time, master.'

'We're off to the Trampled Peacock!'

'Is that such a good idea, master?'

'Well, it wasn't mine, Bugg, but there it is. Please, Rucket, lead the way.'

'Oh, wonderful. I look forward to a night of weathering attacks on my vanity. Come now, all of you, we're wasting time.'

Tehol threw up his hands as soon as they entered the court-yard. 'Extraordinary! Bugg, look who's here! Why, it's Shand and Rissarh and Hejun! Come, let us put two tables together and so make of this a festive gathering of co-conspirators!'

'The coincidence leaves me awed,' the manservant said.

'Who in the Errant's name are those women?' Rucket demanded. 'And why are they all so angry?'

'That's not anger,' Tehol said, approaching, 'that's

recognition. Dear women, how are you all? Faring well, I see. We've decided to join you.'

'Who is this absurd creature at your side?' Shand asked. 'And what's with the cape?'

'Watch who you're calling a creature, cobble-head,' Rucket hissed.

'Tehol's found a woman,' Rissarh said in a snarl. 'Typical. He steals our man then gets himself a woman—'

Hejun grunted. 'I was beginning to suspect him and the dead bitch.'

'Dead bitch?' Rucket's eyes were wild as she looked round. 'He makes love to a dead bitch?'

'One freak accident—' Tehol began.

'If you shaved your head,' Shand said to Rucket, sputtering with rage, 'we'd all see how truly ugly you are!'

The guard was looking alarmed. People at other tables gestured madly at the serving staff.

'Worked hard on that one, did you?' Rucket asked. 'Tehol, what's all this about stealing their man? They were sharing one man? Is he still alive? Still sane? Did he volunteer at the Drownings?'

'You want to see me work hard?' Shand rose to her feet, reaching for the knife at her side.

'Oh, how pathetic,' Rucket said. 'Here, compare that with my rapier here.'

'Get her!' This from Rissarh, as she launched herself across the table. It collapsed beneath her a moment later, but she had managed to wrap her arms about Rucket's thighs. The Chief Investigator made a strange squealing sound as she was pulled over. The rapier sprang free and slapped hard against Shand's out-thrust wrist, sending the knife spinning. Hejun then snagged Rucket's sword-arm and twisted the weapon loose. A finely polished boot shot up to strike Hejun in the belly. She groaned and sagged.

Tehol pulled Bugg back a step. 'I think you were right about this not being a good idea.'

Grunts, meaty thuds and flying fists. Fleeing patrons, the yowl of a cat in the kitchen.

Tehol sighed. 'We should go. But first, arrange with the manager four bottles of fine wine, for when they're finished beating on each other. I predict that by dawn they will all be fast friends.'

'I'm not sure of that—'

'Nonsense, Bugg, it's the way of things. Come on, before they turn on us.'

Not surprisingly, the bodyguard led the way out of the courtyard.

Outside, Tehol brushed imaginary dust from his hands. 'All in all, a fine evening, wouldn't you say? Now, we should see if we can scrounge some firewood – or at least something that burns – on our way home. Roast cat beckons.'

The crashing sounds from the restaurant courtyard suddenly increased.

Tehol hesitated. 'I'm tempted by the sounds of firewood production in there.'

'Don't be a fool, master.'

'Perhaps you're right. Lead us on, Bugg. Home.'

CHAPTER EIGHTEEN

Expectancy stands alone
And crowds the vast emptiness
This locked chest of a chamber
With its false floor the illusory
Dais on which, four-legged
carpentry of stretcher-
bearers, crouches the throne
Of tomorrow's glory when
The hunters come down
From the cut-wood gloom
Stung hard to pursuit
The shadows of potentates
And pretenders but he holds
Fast, the privileged indifference
That is fruitless patience
Expectancy stands ever
Alone before this eternally
Empty, so very empty throne.

Hold of the Empty Throne
Kerrulict

A shes swirling on all sides, the river a snake of sludge
spreading its stain into the dead bay, the Nerek
youth squatted at the edge of the sacred land.
Behind him, the others sat round their precious hearth and
continued arguing. The youth knew enough to wait.

Consecrated ground. They had huddled on it whilst the sorcerous storms raged, destroying the village of the Hiroth, flattening the forests around them, and the fires that burned for days afterwards could not lash them with their heat. And now the cinders had cooled, no more sparks danced in the wind, and the bloated bodies of dead wild animals that had crowded the river mouth had broken loose some time in the night just past, drawn out to the sea and the waiting sharks.

His knife-sharer came to his side and crouched down. 'Their fear holds them back,' he said, 'and yet it is that very fear that will force them to accept. They have no choice.'

'I know.'

'When you first spoke of your dreams, I believed you.'

'Yes.'

'Our people have not dreamed since the Letherii conquered us. Our nights were empty, and we believed they would be so for all time, until the last Nerek died and we were no more a people. But I saw the truth in your eyes. We have shared the knife, you and I. I did not doubt.'

'I know, brother.'

The eldest of the Nerek called out behind them, a voice harsh with anger, 'It is decided. The two of you will go. By the old paths, to make your travel swift.'

Youth and knife-brother both rose and swung round.

The eldest nodded. 'Go. Find Hull Beddict.'

The two Nerek stepped out into the gritty ash, and began the journey south. The birth of dreams had revealed once more the old paths, the ways through and between worlds. It would not take long.

Fear Sengar led him into a secluded glade, the sounds of the readied army distant and muted. As soon as Trull took his first stride into the clearing, his brother spun round. Forearm hard against his throat, weight driving him back until he struck the bole of a tree, where Fear held him.

'*You will be silent!* No more of your doubts, not to anyone

658

else and not to me. You are my brother, and that alone is why I have not killed you outright. Are you hearing me, Trull?'

He was having trouble breathing, yet he remained motionless, his eyes fixed on Fear's.

'Why do you not answer?'

Still he said nothing.

With a snarl Fear drew his arm away and stepped back.

'Kill me, would you?' Trull continued to lean against the tree. He smiled. 'From behind, then? A knife, catching me unawares. Otherwise, brother, you would be hard-pressed.'

Fear looked away. Then nodded. 'Yes.'

'A knife in the back.'

'Yes.'

'Because, if I have my spear, it's equally likely that you would be killed, not me.'

Fear glared at him, then the anger slowly drained from his eyes. 'It must stop, Trull. We are about to go into battle—'

'And you doubt my ability?'

'No, only your willingness.'

'Well, yes, you are right to doubt that. But I will do as you command. I will kill Letherii for you.'

'For the emperor. For our people—'

'No. For you, Fear. Otherwise, you would be well advised to question my ability. Indeed, to remove me from command. From this entire, absurd war. Send me away, to the northernmost villages of the Den-Ratha where there are likely to be a few thousand Edur who chose to remain behind.'

'There are none such.'

'Of course there are.'

'A handful.'

'More than you think. And yes, I have been tempted to join them.'

'Rhulad would not permit it. He would have to kill you.'

'I know.'

659

Fear began pacing. 'The K'risnan. They said Rhulad was killed yesterday. In Trate. Then he returned. There can be no doubt, now, brother. Our emperor cannot be stopped. His power does naught but grow—'

'You are seeing this wrong, Fear.'

He paused, looked over. 'What do you mean?'

'"Our emperor cannot be stopped." I do not see it that way.'

'All right. How do you see it, Trull?'

'Our brother is doomed to die countless deaths. Die, rise, and die again. Our brother, Fear, the youngest among us. That is how I see it. And now, I am to embrace the power that has done this to Rhulad? I am to serve it? Lend it my skills with the spear? I am to carve an empire for it? Are his deaths without pain? Without horror? Is he not scarred? How long, Fear, can his sanity hold on? There he stands, a young warrior bedecked in a gold nightmare, his flesh puckered and mangled, and weapons shall pierce him – he knows it, he knows he will be killed again and again.'

'Stop, Trull.' Like a child, Fear placed his hands over his ears and turned away. 'Stop.'

'Who is doing this to him?'

'Stop!'

Trull subsided. *Tell me, brother, do you feel as helpless as I do?*

Fear faced him once more, his expression hardening anew. 'Voice your doubts if you must, Trull, but only to me. In private.'

'Very well.'

'Now, a battle awaits us.'

'It does.'

A herd of deer had been startled from the forest fringe south of Katter River, darting and leaping as they fled across the killing field. On the earthen ramparts outside High Fort's walls, Moroch Nevath stood beside his queen and his prince. Before them in a motionless row were arrayed the four sorcerors of Janall's cadre, wrapped in cloaks against the morning chill, while to either side and along the length of the fortified berm waited the heavy infantry companies of the queen's battalion. Flanking each company were massive wagons, and on each squatted a Dresh ballista, its magazine loaded with a thirty-six-quarrel rack. Spare racks waited nearby on the ramped loader, the heavily armoured crew gathered round, nervously scanning the line of woods to the north.

'The Edur are moving down,' Prince Quillas said. 'We should see them soon.'

The deer had settled on the killing field and were grazing.

Moroch glanced to the lesser berm to the east. Two more companies were positioned there. The gap between the two ramparts was narrow and steep-sided, and led directly to a corner bastion on the city's wall, where ballistae and mangonels commanded the approach.

The prince's own mage cadre, three lesser sorcerors, were positioned with a small guard on the rampart immediately south of the Dry Gully, tucked in the angular indentation of High Fort's walls. The old drainage course wound a path down from the minor range of hills a thousand paces to the north. Three additional ramparts ran parallel to the Dry Gully, on which were positioned the forward elements of the Grass Jackets Brigade. The easternmost and largest of these ramparts also held a stone-walled fort, and it was there that the brigade commanders had placed their own mage cadre.

Additional ramparts were situated in a circle around the rest of High Fort, and on these waited reserve elements of the brigades and battalions, including elements of heavy cavalry. Lining the city's walls and bastions was High Fort's own garrison.

To Moroch's thinking, this imminent battle would be decisive. The treachery of the Edur that had been revealed at Trate would not be repeated here, not with eleven sorcerors present among the Letherii forces.

661

'Wraiths!'

The shout came from one of the queen's officers, and Moroch Nevath returned his attention to the distant treeline.

The deer had lifted their heads, were staring fixedly at the forest edge. A moment later they bolted once more, this time in a southwest direction, reaching the loggers' road, down which they bounded until lost in the mists.

On the other side of the killing field – pasture in peaceful times – shadows were flowing out from between the boles, vaguely man-shaped, drawing up into a thick mass that then stretched out into a rough line, three hundred paces long and scores deep. Behind them came huge, lumbering demons, near twice the height of a man, perhaps a hundred in all, that assembled into a wedge behind the line of wraiths. Finally, to either side, appeared warriors, Tiste Edur to the right of the wedge, and a horde of small, fur-clad savages on the far left.

'Who are they?' Prince Quillas asked. 'Those on the far flank – they are not Edur.'

The queen shrugged. 'Some lost band of Nerek, perhaps. I would judge a thousand, no more than that, and poorly armed and armoured.'

'Fodder,' Moroch said. 'The Edur have learned much from us, it seems.'

A similar formation was assembling north of the lesser berm, although there both flanking forces were Tiste Edur.

'The wraiths will charge first,' Moroch predicted, 'with the demons behind them seeking to break our lines. And there, signal flags from the Grass Jackets. They have no doubt sighted their own enemy ranks.'

'Were you the Edur commander,' Quillas said, 'what would you do? The attack cannot be as straightforward as it now seems, can it?'

'If the commander is a fool, it can,' Janall said.

'The sorcery will prove mutually negating, as it always does. Thus, the battle shall be blade against blade.' Moroch thought for a moment, then said, 'I would make use of the Dry Gully. And seek a sudden charge against your mage cadre, Prince.'

'They would become visible – and vulnerable – for the last fifty or sixty paces of the charge, Finadd. The bastions will slaughter them, and if not them, then the westernmost company of the Grass Jackets can mount a downslope charge into their flank.'

'Thus leaving their rampart under-defended. Use the Dry Gully as a feint, and a reserve force to then rush the rampart and seize it.'

'That rampart crouches in the shadow of High Fort's largest bastion tower, Finadd. The Edur would be slaughtered by the answering enfilade.'

After a moment, Moroch nodded. 'It is as you say, Prince. I admit, I see nothing advantageous to the Tiste Edur.'

'I agree,' Prince Quillas said.

'Strangely quiet,' Moroch mused after a time as the enemy forces assembled.

'It's the wraiths and demons, Finadd. No soldiers like thinking of those.'

'The mages will annihilate them,' Janall pronounced. She was dressed in elaborate armour, her helm filigreed in silver and gold. Her sword was the finest Letherii steel, but the grip was bound gold wire and the pommel a cluster of pearls set in silver. Beadwork covered her tabard. Beneath, Moroch knew, was steel scale. He did not think she would find need to draw her sword. Even so . . . The Finadd swung about and gestured to an aide, whom he then drew to one side. 'Ready the queen's horses, in the south lee of the west bastion.'

'Yes, sir.'

Something was wrong. Moroch felt it as he watched the aide hurry off. He scanned the sky. Grey. Either the sun would burn through or there would be rain. He returned to his original position and studied the distant ranks. 'They're in position. Where are the chants? The exhortations? The ritual curses?'

'They see the doom awaiting them,' Quillas said, 'and are silenced by terror.'

A sudden stirring among the queen's mages. Alertness. Janall noticed and said, 'Prepare the lines. The Edur have begun sorcery.'

'What kind?' Moroch asked.

The queen shook her head.

'Betrayer's balls,' the Finadd muttered. It felt wrong. Terribly wrong.

Ahlrada Ahn had drawn his cutlass and was grinning. 'I never understood you spear-wielders. This will be close fighting, Trull Sengar. They will hack the shaft from your hands—'

'They will try. Blackwood will not shatter, as you know. Nor shall my grip.'

Standing behind the wedge of demons was a K'risnan. The warlock's comrade was with the other force, also positioned behind a demon cohort. Hanradi Khalag commanded there, and the K'risnan in his charge was his son.

B'nagga and a thousand of his Jheck were just visible in a basin to the west. Another thousand were moving down the gully, whilst the third thousand accompanied the easternmost force along with wraiths and demons.

It occurred to Trull that he knew almost nothing of the huge, armoured demons bound to this war by the K'risnan. Not even the name by which they called themselves.

Warriors of the Arapay and Hiroth were massed along the forest line, less than a third of their total numbers visible to the enemy. Outwardly, the dominant Edur army would appear to be the central one, Hanradi Khalag's eighteen thousand Hiroth and Merude, but in truth Fear's force here in the forest amounted to almost twenty-three thousand Edur warriors. And arrayed among them were wraiths in numbers beyond counting.

Tendrils of grey mist swirled round the nearest K'risnan, forming a fluid web that began to thicken, then rise. Thread-thin strands snaked out, entwining the nearest ranks of Edur. Flowing out like roots, embracing all within sight barring the wraiths and the demons. In a billowing, grey wall, the sorcery burgeoned. Trull felt it playing over him, and its touch triggered a surge of nausea that he barely defeated.

From the Letherii cadre, a wave of raging fire rose in answer, building with a roar directly in front of the rampart, then plunging swift and savage across the killing field.

As suddenly as that, the battle was begun.

Trull stared as the massive wall of flame rushed towards them. At the last moment the grey skein rushed out, colliding with the wave and lifting it straight up in explosive columns, pillars that spiralled with silver fire.

And Trull saw, within the flames, the gleam of bones. Thousands, then hundreds of thousands, as if the fire's very fuel had been transformed. Towering higher, fifty man-heights, then a hundred, two hundred, filling the sky.

The conjoined wave then began toppling. Fiery pillars heaving over, towards the Letherii entrenchments.

Even as they plunged earthward, the wraiths from the forest and those in the foremost line launched into a rushing attack. The wedge of demons promptly vanished.

It was the signal Trull and the other officers had been waiting for. 'Weapons ready!' He had to bellow to make himself heard—

The wave struck. First the killing field, and the ground seemed to explode, churning, as if a multitude of miner's picks had struck the earth, deep, tearing loose huge chunks that were flung high into the air. Dust and flames, the clash of split bones ripping the flat expanse, a sound like hail on sheets of iron. Onward, onto the slopes of the ramparts.

In its wake, a flowing sea of wraiths.

'Forward!'

And then the Edur were running across broken, steaming ground. Behind them, thousands pouring from the forest edge.

Trull saw, all too clearly, as the wave of burning, hammering bones reached the entrenchments. A blush of crimson, then pieces of human flesh danced skyward, a wall, rising, severed limbs flailing in the air. Fragments of armour, the shattered wood of the bulwarks, skin and hair.

The queen's cadre was engulfed, bones rushing in to batter where they had been. A moment later the mass exploded outward in a hail of shards, and of the four sorcerors who had been standing there a moment earlier only two remained, sheathed in blood and reeling.

A demon rose from the ravaged earth in front of them, mace swinging. The mage it struck seemed to fold bonelessly around it, and his body was tossed through the air. The last sorceror staggered back, narrowly avoiding the huge weapon's deadly path. She gestured, even as a hail of heavy quarrels hammered into the demon.

Trull heard its squeal of pain.

Flickering magic swarmed the demon as it spun round and toppled, sliding down the blood-soaked slope, the mace tumbling away.

Other demons had appeared among the remnants of the Letherii soldiery, flailing bodies flying from their relentless path.

Another wave of sorcery, this time from somewhere to the southeast, a rolling column, crackling with lightning as it swept crossways on the killing field, plunging into the advancing ranks of wraiths. They melted in their hundreds as the magic tore through them.

Then the sorcery struck Hanradi Khalag's warriors, scything a path through the press.

The Merude chief's son counter-attacked, another surge of grey, tumbling bones. A rampart to the east vanished in a thunderous detonation, but hundreds of Edur lay dead or dying on the field.

Deafened, half-blinded by dust and smoke, Trull and his warriors reached the slope, scrambled upward and came to the first trench.

Before them stretched an elongated pit filled with un-recognizable flesh, split bones and spilled organs, strips of leather and pieces of armour. The air was thick with the stench of ruptured bowels and burnt meat. Gagging, Trull stumbled across, his moccasins plunging down into warm pockets, lifting clear sheathed in blood and bile.

Ahead, a raging battle. Wraiths swarming over soldiers, demons with mauls and maces crushing the Letherii closing on them from all sides, others with double-bladed axes cleaving wide spaces round themselves. But ballista quarrels were finding them one by one. Trull watched a demon stagger, twice impaled, then soldiers rushed in, swords hacking.

And then he and his company closed with the enemy.

Moroch Nevath stumbled through the dust, the screaming soldiers and the fallen bodies, bellowing his prince's name. But Quillas was nowhere to be seen. Nor was Janall. Only one mage remained from the cadre, launching attack after attack on some distant enemy. A company of heavy infantry had moved up to encircle her, but they were fast dying beneath an onslaught of Tiste Edur.

The Finadd, blood draining from his ears after the con-cussion of the wave of bones, still held his sword, the Letherii steel obliterating the occasional wraith that ventured near. He saw one Edur warrior, the spear a blur in his hands, leading a dozen or so of his kin ever closer to the surviving mage.

But Moroch was too far away, too many heaving bodies between them, and he could only watch as the warrior broke through the last of the defenders and lunged at the mage, driving his spear into her chest, then lifting her entire, the spear-shaft bowing as he flung her spasming body to one side. The iron point of the spear broke free in a stream of blood.

Reeling away, Moroch Nevath began making his way to the south slope of the rampart. He needed a horse. He needed to bring the mounts closer. For the prince. The queen.

Somewhere to the east, a roar of sound, and the ground shook beneath him. He staggered, then his left leg swept out, skidding on slime, and something snapped in the Finadd's groin. Pain lanced through him. Swearing, he watched himself fall, the ruptured ground rising in front of him, and landed heavily. Burning agony in his left leg, his pelvis, up the length of his spine. Still swearing, he began dragging himself forward, his sword lost somewhere in his wake.

Bones. Burning, plunging from the sky. Bodies exploding where they struck. Crushing pressure, the air roiling and screaming like a thing alive. The sudden muting of all noise, the outrageous cacophony of grunts as a thousand men died all at once. A sound that Moroch Nevath would never forget. What had the bastards unleashed?

The Letherii were broken, fleeing down the south slope of the rampart. Wraiths dragged them down. Tiste Edur hacked at their backs and heads as they pursued. Trull Sengar clambered onto a heap of corpses, seeking a vantage point. To the east, on the two berms that he could see, the enemy were shattered. Jheck, veered into silver-backed wolves, had poured up from the gully alongside a horde of wraiths to assault what had survived of the Letherii defences. Mage-fire had ceased.

In the opposite direction, B'nagga had led his own beasts south, skirting the foremost rampart, to attack the reserve positions on the west side of the city. There had been enemy cavalry there, and the horses had been driven to panic by the huge wolves rushing into their midst. A dozen demons had joined the Jheck, forcing the Letherii into a chaotic retreat that gathered up and carried with it the southernmost elements. Companies of Arapay Edur were following in B'nagga's wake.

Trull swung to face north. And saw his brother standing alone above a body, on the far side of the killing field.

The K'risnan.

'Trull.'

He turned. 'Ahlrada Ahn. You are wounded.'

'I ran onto a sword – held by a dead man.'

The gash was deep and long, beginning just below the warrior's left elbow and continuing up into his shoulder. 'Find yourself a healer,' Trull said, 'before you bleed out.'

'I shall. I saw you slay the witch.' A statement to which Ahlrada added nothing.

'Where is Canarth?' Trull asked. 'I do not see my troop.'

'Scattered. I saw Canarth dragging Badar from the press. Badar was dying.'

Trull studied the blood and fragments of flesh on the iron point of his spear. 'He was young.'

'He was blooded, Trull.'

Trull glanced over at High Fort's walls. He could see soldiers lining it. The garrison, witness to the annihilation of the Letherii manning the outer defences. The nearest bastion was still launching quarrels, tracking the few demons still in range.

'I must join my brother, Ahlrada. See if you can gather our warriors. There may be more fighting to come.'

Huddled in the lee of the west wall, Moroch Nevath watched a dozen wolves pad from one heap of corpses to another. The beasts were covered in blood. They gathered round a wounded soldier, there was a sudden flurry of snarls, and the twitching body went still.

All over . . . so fast. Decisive indeed.

He had never found the horses.

On the rampart opposite him, eighty paces distant, a

669

score of Tiste Edur had found Prince Quillas. Dishevelled but alive. Moroch wondered if the queen's corpse lay somewhere beneath the mounds of broken flesh. Beadwork unstrung and scattered in the welter, her jewelled sword still locked in its scabbard, the ambitious light in her eyes dulled and drying and blind to this world.

It seemed impossible.

But so did all these dead Letherii, these obliterated battalions and brigades.

There had been no negation of magic. The eleven mages had been destroyed by the counter-attack. A battle had been transformed into a slaughter, and it was this inequity that stung Moroch the deepest.

He and his people had been on the delivering end, time and again, until it seemed inherently just and righteous. *Something went wrong. There was treachery. The proper course of the world has been . . . upended.* The words repeating in his head were growing increasingly bitter. *It is not for us to be humbled. Ever. Failure drives us to succeed tenfold. All will be put right, again. It shall. We cannot be denied our destiny.*

It began to rain.

An Edur warrior had seen him and was approaching, sword held at the ready. The downpour arrived with vigour as the tall figure came to stand before Moroch Nevath. In traders' tongue he said, 'I see no wounds upon you, soldier.'

'Torn tendon, I think,' Moroch replied.

'Painful, then.'

'Have you come to kill me?'

A surprised expression. 'You do not know? The garrison surrendered. High Fort is fallen.'

'What of it?'

'We come as conquerors, soldier. What value killing all of our subjects?'

Moroch looked away. 'Letherii conquer. We are never conquered. You think this battle means anything? You have revealed your tactics, Edur. This day shall not be repeated, and before long you will be the subjugated ones, not us.'

The warrior shrugged. 'Have it your way, then. But know this. The frontier has fallen. Trate, High Fort and Shake Fort. Your famous brigades are routed, your mage cadres dead. Your queen and your prince are our prisoners. And we begin our march on Letheras.'

The Tiste Edur walked away.

Moroch Nevath stared after him for a time, then looked round. And saw Letherii soldiers, stripped of weapons but otherwise unharmed, walking from the fields of battle. Onto the loggers' road, and south, on the Katter Road. Simply walking away. He did not understand. *We will reassemble. Pull back and equip ourselves once more. There is nothing inevitable to this. Nothing.* Wincing, he forced himself to move away from the wall—

A familiar voice, shouting his name. He looked up, recognized an officer from the queen's entourage. The man bore minor wounds, but otherwise seemed hale. He quickly approached. 'Finadd, I am pleased to see you alive—'

'I need a horse.'

'We have them, Finadd—'

'How was the queen captured?' Moroch demanded. *Why did you not die defending her?*

'A demon,' the man replied. 'It was among us in the blink of an eye. It had come to take her – we could not prevent it. We tried, Finadd, we tried—'

'Never mind. Help me up. We must ride south – I need a healer—'

Trull Sengar picked his way across the killing field. The rain was turning the churned ground into a swamp. The bones of the sorcery had vanished. He paused, hearing piteous cries from somewhere off to his right. A dozen paces in that direction, and he came upon a demon.

Four heavy quarrels had pierced it. The creature was lying on its side, its bestial face twisted with pain.

Trull crouched near the demon's mud-smeared head. 'Can you understand me?'

Small blue eyes flickered behind the lids, fixed on his own eyes. 'Arbiter of life. Denier of mercy. I shall die here.'

The voice was thin, strangely childlike.

'I shall call a healer—'

'Why? To fight again? To relive terror and grief?'

'You were not a warrior in your world?'

'A caster of nets. Warm shoals, a yellow sky. We cast nets.'

'All of you?'

'What war is this? Why have I been killed? Why will I never see the river again? My mate, my children. Did we win?'

'I shall not be long. I will return. I promise.' Trull straightened, went on to where stood Fear and, now, a dozen others. The K'risnan was alive, surrounded by healers – none of whom seemed capable of doing anything for the figure writhing in the mud. As Trull neared, he saw more clearly the young warlock.

Twisted, deformed, his skin peeling in wet sheets, and eyes filled with awareness.

Fear stepped into Trull's path and said, 'It is the sword's sorcery – the gift-giver's own, channelled from the weapon into Rhulad, and from Rhulad to whomever he may choose. Yet . . .' He hesitated. 'The body cannot cope. Even as it destroys the enemy, so it changes the wielder. This is what the women are telling me.'

His brother's face was pale, and nowhere in his expression could Trull see triumph or satisfaction at the victory they had won this day.

'Will he survive?'

'They think so. This time. But the damage cannot be reversed. Trull, Hanradi's son is dead. We have lost a K'risnan.'

'To this?' Trull asked. 'To the sword's power?'

'Partly. The Letherii mages mostly, I think, given how badly burned he was. They resisted longer than we expected.'

672

Trull faced High Fort. 'It has surrendered?'

'Yes, a few moments ago. A delegation. The garrison is being disarmed. I was thinking of leaving Hanradi to govern. His spirit is much damaged.'

Trull said nothing to that. He moved past Fear and strode to the women gathered round the K'risnan. 'One of you, please,' he said. 'There is healing I would have you attend to.'

An Arapay woman nodded. 'Wounded warriors. Yes, preferable. Lead me to them.'

'Not Edur. A demon.'

She halted. 'Don't be a fool. There are Edur who require my skills – I have no time for a demon. Let it die. We can always acquire more.'

Something snapped in Trull, and before he was even aware of it the back of his right hand was stinging and the woman was on the ground, a stunned expression on her suddenly bloodied face. Then rage flared in her eyes.

Fear pushed Trull back a step. '*What are you doing?*'

'I want a demon healed,' Trull said. He was trembling, frightened at the absence of remorse within him even as he watched the woman pick herself up from the mud. 'I want it healed, then unbound and sent back to its realm.'

'Trull—'

The woman snarled, then hissed, 'The empress shall hear of this! I will see you banished!' Her companions gathered, all looking on Trull with raw hatred.

He realized that his gesture had snapped something within them as well. Unfortunate.

'How badly injured is it?' Fear asked.

'It is dying—'

'Then likely it has already done so. No more of this, Trull.' He swung to the women. 'Go among our warriors, all of you. I will see the K'risnan carried to our camp.'

'We will speak of this to the empress,' the first healer said, wiping at her face.

'Of course. As you must.'

673

They stalked off into the rain.

'The battle lust is still upon you, brother—'

'No it isn't—'

'Listen to me. It is how you will excuse your actions. And you will ask for forgiveness and you will make reparations.'

Trull turned away. 'I need to find a healer.'

Fear pulled him roughly round, but Trull twisted free. He headed off. He would find a healer. A Hiroth woman, one who knew his mother. Before word carried.

The demon needed healing. It was as simple as that.

An indeterminate time later, he found himself stumbling among bodies. Dead Edur, the ones killed by the sorcerous attack he recalled from earlier. Scorched, burnt so fiercely their faces had melted away. Unknown to his eyes and unknowable. He wandered among them, the rain pelting down to give the illusion of motion, of life, on all sides. But they were all dead.

A lone figure nearby, standing motionless. A woman, her hands hanging at her sides. He had seen her before, a matron. Hanradi Khalag's elder sister, tall, hawk-faced, her eyes like onyx. He halted in front of her. 'I want you to heal a demon.'

She did not seem to see him at all. 'I can do nothing for them. My sons. I cannot even find them.'

He took one of her hands and held it tight. 'Come with me.'

She did not resist as he led her away from the strewn corpses. 'A demon?'

'Yes. I do not know the name by which they call themselves.'

'Kenyll'rah. It means "To Sleep Peacefully" or something like that. The Merude were charged with making their weapons.'

'They have been sorely used.'

'They are not alone in that, warrior.'

He glanced back at her, saw that awareness had returned

674

to her eyes. Her hand held his now, and tightly. 'You are the emperor's brother, Trull Sengar.'

'I am.'

'You struck an Arapay woman.'

'I did. It seems such news travels swiftly – and mysteriously.'

'Among the women. Yes.'

'And yet you will help me.'

'Heal this demon? If it lives, I shall.'

'Why?'

She did not reply.

It took some time, but they finally found the creature. Its cries had ceased, but the woman released Trull's hand and crouched down beside it. 'It lives still, Trull Sengar.' She laid her palms on the demon's massive chest and closed her eyes.

Trull watched the rain streaming down her face, as if the world wept in her stead.

'Take the first of the quarrels. You will pull, gently, while I push. Each one, slowly.'

'I want it released.'

'I cannot do that. It will not be permitted.'

'Then I want it placed in my charge.'

'You are the emperor's brother. None will defy you.'

'Except, perhaps, one of the emperor's other brothers.' He was pleased to see the crease of a smile on her thin features.

'That trouble will be yours, not mine, Trull Sengar. Now, pull. Carefully.'

The demon opened its small eyes. It ran its massive hands over the places where wounds had been, then it sighed.

The healer stepped back. 'I am done. There are bodies to gather.'

'Thank you,' Trull said.

She made no reply. Wiping rain from her face, she walked away.

675

The demon slowly climbed to its feet. 'I will fight again,' it said.

'Not if I have any say in the matter,' Trull replied. 'I would place you in my charge.'

'To not fight? That would be unfair, Denier. I would witness the death of my kind, yet not share the risk, or their fate. It is sad, to die so far from home.'

'Then one among you must remain, to remember them. That one will be you. What is your name?'

'Lilac.'

Trull studied the sky. It seemed there would be no let-up in the downpour. 'Come with me. I must speak to my brother.'

Tiste Edur warriors were entering the city. No Letherii soldiers were visible on the walls, or at the bastions. The gates had been sundered some time during the battle, struck by sorcery. Twisted pieces of bronze and splintered wood studded the muddy ground, amidst strewn corpses.

The demon had collected a double-bladed axe near the body of one of its kind and now carried it over a shoulder. For all its size, Lilac moved quietly, shortening its stride to stay alongside Trull. He noted that the pattern of its breathing was odd. After a deep breath it took another, shorter one, followed by a faintly whistling exhalation that did not seem to come from its broad, flattened nose.

'Lilac, are you fully healed?'

'I am.'

Ahead lay the rampart where four mages had stood. Three of them had been obliterated in the first wave of sorcery. On the berm's summit now were gathered Fear and a number of officers. And two prisoners.

The slope was treacherous underfoot as Trull and the demon made their ascent. Red, muddy streams, bodies slowly sliding down. Wraiths moved through the rain as if still hunting victims. From the west came the low rumble of thunder.

They reached the rampart's summit. Trull saw that one of

the prisoners was Prince Quillas. He did not seem injured. The other was a woman in mud-spattered armour. She wore no helmet and had taken a head wound, staining the left side of her face with streaks of blood. Her eyes were glazed with shock.

Fear had turned to regard Trull and the demon, his expression closed. 'Brother,' he said tonelessly, 'it seems we have captured two personages of the royal family.'

'This is Queen Janall?'

'The prince expects we will ransom them,' Fear said. 'He does not seem to understand the situation.'

'And what is the situation?' Trull asked.

'Our emperor wants these two. For himself.'

'Fear, we are not in the habit of parading prisoners.'

A flicker of rage in Fear's eyes, but his voice remained calm. 'I see you have had your demon healed. What do you want?'

'I want this Kenyll'rah in my charge.'

Fear studied the huge creature. Then he shrugged and turned away. 'As you like. Leave us now, Trull. I will seek you out later . . . for a private word.'

Trull flinched. 'Very well.'

The world felt broken now, irreparably broken.

'Go.'

'Come with me, Lilac,' Trull said. He paused to glance over at Prince Quillas, and saw the terror in the young Letherii's visage. Rhulad wanted him, and the queen. Why?

They walked the killing field, the rain pummelling down in a soft roar, devastation and slaughter on all sides. Figures were moving about here and there. Tiste Edur seeking fallen comrades, wraiths on senseless patrols. The thunder was closer.

'There is a river,' Lilac said. 'I smelled it when we first arrived. It is the same river as ran beneath the bridge.'

'Yes,' Trull replied. 'The Katter River.'

'I would see it.'

'Why not?'

They angled northwest. Reached the loggers' road that ran parallel to the forest and followed its three-rutted track until the treeline thinned on their right, and the river became visible.

'Ah,' Lilac murmured, 'it is so small . . .'

Trull studied the fast-flowing water, the glittering skin it cast over boulders. 'A caster of nets,' he said.

'My home, Denier.'

The Tiste Edur walked down to the river's edge. He reached and plunged his bloodstained hand into the icy water.

'Are there not fish in there?' Lilac asked.

'I am sure there are. Why?'

'In the river where I live, there are n'purel, the Whiskered Fish. They can eat a Kenyll'rah youth whole, and there are some in the deep lakes that could well eat an adult such as myself. Of course, we never venture onto the deeps. Are there no such creatures here?'

'In the seas,' Trull replied, 'there are sharks. And, of course, there are plenty of stories of larger monsters, some big enough to sink ships.'

'The n'purel then crawl onto shore and shed their skins, whereupon they live on land.'

'That is a strange thing,' Trull said, glancing back at the demon. 'I gather that casting nets is a dangerous activity, then.'

Lilac shrugged. 'No more dangerous than hunting spiders, Denier.'

'Call me Trull.'

'You are an Arbiter of Life, a Denier of Freedom. You are the Stealer of my Death—'

'All right. Never mind.'

'What war is this?'

'A pointless one.'

'They are all pointless, Denier. Subjugation and defeat

678

breed resentment and hatred, and such things cannot be bribed away.'

'Unless the spirit of the defeated is crushed,' Trull said. 'Absolutely crushed, such as with the Nerek and the Faraed and Tarthenal.'

'I do not know those people, Denier.'

'They are among those the Letherii – our enemy in this war – have conquered.'

'And you think them broken?'

'They are that, Lilac.'

'It may not be as it seems.'

Trull shrugged. 'Perhaps you are right.'

'Will their station change under your rule?'

'I suspect not.'

'If you understand all this, Denier, why do you fight?'

The sound of moccasins on gravel behind them. Trull straightened and turned to see Fear approaching. In his hand was a Letherii sword.

Trull considered readying the spear strapped to his back, then decided against it. Despite what he'd said earlier, he was not prepared to fight his brother.

'This weapon,' Fear said as he halted five paces from Trull, 'is Letherii steel.'

'I saw them on the field of battle. They defied the K'risnan sorcery, when all else was destroyed. Swords, spear-heads, undamaged.' Trull studied his brother. 'What of it?'

Fear hesitated, then looked out on the river. 'It is what I do not understand. How did they achieve such a thing as this steel? They are a corrupt, vicious people, Trull. They do not deserve such advances in craft.'

'Why them and not us?' Trull asked, then he smiled. 'Fear, the Letherii are a forward-looking people, and so inherently driven. We Edur do not and have never possessed such a force of will. We have our Blackwood, but we have always possessed that. Our ancestors brought it with them from Emurlahn. Brother, we look back—'

'To the time when Father Shadow ruled over us,' Fear cut in, his expression darkening. 'Hannan Mosag speaks the truth. We must devour the Letherii, we must set a yoke upon them, and so profit from their natural drive to foment change.'

'And what will that do to us, brother? We resist change, we do not worship it, we do not thrive in its midst the way the Letherii do. Besides, I am not convinced that theirs is the right way to live. I suspect their faith in progress is far more fragile than it outwardly seems. In the end, they must ever back up what they seek with force.' Trull pointed to the sword. 'With that.'

'We shall guide them, Trull. Hannan Mosag understood this—'

'You revise the past now, Fear. He was not intending to wage war on the Letherii.'

'Not immediately, true, but it would have come. And he knew it. So the K'risnan have told me. We had lost Father Shadow. It was necessary to find a new source of faith.'

'A faceless one?'

'Damn you, Trull! You knelt before him – no different from the rest of us!'

'And to this day, I wonder why. What about you, Fear? Do you wonder why you did as you did?'

His brother turned away, visibly trembling. 'I saw no doubt.'

'In Hannan Mosag. And so you followed. As did the rest of us, I suspect. One and all, we knelt before Rhulad, believing we saw in each other a certainty that did not in truth exist—'

With a roar, Fear spun round, the sword lifting high. It swung down—

—and was halted, suddenly, by the demon, whose massive hand had closed round Fear's forearm and held it motionless.

'Release me!'

'No,' Lilac replied. 'This warrior stole my death. I now steal his.'

Fear struggled a moment longer, then, seeing it was hopeless, he sagged.

'You can let him go now,' Trull said.

'If he attacks again I will kill him,' the demon said, releasing Fear's arm.

'We followed Hannan Mosag,' Trull said, 'and yet, what did we know of his mind? He was our Warlock King, and so we followed. Think on this, Fear. He had sought out a new source of power, rejecting Father Shadow. True, he knew, as we did, that Scabandari Bloodeye was dead, or, at best, his spirit lived but was lost to us. And so he made pact with . . . something else. And he sent you and me, Binadas and Rhulad and the Buhns, to retrieve the gift that . . . thing . . . created for him. The fault lies with us, Fear, in that we did not question, did not challenge the Warlock King. We were fools, and all that is before us now, and all that will come, is our fault.'

'He is the Warlock King, Trull.'

'Who arrived at absolute power over all the Edur. He held it and would not lose it, no matter what. And so he surrendered his soul. As did we, when we knelt before Rhulad.'

Fear's eyes narrowed on him. 'You are speaking treason, brother.'

'Against what? Against whom? Tell me, I truly want to know. Have you seen the face of our new god?'

'Were Binadas standing here and not I,' Fear whispered, 'you would be dead now.'

'And, in our wondrous new empire, will that be the singular fate of all those who voice dissent?'

Fear looked down at the sword in his hand. Then let it drop. 'Your warriors are awaiting you, Trull. In two days' time we resume our march. South, to Letheras.' He then turned and walked away.

Trull watched him for a moment, then looked out on the

river once more. For every eddy in the current, in the lees of boulders and notches in the bank, the river rushed on, slave to relentless laws. When he had placed his hand in the water, it had quickly grown numb. 'Eventually, Lilac, we will make sense of this.'

The demon said nothing.

Trull walked to a nearby boulder and sat down on it. He lowered his head into his hands and began to weep.

After a time the demon moved to stand beside him. Then a heavy hand settled on his shoulder.

CHAPTER NINETEEN

Invisible in all his portions
This thick-skinned thing has borders
Indivisible to every sentinel
Patrolling the geography of
Arbitrary definitions, and yet the
Mountains have ground down
The fires died, and so streams
This motionless strand of sharp
Black sand where I walk
Cutting my path on the coarse
Conclusions countless teeth
Have grated – all lost now
In this unlit dust – we are not
And have never been
The runners green and fresh
Of life risen from the crushed
Severing extinctions (that one past
this one new) all hallowed and self-sure
But the dead strand moves unseen,
The river of black crawls on
To some wistful resolution
The place with no meaning
Inconsequential in absence
Of strings and shadows
Charting from then to now
And these stitched lines

683

Finding this in that . . .

Excerpt from
The Black Sands of Time
(in the collection *Suicidal Poets of Darujhistan*)
edited by Haroak

The corpse beyond the pier was barely visible, a pallid patch resisting the roll of the waves. The shark that rose alongside it to make a sideways lunge was one of the largest ones Udinaas had yet seen during the time he'd sat looking out on the harbour, his legs dangling from the jetty's edge.

Gulls and sharks, the feast lasting the entire morning. The slave watched, feeling like a spectator before nature's incessant display, the inevitability of the performance leaving him oddly satisfied. Entertained, in fact. Those who owed. Those who were owed. They sat equally sweet in the bellies of the scavengers. And this was a thing of wonder.

The emperor would summon him soon, he knew. The army was stirring itself into motion somewhere beyond Trate's broken gates, inland. An oversized garrison of Beneda Edur was remaining in the city, enforcing the restitution of peace, normality. The once-chief of the Den-Ratha had been given the title of governor. That the garrison under his control was not of his own tribe was no accident. Suspicion had come in the wake of success, as it always did.

Hannan Mosag's work. The emperor had been . . . fraught of late. Distracted. Suffering. Too often, madness burned in his eyes.

Mayen had beaten Feather Witch senseless, as close to killing the slave outright as was possible. In the vast tent that now served as Edur headquarters – stolen from the train that had belonged to the Cold Clay Battalion – there had been rapes. Slaves, prisoners. Perhaps Mayen simply did to others what Rhulad did to her. A compassionate mind might believe so. And as for the hundreds of noble women taken from the Letherii by Edur warriors, most had since been returned at the governor's command, although it was likely that many now carried half-blood seeds within them.

The governor would soon accept the many requests to hear delegations from the various guilds and merchant interests. And a new pattern would take shape.

Unless, of course, the frontier cities were liberated by a victorious Letherii counter-attack. Plenty of rumours, of course. Clashes at sea between Edur and Letherii fleets. Thousands sent to the deep. The storm seen far to the west the night before had signalled a mage-war. The Ceda, Kuru Qan, had finally roused himself in all his terrible power. While Letherii corpses crowded the harbour, it was Edur bodies out in the seas beyond.

Strangest rumour of all, the prison island of Second Maiden Fort had flung back a succession of Edur attacks, and was still holding out, and among the half-thousand convicted soldiers was a sorceror who had once rivalled the Ceda himself. That was why the Edur army had remained camped here – they wanted no enemy still active behind them.

Udinaas knew otherwise. There might well be continued resistance in their wake, but the emperor was indifferent to such things. And the Letherii fleet had yet to make an appearance. The Edur ships commanded Katter Sea as far south as the city of Awl.

He drew his legs up and climbed to his feet. Walked back down the length of the pier. The streets were quiet. Most signs of the fighting had been removed, the bodies and broken furniture and shattered pottery, and a light rain the night before had washed most of the bloodstains away. But the air still stank of smoke and the walls of the buildings were smeared with an oily grit. Windows gaped and doorways that had been kicked in remained dark.

He had never much liked Trate. Rife with thugs and the dissolute remnants of the Nerek and Fent, the market stalls crowded with once-holy icons and relics, with ceremonial artwork now being sold as curios. The talking sticks of chiefs, the medicine bags of shamans. Fent ancestor chests, the bones still in them. The harbour front streets and alleys had been crowded with Nerek children selling their bodies, and over it all hung a vague sense of smugness, as if this was the proper order of the world, the roles settled out as they should be. Letherii dominant, surrounded by lesser creatures inherently servile, their cultures little more than commodities.

Belief in destiny delivered its own imperatives.

But here, now, the savages had arrived and a new order had been asserted, proving that destiny was an illusion. The city was in shock, with only a few malleable merchants venturing forth in the faith that the new ways to come were but the old ways, that the natural order in fact superseded any particular people. At the same time, they believed that none could match the Letherii in this game of riches, and so in the end they would win – the savages would find themselves civilized. Proof that destiny was anything but illusory.

Udinaas wondered if they were right. There were mitigating factors, after all. Tiste Edur lifespans were profoundly long. Their culture was both resilient and embedded. Conservative. *Or, so it was. Until Rhulad. Until the sword claimed him.*

A short time later he strode through the inland gate and approached the Edur encampment. There seemed to be little organization to the vast array of tents. This was not simply an army, but an entire people on the move – a way of life to which they were not accustomed. Wraiths patrolled the outskirts.

They ignored him as he passed the pickets. He had not heard from Wither, his own companion shade, in a long time, but he knew it had not gone away. Lying low with its secrets. Sometimes he caught its laughter, as if from a great distance, the timing always perverse.

Rhulad's tent was at the centre of the encampment, the entrance flanked by demons in boiled leather armour stained black, long-handled maces resting heads to the ground before them. Full helms hid their faces.

'How many bodies have they dragged out today?' Udinaas asked as he walked between them.

Neither replied.

There were four compartments within, divided by thick-clothed walls fixed to free-standing bronze frames. The foremost chamber was shallow but ran the breadth of the tent. Benches had been placed along the sides. The area to the right was crowded with supplies of various sorts, casks and crates and earthen jars. Passage into the main room beyond was between two dividers.

He entered to see the emperor standing before his raised throne. Mayen lounged on a looted couch to the left of the wooden dais, her expression strangely dulled. Feather Witch stood in the shadows against the wall behind the empress, her face swollen and bruised almost beyond recognition. Hannan Mosag and Hull Beddict were facing the emperor, their backs to Udinaas. The Warlock King's wraith bodyguard was not present.

Hannan Mosag was speaking. '. . . of that there is no doubt, sire.'

Coins had fallen from Rhulad's forehead, where the soldier's palm had struck when it broke his neck. The skin revealed was naught but scar tissue, creased where the skull's frontal bone had caved inward – that internal damage had healed, since the dent was now gone. The emperor's eyes were so bloodshot they seemed nothing but murky red pools. He studied Hannan Mosag for a moment, apparently unaware of the spasms crossing his ravaged features, then said, 'Lost kin? What does that mean?'

'Tiste Edur,' Hannan Mosag replied in his smooth voice.

'Survivors, from when our kind were scattered, following the loss of Scabandari Bloodeye.'

'How are you certain of this?'

'I have dreamed them, Emperor. In my mind I have been led into other realms, other worlds that lie alongside this one—'

'Kurald Emurlahn.'

'That realm is broken in pieces,' Hannan Mosag said, 'but yes, I have seen fragment-worlds. In one such world dwell the Kenyll'rah, the demons we have bound to us. In another, there are ghosts from our past battles.'

Hull Beddict cleared his throat. 'Warlock King, are these realms the Holds of my people?'

'Perhaps, but I think not.'

'That is not relevant,' Rhulad said to Hull as he began pacing. 'Hannan Mosag, how fare these lost kin?'

'Poorly, sire. Some have lost all memory of past greatness. Others are subjugated—'

The emperor's head swung round. 'Subjugated?'

'Yes.'

'We must deliver them,' Rhulad said, resuming his pacing, the macabre clicking sounds of coin edges snapping together the only sound to follow his pronouncement.

Udinaas moved unobtrusively to stand behind the throne. There was something pathetic, to his mind, about the ease with which the Warlock King manipulated Rhulad. Beneath all those coins and behind that mottled sword was a marred and fragile Edur youth. Hannan Mosag might have surrendered the throne in the face of Rhulad's power, but he would not relinquish his ambition to rule.

'We will build ships,' the emperor resumed after a time. 'In the Letherii style, I think. Large, seaworthy. You said there were Tiste Andii enclaves as well? We will conquer them, use them as slaves to crew our ships. We shall undertake these journeys once Lether has fallen, once our empire is won.'

'Sire, the other realms I spoke of – some will allow us to

hasten our passage. There are . . . gateways. I am seeking the means of opening them, controlling them. Provided there are seas, in those hidden worlds, we can achieve swift travel—'

'Seas?' Rhulad laughed. 'If there are no seas, Hannan Mosag, then you shall *make* them!'

'Sire?'

'Open one realm upon another. An ocean realm, released into a desert realm.'

The Warlock King's eyes widened slightly. 'The devastation would be . . . terrible.'

'Cleansing, you mean to say. After all, why should the Edur empire confine itself to one world? You must shift your focus, Hannan Mosag. You are too limited in your vision.' He paused, winced at some inner tremor, then continued in a strained tone, 'It is what comes of power. Yes, what comes. To see the vastness of . . . things. Potentials, the multitude of opportunities. Who can stand before us, after all?' He spun round. 'Udinaas! Where have you been?'

'At the harbour front, Emperor.'

'Doing what?'

'Watching the sharks feeding.'

'Hah! You hear that, Hannan Mosag? Hull Beddict? He is a cold one, is he not? This slave of ours. We chose well indeed. Tell us, Udinaas, do you believe in these secret realms?'

'Are we blind to hidden truths, Emperor? I cannot believe otherwise.'

A start from Hannan Mosag, his eyes narrowing.

Mayen suddenly spoke, in a low drawl. 'Feather Witch says this one is possessed.'

No-one spoke for a half-dozen heartbeats. Rhulad slowly approached Udinaas. 'Possessed? By what, Mayen? Did your slave yield that detail?'

'The Wyval. Do you not recall that event?'

Hannan Mosag said, 'Uruth Sengar examined him, Empress.'

'So she did. And found nothing. No poison in his blood.'

Rhulad's eyes searched his slave's face. 'Udinaas?'

'I am as you see me, master. If there is a poison within me, I am not aware of it. Mistress Uruth seemed certain of her conclusion, else she would have killed me then.'

'Then why should Feather Witch make such accusations?'

Udinaas shrugged. 'Perhaps she seeks to deflect attention so as to lessen the severity of the beatings.'

Rhulad stared at him a moment, then swung round. 'Beatings? There have been no beatings. An errant sorcerous attack . . .'

'Now who is seeking to deflect attention?' Mayen said, smiling. 'You will take the word of a slave over that of your wife?'

The emperor seemed to falter. 'Of course not, Mayen.' He looked across to Hannan Mosag. 'What say you?'

The Warlock King's innocent frown managed the perfect balance of concern and confusion. 'Which matter would you have me speak of, sire? The presence of Wyval poison within this Udinaas, or the fact that your wife is beating her slave?'

Mayen's laughter was harsh. 'Oh, Rhulad, I really did not think you believed me. My slave has been irritating me. Indeed, I am of a mind to find another, one less clumsy, less . . . disapproving. As if a slave has the right to disapprove of anything.'

'Disapprove?' the emperor asked. 'What . . . why?'

'Does a Wyval hide within Udinaas or not?' Mayen demanded, sitting straighter. 'Examine the slave, Hannan Mosag.'

'*Who rules here?*' Rhulad's shriek froze everyone. The emperor's sword had risen, the blade shivering as shudders rolled through him. 'You would all play games with us?'

Mayen shrank back on the divan, eyes slowly widening in raw fear.

The emperor's fierce gaze was fixing on her, then the

Warlock King, then back again. 'Everyone out,' Rhulad whispered. 'Everyone but Udinaas. *Now.*'

Hannan Mosag opened his mouth to object, then changed his mind. Hull Beddict trailing, the Warlock King strode from the tent. Mayen, wrapping herself in the silk-stitched blanket from the couch, hurried in their wake, Feather Witch stumbling a step behind.

'Wife.'

She halted.

'The family of the Sengar have never believed there was value in beating slaves. You will cease. If she is incompetent, then find another. Am I understood?'

'Yes, sire,' she said.

'Leave us.'

As soon as they were gone, Rhulad lowered the sword and studied Udinaas for a time. 'We are not blind to all those who would seek advantage. The Warlock King sees us as too young, too ignorant, but he knows nothing of the truths we have seen. Mayen – she is as a dead thing beneath me. We should have left her to Fear. That was a mistake.' He blinked, as if recovering himself, then regarded Udinaas with open suspicion. 'And you, slave. What secrets do you hide?'

Udinaas lowered himself to one knee, said nothing.

'Nothing will be hidden from us,' Rhulad said. 'Look up, Udinaas.'

He did, and saw a wraith crouched at his side.

'This shade shall examine you, slave. It will see if you are hiding poison within you.'

Udinaas nodded. *Yes, do this, Rhulad. I am weary. I want an end.*

The wraith moved forward, then enveloped him.

'*Ohh, such secrets!*'

He knew that voice and closed his eyes. *Clever, Wither. I assume you volunteered?*

'*So many, left shattered, wandering lost. This bastard has used us sorely. Do you imagine we would willingly accede to his*

691

demands? I am unbound, and that has made me useful, for I am proof against compulsion where my kin are not. Can he tell the difference? Evidently he cannot.' A trill of vaguely manic laughter. 'And what shall I find? Udinaas. You must stay at this madman's side. He is going to Letheras, you see, and we need you there.'

Udinaas sighed. *Why?*

'All in good time. Ah, you rail at the melodrama? Too bad, hee-hee. Glean my secrets, if you dare. You can, you know.'

No. Now go away.

Wither slipped back, resumed its swirling man-shape in front of Udinaas.

Rhulad released one hand from the sword to claw at his face. He spun round, took two steps, then howled his rage. 'Why are they lying to us? We cannot trust them! Not any of them!' He turned. 'Stand, Udinaas. You alone do not lie. You alone can be trusted.' He strode to the throne and sat. 'We need to think. We need to make sense of this. Hannan Mosag . . . he covets our power, doesn't he?'

Udinaas hesitated, then said, 'Yes, sire. He does.'

Rhulad's eyes gleamed red. 'Tell us more, slave.'

'It is not my place—'

'We decide what is your place. Speak.'

'You stole his throne, Emperor. And the sword he believed was rightly his.'

'He wants it still, does he?' A sudden laugh, chilling and brutal. 'Oh, he's welcome to it! No, we cannot. Mustn't. Impossible. And what of our wife?'

'Mayen is broken. She wanted nothing real from her flirting with you. You were the youngest brother to the man she would marry. She sought allies within the Sengar household.' He stopped there, seeing the spasms return to Rhulad, the extremity of his emotion too close to an edge, a precipice, and it would not do to send him over it. Not yet, perhaps not at all. *It's the poison within me, so hungry for vengeance, so . . . spiteful. These are not my thoughts, not my inclinations. Remember that, Udinaas, before you do worse than would Hannan Mosag.* 'Sire,' he said softly, 'Mayen is lost. And hurting. And you are the only one who can help her.'

'You speak to save the slave woman,' the emperor said in a rough whisper.

'Feather Witch knows only hatred for me, sire. I am an Indebted, whilst she is not. My desire for her was hubris, and she would punish me for it.'

'Your desire for her.'

Udinaas nodded. 'Would I save her from beatings? Of course I would, sire. Just as you would do the same. As indeed you just did, not a moment ago.'

'Because it is . . . sordid. What am I to make of you, Udinaas? A slave. An . . . Indebted . . . as if that could make you less in the eyes of another slave.'

'The Letherii relinquish nothing, even when they are made into slaves. Sire, that is a truth the Tiste Edur have never understood. Poor or rich, free or enslaved, we build the same houses in which to live, in which to play out the old dramas. In the end, it does not matter whether destiny embraces us or devours us – either is as it should be, and only the Errant decides our fate.'

Rhulad was studying him as he spoke. The tremors had slowed. 'Hull Beddict struggled to say the same thing, but he is poor at words, and so failed. Thus, Udinaas, we may conquer them, we may command their flesh in the manner we command yours and that of your fellow slaves, but the *belief* that guides them, that guides all of you, that cannot be defeated.'

'Barring annihilation, sire.'

'And this Errant, he is the arbiter of fate?'

'He is, sire.'

'And he exists?'

'Physically? I don't know. It doesn't matter.'

Rhulad nodded. 'You are right, slave, it doesn't.'

'Conquer Lether and it will devour you, sire. Your spirit. Your . . . innocence.'

A strange smile twisted Rhulad's face. 'Innocence. This,

from a short-lived creature such as you. We should take offence. We should see your head torn from your shoulders. You proclaim we cannot win this war, and what are we to think of that?'

'The answer lies upon your very flesh, sire.'

Rhulad glanced down. His fingernails had grown long, curved and yellow. He tapped a coin on his chest. 'Bring to an end . . . the notion of wealth. Of money. Crush the illusion of value.'

Udinaas was stunned. *He may be young and half mad, but Rhulad is no fool.*

'Ah,' the emperor said. 'We see your . . . astonishment. We have, it seems, been underestimated, even by our slave. But yours is no dull mind, Udinaas. We thank the Sisters that you are not King Ezgara Diskanar, for then we would be sorely challenged.'

'Ezgara may be benign, sire, but he has dangerous people around him.'

'Yes, this Ceda, Kuru Qan. Why has he not yet acted?'

Udinaas shook his head. 'I have been wondering the same, sire.'

'We will speak more, Udinaas. And none other shall know of this. After all, what would they think, an emperor and a slave together, working to fashion a new empire? For we must keep you a slave, mustn't we? A slave in the eyes of all others. We suspect that, were we to free you, you would leave us.'

A sudden tremble at these words.

Errant take me, this man needs a friend. 'Sire, I would not leave. It was I who placed the coins in your flesh. There is no absolving that, no true way I could make amends. But I *will* stand by you, through all of this.'

Rhulad's terrible eyes, so crimson-bruised and hurt, shifted away from Udinaas. 'Do you understand, Udinaas?' he asked in a whisper. 'I am so . . .'

Frightened. 'Yes, sire, I understand.'

694

The emperor placed a hand over his eyes. 'She is drowning herself in white nectar.'

'Yes, sire.'

'I would free her . . . but I cannot. Do you know why, Udinaas?'

'She carries your child.'

'You *must* have poison blood, Udinaas, to know so much . . .'

'Sire, it might be worth considering sending for Uruth. For your mother. Mayen needs . . . someone.'

Rhulad, face still covered by his mangled hand, nodded. 'We will join with Fear's army soon. Five, six days. Uruth will join them. Then . . . yes, I will speak with Mother. My child . . .'

My child. No, it is impossible. A Meckros foundling. There is no point in thinking about him. None at all.

I am not an evil man . . . yet I have just vowed to stand at his side. Errant take me, what have I done?

A farm was burning in the valley below, but she could see no-one fighting the flames. Everyone had fled. Seren Pedac resumed hacking at her hair, cutting it as short as she could manage with the docker's knife one of Iron Bars's soldiers had given her.

The Avowed stood nearby, his squad mage, Corlo, at his side. They were studying the distant fire and speaking in low tones.

Somewhere south and east of Dresh, half a day from the coast. She could not imagine the Tiste Edur invaders were anywhere near, yet the roads had been full of refugees, all heading east to Letheras. She had seen more than a few deserters among the crowds, and here and there bodies lay in ditches, victims of robbery or murdered after being raped.

Rape, it seemed, had become a favoured pastime among the thugs preying on the fleeing citizens. Seren knew that, had she been travelling alone, she would probably be dead by now. In some ways, that would have been a relief. An end to this sullied misery, this agonizing feeling of being unclean. In her mind, she saw again and again Iron Bars killing those men. His desire to exact appropriate vengeance. And her voice, croaking out, stopping him in the name of mercy.

Errant knew, she regretted that now. Better had she let him work on that bastard. Better still were they still carrying him with them. Eyes gouged out, nose cut off, tongue carved from his mouth. And with this knife in her hand she could slice strips of skin from his flesh. She had heard a story once, of a factor in a small remote hamlet who had made a habit of raping young girls, until the women one night ambushed him. Beaten and trussed, then a loincloth filled with spike-thorns had been tied on like a diaper, tightly, and the man was bound to the back of his horse. The pricking thorns drove the animal into a frenzy. The beast eventually scraped the man loose on a forest path, but he had bled out by then. The story went that the man's face, in death, had held all the pain a mortal could suffer, and as for what had been found between his legs . . .

She sawed off the last length of greasy hair and dropped it on the fire. The stench was fierce, but there were bush-warlocks and decrepit shamans who, if they happened upon human hair, would make dire use of it. It was a sad truth that, given the chance to bind a soul, few resisted the temptation.

Corlo called to the soldiers and suddenly they were running hard down the hillside towards the farm, leaving behind only Seren and Iron Bars. The Crimson Guardsman strode towards her. 'You hear it, lass?'

'What?'

'Horses. In the stable. The fire's jumped to its roof. The farmer's left his horses behind.'

'He wouldn't do that.'

He squinted down at her, then crouched until he was at

696

eye level. 'No, likely the owner's dead. Strange, how most locals around here don't know how to ride.'

She looked down at the farm once again. 'Probably a breeder for the army. The whole notion of cavalry came from Bluerose – as did most of the stock. Horses weren't part of our culture before then. Have you ever seen Letherii cavalry on parade? Chaos. Even after, what, sixty years? And dozens of Bluerose officers trying to train our soldiers.'

'You should have imported these Bluerose horse-warriors over as auxiliaries. If it's their skill, exploit it. You can't borrow someone else's way of life.'

'Maybe not. Presumably, you can ride, then.'

'Aye. And you?'

She nodded, sheathing the knife and rising. 'Trained by one of those Bluerose officers I mentioned.'

'You were in the army before?'

'No, he was my lover. For a time.'

Iron Bars straightened as well. 'Look – they've reached them in time. Come on.'

She hesitated. 'I forgot to thank you, Iron Bars.'

'You wouldn't have been as pretty drowned.'

'No. I'm not ready yet to thank you for that. What you did to those men . . .'

'I've a great-granddaughter back in Gris, D'Avore Valley. She'd be about your age now. Let's go, lass.'

She walked behind him down the slope. Great-granddaughter. What an absurd notion. He wasn't that old. These Avowed had strange senses of humour.

Corlo and the squad had pulled a dozen horses from the burning stable, along with tack and bridles. One of the soldiers was cursing as Seren and Iron Bars approached.

'Look at these stirrups! No wonder the bastards can't ride the damned things!'

'You set your foot down in the crotch of the hook,' Seren explained.

'And what happens if it slips out?' the man demanded.

'You fall off.'

'Avowed, we need to rework these things – some heavy leather—'

'Cut up a spare saddle,' Iron Bars said, 'and see what you can manage. But I want us to be riding before sunset.'

'Aye, sir.'

'A more stable stirrup,' the Avowed said to Seren, 'is a kind of half-boot, something you can slide your foot into, with a straight cross-bar to take your weight. I agree with Halfpeck. These Bluerose horse-warriors missed something obvious and essential. They couldn't have been very good riders . . .'

Seren frowned. 'My lover once mentioned how these saddles were made exclusively for Lether. He said they used a slightly different kind back in Bluerose.'

His eyes narrowed on her, and he barked a laugh, but made no further comment.

She sighed. 'No wonder our cavalry is next to useless. I always found it hard to keep my feet in, and to keep them from turning this way and that.'

'You mean they swivel?'

'I'm afraid so.'

'I'd like to meet these Bluerose riders some day.'

'They are a strange people, Iron Bars. They worship someone called the Black-winged Lord.'

'And they resemble Letherii?'

'No, they are taller. Very dark skins.'

He regarded her for a moment, then asked, 'Faces like the Tiste Edur?'

'No, much finer-boned.'

'Long-lived?'

'Not that I'm aware of, but to be honest, I don't really know. Few Letherii do, nor do they much care. The Blueroses were defeated. Subjugated. There were never very many of them, in any case, and they preferred isolation. Small cities, from what I've heard. Gloomy.'

'What ended your affair?'

'Just that, I suppose. He rarely saw any good in anything. I wearied of his scepticism, his cynicism, the way he acted – as if he'd seen it all before a thousand times . . .'

The stable was engulfed in flames by now, and they were all forced away by the fierce heat. In the nearby pasture they retreated to, they found a half-dozen corpses, the breeder and his family. They'd known little mercy in the last few bells of their lives. None of the soldiers who examined them said a word, but their expressions hardened.

Iron Bars made a point of keeping Seren away whilst three men from the squad buried the bodies. 'We've found a trail,' he said. 'If you don't mind, lass, we want to follow it. For a word with the ones who killed that family.'

'Show me the tracks,' she said.

He gestured and Corlo led her to the edge of a stand of trees on the southeast end of the clearing. Seren studied the array of footprints entering the woodcutters' path. 'There's twenty or more of them,' she pronounced after a moment.

The mage nodded. 'Deserters. In armour.'

'Yes, or burdened with loot.'

'Likely both.'

She turned to regard the man. 'You Crimson Guardsmen – you're pretty sure of yourselves, aren't you?'

'When it comes to fighting, aye, lass, we are.'

'I watched Iron Bars fight in Trate. He's an exception, I gather—'

'Aye, he is, but not among the Avowed. Jup Alat would've given him trouble. Or Poll, for that matter. Then there's those in the other companies. Halfdan, Blues, Black the Elder . . .'

'More of these Avowed?'

'Aye.'

'And what does it mean? To be an Avowed?'

'Means they swore to return their prince to his lands. He was driven out, you see, by the cursed Emperor Kellanved. Anyway, it ain't happened yet. But it will, someday, maybe soon.'

699

'And that was the vow? All right. It seems this prince had some able soldiers with him.'

'Oh indeed, lass, especially when the vow's kept them alive all this time.'

'What do you mean?'

The mage looked suddenly nervous. 'I'm saying too much. Never mind me, lass. Anyway, you've seen the trail the bastards left behind. They made no effort to hide, meaning they're cocksure themselves, aren't they?' He smiled, but there was no humour in it. 'We'll catch up, and then we'll show them what real cavalry can do. Riding horses with stirrups, I mean – we don't often fight from the saddle, but we ain't new to it either.'

'Well, I admit, you've got me curious.'

'Just curious, lass? No hunger for vengeance?'

She looked away. 'I want to look around,' she said. 'Alone, if you don't mind.'

The mage shrugged. 'Don't wander too far. The Avowed's taken to you, I think.'

That's . . . unfortunate. 'I won't.'

Seren headed into the wood. There had been decades of thinning, leaving plenty of stumps and open spaces between trees. She listened to Corlo walking away, back to the clearing. As soon as silence enveloped her, she suddenly regretted the solitude. Desires surged, none of them healthy, none of them pleasant. She would never again feel clean, and this truth pushed her thoughts in the opposite direction, as if a part of her sought to foul her flesh yet further, as far as it could go. Why not? Lost in the darkness as she was, it was nothing to stain her soul black, through and through.

Alone, now frightened – of herself, of the urges within her – she walked on, unmindful of direction. Deeper into the wood, where the stumps were fewer and soft with rot, the deadfall thicker. The afternoon light barely reached through here.

Hurt was nothing. Was meaningless. But no, there was

value in pain, if only to remind oneself that one still lived. When nothing normal could be regained, ever, then other pleasures had to be found. Cultivated, the body and mind taught anew, to delight in a darker strain.

A clearing ahead, in which reared figures.

She halted.

Motionless, half sunk into the ground, tilting this way and that in the high grasses. Statues. This had been Tarthenal land, she recalled. Before the Letherii arrived to crush the tribes. The name 'Dresh' was Tarthenal, in fact, as were the nearby village names of Denner, Lan and Brous.

Seren approached, came to the edge of the clearing.

Five statues in all, vaguely man-shaped but so weathered as to be featureless, with but the slightest indentations marking the pits of their eyes carved into the granite. They were all buried to their waists, suggesting that, when entirely above ground, they stood as tall as the Tarthenal themselves. Some kind of pantheon, she supposed, names and faces worn away by the tens of centuries that had passed since this glade had last known worshippers.

The Letherii had nearly wiped the Tarthenal out back then. As close to absolute genocide as they had ever come in their many conquests. She recalled a line from an early history written by a witness of that war. *'They fought in defence of their holy sites with expressions of terror, as if in failing something vast and terrible would be unleashed . . .'* Seren looked around. The only thing vast and terrible in this place was the pathos of its abandonment.

Such dark moments in Letherii history were systematically disregarded, she knew, and played virtually no role in their culture's vision of itself as bringers of progress, deliverers of freedom from the fetters of primitive ways of living, the cruel traditions and vicious rituals. Liberators, then, destined to wrest from savage tyrants their repressed victims, in the name of civilization. That the Letherii then imposed their own rules of oppression was rarely acknowledged. There was, after all, but one road to success and fulfilment, gold-cobbled and maintained by Letherii toll-collectors, and only the free could walk it.

Free to profit from the same game. Free to discover one's own inherent disadvantages. Free to be abused. Free to be exploited. Free to be owned in lieu of debt. Free to be raped.

And to know misery. It was a natural truth that some walked that road faster than others. There would always be those who could only crawl. Or fell to the wayside. The most basic laws of existence, after all, were always harsh.

The statues before her were indifferent to all of that. Their worshippers had died defending them, and all for nothing. Memory was not loyal to the past, only to the exigencies of the present. She wondered if the Tiste Edur saw the world the same way. How much of their own past had they selectively forgotten, how many unpleasant truths had they twisted into self-appeasing lies? Did they suffer from the same flaw, this need to revise history to answer some deep-seated diffidence, a hollowness at the core that echoed with miserable uncertainty? Was this entire drive for progress nothing more than a hopeless search for some kind of fulfilment, as if on some instinctive level there was a murky understanding, a recognition that the game had no value, and so victory was meaningless?

Such understanding would have to be murky, for clarity was hard, and the Letherii disliked things that were hard, and so rarely chose to think in that direction. Baser emotions were the preferred response, and complex arguments were viewed with anger and suspicion.

She laid a hand upon the shoulder of the nearest statue, and was surprised to discover the stone warm to her touch. Retaining the sun's heat, perhaps. But no, it was too hot for that. Seren pulled her hand away – any longer and she would have burned her skin.

Unease rose within her. Suddenly chilled, she stepped back. And now saw the dead grass surrounding each statue, desiccated by incessant heat.

It seemed the Tarthenal gods were not dead after all.

Sometimes the past rises once again to reveal the lies. Lies that persisted through nothing more than force of will, and collective opinion. Sometimes that revelation comes drenched in fresh blood. Delusions invited their own shattering. Letherii pre-eminence. Tiste Edur arrogance. *The sanctity of my own flesh.*

A sound behind her. She turned.

Iron Bars stood at the edge of the clearing. 'Corlo said there was something . . . restless . . . in this wood.'

She sighed. 'Better were it only me.'

He cocked his head, smiled wryly.

She approached. 'Tarthenal. I thought I knew this land. Every trail, the old barrow grounds and holy sites. It is a responsibility of an Acquitor, after all.'

'We hope to make use of that knowledge,' the Avowed said. 'I don't want no fanfare when we enter Letheras.'

'Agreed. Even among a crowd of refugees, we would stand out. You might consider finding clothing that looks less like a uniform.'

'I doubt it'd matter, lass. Either way, we'd be seen as deserters and flung into the ranks of defenders. This ain't our war and we'd rather have nothing to do with it. The question is, can you get us into Letheras unseen?'

'Yes.'

'Good. The lads are almost ready with the new stirrups.'

She glanced back at the statues.

'Makes you wonder, don't it, lass?'

'About what?'

'The way old anger never goes away.'

Seren faced him again. 'Anger. That's something you're intimately familiar with, I gather.'

A frown. 'Corlo talks too much.'

'If you wanted to get your prince's land back, what are you doing here? I've never heard of this Emperor Kellanved, so his empire must be far away.'

'Oh, it's that, all right. Come on, it's time to go.'

703

'Sorry,' she said as she followed him back into the forest. 'I was prying.'

'Aye, you were.'

'Well. In return, you can ask me what you like.'

'And you'll answer?'

'Maybe.'

'You don't seem the type to end up as you did in Trate. So the merchant you were working for killed himself. Was he your lover or something?'

'No, and you're right, I'm not. It wasn't just Buruk the Pale, though I should have seen it coming – he as much as told me a dozen times on our way back. I just wasn't willing to hear, I suppose. The Tiste Edur emperor has a Letherii adviser—'

'Hull Beddict.'

'Yes.'

'You knew him?'

She nodded.

'And now you're feeling betrayed? Not only as a Letherii, but personally too. Well, that's hard, all right—'

'But there you are wrong, Iron Bars. I don't feel betrayed, and that's the problem. I understand him all too well, his decision – I understand it.'

'Wish you were with him?'

'No. I saw Rhulad Sengar – the emperor – I saw him come back to life. Had it been Hannan Mosag, the Warlock King . . . well, I might well have thrown in my lot with them. But not the emperor . . .'

'He came back to life? What do you mean by that?'

'He was dead. Very dead. Killed when collecting a sword for Hannan Mosag – a cursed sword of some kind. They couldn't get it out of his hands.'

'Why didn't they just cut his hands off?'

'It was coming to that, I suspect, but then he returned.'

'A nice trick. Wonder if he'll be as lucky the next time.'

They reached the edge of the wood and saw the others seated on the horses and waiting. At the Avowed's comment, Seren managed a smile. 'From the rumours, I'd say yes, he was.'

'He was killed again?'

'Yes, Iron Bars. In Trate. Some soldier who wasn't even from Lether. Just stepped up to him and broke his neck. Didn't even stay around to carve the gold coins from his body . . .'

'Hood's breath,' he muttered as they strode towards the others. 'Don't tell the others.'

'Why?'

'I got a reputation of making bad enemies, that's why.'

Eleven Tarthenal lived within a day's walk from the glade and its statues. Old Hunch Arbat had been chosen long ago for the task to which he sullenly attended, each month making the rounds with his two-wheeled cart, from one family to the next. Not one of the farms where the Tarthenal lived in Indebted servitude to a land-owner in Dresh was exclusively of the blood. Mixed-breed children scampered out to greet Old Hunch Arbat, flinging rotten fruit at his back as he made his way to the slop pit with his shovel, laughing and shouting their derision as he flung sodden lumps of faeces into the back of the cart.

Among the Tarthenal, all that existed in the physical world possessed symbolic meaning, and these meanings were mutually connected, bound into correspondences that were themselves part of a secret language.

Faeces was gold. Piss was ale. The mixed-breeds had forgotten most of the old knowledge, yet the tradition guiding Old Hunch Arbat's rounds remained, even if most of its significance was lost.

Once he'd completed his task, a final journey was left to him: pulling the foul cart with its heap of dripping, fly-swarmed waste onto a little-used trail in the Breeder's Wood, and eventually into the glade where stood the mostly buried statues.

As soon as he arrived, just past sunset, he knew that

something had changed. In a place that had never changed, not once in his entire life.

There had been visitors, perhaps earlier that day, but that was the least of it. Old Hunch Arbat stared at the statues, seeing the burnt grasses, the faint glow of heat from the battered granite. He grimaced, revealing the blackened stumps of teeth – all that was left after decade upon decade of Letherii sweet-cakes – and when he reached for his shovel he saw that his hands were trembling.

He collected a load, carried it over to the nearest statue. Then flung the faeces against the weathered stone.

'Splat,' he said, nodding.

Hissing, then blackening, smoke, then ashes skirling down.

'Oh. Could it be worse? Ask yourself that, Old Hunch Arbat. Could it be worse? No, says Old Hunch Arbat, I don't think so. You don't think so? Aren't you sure, Old Hunch Arbat? Old Hunch Arbat ponders, but not for long. You're right, I say, it couldn't be worse.

'Gold. Gold and ale. Damn gold damn ale damn nothing damn everything.' Cursing made him feel slightly better. 'Well then.' He walked back to the cart. 'Let's see if a whole load will appease. And, Old Hunch Arbat, your bladder's full, too. You timed it right, as always. Libations. The works, Old Hunch Arbat, the works.

'And if that don't help, then what, Old Hunch Arbat? Then what?

'Why, I answer, then I spread the word – if they'll listen. And if they do? Why, I say, then we run away.

'And if they don't listen?

'Why, I reply, then I run away.'

He collected another load onto his wooden shovel. 'Gold. Gold and ale . . .'

'Sandalath Drukorlat. That is my name. I am not a ghost. Not any more. The least you can do is acknowledge my existence. Even the Nachts have better manners

706

than you. If you keep sitting there and praying, I'll hit you.'

She had been trying since morning. Periodic interruptions to his efforts. He wanted to send her away, but it wasn't working. He'd forgotten how irritating company could be. Uninvited, unwelcome, persistent reminder of his own weaknesses. And now she was about to hit him.

Withal sighed and finally opened his eyes. The first time that day. Even in the gloom of his abode, the light hurt, made him squint. She stood before him, a silhouette, unmistakably female. For a god swathed in blankets, the Crippled One seemed unmindful of the nakedness among his chosen.

Chosen. Where in Hood's name did he find her? Not a ghost, she said. Not any more. She just said that. She must have been one, then. Typical. He couldn't find anyone living. Not for this mission of mercy. Who better for someone starved of companionship than someone who's been dead for who knows how long? Listen to me. I'm losing my mind.

She raised a hand to strike him.

He flinched back. 'All right, fine! Sandalath something. Pleased to meet you—'

'Sandalath Drukorlat. I am Tiste Andii—'

'That's nice. Now, in case you haven't noticed, I was in the midst of prayers—'

'You're always in the midst of prayers, and it's been two days now. At least, I think two days. The Nachts slept, anyway. Once.'

'They did? How strange.'

'And you are?'

'Me? A weaponsmith. A Meckros. Sole survivor of the destruction of my city—'

'Your name!'

'Withal. No need to shout. There hasn't been any shouting. Well, some screaming, but not by me. Not yet, that is—'

'Be quiet. I have questions that you are going to answer.'

She was not particularly young, he noted as his eyes

707

adjusted. Then again, neither was he. And that wasn't good. The young were better at making friends. The young had nothing to lose. 'You're being rather imperious, Sandalath.'

'Oh, did I hurt your feelings? Dreadfully sorry. Where did you get those clothes?'

'From the god, who else?'

'What god?'

'The one in the tent. Inland. You can't miss it. I don't see how – two days? What have you been doing with yourself? It's just up from the strand—'

'Be quiet.' She ran both hands through her hair.

Withal would rather she'd stayed a silhouette. He looked away. 'I thought you wanted answers. Go ask him—'

'I didn't know he was a god. You seemed preferable company, since all I got from him was coughing and laughter – at least, I think it was laughter—'

'It was, have no doubt about that. He's sick.'

'Sick?'

'Insane.'

'So, an insane hacking god and a muscle-bound, bald aspirant. And three Nachts. That's it? No-one else on this island?'

'Some lizard gulls, and ground-lizards, and rock-lizards, and lizard-rats in the smithy—'

'So where did you get that food there?'

He glanced over at the small table. 'The god provides.'

'Really. And what else does this god provide?'

Well, you, for one. 'Whatever suits his whim, I suppose.'

'Your clothes.'

'Yes.'

'I want clothes.'

'Yes.'

'What do you mean, "yes"? Get me some clothes.'

'I'll ask.'

'Do you think I like standing here, naked, in front of some stranger? Even the Nachts leer.'

708

'I wasn't leering.'

'You weren't?'

'Not intentionally. I just noticed, you're speaking the Letherii trader language. So am I.'

'You're a sharp one, aren't you?'

'I've had lots of practice, I suppose.' He rose. 'It occurs to me that you're not going to let me resume my prayers. At least until you get some clothes. So, let's go talk to the god.'

'You go talk to him. I'm not. Just bring me clothes, Withal.'

He regarded her. 'Will that help you . . . relax?'

Then she did hit him, a palm pounding into the side of his head. She'd caught him unprepared, he decided a moment later, after he picked himself free of the wreckage of the wall he'd gone through. And stood, weaving, the scene around him spinning wildly. The glaring woman who'd stepped outside and seemed to be considering hitting him again, the pitching sea, and the three Nachts on a sward nearby, rolling in silent hilarity.

He walked down towards the sea.

Behind him, 'Where are you going?'

'To the god.'

'He's the other way.'

He reversed direction. 'Talking to me like I don't know this island. She wants clothes. Here, take mine.' He pulled his shirt over his head.

And found himself lying on his back, staring up through the bleached weave of the cloth, the sun bright and blinding—

—suddenly eclipsed. She was speaking. '. . . just lie there for a while longer, Withal. I wasn't intending to hit you that hard. I fear I've cracked your skull.'

No, no, it's hard as an anvil. I'll be fine. See, I'm getting up . . . oh, why bother. It's nice here in the sun. This shirt smells. Like the sea. Like a beach, with the tide out, and all the dead things rotting in fetid water. Just like the Inside Harbour. Got to stop the boys from swimming in there. I keep telling them

. . . oh, they're dead. All dead now, my boys, my apprentices.

You'd better answer me soon, Mael.

'Withal?'

'It's the tent. That's what the Nachts are trying to tell me. Something about the tent . . .'

'Withal?'

I think I'll sleep now.

The trail ran in an easterly direction, roughly parallel to the Brous Road at least to start, then cut southward towards the road itself once the forest on the left thinned. One other farm had been passed through by the deserters, but there had been no-one there. Signs of looting were present, and it seemed a wooden-wheeled wagon had been appropriated. Halfpeck judged that the marauders were not far ahead, and the Crimson Guardsmen would reach them by dawn.

Seren Pedac rode alongside Iron Bars. The new stirrups held her boots firmly in place; she had never felt so secure astride a horse. It was clear that the Blueroses had been deceiving the Letherii for a long time, and she wondered if that revealed some essential, heretofore unrecognized flaw among her people. A certain gullibility, bred from an unfortunate mixture of naivety and arrogance. If Lether survived the Edur invasion and the truth about the Bluerose deception came to light, the Letherii response would be characteristically childish, she suspected, some kind of profound and deep hurt, and a grudge long held on to. Bluerose would be punished, spitefully and repeatedly, in countless ways.

The two women soldiers in the squad had dismantled a hide rack at the first farm, using the frame's poles to fashion a half-dozen crude lances, half again as tall as a man. The sharpened, fire-hardened points had been notched transversely, the thick barbs bent outward from the shaft. Each tip had been smeared with blood from the breeder and his family, to seal the vengeful intent.

They rode through the night, halting four times to rest their horses, all but one of the squad managing a quarter-bell's worth of sleep – a soldier's talent that Seren could not emulate. By the time the sky paled to the east, revealing mists in the lowlands, she was grainy-eyed and sluggish. They had passed a camp of refugees on the Brous Road, an old woman wakening to tell them the raiders had caught up with them earlier and stolen everything of value, as well as two young girls and their mother.

Two hundred paces further down, they came within sight of the deserters. The wagon stood in the centre of the raised road, the two oxen that had been used to pull it off to one side beneath a thick, gnarled oak on the other side of the south ditch. Chains stretched from one of the wheels, along which three small figures were huddled in sleep. A large hearth still smouldered, its dying embers just beyond the wagon.

The Crimson Guardsmen halted at some distance to regard the raiders.

'No-one's awake,' one of the women commented.

Iron Bars said, 'These horses aren't well trained enough for a closed charge. We'll go four one four. You'll be the one, Acquitor, and stay tight behind the leading riders.'

She nodded. She was not prepared to raise objections. She had been given a spare sword, and she well knew how to use it. Even so, this charge was to be with lances.

The soldiers cinched the straps of their helmets then donned gauntlets, shifting their grips on the lances to a third of the way up from the butts. Seren drew her sword.

'All right,' Iron Bars said. 'Corlo, keep them asleep until we're thirty paces away. Then wake 'em quick and panicky.'

'Aye, Avowed. It's been a while, ain't it?'

Halfpeck asked, 'Want any of 'em left alive, sir?'

'No.'

Iron Bars, with Halfpeck on his left and the two women on his right, formed the first line. Walk to trot, then a collected canter. Fifty paces, and no-one was stirring among the deserters. Seren glanced back at Corlo, and he smiled, raising one hand and waggling the gloved fingers.

She saw the three prisoners at the wagon sit up, then quickly crawl beneath the bed.

Lances were levelled, the horses rolling into a gallop.

Sudden movement among the sleeping deserters. Leaping to their feet, bewildered shouts, a scream.

The front line parted to go round the wagon, and Seren pulled hard to her left after a moment of indecision, seeing the glitter of wide eyes from beneath the wagon's bed. Then she was alongside the tall wheels.

Ahead, four lances found targets, three of them skewering men from behind as they sought to flee.

A deserter stumbled close to Seren and she slashed her sword, clipping his shoulder and spinning him round in a spray of blood. Cursing at the clumsy blow, she pushed herself forward on the saddle and rose to stand in her stirrups. Readied the sword once more.

The leading four Guardsmen had slowed their mounts and were drawing swords. The second line of riders, in Seren's wake, had spread out to pursue victims scattering into the ditches to either side. They slaughtered with cold efficiency.

A spear stabbed up at Seren on her right. She batted the shaft aside, then swung as her horse carried her forward. The blade rang in her grip as it connected with a helmet. The edge jammed and she pulled hard, dragging the helm from the man's head. It came free and flew forward to bounce on the road, red-splashed and caved in on one side.

She caught a moment of seeing Iron Bars ten paces ahead. Killing with appalling ease, a single hand gripping the reins as he guided his horse, sword weaving a murderous dance around him.

Someone flung himself onto her sword-arm, his weight wrenching at her shoulder. She shouted in pain, felt herself being pulled from her saddle.

His face, bearded and grimacing, seemed to surge towards her as if hunting some ghastly kiss. Then she saw the features go slack. Blood filled his eyes. The veins on his temples collapsed into blue stains blossoming beneath the skin. More blood, spraying from his nostrils. His grip fell away and he toppled backward.

Drawing in close, a long, thin-bladed knife in one hand, Corlo came alongside her. 'Push yourself up, lass! Use my shoulder—'

Hand fisted around the grip of her sword, she set it against him and righted herself. 'Thanks, Corlo—'

'Rein in, lass, we're about done here.'

She looked round. Three Guardsmen had dismounted, as had Iron Bars, and were among the wounded and dying, swords thrusting down into bodies. She glanced back. 'That man – what happened to him?'

'I boiled his brain, Acquitor. Messy, granted, but the Avowed said to keep you safe.'

She stared at him. 'What sort of magic does *that*?'

'Maybe I'll tell you sometime. That was a nice head-shot back there. The bastard came close with that spear.'

He did. She was suddenly shaking. 'And this is your profession, Corlo? It's . . . disgusting.'

'Aye, Acquitor, that it is.'

Iron Bars approached. 'All is well?'

'We're fine, sir. All dead?'

'Twenty-one.'

'That's all of them,' the mage said, nodding.

'Less than a half-dozen actually managed to draw their weapons. You fouled 'em up nicely, Corlo. Well done.'

'Is that how you soldiers win your battles?' Seren asked.

'We wasn't here to give battle, Acquitor,' Iron Bars said. 'Executions, lass. Any mages among the lot, Corlo?'

'One minor adept. I got him right away.'

Executions. Yes. Best to think of it that way. Not butchery. They were murderers and rapists, after all. 'You didn't leave me any alive, Avowed?'

He squinted up at her. 'No, none.'

'You don't want me to . . . do what I want. Do you?'

'That's right, lass. I don't.'

'Why?'

'Because you might enjoy it.'

'And what business is that of yours, Iron Bars?'

'It's not good, that's all.' He turned away. 'Corlo, see to the prisoners under the wagon. Heal them if they need it.'

He's right. The bastard's right. I might enjoy it. Torturing some helpless man. And that wouldn't be good at all, because I might get hungry for more. She thought back to the feeling when her sword's blade had connected with that deserter's helmed head. Sickening, and sick with pleasure, all bound together.

I hurt. But I can make others hurt. Enough so they answer each other, leaving . . . calm. Is that what it is? Calm? Or just some kind of hardening, senseless and cold.

'All right, Iron Bars,' she said. 'Keep it away from me. Only,' she looked down at him, 'it doesn't help. Nothing helps.'

'Aye. Not yet, anyway.'

'Not ever,' she said. 'I know, you're thinking time will bring healing. But you see, Avowed, it's something I keep reliving. Every moment. It wasn't days ago. It was with my last breath, every last breath.'

She saw the compassion in his eyes and, inexplicably, hated him for it. 'Let me think on that, lass.'

'To what end?'

'Can't say, yet.'

She looked down at the sword in her hand, at the blood and snarled hair along the notched edge where it had struck the man's head. *Disgusting. But they'll expect it to be wiped away. To make the iron clean and gleaming once more, as if it was nothing more than a sliver of metal. Disconnected from its deeds, its history, its very purpose.* She didn't want that mess cleaned away. She liked the sight of it.

They left the bodies where they had fallen. Left the

lances impaled in flesh growing cold. Left the wagon, apart from the food they could transport – the refugees coming up on the road could have the rest. Among the dead were five youths, none of them older than fifteen years. They'd walked a short path, but as Halfpeck observed, it had been the wrong path, and that was that.

Seren pitied none of them.

BOOK FOUR

MIDNIGHT TIDES

Kin mourn my passing, all love is dust
The pit is cut from the raw, stones piled to the side
Slabs are set upon the banks, the seamed grey wall rises
Possessions laid out to flank my place of rest
All from the village are drawn, beating hides
Keening their grief with streaks in ash
Clawed down their cheeks, wounds on their flesh
The memory of my life is surrendered
In fans of earth from wooden shovels
And were I ghostly here at the edge of the living
Witness to brothers and sisters unveiled by loss
Haunters of despair upon this rich sward
Where ancestors stand sentinel, wrapped in skins
I might settle motionless, eyes closed to dark's rush
And embrace the spiral pull into indifference
Contemplating at the last, what it is to be pleased
Yet my flesh is warm, the blood neither still in my veins
Nor cold, my breathing joining this wind
That carries these false cries, I am banished
Alone among the crowd and no more to be seen
The stirrings of my life face their turned backs
The shudders of their will, and all love is dust
Where I now walk, to the pleasure of none
Cut raw, the stones piled, the grey wall rising.

Banished
Kellun Adara

CHAPTER TWENTY

It seemed the night would never end during the war
with the Sar Trell. Before the appearance of Our Great
Emperor, Dessimbelackis, our legions were thrown
back on the field of battle, again and again. Our sons
and daughters wept blood on the green ground, and
the wagon-drums of the enemy came forth in thunder.
But no stains could hold upon our faith, and it shone
ever fierce, ever defiant. We drew our ranks tall,
overlapped shields polished and bright as the red sun,
and the one among us who was needed, who was
destined to grasp the splashed grip of the First Empire's
truthful sword, gave his voice and his strength to lead
us in answer to the well-throated rumble of the Sar Trell
warcries, the stone-tremble of their wagon-drums.
Victory was destined, in the forge-lit eyes of He of
the Seven Holy cities, the fever-charge of his will,
and on that day, the Nineteenth in the Month of
Leth-ara in the Year of Arenbal, the Sar Trell army
was broken on the plain south of Yath-Ghatan, and
with their bones was laid the foundation, and with
their skulls the cobbles of Empire's road . . .

The Dessilan
Vilara

Somewhere ahead, the Royal Colonnade of the Eternal Domicile. Arched, the hemispherical ceiling web-spun in gold on a midnight blue background, diamonds glittering like drops of dew in the streaming strands. The pillars flanking the aisle that led to the throne room were carved in a spiral pattern and painted sea-green, twenty to each side and three paces apart. The passageways between them and the wall were wide enough to permit an armoured palace guard to walk without fear of his scabbard scraping, while the approach down the centre aisle was ten men wide. At the outer end was a large chamber that served as a reception area. First Empire murals, copied so many times as to be stylized past meaning, had been painted on the walls. Traditional torch sconces held crystals imbued with sorcery that cast a faintly blue light. At the inward end stood two massive, bejewelled doors that led to a narrow, low passage, fifteen paces long, before opening out into the domed throne room proper.

The air smelled of marble dust and paint. The ceremonial investiture was three days away, when King Ezgara Diskanar in his robes of state would stride down the length of the Royal Colonnade and enter the throne room, his queen a step behind on his left, his son the prince two paces back and immediately behind his father. Or, rather, that was how it should have been.

A trail of servants and guards had led Brys here, following the seemingly random wanderings of Ceda Kuru Qan. The strange emptiness of the Eternal Domicile on this last stretch unnerved the Finadd, his boots echoing on the unadorned flagstones as he entered the reception chamber.

To find the Ceda on his hands and knees directly in front of him.

Kuru Qan was muttering to himself, tracing his fingertips along the joins in the floor. Beside him was a tattered, paint-spattered basket crowded with scribers, brushes and stoppered jars of pigments.

'Ceda?'

720

The old man looked up, squinting over the tops of the lenses, the contraption having slid down to the end of his nose. 'Brys Beddict? I've been wondering where you've been.'

'In the throne room. The old throne room, where still resides our king. The surviving battalions and brigades are converging to the defence of Letheras. Things have been rather . . . hectic.'

'No doubt. Relevant? Significantly so. Indeed, telling. Now, count the flagstones across this chamber. Width, then length, if you will.'

'What? Ceda, the king is asking for you.'

But Kuru Qan had ceased listening. He had begun crawling about, mumbling, brushing away the grit left behind by the builders.

Brys was motionless for a moment, considering, then he began counting flagstones.

After he was done, he returned to the Ceda's side. Kuru Qan was simply sitting now, appearing wholly consumed in the cleaning of his lenses. Without looking up, he began speaking. 'Battalions and brigades. Yes, most certainly. Assembling in the hills surrounding Brans Keep. Useful? The last of my mages. Tell me the centre flagstone, Brys. Will Merchants' Battalion remain in the city? I think not. It shall be cast upon those hills. All of it. The centre, Brys Beddict?'

'The one before you, Ceda.'

'Ah yes. Good. Very good. And what armies are left to us? How fare the fleets? Oh, the seas are unwelcoming, are they not? Best stay away. Dracons Sea, at the very least, although the protectorates are making noises. Korshenn, Pilott, Descent – they think they see their chance.'

Brys cleared his throat. 'The Artisan Battalion has left the Manse and is marching to Five Points. Riven Brigade withdrew from Old Katter with minimal losses. Snakebelt Battalion has departed Awl, and the Crimson Rampant Brigade has left Tulamesh – the north coast cities have been yielded. Dresh was taken last night, the garrison slaughtered. Whitefinder Battalion are razing the ground on their retreat from First Reach and should be at Brans Keep soon. Preda Unnutal Hebaz will lead the Merchants' Battalion from the city in three days' time. It is anticipated, Ceda, that you will be accompanying her.'

'Accompanying? Nonsense, I am far too busy. Too busy. So many things left to do. She shall have my mages. Yes, my mages.'

'There are only fourteen remaining, Ceda.'

'Fourteen? Relevant? I must needs think on that.'

Brys studied Kuru Qan, his old friend, and struggled against waves of pity. 'How long, Ceda, do you plan on remaining here, on the floor?'

'It is no easy thing, Finadd, not at all. I fear I have waited too long as it is. But we shall see.'

'When can the king expect you?'

'Alas, we do not know what to expect, do we? Barring a few salient truths so painfully gleaned from the chaos. The Seventh Closure, ah, there is nothing good to this turn of events. You must go, now. Care for your brother, Brys. Care for him.'

'Which one?'

Kuru Qan was cleaning his lenses again, and made no reply.

Brys swung about and strode towards the doors.

The Ceda spoke behind him. 'Finadd. Whatever you do, don't kill him.'

He halted and glanced back. 'Who?'

'Don't kill him. You must not kill him. Now, go. Go, Finadd.'

So many alleys in Letheras never knew the light of day. Narrow, with various balconies, ledges and projections forming makeshift roofs, the corridors beneath were twisted and choked with refuse, a realm of rats, slipper-beetles and spiders. And the occasional undead.

Shurq Elalle stood in the gloom, as she had stood most of the previous night. Waiting. The street beyond had wakened with the day, although the crowds were markedly more furtive and tense than was usual. There had been a riot near the West Gate two nights past, brutally quelled by soldiers of the Merchants' Battalion. Curfews had been enforced, and it had been finally noted that the low castes seemed to have virtually vanished from the city, cause for confusion and a vague unease.

Almost directly across from her was a side postern gate leading into Gerun Eberict's estate. The Finadd disliked ceremony upon his return. Modesty was not the issue. More relevant, however, were the innumerable positions from which to stage an attempted assassination near the estate's formal entrance.

None the less, there was some commotion attending Gerun's appearance. Bodyguards drifting into the street announced his imminent arrival. Shurq melted back into the darkness as they scanned the area. Taking defensive positions around the side postern, they waited. Their officer appeared next, striding past them to unlock the gate and push it back, revealing a narrow passage that opened out into the sunlit courtyard. All at once, there were fewer citizens in the area, thinning as if by some prearranged signal until only the guards remained within the range of Shurq's vision.

'Don't make me laugh,' she muttered under her breath.

Gerun Eberict then strode into view, one hand resting on the pommel of the sword scabbarded at his left hip. He did not pause, but continued on directly into the passage. The guards swept in after him, followed at last by the officer, who then slammed the gate shut behind him.

Shurq walked further into the alley until she came to a rusty ladder more or less fixed to the wall of the building on her right. She climbed, ignoring the protests of fittings and weakened metal, until she reached the roof. Clambered up the slope, testing the firmness of each slab of grey slate she set her weight upon, then over the edge. Sidling along until she could look down upon the front entrance of Gerun's house and part of the courtyard. She lowered herself as far as she could on the opposite side, until only her fingers, eyes and top of her head were visible – as unlikely to be noticed as she could manage, should someone in the courtyard glance up in her direction.

Gerun Eberict was standing before the doors, listening to the captain of the house guard, who was speaking at length, punctuating his statements every now and then with gestures indicating bafflement.

His report was cut off when Gerun's right hand snapped out to close around his neck.

Even from this distance, she could see the man's face darken to a curious shade of blue.

Of course, no person with any courage would take much of that, so she was not surprised when the captain tugged a knife from his belt.

Gerun had been waiting for that, having palmed his own knife, with which he stabbed the captain, up under the breastbone, pushing it to the hilt.

The captain sagged. The Finadd released his hold on the man's neck and watched him crumple to the flagstones.

'It's just coin, Gerun,' Shurq said quietly. 'And a missing brother who you killed a long time ago. Your lack of control is dismaying . . . for your other employees, that is. For me, well, little more than confirmation of all my suspicions.'

There would be a bloodbath, if not tonight, then the next night. The city's countless spies and snitches – those who had remained – would be stung into frantic activity, and the great hunt for the thief would begin.

All rather unpleasant.

Gerun's wealth had paid for the exodus of the city's indigents, meaning he would have to make most of his victims Letherii rather than Nerek, Tarthenal or Faraed. Indeed, he might find victims hard to find. Besides which, there was a war, and the Finadd might well find his time

724

otherwise occupied. The man's rage would be apoplectic in no time.

She watched as Gerun stormed into his house, guards scrambling after him, then she lowered herself along the slope, rolled onto her back and slid towards the edge.

There was a balcony directly below—

No, not any more.

She fell, struck a clothes line that snapped with her weight, cannoned off the side of a ledge thick with pigeon droppings, and landed spread-eagled on a heap of rubbish. Where she lay for a time, unmoving.

That was the problem with cities. Nothing ever stayed the same. She'd used that balcony at least a half-dozen times before, when staking out the estate. She lifted an arm. Then the other. Drew her legs beneath her. Nothing broken thus far. And, after a careful examination, nothing overly damaged. Fortunately, she concluded, the dead did not suffer much from pride, said wounding being minimal.

It was then that she discovered the bar of rusty iron projecting from her forehead. Perfumed liquids were leaking out, blurring her vision. She probed the offending object with her fingertips. Punched right through the bone, all the way, in fact, to the back of her skull, if the grating noises the bar made when she wriggled it were any indication.

'I've made a mess of my brain,' she said. 'But was I really using it? Probably not. Still, was I in the habit of talking to myself before? I don't think so.'

She stood, knee-deep in the refuse, contemplating physically removing the bar. But that might make things even messier. Less than a hand's width projected out, after all. Hard not to notice, but far less egregious than, say, an arm's length. A visit to Tehol Beddict seemed incumbent, if only for endless advice she could take pleasure in rejecting.

Alas, she realized, she would have to wait for night, since there was no way she could get to his home without being seen. There had been a time, long ago, when she liked attention. Admiring regards and all that, and it was always satisfying to flaunt her qualities. But a bar in the head took fashion sense to excess by any standard of measure. People would notice, and not in a good way.

Disconsolate, Shurq Elalle sat down in the rubbish. To await the coming of night.

'What happened to the legs of my bed?'

'We needed the wood, master.'

'Yes, but why only three of them?'

'I was saving the other one for later. I found a bag of something that might be tea.'

'Well.' Tehol sat up. 'I'm just amazed I slept through it.'

'You were clearly very tired, master.'

'Yes, which is very understandable, given how busy I've been. I have been busy, haven't I?'

'I could not say, having been too busy myself to take much notice. But I have faith in your proclamations, master. You certainly slept like a man who'd been busy.'

'Seems proof enough, I would say. I'm convinced. Now, while I've been working myself senseless, you make claim to having had many things on your table. Let's hear about them.'

'Very well, master. We're more or less done with the wings of the Eternal Domicile. Dry, foundations restored, my crews cleaning up. There have been some complaints about the cold draughts in the Fifth Wing, but that's not my problem, strictly speaking.'

'Why the cold draughts, Bugg?'

'Presumably related to the shoring methods I employed, but they don't know that.'

'And why should your shoring methods make it cold? Bugg, do I detect some discomfort in your demeanour?'

'Discomfort, master? Not at all. Are you certain you want the details of this matter?'

'When you put it that way, probably not. So, is that all you've been doing?'

'I've also been here and there, working through all the rumours to see if I could glean some truth. I have accordingly assembled a list of facts.'

'A list. Wonderful. I love lists. They're so . . . ordered.'

'Indeed, master. Shall I proceed? Well, the northern frontier belongs to the Tiste Edur, as do all the coastal cities all the way down to Height and possibly Old Gedure. It is believed the Edur fleets are in the Ouster Sea, opposite Lenth and therefore on the edge of Gedry Bay. From this one must assume they intend to sail up Lether River. Possibly with the aim of arriving in concert with the land armies. It is clear that the Tiste Edur are marching on Letheras and are planning to conquer it and take the throne. Whether this will succeed in triggering the capitulation of the entire kingdom remains to be seen. Personally, I believe it will. Nor do I think the protectorates will go much beyond restlessness. To do otherwise would be suicidal.'

'If you say so, Bugg. Are the Tiste Edur that formidable, then?'

The manservant ran a hand through his thinning hair, then glanced over at the bodyguard who was standing, silent as ever, near the hatch. 'Again, master, countless rumours. I would hazard the following observations regarding the Tiste Edur. Their new emperor is in possession of terrible power, but the sorcery the Edur are using does not come from their traditional sources. Not Kurald Emurlahn, although it remains part of their arsenal. In the battles thus far, they have been profligate in their use of shadow wraiths and Kenyll'rah demons, both of whom are reluctant participants.'

'Kurald what? Kenyll who? Who's whispering these rumours anyway?'

'Ah, that brings me to my third set of observations. Having to do with the dead.'

'The dead. Of course. Go on, please.'

'This subcontinent, the region ranging from Tiste Edur

lands to the north, Bluerose and Awl'd'an to the east, and Descent and D'aliban to the south – it is a rather peculiar region, master, and has been since, well, since the earliest times. There are, uh, no pathways. For the dead, I mean. For their spirits.'

'I don't quite understand you, Bugg,' Tehol said, rising from the rickety bed and beginning to pace along the rooftop. The bodyguard's gaze tracked him. 'The dead are just dead. Ghosts linger because they have nowhere else to go and are disinclined to go sightseeing in any case. What kind of pathways are you talking about?'

'Into what could be called the Hold of the Dead.'

'There is no Hold of the Dead.'

'Which is what has been so . . . unusual. There should have been. All along. Those of Kolanse, for example, include in their worship a Lord of Death. You will find something similar in the Bolkando kingdom—'

'The Bolkando kingdom? Bugg, nobody knows *anything* about the Bolkando kingdom. Nobody wants to. You are starting to alarm me, my dear manservant, with the breadth of your knowledge. Unless, of course, you are making it all up.'

'Precisely, master. To continue. There was no Hold of the Dead. It once existed. That is, the original Tiles of the Hold from the First Empire contained one. As well as a number of other Holds, all of which have been discarded by and by. It would be nice, indeed, were a scholar to address this strange diminishment. The passage of time in a culture invites elaboration, not simplification, unless some terrible collapse triggers a fall of sorts, but the only trauma Lether has suffered came with the original fall of the First Empire and the subsequent isolation of these colonies. There was, at that time, some degradation, leading to a short period of independent city-states. And then there were wars with the tribes south and east of Kryn, and with the atavistic Andii remnants of Bluerose. But none of that was culturally disturbing. Possibly because the Hold of the Dead could not

728

manifest itself here. In any case, the closing of the pathways for the dead was already a fact, frozen in the very earth of this region. Worse yet, it was all an accident—'

'Hold on, Bugg. Now I do have some pertinent questions.'

'Your questions are always pertinent, master.'

'I know, but these are particularly pertinent.'

'More so than usual?'

'Are you suggesting that my normal pertinence is less than particular, Bugg?'

'Of course not, master. Now, where was I? Oh yes, the accident. In the earliest texts – those that came with the Letherii from the First Empire – there is the occasional mention made of a race called the Jaghut—'

'There is? You are speaking to a man whose head was filled to bursting with classical education, Bugg. I've never heard of these Jaghut.'

'All right, they were mentioned once, and not specifically by name.'

'Hah, I knew it. Don't try any sleight of hand with me.'

'Sorry, master. In any case, in the most proper sense, the Jaghut are represented by those poorly rendered, stylized images you will find on tiles of the Hold of Ice—'

'Those frog-like midgets?'

'Only the green skin survived, alas. The Jaghut were in fact quite tall and not in the least frog-like. The point is, they manifested their sorcery with ice, and cold. It remains common to this day to consider only four principal elements in nature. Air, Earth, Fire and Water. Absolute nonsense, of course.'

'Of course.'

'There is Light, Dark, Shadow, Life, Death and Ice. There might even be more, but why quibble? The point I am making, master, is that, long ago, a Jaghut did something to this land. Sealed it, in a manner of speaking. Using its aspected sorcery. The effect was profound.'

729

'Making the pathways of the dead snowbound, like a mountain pass in winter?'

'Something like that, yes.'

'So the dead loiter in Lether. Ghosts, shades, and people like Shurq Elalle and Kettle.'

'Indeed. But that is all changing.'

Tehol ceased his pacing and faced Bugg. 'It is?'

'Alas, yes, master. The sorcery is . . . thawing. A Hold of the Dead is manifesting itself. The situation is unravelling. Quickly.'

'Does this mean Shurq is in trouble?'

'No. I suspect the curse on her will remain. But the initial efficacy of that curse derives from the fact of the Hold's having been non-existent in the first place.'

'All right. It's all unravelling. Have you visited Kettle lately?'

'Interesting you should ask, master, for it is at the site of the now-dead Azath tower that the Hold of the Dead is manifesting itself. From that, one might conclude that Kettle is somehow connected with the entire event, but she isn't. In fact, she's no longer dead. Not as dead as she was, that is. It is now clear that her purpose is . . . otherwise. As you know, there's trouble coming from the barrows.'

'What's that smoke? Over there.'

Bugg squinted. 'Another riot, I think. Counters' Quarter.'

'Well, they've been a little skittish ever since the ghosts stormed the Tolls Repository. Besides which, the Tolls themselves have been tumbling with all the bad news from the north. In fact, I'm surprised it's taken this long.'

They could hear bells now, as the city's garrison began responding to the alarm from various stations near the area.

'That won't last long,' Bugg predicted.

'Yes, but I am reminded of something,' Tehol said. 'The time has come, I think, to see Shand, Hejun and Rissarh on their way.'

'Will they complain?'

'Less than one might expect. This is a nervous city. The few non-Letherii remaining are being subjected to harassment, and not just by citizens. The authorities are showing their racist underpinnings with all these suspicions and the eagerness to tread over hard-won rights.'

'Proof that the freedoms once accorded non-Letherii peoples were born of both paternalism and a self-serving posturing as a benign overseer. What is given is taken away, just like that.'

'Indeed, Bugg. Is it because, do you think, at the human core, we are naught but liars and cheats?'

'Probably.'

'With no hope of ever overcoming our instinctive nastiness?'

'Hard to say. How have we done so far?'

'That's not fair. Oh, fine, it's perfectly fair. But it doesn't bode well, does it?'

'Few things do, master.'

'Well, this is uncharacteristically glum of you, Bugg.'

'Alas, I fear the Tiste Edur won't be any better. Coin is the poison, after all, and it infects indiscriminately.'

'As I suspected,' Tehol mused, 'clearly, now is not the time to destroy the economy.'

'Either way, you're right, master.'

'Of course I am. Furthermore, it seems incumbent that, for the moment at least, we should do nothing. About anything. The Rat Catchers' Guild has done a fine job thus far; we need make no adjustments there. I know the details of who owes what from the Tolls Repository and Shand has acted with impressive facility on that information. We know the dire state of the royal treasury. You have been paid for your work on the Eternal Domicile, haven't you?'

'Just yesterday, master.'

'Excellent. Well, that was exhausting. I think I'll go back to bed.'

'Good idea, master.'

731

'After all, this rooftop is probably the safest place in Letheras now.'

'Indeed. Best stay here.'

'And you, Bugg?'

'I thought I'd take a walk.'

'More rumours to track down?'

'Something like that, master.'

'Be careful, Bugg, they're press-ganging recruits with some ferocity.'

'I was wondering about that, master. No-one's paid you a visit?'

'Why, they have. But our silent bodyguard sent them away.'

'He said something?'

'No, it was just a look, I think. They scurried.'

'Impressive. As for me, master, I have ways of making myself unpalatable, even for desperate recruiters.'

'You have always been unpalatable, it's true,' Tehol noted as he gingerly lowered himself onto his bed. 'Even the fleas avoid you. Just one more of those eternal mysteries, Bugg, that so endears you to me. Or is it endears me to you?'

'The former, I think, master.'

'Oh, no. You don't like me. I discover this after all this time?'

'I was only commenting on your usage of the appropriate phrase in the context of your statement and the sentiment you presumably wished to express. Of course I like you, master. How could I not?'

'You have a point there, Bugg. Anyway, I'm going to sleep now, so if you don't want me for anything else . . .'

'Right, master. I'll see you later, then.'

Turudal Brizad was just outside the throne room, leaning against a column, his arms crossed. Brys nodded to him and was about to pass when the Queen's First Consort gestured him over. The Finadd hesitated, then approached.

Turudal smiled. 'Relax. I am no longer as dangerous as I

732

once was, Brys Beddict. Assuming that I was dangerous in the first place.'

'First Consort. Please permit me to express my sympathy—'

'Thank you,' Turudal cut in, 'but it's not necessary. The prince was not the only precipitous member of the royal family. My dear queen was, it is worth recalling, at the forefront of inviting this war against the Tiste Edur. She has the arrogance of her people, after all . . .'

'And are they not your people as well, First Consort?'

The man's smile broadened. 'So much of my life, Brys Beddict – here in this palace – can be characterized as fulfilling the role of objective observer in the proceedings of state, and in the domestic travails upon which, it must be said, my fortune depends. Rather, *depended*. In this, I am no different from my counterpart, the First Concubine. We were present as symbols, after all. And so we behaved accordingly.'

'And now you find yourself without a role,' Brys said.

'I find myself even more objective as an observer than I have ever been, Finadd.'

'To what end?'

'Well, that's just it, isn't it? To no end. None at all. I had forgotten what such freedom felt like. You realize, don't you, that the Tiste Edur will conquer this kingdom?'

'Our forces were divided before, First Consort.'

'So were theirs, Finadd.'

Brys studied the man before him, wondering what was so strange about him, this vague air of indifference and . . . what? 'Why did she want this war, Turudal Brizad?'

He shrugged. 'The Letherii motive was, is and shall ever be but one thing. Wealth. Conquest as opportunity. Opportunity as invitation. Invitation as righteous claim. Righteous claim as preordained, as destiny.' Something dark glittered in his eyes. 'Destiny as victory, victory as conquest, conquest as wealth. But nowhere in that perfect scheme will you find the notion of defeat. All failures are

733

temporary, flawed in the particular. Correct the particular and victory will be won the next time round.'

'Until a situation arises where there is no second opportunity.'

'And future scholars will dissect every moment of these days, assembling their lists of the particulars, the specifics from which no generalization threatening the prime assumptions can ever be derived. It is, in truth, an exquisite paradigm, the perfect mechanism ensuring the persistent survival of an entire host of terrible, brutal beliefs.'

'You do seem to have achieved objectivity, Turudal Brizad.'

'Do you know how the First Empire collapsed, Brys Beddict? I don't mean the revised versions every child is taught by tutors. I mean the truth. Our ancestors unleashed their own annihilation. Through a ritual run wild, the civilization tore itself apart. Of course, in our version, those who came afterwards to clean up were transformed into the aggressors, the outside agency that wrought such destruction as to obliterate the First Empire. And here is another truth: our colonies here were not immune to the effects of that unfettered ritual. Although we succeeded in driving away the threat, as far as we could, into the ice wastes. Where, we hoped, the bastards would die out. Alas, they didn't. And now, Brys Beddict, they're coming back.'

'Who? The Tiste Edur? We share nothing with them, Turudal—'

'Not the Tiste Edur, although much of their history – that of their path of sorcery in particular – is bound with the succession of disasters that befell the First Empire. No, Finadd, I am speaking of their allies, the savages from the ice wastes, the Jheck.'

'An interesting story,' Brys said after a moment, 'but I am afraid I do not comprehend its relevance.'

'I am offering explanation,' the First Consort said, pushing himself from the column and walking past Brys.

'For what?'

734

Without turning, he replied, 'For the imminent failure, Finadd, of my objectivity.'

Moroch Nevath slowed his lathered horse as he neared the gates. To either side of the raised road, what had once been a sprawling confusion of huts and shacks had been razed, leaving only mud, potsherds and slivers of wood. Stains on the city's wall were all that remained of the countless buildings that had leaned against it for support.

The crowds of refugees on the road had thinned the last few leagues, as Moroch outdistanced the leading edges. He'd seen deserters among them, and had struggled against an urge to deliver summary justice upon the cowards, but there would be time for that later. The gates ahead were open, a squad of soldiers from the Merchants' Battalion standing guard.

Moroch reined in before them. 'This road will be packed by dusk,' he said. 'You will need at least four more squads to manage the flow.'

A sergeant scowled up at him. 'And who in the Errant's name are you?'

'Another deserter,' muttered a soldier.

Moroch's uniform was covered in dust and patches of old blood. He was bearded, his hair filthy and unbound. Even so, he stared at the sergeant, shocked that he had not been recognized. Then he bared his teeth, 'There will be deserters, yes. They are to be pulled aside, and all those refugees of acceptable age and fitness are to be recruited. Sergeant, I am Finadd Moroch Nevath. I led the survivors from High Fort down to Brans Keep, where we were attached to the Artisan Battalion. I go now to report to the Preda.'

He was pleased at the sudden deference shown once he identified himself.

The sergeant saluted, then asked, 'Is it true, then, sir? The prince and the queen are prisoners of the Edur?'

'A miracle that they survived at all, sergeant.'

735

A strange expression flitted across the sergeant's features, quickly disguised, yet Moroch had understood it. *Why didn't you fall defending them, Finadd? You ran, like all the others . . .*

'We will get them back, sir,' the sergeant said after a moment.

'Send for your reinforcements,' Moroch said, kicking his horse into motion once more. *You're right. I should have died. But you were not there, were you?*

He rode into the city.

Champion Ormly and Chief Investigator Rucket were sitting on the steps of the Rat Catchers' Guild, sharing a bottle of wine. Both scowled when they saw Bugg, who approached to stand before them.

'We know all about you now,' Rucket said. She sneered, but added nothing more.

'Well,' said Bugg, 'that's a relief. What more have you heard from your agents in the occupied cities?'

'Oh,' Ormly said, 'and we're to reveal all our intelligence to you, simply because you ask for it?'

'I don't see why not.'

'He has a point, the bastard,' Rucket said to the Champion.

Who looked at her in disbelief. 'No he doesn't! You're smitten, aren't you? Tehol and his manservant – both of them!'

'Don't be absurd. It's in the contract, Ormly. We share information—'

'Fine, but what's this man shared? Nothing. The Waiting Man. What's he waiting for? That's what I want to know.'

'You're drunk.'

Bugg said, 'You haven't heard anything.'

'Of course we have!' Ormly snapped. 'Peace reigns. The shops are open once more. Coins roll, the sea lanes are unobstructed.'

'Garrisons?'

'Disarmed. Including local constabulary. All protection

and enforcement is being done by the Edur. Empty estates have been occupied by Edur families – some kind of nobility exists with them, with those tribes. Not so different after all.'

'Curious,' Bugg said. 'No resistance?'

'Their damned shades are everywhere. Even the rats don't dare cause trouble.'

'And how close to Letheras are the Edur armies?'

'That we don't know. Days away, maybe. The situation is pretty chaotic in the countryside north of here. I'm not answering any more questions and that's that.' Ormly took the bottle from Rucket and drank deep.

Bugg looked round. The street was quiet. 'Something in the air . . .'

'We know,' Rucket said.

The silence lengthened, then Bugg rubbed at the back of his neck. Without another word, he walked away.

A short time later, he approached the Azath tower. As he began crossing the street towards the front gate, a figure emerged from a nearby alley. Bugg halted.

'Surprised to see you here,' the man said as he drew nearer to the manservant. 'But a momentary surprise. Thinking on it, where else would you be?'

Bugg grunted, then said, 'I wondered when you'd finally stir yourself awake. If.'

'Better late than never.'

'Here to give things a nudge, are you?'

'In a manner of speaking. And what about you?'

'Well,' Bugg considered, 'that depends.'

'On?'

'You, I suppose.'

'Oh, I'm just passing through,' the man said.

Bugg studied him for a long moment, then cocked his head and asked, 'So, how much of you was at the heart of this mess, I wonder? Feeding the queen's greed, the prince's estrangement from his father. Did the notion of the Seventh Closure simply amuse you?'

'I but watched,' the man replied, shrugging. 'Human nature is responsible, as ever. That is not a burden I am willing to accept, especially from you.'

'All right. But here you are, about to take a far more active role . . .'

'This goes back, old man. Edur or human, I do not want to see a revisiting of the T'lan Imass.'

After a moment, Bugg nodded. 'The Pack. I see. I have never liked you much, but this time I am afraid I have to agree with you.'

'That warms my heart.'

'To be so benignly judged? I suppose it would at that.'

He laughed, then, with a careless wave, walked past Bugg.

The problem with gods, Bugg decided, was the way they ended up getting dragged along. Wherever their believers went. This one had vanished from memory everywhere else, as extinct as the Holds themselves.

So. T'lan Imass, the Pack, and the coming of the Jheck. Soletaken worshippers of their ancient lord, and, from the potential resurrection of that ancient cult, a possible return of the T'lan Imass, to expunge the madness.

What had driven him to act now, then? In this particular matter? The answer came to Bugg, and he smiled without humour. *It's called guilt.*

A metallic tapping woke Tehol Beddict. He sat up, looked round. It was nearing late afternoon. The tapping was repeated and he glanced over to see his bodyguard, weapon drawn, standing at the roof's edge on the alley side. The man gestured him over.

Climbing gingerly from the rickety bed, Tehol tiptoed to the bodyguard's side.

Down in the alley below a shape was crawling along beneath a stained tarp of some sort. Slow but steady progress towards the corner.

'I admit,' Tehol said, 'it's a curious thing. But sufficient cause to wake me up? Ah, there I have doubts. The city is

738

full of crawling things, after all. Well, on a normal day, that is. Here we are, however, so perhaps it might be amusing if we follow its tortured journey.'

The shape reached the corner, then edged round it.

Tehol and his companion tracked it from above. Along the wall, then into the aisle leading to the entrance to Tehol's house.

'Ah, it is paying us a visit. Whatever it's selling, I'm not sure I want any. We are facing a conundrum, my friend. You know how I hate being rude. Then again, what if it is selling some horrible disease?'

It reached the doorway, slipped inside.

The bodyguard walked to the hatch and looked down. After a moment, Tehol followed. As he peered over he heard a familiar voice call up.

'Tehol. Get down here.'

'Shurq?'

A gesturing shape in the gloom.

'Best wait here,' Tehol said to his guard. 'I think she wants privacy. You can keep an eye on the entrance from up here, right? Excellent. I'm glad we're agreed.' He climbed down the ladder.

'I have a problem,' she said when he reached the floor.

'Anything I can do for you, Shurq, I shall. Did you know you have a spike of some sort in your forehead?'

'That's my problem, you idiot.'

'Ah. Would you like me to pull it out?'

'I don't think that's a good idea, Tehol.'

'Not worse, surely, than leaving it there.'

'The issue is not as clear as it appears to be,' Shurq said. 'Something is holding it. It's not nearly as loose as one would hope.'

'Are you concentrating on it?'

She said nothing.

He hastily added, 'Maybe it's bent or something.'

'It goes through to the back of my skull. There may be a flange of some sort.'

739

'Why not push it right through?'

'And leave the back of my head in pieces?'

'Well, the only other possibility I can think of at the moment, Shurq, is to pull it out a little bit, saw it off, then push what's left back in. Granted, you'd have a hole, but you could take to wearing a bandanna or head-scarf, at least until we visit Selush.'

'Not bad. But what if it starts clunking around in my head? Besides, bandannas are pathetically out of date as far as fashion goes. I would be mortified to be seen in public.'

'Selush might well have a solution to that, Shurq. A stopper with a diamond in it, or a patch of skin sewn over the hole.'

'A diamond-studded plug. I like that.'

'You'll launch a new trend.'

'Do you think Ublala will like it, Tehol?'

'Of course he will. As for the clunking, well, that's a definite problem. But it seems evident that you're not using your brain. I mean, that physical stuff in there. Your soul is simply making use of the body, right? Probably out of a sense of familiarity. Given that, maybe we *could* pull it out—'

'No. I like the idea of sawing it. And the diamond stopper. That sounds good. Now, can you bring Selush here?'

'Right now?'

'Well, as soon as possible. I don't like walking around with it the way it is. Tell her I will pay for the inconvenience.'

'I'll try.'

'Needless to say, I'm miserable.'

'Of course you are, Shurq.'

'And I want Ublala. I want him now.'

'I understand—'

'No you don't. I said I want him now. But that's impossible. So you'll have to do.'

'Me? Oh dear. Does it bite?'

'Only one way to find out, Tehol Beddict. Get out of those stupid clothes.'

'So long as you don't poke my eye out.'

'Don't make me – oh, right. I'll be careful. I promise.'

'Just so long as you understand, Shurq, I normally don't do this with my employees. Especially dead ones.'

'I don't see why you had to bring that up. It's not like I can help it.'

'I know. But it's, uh, well . . .'

'Creepy?'

'You're lovely and all that, I mean, Selush was brilliant – the best work she's ever done.'

'Think how I feel, Tehol? Errant knows, you're no Ublala.'

'Why, thank you.'

'Now, take your clothes off. I'm sure it won't take long anyway.'

The street was mostly unobstructed, allowing Moroch Nevath to make good time on his approach to the old palace. His horse would probably never fully recover from the journey down from High Fort. There was a Bluerose trainer in the palace, he had heard – although he had never seen the man – who was said to heal horses. If he found the time, he might hunt him down.

A figure stepped into the street ahead.

Recognizing the man, Moroch reined in. 'Turudal Brizad.'

'Finadd. I barely recognized you.'

'You're not alone in that, First Consort. Now, I am off to report to the Preda.'

'You will find her in the throne room. Finadd, I may have need of you shortly.'

Moroch scowled. 'For what?'

The man smiled. 'Specifically, your skill with the sword.'

'Who do you want me to kill, Brizad? Some irate husband, an outraged wife? I think Gerun Eberict would better suit your requirements in such matters.'

'I wish it were that simple, Finadd. Ideally, I would seek out Brys Beddict, but he has other tasks before him—'

'So do I.'

'The Preda will assign you to protection of the Royal Household, such as it is—'

'That is the task of the King's Champion.'

'Yes. Meaning you will find yourself with some time on your hands.'

Moroch's scowl deepened. 'I intend to accompany the Preda when she marches, First Consort.'

Turudal sighed. 'You are no longer trusted, Finadd. You failed both the prince and the queen. It would have been preferable had you died in the endeavour at High Fort.'

'I was injured. Separated from my charges. I could not even find them once the battle commenced—'

'Tragic, Finadd, but such stones make no splash on a frozen lake. What I offer you is an opportunity for redemption, for your name to be hailed in history. I am certain, Moroch Nevath, that you will receive no comparable offer from anyone else.'

The Finadd studied the man standing before him. He'd always made Moroch's skin crawl. Too slick, too perfumed. Too smug. Now more than ever. 'There is nothing you can offer me—'

'Finadd, I want you to kill a god.'

Moroch sneered, said nothing.

Turudal Brizad smiled, then said, 'The god of the Jheck. And where can you find this god? Why, here in the city. Waiting for the arrival of its savage worshippers.'

'How do you know all this?'

'Kill the god, Moroch Nevath, and the Tiste Edur will lose their allies.'

'We will speak more on this,' the Finadd said in a growl. 'But for now, I must go.'

'Of course. You have my sympathies, by the way. I know you could have done nothing to save Quillas or Janall—'

'Save your breath, First Consort.' Moroch snapped the

742

reins, sending his horse forward, forcing Turudal Brizad to step aside hastily to avoid being knocked down.

Bugg found Kettle hunched against the door of the tower. She was shivering, knees drawn up, her head down.

'Child?'

A muffled reply. 'Go away.'

He crouched beside her. 'How bad is it?'

'I'm hungry. My stomach hurts. The bites itch.'

'You're alive, then.' He saw her head nod. 'And you'd rather be dead.' Another nod. 'We need to get you some new clothes. Some food, and water. We need to find you shelter – you can't stay here any longer.'

'But I have to! He needs my help!'

Bugg rose. 'I think I'll walk the grounds.'

'Don't. It's too dangerous.'

'I'll be all right, lass. No need to worry about Grandfather Bugg. And then I'll come back here, and you and I will head to the Downs Market.'

She looked up then, regarded him with red-rimmed eyes that looked far older than the rest of her face. 'I have no money.'

'Me neither,' Bugg said, smiling. 'But a lot of people owe me.'

He headed into the grounds. The earth was hot beneath his worn sandals. Most of the insects had died or moulted, their bodies crunching underfoot. Withered roots had been pushed to the surface, split and peeling. Stained fragments of bone were visible, pieces of skull and fractured long-bones, the occasional oversized vertebra. The crumpled remains of barrows were on all sides.

So much history had been lost, destroyed beneath this steaming earth. A good thing, too, since most of it was unpleasant. Unfortunately, a few hoary nightmares remained. The meanest of the lot, in fact.

And one of them had sworn to help. Against the others.

All in all, Bugg decided, not a promising situation.

'A stranger among us.'

He halted, frowning. 'Who speaks?'

'My brothers welcome you. I welcome you. Come closer. Hold out your hand, draw us forth. Your rewards will be endless.'

'So will my regret. No, I'm afraid I cannot oblige you, Toblakai.'

'You have taken one step too many, stranger. It is too late. You we shall use—'

A surge of power, rushing into Bugg's mind, seeking domination – then gone.

'No. Not you. Come no closer.'

'I am sorry you found me so unpalatable.'

'Go away.'

'You and your brothers are in for a fight,' Bugg said. 'You know that, don't you?'

'We cannot be defeated.'

'Oh, how often those words are spoken. How many of your fellow prisoners said much the same, at one time or another? Always the conceit of the moment.'

'None of this is your concern.'

'You are right, none of it is. But you should be warned, the child, Kettle, is not to be harmed.'

'She is nothing to us.'

'Good. Make sure it stays that way.'

'Be careful with your threats, stranger.'

'Ah. You don't understand, do you? Attack the child, and the one hiding within her will awaken. And that one will annihilate you, and probably everyone else just for good measure.'

'Who is it that hides within the child?'

'Its name? I don't know. But it is Forkrul Assail.'

'You are lying.'

The manservant shrugged, swung about and made his way back to where Kettle waited. There was time still, he decided, to go shopping.

* * *

King Ezgara Diskanar sat on his throne, motionless, pale as dusted marble, the lids of his eyes half lowered as he regarded First Eunuch Nifadas. The scene belonged to an artist, Brys decided. Heavy with gravitas, the colours dark and saturated, a great fall imminent. All here, in this frozen moment. *The Eve before the Seventh Closure*, the painter might call it, with quiet pleasure at the multitude of meanings hidden in the title.

But there was no artist, no vulture to sit on the wings of civilization's tottering construct, red-eyed and clucking. The audience consisted of Brys, First Concubine Nisall, Preda Unnutal Hebaz and four of the King's Guard.

The sun had dropped low enough outside to send shafts of lurid light through the stained glass panels set in the dome, brushing the motes with ugly hues. The air smelled of sweat and lantern smoke.

'And this,' King Ezgara finally said, 'is what awaits my people.'

The First Eunuch's small eyes blinked. 'Sire, the soldiers do not welcome the notion of new overlords. They will fight to defend you.'

'I have seen scant evidence of that thus far, Nifadas.'

The Preda spoke to that. 'Sire, it quickly became evident that we could not match the enemy in the traditional manner, given the sorcery available to them. It was tactically incumbent that we withdraw, avoiding engagement—'

'But now our backs are to the city's wall, Preda.'

'With time to prepare, as we have been doing since the first unit arrived at Brans Keep. Sire, we have never before fielded such a large army as that which is assembling there right now. Over two thousand trebuchets, fifteen hundred mangonels and three hundred triple-mounted Dresh ballistae. We have dug pits, trenches, traps. The mages have woven rituals across the entire battlefield. Our auxiliaries alone number over ten thousand—'

'Untrained fodder, Preda. A terrible waste of citizenry. Are they even armed?'

'Spears and shields, sire. Leather armour.'

The king leaned back. 'Nifadas. Still no word on the fate of my wife and son?'

'Our emissaries do not return, sire.'

'What does he want with them?'

'I am at a loss to answer that,' the First Eunuch admitted. 'This Tiste Edur emperor is . . . unpredictable. Sire, despite the Preda's confidence, I believe it would be wise to begin plans for your temporary displacement—'

'My *what*?'

'Leaving Letheras, sire. Southeast, perhaps. Tallis on the Isle, or Truce.'

'No.'

'Sire—'

'Nifadas, if I am to fall, then it will be here. I shall not bring destruction upon other cities, for it is destruction my presence will invite. The protectorates, should I be usurped, will fall in line. Peacefully, with no loss of life. This Tiste Edur emperor shall have his empire. For myself, if I must die, it will be here, on this very throne. Or, rather,' he said with a wry smile, 'on the one in the Eternal Domicile.'

Silence. Then the Preda turned slowly to face Brys.

He returned her regard dispassionately. The king had made his wishes known. If he would die on his throne, then his Champion would of necessity already be dead. There was no other path to Ezgara Diskanar, after all.

'It is my intention, sire,' Unnutal said, 'that the situation you describe does not arise. The Tiste Edur will be thrown back. Beaten and broken.'

'As you say,' the king replied.

These were not new considerations for Brys. Ever since the first defeats up north, he had been thinking about a final stand before his king. The passage leading into the throne room in the Eternal Domicile was relatively narrow. With four of his best guards he felt he could hold it for some time. But without relief his death would be inevitable. The least palatable thought of all, however, was the possibility of dying beneath sorcery. Against which he had no defence. The Ceda's seeming descent into madness was the most painful blow of all. Should the enemy reach the palace, the loss of Kuru Qan would be decisive.

Brys wanted to die honourably, but he was helpless to choose, and that stung.

The doors opened behind him and he turned to see a guard step inside.

'What now?' the king asked.

'Finadd Gerun Eberict, my lord,' the guard announced.

'Very well.'

The man entered and bowed before the king. 'Sire, I apologize for arriving late. There were household affairs to attend to—'

'Taking precedence over an audience with your king, Finadd?'

'Sire, in my absence my estate was broken into.'

'I am grieved to hear that.'

'A substantial portion of my wealth was stolen, sire.'

'Careless, Gerun. It is never wise to hoard your coin.'

'My security measures were extreme—'

'Yet insufficient, it seems. Have you any clues regarding the brazen thief?'

Gerun Eberict's eyes flicked to Brys, then away again. 'I have, sire. I believe I shall recover my losses shortly.'

'I trust said activity will not prove too messy.'

'I am confident, sire.'

'And to what extent will this interfere with your duties here in the palace, Finadd?'

'None whatsoever, sire. I am able to resume command of my company.'

'Good. They have been busy quelling riots.'

'I intend to bring an end to those riots, sire. You will have peace in Letheras by this evening.'

'That leaves you little time, Gerun. Off you go, then, but be warned. I do not want a bloodbath.'

'Of course, sire.' Gerun Eberict bowed again, saluted the Preda, then left.

The doors shut, then Ezgara said, 'Brys Beddict, ready two hundred of your soldiers as clean-up crews. Expect at least one bloodbath before the twelfth bell tonight.'

'At once, sire—'

'Not yet. Why did Gerun glance to you when I enquired about the thief who struck his estate?'

'I do not know, sire. I was wondering that myself.'

'I trust your resident brother has not fallen to new depths.'

'I do not believe so.'

'Because Gerun Eberict is a formidable enemy.'

Brys nodded his agreement.

'Sire,' the Preda said, 'it is time for me to join my army.'

'Go then, and may the Errant touch you with mercy.'

As Unnutal bowed and strode towards the doors, Brys said to the king, 'I beg my leave as well, sire.'

'Go on, Champion. Once you have detailed your soldiers return here. I want you close, from now on.'

'Yes, sire.'

In the hall outside the throne room, Unnutal Hebaz was waiting. 'He suspects Tehol.'

'I know.'

'Why?'

Brys shook his head.

'You had better warn him, Brys.'

'Thank you for your concern, Preda.'

She smiled, but it was a sad smile. 'I admit to a certain fondness for Tehol.'

'I was not aware of that,' Brys said.

'He needs some bodyguards.'

'He has them, Preda. The Shavankrats.'

Her brows lifted. 'The triplets?' Then she frowned. 'I've not seen them about for some time, come to think of it. Meaning you have anticipated Gerun Eberict, which in turn suggests you know more than you revealed to the king.'

'My concern was not regarding Eberict, Preda.'

'Ah, I see. Well, you need not inform those brothers to be extra vigilant, since I don't think that is possible.'

'Agreed, Preda.'

She studied him briefly, then said, 'Would that you could join us on the field of battle, Brys.'

'Thank you for that, Preda. Errant be with you.'

'I'd rather the Ceda,' she said, then added, 'I apologize. I know he was your friend.'

'He still is,' Brys said.

She nodded, then departed, her boots echoing in the hallway.

Brys stared after her. *In a few days from now she might be dead.*

So might I.

CHAPTER TWENTY-ONE

The Betrayer stands in the shadow of the Empty Throne.
That is why it is empty.

The Casting of the Tiles
Ceda Parudu Erridict

The mass of refugees had forced them from the main
road, but Seren Pedac was familiar with all the old
tracks winding through the countryside, the herder
paths, quarry and logging roads, the smugglers' trails. They
were skirting an overgrown limestone quarry four leagues
north from Brous as the sun sank behind the trees on their
right.

The Acquitor found herself riding alongside the mage,
Corlo. 'I have been wondering,' she said. 'The sorcery you
use. I have never heard of magic that steals the will from its
victims, that reaches into their minds.'

'Not surprised,' he said in a grunt. 'Here in this back-
water, all the sorcery is raw and ugly. No subtlety, no
refinement of the powers. Yours is a land where most of the
doors are closed. I doubt there's been any innovation in
the study of sorcery in the past ten thousand years.'

'Thank you for those admiring sentiments, Corlo. Maybe
you'd care to explain things for my ignorant self.'

He sighed. 'Where to start?'

'Manipulating people's minds.'

'Mockra. That's the warren's name.'

'All right, bad idea. Go back further. What's a warren?'

'Well, even that's not easy to answer, lass. It's a path of magic. The forces that govern all existence are aspected. Which means—'

'Aspected. In the way the Holds are aspected?'

'The Holds.' He shook his head. 'Sitting in a wagon with square wheels and complimenting each other on the smooth ride. That's the Holds, Acquitor. They were created in a world long gone, a world where the forces were rougher, wilder, messier. The warrens, well, those are wheels without corners.'

'You're not helping much here, Corlo.'

He scratched at his beard. 'Damned fleas. All right. Paths of aspected magic. Like forces and unlike forces. Right? Unlike forces repel, and like forces hold together, you see. Same as water in a river, all flowing the same way. Sure, there's eddies, draws and such, but it all heads down eventually. I'll talk about those eddies later. So, the warrens are those rivers, only you can't see them. The current is invisible, and what you can see is only the effect. Watch a mob in a square, the way the minds of every person in it seem to melt into one. Riots and public executions, or battles, for that matter, they're all hints of Mockra, they're what you can see. But a mage who's found a way into the warren of Mockra, well, that mage can reach deeper, down into that water. In fact, that mage can jump right in and swim with the current. Find an eddy and step back out, in a different place from where he started.'

'So when you say "path" you mean it in a physical sense.'

'Only if you choose to use it that way. Mockra's not a good example; the eddies take you nowhere, mostly. Because it's sorcery of the mind, and the mind's a lot more limited than we'd care to think. Take Meanas – that's another warren. It's aspected to shadows and illusion, a child of Thyr, the warren of Light. Separate but related. Open the warren of Meanas, and you can travel through shadows. Unseen, and fast as thought itself, nearly. And illusions, well, that reveals the sisterhood to Mockra, for it is a kind of manipulation of the mind, or, at least, of perception, via the cunning reshaping of light and shadow and dark.'

'Do the Tiste Edur employ this Meanas?' Seren asked.

'Uh, no. Not really. Theirs is a warren not normally accessible to humans. Kurald Emurlahn. It's Shadow, but Shadow more as a Hold than a warren. Besides, Kurald Emurlahn is shattered. In pieces. The Tiste Edur can access but one fragment and that's all.'

'All right. Mockra and Meanas and Thyr. There are others?'

'Plenty, lass. Rashan, Ruse, Tennes, Hood—'

'Hood. You use that word when you curse, don't you?'

'Aye, it's the warren of Death. It's the name of the god himself. But that's the other thing about warrens. They can be realms, entire worlds. Step through and you can find yourself in a land with ten moons overhead, and stars in constellations you've never seen before. Places with two suns. Or places filled with the spirits of the dead – although if you step through the gates in Hood's Realm you don't come back. Or, rather, you shouldn't. Anyway, a mage finds a warren suited to his or her nature, a natural affinity if you like. And through enough study and discipline you find ways of reaching into it, making use of the forces within it. Some people, of course, are born with natural talent, meaning they don't have to work as hard.'

'So, you reach into this Mockra, and that gets you into the minds of other people.'

'Sort of, lass. I make use of proclivities. I make the water cloudy, or fill it with frightening shadows. The victim's body does the rest.'

'Their body? What do you mean?'

'Say you take two cows to slaughter. One of them you kill quick, without it even knowing what's about to happen. The other, well, you push it down a track, in some place filled with the stench of death, with screams of other dying animals on all sides. Until, stupid as that cow is, it knows what's coming. And is filled with terror. Then you kill it. Cut a haunch from each beast, do they taste identical?'

'I have no idea.'

'They don't. Because the frightened cow's blood was filled with bitter fluids. That's what fear does. Bitter, noxious fluids. Makes the meat itself unhealthy to eat. My point is, you trick the mind to respond to invisible fears, unfounded beliefs, and the blood goes foul, and that foulness makes the fear worse, turns the belief into certainty.'

'As if the slaughterhouse for the second cow was only an illusion, when in truth it was crossing pasture.'

'Exactly.'

Seren studied the back of Iron Bars where he rode ahead, and was silent.

'All right,' Corlo said after a time, 'now tell me what you're really on about, lass.'

She hesitated, then asked, 'Corlo, can you do anything about memories?' She looked across at him. 'Can you take them away?'

In front of them, Iron Bars half turned in his saddle, regarded Seren a moment, then swung back round.

'Ah,' Corlo said under his breath. 'You sure you want that?'

'Can you?'

'I can make you blind and senseless to them, but it'll be in your nature to fret about that strange emptiness. As if you're always on the edge of realization, but never able to reach it. It could drive you to distraction, Acquitor. Besides, the body remembers. You'll react to things you see, smell, taste, and you won't know why. It'll gnaw away at you. Your whole personality will change.'

'You've done it before, haven't you?'

He nodded. Then hesitantly ventured, 'There's another option, lass.'

'What?'

'It's not the memories that are hurting, Acquitor. It's how

753

you feel about them. It's the you, now, warring with the you, then. Can't explain it any better—'

'No, I understand you.'

'Well, I can make you feel, uh, differently about it.'

'How do you mean?'

'End the war, lass.'

'What would I feel, Corlo?'

'I could make you cry it out. All out, Seren.' He met her eyes. 'And when that was done, you'd feel better. Not much better, but some. You release it all, but only once, I promise. There's a risk with crying it all out, mind you. Could be as traumatic as the rape itself. But you won't fall into the trap of cycling through it over and over again. Release gets addictive, you see. It becomes a fixed behaviour, as destructive as any other. Keep repeating the exercise of grief and it loses meaning, it becomes rote, false, a game of self-delusion, self-indulgence. A way of never getting over anything, ever.'

'This sounds complicated, Corlo.'

'It is. You stop the war all in one shot, and afterwards the memory leaves you feeling . . . nothing. A little remorse, maybe. The same as you feel for all the mistakes you left behind you during your whole life. Regrets, but no self-recrimination, because that's your real enemy. Isn't it? A part of you feeling like you somehow deserved it.'

She nodded, not trusting herself to speak.

'Making you want to punish yourself.'

Another nod.

Corlo raised his voice. 'Avowed, we might—'

'Aye,' he said, lifting a gauntleted hand.

The troop halted.

Corlo's hands were there, helping her down from the horse. She glared at him. 'You've started, haven't you?'

'No, lass. You did. Remember what I said about natural talent? You've got it by the bucketful.'

'I never cry,' she said as he led her off the trail into the adjacent forest.

'Of course not,' he replied. 'You've got the warren right there in your head, and you've spent most of your life manipulating it like a High Mage. Anything to keep going, right?'

She pulled up, looked behind them.

Iron Bars was just visible at the trail's edge, watching.

'Don't mind him, he's just worried, lass. He won't be there when you—'

'No,' she said. 'He comes with us.'

'Acquitor?'

'If I start beating on your chest, Corlo, I'm liable to break a rib or two. He's tougher.'

The mage's eyes widened, then he smiled. 'Avowed! Stop hovering, if you please.'

Warrens. It occurred to Seren Pedac, much later, that they were a thing not easily defined, yet simply understood. Forces of nature, proclivities and patterns. Corlo's explanations had worked to illuminate for her those mostly hidden forces, somewhat, but in the end it was the knowledge already within her that offered revelation.

In a simplistic world, four elements are commonly identified, and things are left at that. As if the universe could be confined to four observable, apposite manifestations. But Corlo had mentioned others, and once that notion was accepted, then it was as if the world opened out, as if new colours rose sudden and startling in their terrible beauty.

Time was such an element, she now believed. The stretch of existence between events, consisting of countless other events, all strung together in complex patterns of cause and effect, all laid out like images sewn onto a tapestry, creating a sequence of scenes that, once one stood back, was revealed to be co-existing. Present all at once.

She had been repeating scenes. A grim realization. Repeating scenes for most of her life. She had imposed her own pattern, bereft of nuance, and had viewed her despair

755

as a legitimate response, perhaps the only legitimate response. A conceit of being intelligent, almost preternaturally aware of the multitude of perspectives that was possible in all things. And that had been the trap, all along, the sorcerous incantation called grief, her invitation to the demons of self-recrimination, reappearing again and again on that tapestry – different scenes, the same leering faces.

Unravelling the ritual had proved frighteningly easy, like pulling a single thread. If it had been Corlo's work, then he had been subtle beyond belief, for it had seemed that the effort was entirely her own. He had sat across from her, there in the glade they'd found thirty paces from the trail, his expression both relaxed and watchful, and, oddly enough, she had felt no shame weeping in front of him.

Iron Bars had begun by pacing restlessly, but his motion stilled when her first tears arrived, and eventually she found herself in the half-embrace of one of his arms, her face pressed against his neck.

It might have been sordid, under other circumstances. The critical part of herself could well have sneered at the contrivance, as if the only genuine gestures were the small ones, the ones devoid of an audience. As if true honesty belonged to solitude, since to be witnessed was to perform, and performance was inherently false since it invited expectation.

In the exhausted aftermath of a surprisingly short period of release, when it seemed in truth that she was empty inside, hollowed-out calm, she could explore what was left, without the fetters of emotion. She had chosen to have faith in Buruk the Pale, believed – because it was easy – that he would not give up on life. She never did, after all. She had refused the evidence of his sudden ease, the strange freedom in his words to her during those last few days. When he'd already made up his mind. He'd seen the war coming, after all, and wanted to excise his own role in its making. Cut himself from this particular tapestry. But there had been sorcery in her own self-deceit, the path to grief and guilt, and there had been a comforting familiarity to the ritual.

From her failure sprang the requirement to be punished.

She had not invited the rape. No sane person would do that. But she had woven the scene and all its potential horror.

Not all things about oneself were likeable.

So she had wept for her flaws, for her weaknesses and for her humanity. Before two witnesses who no doubt had their own stories, their own reasons to grieve.

But now it was done. There was no value in repeating this particular ritual. Exhaustion gave way to sleep, and when she awoke it was dawn. The squad had camped in the glade, and all were still asleep with the exception of Iron Bars, who was sitting before a small hearth, intent on stirring the flames to life once more.

A blanket had been thrown over her. The morning air was cool and damp. Seren sat up, drawing the wool about her shoulders, then rose and joined the Avowed at the smouldering fire.

He did not glance up. 'Acquitor. You are rested?'

'Yes, thank you. I don't know if I should apologize—'

'For what? I've been hearing horses, south of here.'

'That would be Brous. There's a garrison there, a small one.'

'Brous is a city?'

'A village, set in the midst of stone ruins. It was once a holy site for the Tarthenal, although they didn't build it.'

'How do you know?'

'The scale is all wrong for Tarthenal.'

'Too small?'

'No, too big.'

He looked up, squinted, then rose. 'Time to prepare a meal, I think.'

'You're a strange officer, Iron Bars,' Seren said, smiling. 'Cooking every breakfast for your soldiers.'

'I always wake up first,' he replied, dragging close a food pack.

757

She watched him working, wondering how often he had done this. How many glades like this one, how many mornings the first to rise among snoring soldiers. So far from anything resembling home. In a way, she understood him in that regard. There were two manifestations in the Empty Hold that spoke to that nature. Walker and Wanderer, the distinction between them a subtle one of motivation.

The Avowed, she realized, was an easy man to watch.

Coughing, the mage Corlo clawed free of his blanket and stumbled over. 'Where's that tea?'

'Almost ready,' Iron Bars replied.

'Got a headache,' Corlo said. 'Something's up.'

'Heard horses earlier,' the Avowed said. 'Screaming.'

'That's brewed enough for me.'

The Avowed dipped a ladle into the pot, filled the tin cup Corlo held out.

Seren saw the mage's hand trembling.

'May need the diadem today, sir.'

'Uh, rather not. Let's try to avoid that if we can.'

'Aye.'

'The diadem?' Seren asked. 'The one you used to open that path in Trate?'

Corlo shot her a sharp look, then nodded. 'But not for that. There's other rituals woven into it. Forty of 'em, in fact. The one we might have to use speeds us up, makes us faster than normal. But we go that way as rarely as we can, since it leaves us with the shakes – and those shakes get worse the more we use it.'

'Is that why you're trembling now?'

He glanced down at his hand after taking a sip of the herbal brew. 'No. That's something else.'

'Whatever's happening right now at Brous.'

'I guess.'

'Wake up the others, Corlo,' Iron Bars said. 'Acquitor, should we be avoiding Brous?'

'Hard to do. There's a ridge of hills to the east of here.

No tracks to speak of across them. We'd lose a day, maybe two, if we went that way.'

'All right.'

'I'll see to the horses,' Seren said after a moment.

The Avowed nodded. 'Then come back and eat.'

'Aye, sir.'

She was pleased at the answering smile, slight though it was.

They were among the ruins well before the village came into view. Most were half buried, rising in humps from the forest floor. Ancient roots gripped the stone, but had clearly failed in forcing cracks into the strange rock. Causeways that had once been raised now formed a crazed web of roads through the forest, littered in dead leaves but otherwise defying intrusion. Reaching the edge of the wood, they could see a scattering of domed buildings in the clearing ahead, and beyond it the palisade wall of Brous, over which woodsmoke hung in a sullen wreath of grey.

The ancient domed buildings possessed formal entrances, a projecting, arched corridor with doorways as wide as they were tall – three times the height of a man.

'Hood's breath,' Corlo hissed, 'these dwarf even K'Chain Che'Malle tombs.'

'Can't say I've ever seen those—' Seren began.

But the mage interrupted. 'Then I'm surprised, since there are plenty of remnants in these lands. They were something between lizards and dragons, walking on two legs. Lots of sharp teeth – Trate's markets had the occasional stall selling the old teeth and bones. K'Chain Che'Malle, lass, ruled this entire continent, once. Long before humans arrived. Anyway, their tombs look something like these ones, only smaller.'

'Oh. It's been assumed that those were Tarthenal. Nothing was ever found inside them.'

'The K'Chain Che'Malle never got the chance to use them, that's why. Most of them, anyway.'

They fell silent as they rode past the first structure, and saw, on the near side of the village, a hundred or more soldiers and workers gathered. It appeared they were excavating into a small, longish hill. A barrow. Capstones had been dragged from the top of the barrow by teams of horses, and crowds of diggers were attacking the sides.

'Don't want to be a part of that, sir,' Corlo said.

They reined in.

'What's in there?' Iron Bars asked.

'Nothing that has anything to do with these ruins, I don't think.'

'Picking up the dock-rat version of our language doesn't serve you well, you know,' Seren said.

'Fine,' Corlo rasped. 'What I meant was, the low barrows belong to something else. And the interment was messy. Lots of wards. There's a mage in that company, Avowed, who's been busy dismantling them.'

'All of them?'

'Almost. Left a couple in place. I think he means to bind whatever's in there.'

'We've been noticed,' Seren said.

A troop of mounted soldiers was riding towards them, an officer in the lead.

'Recognize him?' the Avowed asked her.

'Finadd Arlidas Tullid,' she replied. 'He commands the Brous garrison.'

Iron Bars glanced at her. 'And?'

'He's not a nice man.'

The Finadd's troop comprised sixteen riders. They reined in, and Arlidas nodded at Seren. 'Acquitor. Thought I recognized you. You come from where?'

'Trate.'

'That's a long ride. I take it you left before it fell.'

She did not contradict him.

The Finadd scanned the Crimson Guardsmen, and apparently did not like what he saw. 'Your arrival is well timed,' he said. 'We're recruiting.'

'They have already been recruited,' Seren said, 'as my escort. I am riding to Letheras, for an audience with the king.'

Arlidas scowled. 'No point in that, Acquitor. The man just sits there, cowering on his throne. And the Ceda's lost his mind. That is why I decided to declare our independence. And we intend to defend ourselves against these damned grey-skins.'

Seren's laugh was sudden, instantly regretted. 'Independence, Finadd? The village of Brous? With you in charge? As what, its emperor?'

'You have entered our territory, Acquitor, meaning you and your escort are now subject to me. I am pleased to see you all armed, since I have few spare weapons.'

'You are not recruiting us,' Iron Bars said. 'And I suggest you do not make an issue of it, Finadd, or in a short while you will find yourself with a much smaller army.'

Arlidas sneered. 'The six of you and an Acquitor—'

'Finadd.' A rider nudged his horse from the troop to halt alongside Arlidas. Round, hairy, small-eyed and filthy from crawling tunnels of dirt. 'That one's a mage.' He pointed at Corlo.

'So are you, you damned Nerek halfling,' the Finadd snapped.

'Tell him,' Corlo said to the other mage. 'Your name's Urger, isn't it? Tell your Finadd, Urger.'

The half-Nerek licked his lips. 'He'll kill us all, sir. Every one of us. He won't even break a sweat. And he'll start with you, Finadd. He'll pluck your brain out and drop it in a cauldron of boiling oil.'

Corlo said, 'You'd best return to that barrow, Urger. Your demon's trying to get out, and it just might succeed. You'll lose your chance to bind it.'

The mage twisted round in his saddle. 'Errant take me, he's right! Finadd, I must go! No waiting!' With that he wheeled his horse and drove heels into its flanks.

Arlidas glared at Seren, Iron Bars and Corlo in turn,

then he snarled wordlessly and gestured to his soldiers. 'Back to the barrow. Back, damn you!'

They rode off.

Seren looked over at Corlo. 'You made yourself pretty scary, didn't you?'

The mage smiled.

'Let's get going,' the Avowed said, 'before they gather their wits.'

'I'd like to learn how you do that, Corlo.'

His smile broadened. 'You would, would you?'

'There is always something ominous in dust rising from a distant road, do you not think?'

Trull Sengar squinted eastward until he spied the telltale smear. 'Nothing to worry about, Lilac,' he said. 'It's a column from my father's army, I suspect. A portion of it occupied the Manse not long ago.'

'There was fighting there,' the demon said, then sighed. 'Two of my kin fell.'

'I am sorry for that,' Trull said.

They were camped on the outskirts of Thetil, preparing for the fast, extended march down to First Reach, where their army would join up with the emperor's before striking southeast to Letheras. Tomad's army would march down Mappers' Road to approach the capital city from the north. The Letherii forces were fleeing before them along every approach. Even so, one more battle lay ahead, probably outside the walls of Letheras.

Trull glanced over at his company. A dozen or so warriors were gathered round Sergeant Canarth, who was in the midst of a gesture-filled tirade of some sort. Trull's captain, Ahlrada Ahn, stood nearby, apart yet listening.

Since Trull had acquired his demon bodyguard, the other warriors had kept their distance, the squad leaders reluctant to stand still even when Trull approached with orders. There was something wrong, clearly, with singling out a demon, with making it obvious that the creature was intelligent, an individual. Understandable, given the usual treatment of the Kenyll'rah by their Tiste Edur masters. But, he well knew, there was more to it than that.

During their march down from High Fort, Trull Sengar had found himself mostly shunned by his warrior kin and by the women. No official sanction had yet been pronounced, but silent judgement had already occurred, and it was these unspoken forms of punishment that maintained the necessary cohesion of the Edur tribes – rejection of aberrant behaviour must be seen, the punishment one of public participation, the lesson clear to all who might harbour similar dangerous impulses. Trull understood this well enough, and did not rail against it.

Without the demon at his side, it would have been far more painful, far more lonely, than it was. Yet even with Lilac, there was a truth that stung. The demon was not free, and had it been so it would not now be here, at his side. Thus, the premise of companionship was flawed, and Trull could not delude himself into believing otherwise.

Fear had not spoken to him once since High Fort. Orders were conveyed through B'nagga, who was indifferent to, or unaware of, the tensions swirling about Trull.

Nearby sat their two charges, the queen and her son, for whom Trull and his company had provided escort down from High Fort. They had been carried by ox-drawn wagon, the prince's minor wounds tended to by a Letherii slave, the queen provided with a female slave of her own to cook meals and do other chores as required. An indulgence permitting the king's wife to resume her haughty demeanour. Even so, the two prisoners had said little since their capture.

Ahlrada Ahn made his way over.

Trull spoke first. 'Captain. What has Sergeant Canarth so animated?'

The dark-skinned warrior frowned. 'You, Trull Sengar.'

'Ah, and you've come to warn me of insurrection?'

The suggestion clearly offended him. 'I am not your ally,'

he said. 'Not in this matter. Canarth intends to approach Fear and request a new commander.'

'Well, that would be a relief,' Trull said. 'What is it you want, then?'

'I want you to excuse yourself before Canarth delivers his request.'

Trull looked away. Southward, the sprawl of farms on the other side of Thetil. No livestock, no workers in the fields. The rains had been kind, and all was a luscious, deep green. 'A Bluerose slave, wasn't she? Your mother. Which was why you were always apart from the rest of us.'

'I am ashamed of nothing, Trull Sengar. If you are seeking to wound me—'

He met Ahlrada's hard gaze. 'No, the very opposite. I know you do not like me. Indeed, you never have – long before I struck . . . a woman. Oddly enough, I have always admired you. Your strength, your determination to rise above your birth—'

'Rise above?' Ahlrada's grin was cold. 'I suffered under no such compulsion, Trull Sengar. Before she died, my mother told me many secrets. The Bluerose are the survivors, from a war in which it was supposed there were no survivors. It was believed the Edur had killed them all, you see. It was necessary to believe that.'

'You have lost me, Ahlrada Ahn,' Trull said. 'What war are you speaking of?'

'I am speaking of the Betrayal. When the Edur and the Andii fought as allies against the K'Chain Che'Malle. The Betrayal, which was not as the Edur histories would have it. The Andii were the ones betrayed, not the Edur. Scabandari Bloodeye stabbed Silchas Ruin. In the back. All that you learned as a child and hold true to this day, Trull Sengar, was a lie.' His smile grew colder. 'And now you will accuse me of being the liar.'

'The Bluerose are Tiste Andii?'

'The blood is thinned, but it remains.'

Trull looked away once more. After a time, he slowly

764

nodded to himself. 'I see no reason, Ahlrada Ahn, to call you a liar. Indeed, your version makes more sense. After all, had we been the ones betrayed, then we should have been as the Andii today – mere remnants of a broken people—'

'Not as broken as you think,' Ahlrada said.

'You do not think Bluerose will capitulate? Is it not already a protectorate of the Letherii? A nation of subjugated people?'

'They have been waiting for this, Trull Sengar. After all, the truth cannot be hidden – once the Edur occupy Bluerose, it will be discovered that its ruling class possess Andii blood.'

'Probably.'

They were silent for a time, then Ahlrada Ahn said, 'I hold no particular hatred for you, Trull Sengar. My hatred is for all the Tiste Edur.'

'I understand.'

'Do you? Look upon the shadow wraiths. The ghosts who have been bound to the Edur, who are made to fight this war. To find oblivion beneath swords of Letherii steel, the fatal iron against which they have no defence. They are Tiste Andii, the shades of those who fell in that betrayal, long ago.'

The demon, Lilac, spoke. 'It is true, Trull Sengar. The wraiths are compelled, as much as we Kenyll'rah. They are not your ancestors.'

'To all of this,' Trull said, 'I can do nothing.'

Without another word, he strode away. Through the camp, deftly avoided by all, his path appearing before him devoid of any obstruction, as if by the hand of sorcery. Trull was not immune to regret. He would have liked to have taken back that moment when he'd lost control, when his outrage had broken through. The woman had been right, he supposed. The wounded Edur must be healed first and foremost. There was no time for demons. He should not have struck her.

No-one cared for his reasons. The act was inexcusable, as simple as that.

He approached the command tent.

And saw that the riders they'd seen earlier on the road had arrived. Among them, Uruth, his mother.

She was standing beside her horse.

Fear emerged from the tent and strode to her.

Uruth was speaking as Trull arrived. '. . . I can barely stand. Should we run low on food on our march south, allow me to be the first to suggest we slaughter the horses.' She noted Trull and faced him. 'You have made terrible mistakes, my son. None the less, this over-reaction on the part of the women in this camp will not be tolerated. It is for me to sanction you, not them.' She returned her attention to Fear. 'Are the warriors naught but children? Grubby hands on their mother's skirts? Did your brother Trull reveal cowardice on the field of battle?'

'No,' Fear replied, 'there was no question of his courage—'

'For you and your warriors, Fear, nothing else obtains. I would have thought better of you, my eldest son. Your brother sought the healing of a fallen comrade—'

'A demon—'

'And did not demons fight at High Fort? Did not many of them give their lives to win victory? Healers are to accede to the wishes of the warriors after a battle. They are not to make judgements on who is worthy of healing. Had I been here, I myself might well have struck her for her impudence. Shall every Edur woman now assume the flaws of our Empress Mayen? Not if I have a say in the matter. Now, Fear, you will correct your warriors' attitudes. You will remind them of Trull's deeds during the journey to retrieve the emperor's sword. You will tell them to recall his delivery of the news of the Letherii harvest of the tusked seals. Most importantly, Fear, you will not turn away from your brother. Do you challenge my words?'

It seemed a vast weight lifted from Fear, as he straightened with a wry smile. 'I would not dare,' he said.

Trull hesitated, then said, 'Mother, Fear's anger with me

has been over my disagreement with the necessity of this war. I have been careless in voicing my objections—'

'A crisis of loyalty to the emperor is a dangerous thing,' Uruth said. 'Fear was right to be angry, nor am I pleased by your words. Only the emperor has the power to halt this conquest, and he will not do that. Neither Fear nor I, nor anyone else, Trull, are capable of responding to your doubts. Do you not see that? Only Rhulad, and he is not here.'

'I understand,' Trull said. He looked to Fear. 'Brother, I apologize. I shall save my words for Rhulad—'

'He is not interested in hearing them,' Fear said.

'None the less.'

They studied each other.

Uruth sighed. 'Enough of this. Trull, is that the demon in question?'

Trull swung round to where Lilac stood, five paces back. 'Yes.'

His mother approached the demon. 'Kenyll'rah, do your kin still rule over you in your home realm?'

A deferential nod. 'The tyrants remain, mistress, for the war continues.'

'Yet you were not a soldier.'

Lilac shrugged. 'Even the Kenryll'ah must eat, mistress.'

'We found few soldiers among those we summoned,' Uruth said.

'We are losing the war. Four of the Kenryll'ah towers have fallen. Korvalahrai ships were seen far up the Chirahd River.'

'I must leave to join the emperor tomorrow morning,' Uruth said. 'Which leaves us this night.'

'For what?' Trull asked.

'A conversation with a Kenryll'ah tyrant,' she replied, her regard still on the demon. 'Perhaps the time has come for a formal alliance.'

Lilac spoke. 'They are not pleased with your thefts, Tiste Edur.'

Uruth turned away. 'You are a peasant, demon. All I need from you is the path into your realm. Keep your opinions to yourself.'

Trull watched his mother stride into the command tent. He glanced at Fear and saw his brother staring at him.

'Did you come here to speak to me about something?'

Trull hesitated, then said, 'My warriors are about to come to you seeking a new commander. I thought to anticipate them by resigning.'

Fear smiled. '"Resigning." I suppose we are indeed an army now. In the Letherii fashion. Sergeants, lieutenants, captains.'

'And commanders.'

'There will be no resignations, Trull.'

'Very well. Expect Canarth to request an audience soon.'

'And he shall have one, although he will not leave pleased.' Fear stepped close. 'We will soon be joining our brothers. I know you will have words you will want to say to Rhulad. Be careful, Trull. Nothing is at it once was. Our people have changed.'

'I can see that, Fear.'

'Perhaps, but you do not understand it.'

'Do you?' Trull challenged.

Fear shrugged, made no reply. A moment later, he walked back to his command tent.

'Your mother,' Lilac said, 'would play a dangerous game.'

'This is the emperor's game, Lilac,' Trull said. He faced the demon. 'Your people are at war in your home realm?'

'I am a caster of nets.'

'Yet, should the need arise, your tyrant masters could call you into military service.'

'The Kenryll'ah have ruled a long time, Trull Sengar. And have grown weak with complacency. They cannot see their own impending demise. It is always the way of things, such blindness. No matter how long and perfect the succession of fallen empires and civilizations so clearly writ into the past, the belief remains that one's own shall live

768

for ever, and is not subject to the indomitable rules of dissolution that bind all of nature.' The small, calm eyes of the demon looked down steadily upon Trull. 'I am a caster of nets. Tyrants and emperors rise and fall. Civilizations burgeon then die, but there are always casters of nets. And tillers of the soil, and herders in the pastures. We are where civilization begins, and when it ends, we are there to begin it again.'

A curious speech, Trull reflected. The wisdom of peasants was rarely articulated in such clear fashion. Even so, claims to truth were innumerable. 'Unless, Lilac, all the casters and tillers and herders are dead.'

'I spoke not of ourselves, Trull, but of our tasks. Kenyll'rah, Edur, Letherii, the selves are not eternal. Only the tasks.'

'Unless everything is dead.'

'Life will return, eventually. It always does. If the water is foul, it will find new water.'

'My mother said she would make use of you, to fashion a path,' Trull said. 'How will this be done?'

'I will be sacrificed. My blood shall be the path.'

'I did not have you healed only to have you sacrificed, Lilac.'

'There is nothing you can do, Trull Sengar.'

'There must be. Is there no way of setting you free?'

The demon was silent for a moment, then it said, 'Your blood can create a new binding. Myself to you, in exclusion of all else. Then you could command me.'

'To do what? Return to your realm?'

'Yes.'

'And could you then be summoned again?'

'Only by you, Trull Sengar.'

'You would have me as your master, Lilac?'

'The alternative is death.'

'Which you said earlier you'd prefer to slavery.'

'Between the choices of fighting this war or dying, yes.'

'But returning home . . .'

'That is preferable to all else, Trull Sengar.'

The Tiste Edur drew out his knife. 'What must I do?'

Trull entered the command tent a short while later. He found Fear and Uruth in the centre chamber. 'Mother.'

She turned, frowned. 'What have you done?'

'I sent my demon away. You will have to find another.'

Her gaze dropped to his left hand, narrowed on the broad, still dripping cut across the palm. 'I see. Tell me, son, will your defiance never end?'

'I paid a high price to save that demon's life.'

'What of it?'

'You intended to use him to create your path into his realm—'

'And?'

'To do that, you would have to sacrifice it—'

'The demon told you that? It lied, Trull. In fact, killing it would have severed its link to its own world. It deceived you, son. But you are bound now, the two of you. You can summon it back, and deliver your punishment.'

Trull cocked his head, then smiled. 'You know, Mother, I think I would have done the same, were I in its place. No, I have sent it home, and there it shall stay.'

'Where it may well find itself fighting in another war.'

'Not for me to decide,' Trull said, shrugging.

'You are difficult to understand,' Uruth said, 'and the effort wearies me.'

'I am sorry,' Trull said. 'This alliance you will attempt with the demon tyrants – what is the emperor seeking from it? What does Rhulad plan to offer in return?'

'Are you truly interested, son?'

'I am.'

Uruth shot Fear a glance, then sighed. 'The Korvalahrai are seafarers. They are reaching into the Kenryll'ah lands via a vast river, and even now approach the heart in a fleet carrying all the Korvalahrai. Rhulad's power is such that he can divert that river, for a time. The invading fleet will be destroyed in the conflagration. Achieving such a thing would in turn serve Edur needs, as well. In return, we are given more demons for our war, perhaps a minor Kenryll'ah or two, who are far better versed in the arts of battle than their subject Kenyll'rah.' She turned to Fear. 'I will need another demon.'

'Very well.'

'And then, a place of solitude.'

Fear nodded. 'Trull, return to your company.'

As he was walking back to where his warriors were camped, Trull found himself smiling. Lilac's pleasure, moments before it vanished, had been childlike. Yet the demon's mind was not simple. It must have known there was a risk that, upon discovering the deception, Trull would summon it back in a fit of rage and inflict terrible punishment. For some reason, Lilac had concluded that such an event was unlikely.

My weakness, so plain and obvious even a demon could see it.

Perhaps he was not a warrior after all. Not a follower of commands, capable of shutting out all unnecessary thoughts in service to the cause. Not a leader, either, to stride ahead, certainty a blinding fire drawing all with him.

Worse yet, he was suspicious of Rhulad's transformation. Fear, in his youth, had displayed none of Rhulad's strutting arrogance, his posing and posturing – all of which might well suit a leader of warriors, but not in the manner that Fear led warriors. Rhulad had been bluster, whilst Fear was quiet confidence, and Trull was not sure if that essential character trait had changed in Rhulad.

I do not belong.

The realization shocked him, slowed his steps. He looked around, feeling suddenly lost. Here, in the midst of his own people.

The Tiste Edur have changed. But I haven't.

* * *

South, across the region known as the Swath, a deforested scrubland which had once been part of Outcry Wood, past the burnt-out town of Siege Place, and onto the slowly climbing Lookout Track towards the hills of Lookout Climb. Three days crossing the old hills – a range thoroughly denuded by wild goats – onto Moss Road. Marching northeast along the banks of the Moss River to the ford town of Ribs.

Retreating Letherii forces had stripped the countryside ahead of the emperor and his army. The military food and materiel caches that Hull Beddict knew of were all emptied. If not for the shadow wraiths, supplying the Tiste Edur army would have been impossible – the invasion would have stalled. Unacceptable, Rhulad had decided. The enemy was reeling. It was necessary to keep it so.

Udinaas remembered eating smoked eel from Moss River, one time when the trader ship had docked in Dresh. Delicious, once one got used to the furry skin, which was to be chewed but not swallowed. He had since heard, from another slave, that the eels had been transplanted into Dresh Lake, producing a strain that was both bigger and nastier. It had turned out that those eels captured in Moss River were juveniles, and few ever reached adulthood since there was a razor-jawed species of predatory fish resident in the river. No such fish in Dresh Lake. Adolescent swimmers from Dresh started disappearing before anyone realized the adult eels were responsible. Razor-jawed fish were netted from the river and tossed into the lake, but their behaviour changed, turning them into frenzy feeders. Adult swimmers from Dresh started vanishing. The slave who had been relating all this then laughed and finished with, 'So they poisoned the whole lake, killed everything. And now no-one can swim in it!'

From this, Udinaas surmised, various lessons could be drawn, should one be inclined to draw lessons from multiple acts of stupidity.

They had camped on the road, a day's march west of

Ribs. The emperor was suffering from some kind of fever. Healers were tending to him, and the last Udinaas had heard, Rhulad was sleeping. It was late afternoon, and the sun's light was painting the river's surface red and gold.

Udinaas walked along the stony strand, flinging rocks out onto the water every now and then, shattering the lurid hues. At the moment, he was not feeling anything like a slave, or an Indebted. He marched in the shadow of the emperor, for all to see, for all to wonder at.

He heard boots crunching on pebbles and turned to see Hull Beddict scrambling down onto the strand. A big man, on whom every oversized muscle seemed to brood, somehow. There was fever in his eyes as well, but unlike Rhulad this heat had nothing to do with illness. 'Udinaas.'

The slave watched the man approach, fighting his instinctive urge towards deference. The time for that was past, after all. He just wasn't sure what belonged in its stead.

'I have been looking for you.'

'Why?'

'The emperor's condition . . .'

Udinaas shrugged. 'A marsh fever, nothing more—'

'I was not speaking of that, slave.'

'I am not your slave, Hull Beddict.'

'I am sorry. You are right.'

Udinaas collected another stone. He wiped the grit from its underside before throwing it out over the water. They watched it splash, then Udinaas said, 'I understand your need to distinguish yourself from the other Letherii marching with this army. Even so, we are all bound to servitude, and the varying shades of that are not as relevant as they once were.'

'Perhaps you have a point, Udinaas, but I don't quite understand what you're getting at.'

He brushed the grit from his hands. 'Who better to teach the newly conquered Letherii than the Edur's original Letherii slaves?'

'You anticipate a new status for you and your fellow slaves, then?'

'Maybe. How are the Tiste Edur to rule? Much remains to be answered, Hull Beddict. I gather you intend to involve yourself in that particular reshaping, if you can.'

The man's smile was sour. 'It seems I am to have little or no role in much of anything, Udinaas.'

'Then the Errant looks kindly upon you,' Udinaas said.

'I am not surprised you might see it that way.'

'It is a waste of time, Hull Beddict, to fashion intricate plans for restitution. What you did before, all you did before – the mistakes, the bad decisions – they are dead, for everyone but you. None of it has purchased a future claim to glory, none of it has *earned* you anything.'

'Has not the emperor heeded my advice?'

'In this war? When it suited him. But I trust you are not expecting any consideration in return.' Udinaas turned, met Hull's eyes. 'Ah, I think you are.'

'Reciprocity, Udinaas. Surely the Tiste Edur understand that, since it is so essential within their own culture.'

'There is no reciprocity when you display expectation, Hull Beddict. *Poof!* It vanishes. And that was just my point earlier: there is much that we can teach the future conquered Letherii.'

'I am blood-bound to Binadas,' Hull said, 'yet you accuse me of insensitivity to the mores of the Tiste Edur.' His expression was wry. 'I am not often chastised in such things. You remind me of Seren Pedac.'

'The Acquitor who escorted you? I saw her, in Trate.'

Hull stepped close, suddenly intent. 'During the battle?'

Udinaas nodded. 'She was in bad shape, but alive. She'd found a worthy escort of her own – I have no doubt she still lives.'

'An escort of her own? Who?'

'I'm not sure. Foreigners. One of them killed Rhulad and his chosen brothers.' Udinaas collected another stone. 'Look at that, Hull Beddict, a river of gold. Flowing into the sunset.' He flung the stone, broke the mirrored perfection. Momentarily.

'You witnessed that killing.'

'I did. Whoever that foreigner was, he was terrifying.'

'More terrifying than Rhulad's return?'

Udinaas said nothing for a time, then he stepped away, down to the water's edge. He stared into the shallows, saw the muddy bottom swarming with newborn eels. 'Do you know what is coming, Hull Beddict?'

'No. Do you?'

'Dresh Lake. That's what's coming.'

'I don't understand.'

'Doesn't matter. Don't mind me, Hull Beddict. Well, I'd best return. The emperor is awake.'

Hull followed him up from the strand. 'Things like that,' he said. 'He's awake. How do you know?'

'A stirring in the shadows,' Udinaas said. 'Rhulad sets the world to a tremble. Well,' he amended, 'a small part of it. But it's growing. In any case, his fever has broken. He is weak, but alert.'

'Tell me,' Hull said as they walked into the vast camp, 'about Feather Witch.'

Udinaas grimaced. 'Why?'

'She is no longer Mayen's slave. She now serves the Edur healers. Was that your work?'

'The emperor's command, Hull Beddict.'

'You claim no influence on him? Few would believe that now.'

'Reciprocity.'

'And in return, you give Rhulad what?'

Friendship. 'I do not advise him, Hull Beddict. I do not seek to influence him. I cannot answer your question.' *Rather, I won't.*

'She affects to hold only hatred for you, Udinaas. But I am not convinced.'

'Oh, I am.'

'I think, perhaps, she has given her heart to you. Yet

would fight it, for all the pointless prohibitions and prejudices of our people. What is the extent of your debt, Udinaas?'

'My debt? My father's debt. Seven hundred and twenty-two docks, from the day I was taken as a slave.'

Hull reached out and stopped him. 'That's it?'

'A Beddict might well say that. For most Letherii, that is insurmountable. Especially given the interest.' Udinaas resumed walking.

Hull came up alongside him. 'Who holds it?'

'A minor lender in Letheras. Why are you asking?'

'The lender's name?'

'Huldo.'

'Huldo.' After a moment, Hull snorted.

'You find that amusing?'

'I do. Udinaas, my brother Tehol *owns* Huldo.'

'Maybe once. As I understand it, Tehol owns nothing these days.'

'Let me tell you a story about my brother. He was, I guess, around ten years old, when a family debt was purchased by a particularly unscrupulous lender. The plan was to force us to relinquish a certain holding, and so the debt was called. We couldn't pay, not all at once, and of course the lender knew it. Now, it was at the time assumed by all that Tehol was at school every day during this crisis, and indeed, that, young as he was, he had no idea of the trouble our parents were in. Only much later did certain facts come to light. The fact that Tehol had finessed a debt of his own, over his tutor. Nothing large, but he was able to coerce the tutor into saying nothing about his absences, whilst he operated a business venture of his own down at a flow-out on the river. Two employees, both Nerek, sifting sewage. This particular out-flow issued from an estate district – extraordinary what treasures could be recovered. Jewellery, mostly. Rings, earrings, pearls. In any case, it seemed there was a windfall, a necklace, and the result was Tehol and his two Nerek employees found themselves suddenly flush—'

'By selling the necklace?'

'Oh no, from the reward. Their business was returning lost items. Shortly thereafter, the lender pressuring our family received payment in full on our debt, and was then subsequently financially gutted when a host of holdings on *him* were called.'

Udinaas grunted. 'Grateful patrons, indeed.'

'Probably. We never found out. And Tehol never explained a damned thing. It took me over a year to piece some of it together. My point is, Udinaas, Tehol's genius is of the diabolical kind. Destitute? Not a chance. Retired from business dealings? Impossible. I am now quite skilled at tracking my brother, you see. Huldo's not the only lender Tehol owns.'

'So,' Udinaas said as they approached the emperor's tent, 'I am Indebted to the Beddicts.'

'Not any more,' Hull said. 'I am clearing it. Right now. I am sure Tehol will forgive me, assuming I ever get a chance to corner him.'

Udinaas looked over at the man. Then he nodded. 'I see. Reciprocity.'

'I am without expectation, Udinaas.'

'Good. I knew you were a fast learner.'

Hull Beddict halted outside the entrance. 'I enjoyed speaking to you,' he said.

Udinaas hesitated, then smiled.

Seated on his throne, sweat streaming down between and over the gold coins on his face, neck and chest, some horrible insight burning in his eyes, the emperor trembled as if rabid. 'Udinaas,' he croaked. 'As you can see, we are well.'

'These southlands, Emperor, hold strange diseases—'

'We were not sick. We were . . . travelling.'

They were alone in the chamber. Hannan Mosag was overseeing the warriors, where some old feuds between tribes were threatening to breach the unity. Mayen was

777

cloistered among the women, for it was said that Uruth Sengar was coming, summoned via the K'risnan. The air in the tent smelled of sour sweat.

'A long and difficult journey, then,' Udinaas said. 'Do you wish some wine? Food?'

'No. Not yet. We have ... done something. A terrible thing. To achieve an alliance. When we strike the Letherii army outside Letheras, you shall see what has been won this day. We are ... pleased. Yes, pleased.'

'Yet frightened. By your own power.'

The eyes flickered, fixed on Udinaas. 'We can hide little from you, it seems. Yes, frightened. We ... I ... have drowned an entire world. A fragment of Kurald Emurlahn, upon which our ships will soon travel. Seeking our lost kin. And ... champions.' He clawed at his face. '*I drowned a world.*'

The subject needed deflection, Udinaas decided. 'Champions? I do not understand, Emperor.'

A moment to recover, then a nod. 'Worthy foes, Udinaas. Skilled fighters capable of killing us. They are needed.'

'For your power to grow yet stronger.'

'Yes. Stronger. It is necessary. So many things are necessary, now ...'

Udinaas risked a glance away as he said, 'It is right to fear, then, Emperor.'

'It is? Explain.'

'Fear bespeaks of wisdom. Recognition of responsibility.'

'Wisdom. Yes, it must be so, mustn't it? We had not considered that before. We fear, because we are becoming wise.'

Oh, you poor lad. How can I do this? 'How will you incite these ... champions?'

Rhulad shivered, then raised the sword in his right hand. 'Who among them will turn away from such a challenge? Those who do are not worth fighting. Or, if they are yet reluctant, they will be compelled. This world is vast,

778

Udinaas, far vaster than you might think. There are other lands, other empires. There are formidable peoples, races. We will search far. We will find those useful to us. And then, one day, we will conquer. Every kingdom. Every continent.'

'You will need to deceive those champions, Emperor. Into believing that killing you means their victory. You will have to make it seem that it is your ego that forces such challenges. They must know nothing of the sword's power, of its demands upon you.'

'Yes, you speak true, Udinaas. Together, we will shape the future. You will want for nothing.'

'Emperor, I want for nothing now. I need no promises. Please, I did not mean to offend by that. What I meant was, there is no *need* for promises.'

Sudden pain in Rhulad's dark eyes, a grief and sorrow that rent at Udinaas, somewhere deep inside. It was all he could do to continue meeting the emperor's gaze.

'We would have some wine, now, Udinaas.' A tone of profound sorrow. 'Two goblets, for you and me. We shall drink, and think of nothing. We shall talk, perhaps, of inconsequential matters.'

Udinaas strode to the table where sat a jug of Letherii wine. 'I visited Dresh, once,' he said as he poured out two cups full. 'And ate smoked Moss River eel. Would you like me to tell about Moss River eels, Emperor?' He carried the two goblets over to the Edur seated on the throne.

'Is it inconsequential?'

Udinaas hesitated, then nodded. 'It is.'

'Then, yes, Udinaas. We would.'

Seren Pedac and the Crimson Guardsmen rode at a canter. Half a league ahead was the town of Dissent. It had once been walled, but local builders had dismantled most of the stonework long ago. The town had since grown outward in a mostly chaotic manner, swallowing commons and nearby farms. But now Dissent was barely visible, devoured in turn by at least three encamped armies.

'Crimson Rampant Brigade,' Seren said, scanning the distant banners. 'Snakebelt Battalion, and the Riven Brigade.'

'Can we ride straight through?' Iron Bars asked.

She glanced across at him, then nodded. 'I think so. My apologies. I'm a little shocked, that's all. If this is all that's left of the frontier armies . . .'

'The ground ahead is not ideal for a battle,' the Avowed judged. 'I'd be surprised if the king intended to await the Edur here. Can you think of anywhere else close by that might be better suited?'

'Brans Keep, in the hills a few leagues northeast of Dissent.'

'And Dissent is the nearest major town?'

'Apart from Letheras itself,' Seren said.

'Then this is temporary encampment. When the Tiste Edur draw closer, those three armies will march to Brans Keep. Assuming the warlord commanding them has any wits at all. In any case, Acquitor, other Letherii forces might already be waiting there, at Brans Keep. It's a question of logistics, keeping these ones here.'

'I hope you are right. Then again, I wonder if it will make any difference.'

'We're far from the sea, Seren,' Iron Bars said. 'That demon the Edur have chained can't reach here, and that evens things some.'

A worthy try, Iron Bars. 'Another day to Outkeep, then we should reach Letheras the following day, well before dusk.'

'Could we hasten that, Acquitor? These soldiers camped ahead, might they be prepared to exchange horses?'

'If I insist, yes.'

'Based on your desire to speak to the king.'

'Yes.'

'And will you? Speak to the king, that is.'

'No.'

He said nothing for a time, whilst she waited. Then,

'And in Letheras, what will you do once you've arrived?'

'I expect I will have some dusting to do.'

'Sorry?'

'My house is closed up. I've not had a chance to send a message to my staff – all two of them.'

'That doesn't sound very secure – no-one to guard your possessions.'

She smiled. 'I have nothing of value, Iron Bars. Thieves are welcome to it. Well, I'd prefer if they left me my furniture – my neighbours are diligent enough, I suppose, to prevent anything like that.'

The Avowed stared ahead for a moment. 'We must needs depart your company, then, Acquitor. To make contact with our new employer. Presumably, we'll be shipping out soon after.'

Before the city's occupied and sealed up. 'I imagine so.'

'There might be room aboard . . .'

'I am Letherii, Iron Bars.' She shook her head. 'I am done with travelling for a time, I think.'

'Understandable. Anyway, the offer's open.'

'Thank you.' *So here I run again.*

Corlo, riding behind them, called out, 'Easy on that, lass. Mockra's dangerous when you don't control it.'

The Avowed turned his head, studied her.

She shrugged.

CHAPTER TWENTY-TWO

An old man emerged from the ditch, a creature
Of mud and wild autumn winds capering
Like a hare across a bouldered field, across
And through the stillness of time unhinged
That sprawls patient and unexpectant in the
Place where battle lies spent, unmoving and
Never again moving bodies strewn and
Death-twisted like lost languages tracking
Contorted glyphs on a barrow door, and he
Read well the aftermath, the disarticulated script
Rent and dissolute the pillars of self toppled
Like termite towers all spilled out round his
Dancing feet, and he shouted in gleeful
Revelation the truth he'd found, in these
Red-fleshed pronouncements – 'There is peace!'
He shrieked. 'There is peace!' and it was
No difficult thing, where I sat in the saddle
Above salt-rimed horseflesh to lift my crossbow
Aim and loose the quarrel, skewering the madman
To his proclamation. 'Now,' said I, in the
Silence that followed, 'Now, there is peace.'

The Lay of Skinner
Fisher kel Tath

On facing hills, the smouldering ruins of first reach in the low, flat floodplain between, the two armies of the Tiste Edur came within sight of one another. Wraiths swarmed through the ashes, weapons were lifted high, triumphant cries piercing the still morning air.

The convergence was, of course, incomplete. The third, easternmost force, led by Tomad Sengar and Binadas, was still striking south down Mappers' Road towards White Point. It would join with these two armies, Trull knew, somewhere close to Brans Keep, and there the fate of Lether, and indeed of the Edur empire, would be decided in a single battle.

He stood leaning on his spear, feeling no inclination to join his voice to the fierce tumult buffeting him from all sides. Just north of the ruins in the floodplain below, a hundred or more starlings cavorted and wheeled, their own cries drowned out, a detail that somehow transformed their dance into a fevered, nightmarish display.

In the distant line of warriors opposite, a space was clearing, a single dominant standard bobbing forward, beneath it a figure flashing gold, holding high a sword.

The warcries redoubled.

Trull flinched at the deafening sound. He pulled his gaze away from Rhulad on that far hilltop and saw Fear approaching.

'Trull! B'nagga, you and I – horses await us – we ride now to our emperor!'

He nodded, uneasy with the ferocity evident in Fear's eyes. 'Lead on, brother.'

The ride across to Rhulad's army was a strange experience. Trull did not like horses that much, and liked riding them even less. He was jolted again and again, jarring the scene on all sides. They rode across burnt ground, heaps of the remains of butchered livestock lining the tracks approaching the town. And the roaring of the warriors was a wave at their backs, pushing them onwards.

Then, halfway across, the sensation shifted, spun entirely

round, as the voices of the warriors in the emperor's army engulfed them. Their horses balked, and it was a struggle to make them resume the approach.

As they climbed the slope, Trull could see his brother Rhulad more clearly. He was barely recognizable, hulking now beneath the weight of the coins. His forehead was exposed, revealing skin the colour of dirty snow, the contrast darkening the pits of his eyes. His teeth were bared, but it seemed as much a grimace of pain as anything else. Hannan Mosag stood on the emperor's left, the slave Udinaas on the right. Hull Beddict was positioned three paces behind the Warlock King. Mayen and Uruth were nowhere to be seen.

Arriving, they reined in and dismounted. Slaves appeared to lead the horses away.

Fear strode forward to kneel before the emperor. Across the valley, another surge of sound.

'My brother,' Rhulad said in his rasping, broken voice. 'Rise before us.' The emperor stepped close and settled a coin-backed hand on Fear's shoulder. 'There is much I must say to you, but later.'

'As you command, Emperor.'

Rhulad's haunted eyes shifted. 'Trull.'

He knelt and studied the ground before him. 'Emperor.'

'Rise. We have words for you as well.'

No doubt. 'Mother arrived safely?'

A flash of irritation. 'She did.' It seemed he would say something more to Trull, but then he changed his mind and faced B'nagga. 'The Jheck are well, B'nagga?'

A fierce grin. 'They are, Emperor.'

'We are pleased. Hannan Mosag would speak to you regarding the impending lie of battle. A tent has been prepared for such matters. Hull Beddict has drawn us detailed maps.'

B'nagga bowed, then walked to the Warlock King. The two departed, trailed by Hull Beddict.

'Our brothers,' Rhulad said, the sword shaking in his left hand. 'Come, we will take food and drink in our own tent. Udinaas, precede us.'

The slave strode into the mass of warriors. The Edur melted back before the nondescript Letherii, and into his wake walked the emperor, Fear and Trull.

They reached the command tent a short while later, after traversing an avenue walled in flesh, waving weapons and frenzied warcries. Wraiths stood guard to either side of the entrance. As soon as the slave and the three brothers entered, Rhulad spun round and halted Trull with one hand. 'How far do you intend to push me, Trull?'

He looked down at the hand pressed against his chest. 'It seems you are the one doing the pushing, Rhulad.'

A moment of taut silence, then his brother barked a laugh and stepped back. 'Words from our past, yes? As we once were, before . . .' a wave of the sword, 'all this.' His ravaged gaze fixed on Trull for a moment. 'We have missed you.' He smiled at Fear. 'Missed you both. Udinaas, find us some wine!'

'A Letherii drink,' Fear said.

'I have acquired a taste for it, brother.'

Trull and Fear followed Rhulad into the inner chamber, where the slave was already pouring three cups of dark wine into Letherii-made goblets of silver and gold. Trull felt unbalanced, the sudden breach in Rhulad's façade shocking him, hurting him somewhere inside for reasons he could not immediately fathom.

Eschewing the throne dominating the centre of the room, the emperor settled down in a leather-slung tripod chair near the food-laden table along one wall. Two identical chairs flanked him. Rhulad gestured. 'Come, brothers, sit with us. We know, we understand well, it seemed all we were was but ashes, and the love we shared, as brothers, was so sadly strained, then.'

Trull could see that even Fear was stunned, as they sat down in the low chairs.

'We must not run from our memories,' Rhulad said, as Udinaas brought him his cup. 'The blood of kin need not always burn, brothers. There must be times when it simply . . . warms us.'

Fear cleared his throat. 'We have . . . missed you as well, Emperor—'

'Enough! No titles. Rhulad, so our father named me, as he named all his sons, each in turn from the host of ancestors of the Sengar line. It is too easy to forget.'

Udinaas set a cup into Fear's hand. Fingers closed of their own accord.

Trull glanced up as the slave approached him with the last cup. He met the Letherii's eyes, was startled by what he saw in them. He reached out and accepted the wine. 'Thank you, Udinaas.'

A flinch from Rhulad. 'He is mine,' he said in a tight voice.

Trull's eyes widened. 'Of course, Rhulad.'

'Good. Yes. Fear, I must tell you of Mayen.'

Slowly leaning back, Trull studied the wine trembling in the cup in his hands. The slave's gaze, the message it seemed to convey. *All is well.*

'I did not,' Fear ventured hesitantly, 'see her earlier . . .'

'No, nor our mother. Mayen has been unwell.' Rhulad shot Fear a nervous glance. 'I am sorry, brother. I should not have . . . should not have done that. And now, well, you see . . .' He drained his wine in a single motion. 'Udinaas, more. Tell him. Explain, Udinaas, so that Fear understands.'

The slave refilled the cup, then stepped back. 'She is with child,' he said, meeting Fear's gaze. 'There is no doubt, now, that her heart belongs to you. Rhulad would have wished otherwise. At first, in any case. But not now. He understands. But the child, that has made matters difficult. Complicated.'

The cup in Fear's hand had not visibly moved, but Trull could see that it was close to spilling, as if a numbness was

786

stealing the strength of the limb. 'Go on,' Fear managed.

'There is no precedent, no rules among your people,' Udinaas resumed. 'Rhulad would relinquish his marriage to her, he would undo all that has been done. But for the child, do you see, Fear Sengar?'

'That child will be heir—'

Rhulad interrupted with a harsh laugh. 'No heir, Fear. Ever. Don't you see? The throne shall be my eternal burden.'

Burden. By the Sisters, what has awakened you, Rhulad? Who has awakened you? Trull snapped his gaze back to Udinaas, and mentally reeled in sudden realization. *Udinaas? This . . . this slave?*

Udinaas was nodding, eyes still on Fear's own. 'The warrior that raises that child will be its father, in all things but the naming. There will be no deception. All will know. If there is to be a stigma . . .'

'It will be for me to deal with,' Fear said. 'Should I choose to stand beside Mayen, once wife to the emperor, with a child not my own to raise as my wife's first-born.'

'It is as you say, Fear Sengar,' Udinaas said. Then he stepped back.

Trull slowly straightened, reached with one hand and gently righted the cup in Fear's grip. Startled, his brother looked at him, then nodded. 'Rhulad, what does Mother say to all this?'

'Mayen has been punishing herself with white nectar. It is not an easy thing to defeat, such . . . dependency. Uruth endeavours . . .'

A soft groan from Fear, as he closed his eyes.

Trull watched Rhulad stretch out as if to touch Fear, watched him hesitate, then glance across to Trull.

Who nodded. *Yes. Now.*

A momentary contact, that seemed to shoot through Fear, snapping his eyes open.

'Brother,' Rhulad said, 'I am sorry.'

Fear studied his youngest brother's face, then said, 'We

are all sorry, Rhulad. For . . . so much. What has Uruth said of the child? Is it well?'

'Physically, yes, but it knows its mother's hunger. This will be . . . difficult. I know, you do not deserve any of this, Fear—'

'Perhaps, Rhulad, but I will accept the burden. For Mayen. And for you.'

No-one spoke after that, not for some time. They drank their wine, and it seemed to Trull that something was present, some part of his life he'd thought – not long gone, but non-existent in the first place. They sat, the three of them. Brothers, and nothing more.

Night descended outside. Udinaas served food and still more wine. Some time later, Trull rose, the alcohol softening details, and wandered through the chambers of the tent, his departure barely noticed by Rhulad and Fear.

In a small room walled in by canvas, he found Udinaas.

The slave was sitting on a small stool, eating his own supper. He looked up in surprise at Trull's sudden arrival.

'Please,' Trull said, 'resume your meal. You have earned it, Udinaas.'

'Is there something you wish of me, Trull Sengar?'

'No. Yes. What have you done?'

The slave cocked his head. 'What do you mean?'

'With . . . him. What have you done, Udinaas?'

'Not much, Trull Sengar.'

'No, I need an answer. What are you to him?'

Udinaas set down his plate, drank a mouthful of wine. 'A subject who's not afraid of him, I suppose.'

'That's . . . all? Wait, yes, I see. But then I wonder, why? Why are you not afraid of him?'

Udinaas sighed, and Trull realized how exhausted the slave was. 'You, all the Edur, you see the sword. Or the gold. You see . . . the power. The terrifying, brutal power.' He shrugged. 'I see what it takes from him, what it costs Rhulad. I am Letherii, after all,' he added with a grimace. 'I understand the notion of debt.' He looked up. 'Trull Sengar, I am his friend. That is all.'

Trull studied the slave for a half-dozen heartbeats. 'Never betray him, Udinaas. Never.'

The Letherii's gaze skittered away. He drank more wine. 'Udinaas—'

'I heard you,' the man said in a grating voice.

Trull turned to leave. Then he paused and glanced back. 'I have no wish to depart on such terms. So, Udinaas, for what you have done, for what you have given him, thank you.'

The slave nodded without looking up. He reached down to retrieve his plate.

Trull returned to the central chamber to find that Hannan Mosag had arrived, and was speaking to Rhulad.

'. . . Hull believes it lies near a town downriver from here. A day's journey, perhaps. But, Emperor, a necessary journey none the less.'

Rhulad looked away, glared at the far wall. 'The armies must go on. To Brans Keep. No delays, no detours. I will go, and Fear and Trull as well. Hull Beddict, to guide us. Udinaas, of course.'

'A K'risnan,' the Warlock King said, 'and our new demonic allies, the two Kenryll'ah.'

'Very well, those as well. We shall meet you at Brans Keep.'

'What is it?' Trull asked. 'What has happened?'

'Something has been freed,' Hannan Mosag said. 'And it must be dealt with.'

'Freed by whom, and for what purpose?'

The Warlock King shrugged. 'I know not who was responsible. But I assume it was freed to fight us.'

'A demon of some sort?'

'Yes. I can only sense its presence, its will. I cannot identify it. The town is named Brous.'

Trull slowly nodded. 'Would that Binadas were with us,' he said.

Rhulad glanced up. 'Why?'

Trull smiled, said nothing.

After a moment, Fear grunted, then nodded.

Rhulad matched Trull's smile. 'Yes,' he said, 'would that he were.'

Hannan Mosag looked at the three of them in turn. 'I do not understand.'

The emperor's laugh was harsh, only slightly bitter. 'You send us on another quest, Warlock King.'

Hannan Mosag visibly blanched.

Seeing that, Rhulad laughed again, this time in pure amusement.

After a moment, both Fear and Trull joined him, whilst Hannan Mosag stared at them all in disbelief.

They had drunk too much wine, Trull told himself later. That was all. Far too much wine.

Seren Pedac and the Crimson Guardsmen guided their horses down from the road, across the ditch, and drew rein at the edge of a green field. The vanguard of the Merchants' Battalion had emerged from the city's gates, and the Acquitor could see Preda Unnutal Hebaz at the forefront, riding a blue-grey horse, white-maned, that tossed its head in irritation, hooves stamping with impatience.

'If she's not careful,' Iron Bars observed, 'that beast will start bucking. And she'll find herself on her arse in the middle of the road.'

'That would be an ill omen indeed,' Seren said.

After a moment, the Preda managed to calm the horse.

'I take it we have something of a wait before us,' Iron Bars said.

'King's Battalion and Merchants' Battalion at the very least. I don't know what other forces are in Letheras. I wouldn't think the south battalions and brigades have had time to reach here, which is unfortunate.' She thought for a moment, then said, 'If we cross this field, we can take the river road and enter through Fishers' Gate. It will mean crossing two-thirds of the city to reach my home, but for you, Avowed, well, presumably the ship you're signed on with will be close by.'

Iron Bars shrugged. 'We're delivering you to your door, Acquitor.'

'That's not necessary—'

'Even so, it is what we intend to do.'

'Then, if you don't mind . . .'

'Fishers' Gate it shall be. Lead on, Acquitor.'

The rearguard elements of the King's Battalion had turned in the concourse before the Eternal Domicile and were now marching up the Avenue of the Seventh Closure. King Ezgara Diskanar, who had stood witness on the balcony of the First Wing since his official despatch of the Preda at dawn, finally swung about and made his way inside. The investiture was about to begin, but Brys Beddict knew he had some time before his presence was required.

Four of his own guard were on the balcony with him. Brys gestured one over. 'Find me a messenger.'

'Yes, sir.'

Brys waited, staring out over the city. The air was oppressive with more than just humidity and heat. After the passing of the battalion's rearguard, few citizens ventured into its wake. The battle at Brans Keep was still days away, but it seemed that most of the city's residents – those who remained – had elected to stay in their homes as much as possible.

The messenger arrived, a woman he had employed often and one he knew he could trust.

'Deliver a missive to my brother, Tehol, at his home.'

'He will be on his roof?'

'I expect so, and that is the message – he is to stay there. Now, an additional message, to the Shavankrat brother guarding Tehol. A name. Gerun Eberict. That is all.'

'Yes, sir.'

'Go, then.'

She quickly left. Brys strode into the narrow corridor that tracked the length of the wing on the second tier. At the far end steps descended to an antechamber that was part of the central dome complex. There, he found Finadd Moroch Nevath, sitting on a stone bench.

'Brys, I have been waiting for you.'

'Not too long, I hope. What do you wish of me, Finadd?'

'Do you believe in gods?'

Startled, Brys was silent for a moment, then said, 'I am afraid I do not see the relevance of that question.'

Moroch Nevath reached into a pouch at his hip and withdrew a battered tile, such as might be found among market readers. 'When did you last speak with Turudal Brizad?'

'The First Consort has not been in the palace – either palace, since yesterday,' Brys said. 'First Eunuch Nifadas ordered an extensive search, and it has been concluded that Turudal has fled. Not entirely surprising—'

Moroch tossed him the tile. Instinctively, Brys caught it in his left hand. He looked down at the ceramic plaque. Yellowed at the edges, latticed with cracks, the illustration reduced to a series of stylized scratches that Brys none the less recognized. 'The tile of the Errant. What of it, Moroch?'

The soldier rose to his feet. He'd lost weight, Brys noted, and seemed to have aged ten years since joining the treaty delegation. 'He's been here. All along. The bastard's been right under our noses, Brys Beddict.'

'What are you talking about?'

'The Errant. The First Consort. Turudal Brizad.'

'That is . . . ridiculous.'

'I have a somewhat harsher word for it, Brys.'

The Champion glanced away from the man standing before him. 'How did you come to this extraordinary conclusion, Moroch?'

'There have been Turudal Brizads every generation – oh, different names, but it's him. Scenes on tapestries, paintings. Walk the royal collection, Brys – everything's out in the hallway, about to be moved. It was right there, for anyone to see, should they find reason to look.'

'And what reason did you have, Moroch?'

A grimace. 'He asked me to do something for him.'

Brys grunted. 'He's a god.' *Supposedly.* 'Why should he need your help?'

'Because he says you will be too busy.'

Brys thought back to his last conversation with Turudal Brizad. . . . *the end of my objectivity.* Something like that, as the man was walking away. 'I admit to some . . . scepticism, Moroch Nevath.'

'Set it aside for the moment, Brys. I am here to ask your advice. Assume the worst.'

'A god asks for your help? I suppose one must consider possible motivations, and the consequences of accepting or rejecting the request.'

'Yes.'

'Will doing as he asks be to the benefit of Lether?'

'He says it will.'

'Where is he now?'

'In the city, somewhere. He was watching the last of the refugees allowed in this morning, on the wall, or so one of my guards reported.'

'Then, I would think, Moroth, that you must do as he asks.'

'Over the duty of protecting the king?'

'I imagine the god assumes that task will be mine.'

'We are almost equal, you and I, Brys.'

'I know.'

'You may believe that you are the better between us. I believe otherwise.'

'The decision was not ours to make, Moroch.'

Moroch studied him for a half-dozen heartbeats, then said, 'I thank you for the advice, Finadd.'

'I hesitate to say it, Moroch Nevath, but the Errant be with you.'

'Not funny,' the swordsman muttered as he strode away.

Brys made his way into the dome complex. He came to the main corridor, halting to study the layout once more. The walls had been scrubbed, the dust on the floor mopped away. Guards and functionaries were moving about, readying for the investiture. Many glances were cast in the direction of the figure sleeping halfway down the corridor, curled up on the centre tile.

Sighing, Brys approached Kuru Qan. 'Ceda.'

The old man made a sound, then turned over so that his back was to Brys.

'Wake up, Ceda. Please.'

Head lifting, Kuru Qan groped for the twin lenses lying on the floor nearby, drew them to his face. 'Who calls?'

'It is Brys Beddict.'

'Ah, Finadd.' Kuru Qan twisted round and peered up. 'You look well.'

You do not. 'Ceda, the investiture is about to begin. Unless you would have King Ezgara Diskanar step around you during his solemn march, you will have to move.'

'No!' The old man spread himself out on the flagstone. 'I must not! This is mine. My place.'

'You insist that he step to one side on his approach? Ceda, you risk the king's anger—'

'Relevant? Not in the least.' His fingers scrabbled on the stone. 'This is mine. Warn him, Finadd. Warn the king.'

'About what?'

'I will not be moved. Any who would try will be blasted into ashes. Ashes, Brys Beddict.'

Brys glanced around. A small crowd had gathered to listen to the exchange. The Finadd scowled. 'Be on your way, all of you.' People scrambled.

Temporarily alone once more, Brys crouched down before the Ceda. 'You had paints and brushes with you last time. What happened to them?'

'Paints and brushes?' The eyes blinked behind the lenses. 'Gone. Gone away. The king wants you now, Finadd. He is ready to begin the procession. Nifadas is coming – he will complain, but no matter. It will be a small audience, won't it. Relevant? Oh yes. Best the king ignore me – explain that to him, Brys.'

The Finadd straightened. 'I shall, Ceda.'

'Excellent. Now, be on your way.'

'This doesn't smell right.'

Trull looked over at the Kenryll'ah demon that had spoken. It was taller than the Tiste Edur on their horses. A face of sharper features than those on Lilac, black as chiselled basalt, the upper and lower canines protruding and glinting silver. A fur-lined collar, a vest of bronze scales, salt-rimed and dark with patination. A heavy leather belt on which was slung a huge scabbarded tulwar. Leather leggings, grey and supple. The other demon, standing at its side, differed only in the choice of weapons, a massive matlock gripped in two gauntleted hands.

This second Kenryll'ah bared its teeth. 'Making me hungry.'

'Split bones,' the other said. 'Marrow.'

The stench the two were referring to was that of rotting corpses. They had reached the edge of the clearing, beyond which was the palisade wall of the town of Brous. In the field were barrows, and one long excavated trench. There was no-one in sight.

'Brothers,' the emperor said, 'dismount and ready your weapons.'

Trull swung down from his horse. He turned. 'K'risnan, can you sense anything?'

The young Arapay warlock's face was sickly. He nodded. 'In the town, I think. It knows we're here.'

Rhulad closed both hands on the grip of his sword and raised it to centre guard position. 'Udinaas, remain with the horses. Fear, on my left. Trull, my right. K'risnan, stay behind us five paces. Demons, out to either side.'

'Can't we eat first?'

'Or pee? I need to pee.'

'You should have thought of that before we left,' the first demon said.

'And you should have eaten. We've plenty of spare horses, you know.'

The emperor hissed. 'Silence, both of you. We've had to listen to you the entire journey. No more, lest I decide to kill you first.'

'That wouldn't be wise,' the second Kenryll'ah said. 'I smell more than meat, I smell the one thing still alive in there, and it isn't pleasant.'

'I taste it,' the first demon said. 'And it makes me want to retch.'

'You should have thought of retching before we left,' the second one said.

'I think of retching every time I look at you.'

'Enough!'

'I apologize for my brother,' the first demon said.

'And I for mine,' the second one added.

Strange tyrants. Trull unslung his spear and strode to Rhulad's side.

They made their way across the clearing. Reaching the pit, they saw the first of the bodies. Broken and tossed at the base of the deep, ragged excavation, like an open mass burial. Workers and soldiers. Flesh dark and bloating in the heat. Flies swarmed.

They skirted the pit and approached the town. The gates opposite them had been knocked down, inward, the heavy doors shattered. Somewhere in the town a dog was barking.

The street was strewn with corpses just inside the wall. The doors of every house and building within sight had been stove in. Ahead and to the right, two horses stood yoked to a wagon that had been knocked over. Exhaustion and the strain of the yokes had driven one of the beasts into an awkward sitting position. Trull hesitated, then walked over to them, drawing the knife at his belt. The others paused and watched as he cut the horses loose. Neither animal was in any condition to flee, but they slowly made their way outside on trembling, uncertain legs.

Trull returned to his position beside Rhulad.

'It's coming,' the first demon said.

Further down the main street a flock of starlings swirled into view, spinning between the buildings. In a mass of black, the birds seemed to boil towards the Tiste Edur and the Kenryll'ah. Striding in the midst of the birds, a tall figure, spectral, its skin white, its hair pallid yellow and hanging in limp strands. It was wearing a leather harness that looked wrinkled and blackened with rot. There was something strange about its limbs.

'He is unarmed,' Fear said.

'Yet,' the K'risnan hissed behind them, 'he is the one.'

The starlings spun higher, alighting on roof edges to either side, as the figure halted ten paces away.

'Peaceful,' it said in Letherii, 'is it not?'

Rhulad spoke. 'I am Emperor Rhulad of the Tiste Edur. Who, and what, are you, stranger?'

'I am Forkrul Assail. I am named Serenity.'

'You are a demon, then?'

The head cocked. 'I am?'

'This is not your world.'

'It isn't?'

Rhulad half turned. 'K'risnan, banish him.'

'I cannot, Emperor.'

'The tumult of your presence invites discord,' Serenity said.

Watching the Forkrul Assail's movements, Trull realized that it possessed extra joints in the arms and the legs, and there was some kind of hinge across the creature's breastbone. Its motion was oddly loose.

'Discord?' Rhulad asked.

'I desire peace once more.'

Fear spoke. 'If it is peace you seek, Serenity, then you need only turn and walk away. Leave.'

'To leave here is to arrive elsewhere. I cannot retreat

from disorder, for it shall surely follow. Peace must be asserted where one finds oneself. Only when discord is resolved will there be peace.' The Forkrul Assail then stepped forward.

' 'Ware!' one of the demons snarled.

Serenity surged closer, even as the starlings exploded skyward once more.

Trull's weapon possessed the greatest reach, but he did not attempt to stab the creature. Its arms were lifted to fend off the attack, and Trull chose to batter at those with a high sweep of the spear shaft. Like a serpent, Serenity's right arm writhed around the shaft, binding the weapon. A sudden flex and the Blackwood cracked, then splintered, the red core welling into view down the length of the split. Trull had little time to feel shock, as Serenity's left hand lashed out.

Two fingertips touched Trull's temple—

He was already pitching himself to the side, but at the contact he felt his neck wrenched round. Had he remained standing, had he resisted, his neck would now be broken. As it was, ducking, shoulder dipping, he was flung downward, thrown off his feet.

Fear had charged in low, a beat behind Trull's high attack, slashing diagonally down and in to take the Forkrul Assail at the knee.

But the leg folded back, the knee reversing its angle, whilst at the same time Serenity reached down with his left hand and grasped the sword-blade. The Forkrul Assail plucked it from Fear's hand, fingers clenching, crushing the iron.

For all their failures, Trull and Fear had done what was demanded of them. Their flank attacks had preceded Rhulad's, with the intention of opening Serenity to the emperor's attack. Rhulad's mottled sword was a blur, whistling in the air – yet not once making contact, as the Forkrul Assail seemed to simply flow around it.

Flinging Fear's bent sword aside, Serenity stepped in.

And plunged his fingers like spikes into Rhulad's chest, pushing past the coins, sliding between ribs, and piercing his heart, then snapping back out.

The emperor crumpled.

Serenity swung to face Fear.

Then leapt back, eight paces or more through the air, narrowly avoiding a matlock that struck the dirt of the street and sank deep.

Serenity back-pedalled further as the other demon pursued, the massive tulwar dancing like a dagger in its hands.

Trull scrambled to his feet. He spun, intending to collect another spear from the cache he'd left strapped to his horse—

—and found Udinaas rushing towards him, the weapons cradled in his arms.

Trull pulled one free, then turned once more, leaping over Rhulad's body. Ahead, the Forkrul Assail had darted to the left, ducking beneath a slash of the tulwar, hands lashing out even as the demon kicked it hard in the side.

Serenity was thrown by the blow, thudded on the ground and rolled, twice, before regaining its feet.

But Trull had heard the crack of ribs in that kick.

The demon closed once more from the Forkrul Assail's right.

A moment before they closed, Trull launched his spear.

Serenity did not see it coming. Struck solidly just below the left collarbone, the creature was spun round by the impact. The demon's tulwar chopped down into its right thigh, ringing as it bit into bone. The demon wrenched it loose.

Trull reached back and another spear was placed in his hand. He moved closer.

Staggering back, the Forkrul Assail had plucked the spear from its shoulder and was fending off the tulwar slashes with its hands, pushing against the flat of the blade.

The other demon was rushing in from the other side, matlock raised high.

Pale bluish blood streaming from the two wounds – which seemed to be closing even as Trull watched – Serenity leapt back once more, then turned and ran.

The Kenryll'ah prepared to pursue.

'Halt!' Trull shouted. 'Leave it!'

Udinaas was standing above Rhulad's body. A few paces away stood the K'risnan, his young face frozen into an expression of terror. He was shaking his head in denial, again and again.

'K'risnan.'

Wild eyes fixed on Trull. 'It . . . threw me back. My power . . . when the emperor died . . . all, flung back . . .'

The demons approached.

'Leave it to us,' the first one said, whipping blood from the tulwar.

'Yes,' nodded the other. 'We've never before heard of these Forkrul Assail, but we've decided.'

'We don't like them,' the first demon said.

'Not in the least.'

'We will hunt it down and tell it so.'

Fear spoke. 'Udinaas, how long . . .' His eyes were on Rhulad.

'Not long,' the slave replied.

'Do we wait?'

'It would be best, I think,' said Udinaas.

Rubbing at his face, Fear walked over to his sword. He picked it up, examined it, then tossed it aside. He looked across at Trull.

Trull said, 'It broke Blackwood.'

A grimace. 'I saw. That second spear, that was well thrown, brother.'

Still, the brothers knew. Without the Kenryll'ah, they would now be dead.

The first demon spoke. 'May we pursue now?'

Fear hesitated, then nodded. 'Go.'

800

The two Kenryll'ah swung round and headed up the street.

'We can eat on the way.'

'Good idea, brother.'

Somewhere in the town, the dog was still barking.

'We have to help him,' Sandalath Drukorlat said.

Withal glanced over at her. They were standing on the sward's verge overlooking the beach. The Tiste Edur youth was curled up in the sand below. Still shrieking. 'It's not his first visit,' Withal said.

'How is your head?' she asked after a moment.

'It hurts.'

The Tiste Edur fell silent, shuddering, then the youth's head jerked up. He stared at Withal and the Tiste Andii woman standing beside the Meckros weaponsmith. Then back again. 'Withal!'

The smith's brows rose, although the motion made him wince, and he said, 'He normally doesn't talk to me much.' To the youth, 'Rhulad. I am not so cruel as to say welcome.'

'Who is she? Who is that . . . *betrayer*?'

Sandalath snorted. 'Pathetic. This is the god's sword-wielder? A mistake.'

'If it is,' Withal said in a low voice, 'I have no intention of telling him so.'

Rhulad clambered to his feet. 'It killed me.'

'Yes,' Withal replied. 'It did, whatever "it" was.'

'A Forkrul Assail.'

Sandalath stiffened. 'You should be more careful, Edur, in choosing your enemies.'

A laugh close to hysteria, as Rhulad made his way up from the beach. 'Choose, woman? I choose *nothing*.'

'Few ever do, Edur.'

'What is she doing here, Withal?'

'The Crippled God thought I needed company. Beyond three insane Nachts.'

'You are lovers?'

801

'Don't be absurd,' Sandalath said, sneering.

'Like she said,' Withal added.

Rhulad stepped past them. 'I need my sword,' he muttered, walking inland.

They turned to watch him.

'His sword,' Sandalath murmured. 'The one the god had you make?'

Withal nodded. 'But I am not to blame.'

'You were compelled.'

'I was.'

'It's not the weapon that's evil, it's the one wielding it.'

He studied her. 'I don't care if you crack my skull again. I am really starting to hate you.'

'I assure you my sentiments are identical regarding you.'

Withal turned away. 'I'm going to my shack.'

'Of course you are,' she snapped behind him. 'To beg and mumble to your god. As if it'd bother listening to such pathetic mewling.'

'I'm hoping,' Withal said over his shoulder, 'that it'll take pity on me.'

'Why should it?'

He did not reply, and wisely kept his answering smile to himself.

Standing ten paces to the side of the throne, Brys Beddict watched as King Ezgara Diskanar walked solemnly into the domed chamber. Distracted irritation was on the king's face, since his journey had required a detour around the prone, shivering form of the Ceda, Kuru Qan, but that was behind him now, and Brys saw Ezgara slowly resume his stern expression.

Awaiting him in the throne room was a handful of officials and guards. First Eunuch Nifadas was positioned to the right of the throne, holding the Lether crown on a blood-red pillow. First Concubine Nisall knelt at the foot of the dais, on the left side. Along with Brys and six of his guardsmen, Finadd Gerun Eberict was present with six of his own soldiers of the Palace Guard.

And that was all. The investiture on this, the day of the Seventh Closure – or close enough since no-one could agree on that specific date – was to be witnessed by these few. Not as originally planned, of course. But there had been more riots, the last one the bloodiest of them all. The king's name had become a curse among the citizenry. The list of invitations had been truncated as a matter of security, and even then, Brys was nervous about Gerun Eberict's presence.

The king neared the dais, his robes sliding silken on the polished marble floor in his wake.

'This day,' Nifadas intoned, 'Lether becomes an empire.'

The guards executed the salute reserved for the royal line and held it, motionless as statues.

Ezgara Diskanar stepped up onto the dais and slowly turned round.

The First Eunuch moved to stand before him and raised the pillow.

The king took the crown and fitted it onto his head.

'This day,' Nifadas said, stepped back, 'Lether is ruled by an emperor.' He turned. 'Emperor Ezgara Diskanar.'

The guards released their salute.

And that is it.

Ezgara sat on the throne.

Looking old and frail and lost.

The windows were shuttered tight. Weeds snarled the path, vines had run wild up the walls to either side of the stepped entrance. From the street behind them came the stench of smoke, and a distant roar from somewhere in the Creeper Quarter inland, beyond Settle Lake, indicated that yet another riot had begun.

From the Fishers' Gate, Seren Pedac and the Crimson Guardsmen had walked their horses down littered streets. Signs of looting, the occasional corpse, a soldier's dead horse, and figures scurrying from their path into alleys and side avenues. Burnt-out buildings, packs of hungry feral dogs drawn in from the abandoned farmlands and forests, refugee families huddled here and there, the King's City of Lether seemed to have succumbed to depraved barbarity with the enemy still leagues beyond the horizon.

She was stunned at how swiftly it had all crumbled, and more than a little frightened. For all her disgust and contempt for the ways of her people, there had remained, somewhere buried deep, a belief in its innate resiliency. But here, before her, was the evidence of sudden, thorough collapse. Greed and savagery unleashed, fear and panic triggering brutality and ruthless indifference.

They passed bodies of citizens who had been long in dying, simply left in the street while they bled out.

Down one broad avenue, near the canal, a mob had passed through, perhaps only half a day earlier. There was evidence that soldiers had battled against it, and had been pushed back into a fighting withdrawal. Flanking buildings and estates had been trashed and looted. The street was sticky with blood, and the tracks of dozens of wagons were evident, indicating that here, at least, the city's garrison had returned to take away corpses.

Iron Bars and his Guardsmen said little during the journey, and now, gathered before her home, they remained on their horses, hands on weapons and watchful.

Seren dismounted.

After a moment, Iron Bars and Corlo did the same.

'Don't look broken into,' the mage said.

'As I said,' Seren replied, 'nothing inside is worth taking.'

'I don't like this,' the Avowed muttered. 'If trouble comes knocking, Acquitor . . .'

'It won't,' she said. 'These riots won't last. The closer the Edur army gets, the quieter things will become.'

'That's not what happened in Trate.'

'True, but this will be different.'

'I don't see why you'd think so,' Iron Bars said, shaking his head.

'Go find your ship, Avowed,' Seren said. She turned to the others. 'Thank you, all of you. I am honoured to have known you and travelled in your company.'

'Go safe, lass,' Corlo said.

She settled a hand on the mage's shoulder. Held his eyes, but said nothing.

He nodded. 'Easy on that.'

'You heard?'

'I did. And I've the headache to prove it.'

'Sorry.'

'Try to remember, Seren Pedac, Mockra is a subtle warren.'

'I will try.' She faced Iron Bars.

'Once I've found our employer and planted my squad,' he said, 'I'll pay you another visit, so we needn't get all soft here and now.'

'All right.'

'A day, no longer, then I'll see you again, Acquitor.'

She nodded.

The Avowed and his mage swung themselves back into their saddles. The troop rode off.

Seren watched them for a moment, then turned about and walked up the path. The key to the elaborate lock was under the second flagstone.

The door squealed when she pushed it back, and the smell of dust swept out to engulf her. She entered, shutting the door.

Gloom, and silence.

She did not move for a time, the corridor stretching before her. The door at its end was open, and she could see into the room beyond, which was lit by cloth-filtered sunlight coming from the courtyard at the back. A high-backed chair in that far room faced her, draped in muslin cloth.

One step, then another. On, down the corridor. Just

before the entrance to the room, the mouldering body of a dead owl, lying as if asleep on the floor. She edged round it, then stepped into the room, noting the slight breeze coming from the broken window where the owl had presumably entered from the courtyard.

Ghostly furniture to either side, but it was the chair that held her gaze. She crossed to it, then, without removing the cloth, she sat down, the muslin drawing inward as she sank down into the seat.

Blinking, Seren looked about.

Shadows. Silence. The faint smell of decay. The lump of the dead owl lying just beyond the threshold.

'Seren Pedac's . . . empire,' she whispered.

And she had never felt so alone.

In the city of Letheras, as companies of Gerun Eberict's soldiers cut and chopped their way through a mass of cornered citizens who had been part of a procession of the king's loyalists, on their way to the Eternal Domicile to cheer the investiture, citizens whose blood now spread on the cobbles to mark this glorious day; as starlings in their tens of thousands wheeled ever closer to the old tower that had once been an Azath and was now the Hold of the Dead; as Tehol Beddict – no longer on his roof – made his way down shadowy streets on his way to Selush, at the behest of Shurq Elalle; as the child, Kettle, who had once been dead but was now very much alive, sat on the steps of the old tower singing softly to herself and plaiting braids of grass; as the rays of the sun lengthened to slant shafts through the haze of smoke, the bells began ringing.

Pronouncing the birth of the empire.

The end of the Seventh Closure.

But the scribes were in error. The Seventh Closure had yet to arrive.

Two more days.

Leaning against a wall with his arms crossed, near the old palace, the First Consort, Turudal Brizad, the god known as

the Errant, looked skyward at the cloud of starlings as the
bells sounded, low and tremulous.

'Unpleasant birds,' he said to himself, 'starlings . . .'

Two more days.

A most tragic miscalculation, I fear.

Most tragic.

CHAPTER TWENTY-THREE

A vast underground cavern yawned beneath the basin,
the crust brittle and porous. Could one have stood in
that ancient cave, the rain would have been ceaseless.
Even so, eleven rivers fed into the marshlands that
would one day be the city of Letheras, and the process
of erosion that culminated in the collapse of the basin
and the catastrophic draining of the rivers and swamps,
was a long one. Thus, modest as Settle Lake is,
it is worth reminding oneself of its extraordinary
depth. The lake is, indeed, like a roof hatch with the
enormous cavern the house beneath. So, the pulling
down into the deep of Burdos' fishing boat – the sole
fisher of Settle Lake – nets and all, should come as
no surprise. Nor should the fact that since that time,
when so many witnessed Burdos' demise, no other
fishing boat has plied the waters of Settle Lake. In
any case, I was, I believe, speaking of the sudden
convergence of all those rivers, the inrush of the
swamp's waters, said event occurring long before the
settlement of the area by the colonists. Fellow scholars,
it would have been a dramatic sight, would it not?

Excerpt from *The Geologic History of Letheras*,
a lecture given by Royal Geographer Thula Redsand
at the Cutter Academy 19th Annual Commencement
(moments before the Great Collapse of the Academy Ceiling)
Comments recounted by sole survivor, Ibal the Dart

There was nothing natural in the dust that loomed like a behemoth above the Edur armies as they came down from the north and began moving into positions opposite Brans Keep. The ochre cloud hovered like a standing wave in a cataract, fierce winds whipping southward to either side, carrying ashes and topsoil in a dark, ominous onslaught against the waiting Letherii armies and the barren hills behind them.

The emperor of the Tiste Edur had found the glory of rebirth yet again. Every death was a tier in his climb to unassailable domination. Resurrection, Udinaas now understood, was neither serene nor painless. It came in screams, in shrieks that rent the air. It came in a storm of raw trauma that tore at Rhulad's sanity as much as it would anyone's suffering the same curse. And there was no doubt at all in the slave's mind, the sword and its gift were cursed, and the god behind it – if it was a god in truth – was a creature of madness.

This time, Rhulad's brothers had been there to witness his awakening. Udinaas had not been surprised at the horror writ on their faces with the emperor's first ragged scream, the convulsions racking Rhulad's body of smudged gold and dried blood, the cold unearthly light blazing anew in his terrible eyes. He had seen them frozen, unable to draw closer, unable to flee, standing witness to the dreadful truth.

Perhaps, afterwards, when they had thawed – when their hearts started beating once more – there was sympathy. Rhulad wept openly, with only the slave's arm across his shoulders for comfort. And Fear and Trull had looked on, the K'risnan sitting hunched and mute on the ground behind them, until such time as the emperor found himself once more, the child and brother and newly blooded warrior he'd once been – before the sword found his hands – discovered, still cowering but alive within him.

Little had been said on the return journey, but they had ridden their horses into the ground in their haste, and for all but Udinaas the ride had been a flight. Not from the Forkrul Assail and its immutable fascination for the peace of cold corpses, but from the death, and the rebirth, of the emperor of the Tiste Edur.

They rejoined the army five leagues from Brans Keep, and received Hannan Mosag's report that contact had been established with the K'risnan in the other two armies, and all were approaching the fated battlefield, where, shadow wraiths witnessed, the Letherii forces awaited them.

Details, the trembling skein of preparation, Udinaas was indifferent to them, the whisper of order in seeming chaos. An army marched, like some headless migration, each beast bound by instinct, the imperatives of violence. Armies marched from complexity into simplicity. It was this detail that drove them onward. A field waited, on which all matters could be reduced, on which dust and screams and blood brought cold clarity. This was the secret hunger of warriors and soldiers, of governments, kings and emperors. The simple mechanics of victory and defeat, the perfect feint to draw every eye, every mind lured into the indulgent game. Focus on the scales. Count the measures and mull over balances, observe the stacked bodies like stacked coins and time is devoured, the mind exercised in the fruitless repetition of the millstone, and all the world beyond was still and blurred for the moment ... so long as no-one jarred the table.

Udinaas envied the warriors and soldiers their simple lives. For them, there was no coming back from death. They spoke simply, in the language of negation. They fought for the warrior, the soldier, at their side, and even dying had purpose – which was, he now believed, the rarest gift of all.

Or so it should have been, but the slave knew it would be otherwise. Sorcery was the weapon for the battle to come. Perhaps it was, in truth, the face of future wars the world over. Senseless annihilation, the obliteration of lives in numbers beyond counting. A logical extension of governments, kings and emperors. War as a clash of wills, a contest indifferent to its cost, seeking to discover who will blink first – and not caring either way. War, no different an exercise from the coin-reaping of the Merchants' Tolls, and thus infinitely understandable.

The Tiste Edur and their allies were arraying themselves opposite the Letherii armies, the day's light growing duller, muted by the hovering wave of suspended dust. In places sorcery crackled, shimmered the air, tentative escapes of the power held ready by both sides. Udinaas wondered if anyone, anyone at all, would survive this day. And, among those who did, what lessons would they take from this battle?

Sometimes the game goes too far.

She was standing beside him, silent and small and wrapped in a supple, undyed deerhide. She had said nothing, offered no reason for seeking him out. He did not know her mind, he could not guess her thoughts. Unknown and profoundly unknowable.

Yet now he heard her draw a shuddering breath.

Udinaas glanced over. 'The bruises are almost gone,' he said.

Feather Witch nodded. 'I should thank you.'

'No need.'

'Good.' She seemed to falter at her own vehemence. 'I should not have said that. I don't know what to think.'

'About what?'

She shook her head. 'About what, he asks. For Errant's sake, Udinaas, Lether is about to fall.'

'Probably. I have looked long and hard at the Letherii forces. I see what must be mages, standing apart here and there. But not the Ceda.'

'He must be here. How could he not be?'

Udinaas said nothing.

'You are no longer an Indebted.'

'And that matters?'

'I don't know.'

811

They fell silent. Their position was on a rise to the northwest of the battlefield. They could make out the facing wall of Brans Keep itself, a squat, formidable citadel leaning up against a cliff carved sheer into a hillside. Corner towers flanked the wall, and on each stood large fixed mangonels with their waiting crews. There was also a mage present on each tower, arms raised, and it was evident that a ritual was under way binding the two on their respective perches. Probably something defensive, since the bulk of the King's Battalion was positioned at the foot of the keep.

To the west of that battalion a ridge reached out from the hills a short distance, and on its other side were positioned elements of the king's heavy infantry, along with the Riven Brigade. West of that waited companies of the Snakebelt Battalion with the far flanking side protected by the Crimson Rampant Brigade, who were backed to the westernmost edge of the Brans Hills and to the course of the Dissent River to the south.

It was more difficult to make out the array of Letherii forces east of the King's Battalion. There was an artificial lake on the east side of the keep, and north of it, alongside the battalion, was the Merchants' Battalion. Another seasonal river or drainage channel wound northeast on their right flank, and it seemed the Letherii forces on the other side of that intended to use the dry ditch as a line of defence.

In any case, Rhulad's own army would present the western body of the Edur advance. Central was Fear's army, and further to the east, beyond an arm of lesser hills and old lake beds, approached the army of Tomad and Binadas Sengar, on their way down from the town of Five Points.

The rise Udinaas and Feather Witch stood on was ringed in shadow wraiths, and it was clear to Udinaas that protective sorcery surrounded them. Beyond the rise, out of sight of the facing armies, waited the Edur women, elders and children. Mayen was somewhere among them, still cloistered, still under Uruth Sengar's direct care.

He looked once more at Feather Witch. 'Have you seen Mayen?' he asked.

'No. But I have heard things . . .'

'Such as?'

'She is not doing well, Udinaas. She hungers. A slave was caught bringing her white nectar. The slave was executed.'

'Who was it?'

'Bethra.'

Udinaas recalled her, an old woman who'd lived her entire life in the household of Mayen's parents.

'She thought she was being kind,' Feather Witch continued. Then shrugged. 'There was no discussion.'

'I imagine not.'

'One cannot be denied all white nectar,' she said. 'One must be weaned. A gradual diminishment.'

'I know.'

'But they are concerned for the child she carries.'

'Who must be suffering in like manner.'

Feather Witch nodded. 'Uruth does not heed the advice of the slaves.' She met his eyes. 'They have all changed, Udinaas. They are as if . . . fevered.'

'A fire behind their eyes, yes.'

'They seem unaware of it.'

'Not all of them, Feather Witch.'

'Who?'

He hesitated, then said, 'Trull Sengar.'

'Do not be deceived,' she said. 'They are poisoned one and all. The empire to come shall be dark. I have had visions . . . I see what awaits us, Udinaas.'

'One doesn't need visions to know what awaits us.'

She scowled, crossed her arms. Then glared skyward. 'What sorcery is this?'

'I don't know,' Udinaas replied. 'New.'

'Or . . . old.'

'What do you sense from it, Feather Witch?'

813

She shook her head.

'It belongs to Hannan Mosag,' Udinaas said after a moment. 'Have you seen the K'risnan? Those from Fear Sengar's army are . . . malformed. Twisted by the magic they now use.'

'Uruth and the other women cling to the power of Kurald Emurlahn,' Feather Witch said. 'They behave as if they are in a war of wills. I don't think—'

'Wait,' Udinaas said, eyes narrowing. 'It's beginning.'

Beside him, Ahlrada Ahn bared his teeth. 'Now, Trull Sengar, we stand in witness. And this is what it means to be an Edur warrior today.'

'We may do more than wait,' Trull said. *We may also die.*

The dark dust was spiralling upward in thick columns now, edging forward towards the killing field between the armies.

Trull glanced behind him. Fear stood in the midst of Hiroth warriors. Two K'risnan were before him, one a mangled, hunched survivor from High Fort, the other sent over from Rhulad's army. Grainy streams of what seemed to be dust were rising from the two sorcerors, and their faces were twisted in silent pain.

The crackle of lightning came from the other side of the killing field, drawing Trull's attention round once more. Coruscating waves of blinding white fire were building before the arrayed Letherii mages, wrought through with flashes of lightning that arced among them.

Far to the right, Rhulad began moving the mass of his warriors forward, forming a broad wedge formation at the very edge of the killing field. Trull could see his brother, a hazy, blurred figure of gold. Further right was Hannan Mosag and his companies, and beyond them, already moving south alongside the basin's edge, were thousands of Soletaken Jheck and at least a dozen Kenryll'ah, each leading a score of their peasant subjects. The route they were taking had been noted, and the flanking Crimson

Rampant Brigade was manoeuvring round to face the threat.

There would be nothing subtle in this battle. No deft brilliance displayed by tactical geniuses. The Letherii waited with their backs to the steep hills. The Tiste Edur and their allies would have to come to them. Such were the simple mechanics, seemingly incumbent, and inevitable.

But sorcery spoke with a different voice.

The spiralling pillars of dust towered into the sky, each one keening, the wind shrieking so loud that Edur and Letherii alike began to cower.

The Letherii white fire surged upward, forming its own standing wall of bridled mayhem.

Trull was finding it difficult to breathe. He saw a hapless raven that had made the mistake of flying over the killing field tumble and flutter to the ground, the first casualty of the day. It seemed a pathetic harbinger to his mind. Rather a thousand. Ten thousand ravens, caterwauling through the sky.

The pillars leaned, staggered, lurched forward.

And began toppling.

A rush of wind from behind battered Trull and his fellow warriors, blessedly rich and humid, in the wake of the advancing columns of dust. Faint shouts on all sides, as weapons were readied.

The spiralling pillars were a long time in coming down.

Shadow wraiths were suddenly flowing across the ground, a dark, low flood. Udinaas could feel their terror, and the dread compulsion that drove them forward. *Fodder*. It was too early to launch an attack. They would be beneath the clash of sorcery.

As the columns toppled, the wave of Letherii fire rose to meet them.

Feather Witch hissed. 'The Empty Hold. The purest sorcery of the Letherii. Errant, I can feel it from here!'

'Not enough,' Udinaas muttered.

* * *

Positioned with the King's Battalion, Preda Unnutal Hebaz saw the day's light fade as the shadows of the falling pillars swept over the soldiers. She saw her men and women screaming, but could not hear them, as the roar of the dust thundered ever closer.

The Letherii ritual was suddenly released, the spitting, hissing fire sweeping over the heads of the cowering ranks, the tumbling froth surging upwards to meet the descending pillars.

Rapid concussions, shaking the earth beneath them, tearing fissures up the hillsides, and from Brans Keep a dull groaning. Unnutal spun round even as she was pushed to the ground. She saw, impossibly, the lake beside the keep lift in a mass of muddy water and foam. Saw, as the front wall of the keep bowed inward, pulling away from the flanking towers, dust shooting outward like geysers, and vanishing back into a billowing cloud.

Then the east tower swayed, enough to pitch from the edge the mangonel atop it, taking most of the crew with it. And the mage, Jirrid Attaract. All, plunging earthward.

The west tower leaned back. Its enormous foundation stones pushed outward, and suddenly it vanished into a cloud of its own rubble. The mage Nasson Methuda disappeared with it.

Twisting, Unnutal glared skyward.

To see the white fire shattering, dispersing. To see the pillars plunge through, sweeping the Letherii sorcery aside.

One struck the centre of the Merchants' Battalion, the dark dust billowing out to the sides and rolling up against the hill.

For a moment, she could see nothing, then the pillar began to re-form. Yet not as it had been. Now it was not dust that began spiralling upward, but living soldiers.

Whose flesh blackened like rot even as she watched.

They were screaming as they were lifted skyward, screaming as their flesh peeled away. Screaming—

816

The shadow above Unnutal Hebaz deepened. She looked up.

And closed her eyes.

Whirling in a frenzy, a huge fragment of Letherii sorcery slanted off the side of a collapsing pillar, plunged down and tore a bloody swath through the core of the Merude warriors a thousand paces to Trull's left.

The warriors died where they stood, in red mist.

The white fire, now stained pink, rolled through the press towards the K'risnan on that side. The young sorceror raised his hands at the last moment, then the magic devoured him.

When it dwindled, wavered, then vanished, the K'risnan was gone, as were those Edur who had been standing too close. The ground was blackened and split.

On the other side of the killing field, columns were rising once more filled with spinning bodies. Higher, the mass of writhing flesh dimming into a muddy hue, then giving way to white bone and polished iron. The pillars rose still higher, devouring more and more soldiers, entire companies torn from the entrenchments and dragged into the twisting maw.

Ahlrada Ahn reached out and pulled Trull close. '*He must stop this!*'

Trull pulled savagely away, shaking his head. 'This is not Rhulad! This is the Warlock King!' *Hannan Mosag, do you now vie for insanity's throne?*

Around them, the world was transformed into madness. Seething spheres of Letherii magic were thundering down here and there, tearing through ranks of Tiste Edur, devouring shadow wraiths by the hundreds. One landed in the midst of a company of demons and incinerated every one of them, including the Kenryll'ah commanding them.

Another raced across the ground towards the rise to the west of the emperor's forces. There was nothing to oppose it as it swept up the slope, and struck the encampment of the Edur women, elders and children.

817

Trull staggered in that direction, but Ahlrada Ahn dragged him back.

Letherii soldiers, nothing now but bones, spun in the sky above the hills. The Merchants' Battalion. The Riven Brigade. The Snakebelt Battalion. The King's Battalion. All those lives. *Gone.*

And the columns had begun moving, each one on an independent path, eastward and westward, plunging into the panicked ranks of more soldiers. Devouring, the hunger unending, the appetite insatiable.

War? This is not war—

'We're moving forward!'

Trull stared at Ahlrada Ahn.

The warrior shook him. 'Forward, Trull Sengar!'

Udinaas watched the deadly sorcery cut through the shadow wraiths, then roll towards the rise where he stood with Feather Witch. There was nowhere to run. No time. It was perfect—

A cold wind swept over him from behind, an exhalation of shadows. Rushing forward, colliding with the Letherii magic twenty paces downslope. Entwining, the shadows closing like a net, trapping the wild fire. Then shadow and flame vanished.

Udinaas turned.

Uruth and four other Edur women were standing in a line fifteen paces back. As he stared, two of the women toppled, and Udinaas could see that they were dead, the blood boiled in their veins. Uruth staggered, then slowly sank to her knees.

All right, not so perfect.

He faced the battlefield once more. The emperor was leading his warriors across the blistered, lifeless basin. The enemy positions on the hillsides opposite looked virtually empty. To either side, however, the slave could see fighting. Or, rather, slaughter. Where the pillars had yet to stalk, Letherii lines had broken of their own accord, and soldiers were fleeing, even as Soletaken Jheck dragged them to the ground, as demons ran them down, and squads of Edur pursued with frenzied determination. To the east, the dry river gully had been overrun. To the west, the Crimson Rampant Brigade was routed.

Hannan Mosag's terrible sorcery continued to rage, and Udinaas began to suspect that it was, like the Letherii magic, out of control. Pillars were spawning smaller kin. For lack of flesh, they began tearing up the ground, earth and stones spinning ever higher. Two bone-shot columns clashed near what was left of Brans Lake, and seemed to lock in mutual obliteration that sent thunderous concussions that visibly battered the hills beyond. Then they tore each other apart.

The bases of many of the pillars broke contact with the ground, and this triggered an upward plunge that ended in their dissolution into white and grey clouds.

All at once, even as ragged companies of Tiste Edur crossed the killing field, bones and armour began raining down. Limbs, polished weapons, helms, skulls, plummeting in murderous sweeps across the basin. Warriors died beneath the ghastly hail. There was panic, figures running.

Sixty paces ahead and below, along the very edge of the slope, walked Hull Beddict. He held a sword in one hand. He looked dazed.

A helm-wrapped skull, minus the lower jaw, thumped and bounded across Hull's path, but it seemed he did not notice, as he stumbled on.

Udinaas turned to Feather Witch. 'For Errant's sake,' he snapped, 'see what you can do for Uruth and the others!'

She started, eyes wide.

'They just saved our lives, Feather Witch.' He added nothing more, and left her there, making his way down to Hull Beddict.

Bones were still falling, the smaller pieces – fingers, rib fragments. Teeth rained down thirty paces ahead, covering the ground like hailstones, a sudden downpour, ending as quickly as it had begun.

Udinaas moved closer to Hull Beddict.

'Go no further, Hull!' he shouted.

The man halted, slowly turned, his face slack with shock. 'Udinaas? Is that you? Udinaas?'

The slave reached him, took his arm. 'Come. This is done, Hull Beddict. A sixth of a bell, no more than that. The battle is over.'

'Battle?'

'Slaughter, then. A squalid investment, wouldn't you say? Training all those soldiers. Those warriors. All that armour. Weapons. I think those days are over, don't you?' He was guiding the man back up the slope. 'Tens of thousands of dead Letherii; no point in even burying what's left of them. Two, maybe three thousand dead Tiste Edur. Neither had the chance to even so much as lift their weapons. How many shadow wraiths obliterated? Fifty, sixty thousand?'

'We must . . . stop. There is nothing . . .'

'No stopping now, Hull. Onward, to Letheras, like a rushing river. There will be rearguards to cut down. Gates to shatter. Streets and buildings to fight over. And then, the palace. And the king. His guard – they'll not lay down their weapons. Even if the king commands it. They serve the kingdom, after all, not Ezgara Diskanar. Letheras, Hull Beddict, will be ugly. Not ugly the way of today, here, but in some ways worse, I would—'

'Stop, slave. Stop talking, else I kill you.'

'That threat does not bother me much, Hull Beddict.'

They reached the rise. Feather Witch and a half-dozen other slaves were among the Edur women, now. Uruth was lying prone, suffering convulsions of some sort. A third woman had died.

'What's wrong, Hull Beddict?' Udinaas asked, releasing the man's arm. 'No chance to lead a charge against your foes? Those press-ganged Indebteds and the desperate fools who'd found dignity in a uniform. The hated enemy.'

Hull Beddict turned away. 'I must find the emperor. I must explain . . .'

Udinaas let the man go. The rain of bones had ceased, finally, and now only dust commanded the sky. The ruined keep was burning, heaving black smoke that would be visible from the walls of Letheras.

The slave strode over to Feather Witch. 'Will Uruth live?'

She looked up, her eyes strangely flat. 'I think so.'

'That was Kurald Emurlahn, wasn't it?'

'Yes.'

Udinaas turned away. He studied the basin, the masses of Edur wandering here and there among the burnt bodies of their kin, amongst the bright white bones and shining iron. A bloodless battlefield. Soletaken Jheck ranged the distant hillsides, hunting stragglers, but those who had not already fled were corpses or mere remnants of corpses. A few score wraiths drifted here and there.

He saw Rhulad, surrounded by warriors, marching back across the field. Towards Hannan Mosag's position. The slave set off to intercept the emperor. Words were about to be exchanged, and Udinaas wanted to hear them.

Trull and his company stood at the edge of the dry river gully. The bodies of soldiers littered the other side all the way to the ridge of hills paralleling the course. Fifteen hundred paces to their left, the lead elements of Tomad and Binadas Sengar's army were approaching. There were signs that they had seen battle. In the traditional manner, sword against sword.

'They have captured the Artisan Battalion's standard,' Ahlrada Ahn said, pointing.

Trull looked back to the field east of the gully. 'Who was here, then?'

'Whitefinder and Riven, I think. They broke when they witnessed the fate of Merchants' and the King's, and the pillars began moving towards them.'

Feeling sick, Trull looked away – but there was no direction available to ease him. On all sides, the slowly settling ashes of madness.

'The Tiste Edur,' said Ahlrada Ahn, 'have won themselves an empire.'

His words were heard by Sergeant Canarth, who strode up to them. 'You deny half your blood, Ahlrada? Do you find this victory bitter? I see now why you stand at Trull Sengar's side. I see now – we all see' – he added with a gesture encompassing the warriors behind him – 'why you so defend Trull, why you refuse to side with us.' Canarth's hard eyes fixed on Trull. 'Oh yes, Trull Sengar, your friend here possesses the blood of the Betrayers. No doubt that is why the two of you are such close friends.'

Trull unslung the spear at his back. 'I am tired of you, Canarth. Ready your weapon.'

The warrior's eyes narrowed, then he grinned, reaching for his own spear. 'I have seen you fight, Trull. I know your weaknesses.'

'Clear a space,' Trull said, and the others moved back, forming a ring.

Ahlrada Ahn hesitated. 'Do not do this. Trull – Canarth, retract your accusations. They are unfounded. It is forbidden to provoke your commander—'

'Enough,' Canarth snapped. 'I will kill you next, Betrayer.'

Trull assumed a standard stance, then settled his weight and waited.

Canarth shifted his grip back a hand's width, then probed out, the iron tip at throat-level.

Ignoring it for the moment, Trull slid his hands further apart along the shaft of his spear. Then he made contact, wood against wood, and held it as he stepped in. Canarth disengaged by bringing the iron point down and under, perfectly executed, but Trull was already inside, forcing Canarth to pull his weapon back, even as the sergeant swung the butt-end upward to block an expected up-sweep

– which did not come. Instead, Trull lifted his spear high and horizontal, and drove it forward to crack against Canarth's forehead.

The sergeant thumped onto his back.

Trull stood over him, studying the man's dazed expression, the split skin of his forehead leaking tendrils of blood.

The other warriors were shouting, expressing disbelief with Trull's speed, with the stunning, deceptive simplicity of the attack. He did not look up.

Ahlrada Ahn stepped close. 'Finish him, Trull Sengar.'

All of Trull's anger was gone. 'I see no need for that—'

'Then you are a fool. He will not forget—'

'I trust not.'

'Fear must be told of this. Canarth must be punished.'

'No, Ahlrada Ahn. Not a word.' He raised his gaze, looked northward. 'Let us greet Binadas and my father. I would hear tales of bravery, of fighting.'

The dark-skinned warrior's stare faltered, flickered away. 'Sisters take me, Trull, so would I.'

There were no old women to walk this field, cutting rings from fingers, stripping lightly stained clothing from stiffening corpses. There were no vultures, crows and gulls to wheel down to the vast feast. There was nothing to read of the battle now past, no sprawl of figures cut down from behind – not here, in the centre of the basin – no last stands writ in blood-splashed heaps and encircling rings of bodies. No tilted standards, held up only by the press of cold flesh, with their sigils grinning down. Only bones and gleaming iron, white teeth and glittering coins.

The settling dust was a soft whisper, gently dulling the ground and its random carpet of human and Edur detritus.

The emperor and his chosen brothers were approaching the base of the slope as Udinaas reached them. Their crossing of the field had stirred up a trail of dust that hung white and hesitant in their wake. Rhulad held his sword in his left hand, the blade wavering in the dim light. The uneven armour of gold was dark-tracked with sweat, the bear fur on the emperor's shoulders the muted silver of clouds.

Udinaas could see in Rhulad's face that the madness was close upon him. Frustration created a rage capable of lashing out in any direction. Behind the emperor, who began climbing up the slope to where Hannan Mosag waited, scrambled Theradas and Midik Buhn, Choram Irard, Kholb Harat and Matra Brith. All but Theradas had been old followers of Rhulad, and Udinaas was not pleased to see them. Nor, from the dark looks cast in his direction, were they delighted with the slave's arrival.

Udinaas almost laughed. *Just like the palace in Letheras, the factions take shape.*

As Udinaas moved to catch up to Rhulad – who'd yet to notice him – Theradas Buhn stepped into his path as if by accident, then straight-armed the slave in the chest. He stumbled back, lost his footing, and fell onto the slope, sliding back down to its base.

The Edur warriors laughed.

A mistake. The emperor spun round, eyes searching, recognizing Udinaas through the clouds of dust. It was not difficult to determine what had just happened. Rhulad glared at his brothers. 'Who struck down my slave?'

No-one moved, then Theradas said, 'We but crossed paths, sire. An accident.'

'Udinaas?'

The slave was picking himself up, brushing the dust from his tunic. 'It was as Theradas Buhn said, Emperor.'

Rhulad bared his teeth. 'A warning to you all. We will not be tried this day.' He wheeled round and resumed his climb.

Theradas glared at Udinaas, and said in a low voice, 'Do not believe I now owe you, slave.'

'You will discover,' the slave said, moving past the warrior, 'that the notion of debt is not so easily denied.'

Theradas reached for his cutlass, then let his hand drop with a silent snarl.

Rhulad reached the crest.

Those still below heard Hannan Mosag's smooth voice. 'The day is won, Emperor.'

'We found no-one left to fight!'

'The kingdom lies cowering at your feet, sire—'

'Thousands of Edur are *dead*, Warlock King! Demons, wraiths! How many Edur mothers and wives and children will weep this night? What glory rises from our dead, Hannan? From this . . . dust?'

Udinaas reached the summit. And saw Rhulad advancing upon the Warlock King, the sword lifting into the air.

Sudden fear in Hannan Mosag's red-rimmed eyes.

'Emperor!'

Rhulad whirled, burning eyes fixing upon Udinaas. 'We are challenged by our slave?' The sword-blade hissed through the air, although ten paces spanned the distance between them.

'No challenge,' Udinaas said quietly as he approached. Until he stood directly in front of the emperor. 'I but called out to inform you, sire, that your brothers are coming.' The slave pointed eastward, where figures were crossing the edge of the basin. 'Fear, Binadas and Trull, Emperor. And your father, Tomad.'

Rhulad squinted, blinking rapidly as he studied the distant warriors. 'Dust has blinded us, Udinaas. It is them?'

'Yes, Emperor.'

The Edur wiped at his eyes. 'Yes, that is well. Good, we would have them with us, now.'

'Sire,' Udinaas continued, 'a fragment of Letherii sorcery sought out the encampment of the women during the battle. Your mother and some others defeated the magic. Uruth is injured, but she will live. Three Hiroth women died.'

The emperor lowered the sword, the rage flickering in his frantic, bloodshot eyes, flickering, then fading. 'We sought battle, Udinaas. We sought . . . death.'

'I know, Emperor. Perhaps in Letheras . . .'

A shaky nod. 'Yes. Perhaps. Yes, Udinaas.' Rhulad's eyes suddenly bored into the slave's own. 'Those towers of bone, did you see them? The slaughter, their flesh . . .'

The slave's gaze shifted momentarily past the emperor, found Hannan Mosag. The Warlock King was staring at Rhulad's back with dark hatred. 'Sire,' Udinaas said in a low voice, 'your heart is true, to chastise Hannan Mosag. When your father and brothers arrive. Cold anger is stronger than hot rage.'

'Yes. We know this, slave.'

'The battle is over. All is done,' Udinaas said, glancing back over the field. 'Nothing can be . . . taken back. It seems the time has come to grieve.'

'We know such feelings, Udinaas. Grief. Yes. Yet what of cold anger? What of . . .'

The sword flinched, like a hackle rising, like lust awakened, and the slave saw nothing cold in Rhulad's eyes.

'He has felt its lash already, Emperor,' Udinaas said. 'All that remains is your disavowal . . . of what has just passed. Your brothers and your father will need to hear that, as you well know. From them, to all the Edur. To all the allies. To Uruth.' He added, in a rough whisper, 'They would complicate you, sire – those gathered and gathering even now about you and your power. But you see clear and true, for that is the terrible gift of pain.'

Rhulad was nodding, staring now at the approaching figures. 'Yes. Such a terrible gift. Clear and true . . .'

'Sire,' Hannan Mosag called out.

A casual wave of the sword was Rhulad's only response. 'Not now,' he said in a rasp, his gaze still fixed on his father and brothers.

Stung, face darkening with humiliation, the Warlock King said no more.

Udinaas turned and watched the warriors of the Sengar line begin the ascent. *Do not, slave, deny your own thoughts on this. That bastard Hannan Mosag needs to be killed. And soon.*

Theradas Buhn, standing nearby, then said, 'A great victory, sire.'

'We are pleased,' Rhulad said, 'that you would see it so, Theradas Buhn.'

Errant take me, the lad learns fast.

Reaching the crest, Binadas moved ahead and settled to one knee before Rhulad. 'Emperor.'

'Binadas, on this day were you ours, or were you Hannan Mosag's?'

Clear and true.

A confused expression as Binadas looked up. 'Sire, the army of Tomad Sengar has yet to find need for sorcery. Our conquests have been swift. The battle this morning was a fierce one, the decision uncertain for a time, but the Edur prevailed. We suffered losses, but that was to be expected – though no less regretted for that.'

'Rise, Binadas,' Rhulad said, sighing heavily beneath his gold armour.

Udinaas now saw that Hull Beddict was approaching in the wake of the Sengar warriors. He looked no better than before, walking like a man skull-cracked and half senseless. Udinaas felt some regret upon seeing his fellow Letherii, for he'd been hard on the man earlier.

Tomad spoke. 'Emperor, we have word from Uruth. She has recovered—'

'We are relieved,' Rhulad cut in. 'Her fallen sisters must be honoured.'

Tomad's brows rose slightly, then he nodded.

The emperor strode to Fear and Trull. 'Brothers, have the two Kenryll'ah returned?'

'No, sire,' Fear replied. 'Nor has the Forkrul Assail appeared. We must, I think, assume the hunt continues.'

This was good, Udinaas decided. Rhulad choosing to speak of things few others present knew about – reinforcing once more all that bound him to Fear and Trull. A display for Tomad, their father. For Binadas, who must now be feeling as if he stood on the narrowest of paths, balanced

827

between Rhulad and the Warlock King. And would soon have to choose.

Errant save us, what a mess awaits these Tiste Edur.

Rhulad set a hand on Trull's shoulder, then stepped past. 'Hull Beddict, hear us.'

The Letherii straightened, blinking, searching until his gaze found the emperor. 'Sire?'

'We grieve this day, Hull Beddict. These . . . ignoble deaths. We would rather this had been a day of honourable triumph, of courage and glory revealed on both sides. We would rather, Hull Beddict, this day had been . . . clean.'

Cold anger indeed. A greater mercy, perhaps, would have been a public beating of Hannan Mosag. The future was falling out here and now, Udinaas realized. *And was that my intention? Better, I think, had I let Rhulad cut the bastard down where he stood. Clean and simple – the only one fooled into believing those words is Rhulad himself. Here's two better words: vicious and subtle.*

'We would retire, until the morrow,' the emperor said. 'When we march to claim Letheras, and the throne we have won. Udinaas, attend me shortly. Tomad, at midnight the barrow for the fallen shall be ready for sanctification. Be sure to see the burial done in all honour. And, Father,' he added, 'those Letherii soldiers you fought this day, join them to the same barrow.'

'Sire—'

'Father, the Letherii are now our subjects, are they not?'

Udinaas stood to one side, watching various Edur departing the hilltop. Binadas spoke with Hannan Mosag for a time, then strode to Hull Beddict for the formal greeting of the blood-bound. Then Binadas guided the Letherii away.

Fear and Tomad departed to arrange the burial details. Theradas Buhn and the other chosen brothers set off for the Hiroth encampments.

In a short time, there were only two left. Udinaas, and Trull Sengar.

The Edur was studying the slave from about fifteen paces away, with sufficient intent to make the slave begin to feel nervous. Finally, Udinaas casually turned away, and stared out towards the hills to the south.

A dozen heartbeats later, Trull Sengar came to stand beside him.

'It seems,' the Edur said after a time, 'that you, for all that you are a slave, possess talents verging on genius.'

'Master?'

'Enough of this "master" shit, Udinaas. You are now a . . . what is the title? A chancellor of the realm? Principal Adviser, or some such thing?'

'First Eunuch, I think.'

Trull glanced over. 'I did not know you'd been—'

'I haven't. Consider it symbolic.'

'All right, I understand, I think. Tell me, are you so certain of yourself, Udinaas, that you would stand between Rhulad and Hannan Mosag? Between Rhulad and Theradas Buhn and those rabid pups who are the chosen brothers of the emperor? You would stand, indeed, between Rhulad and his own madness? Sister knows, I'd thought the Warlock King arrogant . . .'

'It is not arrogance, Trull Sengar. If it was, I'd be entirely as sure of myself as you seem to think I am. But I am not. Do you believe I have somehow manipulated myself into this position? By choice? Willingly? Tell me, when have any of us last had any meaningful choices? Including your young brother?'

The Edur said nothing for a while. Then he nodded. 'Very well. But, none the less, I must know your intentions.'

Udinaas shook his head. 'Nothing complicated, Trull Sengar. I do not want to see anyone hurt more than they already have been.'

'Including Hannan Mosag?'

'The Warlock King has not been hurt. But we have seen, this day, what he would deliver upon others.'

'Rhulad was . . . distressed?'

'Furious.' *But not, alas, for admirable reasons – no, he just wanted to fight, and die.* The other, more noble sentiments had been borrowed. *From me.*

'That answer leaves me feeling . . . relief, Udinaas.'

Which is why I gave it.

'Udinaas.'

'Yes?'

'I fear for what will come. In Letheras.'

'Yes.'

'I feel the world is about to unravel.'

Yes. 'Then we shall have to do our best, Trull Sengar, to hold it all together.'

The Tiste Edur's eyes held his, then Trull nodded. 'Beware your enemies, Udinaas.'

The slave did not reply. Alone once more, he studied the distant hills, the thinning smoke from the fires somewhere in the belly of the fallen keep rising like mocking shadows from earlier this day.

All these wars . . .

CHAPTER TWENTY-FOUR

Five wings will buy you a grovel,
There at the Errant's grubby toes
The eternal domicile crouching low
In a swamp of old where rivers ran out
And royal blood runs in the clearest stream
Around the stumps of rotted trees
Where forests once stood in majesty
Five roads from the Empty Hold
Will lay you flat on your back
With altar knives and silver chased
The buried rivers gnawing the roots
All aswirl in eager caverns beneath
Where kingly bones rock and clatter
In the silts, and five are the paths
To and from this chambered soul
For all you lost hearts bleeding out
Into the wilderness.

Day of the Domicile
Fintrothas (the Obscure)

The fresh, warm water of the river became the demon's blood, a vessel along which it climbed, the current pushing round it. Somewhere ahead, it now knew, lay a heart, a source of power at once strange and familiar. Its master knew nothing of it, else he would not have permitted the demon to draw ever closer, for

831

that power, once possessed, would snap the binding chains.

Something waited. In the buried courses that ran ceaselessly beneath the great city on the banks of the river. The demon was tasked with carrying the fleet of ships – an irritating presence plying the surface above – to the city. This would be sufficient proximity, the demon knew, to make the sudden lunge, to grasp that dread heart in its many hands. To feed, then rise, free once again and possessing the strength of ten gods. To rise, like an elder, from the raw, chaotic world of long ago. Dominant, unassailable, and burning with fury.

Through the river's dark silts, clambering like a vast crab, sifting centuries of secrets – the bed of an ancient river held so much, a multitude of tales written in layer upon layer of detritus. Muddy nets snagged upon older wreckage, sunken ships, the sprawl of ballast stones, ragged rows of sealed urns still holding their mundane riches. Bones rotting everywhere, gathered up in sinkholes where the currents swirled, and deeper still, in silts thick and hardening and swallowed in darkness, bones flattened by pressures and transformed into crystalline lattices, arrayed in skeletons of stone.

Even in death, the demon understood, nothing was still. Foolish mortals, short-lived and keen with frenzy, clearly believed otherwise, as they scrambled swift as thought above the patient dance of earth and stone. Water, of course, was capable of spanning the vast range of pace among all things. It could charge, out-running all else, and it could stand seemingly motionless. In this it displayed the sacred power of gods, yet it was, of itself, senseless.

The demon knew that such power could be harnessed. Gods had done so, making themselves lords of the seas. But it was the river that fed the seas. And springs from the layers of rock. The sea-gods were, in truth, subservient to those of the rivers and inland pools. The demon, the old spirit-god of the spring, intended to right the balance once more. With the power awaiting it beneath the city, even the gods of the sea would be made to kneel.

It savoured such thoughts, strange with clarity as they were – a clarity the demon had not possessed before. The taste of the river, perhaps, these bright currents, the rich seep from the shores. Intelligence burgeoning within it.

Such pleasure.

'Nice stopper.'

She turned and stared, and Tehol smiled innocently.

'If you are lying, Tehol Beddict . . .'

Brows lifted. 'I would never do that, Shurq.' Tehol rose from where he'd been sitting on the floor and began pacing in the small, cramped room. 'Selush, you have a right to be proud. Why, the way you tucked in the skin around the gem, not a crease to be seen—'

'Unless I frown,' Shurq Elalle said.

'Even then,' he replied, 'it would be a modest . . . pucker.'

'Well,' Shurq said, 'you'd know.'

Selush hastened to pack her supplies back into the bag. 'Oh, don't I know what's coming? A spat.'

'Express your gratitude, Shurq,' Tehol said.

Fingertips probing the gem in its silver setting in her forehead, Shurq Elalle hesitated, then sighed. 'Thank you, Selush.'

'Not the spat I was talking about,' the wild-haired woman said. 'Those Tisteans. They're coming. Lether has been conquered, and I dread the changes to come. Grey skin, that will be the new fashion – mark my words. But I must maintain my pragmatism,' she added, suddenly brightening. 'I'm already mixing a host of foundations to achieve that ghastly effect.' A pause, a glance over at Shurq Elalle. 'Working on you was very helpful, Shurq. I thought I'd call the first line *Dead Thief of the Night*.'

'Cute.'

'Nice.'

'But don't think that means you're taking a cut of my profits, Shurq.'

'I wouldn't dream of it.'

'I have to be going now,' Selush said, straightening with her bag slung over one shoulder. 'I intend to be hiding in my basement for the next few days. And I would advise the same for you two.'

Tehol looked round. 'I don't have a basement, Selush.'

'Well, it's the thought that counts, I always say. Goodbye!'

A swish of curtain and she was gone.

Shurq Elalle asked, 'How late is it?'

'Almost dawn.'

'Where's your manservant?'

'I don't know. Somewhere, I would think.'

'Really?'

Tehol clapped his hands. 'Let's head onto the roof. We can see if my silent bodyguard changes expression upon seeing your beauty.'

'What has he been doing up there all this time?'

'Probably standing directly above the doorway here, in case some unwelcome visitor arrived – which, fortunately, did not happen. Brys's messenger girl hardly qualified.'

'And what could he have done about some attacker from up there?'

'I imagine he would have flung himself straight down in a flurry of swords, knives and clubs, beating the intruder senseless in an instant. Either that, or he'd shout then run back to the ladder, climb down and exact revenge over our corpses.'

'Your corpse. Not mine.'

'You're right, of course. My mistake.'

'I am not surprised you are confused now, Tehol,' Shurq said, sweeping back her hair with both hands, the gesture admirably flinging out her chest. 'Given the pleasure you discovered in my wares earlier.'

'Your "wares" indeed. A good term to use, since it could mean virtually anything. Now, shall we head up to greet the dawn?'

'If you insist. I can't stay long. Ublala will be getting worried.'

'Harlest will advise him how the dead have no sense of time, Shurq. No need to fret.'

'He was muttering about dismembering Harlest just before I left them.'

They walked to the ladder, Shurq taking the lead.

'I thought he was trapped in a sarcophagus,' Tehol pointed out.

'We could still hear him. Dramatic hissing and scratching on the underside of the lid. It was, even for me, somewhat irritating.'

'Well, let's hope Ublala did nothing untoward.'

They climbed.

The sky was paling to the east, but a chill remained in the air. The bodyguard stood facing them until he had their attention, then he pointed towards the river.

The Edur fleet crowded the span, hundreds of raider craft and transports, a dark sweep of sails. Among the lead ships, oars had appeared, sliding out from the flanks of the hulls. The landings would begin within the bell.

Tehol studied them for a moment, then he faced northwest. The white columns of the battle the day before were gone, although a stain of dark smoke from the keep lingered, lit high above the horizon by the sun's first shafts. Above the west road was a streak of dust, drawing closer as the sun rose.

It was some time before either Tehol or Shurq spoke, then the latter turned away and said, 'I have to go.'

'Stay low,' Tehol said.

She paused at the top of the ladder. 'And you, Tehol Beddict, stay here. On this roof. With that guard standing close.'

'Sound plan, Shurq Elalle.'

'Given the chance, Gerun Eberict will come for you.'

'And you.'

835

From the far west gate, a raucous flurry of bells announced the approach of the Edur army.

The thief disappeared down through the hatch.

Tehol stood facing west. His back grew warmer, and he knew that this day would be a hot one.

One of her hands rested on the king's shoulder, but Brys could see that Nisall was near collapse. She had stood vigil over Ezgara Diskanar most of the night, as if love alone could guard the man against all dangers. Exhaustion had taken the king into sleep, and he now sat the throne like a corpse, slumped, head lolling. The crown had fallen off some time in the night and was lying beside the throne on the dais.

The Chancellor, Triban Gnol, had been present earlier but had left with the last change of guards. Ghost-like since the loss of the queen and the prince, and Turudal Brizad, he had grown suddenly ancient and withered, drifting down corridors speaking to no-one.

Finadd Moroch Nevath had disappeared, although Brys trusted that the swordsman would arrive when the time came. For all that he had suffered, he was a brave man and none of the rumours concerning his conduct at High Fort were, to Brys's mind, worth the spit needed to utter them.

First Eunuch Nifadas, along with Brys Beddict, had assumed the responsibility for what remained of the soldiers in the palace. Each wing entranceway was now barricaded by at least thirty guards, with the exception of the King's Path, where the Ceda in his madness had forbidden anyone to remain, barring himself. In the city beyond, Finadd Gerun Eberict and the city garrison were positioned throughout Letheras, their numbers insufficient to hold the gates or walls yet prepared to fight none the less – at least, Brys assumed that was the case, since he had not left the throne room in some time, and Gerun had not reappeared since the man assumed command of the garrison.

Spelled by Nifadas, the King's Champion had rested

836

on a bench near the throne room's grand entrance, managing a half-dozen bells of surprisingly sound sleep. Servants had awakened him with breakfast, beginning the day to come with surreal normality. Chilled in sweat-damp clothes beneath his armour, Brys quickly ate, then rose and walked to where Nifadas sat at the bench opposite.

'First Eunuch, it is time for you to rest.'

'Champion, there is no need for that. I have done very little and am not in the least fatigued.'

Brys studied the man's eyes. They were sharp and alert, quite unlike the usual sleepy regard with which Nifadas commonly presented. 'Very well,' he said.

The First Eunuch smiled up at him. 'Our last day, Finadd.'

Brys frowned. 'There is no reason to assume, Nifadas, that the Edur will see cause to take your life. As with the Chancellor, your knowledge will be needed.'

'Knowledge, yes. A worthy assumption, Finadd.'

The First Eunuch added nothing more.

Brys glanced back at the throne, then strode towards it. He came close to Nisall. 'First Concubine, he will sleep a while yet.' He took her arm. 'Don't worry,' he said as she began to resist, 'just to that bench over there. No further.'

'How, Brys? How could it all collapse? So fast? I don't understand.'

He remembered back to the secret meetings, where Nisall and Unnutal Hebaz and Nifadas and the king planned their moves and countermoves in the all-devouring games of intrigue within the Royal Household. Her confidence then had seemed unassailable, the cleverness bright in her eyes. He remembered how the Letherii saw the Tiste Edur and their lands, a pearl ripe for the plucking. 'I don't know, Nisall.'

She let him guide her down from the dais. 'It seems so . . . quiet. Has the day begun?'

'The sun has risen, yes.'

'He won't leave the throne.'

'I know.'

'He is . . . frightened.'

'Here, Nisall, lie down here. Use these cushions. Not ideal, I know—'

'No, it's fine. Thank you.'

Her eyes closed as soon as she settled. Brys stared down at her for a moment. She was already sleeping.

He swung round and walked down to the grand entrance, strode into the low-ceilinged corridor where he intended to make his stand. Just beyond, the Ceda was lying, curled up in sleep, on the centre tile.

And standing near Kuru Qan was Gerun Eberict. With sword in hand. Staring down at the Ceda.

Brys edged closer. 'Finadd.'

Gerun looked up, expressionless.

'The King's Leave does not absolve you from all things, Gerun Eberict.'

The man bared his teeth. 'He has lost his mind, Brys. It would be a mercy.'

'Not for you to judge.'

Gerun cocked his head. 'You would oppose me in this?'

'Yes.'

After a moment, the Finadd stepped back, sliding his sword back into the scabbard at his hip. 'Well timed, then. Ten heartbeats later . . .'

'What are you doing here?' Brys asked.

'My soldiers are all in position. What else would you have me do?'

'Command them.'

A whistling snort from him, then, 'I have other tasks awaiting me this day.'

Brys was silent. Wondering if he should kill the man now.

It seemed Gerun guessed his thoughts, for his scarred sneer broadened. 'Recall your responsibilities, Brys Beddict.' He gestured and a dozen of his own estate guards strode into the chamber. 'You are supposed to die defending

838

the king, after all. In any case,' he added as he slowly backed away, 'you have just confirmed my suspicions, and for that I thank you.'

Blood or honour. 'I know what you believe, Gerun Eberict. And so I warn you now, you will not be permitted the Leave in this.'

'You speak for the king? Brys Beddict, that is rather presumptuous of you, don't you think?'

'The king expects you to command the garrison in defence of the city – not abandon your responsibilities in order to conduct your own crusade.'

'Defence of the city? Don't be an idiot, Brys. If the garrison seeks heroic final stands it is welcome to them. I intend to survive this damned conquest. The Tiste Edur do not frighten me in the least.' He turned about then and, surrounded by his guards, left the chamber.

Blood or honour. *I have no choice in this, Tehol. I'm sorry.*

Bugg was not entirely surprised to find himself virtually alone on the wall. His ascent had not been challenged, since it seemed all the garrison guards had withdrawn to various choke-points in the city. Whether those soldiers would rise to stubborn defence remained to be seen, of course. In any case, their presence had kept the streets empty for the most part.

The manservant leaned on a merlon and watched the Edur army approach down the west road. An occasional glance to his left allowed him to monitor the closing of the fleet, and the vast, deadly demon beneath it – a presence spanning the width of the river and stretching back downstream almost half a league. A terrible, brutal creature straining at its sorcerous chains.

The west gate was open and unguarded. The lead elements of the Edur army had closed to within a thousand paces, advancing with caution. Ranging to either side of the column, in the ditches and across the fields, the first of the Soletaken wolves came into view.

Bugg sighed, looked over at the other occupant along the wall. 'You will have to work fast, I think.'

The artist was a well-known and easily recognized figure in Letheras. A mass of hair that began on his head and swept down to join with the wild beard covering jaw and neck, his nub of a nose and small blue eyes the only visible features on his face. He was short and wiry, and painted with agitated capering – often perched on one leg – smearing paint on surfaces that always seemed too small for the image he was seeking to capture. This failing of perspective had long since been elevated into a technique, then a legitimate style, in so far as artistic styles could be legitimate. At Bugg's comment he scowled and rose up on one leg, the foot of the other against the knee. 'The scene, you fool! It is burned into my mind, here behind this eye, the left one. I forget nothing. Every detail. Historians will praise my work this day, you'll see. Praise!'

'Are you done, then?'

'Very nearly, very very nearly, yes, nearly done. Every detail. I have done it again. That's what they will say. Yes, I have done it again.'

'May I see?'

Sudden suspicion.

Bugg added, 'I am something of an historian myself.'

'You are? Have I read you? Are you famous?'

'Famous? Probably. But I doubt you've read me, since I've yet to write anything down.'

'Ah, a lecturer!'

'A scholar, swimming across the ocean of history.'

'I like that. I could paint that.'

'So, may I see your painting?'

A grand gesture with a multicoloured hand. 'Come along, then, old friend. See my genius for yourself.'

The board perched on its easel was wider than it was high, in the manner of a landscape painting or, indeed, a record of some momentous vista of history. At least two arm-lengths wide. Bugg walked round for a look at the image captured on the surface.

And saw two colours, divided in a rough diagonal. Scratchy red to the right, muddy brown to the left. 'Extraordinary,' Bugg said. 'And what is it you have rendered here?'

'What is it? Are you blind?' The painter pointed with a brush. 'The column! Those approaching Edur, the vast army! The standard, of course. The standard!'

Bugg squinted across the distance to the tiny patch of red that was the vanguard's lead standard. 'Ah, of course. Now I see.'

'And my brilliance blinds you, yes?'

'Oh yes, all comprehension has been stolen from my eyes indeed.'

The artist deftly switched legs and perched pensively, frowning out at the Edur column. 'Of course, they're closer now. I wish I'd brought another board, so I could elaborate yet further on the detail.'

'Well, you could always use this wall.'

Bushy brows arched. 'That's . . . clever. You are a scholar indeed.'

'I must be going, now.'

'Yes, yes, stop distracting me. I need to focus, you know. Focus.'

Bugg quietly made his way down the stone stairs. 'A fine lesson,' he muttered under his breath as he reached street level. Details . . . so many things to do this day.

He walked deserted streets, avoiding the major inter-sections where barricades had been raised and soldiers moved about in nervous expectation. The occasional furtive figure darted into and out of view as he went on.

A short time later the manservant rounded a corner, paused, then approached the ruined temple. Standing near it was Turudal Brizad, who looked over as Bugg reached his side.

'Any suggestions?' the god known as the Errant asked.

'What do you mean?'

841

'The mortal I requested for this task has not appeared.'

'Oh. That's not good, since the Jheck are at the gates even as we speak.'

'And the first Edur from the ships have disembarked, yes.'

'Why not act for yourself?' Bugg asked.

'I cannot. My aspect enforces certain . . . prohibitions.'

'Ah, the nudge, the pull or the push.'

'Yes, only that.'

'You have been about as direct as you can be.'

The Errant nodded.

'Well, I see your dilemma,' Bugg said.

'Thus my query – do you have any suggestions?'

The manservant considered for a time, whilst the god waited patiently, then he sighed and said, 'Perhaps. Wait here. If I am successful, I will send someone to you.'

'All right. I trust you will not be overlong.'

'I hope not. Depends on my powers of persuasion.'

'Then I am encouraged.'

Without another word, Bugg headed off. He quickened his pace as he made his way towards the docks. Fortunately, it was not far, and he arrived at Front Street to see that only the main piers had been commandeered by the landing warriors of the Tiste Edur. They were taking their time, he noted, a sign of their confidence. No-one was opposing their landing. Bugg hurried along Front Street until he came to the lesser berths. Where he found his destination, a two-masted, sleek colt of a ship that needed new paint but seemed otherwise relatively sound. There was no-one visible on its deck, but as soon as he crossed the gangway he heard voices, then the thump of boots.

Bugg had reached the mid-deck when the cabin door swung open and two armed women emerged, swords out.

Bugg halted and held up his hands.

Three more figures appeared once the two women stepped to either side. A tall, grey-maned man in a crimson surcoat, and a second man who was clearly a mage of some sort. The third arrival Bugg recognized.

'Good morning, Shand. So this is where Tehol sent you.'

'Bugg. What in the Errant's name do you want?'

'Well said, lass. And are these fine soldiers Shurq Elalle's newly hired crew?'

'Who is this man?' the grey-haired man asked Shand.

She scowled. 'My employer's manservant. And your employer works for my employer. His arrival means there's going to be trouble. Go on, Bugg, we're listening.'

'First, how about some introductions, Shand?'

She rolled her eyes. 'Iron Bars—'

'An Avowed of the Crimson Guard,' Bugg cut in, smiling. 'Forgive me. Go on, please.'

'Corlo—'

'His High Mage. Again, forgive me, but that will have to do. I have very little time. I need these Guardsmen.'

'You need us for what?' Iron Bars asked.

'You have to kill the god of the Soletaken Jheck.'

The Avowed's expression darkened. 'Soletaken. We've crossed paths with Soletaken before.'

Bugg nodded. 'If the Jheck reach their god, they will of course protect it—'

'How far away?'

'Just a few streets, in an abandoned temple.'

Iron Bars nodded. 'This god, is it Soletaken or D'ivers?'

'D'ivers.'

The Avowed turned to Corlo, who said, 'Ready up, soldiers, we've some fighting ahead.'

Shand stared at them. 'What do I tell Shurq if she shows up in the meantime?'

'We won't be long,' Iron Bars said, drawing his sword.

'Wait!' Shand swung to Bugg. 'You! How did you know they'd be here?'

The manservant shrugged. 'Errant's nudge, I suppose. Take care, Shand, and say hello to Hejun and Rissarh for me, won't you?'

843

* * *

Fifty paces' worth of empty cobbled road between them and the yawning gates of Letheras. Trull Sengar leaned on his spear and glanced over at Rhulad.

The emperor, fur-shouldered and hulking, was pacing like a beast, eyes fixed on the gateway. Hannan Mosag and his surviving K'risnan had advanced ten paces in the midst of shadow wraiths, the latter now sliding forward.

The wraiths reached the gate, hovered a moment, then swept into the city.

Hannan Mosag turned and strode back to where the emperor and his brothers waited. 'It is as we sensed, Emperor. The Ceda's presence is nowhere to be found. There are but a handful of minor mages among the garrison. The wraiths and demons will take care of them. We should be able to carve our way through the barricades and reach the Eternal Domicile by noon. A fitting time for you to ascend the throne.'

'Barricades,' Rhulad said, nodding. 'Good. We wish to fight. Udinaas!'

'Here.' The slave stepped forward.

'This time, Udinaas, you will accompany the Household, under Uruth's charge.'

'Emperor?'

'We shall not risk you, Udinaas. Should we fall, however, you will be sent to us immediately.'

The slave bowed and stepped back.

Rhulad swung to where stood his father and three brothers. 'We shall enter Letheras now. We shall claim our empire. Ready your weapons, blood of ours.'

They began moving forward.

Trull's gaze held on Hannan Mosag for a moment longer, wondering what the Warlock King was hiding, then he followed his brothers.

Hull Beddict was among the second company to enter Letheras, and twenty paces in from the gate he stepped to one side and halted, watching as the wary Edur marched on. None paid him any attention. From the nearby buildings, pallid faces looked down from windows and through slightly parted shutters. From out over the docks gulls wheeled and cried out in a cacophony of panic. Somewhere ahead, down the main avenue, the fighting began at the first barricade. There was a thump of sorcery, then screams.

A meaningless waste of life. He hoped not all the garrison soldiers would be so foolishly brave. There was no longer any reason for fighting. Lether was conquered. All that was left was to depose the ineffectual king and his treacherous advisers. The one truly just act of this war, as far as Hull Beddict was concerned.

His grieving for his brother Brys was done. Although Brys was not yet dead, his death was none the less as certain an outcome as could exist. The King's Champion would die defending the king. It was tragic, and unnecessary, but it would be the last tradition acted out by the Letherii, and nothing Hull or anyone else could do or say would prevent it.

All the ashes had settled in Hull's mind. The slaughter behind them, the murder waiting ahead of them. He had betrayed, to see an end to the corrupt insanity of his people. That the victory demanded the death of Brys offered the final layer of ash to shroud Hull's soul. There would be no absolution.

Even so, one responsibility remained with Hull. As the third company of Tiste Edur entered through the gates, he turned and made his way down a side alley.

He needed to speak to Tehol. To explain things. To tell his brother that he knew of the deceptions, the schemes. Tehol was, he hoped, the one man in Letheras who would not hate Hull for what he had done. He needed to speak to him.

He needed something like forgiveness.

For not being there to save their parents all those years ago.

For not being there to save Brys now.

Forgiveness, a simple thing.

Udinaas stood among the other slaves of the Sengar house-hold, awaiting their turn to enter Letheras. Word had already come that there was fighting ahead, somewhere. Uruth stood nearby, and with her was Mayen, wrapped in a heavy cloak, her face looking ravaged, eyes like a thing hunted. Uruth remained close, as if fearing an escape attempt from the younger woman. Not out of compassion for Mayen, however. The child was all that mattered now.

Poor Mayen.

He knew how she felt. Something like a fever gripped him, an urgency in his blood. Sweat trickled down his body beneath his tunic. His skin felt on fire. He held himself still, on the edge, he feared, of losing control.

The sensation had come on suddenly, like an inner wave of panic, a faceless terror. Worsening—

Head spinning, it was a moment before he realized what was happening. Then horror flooded through Udinaas.

The Wyval.

It was coming to life within him.

B'nagga in the lead, the Jheck entered the city. Soletaken, loping with heads sunk low, one and all seeking the scent of their god. And finding it within the fear-sour currents drifting through Letheras, an impatience, a sentience con-sumed with rage.

Gleeful howls, rising to fill the city, reverberating down the streets, from over nine thousand wolves. Striking terror amongst cowering citizens. Nine thousand wolves, white-furred, racing on a score of convergent routes towards the old temple, an inward rush of bestial madness.

B'nagga joined his voice to the chilling howls, his heart filled with savage joy. The Pack awaited them. Demons, wraiths, Tiste Edur and damned emperors were as nothing now. Momentary allies of convenience. What would rise here in Letheras was the ascension of the Jheck. An empire of Soletaken, with a god-emperor upon the throne. Rhulad torn to pieces, every Edur sundered into bloody, sweet-tasting meat, rich marrow from split bones, skulls broken open, brains devoured.

This day would end in such slaughter that none who survived would forget.

This day, B'nagga told himself with a silent laugh, belonged to the Jheck.

Seventy-three of his company's finest soldiers formed a shield wall behind Moroch Nevath. They held the principal bridge crossing Main Canal, a suitable site for this pathetic drama. Best of all, the Third Tiers were arrayed behind them, on which citizens had now appeared. Spectators – a Letherii talent. No doubt wagers were being made, and at least Moroch Nevath would have an audience.

The hooded looks, the rumours of his cowardice at High Fort, would cease this day. It wasn't much, but it would suffice.

He recalled he had promised to do something for Turudal Brizad, but the man's outrageous claims had not quite convinced Moroch. Tales of gods and such, coming from a painted consort at that, well, that would have to wait another day, another lifetime. Leave the foppish lover of the lost queen and that obnoxious chancellor to fight his own battles. Moroch wanted to cross blades with the Tiste Edur.

If they let him. A squalid death beneath a wave of sorcery was more likely.

A grunt from one of his soldiers.

Moroch nodded, seeing the first of the Edur approaching from the main avenue. 'Hold that shield wall,' he said in a growl, moving to stand five paces in front of it. 'It's a small company – let's send their souls to the Errant's piss-hole.'

In answer to his bold words, shouts from the soldiers,

voices made ugly with blood-lust. Swords hammering shield-rims.

Moroch smiled. *They've seen us*. 'Look at them, comrades – see how they hesitate.'

Bellowed challenges from the soldiers.

The Tiste Edur resumed their march. In their lead, a warrior draped in gold.

Whom Moroch had seen before. 'Errant bless me,' he whispered, then spun round. 'The emperor! The one in gold!' And turned back, taking four more strides until he was at the very edge of the bridge. Raising his sword. 'Rhulad of the Edur!' he shouted. 'Come and face me, you damned freak! Come forward and die!'

Bugg pointed down the street. 'See that man? That's Turudal Brizad. That is who you are doing this favour for. If he's not grateful, give him an earful. I have to get going, but I will be back shortly—'

The air filled suddenly with howling, coming from the north and west.

'Oh, damn,' Bugg said. 'You'd better get going. And I'd better stay too,' he added, heading off towards the Errant.

'Corlo,' Iron Bars snapped as they followed the manservant.

'Oh, it's befuddled, some, Avowed. Can't hear a thing besides.'

Iron Bars nodded. 'Weapons ready. We're wasting no time on this. How many in there, Corlo?'

'Six, their favourite number.'

'Let's go.'

Bugg had moved ahead and was fifteen paces from Turudal, who had turned to face him, when the Avowed and his squad thumped past, gaining speed.

As they closed on the Errant the god, brows lifting, pointed towards the entrance to the ruined temple.

The Crimson Guardsmen shifted course, reaching full sprint as they passed Turudal Brizad.

Bugg heard Iron Bars say to the god, 'Pleased-to-meet-you-see-you-later,' and then the Avowed and his soldiers were past. Straight for the dark entrance, then plunging inside.

Bestial screams, human shouts, the deafening thunder of sorcery—

'He's mine!' Rhulad said in a snarl, lifting his sword and stalking towards the lone Letherii swordsman at this end of the bridge.

Hannan Mosag called, 'Emperor! Leave these to my K'risnan—'

Rhulad spun round. '*No!*' he shrieked. 'We shall fight! We are warriors! These Letherii deserve to die honourably! We will hear nothing more from you!' The emperor swung back. 'This, this brave swordsman. *I want him.*'

Beside Trull, Fear muttered, 'He wants to be killed by him. I recognize that Letherii. He was with the delegation.'

Trull nodded. The Finadd, a Letherii captain and bodyguard to Prince Quillas – he could not recall the man's name.

It was clear that Rhulad had not recognized him.

Mottled sword held at the ready, the emperor approached.

Moroch Nevath smiled. Rhulad Sengar, who had died, only to return. If the rumours were true, he had died again in Trate. *But this time, I will make him stay dead. I will cut him to pieces.* He waited, watching the emperor's approach.

Favouring the right side, the right foot edging ahead of the other, a detail telling Moroch that Rhulad had been trained to use a single-handed sword, rather than this two-handed monstrosity now wavering about before him like an oversized club.

The sudden charge was not unexpected, only the speed of that weapon as the blade whirled towards Moroch's head. He barely managed to avoid getting his skull sliced in half, ducking and pitching to his right. A deafening clang, the shock ripping through him as the sword bit into his helmet, caught, then tore it from his head.

Moroch sprang back, staying as low as possible, then straightened once more. The top third of his own sword was slick with blood. He had met the charge with a stop-hit.

Opposite him, Rhulad staggered back, blood pulsing from his right thigh.

The lead leg was always vulnerable.

Let's see you dance now, Emperor.

Moroch shook off the numbing effects of the blow to his head. Muscles and tendons in his neck and back were screaming silent pain, and he knew that he had taken damage. For the moment, however, neither arm had seized in answer to the trauma.

A shriek, as Rhulad attacked once more.

Two-handed thrust, broken timing – a moment's hesitation, sufficient to avoid Moroch's all-too-quick parry – then finishing in a full lunge.

The Finadd twisted his body in an effort to avoid the sword-point. Searing fire above his right hip as the mottled blade's edge sawed deep. A wet, red rush, spraying out to the side. Now inside the weapon's reach, Moroch drove his own sword in from a sharp angle, stabbing the tip into the emperor's left armpit. The bite of gold coin, the grating resistance of ribs, then inward, gouging along the inside of Rhulad's shoulder blade, striving for the spine.

The mottled sword seemed to leap with a will of its own, reversing grip, hands lifting high, point down. A diagonal thrust, entering above Moroch's right hip bone, down through his groin.

Rhulad pushed down from the grip end, the point chewing through the Finadd's lower intestines, until the pommel clunked on the paving stones beneath them, then the emperor straightened, pushing the weapon back up, through Moroch's torso, alongside his heart, through his left lung, the point bursting free just behind his clavicle on that side.

Dying, Moroch threw the last of his strength against his own weapon, seeing Rhulad bow around its embedded point. Then a snap, as the emperor's spine broke.

Crimson smile broadening, Moroch Nevath sagged to the slick stones, even as Rhulad pitched down.

Another figure loomed over him, then. One of Rhulad's brothers.

Who spoke as if from a long distance away. 'Tell me your name, Finadd.'

Moroch sought to answer, but he was drowning in blood. *I am Moroch Nevath. And I have killed your damned emperor.*

'Are you the King's Champion in truth? Your soldiers on the bridge seem to be yelling that – King's Champion . . . is that who you are, Finadd?'

No.

You bastards have not met him yet.

With that pleasing thought, Moroch Nevath died.

So swift the healing, so terribly swift the return of life. Surrounded by the wolf howls reverberating through Letheras in a chorus of the damned, the emperor voiced a scream that tore the air.

The company of soldiers on the bridge were silenced, staring as Rhulad, sheathed in blood, staggered upright, tugging the sword from the Finadd's body, then skidding with a lurch as he stepped to one side. Righting himself, his eyes filled with madness and terror.

'Udinaas!'

Desperately alone. A soul writhing in agony.

'Udinaas!'

Two hundred paces away on the main avenue, Uruth Sengar heard her son's frantic cry. She spun, seeking the slave among those walking in her wake. At that moment,

Mayen shrieked, pushed her way clear of the other women, and was suddenly running – into an alley. And gone.

Frozen, Uruth hesitated, then with a hiss returned her attention to the slaves cowering in front of her.

'Udinaas! Where are you?'

Blank, terrified looks met her. Familiar faces one and all. But among them, nowhere could she find Udinaas.

The slave was gone.

Uruth plunged among them, fists flailing. 'Find him! *Find Udinaas!*'

A sudden hate raged through her. For Udinaas. For all the Letherii.

Betrayed. My son is betrayed.

Oh, how they would pay.

She could hear sounds of fighting now throughout the city, as the invaders poured into the streets and were met by desperate soldiers. Frightened, moving about from one place of cover to the next in the overgrown yard, the child Kettle began to cry. She was alone.

The five killers were almost free. Their barrow was breaking apart, thick fissures welling in the dark, wet earth, submerged rocks grinding and snapping together. The muted sounds of five voices joined in a chant as heavy as drums . . . rising, coming ever closer to the surface.

'Oh,' she moaned, 'where is everybody? Where are my friends?'

Kettle staggered over to the barrow containing her only ally. He was there, so very close. She reached down—

—and was dragged in, a heaving passage of hot soil, then through, stumbling, slipping on a muddy bank. Before her sprawled a fetid swamp beneath a grey sky.

And, almost within arm's reach, a figure was climbing from the dark water. White-skinned, long hair smeared with mud. 'Kettle!' The voice a strained grasp. 'Behind you – reach—'

She turned round.

Two swords, points thrust into the mud.

'Kettle – take them – give them—'

A wet gasp, and she spun back, to see the bared arms of another figure, clawing up to wrap about her friend – a woman's arms, lean, ribboned in muscle. He was dragged back – she saw him drive an elbow into the fiercely twisting, black-streaked face that rose suddenly from the slime. Connecting hard in a splatter of blood. But the clutching hands would not let go.

And they both sank back into the swirling foam.

Whimpering, Kettle crawled over to the swords. She tugged them from the mud, then clambered back to the water's edge.

Limbs appeared amidst the thrashing waves.

Shivering, Kettle waited.

So easy, now, a slave once more, as the Wyval suffused his body, stealing the will of every muscle, every organ, the charging blood in his veins. Udinaas could barely see through his own eyes, as street after street blurred past. Sudden moments of brutal clarity, as he came upon three Soletaken wolves – which turned as one with snarls and bared fangs – and was among them, his hands now talons, the thumb-long claws tearing into wolf-flesh, curling round ribs and ripping them loose. A massive, gnarled fist, slamming into the side of a lunging, snapping head, breaking bone – the wolf's head suddenly lolling, the eyes blank in death.

Then, motion once more.

His master needed him. Needed him now. No time to lose.

A slave. Absolved of all responsibility, nothing more than a tool.

And this, Udinaas knew, was the poison of surrender.

Close, now, and closing.

There is nothing new in being used. Look upon these sprawled corpses, after all. Poor Letherii soldiers lying dead for no reason.

Defending the corpse of a kingdom, citizens once more every one of them. The kingdom that does not move, the kingdom in service to the god of dust – you will find the temples in crooked alleys, in the cracks between cobbles.

You will find, my friends, no sweeter world than this, where honour and faith and freedom are notions levelled one and all, layers as thin as hate, envy and betrayal. Every notion vulnerable to any sordid breeze, stirred up, stirred together. A world without demands to challenge the confused haze of holy apathy.

The god of dust rises dominant—

Ahead, a dozen wolves, charging straight for him.

There would, it seemed, be a delay.

Udinaas bared his teeth.

'How are you managing it?' Bugg asked.

The Errant glanced over. 'The wolves?'

'They're everywhere but here, and they should have arrived long ago.'

The god shrugged. 'I keep nudging them away. It's not as difficult as I feared, although their leader is too clever by far – much harder to deceive. Besides, the beasts keep running into other . . . opposition.'

'What kind of opposition?'

'Other.'

The shouts from within the temple ceased then. Silence, no movement from the dark doorway. A half-dozen heart-beats, then, a muttering of voices and swearing.

The mage, Corlo, appeared, backing out and dragging a limp body in his wake, a body leaving twin trails of blood from its heels.

Concerned, Bugg stepped forward. 'Is she alive?'

Corlo, himself a mass of cuts and bruises, cast the manservant a slightly wild look. 'No, dammit.'

'I am sorry for that,' the Errant murmured.

More Guardsmen were emerging from the doorway. All were wounded, one of them badly, his left arm torn loose at the shoulder and dangling from a few pink-white tendons. His eyes were glazed with shock.

Corlo glared at Turudal Brizad. 'Can you do any healing? Before the rest of us bleed out—'

Iron Bars stepped from the ruined temple, sheathing his sword. He was covered in blood but none of it was his. His expression was alarmingly dark. 'We were expecting wolves, damn you,' he said in a low growl as he stared at the Errant, who had closed to lay hands upon the most grievously injured soldier, raising new flesh to bind the arm once more to the shoulder as the soldier's face twisted with pain.

Turudal Brizad shrugged. 'There was little time to elaborate on what you were about to fight, Avowed. In case you have forgotten.'

'Damned cats,' he said.

'Lizard cats, you mean,' one of the Guardsmen said, spitting blood onto the street. 'Sometimes I think nature is insane.'

'You got that right, Halfpeck,' Corlo said, reaching down to close the eyelids of the dead woman lying at his feet.

Iron Bars suddenly moved, a blur, past the Errant, both hands lifting—

—as a huge white wolf, claws skittering, pitched round from an alley mouth and, head ducking, lunged towards Turudal Brizad, who had only just begun to turn round.

The Avowed caught it in mid-leap, left hand closing on its right leg just beneath the shoulder, right hand clutching its neck beneath the beast's jaws. He heaved the wolf high, pivoted and smashed it head first onto the street. Crushing snout, skull and shoulders. Limbs kicking spasmodically, the Soletaken flopped onto its back, yellow vomit spurting, urine arcing as it died. A moment later, all movement from the limbs ceased, although the urine continued to stream, the arc dwindling, then collapsing.

Iron Bars stepped back.

Halfpeck suddenly laughed. 'It pissed on you!'

'Be quiet,' Iron Bars said, looking down at his wet legs. 'Hood take me, that stinks.'

'We should get back to the ship,' Corlo said. 'There's wolves all over the place and I don't think I can keep them away much longer.'

Turudal Brizad; 'But I can. Especially now.'

Bugg asked, 'What's changed, apart from the Pack getting chopped to pieces?'

The Errant pointed down at the dead Soletaken. 'That was B'nagga, the leader of the Jheck.' He shot Bugg a look, astonished and half disbelieving. 'You chose well,' he said.

'This squad managed to escape Assail,' Bugg said, shrugging.

The god's eyes widened. He turned to Iron Bars. 'I will ensure you a clear path to your ship—'

'Oh, damn,' Bugg cut in, slowly turning. 'They're getting out.'

'More trouble?' Iron Bars asked, looking round, his hand drifting close to the sword at his hip.

'Not here,' Bugg said. 'But not far.' He faced the Avowed, gauging.

Iron Bars frowned, then said, 'Corlo, take the squad back to the ship. All right, old man, lead the way.'

'You don't have to do this—'

'Yes I do. With that wolf pissing on me I feel the need to lose my temper. It's another fight, isn't it?'

Bugg nodded. 'Might make the Pack seem like kittens, Iron Bars.'

'Might? Will it or won't it?'

'All right, we might well lose this one.'

'Fine,' the Avowed snapped. 'Let's get it over with.'

The manservant sighed. 'Follow me, then. It's a dead Azath House we're heading to.'

'Dead? Hood take me, a garden fête.'

A garden fête? Dear me, I like this man. 'And we're inviting ourselves, Avowed. Still with me?'

Iron Bars looked across at Corlo, who had stopped to

listen, his face bloodless as he repeatedly shook his head in denial. The Avowed grunted. 'Once you've dropped 'em off, come and find us, Corlo. And try and make your arrival timely.'

'Avowed—'

'Go.'

Bugg glanced at the Errant. 'You coming?'

'In spirit,' he replied. 'There is another matter I must attend to, I am afraid. Oh,' he added as Bugg and Iron Bars turned to go, 'dear manservant, I thank you. And you as well, Avowed. Tell me, Iron Bars, how many of the Avowed remain among the Crimson Guard?'

'No idea. A few hundred, I'd imagine.'

'Scattered here and there . . .'

The grey-haired soldier smiled. 'For the moment.'

Bugg said, 'We shall have to run, I think.'

'Can you keep up?' Iron Bars asked.

'As swift as a charging wave, that's me,' Bugg said.

Brys stood alone in the corridor. The howling was, thankfully, over. It was the only sound that had managed to penetrate the walls. There was no way to know if the garrison was fighting in the city beyond the Eternal Domicile. It seemed such a pointless thing . . .

His breath caught upon hearing a strange sound. Brys lowered his gaze, fixed it upon the Ceda, who was lying curled tight in the chamber beyond, with his back to Brys and the throne room behind him.

Kuru Qan's head shifted slightly, then rose a fraction from the floor.

And, from the Ceda, there came low laughter.

The path was unmistakable. Keening with glee, the demon drew itself to the cave's entrance, contracting its massive, corpulent presence, the bloated flesh of its body, away from the river's broad span. Inward, gathering, hovering before the tunnel beneath the city, where old swamp water still flowed, putrid and sweet, a flavour like sweet nectar to the demon.

Ready now, at last, for the lunge, the breaking away from the grip of its master. Who was so regrettably preoccupied at the moment.

Now.

Surging forward, filling the cave, then into the narrow, twisting tunnel.

To the heart. The wondrous, blessed heart of power.

Joy and hunger burning like twin fires within it. Close, so close now.

Squirming down, the path narrowing, squeezing with the vast pressure of overlying stone and earth. A little further.

Reaching out, the space suddenly opening, blissfully wide and high, spreading out to all sides, the water welcoming in its warmth.

A storm of long-still silts sweeping up, blinding, shadows of dead things cavorting before its countless eyes.

The heart, the enormous cavern beneath the lake, the city's very soul – the power—

And Brys heard Kuru Qan speak.

'Now, friend Bugg.'

Thirty paces from the overgrown yard of the Azath tower, Bugg skidded to a halt. He cocked his head, then smiled.

Ahead, Iron Bars slowed, then turned round. 'What?'

'Find the girl,' the manservant said. 'I'll join you when I can.'

'Bugg?'

'In a moment, Avowed. I must do something first.'

The Crimson Guardsman hesitated, then nodded and swung back.

Bugg closed his eyes. *Jaghut witch, hear me. Recall my favour at the quarry? The time has come for . . . reciprocity.*

She replied in his mind, distant, yet swiftly closing. *'I*

hear you, little man. I know what you seek. Ah, you are a clever one indeed . . .'

Oh, I cannot take all the credit, this time.

The demon expanded to fill the cavern. The heart was all about, the power seeping in to enliven its flesh. The chains of binding melted away.

Now, it need only reach out and grasp hold.

The strength of a thousand gods awaited it.

Reaching.

Countless grasping, clutching hands.

Finding . . . *nothing*.

Then, a mortal's voice—

From the Ceda, two more words, uttered low and clear, *'Got you.'*

A lie! Illusion! Deceit! The demon raged, spun in a conflagration of brown silt, seeking the way out – only to find the tunnel mouth sealed. A smooth surface, fiercely cold, the cold burning – the demon recoiled.

Then, the lake overhead. Upward – fast, faster—

Ursto Hoobutt and his sometime lover, Pinosel, were both drunk as they awaited the fall of Letheras. They had been singing, celebrating the end of their debts, sprawled on the mouldy walkway surrounding Settle Lake amidst nervous rats and head-jutting pigeons.

When the wine ran out, they began bickering.

It had begun innocently enough, as Pinosel loosed a loud sigh and said, 'And now you can marry me.'

It was a moment before her words registered, upon which, bleary-eyed, he looked over in disbelief. 'Marry you? Wha's wrong wi' 'ow it is now, Cherrytart?'

'What's wrong? It's respectable I want, you fat, flea-bit oaf. I earned it. Respectable. You marry me, Ursto Hoobutt, now that the Edurians done conquered us. Marry me!'

'All right, I will.'

'When?' she demanded, sensing the out he was angling towards.

'When . . . when . . .' Hah! He had his answer—

And, at that instant, the fetid green water of Settle Lake, sprawled out before them like a turgid plain of seaweed fertilizer, paled into murky white. And clouds began rising from its now frozen surface.

An icy breeze swept over Ursto Hoobutt and Pinosel.

There was a sudden deep thump from somewhere beneath the frozen lake's ice, although not a single crack showed.

Ursto Hoobutt stared, disbelieving. Opened his mouth, then closed it.

Then his shoulders sagged. 'Today, love. I'll marry ya today . . .'

860

CHAPTER TWENTY-FIVE

When the gods of dust were young
They swam in blood.

Whiteforth's Dream on the Day of the
Seventh Closure
Fever Witch

Shurq Elalle walked down the tunnel to the crypt door. her thoughts were on Gerun Eberict; her concern was for Tehol Beddict. The Finadd was of the most vicious sort, after all, and Tehol seemed so . . . helpless. Oh, fit enough, probably quite capable of running fast and far should the need arise. But it was clear that Tehol had no intention of running anywhere. The silent bodyguards Brys had assigned to him were some comfort, although, the way Gerun worked, they might prove little more than a minor inconvenience.

If that was not troubling enough, there was the ominous silence from Kettle at the dead Azath tower. Was that a result of the child's returning to life, thus severing the link that bound the dead? Or had something terrible happened?

She reached the portal and pushed it open.

Light flared from a lantern, and she saw Ublala seated on the sarcophagus, the lantern on his lap as he adjusted the flame.

She saw his expression and frowned. 'What is wrong, my love?'

'There's no time,' he said, rising, bumping his head on the ceiling, then ducking into a hunch. 'Bad things. I was about to go.' He set the lantern down on the lid. 'Couldn't wait for you any longer. I've got to go.'

'Where?'

'It's the Seregahl,' he mumbled, hands wringing. 'It's bad.'

'The Seregahl? The old Tarthenal gods? Ublala, what are you talking about?'

'I have to go.' He headed for the doorway.

'Ublala, what about Harlest? Where are you going?'

'The old tower.' He was in the tunnel, his words dwindling. 'I love you, Shurq Elalle . . .'

She stared at the empty doorway. Love? That sounded . . . final.

Shurq Elalle went to the sarcophagus and slid the lid to one side.

'Aarrgh! Hiss! Hiss! Hiss—'

'Stop that, Harlest!' She batted the clawing hands away. 'Get out of there. We have to go—'

'Where?' Harlest slowly sat up, practising baring his long fangs and making growling sounds.

She studied him for a moment, then said, 'A cemetery.'

'Oh,' Harlest sighed, 'that's *perfect.*'

Sitting in the street, in a pool of darkening blood, the emperor of the Tiste Edur had one hand held against his face and seemed to be trying to claw his eyes out. He still screamed every now and then, a shrill, wordless release of raw anguish.

On the bridge, thirty paces distant, the Letherii soldiers were silent and motionless behind their shields. Other citizens of the city were visible along the edge of the canal on the other side, a row of onlookers, their numbers growing.

Trull Sengar felt a hand settle on his shoulder and he turned to find Uruth, her face twisted with distress.

862

'Son, something must be done – he's losing his mind—'

Udinaas, the damned slave who had become so essential, so integral to Rhulad – to the young Edur's sanity – had vanished. And now the emperor railed, recognizing no-one, froth on his lips, his cries those of a panicked beast. 'He must be hunted down,' Trull said. 'That slave.'

'There is more—'

Hannan Mosag had moved to stand close to Rhulad, and now spoke, his words carrying easily. 'Emperor Rhulad, hear me! This is a day of dark truths. Your slave, Udinaas, has done what we would expect of a Letherii. Their hearts are filled with treachery and they serve none but themselves. Rhulad, Udinaas has run away.' He paused, then said, 'From you.'

The triumph was poorly hidden as the Warlock King continued. 'He has made himself into your white nectar, and now leaves you in pain. This is a world without faith, Emperor. Only your kin can be trusted—'

Rhulad's head snapped up, features ravaged with hurt, a dark fire in his eyes. 'Trusted? You, Hannan Mosag? My brothers? Mayen?' Blood-smeared gold, matted bear fur, sword-blade threaded through bits of human meat and intestines, the emperor staggered upright, chest heaving with emotion. 'You are all as *nothing* to us. Liars, cheats, betrayers! All of you!' He whipped the sword, spattering red and pink fragments onto the cobbles and against the shins of those standing nearest him, and bared his teeth. 'The emperor shall reflect his people,' he rasped, an ugly grin spreading. 'Reflect, as it must be.'

Trull saw Fear take a step forward, halting as Rhulad's sword shot upward, the point hovering at Fear's throat.

'Oh no, brother, we want nothing from you. We want nothing from any of you. Except obedience. An empire must be shaped, and that shaping shall be by the emperor's hands. Warlock King!'

'Sire?'

The sword slid away from Fear's throat, waved carelessly

towards the soldiers blocking the bridge. 'Get rid of them.'

Binadas among them, the K'risnan shambled forward at Hannan Mosag's gesture. Behind them were four slaves with two large leather sacks which they dragged over the cobbles to where the K'risnan waited in a row. Noting the sacks, the Warlock King shook his head. 'Not here, I think. Something . . . simpler.' He faced the emperor. 'A moment, sire, in which to prepare. I shall do this myself.'

Uruth tugged Trull round again. 'It is more than just Udinaas,' she said. 'Mayen has escaped.'

He stared at her, not quite comprehending. 'Escaped?'

'We must find her . . .'

'She ran away . . . from us? From her own people?'

'It is the hunger, Trull. Please.'

After a moment, he pulled away, looked round until he saw a company of warriors grouped behind Theradas and Midik Buhn. Trull walked over to them.

Theradas scowled. 'What do you want, Trull Sengar?'

'The emperor's mother has orders for you and your warriors, Theradas.'

His expression lost its ferocity, was replaced with uncertainty. 'What are they?'

'Mayen is lost, somewhere in the city. She must be found. As for Udinaas . . . if you see him . . .'

'If we see him he will die terribly, Trull Sengar.'

He betrayed Rhulad. When I warned him . . . Trull glanced over at Rhulad. A return from this madness? Not likely. It was too late. 'As you like, Theradas. Just find Mayen.'

He watched them head off, then turned and met Uruth's eyes. She nodded.

The soldiers on the bridge knew what was coming. He saw them duck lower behind their shields. Pointless. Pathetic, yet there was courage here, among these Letherii. *Udinaas, I did not . . . did not think you would—*

A seething, spitting grey wave rose suddenly at the foot of the bridge, churning higher.

The shield wall flinched back, contracted.

The wave plunged forward.

From the banks of the canal to either side citizens shrieked and scattered—

—as the sorcery rushed over the bridge, striking the soldiers in a spray of blood and strips of flesh. A heartbeat, then past, spreading out to wash over the fleeing citizens. Devouring them in writhing hunger.

Trull saw it strike nearby buildings, smashing down doors and bursting through shuttered windows. Screams.

'Enough!' Rhulad roared, stepping towards Hannan Mosag, who lowered his arms, which looked twisted and gnarled.

The sorcery vanished, leaving only heaps of bones, polished shields and armour on the bridge. From the sundered buildings, silence. Hannan Mosag sagged, and Trull saw how misshapen he had become beneath his furs.

The emperor suddenly giggled. 'So eager, Hannan Mosag! Your secret god is *so eager!*'

Secret god? Trull looked over at Fear, and found his brother staring back.

'Brothers,' the emperor cried, waving his sword, 'we march to the Eternal Domicile! To the throne! None can deny us! And should they dare, their flesh shall be rendered from their bones! They will know pain. They will suffer! Brothers, this shall be a day of *suffering*' – he seemed to find sweetness in tasting the word – 'for all who would oppose us! Now, walk with your Sire!'

He is . . . transformed. Lost to us. And all for the treachery of a slave . . .

An overgrown yard, just visible through the old, battered stones of the gateway. From the skeletal, twisted branches of leaning trees, something like steam billowed upward. There was no-one about. Iron Bars slowed his steps and looked back up the street. That manservant had yet to appear from beyond the corner of the building he had jogged round moments earlier.

'Fine, then,' the Avowed muttered, drawing his sword, 'we'll just have to see for ourselves . . .' He approached the gateway, strode onto the winding stone path. The squat, square tower was opposite, stained and leaning and dead. From his left, the sounds of stones grinding together, the snap of wood, and thumps that trembled the ground beneath his feet. *Over there, then.*

Iron Bars walked into the yard.

Round a mud-smeared barrow, over a fallen tree, to come to a halt ten paces from what had once been an extensive, elongated mound, now torn apart and steaming, mud sliding down as five huge figures dragged themselves free. Flesh darkened by peat, skin mapped by the tracks of countless roots, dangling hair the colour of copper. Tugging weapons free – massive two-handed swords of black, polished wood.

The five were chanting.

Iron Bars grunted. 'Tartheno Toblakai. Hood-damned Fenn. Well, this won't be fun.'

One of the warriors heard him and fixed black, murky eyes on the Avowed. The chant ceased, and it spoke. 'A child, my brothers.'

'The one who spoke through the earth?' another asked.

'I don't know. Does it matter?'

'It would not help us, that child. We have promised a terrible death.'

'Then let us—'

The Toblakai's words were cut short as Iron Bars rushed forward.

A roar, a keening sweep of a wooden sword flung into the path of the Avowed's own weapon, which slid under, point gliding back round and over the warrior's enormous wrist, following in its swishing wake, to intercept the instinctive back-swing. Slashing through hard, thick skin, the edge scoring against muscle tough as wood.

A huge presence lunging in from the Avowed's right. But Iron Bars continued forward, ducking beneath the first

Toblakai's arm, then pivoting round as the second attacker slammed into the first warrior. Disengaging his sword, thrusting upward, seeking the soft space between the lower mandibles – a jerk of the giant's head, and the Avowed's sword point speared its right eye, plunging deep in a spurt of what seemed to be swamp water.

A shriek.

Iron Bars found himself scrambling over the ruined barrow, the other Toblakai stumbling as they swung round to face him again – with a heap of boulders, mud and ripped-up roots in the way.

The Avowed leapt down onto level ground once more.

Black blood dripping from one arm, a hand pressed over a gouged socket and burst eye, the Toblakai he had attacked was staggering back.

The other four were spreading out, silent now, intent.

Until they could edge round the entire barrow, their approach would be difficult, the footing treacherous.

One down. Iron Bars was pleased—

And then the fifth one shook itself and straightened. One-eyed, but turning to face the Avowed once more.

'You hurt our brother,' one said.

'There's more to come,' Iron Bars said.

'It's not good, hurting gods.'

Gods?

'We are the Seregahl,' the lead Toblakai said. 'Before you hurt us, you might have begged for mercy. You might have knelt in worship, and perhaps we would have accepted you. But not now.'

'No,' the Avowed agreed, 'I suppose not.'

'That is all you would say?'

He shrugged. 'Nothing else comes to mind.'

'You are frowning. Why?'

'Well, I've already killed a god today,' Iron Bars said. 'If I'd known this was going to be a day for killing gods, I might have paced myself better.'

The five were silent for a moment, then the first

one said, 'What god have you killed this day, stranger?'

'The Pack.'

A hiss from the Toblakai on the far right. 'The ones that escaped us! The fast ones!'

'They were fast,' Iron Bars said, nodding. 'But not, it seems, fast enough.'

'D'ivers.'

'Yes,' the Avowed said. 'Six of them . . . and only five of you.'

The first Toblakai said to its brothers, 'Careful with this one, then.'

'We are free,' the one-eyed one growled. 'We must kill this one to remain so.'

'True. This is cause enough.'

They began advancing again.

Iron Bars inwardly sighed. At least he'd made them nervous. And that might serve to keep him alive a little while longer. Then again, he reminded himself, he'd faced worse.

Well, maybe not. Maybe? Who am I kidding?

He shifted his weight, rising to the balls of his feet, readying himself to begin the dance. The dance of staying alive.

Until help came.

Help . . . from a short, pudgy, balding man. Oh, Hood, Iron Bars, just try and stay alive as long as you can – maybe they'll die of exhaustion.

'Look,' one whined, 'he's smiling.'

Unseen storms, raging through the streets, battering the city. Bugg's head was aching with the chaos of power, of the clash of fierce wills. He could still feel the impotent fury of the ancient god trapped beneath the ice of Settle Lake – the Ceda's trap had worked well indeed, and even now the ice was slowly thickening, closing in around the creature in the sealed cavern, and before the sun set it would find itself encased in the ice, feeling the unbearable cold seeping into its being, stealing sensation, stealing its life.

Good things came of being nice to a Jaghut, something the T'lan Imass never understood.

Bugg made his way towards the end of the alley beyond which the old Azath tower was visible. He hoped Iron Bars had not done anything precipitous, such as entering the yard alone. Kettle would have warned him against that in any case. With luck, the child's buried ally was buried no longer. The Avowed was intended to give support, that was all, and only if necessity demanded it. This wasn't that man's fight, after all—

His steps slowed suddenly, as a cold dread swept through him. He quested out with his senses, and detected movement where there should not be movement, an awakening of wills, intentions burning bright, threads of fate converging . . .

The manservant turned round, and began running.

Four of his ablest killers approached Gerun Eberict from up the street. The Finadd raised a hand to halt those behind him.

'Finadd,' the squad leader said upon arriving, 'we had some luck. The brother at the far lookout was flushed out into the street by a pack of Edur. He took six of the bastards down with him. Once the Edur left I sent Crillo out to make sure he was dead—'

'He was cut to pieces,' Crillo interrupted, grinning.

'—and he was at that,' the squad leader resumed, with a glare at Crillo, whose grin broadened.

'And the other?' Gerun asked, scanning the vicinity. It wouldn't do to run into a company of Tiste Edur right now.

The squad leader scowled. 'Crillo got 'im. A damned lucky knife-throw—'

'No luck at all,' Crillo cut in. 'Poor bastard never knew it was coming—'

'Because he'd caught out the rest of us—'

'They're both dead?' Gerun asked. Then shook his head.

'Luck indeed. It should not have been that easy. All right, that leaves the one on the roof. He'll have been looking for signals from his brothers and he won't be seeing them now. Meaning, he'll know we're coming.'

'It's just one man, Finadd—'

'A Shavankrats, Crillo. Don't get overconfident just because the Errant's nudged our way so far. All right, we stay as a group now—' He stopped, then gestured everyone low.

Thirty paces ahead and coming from a side alley, a lone figure ran into the street. A Tiste Edur woman. Like a startled deer she froze, head darting. Before she had a chance to look their way, she heard something behind her and bolted. A metallic flash in her right hand revealed that she carried a knife of some sort.

Gerun Eberict grunted. She was heading the same direction as he was. An undefended Tiste Edur woman. He would enjoy her before killing her. Once his other business was out of the way, of course. Might let the lads have a go, too. Crillo first, for the work he'd already done getting rid of Brys's damned guards.

The Finadd straightened. 'After her, then, since it's on the way.'

Dark laughs from his troop.

'Take point, Crillo.'

They set out.

Faces behind shutters at second floor windows – the whole city cowered like half-drowned rats. It was disgusting. But they were showing him, weren't they, showing him how few deserved to live. This new empire of the Tiste Edur would be little different, he suspected. There would need to be controllers, deliverers of swift and incorruptible justice. People would continue to be rude. Would continue to litter the streets. And there would still be people who were just plain ugly, earning the mercy of Gerun's knife. He would have his work, as before, to make this city a place of beauty—

870

They had reached the place where the woman had emerged from the alley. Crillo was turning round, pointing in the direction she had run, when a spear struck his head, spinning him round in a mass of blood, brain and shattered bone.

From the alley rushed a score or more Tiste Edur warriors.

'Take them!' Gerun Eberict commanded, and was pleased to see his men surge forward.

Past the Finadd, who then stepped back.

I can always get more men.

And ran.

Onto the trail of the woman. Coincidentally, of course. His real target was Tehol Beddict. He'd take her down first, leave her trussed and gagged close by, to await his return. More difficult, now, since he was alone. Tehol's bodyguard would be a challenge, but when one's sword edges were painted with poison, even the slightest cut would be sufficient to kill the man. Quickly.

There!

The woman had been hiding in a niche twenty paces ahead. She bolted at his approach.

Gerun broke into a sprint.

Oh, he wanted her now. She was beautiful. He saw the knife in her hand and laughed. It was a fish knife – he'd seen the Letherii slaves using them in that Hiroth village.

Running hard, he quickly gained on her.

Across another street, into another alley.

Close, now, to Tehol Beddict's home. But he could reach her in time – five more steps—

'There's trouble.'

Stunned, Tehol Beddict turned. 'Not mute after all . . .' His words trailed away at seeing the unease in the body-guard's eyes. 'Serious trouble, then.'

'My brothers are both dead. Gerun Eberict is coming.'

'This city's full of Edur,' Tehol said, throwing both hands

up to encompass a vast sweep of rooftops, tiers and bridges. 'Ranging round like wolves. And then there's those real wolves—'

'It's Gerun.'

Tehol studied the man. 'All right. He's on the way for a visit. What should we do about it?'

'They can come up the walls, the way your thief friend does. We need to get below. We need a place with one door and only one door.'

'Well, there's the warehouse opposite – I know it quite well—'

'Let's go, then.'

The guard went to the hatch, knelt at its edge and cautiously looked down into the room below. He waved Tehol forward, then began the descent.

Moments later they stood in the room. The guard headed to the entrance, tugged the hanging back a fraction and peered outside. 'Looks clear. I'll lead, to that wall—'

'The warehouse wall. There's a watchman, Chalas—'

'If he's still there I'd be surprised.'

'You have a point. All right. When we get to the wall, we head right. Round the corner and in through the office door, the first one we'll come to. The main sliding doors will be barred.'

'And if the office door is locked?'

'I know where the key's hidden.'

The guard nodded.

They stepped into the narrow corridor, turned left and approached the street.

Three more strides.

She threw a desperate look over her shoulder, then lunged forward in a sudden burst of speed.

Gerun snarled, reaching out with one hand.

A whimpering sound escaped her, and she raised the knife just as she reached the mouth of the alley.

And thrust it into her own chest.

Gerun was a hand's width behind her, coming opposite a side corridor between two warehouses, when he was grasped hard, pulled off his feet, and yanked into the dark corridor.

A fist crashed into his face, shattering his nose. Stunned, he was helpless as the sword was plucked from his hand, the helmet dragged from his head.

The massive hands lifted him and slammed him hard against a wall. Once, twice, three times, and with each impact the back of Gerun's head crunched against the cut stone. Then he was smashed onto the greasy cobbles, breaking his right shoulder and clavicle. Consciousness slipped away. When it returned a moment later he was vaguely aware of a huge, hulking figure crouched over him in the gloom.

A massive hand snapped down to cover Gerun's mouth and the figure froze.

The sound of running feet in the alleyway, a dozen, maybe more, all moccasined, the rasp of weapons. Then past.

Blearily, Gerun Eberict stared up at an unfamiliar face. A mixed blood. Half Tarthenal, half Nerek.

The huge man crouched closer. 'For what you did to her,' he said in a hoarse whisper. 'And don't think it'll be quick . . .'

The hand over his mouth, Gerun could say nothing. Could ask no questions. And he had plenty of those.

It was clear, however, that the mixed blood wasn't interested.

And that, Gerun said to himself, was too bad.

Tehol was three paces behind the guard, who was nearing the warehouse wall, when a scraping noise alerted him. He looked to his right, in time to see an Edur woman stagger out from an alley. A knife handle jutted from her chest, and blood was streaming down.

Dumb misery in her eyes, she saw Tehol. Reached out a

red-stained hand, then fell, landing on her left side and skidding slightly on the cobbles before coming to a stop.

'Guard!' Tehol hissed, changing direction. 'She's hurt—'

From the warehouse wall: 'No!'

As Tehol reached her, he looked up to see Tiste Edur warriors rushing from the alley mouth. A spear sailed towards him—

—and was intercepted by the guard lunging in from Tehol's left side. The weapon caught the man under his left arm, snapping ribs as it sank deep into his chest. With a soft groan, the guard stumbled past, then sprawled onto the street, blood pouring from his mouth and nose.

Tehol went perfectly still.

The Edur ranged out cautiously, until they formed a rough circle around Tehol and the dead woman. One checked on the bodyguard, turning the man over with one foot. It was clear that the man was also dead.

In trader tongue, one of the Tiste Edur said, 'You have killed her.'

Tehol shook his head. 'No. She ran into view, already wounded. I was coming to . . . to help. I am sorry . . .'

The warrior sneered, then said to the younger Edur beside him, 'Midik, see if this Letherii is armed.'

The one named Midik stepped up to Tehol. Reached out to pat him down, then snorted. 'He's wearing rags, Theradas. There is no place he could hide anything.'

A third warrior said, 'He killed Mayen. We should take him back—'

'No,' Theradas growled. He sheathed his sword and pushed Midik to one side as he came close to Tehol. 'Look at this one,' he said in a growl. 'See the insolence in his eyes.'

'You do poorly at reading a Letherii's expression,' Tehol said sadly.

'That is too bad, for you.'

'Yes,' Tehol replied, 'I imagine—'

Theradas struck him with a gloved fist.

Pitching Tehol's head back, his nose cracking loudly. He bent over, both hands to his face, then a foot slammed down diagonally against his right shin, snapping both bones. He fell. A heel crunched down on his chest, breaking ribs.

Tehol could feel his body trying to curl up as heels and fists battered at him. A foot smashed down on his left cheek, crushing bone and bursting that eye. White fire blazed in his brain, swiftly darkening to murky black.

Another kick dislocated his left shoulder.

Beneath yet another heel, his left elbow was crushed. As kicks hammered into his gut, he tried to draw his knees up, only to feel them stamped on and broken. Something burst low in his gut and he felt himself spilling out.

Then a heel landed on the side of his head.

Fifty paces up the street, Hull Beddict approached. He saw a crowd of Tiste Edur, and it was clear they were kicking someone to death. A sudden uneasiness in his stomach, he quickened his pace. There were bodies, he saw, beyond the circle. A soldier in the garb of a palace guard, the shaft of a spear jutting from him. And . . . an Edur woman.

'Oh, Errant, what has happened here?'

He made to run—

—and found his path blocked.

A Nerek, and a moment later Hull Beddict recognized him. One of Buruk the Pale's servants.

Frowning, wondering how he had come to be here, Hull moved to step around the man – who sidestepped once more to block him.

'What is this?'

'You have been judged, Hull Beddict,' the Nerek said. 'I am sorry.'

'Judged? Please, I must—'

'You chose to walk with the Tiste Edur emperor,' the Nerek said. 'You chose . . . betrayal.'

'An end to Lether, yes – what of it? No more will this

875

damned kingdom destroy people like the Nerek, and the Tarthenal—'

'We thought we knew your heart, Hull Beddict, but now we see that it has turned black. It is poisoned, because forgiveness is not within you.'

'Forgiveness?' He reached out to push the Nerek aside. *They're beating someone. To death. I think*—

From behind, two knives slid into his back, one under each shoulder blade, angling upward.

Arching in shock, Hull Beddict stared at the Nerek standing before him, and saw that the young man was weeping. *What? Why*—

He sank to his knees, weakness rising through him, and the storm of thoughts – the emotions and desires that had haunted him for years – they too weakened, fell away into a grey, calm mist. The mist rising yet higher, a sudden coldness in his muscles. *It is . . . it is . . . so . . .*

Hull Beddict pitched forward, onto his face, but he never felt the impact with the cobbles.

'Stop. Please—'

The Tiste Edur turned, to see a Letherii step from where he had been hiding, round the corner of the warehouse. Nondescript, limping, a knout tucked into a rope belt, the man edged forward and continued in the trader tongue, 'He's never hurt no-one. Don't kill him, please. I saw, you see.'

'You saw what?' Theradas demanded.

'The woman, she stabbed herself. Look at the knife, see for yourself.' Chalas wrung his hands, eyes on the bleeding, motionless form of Tehol. 'Please, don't hurt him no more.'

'You must learn,' Theradas said, baring his teeth. 'We heed our emperor's words. This shall be a day of suffering, old man. Now, leave us, or invite the same fate.'

Chalas surprised them, lunging forward to drape himself over Tehol, shifting to protect as much of him as he could.

Midik Buhn laughed.

Blows rained down, more savage than ever, and it was not long before Chalas lost consciousness. A half-dozen more kicks dislodged the man from Tehol, until the two were lying side by side. With sudden impatience, Theradas slammed his heel down on a head, hard enough to collapse the skull and crush the brain.

Standing on the far side of the bridge, Turudal Brizad felt the malign sorcery wash over him. The soldiers barricading the bridge had died in the grey conflagration a moment earlier, and now it seemed the terrible sorcery would reach out into the rest of the city. Into the nearby buildings, and, for the Errant, enough was enough.

He nudged the wild power coursing through those buildings, angling it ever downward, slipping it past occupied rooms, downward, past the hidden tunnels of the Rat Catchers' Guild where so many citizens huddled, and into the insensate mud and clays of the long dead swamp. Where it could do nothing, and was slowed, slowed, then trapped.

It was clear, a moment later, that the Warlock King had not detected the manipulation, as the magic was surrendered, the poisoning conduit from the Crippled God closed once more. Hannan Mosag's flesh would not suffer much more of that, fortunately.

Not that it would matter.

He watched as a score of Tiste Edur set off into the city, seeking, no doubt, the fleeing woman from their tribe. But nothing good would come of it, the Errant knew. Indeed, a most egregious error was in the offing, and he grieved for that.

Reaching with his senses, he gained a vision of an overgrown, broken-up yard surrounding a squat tower, and watched in wonder and awe as a lone figure wove a deadly dance in the midst of five enraged Toblakai gods. Extraordinary – a scene the Errant would never forget. But it could not last much longer, he knew.

877

Nothing good ever did, alas.

Blinking, he saw that the Tiste Edur emperor was now leading his kin across the bridge. On their way to the Eternal Domicile.

Turudal Brizad pushed himself into motion once more.

The Eternal Domicile, a conjoining of destinations, for yet another sequence of tragic events to come. *Today, the empire is reborn. In violence and blood, as with all births. And what, when this day is done, shall we find lying in our lap? Eyes opening onto this world?*

The Errant began walking, staying ahead of the Tiste Edur, and feeling, deep within him, the lurching, stumbling measure of time, the countless heartbeats, merging one and all – no need, finally, for a nudge, a push or a pull. No need, it seemed, for anything. He would but witness, now.

He hoped.

Seated cross-legged in the street, the lone High Mage of the Crimson Guard present in this fell city, Corlo Orothos, once of Unta in the days before the empire, cocked his head at the heavy, thumping feet of someone approaching from behind. He risked opening his eyes, then raised a hand in time to halt the newcomer.

'Hello, half-blood,' he said. 'Have you come to worship your gods?'

The giant figure looked down at Corlo. 'Is it too late?' he asked.

'No, they're still alive. Only one man opposes them, and not for much longer. I'm doing all I can, but it's no easy thing to confuse gods.'

The Tarthenal half-blood frowned. 'Do you know why we pray to the Seregahl?'

An odd question. 'To gain their favour?'

'No,' Ublala replied, 'we pray for them to stay away. And now,' he added, 'they're here. That's bad.'

'Well, what do you intend to do about it?'

Ublala squinted down at Corlo, said nothing.

After a moment, the High Mage nodded. 'Go on, then.'

He watched the huge man lumber towards the gateway. Just inside, he paused beside a tree, reached up and broke free a branch as thick as one of Corlo's thighs. Hefting it in both hands, the half-blood jogged into the yard.

It was tearing him apart, striving to burst free of his skeletal cage, the minuscule, now terribly abused muscles. In their journey across Letheras, they'd left thirty or more dead Soletaken in their wake. And six Tiste Edur who'd come up from the docks eager for a fight.

They'd taken wounds – *no,* the remnant that was Udinaas corrected, *I've taken wounds. I should be dead. I'm cut to pieces. Bitten, torn, gouged. But that damned Wyval won't surrender. It needs me still . . . for a few moments longer.*

Through a red haze, the old Azath tower and its yard came into view, and a surge of eagerness from the Wyval flooded him.

The Master needed help. All was not yet lost.

In a blur of motion, Udinaas was past the strange man sitting cross-legged on the street – he caught the sudden jerk of surprise from the man as they swept by. A moment later, plunging through the gateway.

Into the yard.

In time to see a mortal Tarthenal half-blood rushing to close on a fight where a lone swordsman was surrounded by the Toblakai gods, moments from buckling under a hail of blows.

Then, past them all.

To the barrow of the Master. The churned, steaming earth. Diving forward with a piercing, reptilian scream – and into the hot darkness, down, clawing, scraping – tearing clear from the mortal's flesh, the body the Wyval had used for so long, the body it had hidden within – clambering free at last, massive, scaled and sleek-hided, talons plunging into the soil—

* * *

The child Kettle squealed as the creature, winged and as big as an ox, rushed past her on all fours. A thumping splash, water spraying in a broad fan that rose, and rose, then slapped down on the now churning pool. Foam, a snaking red-purple tail slithering down then vanishing in the swirling maelstrom.

She then heard a thud behind her and spun on the slick mud of the bank, the two swords still in her hands—

—to see a badly torn body, a man, lying face down. The shattered ends of long bones jutting from his arms and legs, blood pulsing slowly from ruptured veins. And, settling atop him, a wraith, descending like a shadow to match the contorted body beneath it. A shadowy face looking up at Kettle, the rasp of words—

'*Child, we need your help.*'

She looked back over her shoulder – the surface of the pool was growing calm once more. 'Oh, what do you want me to do? It's all going wrong—'

'*Not as wrong as you think. This man, this Letherii. Help him, he's dying. I cannot hold him together much longer. He is dying, and he does not deserve to die.*'

She crawled closer. 'What can I do?'

'*The blood within you, child. A drop or two, no more than that. The blood, child, that has returned you to life. Please . . .*'

'You are a ghost. Why would you have me do this for him – and not for you?'

The wraith's red eyes thinned as it studied her. '*Do not tempt me.*'

Kettle looked down at the swords in her hands. Then she set one down and brought the freed hand to the gleaming blue edge of the one she still held. Slid her palm a bit along the edge, then lifted her hand to study the result. A long line of blood, a deep, perfect cut. 'Oh, it's sharp.'

'*Here, push him onto his back. Lay your wounded palm on his chest.*'

Kettle moved forward.

* * *

880

A blow had broken his left arm, and the agony as Iron Bars dodged around and between the bellowing Seregahl sent white flashes through his brain. Half blinded, he wielded his battered, blunted sword on instinct alone, meeting blow after blow – he needed a moment free, a few heartbeats in which to recover, to clamp down on the pain—

But he'd run out of that time. Another blow got through, the strange wooden sword slicing as if glass-edged into his left hip. The leg on that side gave out beneath the biting wound. He looked up through sweat-stinging eyes, and saw the one-eyed Seregahl towering directly over him, teeth bared in triumph.

Then a tree branch struck the god in the head. Against its left temple, hard enough to snap the head right over to bounce from the opposite shoulder. The grin froze, and the Toblakai staggered. A second impact caught it, this time coming from behind, up into the back of the skull, the branch exploding into splinters. The god bent forward—

—as a knee drove up into its crotch – and forearms hammered its back, pushing it further down, the knee rising again, this time to crunch against the god's face.

The grin, Iron Bars saw from where he crouched, was entirely gone now.

The Avowed rolled to one side a moment before the Toblakai landed atop him. Rolled, and rolled, stumbling to his feet finally to pivot round. And, rising to his name above the agony in his hip, straightening. Once more facing the Seregahl.

Where, it seemed, one of their own kind was now fighting them – a mortal Tarthenal, who had wrapped his huge arms around one of the gods from behind, trapping its arms to its sides as he squeezed. The remaining three gods had staggered back, as if in shock, and the moment was, to the Avowed's eyes, suddenly frozen.

Two, then three heartbeats.

The cloudiness cleared from the Avowed's eyes. A flicker

of energy returned to his exhausted limbs. The pain faded away.

That mortal Tarthenal was moments from dying, as the other three stirred awake and moved forward.

Iron Bars raced to intercept them.

The odds were getting better.

Two huddled shapes on the street. Tiste Edur standing around, still kicking, still breaking bones. One stamped down, and brains sprayed out onto the cobbles.

Bugg slowed to a stagger, his face twisting with grief, then rage.

He roared.

Heads turned.

And the manservant unleashed what had remained hidden and quiescent within him for so long.

Fourteen Tiste Edur, standing, all reached up to clamp their ears – but the gesture was never completed, as thirteen of them imploded, as if beneath vast pressure, in horrible contractions of flesh, the wild spurt of blood and fluids, skulls collapsing inward.

Imploded, only to explode outward a moment later. In bloody pieces, spattering the warehouse wall and out across the street.

The fourteenth Tiste Edur, the one who had just crushed a head beneath his heel, was lifted into the air. Writhing, his eyes bulging horribly, wastes streaming down his legs.

As Bugg stalked forward.

Until he was standing before Theradas Buhn of the Hiroth. He stared up at the warrior, at his bloated face, at the agony in his eyes.

Trembling, Bugg said, 'You, I am sending home . . . not your home. My home.' A gesture, and the Tiste Edur vanished.

Into Bugg's warren, away, then down, down, ever down.

Into depthless darkness, where the portal opened once more, flinging Theradas Buhn into icy, black water.

Where the pressure, immense and undeniable, embraced him.

Fatally.

Bugg's trembling slowed. His roar had been heard, he knew. Upon the other side of the world, it had been heard. And heads had swung round. Immortal hearts had quickened.

'No matter,' he whispered.

Then moved forward, down to kneel beside the motionless bodies.

He gathered one of those bodies into his arms.

Rose, and walked away.

The Eternal Domicile. A title of such profound conceit, as thoroughly bound into the arrogance of the Letherii as the belief in their own immutable destiny. Manifest rights to all things, to ownership, to the claiming of all they perceived, the unconscionable, brazen arrogance of it all, as if a thousand gods stood at their backs, burdened with gifts for the chosen.

Trull Sengar could only wonder, what bred such certainties? What made a people so filled with rectitude and intransigence? *Perhaps all that is needed . . . is power.* A shroud of poison filling the air, seeping into every pore of every man, woman and child. A poison that twisted the past to suit the mores of the present, illuminating in turn an inevitable and righteous future. A poison that made intelligent people blithely disregard the ugly truths of past errors in judgement, of horrendous, brutal debacles that had stained red the hands of their forefathers. A poison that entrenched the stupidity of dubious traditions, and brought misery and suffering upon countless victims.

Power, then. The very same power we are about to embrace. Sisters have mercy upon our people.

The emperor of the Tiste Edur stood before the grand entrance to the Eternal Domicile. Mottled sword in his right, glittering hand. Dusty bearskin riding shoulders grown massively broad with the weight of gold. Old blood staining his back in map patterns, as if he was redrawing the world. Hair now long, ragged and heavy with oily filth.

Trull was standing behind him, and so could not see his brother's eyes. But he knew, should he look into them now, he would see the destiny he feared, he would see the poison coursing unopposed, and he would see the madness born of betrayal.

It would have taken little, he knew. The simple reaching out for a nondescript, sad-eyed slave, the closing of hands, to lift Rhulad upright, to guide him back into sanity. That, and nothing more.

Rhulad turned to face them. 'The doors stand unbarred.'

Hannan Mosag said, 'Someone waits within, sire. I sense . . . something.'

'What do you ask of us, Warlock King?'

'Permit me and my K'risnan to enter first, to see what awaits us. In the corridor . . .'

Rhulad's eyes narrowed, then he waved them forward, and added, 'Fear, Trull, Binadas, join us. We shall follow immediately behind.'

Hannan Mosag in the lead, the K'risnan and the slaves dragging the two sacks immediately behind him, then Rhulad and his brothers, all approached the doors of the Eternal Domicile.

Standing just outside the throne room's entrance, Brys Beddict saw movement down the corridor, on this side of the motionless form of the Ceda. The Champion reached for his sword, then let his hand fall away as the First Consort, Turudal Brizad, emerged from the shadows, approaching nonchalantly, his expression calm.

'I did not,' Brys said in a low voice, 'expect to see you again, First Consort.'

Turudal's soft eyes lifted past Brys to look into the throne room beyond. 'Who waits, Champion?'

'The king, his concubine. The First Eunuch and the Chancellor. And six of my guards.'

Turudal nodded. 'Well, we will not have to wait much longer. The Tiste Edur are but moments behind me.'

'How fares the city?'

'There has been fighting, Brys Beddict. Loyal soldiers lie dead in the streets. Among them, Moroch Nevath.'

'And Gerun Eberict? What of him?'

Turudal cocked his head, then frowned. 'He pursues . . . a woman.'

Brys studied the man. 'Who are you, Turudal Brizad?'

The eyes met his own. 'Today, a witness. We have come, after all, to the day of the Seventh Closure. An end, and a beginning—'

Brys raised a hand to silence the man, then took a step past him.

The Ceda was stirring in the hallway beyond. Then, rising to his feet, adjusting his grimy, creased robes, he lifted the lenses to his face and settled them in place.

Turudal Brizad turned to join Brys. 'Ah, yes.'

The silhouettes of a group of tall figures had appeared at the distant doors, which were now open.

'The Ceda . . .'

'He has done very well, thus far.'

Brys shot the First Consort a baffled look. 'What do you mean? He has done . . . nothing.'

Brows rose. 'No? He has annihilated the sea-god, the demon chained by Hannan Mosag. And he has been preparing for this moment for days now. See where he stands? See the tile he has painted beneath himself? A tile from which all the power of the Cedance shall pass, upward, into his hands.'

The gloom of the hallway vanished, a white, glowing light suffusing the dusty air.

Revealing the row of Tiste Edur now facing the Ceda, less than fifteen paces between them.

The Edur in the centre of the row spoke. 'Ceda Kuru

Qan. The kingdom you serve has fallen. Step aside. The emperor wishes to claim his throne.'

'Fallen?' The Ceda's voice was thin in comparison, almost quavering. 'Relevant? Not in the least. I see you, Hannan Mosag, and your K'risnan. I feel you gathering your power. For your mad emperor to claim the throne of Lether, you shall have to pass through me.'

'It is pointless, old man,' Hannan Mosag said. 'You are alone. All your fellow mages are dead. Look at you. Half blind, barely able to stand—'

'Seek out the demon you chained in the sea, Warlock King.'

From this distance, Trull could not make out Hannan Mosag's expression, but there was sudden fury in his voice. 'You have done this?'

'Letherii are well versed in using greed to lay traps,' Kuru Qan said. 'You'll not have its power today, nor ever again.'

'For that,' the Warlock King said in a growl, 'you will—'

The white mist exploded, the roar shaking ceiling and walls, and thundered forward, striking the Tiste Edur warlocks.

Ten paces behind Hannan Mosag and his K'risnan, Trull Sengar cried out, ducking away at the blazing concussion, his brothers following suit. He heard screams, cut short, then a body skidded across the polished floor to thud against Trull's feet, knocking him down—

He found himself staring at a K'risnan, burnt beyond recognition, blackened slime melting away from split bones. Rising to his hands and knees, Trull looked up.

Only two Edur remained standing, battling the raging sorcery of the Ceda. Hannan Mosag and Binadas. The other K'risnan were all dead, as were the four slaves who had been crouching beside the two sacks.

As Trull stared, he saw Binadas flung to the ground as if by a thousand fists of light. Blood sprayed—

Then Fear was diving forward, skidding on the bucking

tiles to within reach of his brother. Hands closed on a wrist and an ankle, then Fear was dragging Binadas back, away from the conflagration.

Hannan Mosag bellowed. Swirling grey tendrils sprang up from the floor, entwining the raging motes of fire. A blinding detonation—

Then darkness once more, slowly giving way to gloom.

Hannan Mosag, standing alone now, facing the Ceda.

A heartbeat—

Kuru Qan struck again, a moment before Hannan Mosag's own attack. The two powers collided three paces in front of the Warlock King—

—and Trull saw Hannan Mosag stagger, sheathed in blood, his hands reaching back, groping, the left one landing atop one of the sacks and clutching tight. The other hand then found the other and grasped hold. The Warlock King steadied himself, then began to straighten once more against the onslaught.

The sorcery pouring from the Ceda had twisted the marble walls, until they began to bleed white liquid. The ceiling overhead had sagged, its paints scorched away, its surfaces polished and slick. Brys had stared, disbelieving, as the magic swatted away whatever defensive spells the K'risnan had raised before themselves, swatted it away in an instant, to rush in and slaughter them.

Against Hannan Mosag himself, it battered again and again, driving ever closer.

Then the Warlock King riposted, and the pressure in that hallway pushed Brys and Turudal back a step, then two.

All at once, the two battling powers annihilated each other in a flash, the thunder of the detonation sending cracks through the floor, bucking tiles into the air – everywhere but where the two sorcerors stood.

Dusty silence.

The marble columns to either side were burning in

patches, melting from the top down like massive tallow candles. Overhead, the ceiling groaned, as if moments from collapse.

'Now,' Turudal Brizad hoarsely whispered, 'we will see the measure of Hannan Mosag's desperation . . .'

The sorceries roared to life once again, and Brys saw the Warlock King stagger.

The Ceda, Kuru Qan, the small, ancient man, stood unscathed, and the magic raging from him in wave after wave seemed to Brys to be that of a god.

The Warlock King would not survive this. And, once he fell, this ancient, primal sorcery would sweep out, taking the emperor and his kin, devouring them one and all. Outward, into the city. An entire people, the Tiste Edur, would be annihilated – Brys could sense its hunger, its outrage, its cold lust for vengeance – this was the power of the Letherii, the Cedance, the voice of destiny, a thing terrible beyond comprehension—

Trull saw the Warlock King steady himself, his hands gripping the sacks, and power began to flow from them, up his arms, as he began, slowly, to push back the Ceda's attack.

Those arms twisted, grew into horrific, misshapen appendages. Hannan Mosag's torso began to bend, the spine curving, writhing like a snake on hot stones, new muscles rising, knobs of bone pushing at the skin. He shrieked as the power burgeoned through him.

A grey wave rising, battering at the white fire, tearing its edges, pushing harder, filling half the long, colonnaded hallway, closing on the Ceda, who stood unmoving, head tilted up, the strange lenses flashing before his eyes. Standing, as if studying the storm clawing towards him.

Brys stared in horror as the foul sorcery of the Edur edged ever closer to the Ceda, towering over the small man. He saw a nearby column turn porous, then crumble to dust. A section of the ceiling it had been supporting collapsed downward, only to vanish in a cloudy haze and land in a thud of billowing dust.

Kuru Qan was looking up at the raging wall looming over him.

Brys saw him cock his head, the slightest of gestures.

A renewed burst of white fire, expanding outward from where he stood, surging up and outward, hammering into the grey wall.

Driving fissures through it, tearing enormous pieces away to whip like rent sails up towards the malformed ceiling.

Brys heard the Warlock King's shriek, as the white flames roared towards him.

Trull felt himself dragged to his feet. He turned, stared into Fear's face. His brother was shouting something—

—but the Warlock King was failing. Crumbling beneath the onslaught. Whatever energies he had drawn upon from what was hidden within the sacks were ebbing. Insufficient to counter the Ceda. The Warlock King was about to die – and with him – *all of us* . . .

'Trull!' Fear shook him. 'Along the wall.' He pointed. 'There, edge forward. For a throw—'

A *throw*? He stared at the spear in his hands, the Blackwood glistening with beads of red sweat.

'From the shadows, Trull, behind that pillar! From the *shadows*, Trull!'

It was pointless. Worse, he did not want to even try. What if he succeeded? What would be won?

'Trull! Do this or we all die! Mother, Father – Mayen – her child! All the children of the Edur!'

Trull stared into Fear's eyes, and did not recognize what he saw in them. His brother shook him again, then pushed him along the wall, into the bathing heat of the sorcery battering down at Hannan Mosag, then behind a friable column of what had once been solid marble.

Into cool shadow. Absurdly cool shadow. Trull stumbled forward at a final push from his brother. He was brought up against a warped, rippled wall – and could see, now, the Ceda. Less than seven paces distant. Head tilted upward, watching his assault on the Warlock King's failing defences.

Tears blurred Trull's eyes. He did not want to do this. *But they will kill us all. Every one of us, leaving not a single Tiste Edur alive. I know this. In my heart I know this. They will take our lands, our riches. They will sow salt on our burial grounds. They will sweep us into history's forgotten worlds. I . . . I know this.*

He raised his spear, balanced now in his right hand. Was still for a moment, breath held, then two quick strides, arm flashing forward, the weapon flying straight and true.

Piercing the Ceda in his side, just below his left ribs, its solid weight and the momentum from Trull's arm driving the point deep.

The Ceda spun with the impact, left leg buckling, and fell – away from the painted tile—

—that suddenly shattered.

The white fire vanished, and darkness swept in from all sides.

Numbed, Brys stepped forward—

—and was stayed by the hand of Turudal Brizad. 'No, Champion. He's gone.'

The Ceda. Kuru Qan. My friend . . .

Kettle sat in the mud, staring down at the man's face. It looked to be a kind face, especially with the eyes closed in sleep. The scars were fading, all across his lean, tanned body. Her blood had done that. She had been dead, once, and now she had given life.

'You're a strange one,' the wraith whispered from where it crouched by the water.

'I am Kettle.'

A grunted laugh. 'And what boils within you, I wonder?'

'You,' she said, 'are more than just a ghost.'

'Yes.' Amused. 'I am Wither. A good name, don't you

think? I was Tiste Andii, once, long, long ago. I was murdered, along with all of my kin. Well, those of us that survived the battle, that is.'

'Why are you here, Wither?'

'I await my lord, Kettle.' The wraith suddenly rose – she had not known how tall it was before. 'And now . . . he comes.'

An up-rush of muddy water, and a gaunt figure rose, white-skinned as a blood-drained corpse, long pale hair plastered across its lean face. Coughing, pulling itself clear, crawling onto the bank.

'The swords,' he gasped.

Kettle hurried over to him and pushed the weapons into his long-fingered hands. He used them, points down, to help himself to his feet. Tall, she saw, shrinking back, taller even than the wraith. And such cold, cold eyes, deep red. 'You said you would help us,' she said, cowering beneath his gaze.

'Help?'

The wraith knelt before his lord. 'Silchas Ruin, I was once Killanthir, Third High Mage of the Sixth Cohort—'

'I remember you, Killanthir.'

'I have chosen the new name of Wither, my lord.'

'As you like.'

The wraith glanced up. 'Where is the Wyval?'

'I fear he will not survive, but he keeps her occupied. A noble beast.'

'Please,' Kettle whimpered, 'they're out. They want to kill me – you promised—'

'My lord,' Wither said, 'I would help the Wyval. Together, we can perhaps succeed in driving her deep. Even in binding her once again. If you would give me leave . . .'

Silchas Ruin was silent for a moment, staring down at the kneeling wraith. Then he said, 'As you like.'

Wither bowed his head, paused to glance over at Kettle, and said, 'Leave the Letherii to me. He will not awaken for some time.' Then the wraith flowed down into the swirling water.

Silchas Ruin drew a deep breath, and looked down at the swords in his hands for the first time. 'Strange, these. Yet I sense the mortal chose well. Child, get behind me.' He regarded her, then nodded. 'It is time to fulfil my promise.'

Corlo had no idea what would come of this. An Avowed could indeed die, if sufficiently damaged. It was, he believed, a matter of will as much as anything else. And he had known Iron Bars for a long time, although not as long as he had known other of the Avowed. To his mind, however, there was no other who could compare with Iron Bars, when it came to sheer will.

The High Mage was exhausted, used up. No longer could he deftly manipulate the four remaining gods, although, luckily, one of those was in enough trouble all on its own, with a crazed Tarthenal seemingly doing the impossible – squeezing the very life out of it. Talk about stubborn.

He had been beaten on, again and again, yet he would not relax his deadly embrace. Iron Bars had fought brilliantly, distracting the remaining three repeatedly, sufficient to keep the Tarthenal alive, but the Avowed was very nearly done. Corlo had never before seen such fighting, had never before witnessed the fullest measure of this Avowed's ability. It had been said, by Guardsmen who would know, that he was nearly a match to Skinner. And now Corlo believed it.

He was more than a little startled when two corpses walked past him towards the gateway, one of them clawing the air and hissing.

They halted at the entrance to the yard, and he heard the woman swear with admirable inventiveness, then say, 'I don't know how we can help them. Oh, Ublala, you big, stupid fool.'

The other said, 'We must attack, Shurq Elalle. I have fangs and talons, you know.'

'Well, go on then.'

Shurq Elalle? The captain of the ship we've signed on with?

Our . . . employer? Corlo pried his legs loose from their crossed position, wincing in pain, and pushed himself to his feet. 'Hey, you.'

Shurq Elalle, standing alone now, slowly turned. 'Are you addressing me?'

Corlo hobbled over. 'Corlo, ma'am. Crimson Guard. We signed on with you—'

'We?'

'Yes, the one helping your big, stupid friend. That's Iron Bars, my commander.'

'You're supposed to be waiting onboard!'

He blinked.

She scowled. 'Your commander is about to die.'

'I know – wait—' He stepped past her, onto the track. 'Wait, something's coming – quick!' He ran into the yard, Shurq Elalle following.

The Toblakai in the Tarthenal's arms sagged, and Iron Bars heard the cracking of ribs – a moment before one of the gods slipped past the Avowed and slammed the side of his wooden sword into the Tarthenal's head. The huge man toppled, dragging down with him the dead god in his arms.

Stunned, the Tarthenal tried feebly to extricate himself from the corpse.

With the last of his failing strength, Iron Bars leapt over to position himself above him, arriving in time to deflect a sword-blow and counter with a slash that forced the attacker back a step. From the right, another lunged, then spun away of its own accord, wheeling towards a thunderous concussion from a nearby barrow.

Where a tall, pale figure strode into view through a cloud of steam, a sword in each hand.

The Avowed, momentarily distracted, did not even see the sword-blade that slipped over his guard and, deflected at the last moment by clipping the hilt of his sword, slammed flat like a paddle into his right shoulder, breaking everything it could. The impact sent him flying, crashing down into the earth, weapon flying from a senseless hand. He ended up lying on his back, staring up through straggly black tree branches. Too hurt to move. Too tired to care.

From somewhere to his right he heard fighting, then a grunting bellow that sounded a lot like a death-cry. A Toblakai staggered, almost stumbling over Iron Bars, and the Avowed's eyes widened upon seeing blood spurting from two stabs in the god's neck, and a man gnawing on its left calf, being dragged along by its teeth, its taloned hands clawing up the god's thigh.

Well, he'd seen stranger things, he supposed – *no, not a chance of that*—

The ground shook as another body thumped to the ground. A moment later, there was another dying groan.

Then footsteps slowly approached Iron Bars where he lay, staring up at the sky. A shadow fell over him. The Avowed blinked, and found himself looking up at a pallid, lean face, and two red, very red, eyes.

'You did passably well,' the stranger said.

'And my Tarthenal friend?'

'Struck in the skull. He'll be fine, since I doubt there's much inside it.' A pause, then, 'Why are you still lying there?'

Dust and smoke drifted out from the dark corridor. Turudal Brizad had drawn Brys back into the throne room, and the Champion now stood in the clear space before the dais.

From the throne behind him came a weary voice, 'Finadd? The Ceda . . .'

Brys simply shook his head, unable to speak, struggling to push aside his grief.

From the gloom of the corridor, there was silence. Heavy, ominous.

Brys slowly drew out his sword.

A sound. The grate of footsteps dragging through dust and rubble, the scrape of a sword-tip, and a strange series of dull clicks.

The footsteps halted.

Then, a coin. The snap of its bounce—

—rolling slowly into the throne room.

Brys watched it arc a lazy, curling path over the tiles. Gold, blotched with dried blood.

Rolling, tilting, then wobbling to a stop.

The sounds resumed from the corridor, and a moment later a hulking figure shambled out from the shadows and roiling dust.

No-one spoke in the throne room as the emperor of the Tiste Edur entered. Three steps, then four, then five, until he was almost within sword-reach of the Champion. Behind him, Hannan Mosag, almost unrecognizable, so twisted and bent and broken was the Warlock King. Two more Edur warriors, their faces taut with distress, appeared in Hannan Mosag's wake, dragging two sacks.

Brys spared the others the briefest of glances, noting the blood-smeared spear in the right hand of one of the warriors. *The one who killed the Ceda.* Then he fixed his attention once more on the emperor. The sword was too large for him. He walked as if in pain. Spasms flickered across his coin-studded face. His hooded eyes glittered as he stared past Brys . . . to the throne, and the king seated upon it.

A racking cough from Hannan Mosag as he sagged to a kneeling position, a gasp, and, finally, words. 'King Ezgara Diskanar. I have something . . . to show you. A . . . gift.' He lifted a mangled hand, the effort sending a shudder through him, and gestured behind him.

The two warriors glanced at each other, both uncertain.

The Warlock King grimaced. 'The sacks. Untie them. Show the king what lies within them.' Another hacking cough, a bubbling of pink froth at the corners of Hannan Mosag's mouth.

The warriors worked at the knotted ropes, the one on the left pulling the strands loose a moment before the other one. Drawing the leather mouth open. The Edur, seeing

895

what was within, suddenly recoiled, and Brys saw horror on the warrior's face.

A moment later the other one cried out and stepped back.

'*Show them!*' screamed the Warlock King.

At that, even the emperor turned, startled.

The warrior on the left drew a deep, ragged breath, then stepped forward until he could grip the edges of the sack. With strangely gentle motions, he tugged the leather down.

A Letherii, bound tight. Blistered, suppurating skin, fingers worn to stubs, lumps and growths everywhere on his naked body. He had lost most of his hair, although some long strands remained. Blinking in the light, he tried lifting his head, but the malformed tendons and ligaments in his neck forced the motion to one side. The lower jaw settled and a thread of drool slipped down from the gaping mouth.

Then Brys recognized him.

Prince Quillas—

A cry from the king, a terrible, animal wail.

The other sack was pulled down. The queen, her flesh as ruined as that of her son. From her, however, came a wet cackle as if to answer her husband's cry, then a tumbling of nonsensical words, a rush of madness grating out past her swollen, broken lips. Yet, in her eyes, fierce awareness.

Hannan Mosag laughed. 'I used them. Against the Ceda. *I used them.* Letherii blood, Letherii flesh. Look upon the three of us. See, dear king, see the glory of what is to come.'

The emperor shrieked, 'Take them away! Fear! Trull! Take them *away*!'

The two warriors closed on the huddled figures, drawing the sacks up to what passed for shoulders, then dragging the queen and her son back towards the corridor.

Trembling, the emperor faced the king once more. He opened his mouth to say something, winced, then shut it again. Then he slowly straightened, and spoke in a rasping voice. 'We are Rhulad Sengar, emperor of the Tiste Edur. And now, of Lether. Yield the throne, Diskanar. Yield . . . to us.'

From Brys's left the First Eunuch strode forward, a wine jug and two goblets in his hands. He ascended the dais, offered Ezgara one of the goblets. Then he poured out the wine.

Bemused, the Champion took a step to his right and half turned to regard his king.

Who calmly drank down the wine in three quick swallows. At some time earlier the crown had been placed on his brow once again. Nisall was standing just behind the throne, her eyes narrowed on the First Eunuch, who had finished his own wine and was stepping back down from the dais, making his way to stand near the Chancellor at the far wall.

Ezgara Diskanar fixed dull eyes on Brys. 'Stand aside, Champion. Do not die this day.'

'I cannot do as you ask, my king,' Brys said. 'As you well know.'

A weary nod, then Ezgara looked away. 'Very well.'

Nifadas spoke. 'Champion. Show these savages the measure of a Letherii swordsman. The final act of our kingdom on this dark day.'

Brys frowned, then faced Rhulad Sengar. 'You must fight me, Emperor. Or call upon more of your warriors to cut us down.' A glance at the kneeling Hannan Mosag. 'I believe your sorcery is done for now.'

Rhulad sneered. 'Sorcery? We would not so discard this opportunity, Champion. No, we will fight, the two of us.' He stepped back and raised the mottled sword. 'Come. We have lessons for one another.'

Brys did not reply. He waited.

The emperor attacked. Surprisingly fast, a half-whirl of the blade high, then a broken-timed diagonal downward slash intended to meet the Champion's sword and drive it down to the tiles.

Brys matched the momentary hesitation and leaned back, drawing his sword round as he side-stepped to his right. Blade now resting on the top of Rhulad's own as it flashed downward, the Champion darted the tip up to the emperor's left forearm and sliced through a tendon near the elbow.

He leapt back, thrusting low as he was pulling away, to push the tip of his sword between the tendon and kneecap of Rhulad's left leg.

Snip.

The emperor stumbled forward, almost to the edge of the dais, then, astonishingly, righted himself to lunge in a two-handed thrust.

The mottled blade seemed to dance of its own accord, evading two distinct parries from Brys, and the Champion only managed to avoid the thrust by pushing the heavy blade aside with his left hand.

The two lower fingers spun away from that hand, even as Brys back-pedalled until he was in the centre of the space once more, this time with Rhulad between himself and the king on his throne.

Ezgara was smiling.

As Rhulad wheeled to face him once more, his weapon dipping low, Brys attacked.

Leading foot lifting high, stamping down on the emperor's wavering sword-blade – not a perfect contact, but sufficient to bat it momentarily away – as he drove his point into Rhulad's right kneecap. Slicing downward from the upper edge. Biting deep into the bone near the bottom edge. Twisting withdrawal, pulling the patella out through the cut.

A shriek, as Rhulad's leg shot out to the side.

The kneecap still speared on Brys's sword-point, he darted in again as the emperor drove his own sword down and to the left in an effort to stay upright, and slashed lightly across the tendons of the Edur's right arm, just above the elbow.

Rhulad fell back, thudded hard on the tiles, coins snapping free.

The sword should have dropped from the Edur's hands, yet it remained firm within two clenched fists.

898

But Rhulad could do nothing with it.

Trying to sit up, eyes filling with rage, he strained to lift the weapon.

Brys struck the floor with his sword-tip, dislodging the patella, stepped close to the emperor and severed the tendons and ligaments in the Edur's right shoulder, sweeping the blade across to slice a neck tendon, then, point hovering a moment, thrusting down to disable the left shoulder in an identical manner. Standing over the helpless emperor, Brys methodically cut through both tendons above Rhulad's heels, then sliced diagonally across his victim's stomach, parting the wall of muscles there.

A kick sent Rhulad over, exposing his back.

Slashes above each shoulder blade, two more neck tendons. Lower back, ensuring that the sheets of muscle there fully separated, rolling up beneath the coin-studded skin. Back of shoulders, coins dancing away to bounce across the floor.

Brys then stepped back. Lowered his sword.

Rebounding shrieks from the emperor lying face down on the floor, limbs already curling of their own accord, muscles drawing up. The only movement in the chamber.

A slow settling of dust from the corridor.

Then, from one of the Edur warriors, 'Sisters take me . . .'

King Ezgara Diskanar sighed, leaned drunkenly forward, then said, 'Kill him. *Kill him.*'

Brys looked over. 'No, sire.'

Disbelief on the old man's face. 'What?'

'The Ceda was specific on this, sire. I must not kill him.'

'He will bleed out,' Nifadas said, his words strangely dull.

But Brys shook his head. 'He will not. I opened no major vessels, First Eunuch.'

The Edur warrior named Trull then spoke. 'No major vessels . . . how – how could you know? It is not possible . . . so fast . . .'

Brys said nothing.

The king suddenly slumped back on his throne.

Rhulad's shrieks had fallen away, and now he wept. Heaving, helpless cries. A sudden gasp, then, 'Brothers! Kill me!'

Trull Sengar recoiled at Rhulad's command. He shook his head, looked across at Fear, and saw a terrible realization in his brother's eyes.

Rhulad was not healing. Leaking blood onto the polished tiles. His body . . . destroyed. And he was not healing. Trull turned to Hannan Mosag, and saw the ugly gleam of satisfaction in the Warlock King's eyes.

'Hannan Mosag,' Trull whispered.

'I cannot. His flesh, Trull Sengar, is beyond me. Beyond all of us. Only the sword . . . and only *by* the sword. You, Trull Sengar. Or Fear.' A weak wave of one hand. 'Oh, call in someone else, if you've not the courage . . .'

Courage.

Fear grunted at that. As if punched in the chest.

Trull studied him – but Fear had not moved, not a single step. He dragged his eyes away, fixed them once more on Rhulad.

'My brothers.' Rhulad wept where he lay. 'Kill me. One of you. *Please.*'

The Champion – that extraordinary, appalling swordsman – walked over to where the wine jug sat near the foot of the throne. The king looked half asleep, indifferent, his face flushed and slack. Trull drew a deep breath. He saw the First Eunuch, sitting on the floor with his back to the wall. Another man, elderly, stood near Nifadas, hands to his eyes – a posture both strange and pathetic. The woman standing behind the throne was backing away, as if in sudden realization of something. There had been another man, young, handsome, but it seemed he had vanished.

Along the walls, the six palace guards had all drawn their weapons and held them across their chest, a silent salute to the King's Champion. A salute Trull wanted to match. His gaze returned once more to Brys. So modest in appearance, so . . . *his face. Familiar . . . Hull Beddict. So like Hull Beddict.*

Yes, his brother. The youngest. He watched the Letherii pour wine from the jug into the goblet the king had used earlier.

Sisters, this Champion – what has he done? He has given us this . . . this answer. This . . . solution.

Rhulad screamed. 'Fear!'

Hannan Mosag coughed, then said, 'He is gone, Emperor.'

Trull spun round, looked about. *Gone? No*— 'Where? Hannan Mosag, where—'

'He . . . walked away.' The Warlock King's smile was bloodstained. 'Just that, Trull Sengar. Walked. You understand, now, don't you?'

'To call the others, to bring them here . . .'

'No,' Hannan Mosag said. 'I do not think so.'

Rhulad whimpered, then snapped, 'Trull! I command you! Your emperor commands you! Stab me with your spear. Stab me!'

Tears filled Trull's eyes. *And how shall I look upon him . . . now? How? As my emperor, or as my brother?* He tottered, almost collapsing as anguish washed through him. *Fear. You have left. Left us. Me, with . . . this.*

'Brother! Please!'

From the entrance came a low cackle.

Trull turned, saw the bound forms of the queen and the prince, leaning against the wall like two obscene trophies. The sound was coming from the queen, and he saw a glitter from her eyes.

Something – something else – there's more here . . .

He turned. Watched as the Champion straightened, goblet in his hand. Watched, as the man lifted it to his lips.

Trull's gaze flicked to the king. To that half-lidded stare. The senseless eyes. The Edur's head snapped round, to where the First Eunuch sat. Chin on chest, motionless.

'No!'

As the Champion drank, head tilting back. Two swallows, then three. Lowering the cup, he turned to regard Trull. Frowned. 'You had better leave,' he said. 'Drag your

901

warlock with you. Approach the emperor and I will kill you.'

Too late. All . . . too late. 'What – what do you intend?'

The Champion looked down at Rhulad. 'We will . . . take him somewhere. You will not find him, Edur.'

The queen cackled again, clearly startling the swordsman.

'It is too late,' Trull said. 'For you, in any case. If you have any mercy in you, Champion, best send your guards away now. And have them take the woman with them. My kin will be here at any moment.' His gaze fell to Rhulad. 'The emperor is for the Edur to deal with.'

The quizzical expression in the Champion's face deepened. Then he blinked, shook his head. 'What . . . what do you mean? I see that you will not kill your brother. And he must die, mustn't he? To heal. To . . . return.'

'Yes. Champion, I am sorry. I was too late to warn you.'

The swordsman sagged suddenly, and he threw a bloody hand out to the edge of the throne for balance. The sword, still in the other hand, wavered, then dipped until the point touched the floor. 'What – what—'

Trull said nothing.

But Hannan Mosag cared nothing for compassion, and he laughed once more. 'I understood your gesture, Champion. The coolness to match that of your king. Besides—' His words broke into a cough. He spat phlegm, then resumed. 'Besides, it hardly mattered, did it? Whether you lived or died. That's how it seemed, anyway. At that brazen, fateful moment, at least.'

The Champion sank down to the floor, staring dully at the Warlock King.

'Swordsman,' Hannan Mosag called out. 'Hear me, these final words. You have lost. Your king is dead. He was dead before you even began your fight. You fought, Champion, to defend a dead man.'

The Letherii, eyes widening, struggled to pull himself round, striving to look up, to the throne, to the figure

902

seated there. But the effort proved too great, and he slid back down, head lolling.

The Warlock King was laughing. 'He had no faith. Only gold. No faith in you, swordsman—'

Trull stalked towards him. 'Be silent!'

Hannan Mosag sneered up at him. 'Watch yourself, Trull Sengar. You are as nothing to me.'

'You would claim the throne now, Warlock King?' Trull asked.

An enraged shriek from Rhulad.

Hannan Mosag said nothing.

Trull looked back over his shoulder. Saw the Champion lying sprawled on the dais, at the king's slippered feet. Lying, perfectly still, a mixture of surprise and dismay on his young face. Eyes staring, seeing nothing. *But then, there could be no other way. No other way to kill such a man.*

Trull swung his gaze back down to the Warlock King. 'Someone will do as he commands,' he said in a low voice.

'Do you really think so?'

'His chosen kin—'

'Will do . . . nothing. No, Trull, not even Binadas. Just as your hand is stayed, so too will theirs be. It is a mercy, don't you see? Of course you do. You see that all too well. A mercy.'

'Whilst you heave that ruin of a body onto the throne, Hannan Mosag?'

The answer was plain in the eyes of the Warlock King. *It is mine.*

A hoarse whisper from Rhulad, 'Trull . . . please. I am your brother. Do not . . . do not leave me. Like this. Please.'

Everything was breaking inside him. Trull stepped away from Hannan Mosag, and sank slowly to his knees. *I need Fear. I need to find him. Talk.*

'Please, Trull . . . I never meant, I never meant . . .'

Trull stared down at his hands. He'd dropped his spear – he did not even know where it was. There were six Letherii guards – he looked up – no, they were gone. Where had

903

they gone? The old man standing beside the body of the First Eunuch – where was he? The woman?

Where had everybody gone?

Tehol Beddict opened his eyes. One of them, he noticed, did not work very well. He squinted. A low ceiling. Dripping.

A hand stroked his brow and he turned his head. *Oh, now that hurts.* Bugg leaned forward, nodded. Tehol tried to nod back, almost managed. 'Where are we?'

'In a crypt. Under the river.'

'Did we . . . get wet?'

'Only a little.'

'Oh.' He thought about that for a time. Then said, 'I should be dead.'

'Yes, you should. But you were holding on. Enough, anyway, which is more than can be said for poor Chalas.'

'Chalas?'

'He tried to protect you, and they killed him for it. I am sorry, Tehol. I was too late in arriving.'

He thought about that, too. 'The Tiste Edur.'

'Yes. I killed them.'

'You did?'

Bugg nodded, looked briefly away. 'I am afraid I lost my temper.'

'Ah.'

The manservant looked back. 'You don't sound surprised.'

'I'm not. I've seen you step on cockroaches. You are ruthless.'

'Anything for a meal.'

'Yes, and what about that, anyway? We've never eaten enough – not to have stayed as healthy as we did.'

'That's true.'

Tehol tried to sit up, groaned and lay back down. 'I smell mud.'

'Mud, yes. Salty mud at that. There's footprints here,

904

were here when we arrived. Footprints, passing through.'

'Arrived. How long ago?'

'Not long. A few moments . . .'

'During which you mended all my bones.'

'And a new eye, most of your organs, this and that.'

'The eye doesn't work well.'

'Give it time. Babies can't focus past a nipple, you know.'

'No, I didn't. But I fully understand the sentiment.'

They were silent for a time.

Then Tehol sighed and said, 'But this changes everything.'

'It does? How?'

'Well, you're supposed to be my manservant. How can I continue the conceit of being in charge?'

'Just the same as you always have.'

'Hah hah.'

'I could make you forget.'

'Forget what?'

'Very funny.'

'No,' Tehol said, 'I mean specifically.'

'Well,' Bugg rubbed his jaw, 'the events of this day, I suppose.'

'So, you killed all those Tiste Edur.'

'Yes, I am afraid so.'

'Then carried me under the river.'

'Yes.'

'But your clothes are dry.'

'That's right.'

'And your name's not really Bugg.'

'No, I guess not.'

'But I like that name.'

'Me too.'

'And your real one?'

'Mael.'

Tehol frowned, studied his manservant's face, then shook his head. 'It doesn't fit. Bugg is better.'

'I agree.'

'So, if you could kill all those warriors. Heal me. Walk under a river. Answer me this, then. Why didn't you kill all of them? Halt this invasion in its tracks?'

'I have my reasons.'

'To see Lether conquered? Don't you like us?'

'Lether? Not much. You take your natural vices and call them virtues. Of which greed is the most despicable. That and betrayal of commonality. After all, whoever decided that competition is always and without exception a healthy attribute? Why that particular path to self-esteem? Your heel on the hand of the one below. This is worth something? Let me tell you, it's worth nothing. Nothing lasting. Every monument that exists beyond the moment – no matter which king, emperor or warrior lays claim to it – is actually a testament to the common, to co-operation, to the plural rather than the singular.'

'Ah,' Tehol interjected, managing to raise a finger to mark his objection, 'without a king, general or whomever – without a *leader*, no monument gets built.'

'Only because you mortals know only two possibilities. To follow or to lead. Nothing else.'

'Hold on. I've seen consortiums and co-operatives at work, Bugg. They're nightmares.'

'Aye, breeding grounds for all those virtues such as greed, envy, betrayal and so on. In other words, each within the group seeks to impose a structure of followers and leaders. Dispense with a formal hierarchy, and you have a contest of personalities.'

'So what is the solution?'

'Would you be greatly disappointed to hear that you're not it?'

'Who? Me?'

'Your species. Don't feel bad. None have been, as of yet. Still, who knows what the future will bring.'

'Oh, that's easy for you to say!'

'Actually, no, it isn't. Look, I've seen all this again and

again, over countless generations. To put it simply, it's a mess, a tangled, irreparable mess.'

'Some god you are. You are a god, aren't you?'

The manservant shrugged. 'Make no assumptions. About anything. Ever. Stay mindful, my friend, and suspicious. Suspicious, but not frightened by complexity.'

'And I've some advice for you, since we're doling it out here.'

'And that is?'

'Live to your potential.'

Bugg opened his mouth for a retort, then shut it again and narrowed his gaze.

Tehol gave him an innocent smile.

It was momentary, as more of the memories of this day stirred awake. 'Chalas,' he said after a moment. 'That old fool.'

'You have friends, Tehol Beddict.'

'And that poor guard. He threw himself in front of that spear. Friends – yes, what's happened to everyone else? Do you know? Is Shurq all right? Kettle?'

Bugg grunted, clearly distracted by something, then said, 'I think they're fine.'

'Do you want to go and see for certain?'

He glanced down. 'Not really. I can be very selfish at times, you know.'

'No, I didn't. But I admit, I do have a question. Only I don't know how to ask it.'

Bugg studied him for a long moment, then he snorted, said, 'You have no idea, Tehol, how boring it can be . . . existing for all eternity.'

'Fine, but . . . a *manservant*?'

Bugg hesitated, then slowly shook his head, and met Tehol's gaze. 'My association with you, Tehol, has been an unceasing delight. You resurrected in me the pleasure of existence, and you cannot comprehend how rare that is.'

'But . . . a manservant!'

Bugg drew a deep breath. 'I think it's time to make you forget this day, my friend.'

'Forget? Forget what? Is there anything to eat around here?'

He'd wanted to believe. In all the possible glories. The world could be made simple, there need be no complexity, he'd so wanted it to be simple. He walked through the strangely silent city. Signs of fighting here and there. Dead Letherii soldiers, mostly. They should have given up. As would anyone professing to some rationality, but it seemed this was not the day for what was reasonable and straight-forward. On this day, madness held dominion, flowing in invisible currents through this city.

Through these poor Letherii. Through the Tiste Edur.

Fear Sengar walked on, unmindful of where his steps took him. All his life, he had been gifted with a single, easily defined role. To fashion warriors among his people. And, when the need arose, to lead them into battle. There had been no great tragedies to mar his youth, and he'd stridden, not stumbled, into adulthood.

There had been no time when he'd felt alone. Alone in the frightened sense, that is. Solitude was born of decision, and could be as easily yielded when its purpose was done. There had been Trull. And Binadas, and then Rhulad. But, first and foremost, Trull. A warrior with skill unmatched when it came to fighting with the spear, yet without blood-lust – and blood-lust was a curse, he well knew, among the Edur. The hunger that swept away all discipline, that could reduce a well-trained fighter into a savage, weapons swing-ing wild, that strange, seething silence of the Tiste Edur pulled from cool thought. Among other peoples, he knew, that descent was announced with screams and howls and shrieks. An odd difference, and one that, for some unknown reason, deeply troubled Fear Sengar.

And then, looking upon this Champion of the Letherii king, this brother of Hull Beddict – Fear could not recall if he'd ever heard his name, but if he had, he'd forgotten it. That itself was a crime. He would have to learn that man's name. It was important to learn it.

Fear was skilled with his sword. One of the finest sword-wielders among the Tiste Edur, a truth he simply accepted, with neither pride nor affected modesty. And, he knew, had he stood face to face with that Champion in the throne room, he would have lasted some time. Some fair time, and might well have, on occasion, surprised the Letherii. But Fear had no illusions about who would have been left standing when all was done.

He wanted to weep. For that Champion. For his king. For Rhulad, the brother he'd failed again and again. For Trull, whom he had now abandoned – to a choice no warrior should be forced to make.

Because he had failed Rhulad yet again. Trull could see that, surely. There was no way to hide the cowardice raging through Fear. Not from his closest, most cherished brother. *Who gave voice to all my doubts, my terrors, so that I could defy them – so that I could be seen to defy them.*

Shaped by Hannan Mosag . . . all of this. He understood that now. From the very first, the brutal unification of the tribes, the secret pact with the unknown god had already been made. So obvious, now. The Warlock King had turned his back on Father Shadow, and why not, since Scabandari Bloodeye was gone. Gone, never to return.

Not even Hannan Mosag, then, but long ago. That was when this path first began. Long, long ago.

There had been a moment, back then, when everything was still simple. He was certain of it. Before the fated choices were made. And to all that had occurred since, there was only one who could give answer, and that was Father Shadow himself.

He walked the dusty streets, past corpses lying here and there like passed-out revellers from some wild fête the night before. Barring the blood, the scattered weapons.

He was . . . lost. They had asked too much of him, far too

much. There in that throne room. *We carried his body back. Across the ice wastes. I thought I had sent Trull to his death. So many failures, and every one of them mine. There must be other ways . . . other ways . . .*

Motionless, now, looking down upon a body.

Mayen.

The hunger, he saw, was gone from her face. Finally, there was nothing but peace there. As he'd seen before, when he'd looked upon her sleeping. Or singing with the other maidens. When he'd carried the sword which she then took into her hands. To bury at the threshold of her home. He would not think of other times, when he caught a certain darkness in her eyes, and was left wondering on the twisting of her mind – such things a man could not know, could never know. Fearful mysteries, the ones that lured a man into love, into fascination and, at times, into trembling terror.

Her face held none of that now. Only peace. Sleeping, like the child within her, here on this street.

Fear crouched, then knelt beside her. He closed a hand on the horn grip of the fisher knife, then pulled it from her chest. He studied the knife. A slave's tool. A small sigil was carved near its base, one he recognized.

The knife had belonged to Udinaas.

Was this his gift? An offering of peace? Or simply one more act of deadly vengeance against the family of Edur who had owned him? Who had stolen his freedom? *He abandoned Rhulad. As I have done. For that, I have no right to hate. But . . . what of this?*

He rose, tucking the knife into his belt.

Mayen was dead. The child he would have loved was dead. Some force was here, some force eager to take everything away from him.

And he did not know what to do.

Weeping, ceaseless, weeping from the blood-spattered, twisted form lying on the floor of the throne room. On his

910

knees ten paces away, Trull had his hands to his ears, wanting it to end, wanting someone to end it. This moment . . . it was trapped, deep within itself. It would not end. An eternal chorus of piteous crying, reaching into his skull.

Hannan Mosag was dragging himself towards the throne, so bent and mangled he was barely able to move more than a few hand's widths at a time before the pain in his body forced him to pause once again.

Among the Letherii, only one remained, his reappearance a mystery, yet he stood, expression serene yet watchful, near the far wall. Young, handsome and somehow . . . soft. Not a soldier, then. He had said nothing, seeming content to observe.

Where were the other Edur? Trull could not understand. They had left Binadas, unconscious but alive, at the far end of the corridor. He turned his head in that direction, saw the huddled shapes of the queen and her son beside the entranceway. The prince looked either dead or asleep. The queen simply watched Hannan Mosag's tortured progress towards the dais, teeth gleaming in a wet smile.

I need to find Father. He will know what to do . . . no, there is nothing to know, is there? Just as there is . . . nothing to do. Nothing at all, and that was the horror of it.

'Please . . . Trull . . .'

Trull shook his head, trying not to hear.

'All I wanted . . . you, and Fear, and Binadas. I wanted you to . . . include me. Not a child any longer, you see? That's all, Trull.'

Hannan Mosag grunted a laugh. 'Respect, Trull. That is what he wanted. Where does that come from, then? A sword? A wealth of coins burned into your skin? A title? That presumptuous, obnoxious *we* he's always using now? None of those? How about stealing his brother's wife?'

'Be quiet,' Trull said.

'Do not speak to your king that way, Trull Sengar. It will . . . cost you.'

'I am to quail at your threats, Warlock King?'

Trull let his hands fall away from his ears. The gesture had been useless. This chamber carried the slightest whisper. Besides, there could be no deafness without when there was none within. He caught slight movement from the Letherii at the far wall and looked over to see that he had turned his head, attention fixed now upon the entranceway. The man suddenly frowned.

Then Trull heard footsteps. Heavy, dragging. A sound of metal, and something like streaming water.

Hannan Mosag twisted round where he lay. 'What? What comes? Trull – find a weapon, quickly!'

Trull did not move.

Rhulad's weeping resumed, indifferent to all else.

The thudding footsteps came closer.

A moment later, an apparition shambled into view, blood pouring down from its gauntleted hands. Nearly the size of a Tarthenal, it was sheathed in black, stained iron plates, studded with green rivets. A great helm with caged eye-slits hid the face within, the grille-work hanging ragged on its shoulders and beneath its armoured chin. The figure was encrusted with barnacles at the joins of its elbows, knees and ankles. In one hand it carried a sword of Letherii steel, down which the blood flowed ceaselessly.

Rhulad hissed, 'What is it, Trull? What has come?'

The monstrosity paused just within the entrance. Head creaking as it looked round, it fixed its focus, it seemed, on the corpse of the King's Champion. It resumed walking forward, leaving twin trails of blood.

'Trull!' Rhulad shrieked.

The creature halted, looked down at the emperor lying on the floor. After a moment, a heavy voice rumbled from within the helm. 'You are gravely injured.'

Trembling, Rhulad laughed, a sound close to hysteria. 'Injured? Oh yes. *Cut to pieces!'*

'You will live.'

Hannan Mosag said in a growl, 'Begone, demon. Lest I banish you.'

912

'You can try,' it said. And moved forward once more. Until it stood directly in front of the Champion's body. 'I see no wounds, yet he lies dead. This honourable mortal.'

'Poison,' said the Letherii at the far wall.

The creature looked over. 'I know you. I know all your names.'

'I imagine you do, Guardian,' the man replied.

'Poison. Tell me, did you . . . push him in that direction?'

'It is my aspect,' the Letherii said, shrugging. 'I am driven to . . . poignancy. Tell me, does your god know you are here?'

'I will speak to him soon. Words of chastisement are necessary.'

The man laughed, crossing his arms as he leaned back against the wall. 'I imagine they are at that.'

The Guardian looked once more upon the Champion. 'He held the names. Of all those who were almost forgotten. This . . . this is a great loss.'

'No,' the Letherii said, 'those names are not lost. Not yet. But they will be . . . soon.'

'I need . . . someone, then.'

'And you will find him.'

The Guardian regarded the Letherii once more. 'I am . . . pushed?'

The man shrugged again.

The Guardian reached down, closed a firm grip on the Champion's sword-belt, then lifted him from the floor and slung him over its left shoulder. Standing in a spreading pool of blood, it turned about.

And looked upon Rhulad Sengar. 'They show no mercy, your friends,' it said.

'No?' Rhulad's laugh became a cough. He gasped, then said, 'I am beginning to see . . . otherwise—'

'I have learned mercy,' the Guardian said, and thrust down with his sword.

Into Rhulad's back, severing the spine.

Trull Sengar lurched to his feet, stared, disbelieving—

913

—as the Letherii man whispered, 'And . . . once more.'

The Guardian walked towards the entrance, ignoring Hannan Mosag's enraged bellow as it passed the Warlock King.

Trull stumbled forward, around the motionless form of his brother, until he reached Hannan Mosag. Snapped a hand down and dragged the Warlock King up, until he held him close. 'The throne?' Trull asked in a rasp. 'You just lost it, bastard.' He flung Hannan Mosag back down onto the floor. 'I need to find Fear. Tell him,' Trull said as he walked to the entranceway, 'tell him, Mosag, that I went to find Fear. I am sending in the others—'

Rhulad spasmed behind him, then shrieked.

So be it.

The Wyval clawed its way free from the barrow, dripping red-streaked mud, flanks heaving. A moment later the wraith appeared, dragging the unconscious form of a Letherii man.

Shurq Elalle rose from where she had crouched beside Ublala, stroking his brow and wondering at the stupid smile plastered on his features, and, placing her hands on her hips, surveyed the scene. Five sprawled bodies, toppled trees, the stench of rotting earth. Two of her employees near the facing wall of the Azath tower, the mage tending to the Avowed's wounds. *Avowed. What kind of title is that, anyway?*

Closer to the gate, Kettle and the tall, white-skinned warrior with the two Letherii swords.

Impressively naked, she noted, walking over. 'If I am not mistaken,' she said to him, 'you are of the same blood as the Tiste Edur.'

A slight frown as he looked down upon her. 'No. I am Tiste Andii.'

'If you say so. Now that you have finished off those . . . things, I take it your allegiance to the Azath tower is at an end.'

He glanced over at it with his strange, red eyes. 'We were never ... friends,' he said, then faintly smiled. 'But it is dead. I am not bound to anyone's service but my own.' Studied her once again. 'And there are things I must do ... for myself.'

Kettle spoke. 'Can I come with you?'

'That would please me, child,' the warrior said.

Shurq Elalle narrowed her eyes. 'You made a promise, didn't you?' she asked him. 'To the tower, and though it is dead the promise remains to be honoured.'

'She will be safe, so long as she chooses to remain with me,' the warrior said, nodding.

Shurq looked round once more, then said, 'This city is now ruled by the Tiste Edur. Will they take undue note of you?'

'Accompanied by a Wyval, a wraith and the unconscious slave he insists on keeping with him, I would imagine so.'

'Best, then,' she said, 'you left Letheras without being seen.'

'Agreed. Do you have a suggestion?'

'Not yet—'

'I have ...'

They turned to see the Avowed and his mage, the latter lending the former his shoulder as they slowly approached. It had been Iron Bars who had spoken.

'You,' Shurq Elalle said, 'work for me, now. No volunteering allowed.'

He grinned. 'Aye, but all I'm saying is they need an escort. Someone who knows all the secret ways out of this city. It's the least I can do, since this Tiste Andii saved my life.'

'Thinking of things before I do does not bode well for a good working relationship,' Shurq Elalle said.

'Apologies, ma'am. I won't do it again, I promise.'

'You think I'm being petty, don't you?'

'Of course not. After all, the undead are never petty.'

She crossed her arms. 'No? See that pit over there?

There's an undead man named Harlest hiding in it, waiting to scare someone with his talons and fangs.'

They all turned to study the pit in the yard of the Azath tower. From which they could now hear faint singing.

'Hood's balls,' Iron Bars muttered. 'When do we sail?'

Shurq Elalle shrugged. 'As soon as they let us. And who is Hood?'

The white-skinned warrior replied distractedly, 'The Lord of Death, and yes, he has balls.'

Everyone turned to stare at the warrior, who shrugged.

Shurq grunted, then said, 'Don't make me laugh.'

Kettle pointed up. 'I like that. In your forehead, Mother. I like that.'

'And let's keep it there, shall we?' Fortunately, no-one seemed to grasp the significance of her comment.

The warrior said to Iron Bars. 'Your suggestion?'

The Avowed nodded.

Tehol Beddict, lying atop the sarcophagus, was sleeping. Bugg had been staring down at him, thoughtful, when he heard the sound of footsteps almost directly behind him. He slowly swung about as the Guardian emerged from the wall of water that marked the tunnel mouth.

The apparition was carrying a body over one shoulder. It halted and was silent as it studied the manservant.

Here, in this tomb emptied of water, in this place where an Elder god's will held all back, the Guardian did not bleed.

Bugg sighed. 'Oh, he will grieve for this,' he said, finally recognizing the Letherii on the Guardian's shoulder.

'The Errant says the names remain alive within him,' the creature said.

'The names? Ah, yes. Of course.'

'You abandoned us, Mael.'

'I know. I am sorry.'

The Guardian stepped past him and stopped beside the sarcophagus. Its helmed head tilted down as it observed Tehol Beddict. 'This one shares his blood.'

916

'A brother, yes.'

'He shall carry the memory of the names, then.' It looked over. 'Do you object to this?'

Bugg shook his head. 'How can I?'

'That is true. You cannot. You have lost the right.'

The manservant said nothing. He watched as the Guardian grasped hold of one of Brys's hands and set it down upon Tehol's brow. A moment, then it was done. The apparition stepped away, headed towards the far wall of water.

'Wait, please,' Bugg said.

It paused, looked back.

'Where will you take him?'

'Into the deep, where else, Elder One?'

Bugg frowned. 'In that place . . .'

'Yes. There shall be two Guardians now and for ever more.'

'Will that eternal service please him, do you think?'

The apparition cocked its head. 'I do not know. Does it please me?'

With that ambiguous question hanging in the still air, the Guardian carried the body of Brys Beddict into the water.

After a long moment, Bugg turned back to regard Tehol. His friend would wake with a terrible headache, he knew.

Nothing to be done for it, alas. Except, perhaps, for some tea . . . I've a particularly nasty herbal mix that'll make him forget his headache. And if there is anyone in the world who will appreciate that, it is Tehol Beddict of Letheras.

But first, I'd better get him out of this tomb.

There were bodies lying in the throne room of the Eternal Domicile. The one halfway down the dais, face to the bloody tiles, still made Feather Witch's breath catch, her heart thud loud in her chest. Fear or excitement, she knew not which – perhaps both. King Ezgara Diskanar, flung down from the throne, where Rhulad Sengar of the Tiste

917

Edur now sat, and the darkness in the emperor's eyes seemed beyond measure.

There had been pain in this chamber – she could feel its bitter wake, hanging still in the air. And Rhulad had been its greatest fount. Betrayals, more betrayals than any mortal could bear. She knew this was truth, knew it in her heart.

Before the emperor stood Tomad and Uruth, flanking the trembling, huddled form of Hannan Mosag, who had paid a dear price for this day of triumph. It seemed that he awaited something, a posture of terrified expectation, his eyes downcast. Yet Rhulad appeared content to ignore the Warlock King. For now, he would indulge his sour triumph.

Even so, where was Fear Sengar? And Trull? Feather Witch had assisted Uruth in tending to Binadas, who remained unconscious and would continue so until the healing was done. But, apart from Rhulad's parents, the only others of the emperor's inner court present were a handful of his adopted brothers, Choram Irard, Kholb Harat and Matra Brith. The Buhns were absent, as was the Jheck warchief, B'nagga.

Two Letherii remained, apart from the pathetic wreckages of Queen Janall and Prince Quillas. And already the Chancellor, Triban Gnol, had knelt before Rhulad and proclaimed his eternal service. The other Letherii drew Feather Witch's attention again and again. Consort to the queen, Turudal Brizad gave the appearance of being almost indifferent to all he was witnessing here in the Eternal Domicile.

And he was handsome, extraordinarily handsome.

More than once, she had met his gaze, and saw in his eyes – even from across the room – a certain avid interest that sent tremors through her.

She remained a step behind Uruth, her new mistress, ever attentive, whilst commanders came and went with their irrelevant reports. Fighting here, an end to fighting there, the docks secured. The first of the emissaries from the protectorates eagerly awaited audience in the ruined hallway beyond.

The empire was born.

And she had witnessed, and more than witnessed. A knife, pushed into the hands of Mayen, and word had come that she had been found. Dead. No more would Feather Witch cower beneath her fury. The whore was dead.

Rhulad's first command was to begin a hunt. For Udinaas. His adopted brothers were given a company of warriors each and sent out to find the slave. The search would be relentless, she knew, and in the end, Udinaas would be captured. And made to pay for his betrayal.

She did not know what to think about that. But the thought had run through her once – and only once, quickly driven away afterwards – a hope, a fervent prayer to the Errant that Udinaas would escape. That he would never be found. That at least one Letherii would defy this emperor, defeat him. And in defeating him thus, would break Rhulad's heart yet again.

The world has drawn breath . . . and now breathes once more. As steady as ever, as unbroken in rhythm as the tides.

She could see, through the cleverly fashioned, slitted windows high in the dome overhead, the deepening of the light, and she knew the sun was setting on this day.

A day in which a kingdom was conquered, and a day in which that which was conquered began its inevitable destruction of the conquerors.

For such was the rhythm of these particular tides. Now, with the coming of night, when the shadows drew long, and what remained of the world turned away.

For that is what the Tiste Edur believe, is it not? Until midnight, all is turned away, silent and motionless. Awaiting the last tide.

On his throne, Rhulad Sengar sat, draped in the gold of Lether, and the dying light gleamed in his hooded eyes. Darkened the stains on the sword held in his right hand, point to the dais.

And Feather Witch, her eyes cast downward once more after that momentary glance, downward as required, saw, lying in the join of the dais, a severed finger. Small, like a child's. She stared at it, fascinated, filled with a sudden desire. To possess it. There was power in such things, after all. Power a witch could use.

Assuming the person it had belonged to had been important.

Well, I shall find that out soon enough.

Dusk was claiming the throne room. Someone would have to light lanterns, and soon.

She had not left the room. There had been no reason to. She had sat, motionless, empty, numb to the sounds of fighting, to the howling wolves, to the distant screams in the city beyond. And told herself, every now and then, that she waited. The end of one thing brought the birth of another, after all.

Lives and loves, the gamut of existence was marked by such things. A breaking of paths, the ragged, uneven ever-forward stumble. Blood dried, eventually. Turned to dust. The corpses of kings were laid down and sealed in darkness and set away, to be forgotten. Graves were dug for fallen soldiers, vast pits like mouths in the earth, opened in hunger, and all the bodies were tumbled down, each exhaling a last gasp of lime dust. Survivors grieved, for a time, and looked upon empty rooms and empty beds, the scattering of possessions no-one possessed any longer, and wondered what was to come, what would be written anew on the wiped-clean slate. Wondering, *how can I go on?*

Kingdoms and empires, wars and causes, she was sick of them.

She wanted to be gone. Away, so far away that nothing of her life from before mattered in the least. No memories to drive her steps in this direction or that.

Corlo had warned her. Not to fall into the cycle of

weeping. So now she sat dry-eyed, and let the city beyond weep for itself. She was done with such things.

A knock upon the door.

Seren Pedac looked down the hallway, her heart lurching.

A heavy sound, now repeated, insistent.

The Acquitor rose from the chair, tottering at the tingling in her legs – she had not moved in a long time – then made her way unevenly forward.

Dusk had arrived. She had not noticed that. *Someone has decided. Someone has ended this day. Why would they do that?*

Absurd thoughts, pushed into her mind as if from somewhere outside, in tones of faint irony, drawled out like a secret joke.

At the door now. Flinching as the knock sounded again, at a level opposite her face.

Seren opened it.

To find, standing before her, Fear and Trull Sengar.

Trull could not understand it, but it had seemed his steps were being guided, down this alley, along that street, through the vast city with unerring precision until he saw, in the gloom ahead, his brother. Walking with purpose over a minor bridge of the main canal. Turning in surprise at Trull's hoarse shout. Then waiting until his brother caught up to him.

'Rhulad is resurrected,' Trull said.

Fear looked away, squinted into the shadows of the seemingly motionless water of the canal. 'By your hand, Trull?'

'No. I . . . failed in that. Something else. A demon of some sort. It came for the Champion – I don't know why, but it carried the man's body away. After killing Rhulad in what it saw as an act of mercy.' Trull grimaced. 'A gift of the ignorant. Fear—'

'No. I will not return.'

Trull stared at him. 'Listen to me, please. I believe, if we work together, we can guide him back. From madness. For the Sisters' sake, Fear, we must try. For our people—'

'No.'

'You . . . would leave me to this?'

Sudden pain in Fear's face, but he refused to meet his brother's eyes. 'I must go. I understand something now, you see. This is not of Rhulad's making. Nor Hannan Mosag's. It is Father Shadow's, Trull.'

'Scabandari Bloodeye is dead—'

'Not his spirit. It remains . . . somewhere. I intend to find it.'

'To what end?'

'We have been usurped. All of us. By the one behind that sword. No-one else can save us, Trull. I mean to find Scabandari Bloodeye. If he is bound, I mean to free him. His spirit. We shall return together, or not at all.'

Trull knew his brother well enough to cease arguing. Fear had found a new purpose, and with it he intended to flee . . . from everything, and everyone, else. 'How will you get out of the city? They will be looking for us – it's probable they are doing so even now.'

'Hull once told me that Seren Pedac had her home here.' Fear shook his head. 'I don't know, I don't understand it myself, but I believe she might help.'

'Why?'

Fear shook his head.

'How do you know where she lives?'

'I don't. But it's . . . this way.'

He began walking. Trull quickly caught up to him and gripped his arm. 'Listen – no, I don't mean to prevent you. But listen to me, please.'

'Very well, but let us walk in the meantime.'

'All right. Do you not wonder at all this, Fear? How did I find you? It should have been impossible, yet here we are. And now you, and this house – the Acquitor's house – Fear, something is guiding us. We are being manipulated—'

His brother's smile was wry. 'What of it?'

922

To that, Trull had no answer. Silent, he walked with Fear. Coming upon a score of dead Letherii, he paused to collect a sword and scabbard. He strapped it on, ignoring Fear's raised brows, not out of some ambivalent emotion, but because he himself did not know why he had picked up the weapon. They walked on.

Until they came to a modest house.

Trull's chest seemed to clench tight upon seeing her standing in the doorway. He could not understand it – no, he could, but it was impossible. Absurd. He'd only seen Seren Pedac a few times. Had but exchanged a few score words, if that. Yet, as he studied her face, the shock writ there, so at odds with the appalling depth in her eyes, he felt himself falling forward in his mind—

'What?' she asked, gaze darting between him and Fear. 'What are you . . .'

'I need your help,' Fear said.

'I cannot . . . I don't see how . . .'

Sisters take me, I would give my heart to this woman. This Letherii . . .

Fear said, 'I am fleeing. My brother, the emperor. I need a guide to take me through the city unseen. Tonight.'

'How did you find me?'

'I don't know. I don't even know why . . . why I have this belief that only you can help me.'

She looked then at Trull, and he saw her eyes hold on his for what seemed a long moment, slowly widening. 'And you, Trull Sengar?' she asked. 'Are coming with us?'

With us. She will do this. Why? What need within her does this answer? The pressure in his chest constricted suddenly, even as the fateful words left him. 'I cannot, Acquitor. I failed Rhulad this day. I must try . . . again. I must try to save him.'

Something like resignation filled her eyes.

As if he had wounded something that already bore a thousand scars.

923

And Trull wanted to cry out. Instead, he said, 'I am sorry. But I will await your return – both of you—'

'We shall return here?' she asked, glancing at Fear. 'Why?'

'To end this,' Fear said.

'To end what?'

'The tyranny born here tonight, Seren Pedac.'

'You would kill Rhulad? Your own brother?'

'Kill him? That would not work, as you know. No. But I shall find another way. I shall.'

Oh, who has grasped hold of my soul this night? He found himself unhitching the sword, heard himself saying, 'I don't know if you have a weapon, Acquitor,' and knew his own disbelief at the absurdity of his own words, the shallowness of his reasoning, 'so I will give you mine . . .' And he was holding the sheathed sword out to her.

At the threshold of her home.

Fear turned, studied him, but Trull could not look away from her, not even to see what must be realization dawning in his face.

Letherii though she was, Seren Pedac clearly understood, her gaze becoming confused, then clearing. 'Just that, I take it. A weapon . . . for me to use.'

No. 'Yes . . . Acquitor. A weapon . . .'

She accepted it, but the gesture was without meaning now.

Trull found himself stepping back. 'I have to go now. I will tell Rhulad I saw you, Fear, down at the docks.'

'You cannot save him, brother,' Fear said.

'I can but try. Go well, Fear.'

And he was walking away. It was best, he decided through sudden tears. They would probably never return. Nor would she have accepted the sword. Which was why she asked him before reaching out for it. A weapon to use. Only that.

He was being a fool. A moment of profound weakness, a love that made no sense, no sense at all. No, better by far

924

the way it had played out. She'd understood, and so she'd made certain. No other meaning. No proclamation. Simply a gesture in the night.

A weapon to use. Only that.

They remained standing at the threshold. Trull was gone, his footsteps swallowed by distance. Fear studied Seren Pedac as she looked down at the sword in her hands. Then, glancing up, she saw his fixed regard and smiled wryly.

'Your brother . . . startled me. For a moment, I thought . . . never mind.'

Then why, Seren Pedac, is there such pain in your eyes? Fear hesitated, was about to speak, when a child's voice spoke behind him.

'Are you Seren Pedac?'

He spun round, sword hissing from its scabbard.

The Acquitor stepped past, holding out a hand to stay him. 'Do I know you?' she asked the small girl standing at the gate.

'I am Kettle. Iron Bars said you would help us. We need to leave the city. With no-one seeing.'

'We?'

The girl walked forward, and behind her came a tall, robed and hooded figure. Then a shadow wraith, dragging a body.

A startled sound from Seren. 'Errant fend, this is about to get a lot harder.'

Fear said to her, 'Acquitor, I would berate you for your generosity this night, had it not included me. Can you still manage this?'

She was studying the tall, hooded figure as she replied, 'Probably. There are tunnels . . .'

Fear faced the girl and her party once more. His gaze focused on the wraith. 'You, why are you not serving the emperor this night?'

'I am unbound, Fear Sengar. You are fleeing? This is . . . unexpected.'

He disliked the amusement in its voice. 'And who is that you are pulling behind you?'

'The slave Udinaas.'

Fear said to Seren, 'They will be hunting in earnest for these ones, Acquitor. For that slave.'

'I remember him,' she said.

'His betrayal of the emperor has exacted a high price,' Fear said. 'More, I believe he killed Mayen—'

'Believe what you like,' the wraith said, 'but you are wrong. You forget, Fear Sengar, this man is a *slave*. A thing to be used, and used he has been. By me, by the Wyval that even now circles us in the dark overhead. For what befell Rhulad, for Mayen – neither of these tragedies belong to Udinaas.'

As you say.

'We can argue this later,' Seren said. 'Kettle, who is this disguised man?'

She was about to answer when the figure said, 'I am Selekis, of the Azath tower.'

'From the Azath tower?' Seren asked. 'Amusing. Well, you're as tall as an Edur, Selekis. Can we not see your face?'

'I would rather not, Seren Pedac. Not yet, in any case.' It seemed its hidden gaze was on Fear as it continued, 'Perhaps later, once we have quitted this city and have the time to discuss our eventual destinations. It may be, indeed, that we will travel together for some time.'

'I think not,' Fear said. 'I go to find Father Shadow.'

'Indeed? And Scabandari Bloodeye still lives?'

Shocked, Fear said nothing. *He must be a Tiste Edur. One of the other tribes, perhaps. Also fleeing. No different from me, then.*

'All of you,' Seren said, 'inside. We should scrape together some supplies, although I am certain the Rat Catchers' Guild will be able to supply us . . . for a price.'

The wraith softly laughed. 'It is the Letherii way, of course . . .'

Shurq Elalle stepped clear of the ladder and onto the roof. The sun was up, and people could be seen on the tiers, a little slower in their walking than was usual. Uncertain, filled perhaps with some trepidation. There were Tiste Edur, after all, patrolling in squads. Whilst yet others, in larger groups, were moving through the city as if looking for someone in particular.

Tehol Beddict and his manservant were standing on the side overlooking the canal, their backs to Shurq as she approached. Tehol glanced over a shoulder and gave her a warm smile. He looked . . . different.

'Tehol Beddict,' she said as she came to stand beside him, 'one of your eyes is blue.'

'Is it? Must be some kind of nefarious infection, Shurq, since I can barely see with it besides.'

'It'll clear up in time,' Bugg said.

'So,' Shurq said, 'have you resumed plotting the end of civilization, Tehol?'

'I have, and a delicious end it will be.'

She grunted. 'I'll send you Shand, Hejun and Rissarh, then—'

'Don't you dare. Deliver them to the islands. I work better alone.'

'Alone?'

'Well, with Bugg here, of course. Every man needs a manservant, after all.'

'I imagine so. Well, I am here, then, to say goodbye.'

'Off for some pirating, are we?'

'Why not? I'm simply elaborating on a well-established career.'

Tehol looked to Bugg, and said, 'The thief who sank . . .'

'. . . has resurfaced,' Bugg finished.

The two men smiled at each other.

Shurq Elalle turned away. 'Well, that's one thing I won't miss.'

* * *

After she was gone, Tehol and Bugg stared out for a while longer at the reawakening city of Letheras. The city occupied, the throne usurped, strangers in the streets looking rather . . . lost.

The two-headed insect clung to Tehol's shoulder and would not move. After a time, Tehol rubbed at his weak eye and sighed. 'You know, Bugg, I am glad you didn't do it.'

'Do what?'

'Make me forget.'

'I figured you could handle it.'

'You're right. I can. At least, this way, I can grieve.'

'In your own way.'

'In my own way, yes. The only way I know how.'

'I know, master.'

A short while later, Bugg turned about and walked towards the hatch. 'I'll be back shortly.'

'Right. And when you do, clean up down there.'

The manservant paused at the hatch, considered, then said, 'I think I will find the time to do just that, master.'

'Excellent. Now I'm going to bed.'

'Good idea, master.'

'Well, of course it is, Bugg. It's mine, isn't it?'

EPILOGUE

And it is this moment, my friends,
When you must look away,
As the world unfurls anew
In shapes announced both bright
And sordid, in dark and light
And the sprawl of all existence
That lies between.

Fisher kel Tath

The hole was vast and deep. The two Kenryll'ah demon princes stood at its edge, staring down into it, as they had been for some time.

Finally, one said, 'How far down do you think it goes, brother?'

'I suspect, brother,' the other replied, 'if we were to vacate our bladders into this abyss the streams would fray into mist long before they reached bottom.'

'I suspect you are right. And that Forkrul Assail went down there, didn't he?'

'He did. Head first.'

'You shouldn't have thrown him, then.'

'You are wrong, brother. I simply threw him in the wrong direction.'

'That, or the world suddenly turned.'

'Unlikely. This place doesn't do things like that.'

'You're right. It is proving exceedingly dull, isn't it?'

929

'Exceedingly.'

'Well, shall we?'

'Why not?'

The two demons began loosening straps on their ornate baldrics. Dropping flaps. Shifting their stances to adequate width.

And they stood there, side by side, until, perfectly timed, their flows were done.

The storm had risen sudden, impressively fierce as it raged on the seas. Three Nachts huddled at his feet, Withal stood on the beach, feeling the faint wisps of wind that managed to reach through the sorcerous barrier surrounding the island, brushing against his face like a woman's breath.

A sweet woman, to be more precise. Unlike the one standing beside him. This tall, iron-eyed, foul-mouthed, humourless apparition who followed him around and never seemed to sleep and certainly would not let *him* sleep, not a single damned night the whole night through, not once. Always asking, asking and asking. *What are you going to do? Besides praying?*

Well, what else could he do?

Rhulad Sengar came and went, more insane with each time. Shrieks, laughter, screams and wails. How many times could a man die?

We'll see, I suppose.

'That storm,' Sandalath said, 'it wants to get through, doesn't it?'

He nodded. He could feel its wrath, and its impotence.

'It's waiting for something,' she continued. 'Waiting for someone . . . to do something.'

He repressed the urge to hit her – she'd kill him if he did – wait. *Wait. Wait.* 'Hold on,' he whispered. 'Hold on . . . I've thought of something . . .'

'A miracle!' she shouted, throwing up her hands. 'Oh, I know! *Let's pray!*'

And now he saw it, on the very edge of the thrashing waves beyond the reef. Saw it, and pointed. 'There! A boat, you black-hearted witch! A boat!'

'So what? So what? Why don't you *do something?*'

He spun round, startling the Nachts, and began running.

There was anger, plenty of anger, giving strength to his strides. Oh, so much anger. Deliverers of suffering deserved what was coming to them, didn't they? Oh yes, they surely did. The Nachts had been showing him. Over and over again, the mad grinning apes. Over and over.

Build a nest.

Kick it down.

Build a nest.

Kick . . . it . . . . down!

He saw the hut, that squalid, insipid hovel crouched there on the dead plain. Sensed the Crippled God's sudden awareness, sudden probings into his mind. But oh no, he laughed silently, it couldn't work it out. Couldn't fathom the endless refrain filling his skull.

Build a nest! Kick it down!

He reached the hut, not where the doorway made its slash in the wall, but from a blind side. And, with all his weight, the swordsmith flung himself into that flimsy structure.

It collapsed inward, Withal on top, landing upon a squawking figure beneath. Spitting, hissing with rage and indignation.

Withal grasped handfuls of rotten canvas, heaved himself back upright, and dragged the tent away. Pegs snapping, ties breaking. Dragged it away from that horrid little bastard god.

It shrieked, the brazier tumbling, coals spilling out, sparks lodging in the god's ratty robes, where they smouldered—

'You will die for this, mortal!'

Withal stumbled back, laughing.

And, from behind, the wind suddenly arrived.

931

Almost knocking him down.

He turned into it, facing the beach once more, and saw the stormclouds billowing, rushing in, growing ever higher, towering, spreading their shadow upon the island.

Leaning into the gale, Withal ran back to the beach.

Thrashing, foaming waves on all sides, but there, before him, a stretch of calm. A stretch opposite Sandalath and the capering, dancing Nachts.

Along which the boat slid gracefully through the reef, its lone sail luffing lightly as it glided to shore, grating to a halt five paces from the waterline.

Withal reached the sand in time to see a squat, non-descript man clamber down from the side and wade ashore.

'This,' he said to Withal in the Letherii trader's tongue, 'is for you. Take your friends and make sail.'

'Who are you?' Sandalath demanded.

'Oh, be quiet!' Withal snarled. 'Climb in, woman!'

The Nachts had already done so, and were scrambling about the rigging.

Scowling, the Tiste Andii woman hurried towards the boat.

Withal stared at the man.

Who grimaced, then said, 'Aye, Withal of Meckros, you pray hard enough . . .'

'I knew it.'

'Now, get going. You'll find a way of calm through.'

'And you, Mael?'

'I'll drop in later. I've things for you to do, Withal. But for now,' he faced inland, 'I am going to beat a god senseless.'

This ends the fifth tale of the
Malazan Book of the Fallen

GLOSSARY

Letherii Titles

Acquitor: a sanctioned position as guide/factor when dealing with non-Letherii peoples

Atri-Preda: military commander who governs a city or town

Ceda: title of King's own mage

Finadd: equivalent of captain in the military

Preda: equivalent of commander or general in the military

Sentinel: the King's Voice in establishing first contact with non-Letherii peoples

The King's Leave: a title relieving the holder of all criminal convictions

Lether Place Names

Burl Square: a square in Letheras

Cedance: the dominant set of Tiles (see the Holds)

Cul Street: a street in Letheras

Down Markets: a district in Letheras

Errant's Heel: an alley in Letheras

Eternal Domicile: the new palace under construction in Letheras

Huldo's: a restaurant in Letheras

Katter Bight: a stretch of water outside Old Katter

Kraig's Landing: upriver from the city of Trate

Lether: the kingdom and its protectorates
Letheras: the capital city of Lether
Merchants' Tolls: equivalent of a stock market in Lether
Purser's District: a district in Letheras
Quillas Canal: one of the main canals in Letheras
Rat Catchers' Guild: a mysterious guild active throughout Lether
Red Lane: a lane in Letheras
Rild's: a restaurant in Letheras
Scale House: headquarters of the Rat Catcher's Guild, Letheras
Sherp's Last Lane: a lane in Letheras
Soulan Bridge: a bridge in Letheras
Stinking House: abode of Selush the Dresser of the Dead
Tarancede Tower: a watchtower overlooking Trate Harbour
Temple School: an educational institution in Letheras
The Temple: a high-end brothel in Letheras
Urum's Lenders: an establishment in Letheras
Windlow's Meatgrinders: an abattoir in Letheras

Letherii Cities, Villages and Forts

Awl
Brans Keep
Bridle
Cargo
Desden
Dissent
Dresh
Fent Reach
First Maiden Fort
First Reach
Five Points

Fort Shake
Gedry
Harness
High Fort
Letheras
The Manse
Miner Sluice
Old Gedure
Old Katter
Second Maiden Fort
Thetil
Third Maiden Fort
Trails
Trate
Truce

Letherii Protectorates

Bluerose
Karn
Korshenn
Pilott
Pockface Islands

Neighbouring Kingdoms

Kolanse

Letherii Military

Artisan Battalion
Bluerose Battalion
Cold Clay Battalion

Crimson Rampant Brigade
Fent Garrison
Grass Jackets Brigade
Harridict Brigade
Katter Legion
Maiden Garrison
Merchants' Battalion
Shake Legion
Trate Legion
Wave Wake Brigade
Whitefinder Battalion

Letherii Phrases

Blue Style Steel: an earlier method of ironmongery
Docks: commonest denomination of Lether money
Dresh Ballista: a multi-quarrel war weapon
Letheran Steel: a secret method of ironmongery
Letherii: that of Lether, also the name of the language and of the people
Levels: the coin of the wealthy of Lether
Lupe Fish: a large carnivorous fish resident in Lether River and the canals of Letheras
Ootooloo: a primitive but singular sea-creature from Bluerose
Peaks: the coin of the filthy rich in Lether
(The) Seventh Closure: prophesied renaissance
(The) Shrouded Sisters of the Empty Throne: Educators
Stripling: lowest denomination of Lether money
Truce Fever: a common, curable fever
Tusked Milk: an alcoholic beverage

Tiste Edur Places and Names

Arapay: subjugated and easternmost tribe of Tiste Edur
Beneda: subjugated tribe of Tiste Edur
Calach Breeding Beds: coastline where Tusked Seals breed
Den-Ratha: subjugated, northernmost tribe of Tiste Edur
Hasana Inlet: an inlet claimed by the Tiste Edur
Hiroth: dominant tribe of the Tiste Edur
Kaschan Inlet: an inlet claimed by the Tiste Edur
Knarri: a whaling and fishing craft
K'orthan: raider longboats
K'risnan: the Warlock King's cadre of sorcerors
Merude: subjugated tribe of Tiste Edur
Morok Tree: a blue-leafed tree used in funeral practices
Sollanta: subjugated tribe of Tiste Edur
Stonebowl: a natural depression at the base of a gorge north of the main Hiroth village

Other Names, Titles and Terms

(The) Eres'al: the spirit goddess of the Nerek
Faraed: an assimilated people in Lether
Fent: an assimilated people in Lether
Jheck: a northern tribe
Ken'ryllah: a type of demon
Kenyll'rah: a type of demon
Khalibaral: a type of demon
Meckros: a civilization of mobile, floating cities
N'purel: the Whiskered Fish of the Kenyll'rah homeworld
Nachts: Jaghut-bred versions of bhoka'rala
Nerek: an assimilated people in Lether
Onyx Wizards: sorcerors of Bluerose (defeated in conquest)
Tarthenal: an assimilated people in Lether
The Seregahl: the five gods of the Tarthenal

Mythos (Letherii, Edur and other)

(The) Black Winged Lord: divinity worshipped in Bluerose
Kilmandaros: an Elder Goddess
Mael: an Elder God
Menandore (Betrayer, Dawn)
Scabandari Bloodeye (Father Shadow, Emurlahnis)
Sheltatha Lore (Daughter Dusk)
Silchas Ruin (The Betrayer)
Sukul Ankhadu (The Fickle, Dapple)

The Holds

The Tiles

The Beast Hold
Bone Perch
Elder
Crone
Seer
Shaman
Hunter
Tracker

The Azath Hold
Heartstone
Keeper
Portal
Path
Mason
Tomb
Guest
Barrow
Root
Wall

The Dragon Hold
Queen
Consort
Liege
Knight
Gate
Wyval
The Lady
Blood-Drinker
Path-Shaper

The Ice Hold
Ice Throne
Walker
Huntress
Shaper
Bearer
Child
Seed

The Empty Hold
Empty Throne
Wanderer
Mistress
Watcher
Walker
Saviour
Betrayer

The Fulcra (unaligned)
Shapefinder
The Pack
The Errant
Axe (Eres)

STEVEN ERIKSON

THE MALAZAN BOOK OF THE FALLEN

The epic, genre-defining series

'Homeric in scope and vision . . . a story that never
fails to thrill and entertain . . . a saga that lives up
to its name, both intellectually and in its dramatic,
visually rich and lavish storytelling'
SF SITE

GARDENS OF THE MOON
Bled dry by interminable warfare, infighting and
confrontations with Anomander Rake and his Tiste
Andii, the Malazan Empire simmers with discontent.
Sinister forces gather as the gods themselves
prepare to play their hand . . .

DEADHOUSE GATES
In the Holy Desert Raraku, a long prophesied uprising
has begun and an untried commander battles to save
the lives of thirty thousand refugees. War and betrayal,
intrigue and roiling magic collide as destinies
are shaped and legends born . . .